The Dragon Corps

To Sarah,
Dale Yates

DALE YATES

The cover's background image is of the Coma Cluster of galaxies with credit to NASA, ESA and The Hubble Heritage Team (STScI/AURA), and with acknowledgments to D. Carter (Liverpool John Moores University) and the Coma HST ACS Treasury Team. There is no endorsement stated or implied.

International Standard Book Number (ISBN): 1-4392-2744-6

Library of Congress Control Number (LCCN): 2009901162

First Edition

Proudly Self-Published and Printed in the United States of America.

To order more copies, visit BookSurge at http://www.booksurge.com or call 1-866-308-6235.

For more information on the Dragon Corps universe, visit
http://www.TheDragonCorps.com

Please Be Kind to the Environment.
Conserve Energy, Recycle More, Use Less.

Dedication

My Closest Confidant
My Dearest Friend
My Loving Wife
Theresa

TYFBTC
Thank You For Breaking The Chopsticks

Special Thanks

Jess H.—For getting me killed, again and again and again...
Jessica H.—For provoking my drunk conversations
Carla P.—For friendship and support when life dished its worst
Michael S.—For drawing life into the character
Kelly T.—For defining the line between smart-ass and Cajun
Brian B.—For the twisted, warped and all-around disturbed view
Kaleb A.—For the Cornelius experience
Jim A.—For the critical review and encouragement
Dan E.—For molding me into the last of a dying breed
Lakiesha O.—For evenings of introspective psychology
Kathy B.—For the shoulder and ear when I needed it
Heather C.—For the calm, storm-blue confidence
Dawn A.—For the company and conversation
Kelly S.—For your unforgettable smile
Christine P.—For the muffins
Craig M.—For keeping my childhood real
Sean & Marty W.—For years of camaraderie
Bruce B.—For lecturing me to get up off the chair
Di T.—For the frank, Jewish honesty
Lisa R.—For the inspiration
Carl S.—For the algorithms
Steve P.—For the attitude
Lenny M.—For just being *Lenny*
Excalibur Gang—For the late nights and friendship

A final salute goes to
Sarah Small
Thank you for the laughter and "small" dramas.
You will not be forgotten.

Prologue

It began unknowingly with the rebirth of the Fourth Universe. As the gaseous afterbirth coalesced around minuscule black holes, countless fusion reactions began the chain of events that would create life as it had countless times before.

But this time, something was different.

Fate, in all its mystery, produced sentient life. And it flourished in abundance.

Sentient beings arose to take command of planets, systems and even galaxies. Most died off by either self-destruction or natural phenomenon. But with some luck and quick advancement, a few species survived long enough to defend themselves from the volatile, newborn universe.

Meanwhile, Fate kept busy. Stellar explosions, colliding planets, careening asteroids and rampaging comets sparked the birth of more intelligent life. Over time, sentience speckled the universe.

Eons later, the scattered races found each other. Some encounters created peaceful factions; others fueled bloodshed. Unrelated wars burned bright in the darkness of space.

A few millennia ago, two major factions in the universe clashed: the Federal Kingdom, a relatively new alliance; and the Korac Council, with a history spanning millions of years. Both were very explorative governments. When they found each other, they were initially ecstatic. The joy was short-lived as governing and cultural differences clouded judgment.

Walls began to rise. Massive minefields were built in space in an attempt to define and defend a shapeless border. After countless years of peace, bitterness swelled. Hatred grew.

What happened next is unclear. The details have been lost in the fog of war and remain trivial.

Yet most historians agree that it likely began in a particular twin quasar system, which remained unclaimed at the time. Deep space fleets from the two factions ran into each other. Someone spouted a cross word or fired a shot, and battle commenced and consumed. The ensuing devastation became known as the Twin Quasar War, and it spewed death like a plague.

Both governments poured all resources into vanquishing the other. Industrial infrastructures shifted to delivering war to countless unknown, yet inhabited, planets as the governments fought back and forth from system to system. Some of the unwilling combatants had the ability to fight back; a few did so viciously. But most faced death before they even knew they were not alone in the universe.

Thc Korac Council began to make significant wins as the Federal Kingdom focused its resources on research and development. But the

Kingdom's R&D gave birth to the first and only known Horizon class starship, the "Purusha." With the same mass of a class ten planet, the Purusha hid a secret: A captured dwarf star sat in its heart.

Using the experimental power source, the Purusha's shields were undefeatable, its cannon fire unlimited, its range infinite. The Federal Kingdom's leaders were sure the Purusha could waste the entire Korac Council fleet. They were probably right, but that vision would never take shape because Fate had other plans.

The Korac Council suffered great losses to the Purusha. But the Council scrambled quickly to turn the tables.

Hailed as history's most mysterious military move, because no one has yet been able to duplicate the science behind it, the Korac Council somehow created—or captured—and masked a class seven black hole.

Then, after massing a battle fleet in a nearby parsec, Korac Admiral Huj Ik Et'Lar waited for the Purusha to crash the party. After losing half of his fleet in a vicious battle, Et'Lar ran for the hidden black hole. The Purusha commander, Lord Kokhba, pursued.

Soon, the remaining ships of the Korac fleet disappeared, evaporating in spectacular explosions that shattered the shroud around the black hole. By that time it was too late for the doomed Purusha. The black hole quickly took hold of the immense spaceship.

Scientists theorize that as the black hole consumed the Purusha, the ship's dwarf star collapsed. Already straining to fight the overwhelming pull of gravity, the star flared into another black hole. The new, larger black hole had such an outburst of energy it overtook and consumed the first black hole. As the singularities united, the gravitational processes of the black holes increased at an exponential rate.

At least that's one theory.

Regardless of how it happened, the resulting explosion sent destructive waves across the universe that rained devastation, annihilated many systems and deformed the nearby Mirror Tree Galaxy, which held the main battle front, bringing the two great governments to their knees.

Economic crisis and despair forced the two factions to see their follies and call a truce.

Following the Twin Quasar War, outlaws, mercenaries and pirates emerged to raid throughout the known, and at times unknown, sections of the universe.

The raiders largely got away with their crimes because the Korac Council and Federal Kingdom were still recovering from the Twin Quasar War and couldn't adequately defend themselves or anyone else.

When one faction would track down a group of raiders, the pirates darted for another government's territory. The tense political debates over jurisdiction and extradition always conveniently created cloud cover for the criminals' disappearance.

That all changed when the daughter of Prime King Horakhty of the Federal Kingdom fell victim to an outlaw raid. She had been on a humanitarian mission at Octianon, Dervan Four, helping the agricultural city get back on its feet, when the rampage began.

Horakhty learned of the incident a quarter of a year later, when he also learned that his daughter's attackers ran and hid in Korac space. In his rage, Horakhty immediately called for an emergency meeting with the Korac Council.

After months of intense, nonstop negotiations, both governments agreed on a solution to the marauders: an ultimate law enforcement group, an agency that would have authority across the universe. The main drawbacks were the time and resources needed to establish the agency.

Because of the cost, many other smaller governments hesitated to adopt the idea. The Federal Kingdom, eager to begin restoring peace, had no other option than to announce it would provide the initial funding. After such a bold statement, the lesser governments glimpsed hope and quickly pledged their support.

The Dragon Corps was born.

Soon, many sentient beings joined from throughout the universe, taking oaths to protect peace at any cost. The Corps grew rapidly and branched into five specialized sections, taking on the basic design of the Federal Kingdom's military.

The Dragon Corps remained as the command agency that focused on the creation, interpretation and prosecutorial judgment of interstellar law.

Force Grey Wolf, the largest branch, took control of all mechanized land, sea, air, space, interplanetary, interstellar, intragalactic, intergalactic, extragalactic and intraspace forces.

As the second largest part of the Corps, the Harquebus represented the mass infantry and occupation force with the side task of being the Corps' weapon experts.

House Bravo assumed the role of special operations, to include the fine arts of manual combat, assassination, psychogenics and mana manipulation.

The last group also became the Dragon Corps' most feared agency: the Silver Knights. The Silver Knights served as a covert society of specialized combat engineers and tacticians.

Before the agency could even begin its mammoth task, the Dragon Corps bulged at the seams with volunteers. Thousands, tired of seeing worlds raped and pillaged, wanted to help restore the peace. The Federal Kingdom kept its promise and provided, at great expense, the resources and space fleet needed to start the new agency in its own system.

After a long search, the Federal Kingdom found a three-planet system deep within a previously unexplored territory. The Kingdom quickly sent armadas of terraforming spacecraft with equipment, supplies and factories. The members of the new agency soon followed.

The age of universal law enforcement had begun, and life was never the same.

PART ONE

STORMS IN MYTH

Chapter 1

Except for the distant, dull roar of traffic, the night was silent. Patches of glowing moon and star light randomly pierced the grey veil of scattered clouds.

Salt started to saturate the air as Lyon approached the outskirts of the seaport district. Most of the nearby buildings had been abandoned for years. The port was less important to the city now. Because of that, the area suffered. Even the streets were empty unless you were looking for litter. It seemed ironic how the city gave itself a black eye without even noticing.

He shook his head at the thought and dipped into a pocket of his black overcoat to retrieve a pair of dark sunglasses.

A worn hand with a butchered self-manicure pushed his dirty blond hair from over his ears as the glasses covered oak-brown eyes. As the earpieces made contact with his head, sparks danced from his sub-dermal connectors to the glasses. For a second he almost regretted not getting that modification when they offered it, but for now, these glasses would have to do.

Streaks of light brightened as the glasses slowly came online. Black gave way to a lightened daytime effect. Ensured the specs were working, he pulled his left sleeve up half the length of his forearm to reveal a form-fitting computer. Lyon tapped the diagnostics button. With the tiny screen on his wrist overridden, various gauges became visible in his glasses. Everything appeared to be in order, so he let the sleeve fall back over the computer.

Lyon glanced at the corner's street signs: Jackson Avenue and Fannin Street. Turning right down Fannin, he began to soften his steps on the cracked sidewalk.

"Mac, what's the current situation?" Lyon mentally spoke to the computer. With no reply, he grabbed his arm to check that the wrist computer was seated properly. It was, so he tried again. *"Mac, are you there?"*

"I'm here. Sorry about the delay," his home-based computer replied through the wrist computer's sub-dermal connection straight to Lyon's brain. *"I was in the middle of watching a fascinating display of social dysfunction."*

"What's the current situation?"

"So far the sub-nuclear flux signal is still there, but it's fading rapidly; the last yofeeti transmission was three hours ago." Mac paused for a second. *"Nine hundred forty-seven feet, eight inches and thirteen degrees northeast."*

"Give me a map."

After a couple of seconds, a crackle came from the glasses. *"There you go."*

Lyon stopped and leaned his back against the side of a dilapidated, one-story office complex. He scratched the bristles on his right cheek as the holographic map in his glasses expanded, starting as two-dimensional then rotating and projecting three-dimensionally outward as if it floated two feet in front of him. He looked around the corner over his right shoulder, and the map moved to represent his current visual direction.

There it was.

A red, pulsing globe overlaid the three-dimensional color image. Technical data formed lines that filled the left side of the screen. The flux was less than three feet in diameter, but Lyon knew the globe held more than enough energy to represent a transporter shift.

"Actual vision. Follow me," Lyon told Mac. *"Outlines only."*

The map in front of him, except for the glowing red flux, turned into a green wire frame drawing. Then the map moved toward him until it filled the visual area on the glasses and the wire frame images matched the buildings. Lyon began walking again toward the warehouse that encased the pulsing orb.

He made an early turn and circled around. As he reached the rear of the warehouse, a device appeared from his pocket, and he plugged its short cable into the arm computer. Numerous buttons lined the grip, and a ball rested on top.

Control device in hand, Lyon slid his hand over the computer, again tapping a few buttons. A slight electrical crackling, like a cross between a hum and a snap, sounded before fading. Using the controlling device in his left hand, Lyon started floating to the top windows of the warehouse.

A gradual peak of metal topped the warehouse and sloped to a smaller second roof that jutted from the center and ran the length of the building. The second roof had sides lined with windows in various states of disrepair.

The windows could provide an advantage, so Lyon guided himself over and landed next to them, toward the center of the building. After touching down, he turned off the geomagnetic field and put the controller back into his pocket. Lyon crept on his hands and knees toward the windows and peered into the warehouse.

Only every fourth light glowed, providing just enough illumination for a guard walking through the center of the warehouse. Various crates cluttered the floor. Most formed towers of uneven groupings that bordered the guard's path. One of these groups just happened to form a pile around the location of the flux still pulsing red in the glasses.

But another light seeped from the office door and window in the back.

"Camera, zoom," Lyon mentally ordered.

The outlined hologram on the glasses cleared, and the world in front of him changed as the mini-camera came to life and zeroed on the office window. When the office filled the frame, Lyon commanded, *"Stop."*

Dark hair in a dark suit summed all Lyon could see. The man, assuming only a man would cut his hair that short, had his back to the window and a phone in his ear.

"Mac, patch it in."

"Working on it," the computer replied.

Lyon shifted his body to check on the guard when one of the roof's metal sheets slipped from under his feet, and he starting sliding. Screeching sliced the quiet as the loose sheet grated against the rest of the metal roof. Lyon fumbled to get a grip, causing more of a clatter, but he finally locked on as the rest of his body dangled off the edge some thirty feet from the concrete surface below.

"I've got the link," Mac mentioned as the conversation entered straight into Lyon's head.

"I'll call you back," a voice insisted.

"Is there something wrong?" asked a second voice.

"I don't know yet; there's some noise on the roof." The first voice paused. *"Go ahead and send Kenji's crew, just in case."*

"*Hai! He's not too far from there,"* came the reply.

The conversation ended with clicks of hanging phones.

"Is there something wrong?" The question came from Mac.

"Only if you want to call almost falling off the roof a problem, yes."

"Well, it appears they heard you." The computer remained rather calm.

"Oh." Lyon grunted as he tried to pull himself up. *"You got that too, did you? Nothing gets past you, does it?"*

As he tried to lift himself again, another metal sheet gave way, and Lyon fell. His overcoat flapped in the tumble until he connected with the concrete. Bright circles of pain flashed in his head.

Lyon grunted and mumbled as he started prying himself from the hard surface.

Toward the rear of the warehouse, a door rattled as it slammed open. In the midst of the door's continued vibration, the sound of a charging shotgun echoed.

Lyon leaped to his feet. The electronic enhanced view was gone. *"Mac, what's the situation?"*

No reply.

"Mac, where the hell did you go?"

Still no reply.

Lyon's hand flew up his left sleeve and felt the shattered casing of the wrist computer and some loose wires.

A backlit attacker stuck his head around corner and saw Lyon. In one smooth motion, he brought his massive body around and raised the shotgun to his shoulder.

"Sorry," Lyon said, smiling. "I can't stay and play; my mom's calling."

Lyon tore the useless glasses from his nose and blasted into a run just as a shot thundered down the alley. The gunman saw nothing more than a blur as the shotgun slug tore away a chunk of a brick wall.

The ridiculously fast run lasted for about eight city blocks as Lyon weaved in and out of the buildings. Then he made it to a slightly busier side of town and slowed to a walking pace.

Lyon's breathing remained steady, which allowed him to start focusing on a different attack plan. He unclenched his hand around the glasses and slid them back in a coat pocket.

Another turn into an alley began a shortcut home when an eerie feeling began to tug at him. Training told him what it represented, but he shrugged it off. At a mile a minute, no one had a chance.

Then the feeling became more intense; somebody *was* watching him.

Another shotgun charge rang off the stone alley. Lyon spun and withdrew his pistol. The silhouetted attacker dove for a dumpster, but before it could reach cover, Lyon exploded three rounds into the shadow.

The figure bellowed a short, deep howl of pain almost like that of a bear. The yell rattled nearby windows as the echo of the discharged shots began to lessen to a dull hum.

Solid. He knew each round hit.

Lyon kept the pistol drawn and cautiously approached the body while scanning the nearby area. Once in the light, he took pride in his marksmanship. Two bullets went in the chest and forced the remains of the heart and lungs out the back.

The other round struck the head, causing the skull to implode and splattering cranial fluid and grey matter over the pavement, where it blended with the victim's blood.

Lyon smiled in confidence then noticed something strange.

Part of the dead man's jacket glowed, so Lyon bent down and moved the jacket out of the way with the point of his weapon. On the victim's belt sat a small brown box with a green light on top.

Lyon returned his pistol to the small of his back and unclipped the device from the corpse and opened its front panel. Amid numerous small buttons a screen displayed "2086.54 75LyV."

He'd never seen anything quite like it, but he didn't want to take any chances. The mechanism fell in a clatter on the pavement right before Lyon's heavy boot splintered it.

But if this guard could keep up with Lyon, he deserved a closer examination.

Lyon withdrew a pen and began poking the skin remaining on the face. He never claimed to be a xenobiologist, but he had taken a few science and first aid classes, enough that it didn't take him long to notice it.

This thing's not terran! The thought startled him. *What the hell is he doing here!?*

He left the face and continued to examine the body. An almost nonexistent small intestine and two stomachs confirmed the suspicions. The fact the guard was an alien explained how he kept up with Lyon, but that didn't make Lyon feel any better. He wanted to know what race and, more important, why here.

Suddenly the sound of several startled birds drew his attention from the autopsy to the top of a nearby, three-story building. An armed shadow crept across the rooftop.

Lyon dove farther into the alley as the sound of an approaching vehicle reminded him of the situation he faced.

Thoughts returned to the device he crushed. A locator beacon. *Damn!*

His eyes darted about for an escape route; then he saw it. The alley concealed a doorway into the back of a store. Lyon wasn't a coward, but neither was he a complete idiot. A good run was better than a bad stand any day.

With only the rustling of his overcoat, he slipped over to the door and punched it open. The door swung into a rear storage room. He slipped in and closed the door the best he could.

The room remained rather poorly lit at the moment with only a few rays of light from the street seeping through the cracks in the paint that covered the windows. Lyon wasn't about to turn on the lights, so he fumbled his way about the room. He discovered a door and decided he might as well keep moving.

As Lyon stepped through the door, a spotlight from the street glared through the glass storefront, brightly lighting everything, from the low racks of clothing to him. He briefly stood like a captured deer in the car's spotlight before hitting the floor.

Just as Lyon plunged behind the cashier's counter, a figure rose through the car's sunroof and the rear window slid down. The glass storefront provided no protection from the spray of ammunition as it shredded the racks of clothing and complicated Lyon's attempts to think of a way out. So much for a good run.

Ricocheting bullets began to dance behind the counter, forcing Lyon to move. As he crawled toward the rear corner of the store, the onslaught ceased; they would advance the battle into the store soon.

He took some nearby stairs, four steps at a time. By using the building tops he might increase his chances, or at least he hoped.

The large, metal door slammed against the concrete housing and twanged as Lyon scrambled from the opening toward the rear of an air conditioning vent.

His mind raced. *Keep going. I can't be caught.*

Trying not to waste time, he darted toward the edge of the building and leapt to the next building, two stories shorter.

While in midair, sounds from around the roof entrance broke the silence. A loading magazine snapped. With a roar, a blanket of lead filled the air above Lyon's head as he descended to the other roof.

Upon landing, loose gravel came from nowhere and caused his ankles to buckle, and his entire body lost balance. He screamed just as he smashed into more gravel littering the roof. He didn't have time to think of the pain because the sound of the assailant's boots striking the roof filled his ears.

Lyon dove behind the far end of other building's roof entrance. Sliding down the wall, he reached for his pistol.

"Tomare!" The attacker's declaration spouted like a weapon of its own. Then he muddled, "Sou dewa nai deshou."

Before Lyon could think to ask *"Was that Japanese?"* the assassin put the weapon to his shoulder, and a red bolt shot through the midnight air sizzling past Lyon and striking an air duct. The bolt consumed the unit in electrostatic sparks.

"What the—" Lyon grabbed his composure and shook it back to life. No doubt—that bolt came from a Quazi cannon. Those were only made in the Yarri system about forty, maybe fifty, years ago. Apparently the child's game ended. If he ran, he would soon be toast. But why Japanese?

Another red bolt snapped in his direction. Perfect. It would take a little while for the Quazi to recharge. Lyon swung around the entrance housing and released two rounds—one in each of the attacker's legs. The slugs exploded in plumes of red.

The unknown assailant crashed to the roof with screams of pain. With him immobilized, it was time to move.

Lyon darted around the rooftop, bringing him to its far side. Using the location of the screams, he could tell the individual hadn't moved. He ran for the far edge. Toward the end of his run, he fell forward just in time for his left hand to hook the edge of the lower building and flip himself backwards in the air so his legs had a better chance of striking the roof top. He twisted, and his feet landed flat as he still propelled his body upward until vertical.

Weapon in hand, he immediately obtained a target picture through the pistol's sights and looked straight at a shaking body. Then, movement at the roof entrance drew Lyon's attention, and a quick snap of the pistol blasted the shadow back headfirst. The would-be attacker's weapon rattled down the stairs as the body thudded its way to the next landing. A sure kill. Lyon went back to the first attacker.

The cannon was knocked out of reach, and its previous owner convulsed in shock. Gasping for air, the attacker flopped like a fish out of water while attempting to clasp hands around his shattered legs.

Lyon stared briefly at the terran just long enough to register that the attacker appeared Asian. Lyon filed that thought as he released another round from his pistol to cease the man's misery in a bloody ritual. With one kick, the carcass sailed over the edge of the building toward the empty alley. He grabbed the Quazi cannon and headed for the ledge.

Raising the weapon to his shoulder, he looked through the scope, taking a sweeping view of the street below.

There it sat. The thermograph scope registered a vehicle still warm with three bodies in it.

Two green lights in the scope indicated both cells were now charged. He slid the switch to kill and squeezed slowly on the release. Two blue bolts crackled toward the unsuspecting victims in the car.

The bolts bored through the vehicle and sent a cascade of electrical sparks dancing over the car and the nearby lamppost. Electrical overload forced the light to explode and give way to the night, which immediately consumed the area. Frigid air sucked the heat from the bodies, and Lyon noticed the scope's thermal level already registering a gradual temperature decrease.

He dropped behind the ledge and looked at the weapon. The Quazi cannon had been modified enough to fit a native weapon under its barrel. Lyon unclasped the native weapon and checked the magazine. Empty. He tossed both with a clank of metal.

An infrared stream screamed over his head and singed the top of Lyon's hair, giving off the smell of a particle laser.

"Crap!" Lyon dropped flat and rolled to the left, sprang to his knees, targeted and fired. The bolt, only half charged, slapped the individual in the arm. His weapon dropped to the street three stories below.

Lyon leapt to his feet, dove into the stairwell and raced to the bottom floor, jumping over the mess of a body that remained on the stairwell landing. All the way, it bothered him that he had forgotten about the shooter he had seen first, the one on the roof. He released his anger on the clothing racks that he knocked out of his way before smashing through the remains of the store's display window.

The attacker's weapon had bounced off of a fire hydrant and now rested in the street. Lyon recognized it as a Gortek particle laser. Another piece of a very scattered puzzle.

He grabbed the weapon and slung its strap like a bandoleer over his left shoulder. He stole another look at the rooftop, but there was no sign of the attacker. He caved in the front door with the butt of the Quazi cannon and barreled through the aisles of a pharmacy to the stairwell near the back.

Lyon exploded onto the roof aiming the cannon straight at the attacker, but he was face down and out cold—a terran again, but this one had darker skin.

"If this doesn't beat all." Lyon hung the Quazi on his right shoulder and drew his pistol. Stepping toward the body, he noticed a pack of some sort hanging off the belt, so he flipped the unconscious attacker over with his foot to get a better look at the device.

"A mew." Lyon gritted his teeth. An electro-geomagnetic unit to be more precise, and as MUs go, this one was a lower tech version of the one Lyon used to soar to the warehouse roof. He paused trying to put the pieces together. Nothing seemed to fit.

First he had detected non-native transporter transmissions. An unknown alien with a native weapon chased him. Then native terrans sporting alien technology attacked him. Now he was developing a headache.

Lyon grumbled as he ripped the pack off the belt, played with the controls and tossed it over the edge. As its gravity field fell upon itself, the core crushed in a flash of black.

Lyon sat on the body with his knees pinning down the arms. He grabbed a pencil-like object from an inside pouch of his coat. He had no idea if it would work on a terran; he had nothing to lose either. It only took light pressure against the neck for the needle to fire and inject the fluid.

With a flick, the needle retracted, and he slipped it back into his coat. Then he drew back his hand. His palm struck the man's cheek as Lyon kept the pistol targeted on the head.

The victim didn't show signs of reviving. Lyon smacked him again.

Sluggishly, eyes began to open. They popped open as the helpless man looked down the lethal barrel in much the same way a gazelle might eye a cheetah. His eyes gradually followed the barrel all the way to its owner's face. Amid the well-worn features were two, very calm wood-grained eyes. Slowly Lyon's lips formed a broad smile, a malicious smile. He could feel the terran shiver a bit before trying to put on a tough guy façade.

Beads of sweat forming on the terran's forehead gave away the fact that he was actually in fear for his life.

"After everything we've been through, all I get is the silent treatment?" Lyon's eyes seemed sad, but then hardened until it looked like they could cut through steel. His finger tightened on the trigger. "Who in the hell are you?"

The victim's eyes peeled back farther. Nothing left the tightly held lips. They had trained him well. He gave his oath, and he would say nothing.

Without looking, Lyon swung the pistol behind him and fired a round in the left leg.

The individual released a piercing scream.

"At least I know your vocal cords work. So answer my question before it's the other leg."

"Jay, Big Jay, you fuck!" The victim screamed the last bit, and it helped him deal with the pain as it struck again.

"Good. Good. You're doing good. It's 'well' actually. You're doing well, but I don't care for your attitude." Lyon brought the pistol back around. "Now, Jay—you don't mind if I just call you Jay, do you?" He paused but not long enough to wait for an answer. "Where did you get this weapon?"

"Issued to..." He wavered on the answer. He had to maintain loyalty; otherwise, they would kill him in a most unpleasant way. So with a spit, he took a deep gulp to gather his strength. "...to kill dicks like you!"

Lyon whipped the pistol around and blasted the other leg. "Damn, Jay, you've got a whole lot of nerve to spout shit in your current state of despair."

"Oh, dear God!" Tears formed rivers on Jay's face as he retched in pain. His eyes twitched feverishly.

"Now you're begging to your maker." Lyon pointed the pistol to the sky then leaned closer to Jay's right ear and began whispering slowly. "Want to know a secret? Your makers are much like vicious parents; they brought you into this world, and they *will* take you out. But they won't directly get this particular pleasure with you if I don't get the information I want."

Jay's glazed eyes twitched as they remained affixed on Lyon. "P-please—"

"Shisssss," Lyon whispered as he leaned back and pressed the pistol against Jay's jaw to shut his mouth. "Don't beg; it irritates me."

Lyon paused, mentally examining the feeling that had come over him. It almost disturbed him, this feeling from the recesses of his mind. Was he losing it? He could never tell. Mental searches for fragments of his past to blame revealed little that he would consider the spark. Maybe he could finger training as the culprit; then again, what he felt may simply be natural and all the other emotions were fabrications of society.

He could never bring himself to follow the theory to its conclusion. Fear of the hypothesis alone kept him from it. But now he could not ignore this ultimate destructive lack of sympathy.

An attempt by Big Jay to open his mouth set off Lyon's reflexes to push the pistol hard against the jaw.

"Now, Jay," Lyon's voice was much louder, "personally you don't look very big, but you seem to be an *upstanding* citizen. I'm also an upstanding citizen, so," Lyon moved the pistol away from Jay's chin, "where might upstanding citizens such as ourselves get a unique weapon such as the one you were so casually sporting this fine evening?"

Jay's pain caused most of his body to twitch, but his legs didn't move very much. He knew his options were growing short. This nutcase would keep shooting until he said something. Maybe he *could* say something, enough to get this wacko to leave. He'd just tell his bosses he said nothing. They wouldn't be able to prove otherwise.

"Yakuza," he gargled from the pain he was trying to hold in.

"That's interesting. Go on."

Reluctance returned as Jay's lips tightened.

"Tsk, tsk." Lyon swung the pistol around and planted the barrel on Jay's left hand. "I'm going to need more than that, Jay." Lyon paused as if gathering an afterthought. "I sure hope you're not left-handed. I would hate to see an upstanding, artistic citizen lose his dominant hand."

Jay began spouting strings of obscenities, which stopped when Lyon snapped the pistol's trigger and crammed the blood-coated muzzle in Jay's mouth.

Lyon leaned closer again and struck another smile. Actually, Lyon looked rather happy. "You're not being nice. I'm trying to give you a chance. All I want is information."

In the midst of his enjoyment, Lyon's mind raced. He was almost certain he knew the what, where and how; it was the who and why that bothered him. Lyon then got a hunch and decided to play it.

"Jay," Lyon began easing the pressure that the gun had on Jay's palate, "I'm starting to like you, so I'm going to give you one more chance." He leaned in even closer and began to whisper as if it was essential that no one else hear the conversation.

Just then Jay tried to bite Lyon, who whipped his head back and jammed the barrel farther.

"That was your last try, Jay," Lyon declared. "Sleep tight."

Jay realized his folly only too late. Strips of flesh and tissue blasted in a mist of blood from the top of his head.

"Stubborn punk." Lyon wiped the pistol and his hands on Jay's shirt before holstering the weapon and standing. He looked down at his victim and shook his head.

It was just a simple question, he thought. *Why did you have to piss me off?*

Chapter 2

Leaving through the busted door of the pharmacy, Lyon approached the remains of the black car, full-sized and a bit aged.

The bolts he had slammed into it earlier dented the roof as they penetrated. Human mush coated the inside. The bolts didn't leave much, not much more than one could successfully lift with a fork.

Just then, he heard police sirens approaching. Too late as usual. Lyon turned to stare into the distance before disappearing like a streak of lightning as he blasted into a run. If he had one advantage, it was being born and trained on a larger planet.

The streets in this part of town remained rather barren so early in the morning. Only an occasional car would zip by. The neighborhood of slums and bums gave him a good cover. Not many people would report seeing a real live superhero running faster than a car. Everyone, including the local cops, would urge the witness to lay off the liquor and stop freebasing everything in sight.

The only people who would buy the story were tabloid journalists, leaving the eyewitness accounts to be read primarily by that segment of the population not well known for its intellectual prowess. But most would just laugh at the witnesses imagining something so outrageous. This, too, gave Lyon something to laugh about. If only they knew.

He whipped around a crumbling building and darted across the street. A wooden fence stretched for half the block, broken by a vehicle gate with a smaller door to the left. Lyon unlocked the door and stepped into a large parking lot used by the owners of the surrounding, barely surviving businesses.

Lyon locked the fence door and walked to the back of his corner grocery store. A black cat meowed at him as it jumped down from the top of a dumpster. Lyon ignored the stray as it purred deeply and rubbed against his left leg.

The keys tinkled in his hand as he switched from one to another, finally finding the right match to unlock the building's door. Stepping through, he turned on the stairwell light. The feline stood clear of the door, staring at Lyon. Meows continued as the door closed. Lyon ignored the cat and headed down the split-level stairs.

At the end of the stairs, shrouded in darkness, a brick alcove framed a large metal door. Lyon stood motionless while the door's independent computer verified his identity. Invisible sensors scanned his features and probed deep enough to make retinal and nerve maps. The door split open, granting him access.

Immediately the darkness gave way to a white and grey room. A work bench, crowded with projects, lined the left wall. Three doors stood in the otherwise barren far wall. The far right corner gave way to a hallway. The right wall was covered by various computer equipment and terminals, and a large video screen marked its left. Against the descending stairs that followed the remaining wall, numerous cabinets covered everything except the stairs' exit, which made a ninety degree turn to empty onto the room's stained, grey concrete floor. In the center of the floor sat a large table.

As Lyon descended and walked into the room, his body adjusted slightly to the more natural, increased gravity. Though artificially created, it felt oddly good, and Lyon let a sigh slip. He approached the center table and laid the two captured weapons down on top of it.

"Mac."

The computer screen to his right lit up. "Glad to see you made it back," the completely neutral, but natural, male voice said.

Mac's screen only showed lines of calculations and data, followed every so often by a fluctuating graph. Strangely, Mac appeared to be occupied with something other than television shows. "After I detected the laser fire, I began contemplating how to cover up the existence of this station."

"Oh, don't we have a lot of faith?" Lyon asked sarcastically.

"Only looking at the most likely situation. I don't remember 'and then there will be a firefight' in the mission planning."

Lyon paused for a moment, ignoring the computer as he let his eyes wander around the room randomly. "Find the space traffic logs near this area for the past five years. Give me projections for the next five. Scan the whole globe for unusual transmissions, even if it might seem natural. Find what you can on the meaning of the word 'yakuza.' Give me a secure line to Dragoon W'Lowe. Prepare the scan and maps of the warehouse for transmission. Scan these weapons and cross check their codes with all criminal files. Open weapons locker two and make me a drink."

The computer didn't reply but went straight to work. As Lyon walked to the now open cabinet to rearrange the weapons inside to make room for the two new ones, the table behind him glowed. At the near end, a red laser-like light with no apparent source covered the weapons, while the far end of the table glowed blue-white. When the lights faded, a glass of water replaced the blue-white light. Meanwhile, a cooling unit purred to life on one of the computer's subprocessors as it began trying to find a match for the weapons.

"I've got that secure line for you," Mac said. "Sherri said he is talking with someone else and estimates he will be ready to speak to you in about five and a half minutes."

"Thank you."

Lyon placed the weapons into the locker and securely fastened them.

"Close the locker."

The cabinet closed. The sound of whirring gears could be heard from inside, followed by five clicks.

Lyon walked to the glass, drank the water and set the container back down. The blue-white light flashed again, and the glass refilled.

"Chair," he said. A short crackle came from a chair parked next to the screen. It moved away from the terminal, floated across the room and stopped right behind him. Lyon paid no attention to the action, but in faith, he just sat. His arms rested on the chair's controls. With a quick blur of fingers on the left and right keypads, the table glowed with a blue light from within. The chair floated over to an inset in the end of the table.

Lyon's fingers began tapping a series of commands, and thc table morphed slightly, moving upwards in three sections around him. Each section produced a hologram that blazed with various screens of information being scanned, crosschecked, calculated and predicted. Like slot machines, one screen after another slowed down and stopped.

The right hologram showed a generic personnel roster, while the center screen showed a three-dimensional view of the warehouse he had just visited, as the computer played war games to find the best way to infiltrate the building. The final hologram listed skills and equipment needed for the maneuvers playing out on the second screen.

He looked over the tactics hologram as it played the war scenario, scanned the requirements screen, thought for a moment, then entered some new variables on the chair's keypads. The computer began reprocessing.

"Lyon, you may find this interesting."

"What's that?" He entered a few more key commands.

"Those weapons were tagged as being destroyed about thirty years ago."

Lyon paused. The information was interesting but didn't help him fit any of the puzzle pieces together. As a matter of fact, damn few of the pieces were fitting, and that disturbed him.

"Destroyed by?" he asked.

"By the Korac Council as part of the Treaty of Barguth. The weapons were shipped to a reclamation facility on Hya Eight."

Lyon went back to tapping on the keypads.

"This is getting better," Mac continued. Lyon said nothing.

"Looks like Hya Eight was destroyed twenty-six years ago in a freak neutrino explosion that went nuclear. The investigation report states the faulty neutrino reactor was the one powering the reclamation facility these weapons were sent to."

Lyon sat back in the chair as if thinking about the new piece of information, but in reality, he was busy thinking about how to rip the warehouse to pieces. He just stored Mac's discovery for later use.

"How quickly could we get a combat team here?"

"About three to four days, and that's only if you beg. Personally, I think you're jumping—"

Mac paused for a moment, and the screen shifted from data to the face of a very large man. "Hello, Dragoon W'Lowe," the computer greeted. "How are you today?"

"Fine. How are you?" a stern voice replied.

"About as good as a computer can be. Thanks. Knight Kendrick wishes to speak to you, sir."

"Great." The dragoon's eyes moved from the corner of the screen to look at Lyon as he swiveled in his chair. Dragoon Chrodium W'Lowe's face exhibited very similar features to the faces of the beings that inhabited Lyon's currently assigned planet. The few differences would be undetectable to most, but Lyon noticed them. After all, they were both the same race. Under W'Lowe's white hair and brow, his brown, almost red, eyes mirrored the sternness of his voice. "Looks like you're busy. What do you have? But do make it quick; I just got word to be in a meeting as soon as I can."

Lyon glanced over his shoulder quickly and said, "Mac, send the transmission, along with the findings of the weapons search."

W'Lowe's face moved forward as he reviewed the information now on his hologram.

Lyon began to explain. "Someone is smuggling illegal weapons on this planet. I got these from some punks who shot at me."

W'Lowe looked up, his expression quizzical. "The p'tahians?"

"I doubt it. It's most likely some pirates, but I haven't figured out how they got here or even why they would bother." Lyon looked at the holograms behind him again, entered some more variables then returned to the conversation. "I want a team to stop the smuggling before it attracts attention. And if it is the p'tahians, it may be all we need."

"Wait one minute," W'Lowe paused as his eyes grew even colder. "No one else should even know that planet exists. If we go in force, it's an act of war, and you know it. If for some bizarre reason the p'tahians are doing this, it's still not enough. Remember, there's more than your mission on the line here. If you're marked, that planet and three others are in danger. We're supposed to stop wars, not start them."

"Sir, I understand your reluctance, but from the transmissions we've detected, it looks like they're moving the weapons by transporters. They can't ship bio-weapons that way, so everything making its way here is low grade. But these weapons are still generations beyond this planet. Sooner or later, they'll detect the shipments."

"That's an odd way for pirates to ship." W'Lowe whispered the comment and appeared to look behind Lyon. "Regardless, I'm not going to bless a raiding party and sacrifice the secrecy we've maintained so far."

Lyon squinted. Score one for Mac for correctly predicting that he would have to fight for approval.

"I understand, sir, but this is our—"

"I don't want to hear it again, Kendrick." W'Lowe sat back then glanced at something to his left. "I'm going to be late. Kendrick, do your job and get some hard proof first."

The screen went blank.

Lyon scowled and clenched his jaw. As if two illegal weapons weren't proof enough. What did W'Lowe want before doing something? Lyon dead? He jumped out of the chair to get back to work and get his mind off the annoyance of bureaucratic bullshit.

"Mac, open locker one. What information were you able to gather from the warehouse?"

"Not much. There's still too much interference, but let me go back and check the signals I received from your wrist computer." The computer went to work as it talked. "If I run a few filters and boost the remaining signal, I might be able to detect—bingo! Well, well...."

"Is this when I begin to guess or should I threaten to cut your power?"

"Hey! No need for that; I was going to share." Mac attempted a melodramatic pause but failed. "Of the three people at the warehouse, I got readings on two, neither a terran."

Lyon took off his jacket and other equipment, except for the arm computer, and placed it all in the locker. "Mac, would you get to the point sometime?"

"The one that followed you was assuredly not terran, but I can't get a species match. However, there was a piolant in the...bathroom, I think."

"The piolanese are part of the Korac Council." Lyon squinted and rapped his fingers against his thumbs. "Then again they could still be pirates."

"Well, yes, and I deduct the piolant stayed to protect the transporter or the owner of the voice on the phone. About that voice, by the way, there's still too much interference, so I can't determine a race."

Lyon deactivated the sub-dermal pads on his left forearm, wrenched the busted computer free and placed it on the table. "Here's the communications problem."

Mac went straight to work, manipulating beams of light that bounced off the table.

"In addition to the fire detected from the weapons you brought in, there was a slight disturbance in the geomagnetic force. Oh, and some of the conventional fire was denser than normal, but my readings could be wrong."

The light on the table stopped dancing, and Lyon picked the repaired computer off the table and put it in the locker. "Close locker one. Your distortion came from a MU I found on my reluctant informant. I reversed it."

There was a pause as Lyon thought.

"How dense?"

"Excuse me?" Mac was caught off guard while he finished compiling information from some satellites.

"How dense?" He repeated. "You said some of the conventional fire was denser than normal."

"Yes, but modifying the sensors from existing satellites isn't the most exact science. I could be wrong."

"Sure, and this moon is really made of cheese. How dense?"

"Actually," Mac went searching in the files, and Lyon thought the computer was retrieving data on the density of the bullets. Then Mac said, "The huyin race does use a glass-like substance similar to that found on the moon in an equivalent manner of how terrans use cheese."

Mac hoped to get a response from his attempt at comedy, but Lyon just stood there with his eyes half closed. His mouth twitched to one side as he took a deep breath, pretending not to hear this.

"Two point three GUs, which would be the equivalent of kadious." Mac answered in what almost resembled a bashful voice.

"Thanks." Lyon let the word slip under a coat of sarcasm as he woke from the self-induced trance.

"Because the other weapons are a couple of decades old, kadious makes sense to some degree," Mac continued. "Kadious bullets became practically ineffective some hundred years ago, but the material is roughly five times better than any native equivalent. The question is why would someone go through the trouble of making terran bullets out of kadious?"

Lyon felt the question was relevant enough to merit acknowledgment. He stepped over to his chair and slipped into it. Rocking back, he started fidgeting with his fingers. "Would the piolanese break away from the Korac Council?"

"Regardless how slim, the possibility does exist."

"Then consider this: After countless centuries of solitude, what if the p'tahians actually returned a piolanese request for an alliance?"

"Now wait," Mac interrupted, "the p'tahians don't want anything to do with any being. These must be pirates; they're just lucky they have survived this long without being discovered."

"But what if there is an alliance?"

"Stop right there!" the computer commanded much like the dragoon had earlier. "Nothing is positive yet, and an alliance is highly improbable; we both know that. Just take this slow. A small and tactical investigation—one that won't be detected—will prove these are just lucky pirates. Then we plan from there. Hopefully, we can remove them before they draw attention."

Lyon continued to fidget with his fingers. Mac always thought logically and generally was right. But Lyon refused to forfeit and decided to argue anyhow. "Heavily armed."

"Lightly armed," Mac counter-offered.

"Deal." Lyon now felt a slight level of satisfaction that he had won something, regardless of how intangible it may have been.

"Heavily armed only if you can get proof."

"Oh, I'll get proof." He then added the thought, *I hope.*

Everything seemed to flood Lyon's mind. This could mean war if he fumbled, and a part of him didn't like that feeling. He earned his promotion to knight only recently, and this ten-year tour served as his first solo mission.

An important outpost that had remained quiet for decades, this was supposed to be an easy step up the career ladder. So he accepted it. Heck, he thought he might even be able to turn it into a well-deserved vacation. So much for his vacation, but now he needed some sleep.

Chapter 3

Just when he thought the intelligence reports couldn't get weirder, this one arrived on his desk. Jordan didn't want to read the file at first, but he had to. He didn't see Alpha-classified information very often, maybe only once or twice a week. Generally when he did, it wasn't good news, and this one beckoned him with its flashing icon.

He highlighted the message with a touch on the screen built into the top of his desk, took a sip of his drink and kicked back in the chair. Jordan returned the copper mug to the table. "Sarah, read the priority message."

A female voice, appearing to come from nowhere in particular, started speaking. "The following intelligence report is classified Alpha White," it said. "In summary, intelligence has been gathered that indicates possible terrorist transactions spreading in the Vurdoo Parsec of the Miica Galaxy. The action extends beyond the interplanetary war in that sector and is taking a direction that gives strong indications that the trilom people are in danger."

Jordan dropped his feet and leaned forward. If it wasn't one thing, it was another. There was always some race out there trying to do something stupid.

But it did make sense to attack the trilom, from a pirate's mind. The Corps had just hoped it wouldn't happen; they were already stretched thin and didn't have an outpost in that sector yet. That bit of data meant an entire fleet would be needed in the area to keep the trilom safe. And Jordan didn't know if the Corps could pull one together in time.

The voice continued. "The following transmission logs filed by computer transshipment centers in the area show a definite gap in some cargo ships' transmission logs as if jamming, falsifying or hacking the log entries."

Projectors hummed to life, displaying graphics of the logs and other information on the far wall as the voice went on. "As you can see, in the third column, the ships' signal code is highlighted to better display the gaps. To continue, the fourth column—"

"Beep, beep, beep...beep, beep, beep."

"Halt message," Jordan commanded then shifted his attention. "Answer."

A holographic flat screen sizzled to life at the far edge of his desk, and a familiar face became visible. "Good day, my lord. I do believe you will find today's mail quite interesting," the individual announced.

"Ah! Jerry, are you responsible for brightening my morning?" Jordan replied sarcastically.

"Sorry, just doing my job." Jerry shifted a little, then asked, "My lord, please secure your signal."

Jordan pressed his finger against a top right corner of his screen, waited for a confirmation then said, "I'm secure. So tell me the secret stuff."

Jerry leaned toward the screen, "Well, it's just that you have to be in the Cube in fifteen minutes. Ambassador Koine has asked to speak with you and the branch commanders again. I will be notifying them shortly."

Jordan slowly raised an eyebrow. "He didn't leave any clue as to about what, did he?" The question sounded more like a statement of fact.

"Nothing," Jerry replied. "He gave me some files, but I'm not supposed to open them until everyone gets here. You know Koine."

"Yes. I'll see you then." A nod preceded the disconnect order, and the picture disappeared in floating pixels that fizzled into the void.

Jordan paused for a second with thoughts screaming through his mind on what the ambassador wanted now. There was one standard fact: Koine never visited unless he wanted something. It had been that way for the past five years, since Jordan had taken over as lord of the Dragon Corps.

From what Jordan could tell, Koine served well as the representative of the rolbrid people of the Geeka system, but he didn't hesitate to ask for help whenever the rolbrids felt threatened. Once again, the ambassador was probably going to ask for aid to stop a "war." Every time, it turned out to be more of a misunderstanding in a border skirmish than a true act of war.

It's not like the Corps had anything else to do, with the possible exception of a couple hundred other missions. Personally, it sickened Jordan to rush his best forces to an area just to act as translators. Unfortunately, Koine was treated with the same respect as any of the thousands of other ambassadors. Jordan just hoped the meeting wouldn't take too long.

"Sarah?" Jordan got up from his chair and stared out the window behind his desk. He watched the sunset and the moon Sakra slowly change from orange to a blue-white.

"Yes," a voice replied from his desk.

"Scramble the priority message."

"Provide code, series and step," the voice requested.

"Nickel niner seven delta five, series beta seven kilo, step thirteen point niner."

After a couple of seconds the computer replied, "Complete. Would you like the file transferred to the safe?"

"Yes."

The desk's screen flickered then went blank.

"Done." The voice paused for a moment then continued. "I have just received some more mail from distribution."

"Anything register important?"

"No. But one item is marked immediate."

"Very well." Immediate, in his priority system, meant he would get to it sometime in the next couple of days. His computerized administrative assistant had more than enough skill to handle everything else.

Jordan walked in front of his desk and through his long, spacious office toward the coat rack in the far corner. "Start my shuttle and bring it to the front."

"Under way."

Jordan slipped into his formal jacket, black with silver braids and insignia. In the otherwise white office, a grey, vertical rectangle sat in the center of the wall. As he approached it, the door disappeared. It didn't go anywhere, it just disappeared. The opening revealed halls of light-blue walls spotted with various sets of glass doors. Hall traffic was light, and the few people Jordan did see didn't say anything; they just made a path as the lord wound his way through the maze to a set of large doors that led into the docking bay.

The clear doors disappeared altogether and gave way to the immense bay. Various shuttles littered the parking slots.

His mind strayed as he walked to his shuttle sitting across from the now reappearing doors, and before he knew it, he was sitting down. Time to shake away the other thoughts troubling him.

Jordan didn't like the automatic driver. For him, driving provided a way to forget everything else. He tapped a button on the dash and a control panel folded out. With a bit more typing, the shuttle's door slid shut. The landing struts retracted as light-blue fields formed under the shuttle, keeping it level but at a fair distance from the metal ground. Then at the end of the long, dark-blue shuttle another light-blue field formed, pushing the shuttle forward.

Jordan piloted the shuttle to the departure end of the dock. "Dragon Control," he spoke, "Lord Haddox departing Dock One."

"Confirmed, my lord," a voice sounded in the vehicle. The dock controller paused as he started the departure sequence. "Have a safe trip."

Yellow lights flashed madly as an invisible field surrounded the section of the dock containing Jordan's shuttle. Above, the ceiling lifted away to the night.

The ground sank below as the shuttle rose, and the skyline of the planet Dragon filled the view below. Stretched across the scene was an orange-bordered horizon now barely lit by the setting sun. About thirty degrees from Sakra, and closer to the sky's apex, sat the misty-green moon Kerr.

Jordan directed the shuttle's fields forward, and on the windscreen, holographic sky streets came to life. Green points of light marked the roads as they stretched to form a massive traffic network winding around the metroplex's skyscrapers. It gave the appearance of floating runways that never ended.

Every so often, the roads rose to dodge the tops of buildings, in the process affording drivers and passengers a wonderful view.

For miles, the metroplex stretched in every direction, and lights from landing pads, air terminals and science stations dotted the cityscape. The buildings varied in height, but they all tapered visibly. The two highest buildings were near the center of he city—both three miles high.

Shuttles darted back and forth on invisible overpasses and underpasses. Jordan's navigation screen flashed a warning, and the shuttle in front of him shot down one of the transparent off-ramps to an air terminal directly below, between two buildings.

As he sped toward the Cube, the holographic lights doubled to make the invisible road an eight-lane super skyway with drop and lift exits. Jordan gazed over his left shoulder to see the familiar port for the Cube. He took a drop exit, gliding straight down through multiple layers of scurrying traffic.

He steered the shuttle to within a couple of yards of the port. "Cube Control, Lord Haddox requesting entrance at the main dock."

"Welcome, my lord," Jerry's voice returned. "Stand by."

The shuttle's onboard computer started communicating with the security system to verify Haddox's identity. Confirmed, the port doors slid open and Jordan's shuttle shot down the miles of metal that transitioned to rock. The view of the closing doors above him shrank to a speck. Approaching the underground floor, the vehicle's fields began to slow him down.

The end of the tunnel gave way to a miniature underground docking port. Jordan moved the shuttle forward to his parking slot in front of the Cube. Technically, it was the Command and Control Center or "C3," but during its construction, one of the mathematicians hired to assist the architects in locating stress points began calling it cubed, as in C to the third power. The name, shortened to Cube, just stuck.

Landing struts extended as the shuttle lowered. Then the geomagnetic field slowly dissipated as the generators quieted.

Jordan's shuttle door flew open just in time for him to see Commander Scda Oj's shuttle fall through the hatch and glide toward him. Lord Jordan Haddox decided to wait for his counterpart, so he closed his door, stood by the building and watched the descent.

Scda was of an interesting insectoid race. Due to his size, Scda's shuttle had to be three times the size of Jordan's, and it looked like a large van, grey with a full-color Harquebus emblem painted on the side—a silver arrowhead in a hexagonal field of green. Instinctively, Jordan glanced at the Dragon Corps symbol painted on the side of his squat, long shuttle.

The crystal blue pentacle always reminded Jordan of the unity shared by the five branches. Together, they formed the Corps, and it was Jordan's job to keep the whole agency focused. The governments of the universe endowed the Corps with the power and responsibility to enforce the law.

It was an awesome responsibility at times, but Jordan tried not to let it get to him. The Corps was still very young. Because of that, many still didn't recognize the agency's authority. After the war, the universe changed. The resulting chaos kept the Corps busy.

The second shuttle landed much like Jordan's had. As the shuttle's door slid open with a hiss, green smoke billowed onto the metal floor. Scda's chair slid back and turned to grant him easier access through the now open door.

Jordan quietly watched as the insectoid prepared to leave his shuttle. Two oblong compound eyes almost covered Scda's grey head. Small mandibles protruded from the front, and four antennae extended from the sides of what one may call a mouth. In a way, the antennae looked more like whiskers.

Scda's massive forearms unfolded from his enormous thorax and extended to the ground. With a liquid movement, Scda lifted himself from inside the shuttle and placed his four-legged abdomen on the ground.

As Scda raised his thorax and head and refolded his arms, Jordan looked up at the ten-foot-high being. They called themselves jexans. Their home planet, Jex, was the fourth planet of the Niw star.

Scda was held in high regard for his combat skills during the Twin Quasar War. His battle skills now served an instrumental role within the Corps.

"How's it going?" Jordan began.

"As expected until Earl Harrington called." Scda's rough voice seemed to reverberate in the air. As Scda spoke Jordan looked away; it still gave him the creeps that nothing seemed to move when a jexan spoke.

Scda noticed Jordan's actions but had grown accustomed to the response. With his unblinking, compound eyes, Scda missed very little.

They both entered the first set of disappearing doors and headed down a blank hall to another set.

"Lord, it appears that your hair is slowly changing color." Scda found it rather interesting, at least interesting enough to mention. "There's less brown than the last we met."

"It's called going grey," Jordan half mumbled. He reflexively ran his left hand through his hair. "It tends to happen to us atlantians as we age."

"How old are you?"

"I'd rather not say." It irritated him slightly that after only a hundred and thirty-two years his hair started going grey. Too much stress, Jordan told himself.

They reached the door and stood side-by-side as a green light scanned them. After a few seconds the door opened into an almost empty white room. A long rug led from the door they just came through to another one.

Both looked at the camera. It was hidden, but they knew roughly were it sat in the wall.

"Good evening, gentlemen." Jerry's voice rang in the room. "Ambassador Koine is waiting on the command floor, and Leader Kawka is already here."

The far door opened. Jordan and Scda made their way through the cave hallways. The chiseled rock gleamed with a smooth finish that closely resembled wood grain. Various office doors and glass windows marred the surfaces.

A bank of elevators lined the far wall, and stairs on both sides led down. They headed to the left. The stairs descended to a short landing that had glass doors on both sides.

The left door led to the command cab, and Jordan saw Jerry standing in the center, a microphone extending from his ear. Numerous manned stations and large screens displaying various forms of data lined the front of the cab. The staff, consisting of several races, zipped around the cab answering incoming calls and messages and transferring them appropriately.

Quietly, Jordan and Scda continued down to the command floor. In the middle of the room sat a double set of half circle tables that faced a wall of screens and holograms. Built-in computers marked the tables' smooth surfaces.

At one of the computer stations stood Leader Dars Kawka, of Force Grey Wolf. She appeared to be in the middle of a conversation she'd rather not be having with Ambassador Koine, who stood on the other side of the table. Jordan mentally chuckled at the thought of Ambassador Koine standing.

What made it funny was that the ambassador was just shy of four feet tall. With a race such as rolbrid, that was normal. He wore a kimono-type outfit that dragged slightly on the floor. His short, squat head was hairless. Other than that, his features were rather humanoid.

But Leader Kawka was a different story. The marselian stood about eight feet high with four arms; the lower two were much shorter than the upper set. Her short hair displayed an odd shade of green, but only those able to see the infrared spectrum could appreciate its actual color. On the rich-blue face, her two solid-black eyes must have given some hint that she had glanced at the entrance, because the ambassador turned to face the arrivals.

"Nice to see you again, Lord Haddox." Ambassador Koine's voice sounded like he was gargling broken glass. "I hope I'm not disturbing you at such a time."

"Not at all, ambassador." Not like they had much of a choice, Jordan thought as they quickly shook hands. "I hope we may be of assistance. You remember Commander Oj."

"But of course." The ambassador instinctively held out his hand, but Scda didn't move. Koine stared for a while until he took the offered hand back. Just then he remembered that shaking hands with a jexan could leave a person with a very bloody stub.

"Right...quite right. I forgot. Excuse me. How are we, commander?"

"As well as expected, ambassador." Scda's head gave a short nod.

Jordan placed one hand on the ambassador's shoulder and led him to the center of the room. "Sir, why don't we get ready as the others arrive?"

Koine kept looking over his other shoulder at Scda for a short while. Scda moved to take his seat and adjust himself for comfort. He then looked at Dars who sat down and returned a raised brow that transmitted the thought, *Here we go again.*

As Jordan and the ambassador neared the center of the room, Jordan turned around and looked up to Jerry, who was visible in the glass wall that covered the command cab. "Go ahead and drop the second table and give us a center desk."

The inner half-circle table sank into the floor and another short one rose about two feet in front of Jordan. Subtly, the floor around the desk rose as well, about two feet. Jordan nodded at Jerry for making the compensation for the ambassador's height.

"Thank you very much," the ambassador commented about his separate desk.

Jordan looked down at him. "Sir, do my people have all your data?"

"Yes they do. That Jerry is a very efficient person." Koine took his seat. "I wish I had a couple of him working for me. Say, you wouldn't want to—"

Koine's voice trailed as everyone's attention shifted to the entrance. The person entering just had that kind of presence.

Though shaded faintly white, he mostly remained invisible. The armless, legless shape assumed a somewhat humanoid appearance but seemed to fluctuate as it glided along the floor. The figure moved three feet into the room, then halted and made a deep bow.

"Behalf of Grand Master Hiom, apologize he currently unavailable." The voice wailed like a faint air raid siren.

"That's quite all right," Jordan replied then turned to Koine. "Ambassador Koine, this is Master Holly from House Bravo."

The ambassador stiffened, then forced himself to say...something. "Good to meet...you." Koine slightly tilted his head to the left and just stared.

Holly then floated to his chair next to Dars. As a member of a still widely unknown race, Holly became familiar with such responses and ignored them. They joined a long list of strange things to which Holly had grown accustomed, much like his name. Holly's true name could only be properly represented as a telepathic thought, so he just chose the spoken name of Holly because he liked the sound of it, not because he cared one way or another for the name itself.

"Excuse me, sir," Jerry's calm voice sounded in the room. "Dragoon W'Lowe just called in and said he'll be running a little late and would like for you to go ahead with the meeting."

"Very well." Jordan shifted his gaze from the command cab windows to Koine. "If you don't mind, ambassador."

"Ah," Koine started, still in a little shock after seeing what he would simply call a ghost. But he quickly regained his composure. "Yes, let's begin. We have much to discuss."

Chapter 4

Jordan quietly took the chair at the center of the larger semi-circular desk. He briefly looked at Dars and Holly on his left, then glanced at Scda on his right and the empty chair at the far end of the table. Then the lord began the meeting.

"Ambassador Koine, how may the Dragon Corps be of assistance to your people?"

Koine's gregarious demeanor gave way to absolute solemnity. He rested his arms on his desk and leaned forward. Now on the raised platform, he could look almost everyone in the eyes. Scda, with his extra height, was one exception. Holly didn't have any eyes.

The ambassador's serious gaze glided from one attendee to the next. "Most of you have met me before. We've had a few dealings with pleasing results, but this gathering is much different, I'm afraid."

The ambassador paused, letting the last phrase soak into the room. Jordan, Dars and Scda all had a not-so-fond familiarity with Koine's flair for melodramatic presentations and still expected to hear about a standard border skirmish.

After the quiet held for a while, Koine continued.

"Unlike past occasions when I've come to you representing my people, I now come as a sole representative acting on behalf of the entire Korac Council."

That statement rattled the members noticeably. Scda made a short clicking sound, and Jordan's eyes widened slightly as he leaned forward. Dars folded both sets of arms and leaned back, and a ripple shot through Holly, who had just realized this situation probably required greater attention to detail than he had originally believed.

A tense silence filled the room and Koine knew he had their attention. With that secured, he now continued with *his* meeting.

"I consider you my friends; therefore, I'm going to be completely frank with you." Koine shifted his weight from one arm to the other. "All these minor missions I've come to you with in the past were arranged tests."

Jordan squinted his steel-grey eyes, and his jaw muscles rippled as he clenched his teeth.

"Unfortunately," Koine continued, "it was necessary. The Korac Council doesn't completely trust the Corps yet, especially with the information I'm about to present. Though we partnered with the Federal Kingdom to create the Dragon Corps, we still like to keep our business ours.

"The Council chose me many years ago to test you. We needed to know if you could truly be trusted if, in the future, we may have need to share with you some of our most secure secrets. Judge for yourself the outcome of those tests."

Koine paused again as he shifted his gaze from one person to the next, always having a problem keeping his sight on Holly for any longer than a second. He then pushed himself from the desk and hopped down to walk in front of it, looking up to the command cab.

"Jerry, start the program."

Jerry, mesmerized by the conversation below, shook himself back to attention, pushed a controller from her panel and started typing commands.

The room's hologram projectors centered on the middle of the room and came to life. As the three-dimensional pixels aligned, a rotating bust became visible. The being had a rather humanoid head with very rough brownish-orange skin that seemed to lie in layers. Dual pupils dotted two iris-less green eyes that sat deep in the skull, and mossy-green bony plates covered the top, back and side portions of the head. The lips were split down the center in such a manner that they appeared to be four. The bottom split in the lips merged into a ridge of skin that ran down the chinless neck.

The only mar on an otherwise perfect piolanese face was a blackened circular pattern on the right cheek. The dark pattern mirrored the appearance of a laser pistol blast at close range, because a laser pistol at close range had caused it.

Most had heard the rumors of how the assassin who failed in that attempt spent the next five months in a living hell of torture, much to the pleasure of the being who was supposed to have been the victim. When the torture became boring and he couldn't get any more information from the assassin, he ordered the surgical removal of the would-be assassin's memories while alive, no anesthesia. Doctors then sifted through the retrieved tissue to salvage any possible information the assassin held back. It soon led to the capture and torture of four others.

Everyone on the command floor recognized the face floating in the middle of the room, and Koine knew it. That was why he said nothing as he paced back and forth on his platform. Jordan killed the silence by quietly saying the name "Horwhannor."

That was the cue the ambassador wanted.

"From House Hakkon, Horwhannor was promoted as a senior representative to the Council of Houses approximately fifty years ago. Please excuse me for being blunt, but Horwhannor was one of our best warriors. His sharp mind almost put an end to the Federal Kingdom. Toward the end of the Twin Quasar War, everybody got to know Horwhannor as one of the greatest combat tacticians of all time."

The Dragon Corps members at the long table started seeing a side of the ambassador they never knew existed. He appeared now more as a methodical leader and dedicated patriot than a second-rate politician. For Jordan this meant Koine was more dangerous than he had ever expected.

The hologram started flipping through footage of Horwhannor's press conferences and meetings with other leaders and patriots. The images matched the ambassador's speech.

"For forty years, Horwhannor served our government well. With the war over, he retired from the senior staff. He was still respected by the Council and remained in close confidence. Horwhannor continued to serve by running mining operations, construction factories and training facilities for the Council's military.

"With the universe changed, the Council childishly thought its leaders would change, too. There was no doubt that Horwhannor was patriotic, but the Council misunderstood exactly how devoted a patriot he really was."

Koine shifted his eyes to the room's entrance where Dragoon W'Lowe entered. Cold looks from the table grabbed his attention. Jordan's brow sat low and curled at the ends, and he shot W'Lowe a look that said "sit down and shut up." W'Lowe did as silently instructed.

Normally, Jordan didn't mind if someone was late, especially when it was a meeting with the likes of Ambassador Koine, but this wasn't the same ambassador he thought he knew. Call it a bad feeling, but he disliked the direction of this meeting and definitely wasn't enjoying the ride.

W'Lowe took his seat before he saw the holographic pictures of Horwhannor. When he saw them, he shot a wide-eyed look to Scda on his left.

The ambassador noticed. "May I continue, Dragoon W'Lowe?"

W'Lowe didn't expect such a stern voice from Koine. *What the hell is going on?* he thought.

"Well?" Koine's impatience was evident.

W'Lowe started to stutter but soon grabbed on to the only thing he could. "Nothing, sir, please continue. I apologize for my late arrival and for interrupting."

Koine didn't acknowledge the apology but just continued.

"That was a mistake the Council regrets terribly. Ten years ago, he disappeared."

The ambassador paused again. Dars made a hand gesture as if about to ask, "How is it possible that his disappearance was kept secret?" Koine quickly countered the unspoken question with an answer.

"As I said, the Council keeps its secrets to itself. We all know who Horwhannor is because of the war, but have you seen him in the news in the past ten years?"

He loved his pauses; Koine only broke this one by continuing to pace back and forth on the raised platform. The hologram went back to the bust.

"We knew he was one of our best tacticians but never thought he would turn against us. That's the last thing we expected, so we began searching for him as a missing person. Maybe it was abduction, a *successful* assassination; no one knew. We were expecting anything from a ransom message to a body showing up in some space wreckage. But—" Koine's voice became remorseful as his hand firmly landed on top of his small desk. He had the rapt attention of everyone in the room. His eyes seemed to disappear as his face grimaced in a rolbrid response of trying to hold back anger. "We weren't expecting this."

The holographic projection switched to the vision of countless space vehicles in the midst of a nebula of some sort. They were of Korac Council design and appeared to be conducting battle maneuvers.

"At about the same time Horwhannor disappeared," Koine continued, "most of our Eighth Space Force also disappeared. They were training in the Stagenisis cloud. Among them was the Trioki."

The hologram shifted briefly to a schematic of the Trioki. The massive Envoy class ship toted a wide array of heavy cannons and could carry six complete wings of spacecraft, several battalions of ground troops and an entire regiment of mechanized forces.

"Another one of our best. We started producing these at the end of the war." Koine kept referring to the war but caught himself this time and shifted his comments back to the subject at hand. "In the middle of the Eighth's exercises, we stopped receiving transmissions from them."

Once again, the hologram shifted to a view of the same cloud; this time, debris sprinkled the area.

"When our rescue squadron made it, this was all we found. Among the remains was the training footage you saw. No one could explain it, but we weren't without our theories. Computer glitch on the new ship caused mass fratricide? Maybe the cloud had an unexpected flux and just obliterated the fleet? But we were certain the entire force was in pieces."

Another pause gave time for the picture to change to some kind of bridge. People moved about in Korac uniforms tending to their jobs.

"Welcome to the Ranklin." Koine pointed to the hologram. "A mobile battle station, the Ranklin was able to relieve a Dragon Corps fleet in the area and take over the mission of protecting Umo Bakanu, one of our agricultural planets, from constant raids." The ambassador didn't wait or ask if anyone remembered it. "They had only been there for about three months, but they were doing a great job stopping all attempts to raid the planet. Most of the raiders just stopped trying.

"Keep in mind this was about a year after Horwhannor and the Eighth Space Force disappeared."

Koine stopped to lean against the desk and watch the hologram play.

Suddenly, flashing blue lights filled the bridge on the hologram, and beings of various Korac races started scrambling about.

"Commander," a definite sense of urgency filled the attendant's voice as he turned around to the being who stood in the center, "we've got what looks like an entire fleet massing out of intraspace, eight thousand seven hundred miles out, north southeast sector thirty-four point five by seventy-eight. And more keep appearing every second!"

"Batcon One. Launch all squadrons. Get sector command on the comm." The commander barked the orders as he walked to the edge of the bridge.

The blue lights stopped, and the walls of the spherical room seemed to disappear as the bridge's holographic battle systems kicked in. The bridge now appeared to float in space, in orbit around the planet, but a faint outline of the station remained visible.

"Rotate on that point."

Space moved around the bridge to bring the massing point in front of them. When it did Scda pushed against the table as not to lose his balance on his chair. Most jexans suffered from severe vertigo.

Now the station's fighters began appearing as they launched from their bays. Beyond them were tears in space that appeared as massive lighting bolts flashing in frantic patterns.

"What the hell?" the commander yelled. "Friend or foe, people?"

"We're getting nothing, sir. They're almost within firing range, and we're getting nothing. Scanners aren't locking. I can't even tell if they're receiving our transmissions. I'm not detecting a spike, and the dimensional frequencies are silent."

The fighters now formed a cloud surrounding the station.

"Heavens be with us; I don't like what I'm seeing. That was not a spike like I've ever seen. Ideas anyone?"

"Seven thousand miles," one of the attendants gave an update.

"It didn't look anything like a spike, more like someone tore a hole in space," another replied. "I would guess they're not a known enemy or friend."

The commander stared at nothing while walking back to the center of the bridge. "As long as I'm not alone."

"Six thousand miles."

"Fire at will," the commander barked.

The darkness of space gave way to a multitude of lights from the fighters and the massive cannons of the battle station. Numerous missiles launched from the station and joined in the barrage sailing toward the oncoming fleet.

Oddly, the approaching ships didn't return fire; then it became apparent why. The shots seemed to fizzle into non-existence when they reached about a hundred miles from the fleet. The missiles, meanwhile, hit and exploded against the invisible wall. The spectacle shocked everyone, on the station and in the fighters, to the point that they stopped firing, and the darkness of space consumed the scene again.

"I'm not reading a shield, sir. Hell, I'm only reading an arrival. I can't pickup anything else. I don't like this!"

"Welcome to the battle," he retorted. "Open the gates!"

The barrage resumed, ending in nothing more than bolts and missiles crashing into the barrier. Suddenly, cannon fire from the station stopped.

"Ready, commander," an attendant said.

"Give them hell!"

Three massive lasers shot from the station and peaked at a point thirty miles out. At the sight, the fighters cleared a path as a spark jumped from the center of the station to the apex. Suddenly a chaotic blue stream writhed from that point and whipped its way toward the enemy fleet. At times the stream spouted vents of purple fire as it cut a swath through space.

It slammed against the invisible wall and appeared to be getting nowhere until it flared and purple fire started caressing the shield's surface. Then with a loud crack of lightening, the shield visibly dissipated in a shroud of sparkling lights.

The writhing bolt stopped, and thc bridge crew cheered.

"Composure people," barked the commander. "It's not over; we —"

Just then, the center vessel—the largest of the approaching fleet—took on the appearance of a mushroom exploding its spores. But these weren't spores; they were fighters, a thick blanket of fighters—at *least* twice as many fighters as the station could muster on a *good* day. This wasn't a good day, by far.

The enemy vessel held its position too far out to make any details, but its identity was now too clear to both the bridge crew of the doomed battle station and the Dragon Corps members watching at the meeting.

The bridge commander stumbled over the words but whispered, "The Trioki?"

The Trioki's fighters began returning fire.

"Power returned," a station attendant said. "Beginning firing sequence." The station's regular cannons joined in the multi-colored battle. "Cells will be charged in four minutes."

"What the—" The commander watched one of the oncoming fleet's smaller battleships turn broadside to better provide cover fire for the fighters. Then he squinted and walked to the edge of the bridge again. "It looks like—there's a Hakkon crest on that destroyer!"

Just then a pinpoint of white light from the Trioki grew until it swallowed the bridge, and the hologram on the Dragon Corps' command floor fell upon itself. Pixels bounced around like rubber balls then disappeared.

Chapter 5

"Once again, that footage was the only thing that could be salvaged by our rescue squadron." Koine straightened from the leaning stance he had assumed and resumed pacing along the top of the platform.

"The House Hakkon crest." Koine tightened his thin lips, and they seemed to disappear into his flat head. "That bit of information irritated the Korac Council because things started becoming unpleasantly clear. We were being attacked by one of our own, one of our most trusted.

"The Council dove into Horwhannor's past. We needed everything we could gather to get him. But we didn't like what we found, what we overlooked before. It was so obvious this time."

The desk computers came to life in front of each person sitting at the curved table. Holographic screens at each station began listing line after line of data.

"He undermined the Council on almost all levels," the ambassador explained. "When he was in charge of mining, the accounts reflect missing resources, possibly reallocated to an unknown location. When in charge of weapon destruction in accordance to the Barguth Treaty, there were forged destruction certifications. It's all there, everything we found."

"And you expect us to believe you?" Jordan asked angrily, expressing the thought shared by the other commanders. "You just admitted to lying to us!"

"I understand your trepidation, Lord Haddox. I don't blame you, but please believe me when I tell you that our friendship was not false. I grew to respect this organization; ergo, I'm presenting you with this information. This is a dark stain on the Council, so dark that we've kept this from our citizens.

"We are a proud people, and much of that pride comes from Horwhannor's victories. That traitorous bastard must be caught." Koine began grinding his teeth and grabbing his torso tightly with folded arms.

"Otherwise a liability," Holly finished the thought in his wailing voice.

The ambassador stared at the phantom this time. "Yes," he grunted as if not wanting to admit it.

"He's got one of your most powerful fleets and possibly a mobile staging point with that fancy battle station of yours," Dars piped in. She added with a mild smirk. "With the right move he could have another government declare war against the Korac Council or, worse yet, start taking down the very government he once served."

Koine slammed his hand down again. "Stop stating the obvious."

"Okay, calm down." Jordan reasserted his composure and stood to get the others to focus on his calm demeanor. "This doesn't look good to any of us, but let's look at it piece by piece."

Jordan sat down and turned off the computer in front of him. "From what you say, ambassador, Horwhannor has been on a rogue journey for nine years. No one's seen him?"

"Well...not exactly." Reluctance filled Koine's voice. "One of our search wings reported that they might have found the fleet, but shortly after it massed out of intraspace, we lost its signal. Oncc again, only wreckage remained. This time, though, we didn't even find a ship's log intact."

"Chalk up one more wing for Horwhannor," Dars snapped.

The comment generated a joint ugly glare from Koine and Jordan. Dars sat back and half closed her eyelids into vertical daggers of darkness.

"Since I trust all the information the Korac Council has on Horwhannor is now in our hands, we will begin our investigation." Jordan walked around the table as he spoke. "But before we do, what is the Council's wish on Horwhannor's terms of arrest?"

Koine stared through Jordan with another cold, methodical look. "If you are able to kill him without leaking a word and provide proof of his death to the Council, do so, *immediately*. He'll just disappear for good, and in the history books he will always be remembered as a great leader who mystically vanished."

"Very well." Jordan now stood next to Koine on the platform. He looked down at the ambassador while raising his arm toward the room's entrance. "If you don't mind, we have a lot to talk about."

"Yes, I suppose you do."

The platform lowered, and Koine walked to the door. An escort stood nearby waiting to show the ambassador to his shuttle.

Koine stopped and turned to face Jordan, who remained in the center of the room. "Once again, I apologize for my earlier deception. I hope you see it was necessary for the Council to trust you. And you did, indeed, earn that trust." Koine returned to the entrance and disappeared through the door.

Jordan sat on the small desk, looked first at the floor and then up to the command cab. "Are we secure?"

"Yes," Jerry replied.

"Okay." Jordan began immediately. "This isn't going to be easy. Possibility one, we still have a lot of raiding going on, and we haven't found traces of most of the raiding parties. Horwhannor could be joy riding. Possibility two, he could be in Miica Vurdoo; he seems to be the type who would like—"

"Excuse me," interrupted W'Lowe. He didn't want the discussion to get too far off track. "You may not believe this, but we may already know where he is."

That got everyone's attention, and they kept their eyes on him, waiting for more information.

"I received a call right before this meeting from Knight Lyon Kendrick, who's currently assigned to Terra Four."

The mention of that planet stopped Jordan cold, and he pushed away from the desk and stood straight.

W'Lowe tapped the holographic screen jutting up from the table. "Connect to Sherri."

After a couple of seconds, the female voice of his computerized secretary replied. "Yes, Dragoon W'Lowe."

"Retrieve the data that Knight Kendrick sent. Single out the weapons information and display it on the wall."

The room's hologram projectors shifted and the schematics and data came to life for everyone in the room to see. Outlines of the weapons rotated as the word "Destroyed" appeared in the lower right.

"He found these weapons on Terra Four. As you can tell, they were supposed to be destroyed. Something tells me that was supposed to happen when Horwhannor was commanding the facility." W'Lowe shifted toward Scda, who he knew would be a step ahead.

"Correct," Scda commented while scrolling through the data they just gained from the ambassador.

The emotion in the room was an odd mixture of ecstasy in having such a good lead and pure bewilderment as to the source of the lead's origin.

"Why Terra Four?" Jordan let the rhetorical question hang in the air.

"Isn't that supposed to be your home planet?" Dars asked, directing the question to Jordan and W'Lowe.

"We don't know yet," replied W'Lowe. "The planet's description does match our legends, but so do the descriptions of six other planets. Kendrick only knows about three others, but he's convinced. Regardless, we can't tell the Korac Council."

Dars raised her larger right arm in a swinging motion to help drive her point. "Hello? If Horwhannor is poking around Terra Four, why haven't the p'tahians wiped his forces out?"

"Advanced technology." Holly's words floated across the room.

"Possibly," Scda agreed. "That spike and shield demonstrated unknown technology. The p'tahians might not be able to detect the fleet; the Ranklin couldn't."

"Sure, and maybe the p'tahians will free all seven systems without a question asked," Dars blurted. "That whole race is full of supreme nuts. They're always patrolling their borders looking for a fight. They wouldn't wait two seconds to start wiping out the entire Korac Council if they found one of Horwhannor's ships poking around one of their planets. They're war crazy."

"You did say Horwhannor might want to use the captured fleet to start a war."

Jordan's statement gave Dars something to think about.

"What about storming the system? If we take Horwhannor quickly enough, maybe they'll see we're trying to eliminate their 'infection' for them." W'Lowe tossed the idea out, knowing it didn't have a chance.

So the lord shot it down.

"No." Jordan waved his hand. "This is too delicate. Dars is right; they are nuts. We have to be certain of Horwhannor's location before we do anything."

"Exactly," Holly's wailing voice drew attention. "Too many risks to charge now. Know exact moves."

Scda briefly extended an arm to rap on the desk. "We must also think about what that space armada might do after Horwhannor's death. It is a martyr we might create."

With that last thought banging around his brain, Jordan walked around the table to his seat. The needs of the Korac Council were straightforward, but he didn't want the Corps doing more damage than good. For him, Terra Four itself was more important than completing this mission. It was an illogical thought, and he knew it. At the same time, he couldn't shake it.

Terra's more valuable than the Korac Council's ego, Jordan thought. But if Horwhannor was polluting the planet, Jordan might have to break contact protocol just to save it. The burden of leadership was heavy, but Jordan planned to keep both sides happy.

"Connect us with Knight Kendrick." Jordan didn't look at anyone when he spoke, but Jerry went to work. "I will control this. For now, Kendrick only needs to know the information I'm going to give him."

Everyone quietly agreed.

The hologram on the wall came to life with a face that was strange to everyone in the room. It was the rough face of a terran wearing a smoky-grey golf cap, half of an unlit cigar held tight in the teeth and a chin marked with a five o'clock shadow from two days ago.

"Mac, here." The cigar flipped up and down as the face spoke.

"Yes." Jordan gave W'Lowe an interesting look. "This is Lord Haddox; is Knight Kendrick there?"

In a smooth but fast transition, Mac's face changed to his standard featureless, yet humanoid, silver face. Then Mac made a note to learn better when to goof around and when not to. Then he forgot the note. "Yes, sir. Stand by."

Mac's face disappeared, replaced with a view of Lyon rolling out of bed and rubbing his eyes as he stood. Lyon looked down at the screen and blinked, unbelieving, at seeing the command floor with representatives from each branch. He noticed Dragoon W'Lowe but quickly shifted his gaze toward Jordan.

"At your service, my lord."

"As always." Jordan gave a reassuring reply. "Please, sit down."

Lyon did just that as Jordan continued.

"I understand you have an interesting situation on Terra Four. Quite unexpected, but while we are together, how can we help?" Jordan rocked back on his seat.

Lyon took a deep breath to clear his head and began his answer.

"As I'm sure you already know, I haven't fully established the station here. Mac was experimenting with this planet's artificial satellite systems. He was testing how much he could manipulate them. His success was greater than expected.

"About a week ago we started noticing some yofeeti transmissions. Oddly, the transmissions only went one way, from space to the planet. Mac was damn lucky to even notice them. It took us a couple of days to pinpoint a location. Following each transmission, a sub-nuclear flux appeared at that location but faded in about four hours.

"During my initial investigation, some of my equipment failed, which got me noticed. I was chased by an alien guard, who I had to kill. Then I was shot at with a Gortek laser and a Quazi particle cannon. Before I killed the last terran, he said he was armed with these weapons from a native organization; we're investigating the name."

A rustling sound filled the command floor as people shifted in their seats.

"Also," Lyon continued, "we later deciphered life signs, and a piolant remained behind in the warehouse."

"Quite an interesting situation you have there, Kendrick." Jordan tapped his fingers on the desk before him. *Horwhannor is piolanese; he may have lieutenants doing some dirty work on Terra Four.* "You would like to lead an investigation?"

"Well—" Lyon was caught a little off guard. "If you wish, my lord. Yes, I would like to request a lightly armored scout team."

Lyon didn't see an immediate response and doubted he would have his request filled. Even though he would love to have peace return to his station, he missed combat.

"Done," Jordan's simple reply hung in the air for a while, "but with a few modifications. We'll send some slightly heavier firepower, since you appear to be dealing with weapons smugglers. I'm not going to send a count; you take the lead on this one. Continue to report to Dragoon W'Lowe. I will replace the count with an extra person from House Bravo. It is extremely important to keep low as long as possible."

"Understood, my lord."

"Very well," Jordan said. "I have confidence in you. Find out where those weapons are coming from, and shut the source down. If possible, do it without compromising the planet, but keep Dragoon W'Lowe apprised of any changes."

The other occupants at the table didn't like the amount of information Jordan withheld. They felt Lyon needed as much information as possible to do the job well.

"I'm sure you have a requirements list worked out already."

Lyon gave a quick nod.

"Good, then send it to the Cube, and we'll get you that team as soon as we can."

"As you wish, my lord."

The hologram sparkled into nothing, and the room went quiet.

Eyes followed Jordan as he stood. His furrowed brow appeared heavy again with the weight of leadership.

"I didn't like that any more than you did." Jordan's arms crossed his chest. "I don't like this entire situation. We're missing something, and I hope Kendrick can find it. We must find out what Horwhannor is doing with that space armada and exactly were it is before we take him out."

"While covering your ass," Dars fired back.

Doubt appeared on Jordan's face as he thought about that while heading for the door.

Jordan couldn't bring himself to acknowledge Dars' observation. Instead he just stopped short of the door. "Keep me updated."

Dars began to debate but stopped herself. Then Jordan disappeared through the exit.

The remaining four stared at each other for a while, collectively sharing a thought none of them wanted. Finally they broke and headed to their shuttles preparing to take the actions needed.

Chapter 6

In an explosion of light, the sun slipped past the moon. The rays began refracting in the atmosphere, playing color games with the sky. At first, the sky would appear as bright purple with tints of red scattered around the clouds. Then, it would blast into neon yellow tiger stripes with orange trim.

The spectacular sunset went unviewed by the being meditating on a stone ledge, but he felt it. He also absorbed the essence of the forest below the cliff as it responded to the rapid sunset. Three elaborately crafted stone pillars surrounded him, helping him gain the concentration needed to blend his mind with nature itself.

With his feet folded under him and his arms resting on his lap, he remained motionless except for an occasional rise in his chest. It took him about two minutes to complete the link this time. After constant practice, he would soon have it down to mere seconds.

Roaming mentally through the ebb and flow of nature, he stopped every so often to more closely feel a part of it, such as when a plant closed for the night. He joined a small primate swinging back and forth on a branch in an attempt to reach some fruit. When the primate succeeded, it leapt to the ground and scurried away with the prize.

But nothing was more exhilarating to him than being able to see through an avian's eyes. Drifting above the clouds, he enjoyed the sensation of rising, lowering and dodging the fluffed vapor as the wind gusted about.

"Hitook, I need your attention now."

The thought pierced his concentration, and his link broke as the feel of nature's force began to fade away. His long, slender ears swayed as he turned to look behind him. There, floating about three feet above the ground, was a four-armed, legless torso wrapped in a red cape. The long head that sat directly on top of the body bore four eyes that peered at Hitook.

"There is a call for you," the small man said. "It's Grand Master Hiom. He wishes to speak to you."

"Yes, Master Gon."

Hitook held out his massive arms parallel to the ground as he slowly rose from the ground. He then lowered his thick legs until their oversized feet struck the ground with slapping thuds.

"It's good to see you constantly studying," Gon commented.

Hitook stretched to his full eight-foot height, brushed his fur-covered legs with pawed hands and followed his master back to the school. "I have to. It is the only way I will become as good as you, master."

Gon smiled as he floated next to Hitook. "How good you are is not to be judged against anyone else. We are all different; therefore, you must be judged by your own abilities, not against someone else's accomplishments.

"If the snake attempts to be as clever as the wolf, the snake is sure to fail. But if the snake tries only to be as clever as the snake, he will surely succeed. Remember that."

"Yes, master."

Hitook stepped up to the front door as his master glided next to him. The large beast became reverent as he stood next to the door, putting his paws behind him and dipping his head. Gon accepted the show of honor and drifted through the door.

Before he followed his master, Hitook untied some red cloth from around his left bicep and folded his ears down the nape of his neck. He then tied the cloth around his head to keep his ears back and together in what took the appearance of a ponytail.

As he ducked to enter the doorway, he caught the scent. His gaze whipped around the rear of the foyer to look into the massive meeting room.

Windows covered the far wall, and a large fireplace sat in the left wall. To the right, under the crossed twin hand blades positioned above the House Bravo shield, sat a slightly overweight rolbrid. The three and a half foot high being rocked in a chair and slowly rotated his bald head toward the white-furred beast entering the room.

"Grand Master Hiom," Hitook almost yelled. He quickly stood as straight as he could with his paws in front of his waist and head bowed. "Forgive me, for I was not expecting to see you in person."

"That's quite all right, Mif Riqhim." Hiom's rough rolbrid voice seemed to grind on Hitook's formal native title and last name. Acolytes like Hitook were rarely addressed by rank. "Relax. Please sit down."

Hitook slowly approached Hiom and sat on the floor in front of him. Gon drifted to the kitchen and returned with some herbal drinks and bread. Hiom nodded with pleasure, took a cup and started filling it.

"Mif Riqhim, you were expecting a video call, but what I have to say, I felt I have to say in person." Hiom sipped some of the drink then continued, commanding every bit of Hitook's attention.

"What I am about to say is classified Alpha Blue. About eight days ago, a knight discovered some abnormal yofeeti transmissions on a restricted planet. During an initial investigation, the knight found illegal weapons far beyond the planet's technology.

"The Corps is sending a team in to assist in a covert investigation. The planet has not been officially contacted, and we have to conduct this investigation without disrupting the planet's innocence."

Hiom reached for some bread and began to eat. Gon slid to the grand master's left side, and his legless body lowered to rest on the ground. Hitook's small nose twitched, sending his whiskers waving about. Then Hiom finished the slice of bread.

"I was unable to attend the meeting, but Master Holly chose you as a member of the team. I agree. I want you on this assignment."

"It would be my honor, grand master." Hitook bowed his head again. "But—"

"What is your doubt?" The grand master expected it.

Hitook gave a very worried expression for a second then it changed to concern. He stood and walked to the long window covering the one wall to view some twenty students training with their masters in the yard outside. Twelve years ago Master Holly tested Hitook in that same yard. Hitook felt he had failed, but Master Holly granted him admittance in House Bravo. Everybody seemed to approve of his progression, but Hitook had kept a feeling of inadequacy he'd never been able to shake.

The grand master watched Hitook and waited quietly.

"It—" Hitook stopped himself and turned to look at the grand master. "There are people more qualified than me to complete this mission. Why me, am I expected to fail?"

"Hitook!" Gon quickly reprimanded. "How dare you question—"

The grand master raised his hand, and Gon silenced.

"He has a good reason to question." Looking back at Hitook, he continued, "On the contrary. Even though it is your first assignment, your training has honed your skills to a point beyond anyone's expectations." Hiom paused for a moment remembering. "You even completed the art of *lho gin vi* in three weeks, when it took me two months, once a record."

Hiom returned to enjoying some of the herbal drink and bread.

"I do not believe I would fit in very well."

The fat rolbrid nodded in agreement. "But you are nonetheless perfect for the mission. I am also sending Ninja Ky Adian; she will assist you. You will be the first liqua to be sent on a Corps mission."

Hitook's brow lowered. "What about my brother?"

The grand master jiggled as he laughed and placed his drink on the table. "Your brother is giving the Harquebus a devil of a time. He has yet to learn how to control his rage as you have, still refusing to join meditation sessions. Since he has remained too unpredictable, he has never been sent on a mission yet."

Hitook looked out the window again to watch the sparring. Gon gave Hiom a look of concern, but Hiom's returned a silent reply, *He will be all right.*

"Well, enough talk here; we must be going." Hiom pushed himself from the chair, stood with a rocking motion and stared up at Hitook.

Hitook felt the look. "Do you mean I am to go now, grand master?"

"Time flees too quickly to be wasted. You will be completely equipped when you meet the others." Hiom started toward the door.

"It was nice to see you again, Pytin," Gon said as he rose in the air to see his old friend to the door.

"You still have a way with herbs, Kio." Hiom patted Gon on the shoulder. "Do not worry; you have trained him well."

Gon nodded. Hiom returned it.

Hiom walked out the door as his shuttle landed. He then peered back at Hitook, "Let's get going, my liqua friend."

Hitook faced the door then blinked as if trying to wake from a dream. It wasn't helping.

Gon floated to Hitook. "You must be going."

Hitook's light trance lasted one moment more, then he snapped out of it. "Farewell, master. I'll be back soon." Then he nodded.

Gon stopped Hitook with a hand. "We will see each other again, but right now, you have a long journey that lies before you."

"What do you mean, master?"

"He's right," Hiom interrupted. "Let's go."

Gon lowered his hand as Hitook followed Hiom to his vehicle. The grand master answered the question. "Journeys are more like destinies. Don't fight destiny. Seize it; make it your own."

The shuttle door slid open and Hiom stepped in and took his seat. Hitook took the seat next to him as the door closed.

Hiom leaned forward and spoke to the driver. "Back to the temple."

"Yes, grand master." The driver guided the shuttle into the sky.

Hiom's attention then returned to Hitook. The liqua's face showed signs of worry again. The grand master wanted much to tell Hitook everything he knew, but Lord Haddox was specific about what the team would know.

It wasn't just that, though. Being a rolbrid, his race formed part of the Korac Council. This caused many feelings in Hiom to surface about the traitorous Horwhannor, but the grand master kept those thoughts private. Regardless, this mission was important, and Hiom was sure that Hitook would become an essential part.

"The journey will be long." Hiom folded his arms and noticed Hitook facing him. "Do not be anxious. Your destiny will reveal itself in due time."

The phrase hung in the air of the shuttle, and no one spoke for the rest of the trip.

Chapter 7

Julie clung tightly to the tree limb. From within her black cat suit, only her almond-shaped, coal eyes glinted in the moonlight. They were sharp and tuned to movement in the shadowed forest twenty feet below. Her clever opponent was creating quite the challenge.

Where are you? The question filled her thoughts. Then came the answer.

In a split second, Julie saw it out of the corner of her eye as it left a concealed bow. She rolled back from the limb and flipped to the ground. The arrow stuck in timber with a sharp twang.

I hate archers. The thought surfaced again as it had every time she confronted one.

"You're getting slow," the female attacker's voice taunted from the trees. "The next one will be true."

Julie's eyes closed to slits of ebony. "Don't bet on it."

Suddenly, both started darting about the shadows with only the slightest rustle of leaves whispering from the woodland floor to mark their passing. Both were dressed head to tail in black but appeared as blurs as they disappeared in and out of shadows. Each combatant's weapon hung from it owner's body but blended into part of the fluid motion.

From ground to treetop, it was a frantic but quiet chase.

Finally, Julie evaded the assailant. Waiting behind a tree she paused for a second to catch her breath. She peered around the tree to see the archer's silhouette squatted on the tip of a limb eight feet up, a tail dangling and swaying slowly.

Pulling the assailant from her perch with a painful yank on her tail would be too easy. That didn't keep Julie from thinking about it for a moment. The swish of the tail made it extremely tempting. But the thought made Julie's own tail ache. Instead, Julie smiled with the thought of a new plan, then whipped into action.

With fluid movements, Julie darted from around the tree, pounced ten feet into the air, unsheathed her battle sword and flipped in the air to provide momentum. Her blade bit into the tree and shattered the limb where the archer crouched.

The archer screamed, then hit the ground face first, forcing out a muffled grunt.

Julie bounced off the ground toward another limb. Her tail whipped around to grip the sword's hilt as she grabbed the limb with both hands, swinging up and landing squatted on the branch. Facing the victim on the ground, she uncoiled her tail to wield the sword in her hands again and leapt at the attacker in a stance to pierce the body's center.

The plan went sour when the archer snapped a back flip, leapt to the nearest limb then swung to another. The archer stood on top of the limb, bent her knees and placed a hand against the trunk. She just remained there, motionless, watching and waiting to see what Julie would do next.

As Julie glided to the ground, she thought, *Great move.*

There was one flaw; the archer let her once slung crossbow come free and fall to the ground.

Julie landed, sticking the sword in the ground, grabbed the crossbow and raised it to her shoulder.

Quickly targeting the archer, Julie released the bolt.

Once the bolt pierced the air with a slight whine and reached its target, nothing seemed to move except for a slight twitch in the archer's shadow.

Shaking the crossbow in the air, Julie jumped around in her victory dance and began to mock the archer. "You were right; the next one was true," she laughed.

"Not true enough."

"What!?" Julie stopped jumping and stared at the shadow.

"As matter of fact, I would even call it one hell of a bad shot," the archer mumbled. Through the moonlight, the archer's smooth-red lips formed a smile showing the bolt held tightly in slightly elongated canines that gleamed in a ray of light.

Julie couldn't believe it.

The archer made the most of Julie's shock, using the brief pause to spring from the limb and slam Julie to the ground. Julie lost her grip on the crossbow as it flew twelve feet away.

Now the archer held a dagger in her right hand, Julie's throat in the other.

"Beep, beep, beep."

The archer stopped; everything went quiet.

"Beep, beep, beep."

Julie strained through the pressure on her throat. "Shouldn't you get that?"

The attacker grunted, spat the bolt from her teeth and released her grip, but kept Julie pinned to the ground with her knees. "You're lucky."

The archer sheathed the dagger and pulled off her black hood. With a slight shake, her strawberry hair fell, gliding straight to tap the small of her back. The tips of her pointed ears peeked from the layers of flowing hair. She then lifted her left wrist phone. "Ky, here."

"Yes," a voice replied. "You are to report to Master Incana immediately."

"Message received."

Ky's emerald eyes looked down at Julie. "Sorry to have to cut it short." She stood and held out a hand for Julie. "Maybe next time. What's a sister for, right?"

Julie accepted the hand and got on her feet. She then removed her hood to reveal her deep black hair cut short enough to leave her small pointed ears fully visible. "What do you mean next time? I was about to turn the tables. I would've had you."

"You've said that before." Ky pulled the sword out of the ground and handed it to her birth twin. "You want to run back to the temple?"

Julie tapped the blade against her foot to knock off the dirt, then sheathed the sword. "Sure, I can always beat you in a run." Julie blasted away in a head start.

Ky tightened her thin brow and leapt for her crossbow. "That's because you cheat." Ky's reply faded as she sprang into an equally quick start.

The two tore through the heavy underbrush. Small tornadoes of leaves whipped around their feet as Julie soared along with Ky close behind. Ky could keep the distance, possibly, but she knew the chances of closing it were slim. Julie knew that as well; that's why she tried to remain focused in front of her.

The ravine. The thought flared in both minds.

Sixty feet deep and forty feet wide, it was about a quarter-mile ahead, but the bridge was at least a mile away. Meanwhile, they closed on the ravine fast. Julie wasn't about to slow down and lose any ground, and Ky had to keep going to take any available opportunity to narrow the distance.

There it was. The gaping maw of the ravine caused a visible gap to appear in the horizon of vegetation. No turning back; neither runner dared slow down. And neither wanted to head for the bridge and lose.

Ky brought the crossbow across her chest with her right arm. *This is crazy.* The thought didn't keep her from trying to time her left hand with the movement of her legs. With a quick flick, she pulled out a grappling bolt from her boot. *This is real crazy.*

Ah, hell, Julie thought. She drew the massive sword again and held it flat against her forearm.

The underbrush thinned as they approached the ravine at breakneck speed.

Ky whipped the new bolt into the crossbow and locked it in.

Julie scanned the ravine's edge to find the highest point; she chose the stump of a fallen tree. A leap, and Julie was airborne. With a flip, her legs pointed at the top of the stump.

Relaxed, her knees and ankles bent as she landed. Every muscle and tendon stretched, absorbing the kinetic energy. With a sudden release, Julie flung herself forward looking down at the ravine that now opened below, her tail flapping in the wind.

Just then, Ky's bolt sizzled through the air past Julie and toward the high treetops on the ravine's far end. As the bolt sailed, it uncoiled a cable still held secure to the bow.

Julie executed another flip as she crested her arch over the ravine. Her tail formed a circle in the air as she rotated to point her feet down and hold her arms up and wide.

The bolt struck home. Ky grabbed the crossbow with her left hand and flipped on the coiling motor. The cable twanged taut as Ky flew over the edge.

Julie wasn't going to make it. Close, but it was too far. She flung the battle sword down from its extended position and held it in front of her. Both hands joined in a tight grip on the hilt, and she locked her shoulders.

Pain exploded throughout her body as the blade bit into the hard earth that formed the wall on the far side of the ravine. Chunks of rock and packed dirt pelted Julie as her descent along the ravine wall slowed. She reached out to grip a passing protrusion from the wall. Nerves screamed as her body stopped about twenty-two feet from the top of the ravine.

Concentration reduced the pain. Julie yanked the sword from the rock and sheathed it. With all four limbs, she raced up the side as if gravity no longer worked against her.

Julie crested the rim just as Ky sailed overhead. Julie flung herself onto the top, then began running again.

Ky looked down, saw she was well past Julie now and thumbed the release switch. The cable whistled out of the crossbow as Ky slid to the ground. She hit, rolled forward and was back on her feet running.

"And you have the nerve to call me a cheat?"

Julie's comment just gave Ky a smile. Ky thought she had just made things even. Her sister should be happy.

The recent distraction of the ravine kept both from noticing the brook ahead.

Ky hit the water so fast its coldness didn't bite until she was half way across. Her pace tossed spouts of water everywhere.

In a flash Julie noticed the flailing water and applied some quick thinking to the obstacle.

Ky stood drenched and angry, the race forgotten. She was wet and pissed! Her hair now formed a solid, soaked strand that fell upon her neck and sent another cold shiver down her spine. Ky's thin brows came together to form one at the top of her nose, and her lips disappeared in a clenched mouth as she saw Julie leap over the embankment and prance on the tops of boulders penetrating the water's surface.

A pleased smile stretched on Julie's face.

Ky screamed a torrent of unrecognizable phrases as she kicked ferociously in the water. Meanwhile, Julie seemingly glided over the brook to land on the other side, dry.

Julie paused on the embankment to re-enact her victory dance with a loud chuckle. She knew it would just stoke Ky's anger, so she didn't stay long before she took off running again.

Ky was on her heels and screaming more unintelligible phrases. No one knew what they meant, not even Ky. Her anger just made her want to scream.

The forest began to lighten as the sisters, just feet apart, hopped over a fallen tree. Before they knew it, the tree line broke and gave way to a large field of grain.

Five feet high, the grain covered all but the runners' heads. Its sway mimicked an ocean as wakes split from the runners. On the far end of the field, a towering pyramid temple sat not far from an actual beach.

Their bobbing heads continued to sail on top of the grain sea. Still moving frantically, neither gained nor lost ground. The distance between them remained. The twins were always close competitors; that's why they liked to challenge one another.

In a light brown plume, both blasted from the edge of the grain onto a freshly cut grass field. Bent stalks of wheat trailed from the runners, their once black suits now speckled with tan flecks.

Both headed for the cobblestone walkway that led to the temple's entrance gate. A ten-foot wall stretched around the compound with its only arched opening marking the end of the stone path.

The twins used every last bit of their energy as they neared the race's finish. Their speed quickened, evenly. It was too close to call now.

Julie stretched her arms out as she hit the archway then leapt forward into a summersault, laughing. She landed and started her victory dance just as Ky barreled into her.

Dust clouded the area as the two rolled around in a flurry of tails. The rustling stopped, letting the dust settle, revealing Ky pinning Julie, face down, to the gritty ground.

Muffled, Julie's laugh blew small dust plumes from around her cheeks.

Hunched over her victim, Ky panted and let her anger growl into existence.

"Ky!"

Her breathing and growling stopped as she sat up.

"Finished!?"

She snapped her head to the side so fast that the clinging hair whipped in the wind as it flung over her shoulder to rest on her chest. Ky's emerald eyes disappeared in white as they widened.

"Master Incana!" Ky jumped to her feet, placed her legs together and pinned her arms to her side. Her tail tucked between her legs and coiled down her left calf.

Julie fumbled at first but soon joined her twin in the same pose.

From fifty feet away, a rather lanky being walked toward them. He sported two short legs but two very long and thin arms that were clasped behind his wide and long torso. As he moved, his blue robe glistened as if in rhythm to his continually blinking, three solid orange eyes. The tall and flat face appeared as marbled granite that had no visible nose or ears and featured a small mouth, which moved rapidly as he spoke.

"Done we are?" Incana now stood in front of them and looked down at them.

"Master Incana," Julie began, "I can explain—"

Incana silenced her with a raised hand of three elongated fingers.

Dust shook from Julie as she snapped her head back. The twins stood silent, keeping their eyes straight ahead and unfocused. They tried not to let the itchy dust get to them. Very little of their suits remained black through the new coat of patched brown-grey dust and specks of grain.

"All I wish of you two is an explanation." Separate eyes seemed to watch both. "But your explanations always rather confuse I."

The long arm fell to join the other behind Incana's back. His eyes now focused on Julie. "Go explain to Master Tidgato yourself and the damaged grain."

"Yes, master." Julie stepped back, turned around and walked toward the mill as her tail slowly uncoiled but stayed low to the ground.

Incana's other hand came around and delivered a data pad to Ky. She gazed at it briefly before accepting it.

"The Corps requires you." Incana turned sideways. "It is immediate."

For the first time, Ky's eyes focused on a shuttle parked in the temple's yard behind Incana. Next to it stood something she never thought she would see. For a while, people thought them extinct, another victim of the lawlessness that flourished after the war. She leaned to the right to get a better look.

Wow, she thought. Then before she knew she had engaged her vocal cords she said, "A liqua?"

"Yes," Incana replied calmly.

Ky straightened and became rather embarrassed when she realized she had said that aloud. Ky had heard of them but never saw one.

"He is Hitook Riqhim, an acolyte of Master Gon's."

She leaned out again and instinctively gave a smile. As if uncontrollably, her tail began to relax and uncoil itself. After all, it seemed cute, in a pet animal sort of way.

Hitook had been watching with much concern at the strange antics of the ninja. Now she smiled at him rather oddly. Just then he thought she seemed slightly attractive but debated whether she was actually attractive for her race or if it came from the coat of dust that gave her an appearance similar to fur.

Probably a mixture of both, he decided.

"Ky!" Incana grabbed her attention. "Grand Master Hiom specified that Hitook is still in training and to be sensitive of that."

Oh, great, she thought. Not only did she have a no-notice mission, but it came with a personal acolyte. Trainees bothered her. People who seemed unable to handle things themselves just bothered her.

"There is a meeting already planned on Dolphin Station. Ky?"

Incana's tone of voice drew her attention to his face. That's when she noticed his "What are you waiting for?" look, which was a challenge for a being without eyebrows.

Ky began walking toward the shuttle.

Hitook opened the shuttle's door and stood by quietly. As Ky approached, Hitook dipped his head out of respect. "Ninja Adian."

A shudder ripped through her at the formality. Ky struggled to keep it bottled. She tossed her crossbow in the shuttle and picked up her tail as she took a seat.

Hitook silently slid in the oversized seat behind her. He began to think he might have done something offensive.

The door slid shut on the vision of Ky concentrating too much on staring out the window. With crackling energy, the shuttle lifted, then veered over the wall and soared toward the atmosphere.

Incana turned away from watching the departure and strolled toward the temple shaking his head from side to side ever so slightly.

Chapter 8

Hunter Paloon Osluf repeatedly rapped his rough fingers against the throttle handle. *So far he's good, but I'll wait.*

The view from the droid's cockpit held nothing but trees and other scattered vegetation. High trees formed a tight canopy over the forest, but the early morning sun occasionally forced a beam between the cracks, streaking through the dense moisture that filled the air.

A bird flock darted to the treetops, sending an echoing rustle bouncing off the trees. Paloon slid his grey eyes in that general direction. A tree blocked his line of sight to the noise.

I've got him. The thought elated Paloon. *This is too simple, but rookies always did do stupid stunts.*

He took his hand off the throttle, and it glided over the control panel to tap a button. Shivers shot down his spine as the electric flow adjusted through the panel, which was magnetically sealed to the subdermal control jacks in his neck.

In a millisecond of thought, he called up a digital representation of the scene in front of him, and the computer responded with the calculations he wanted. There it was: an almost sixty-eight degree angle off the third trunk from the right. A line flashed on his retinas showing the trajectory. He focused on the trunk and fired a low-level sonic beam.

A smaller screen displayed the results in his upper left viewing area. Bingo. Solid droid shape. Weapon systems ready, grav engine in the blue, path set, three o'clock, eighty-nine yards.

Paloon called for the engines to tighten up, and they responded, slowly pushing at the ground, packing it tighter.

Now.

The four stubby engine cannons snapped toward the rear and whined. The ground roared as chunks of turf took flight. The droid shot forward, shedding its electrical cloak as the under turret rotated to the right. Paloon's right eye assumed the view down the turret's barrel. The engine cannons shifted forward and ripped up the ground in front, bringing the war machine to a halt; the turret locked and fired without hesitation.

The turret recoiled on its undercarriage. Streams of electricity crackled from the grav engine cannons pushing against the ground to compensate for the kick. The turret's barrel slammed forward and bashed another round as the left rear grav cannon split a nearby twenty-foot trunk.

"Eat death, rookie!" Paloon let the comment go over the radio. Two rounds were plenty, but with a shrug of his shoulder, a third volley streaked from the cannon. The silver capsule buzzed through the air and clanked against the object to join the other two rounds.

Electricity penetrated the air, forming a cloud of electrons around the area. As it dissipated, a large rock appeared where the droid should have been.

Oh, crap! Paloon knew his overconfidence now made him a target since he had waited around to watch the fireworks of the shells just sucking the electricity from each other.

"Look what I've got for teacher," a voice cracked over the radio.

Paloon threw his droid into overdrive. It shot forward, whipping back and forth through the trees.

The radio silence was broken again. "Where are you going, teach?"

Paloon messed up, and he knew it. Eight years in teaching droid tactics, and he screwed up by expecting Ihm Okliu to make a basic mistake like most recruits. Unlike most new troops to Force Grey Wolf, Ihm listened in class, and that stacked the odds against the teacher.

Paloon's head rocked between the padded brackets in the headrest as he slipped the droid between the trees, darting back and forth trying to keep Ihm from locking on. There it was. Five hundred yards ahead to the left rose a rather steep hill, meaning both of them would have to dart to the right.

The speed of the turret rotating to the rear was too slow to suit Paloon, and he became visibly agitated because of it. His plan would have to work.

He increased the altitude, three hundred feet to the hill. Ihm right on his tail.

Down and to the left—one hundred and fifty feet. Ihm held.

Paloon slid lower and to the right getting ready to move around the hill, fifty feet.

Bursts away. Doors on the bottom of Paloon's droid popped open as glowing red charges shot into the ground. Each fired upon impact, creating craters of different shapes and sizes across the terrain.

Paloon switched his left eye to the rear camera, hoping to see Ihm's droid slam into the ground.

But Ihm caught on to the ploy at the last second and shot upwards but almost lost it. As Ihm's droid hit the crater field, it rocked back and forth, its grav engines trying to compensate for the widely varying distances to the ground.

First the nose dipped, then suddenly the left side fell then the rear almost hit the ground. Ihm lucked out by getting enough altitude before hitting the trap.

Paloon's mind started racing. With the momentary lapse in Paloon's thought, his computer spoke in a rather calm voice, "You have been acquired."

Crack! Thoom! Thoom! Ihm's two side turrets released shells. Both slammed into Paloon's droid.

A shroud of electricity surrounded the ship. The panels started flickering, and Paloon's view went to static.

Paloon screamed as the feedback shot into his cranium and his powerless craft carved a trail in the dirt as it ground to a halt. Like a drunk, he fumbled for the pad on the back of his neck and pried if off.

With all of the electricity being sucked into the shells, the electromagnetic seal around the canopy gave way. As the glass rose, Paloon could faintly hear Ihm's droid as it flew past and slowed down to turn around.

Paloon's body was an internal wreck. He knew Ihm would be coming back, but he now felt like he hadn't slept for a week. Paloon fought to command his mind to do something, but he got little response. He slowly raised his head and attempted to see through half-lidded eyes.

He flopped his right hand over to a leg pocket and fumbled with its buttons. The pocket finally came open. His fingers began to fidget with a short, white tube he pulled from the pocket as he slowly placed it behind his right ear and slid it back and forth across his neck until it finally clicked over a data port. With a slight thrust, the tube slipped into the port.

Eyes shot wide open, and his body snapped rigid.

"Damn!" Then his muscles released. "I may have to change my pants."

Paloon threw himself out of the cockpit and slid down the side of the droid. He shoved his hand in the side of the craft, pulling open a panel to reveal a pack. He hastily grabbed the pack, ran into the woods mumbling, "They shouldn't make those damn boosters so strong," and then dove in some bushes.

Still, completely still. Paloon watched the searching craft slowly rustling the underbrush as it circled the downed droid, and sensor systems began scanning the area.

"Come on, hunter," the student sounded through his droid's address system. "You've lost. Let's go back so I can get something to drink, and you can take Jol out. She'll probably take you down as well." Ihm's laughter echoed for what seemed to be an entire minute.

Paloon took advantage of Ihm's attempted distraction. Ever so slowly, he slipped his hand into one of the backpack's pouches and selected a square device that rested nicely inside his palm.

"Where are you?" Worry began to slip into Ihm's voice. "Let's go; it's over."

Paloon clipped the square onto his belt then tapped it for activation. Two black gloves came out of the pack next. He slipped them on while watching the droid circle around. The radius increased in size with each pass.

Paloon closed the clasp on each glove, making sure they were lined with his sub-dermal pads. He activated the pads, and they magnetically snugged the gloves closer for a better data transfer. Then he placed one of the backpack's straps in his teeth and waited.

The searching droid came by for another pass as the predator remained still. He could almost see Ihm's face that time.

With the speed of a cheetah, he leapt into the air and clasped his hands on the nearby tree.

Hanging on by the gloves, he began to rapidly climb the tree. He preferred to have the boots as well, but he didn't have time to get them out of the pack yet.

About fifty feet up the tree, the instructor crouched on a wide branch and started digging in the backpack again while watching the student's movements.

"Hunter Osluf, are you even out there?" Ihm was audibly shaken. He began to think that maybe his teacher was thrown from the craft. "That's it; I going back for—"

"Class is not over, pup." Paloon transmitted with a radio he just clipped to his shoulder and jacked in. "Matter of fact, it's just beginning."

"Teach," Ihm exclaimed over the radio. "You're alive and still want to play. This *will* be fun." His voiced sounded better now that he knew he didn't have to explain a death to the elders.

"You didn't actually think you might have killed me, did you?" Paloon continued to pull items from the backpack and attach them to his uniform. "You either think very little of me or you're too cocky. It had better be the latter."

"But a lone man against an excellently piloted Centurion? Give up, teach."

"Correction, a Centurion piloted by a pup." Paloon's eyes grew very large as he saw the droid stop and begin to rotate in his direction. He threw himself off the branch toward another, grabbed on, then jumped to another and kept moving that way. With the matching boots on now, it made his prance through the treetops much easier.

Ihm stopped the droid in line to where Paloon had been a moment before and fired a stun laser that went off into the forest canopy, giving a distant tree a weird "asleep" feeling in one of its branches. "Oh, you are fast. Didn't think I would have been monitoring the channels to get a triangulation on you, did you?"

Students like him are scary, Paloon thought. *All the right skills, just the wrong attitude.*

"Come on, say something."

Paloon continued swinging through the trees like a primate while keeping a watch on the droid. Then he stopped at one tree and planted a small transmitter on the trunk, then swung a couple of trees away, toward the droid. Hanging from a branch with both hands, he coiled his body to plant his feet squarely on the branch then let his hands go. He hung down and began to swing back and forth as the boots kept grip.

"My thermal and sonic sensors are going to get you," Ihm boasted about his technological edge.

Not with my personal deflector they won't. The hunter lightly tapped the first device he attached to his belt. "You're too narrow-minded, Ihm."

The roaming droid stopped and slipped into cloak, which began at the rear of the craft with waves of energy that completely masked all visual evidence of the droid's existence. Ihm frantically paced through the systems to find the his teacher's location. Nothing. But maybe if he kept him talking?

"Why...why do you say that? I've got the droid."

"What's the only law of the battlefield?"

Ihm started getting distracted with this classroom in the field. Then the answer hit him. "There is none."

"Right, so what does that mean to you?"

Ihm hummed at the question while wondering why the droid couldn't lock on to the transmission signal like it should. He kept inching the droid closer to the vicinity. "Gravity doesn't always work."

"Close," the instructor replied as he looked through the approaching, cloaked droid. Paloon studied the underbrush movements the grav cannons made. "When you land on a planet, you might not know the adversary's capabilities and tactics. It's your job to be completely flexible. Anything goes. Always remember, the enemy will attack you where you don't expect it, no exceptions. There are no rules."

The droid floated now almost directly under the dangling Paloon.

"That doesn't make sense." Ihm, now challenged with the lesson, had little concentration left to focus on why the sensors weren't locking. "Are you going to tell me that even you, with more than twenty years of combat experience, can never tell what the enemy is going to do?"

With a quick mental command, the boots released. Paloon fell down on the droid, planting his hands and turning on the gloves' grip. "No, but you're just a predicable pup."

Upon the thud of Paloon's landing, Ihm kicked the throttle full, and the droid shot into a run, dangling Paloon like a clothesline in a typhoon.

As they darted about, the instructor's legs swung sporadically as his hands remained firmly planted on the invisible craft. Paloon wasn't about to turn on his boots and risk the chance of them attaching to one of the nearby trees that he kept barely missing. He didn't feel like being torn in half. His only option forced him to attempt this one-handed.

"You're crazy, teach."

"I'm crazy!?" Paloon huffed. "You're trailing your instructor going a hundred and ninety klicks, and you want to pass this class!?"

Paloon let his right hand grip go just to start his body whipping around more wildly. He pulled a tubular tool off his belt, then used it to feel around the cloaked ship for the joints. As he fumbled around, Paloon had to unfocus his eyes from the ground flying below him. It messed with his depth perception too much.

There's a joint. He slammed the tool in, locked it and began the drill to shatter the joint. Then he found the next one; it soon shattered; then the next. The final bolt shattered, and the invisible metal plate began to rattle. Paloon sheathed the tool, planted his loose hand on the plate, turned on the grip and yanked.

As the plate lost contact with the ship, it crackled back into a bright white triangle that snapped Paloon's arm back in the rushing wind. The now open panel remained cloaked with only the moving ground visible below. He looked behind him to carefully position his arm to release the plate just right so he didn't lose a foot. Again.

His arm parallel to his back, he let the glove's grip go, and the plate soared horizontally. With that out of the way, Paloon looked back to see where Ihm had been speeding off to in the meantime. He swallowed hard.

Through the invisible craft, Paloon saw the ground give way to the bottom of a five hundred foot chasm. With a quiet whistle the grav engines cut off.

Paloon appeared to be in a single-hand stand as the droid shot for the creek bellow. "Oh, shhhiiiiiiiit!"

"Hey, buddy? You didn't fall asleep on me, did you?"

Ihm's question received no reply while the hunter debated on whether Ihm had lost his mind. Trusting that he didn't let a loose gun this far into the course, Paloon held on as he gazed at the ground rapidly rising to meet him.

The radio cracked, "Waaaaa hoooooooooooo!"

At about one hundred feet, Ihm fired the grav engines again. The wind pushed away from below the droid, as the cannons forced a cushion of geomagnetic electricity toward the ground.

A slight buzz sounded the Centurion's deceleration; then it shot forward before Paloon could get a grip inside the access port.

"You are as crazy as they say," Ihm charged. "Only a nut would have kept hanging on."

"Insanity is nothing more than a state of mind." The hunter tried never to waste an educational opportunity. "Once you've understood all states, then you will become lycan." He also used the time while Ihm flew straight through the chasm to plant the tips of his boots on the body of the droid.

"But you said senses were what truly made one survive against the enemy." Ihm replied attentively as Paloon struck a knowledge nerve. "Wouldn't insanity cloud your judgment of the senses?"

"You fail to see the point, pup." In a blink, Paloon turned his boots on and glove off. The wind snapped him straight as the soles of the boots grasped squarely on the hull. "If you master insanity, it won't cloud your judgment but improve skills."

"By letting you do things a sane person would otherwise not."

"Omega Okliu, you're closer to making lycan than you think. Now land the droid; class is over."

"Oh, no you don't. I want another chance at shaking you off; then I'm going to tag—"

A thundering sizzle rang off the chasm walls, then Ihm's retinal display starting flashing warnings. "My vector core just went! That's going to take me a whole day to fix."

Paloon stood on the droid, holstering his particle cannon. "Ihm, when I say class is over and land, I mean it. Now that I landed it for you, the least you can do is try to get us in the water so you don't damage the grav cannons too badly."

Ihm slightly bowed his head in shame at Paloon's words as the now defunct craft glided into the creek. Landing skids descended into the water, causing the droid to skip for a short distance. Ihm commanded the forks to extend, and the saw-toothed duress gear shot into the creek bed, bringing the droid to a sudden stop.

Paloon released his boots' grip when he heard the forks and kept the momentum by running off the nose of the droid and jumping into the three-foot deep creek.

The flowering spray of water from Paloon's landing cooled him off. It felt quite nice. As the water settled, he trudged out of the creek to the bank then ran a hand through his stubby, white hair.

Paloon spoke into his wrist unit. "Jungle Comm, this is Tran Five."

The triangle-shaped canopy opened. Ihm sat inside releasing the data pads that connected to his neck, head and hands.

"Jungle Comm here."

The hunter focused back to the transmission. "Send a white rescue on my personal beacon for two, and launch droid recovery drones on my ship's beacon and for Omega Okliu's droid."

"On their way."

Ihm rolled out of the cockpit, jumped into the creek and made his way to the bank. He kept quiet as he paced near Paloon who now sat on a rock. Other than the birds chirping, wind rustling the leaves and the bubbling creek, not much else made a sound. They both just watched the slowly moving water.

Paloon felt it wasn't necessary to start teaching again because he could tell by the look on Ihm's face and his silence that the last lesson was still sinking in. That's what he liked about teaching someone of his own race; he could always tell when the lesson caused gears to turn. Unless you spent much time studying the other races, you could never tell if they were focused on the lesson or on some internal mental journey.

But Paloon and Ihm were both atlantian. Ihm stood about four inches higher than Paloon's five foot, three inches. Amid Ihm's light-brown skin sat black eyes that matched the color of his straight shoulder-length hair.

Ihm held much promise. Paloon hadn't decided if it was favoritism because they were of the same race or if it was a true feeling. Paloon combed his fingers through his bearded neck as he thought about it.

About fifteen minutes had passed when the sound of the approaching rescue could be heard.

First the drone appeared, casting its web-like shadow into the chasm. Both onlookers began walking farther up the creek as the ship descended.

"All life forms, please keep a minimum distance of five hundred feet." The request bellowed from the descending ship.

"Electrostatic field commencing in four—"

Paloon turned away from the operation and closed his eyes while Ihm continued to watch. The student didn't have the kind of retinal upgrades as did his teacher.

"—three—"

The frail-looking drone landed on top of the disabled ship with a clank.

"—two—"

An audible snap startled Ihm as the drone's grip pads fired and drew in the Centurion.

"—one—"

The recovery craft shifted to prepare for the field. Then with a bright crack of light and a whoosh of air through the chasm, a purple electric field formed around Ihm's craft, and a red light began flashing on top of the recovery drone.

Slowly the pair of ships rose then turned to creep back toward the base.

"Amazing craft," Ihm commented. "Nothing but engine."

On those words Paloon opened his eyes to see the rescue craft landing farther up the creek. He turned to tap Ihm on the shoulder, and they both walked to the ship. Appearing like a large helicopter without the rotors, the vessel steadied, and a huge side door slid open. The teacher and pupil stepped in and took the folded seats next to the door.

When the door shut, the craft began by gliding forward and then sped toward the base in a ten-minute flight. A quiet flight. As Paloon changed his clothes, Ihm remained in thought.

Near the base, the view remained that of a forest canopy that suddenly opened to reveal the compound. As if carved into the landscape, the base blended with the hills, valleys and creeks that ran through it almost as if they were untouched.

"Drop me off at the command bay," Paloon told the solo pilot he couldn't see behind the cabin wall. "Then take Ihm to Pad Five."

"Will do." The pilot replied as he started the descent to the base.

"Ihm," Paloon turned to him, "tell Jol to prep her droid and tell Julp and Oi to get a Centurion from Bay Four and prep it for my use. I'll only be borrowing it for today."

Ihm nodded his head. "Will do."

The craft came to a whistling halt. As the side door slid open, the pilot mentioned they were at the command bay. Paloon stepped out onto the metal links of the command bay floor. Behind him the rescue craft rose and vectored away.

Paloon took a quick glance around the bay as he made his way toward the center door. The bay was smaller than most as it was designed only to house small personal ships, but the hundred foot ceiling still gave the impression of a great deal of openness. His boots clanked against the metal floor as he wormed his way around some parked ships.

He entered the archway as the electric door sizzled around him. Ahead sat a large square counter with numerous clerks moving busily about, helping people with filing and requesting operations. A large, rectangular screen hung from the ceiling and displayed information on the various current operations.

Paloon stepped toward the counter, turned right and walked past it down a hall. The hall opened on the right to a line of computer banks with two other people jacked in. He approached one of the computers, reached next to the monitor and pulled out a cable that he plugged behind his ear.

The computer ran a bio search then displayed the verified identity. Once the computer gave him access, Paloon stared at the screen as he started downloading the field report, requisition for new parts and updated data on Ihm's files.

About the time Paloon began downloading, he heard footsteps approach. The owner of the footsteps went over to the terminal next to him, and it sounded as if their owner just stood there. Paloon didn't look and kept focused on downloading the information.

After two minutes passed, he finished his updates, unplugged the jack and looked over at the stalker. There stood a tall, older man with long white hair that barely covered his long, pointed ears. Very fit, the man's muscular build could even be seen through the grey uniform cluttered with various awards.

"Elder Lawkin," Paloon began his question at the gentleman, "may I guess you wish to talk to me?"

"Yes, you may." Lawkin extended his right arm to generally point in the correct direction and welcoming Paloon to go first. The elder's light-grey eyes followed Paloon as he headed back toward the busy counter.

They crossed the foyer in front of the counter and entered another hallway. The left wall opened into a waiting area with very comfortable seating, but Paloon steered toward the hall to the right.

At the far end of that hall, the wall held a set of glass doors that Paloon recognized as the elder's office. They entered, and Paloon stepped to the left, letting Lawkin walk past and around to the rear of his desk.

Lawkin apparently forgot about Paloon temporarily as he tapped at the keys on his desk.

"Yes, Elder Lawkin," came a voice into the room.

"Prepare a shuttle, and have it waiting in the command bay."

"Will do, sir."

Paloon knew what that meant. It had been awhile since he worked a special ops mission, and this began to reek of it. But why him?

"There's no one else." Lawkin answered the unspoken question.

That's not what Paloon wanted to hear. At least his ego didn't want to hear it.

Then Lawkin seemed to ignore Paloon again as he stared at data streaming on his desk's holographic monitor. The elder tried to search for the right reply. There wasn't much he was allowed to say. Pathetically, he didn't even know much. Maybe Leader Kawka distrusted him.

"The mission calls for an instructor." Lawkin leaned back and for the first time looked Paloon in the eyes. "For some reason, it also specifically asked for an atlantian. Don't ask me why."

Lawkin raised a finger briefly to drive home the point. Then he settled down and folded his arms. Paloon could hear the agitation rise in Lawkin's voice, and that kept Paloon's mouth shut.

"I know you're in the middle of a class, but K'Nartuk can take over."

"But—"

"Don't even go there again." Lawkin rose to his feet. "You may not trust her, but I do, and you don't have a choice."

Paloon almost stepped back. He's always known Lawkin as mostly a calm-headed person. Something must really be bothering him.

"Yes, sir."

Paloon's calm reply temporarily broke Lawkin's gruffness. The elder relaxed, unfolded his arms and tapped his fingers on the desk. His eyes shifted from Paloon to the screen behind him. The monitor displayed a shuttle landing in the bay.

"Your shuttle's here." Lawkin's eyes pointed at the screen, and Paloon turned to look at it. "You're to report to Dolphin Station."

Paloon's eyes slid back toward Lawkin who now watched his reaction. *Why there? What the hell is this mission?* He didn't vocalize the thoughts because he could tell those were the same questions on Lawkin's face.

"Hurry up. You don't have much time."

Paloon turned and opened the door.

"And Paloon—"

The hunter stopped and looked back over his shoulder.

"Watch your back."

Paloon nodded, walked from the room and began making his way toward the waiting shuttle.

I don't like this either, old friend.

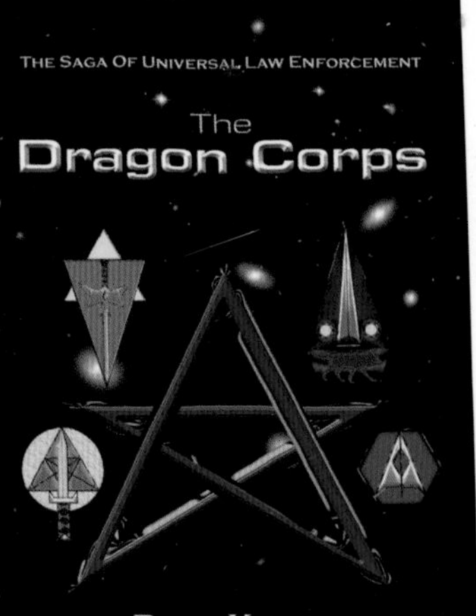

While investigating the innocent planet of Terra, a mildly dysfunctional band of reluctant protectors soon find themselves between saving the planet and starting an intergalactic war.

The Dragon Corps

Dale Yates
www.TheDragonCorps.com
E-mail: info@TheDragonCorps.com

Fate Waits For No One

In a galaxy owned by a race of narcissistic warmongers known as the p'tahians, the residents of Terra go about their daily routines blissfully ignorant of the alien pirates nefariously smuggling weapons onto their planet.

As a representative of the Dragon Corps, the universal law enforcement agency, Lyon is on a covert mission behind enemy lines for a different reason: Terra is believed to only exist in myth.

When Lyon uncovers signs that pirates are transporting illegal weapons onto an undeveloped planet in restricted space, he calls for backup. Lyon's new team of non-volunteers hopes to quietly shut down the operation before the criminals draw the p'tahian's unmitigated wrath, which would bring about the immediate extinction of all life on Terra.

The resulting investigation unravels connections between the yakuza, a psychic grandmother, the mob, local police, the military, rouge aliens, federal agents, mythology, secret charters and one terran who should be dead. This mildly dysfunctional band of reluctant protectors soon find themselves between saving the planet and starting an intergalactic war.

ISBN-13: 978-1419644658
$30.99 Trade Paperback

ISBN-13: 978-1-4392-6405-8
$43.99 Hard Cover

Chapter 9

Larin sat on the ground at the front of the outdoor firing range. Using an unsheathed multi-tool, he busied himself cleaning the numerous probes that protruded from the bottom of the small, grey box in his hands.

When the last probe was cleaned to a sparkling gold just like the others, he folded his multi-tool and slapped it into a chest pocket on his jacket. Another flick of the wrist withdrew a power meter, and he tapped each probe with it. All probes passed inspection, so he flicked his wrist, and the meter disappeared into a pocket under his arm.

Larin kept his yellow eyes on the mounted weapon next to him as he stood to his five-foot height. Five feet was unusually tall for a rolbrid, but over the years, Larin had found his height quite beneficial, even though most of his race laughed and pointed at him.

The two-foot long weapon boasted an impressive particle cannon fueled by a generator in the rear, but Larin's interest was held by the under-barrel mount. He slid the box he had been cleaning across the top of the weapon and snapped it down so only a sliver remained visible.

"We've got power." Larin's comment seemed to be directed at no one. The words rattled around in his throat as if he had thousands of vocal cords that continually crashed into each other. "Let's have the magazine."

With his eyes now focused down range, the comment just floated in the quiet air of the surrounding forest. Larin ignored the buzzing in his ears as he scratched the thick, black bristles of hair that stood on top of his flat skull.

"Hey, El-tee."

Larin whipped his head around just in time to spot the magazine flying toward him. He extended an arm and positioned his hand to catch the item with a snap.

"Thanks," Larin said, keeping his arm extended to point his index finger at the baby-blue marselian standing three hundred yards away behind a solitary control panel.

Larin turned back to the mounted weapon and looked at the item he caught. The magazine was rectangular in shape with an apparent but small mechanical device attached to it, and it looked hollow. Larin knew it wasn't hollow but rather filled with tightly packed slats of clear, manufactured allaric crystal.

He slid the magazine into place in front of the weapon's trigger. Immediately, the weapon made a faint buzz and click as it loaded and prepped the first round.

Larin removed another tool from his belt as he stepped around the weapon. After some precise movements that didn't seem to accomplish anything, a side panel popped off the rear. Larin snatched it in its fall to the ground and slipped it into a leg pocket.

Lying a couple of feet from Larin, some coiled optical cables wound their way through the grass back toward the console panel. Larin grabbed the cables and dragged them toward the weapon.

Before he made any connections, Larin's eyes pointed toward the marselian, who was completely focused on the console in front of him. "Nux, ready?"

The four arms paused as Nux raised his head. "Systems are good." His smaller left arm reached to tap a few more buttons. "On standby. Ready when you are, sir."

Each cable's tip slid easily into the now revealed ports. Even with all the cables in place, many unused ports remained, dotting the interior of the weapon.

"Go," Larin ordered.

Nux tapped some buttons, and before Larin could ask, Nux offered the answer.

"We're a go except for the targeting cam."

With a slight nod of his head, Larin began his examination of the connections. His thick fingers roamed through the cables, confirming each connection by touch. When he found it, his coca-colored skin almost flushed white. Larin felt embarrassed at the very stupid mistake—at least that's how he saw it.

"Standby for reconnect." With a subtle move, he slipped the cable into the proper port.

Nux's arms moved again. "Ready."

Larin pointed toward Nux. The targeting camera came to life with its green light reflecting off of Nux's solid grey eyes.

"Activate the range," Larin ordered as he stepped over the cables to the other side of the weapon, fishing through his pockets.

Recessed bays along the range's rim opened with slight hisses. Five globe-shaped drones sailed into the air and took their positions. As each locked into its floating position, a screen on Nux's console turned on with a visual view.

"Drones are online," Nux said as he continued double-checking the systems. "Range is clear."

Larin gave up the search through his pockets and stepped behind the weapon. "Lower the mount one foot."

The weapon jerked down with a single blast of escaping air.

With the weapon at a more comfortable height, Larin leaned forward to look into one of the targeting sights mounted on its sides. The view allowed him to see straight down the barrel.

The rolbrid pushed away from the weapon to peer downrange. About a thousand feet downrange, five black cubes rested on stands positioned in a concave arc.

"Give me target one."

With a quick whiz, the mount snapped the weapon to point at the far left block. Larin moved forward again to verify it was on target.

The weapon's screen showed the block with faint green crosshairs dissecting the cube perfectly. He then stepped away from the weapon.

"Fire a point through the block."

The wide, snubbed-nose barrel rotated with a whirl as it extended from the weapon, and its rear matter coil hummed to life. Extended eight inches, the barrel clicked to a stop. Then both beings waited patiently.

Larin gazed into the nearby woods. The quiet seemed to release some of the stress Larin had let build. After a deep breath, his shoulders drooped a bit.

"Cells are charged," Nux announced. "Firing."

Reluctantly, Larin brought his attention back to the work at hand and watched the dark cube.

The weapon rocked smoothly in the mount as a faint red bolt zipped toward the block. Except for a gelatin-like jiggle in the block, the blast didn't leave a visible mark of its hit.

Nux's arms glided across the console. Camera views replayed as Nux zoomed onto the cube. He could now see the bolt seep into the cube.

"Direct hit," Nux reported.

"Target two," Larin said.

They repeated the steps for each target. As they went along, Larin became more disinterested. Nux, on the other hand, kept his attention focused.

Disbelief filled Larin's head. He didn't know how Nux could stay interested in the midst of all this procedure. Larin loved testing weapons, but he preferred just firing the weapon instead of going through the hour or so it took to prepare a range *properly*.

All five tests turned out perfect, so Larin sat on the ground with his back to the range, his head resting on the mound of dirt that ran the length of its front. He slipped a data pad from a pocket on his left upper arm.

"Go back to target one," Larin ordered as his punched in various numbers.

The cannon whipped around as Larin thought, *Now comes the real test.*

"Let's try fifty-three by twenty-one at a hundred and twenty cycles by three." Larin maintained a grip on the data pad as he dropped his arm. "Three round burst."

Nux rapped on the console then looked toward Larin. "Ready."

Larin rolled over on his belly, keeping his eyes on the first cube. "Fire."

From the flat orifice under the weapon's cannon barrel blasted three streaks of green light that sizzled toward the target. Larin watched attentively as the charged crystal slats closed the distance.

Then each hit, and before the cube could begin to give, they splintered into thousands of crystal slivers. As each slat broke, green bolts of lighting writhed in the air. The slivers reversed direction, soaring back toward Larin, only making it about six hundred feet before embedding themselves in the ground with wisps of noise.

Larin lowered his brow and tightened his lips. He then flipped over on his back and began entries in the data pad.

Well, hell. Larin tapped the pad on his knee as he gave the situation some thought. He wanted a flux that would cause the manufactured allaric to shatter prematurely. Unfortunately, the flux didn't seem to do anything; the crystal flats acted normally. In a way, it pissed him off. *Let's go extreme.*

"Same power, but change the flux to eight hundred and thirty by three. Three rounds."

With the order Larin rolled over again as Nux entered the change.

"Ready," Nux began, and without too much wait, "Firing."

The three green slats crackled from their under-barrel carriage and, much to Larin and Nux's amazement, slipped into the second black cube with no effect. The cube just shook back and forth as if about to hop off its stand.

Larin folded his legs under him and pushed away from the mound of dirt. He sat there for a while, staring at the dancing cube in amazement. Then he looked over his shoulder to Nux.

Nux stood transfixed as well. His befuddlement was apparent when his eyelids gave a quick blink. Blinking wasn't something marselians did very often, but Nux didn't believe what he saw either.

"Well?"

Larin's stern question shook Nux, and the marselian searched the console's controls.

"The crystals never left," Nux said as he recovered the data. "They did hit the target.

"Uh—" Nux's voice changed tones. "El-tee, I'm picking up some increasing vibrations."

Larin jerked his gaze back toward the cube and realized what he hadn't noticed before: It had never stopped jiggling. Matter of fact, it was moving faster and more erratically.

In a thunderous blast, the cube splattered in all directions.

Reflexes threw Larin on his back as he yelled, "Blessed frapping hell!"

Pain began blaring in Larin's head as he stood. He rubbed the back of his head and wondered if the ringing in his ears came from the explosion of the cube or the collision of his head against the ground.

Tips of Nux's royal-blue hair were the only things visible from behind the console. His head slowly rose until solid-grey eyes took in the damage to the range.

Fragments of the gelatin substance lay haphazardly around the range, dotting the grass with spots of black.

Sure of his safety, Nux rose to his full seven-foot height. His smaller right hand scratched at his hip as the rest of the arms began dancing on the console controls.

It was probably the shock that kept Larin from realizing the possible applications. Authentic allaric crystal is virtually unbreakable unless charged with an electrical current, after which it shatters violently. Manufactured allaric is almost the same except that it stays charged until it hits something more substantial than air. Never had a charged allaric crystal, manufactured or otherwise, withstood hitting something only to detonate later.

The thought slowly sunk in. Larin knew that his little mistake meant something, but his train of thought derailed as Nux broke the quiet.

"Lieutenant Mulkin, mind if I offer a suggestion?"

Larin jerked, pulling his mind out of its trance. *Sure, why not?* He maintained a grip on the data pad as he pointed two fingers in the air in a quiet motion that projected the thought, "Let's have it."

"What if we drop the power, maintain the cycles but increased the rate to, uh...five?" Nux was busy conducting his own calculations at his console.

Larin tried to ignore the tapering ringing in his ears and gave the idea a once over. It was bold. He hadn't thought about what increasing the rate would do versus just increasing the cycles. *He may destroy the weapon, but he may also have something there.*

Larin tossed his hand in the air. "Go for it. Let's see what it will do."

The mount clanked as the cannon took aim at the third target.

"Ready," Nux said as he saw Larin lie down next to the weapon again. "Firing."

This time, the green lights exploded midway to the target. Volatile green bolts shot into the ground as slivers of crystal flew wildly to the far end of the range.

A smirk crept across Larin's lips as he got to his feet. *Damn, sergeant, if you don't have something there.*

Larin looked back at Nux, who had bared his large, yellow teeth in a full smile.

"You ought to be proud," Larin began. "My theory, but hell if you didn't figure it out. You're—"

Larin's voice trailed to nothing as he noticed a shuttle resting in the grass behind Nux. An atlantian in an officer's uniform ran from it toward Larin.

Larin slapped his data pad in his hand as he watched then slid it back into the arm pocket. *What now?*

The runner stopped in front of Larin and began, "Lieutenant Mulkin?"

"Yes," Larin replied, stretching the "s" as he squinted.

"Officer Jefferies, sir." The young man saluted as he introduced himself and offered a data pad. "Chief Gogra requests your immediate departure, sir."

"What kind of frapping bullshit is—" Larin tightened his lips to keep from continuing into a rant. He and Chief Gogra never saw eye to eye, and he tried to not let it get to him, but it did. *No sense in yelling at the messenger.*

"I...I apologize, sir." The subordinate tried to patch the problem, which for some reason he felt responsible. "The chief said you were looking for a deployment—"

"Like hell, I am!" Larin let his frustration slip again and grabbed the data pad from the officer's hand.

His thumb tapped through the buttons. It was authentic, but half of the information such as departure and destination were marked through with the word "Classified" next to it.

"Why frapping bother?" he mumbled at the senseless information and handed the pad back.

"Excuse me, sir?"

"Nothing." Larin pointed his arm toward the shuttle. "Let's get going."

"Right, sir." The officer jogged back toward the shuttle that began firing its engines.

"Sergeant Lufafta," Larin spoke to Nux, "pack everything up and take it back to the shop. Hell knows when I'm getting back."

Nux quietly got to work. Larin reached for the data pad in his arm pocket and tossed it toward him.

"Put this with my stuff as well."

Nux was carrying the weapon's packing crate, so he turned his back to the flying data pad and caught it with his smaller right arm. He then headed toward the cannon with the crate.

Larin turned away and slowly walked to the shuttle. He didn't want to go, so he damn sure wasn't going to do it quickly.

Chapter 10

Intense laughter blared as the speaker in the small clock radio rattled.

"Ha, ha, ha! Ahhh. Oooo, boy." The DJ calmed as his female assistant continued snickering in the background. "And as if that weren't enough, our intrepid police chief then gave the entire city council the finger!"

The roaring laughter resumed, reaching annoying levels as a hand shot from the bed covers and pounded the clock radio like a judge's gavel. When the fist finally struck the snooze button, it unfolded and rested wearily on top of the radio. Mission completed.

Strangely enough, a complete thought penetrated the sleepy fog in Lyon's head. It only succeeded because it had become an instinctive reaction, the result of countless repetitions of mornings just like this. The successful thought summoned barely enough energy to force one of the resting fingers to drag itself over to the off switch and push it two notches.

With the sound of the last click, Lyon uncontrollably relaxed further than he even thought possible.

While the body lay motionless, his mind screamed in agony; it wanted more sleep. Lyon was inclined to agree, but he fought for control. It was a losing battle, but his unconscious continued to silently scream as it was pushed back into the recesses of the mind.

I don't want to be awake. Lyon's now conscious mind shared the same sentiment as his unconscious one did.

As if disregarding the pleas, his hand slid off the radio in search of the remote. Along the way, he knocked over a drinking glass, and it fell to the carpet with a muffled thud. *It was empty,* jumped into Lyon's mind, and he soon forgot about it as he found the remote and gripped it.

His hand fell off the nightstand and dangled from the bed as the index finger felt its way to the power button.

With a short crackle followed by a buzzing, the television came to life, resting on the chest of drawers a couple of feet from the bed. The sound from the early news program was oddly soothing, but the associated and slowly increasing light was harsh as it seemingly cut through Lyon's eyelids to poke at the heart of his mind.

His eyebrows slammed into each other and clashed with wrinkles on the top of his nose. Lyon's eyes almost disappeared in his checks as he tried feebly to close his eyes tighter to stop the burning light. In a rustling flurry, Lyon twisted his head and buried it in the pillow. Now *that* stopped the infiltrating light.

Even though he temporarily halted the light, he knew he wasn't going to stop the morning from coming, and he had to get up. But that would be an accomplishment requiring time.

While he continued his battle to wake, the morning program rambled on about events that occurred yesterday. There were some more shootings and a robbery. The female anchor's male assistant tied the crimes into the city council's meeting with police department heads.

Apparently the council had a plan to reallocate money to give the department an extra five hundred thousand dollars a year, but it came with the stipulation that it must be used for vehicle purchases. The police chief claimed the city needed more officers, not more vehicles, and criticized the reallocation as a political maneuver to line the pockets of the local car factory and dealerships, a few owned by council members. Predictably, an argument ensued.

The assistant anchor almost gave a slight snicker as he tried to explain the event.

Hell, I'd give them the finger too, Lyon thought as he sat up. *Actually, I'd give them more than just a finger.* His legs slipped from the covers, and Lyon sat on the edge of the bed, his head resting in hands offered from arms propped on his knees.

Lyon's ears tuned out the news broadcast. He gave a long yawn and let his head slip down so his fingers ran through his hair that twisted in all directions.

Both arms were flung wide, and another yawn slipped as he stretched. Following the invigorating maneuver, Lyon stood and strolled across the loft toward the open bathroom door. He thumbed the switch and shut the door. Soon the sound of a shower rung throughout the floor.

Strips of golden light painted the stairs that Lyon descended. Wood planks creaked in resistance to both the weight and at being disturbed so early in the cool morning.

When Lyon reached the bottom, a finger flipped a switch on the right wall of the stairs, and hanging florescent lights flickered into life.

He turned around to quickly scan the small store. He stood on a raised platform lined with a simple banister that angled down with the steps to his right, which faced the end of a glass-covered meat counter. The counter stretched along a wall that gave way at the end to an open entryway leading into a tiny freezer area.

Facing him from the far wall were two pane windows covered on the outside with a latticework of metal links. Blue letters outlined in white, arched and read "McAndrew Street" on one window and "Grocery" on the other. The chipped paint showed signs of extreme fading that left only a dull glimmer of its original brilliance. Between the windows rested a wood-framed glass door—also protected by metal links—plastered with multi-colored posters, everything from missing pets to an upcoming circus.

In front of the left window rested a short, L-shaped checkout counter corralling three tiny shopping carts and a stool. Shelves lined the remaining wall and the landing on which Lyon stood. In the center, four head-height aisles striped the black-and-white checkered floor.

It wasn't a glorious life. As a matter of fact, a storekeeper's income really didn't hold much promise as a living, period. But the store provided a good cover.

As important as that cover was, Lyon also enjoyed watching the terran race from this angle. Regardless, Mac thought Lyon was out of his mind for going with the job of storekeeper. Mac preferred a university professor or director of a museum. Mac could be quite persuasive, but this choice was uniquely Lyon's. The decision remained Lyon's mainly because he made it before he had created Mac; nevertheless, the thought that the choice was solely his made Lyon smile.

He strolled across the landing, down the few remaining steps and toward the front door. Five locks of assorted types lined the right edge of the door. Lyon leaned over the counter and placed his hand underneath it to rest his index finger on a sharply cold glass plate.

After a quick scan of his fingerprint, the five locks clicked in sequence and metal plates loosened their grips on the door and retracted into the floor and ceiling. He may not live in a mansion, but Lyon refused to be without his security.

Lyon pulled opened the door, which struck a rust-speckled, golden bell that hung from the wall. As he pushed at the screen door, it skittered on the uneven concrete below. He paused for a moment to take a breath of fresh air—or as fresh as it got in the city.

The morning sun glowed around the skyline. Lyon's store sat on the outskirts, so the buildings around here were only three to five stories high. The tips of skyscrapers loomed in the distance.

Across the street sat an abandoned service station that Lyon acquired with the store. He got lucky. The same guy owned both and wanted to get rid of both. Fortunately enough, Lyon needed both. As if he forgot, the thought reminded him to prepare the station to be occupied. He'd need it for his team's arrival.

A light post on the corner blinked off; its hanging cover seemed to loosen further with the light's retreat. Oddly, that reminded Lyon that he still had much to do.

He stepped over the bundles of newspapers at his feet and went to the left window. His hand gripped the base bar that held tightly to the sill. Again, a hidden glass plate scanned his finger, and the bar clicked its response. The latticework collapsed effortlessly as it bunched at the top of the window.

Lyon walked over to the other window to perform the same maneuver. As he did, a deep purple car with a flawless paint job and chrome mag wheels roared to life from the corner a block away. Its trunk hung dangerously close to the pavement and actually scraped the asphalt as the car rattled away down the road.

The barrier on the second window lifted as Lyon scooped up the two bundles of papers and stepped back inside. He kicked the door shut behind him, setting off the bell again, and flopped the newspapers into the rack that capped the end of the aisle across from the checkout counter. The local newspaper landed in the bottom rack, and the tabloid slid into one of the top racks.

With a firm tug, Lyon popped the bindings on the bundles. He wadded the plastic in his left hand and peeled an issue off of each stack with his right. He turned to slap the papers on the counter. As he tossed the plastic bindings at the trash can behind the counter, they sprang out to grip the top of the can in a desperate attempt to keep from falling in.

Lyon walked behind the meat counter and kicked over a toggle switch. The coolant system rattled and hummed as the lights buzzed to a pinkish white.

He stepped back around the counter and down the ramp into the freezer room. A permanently barred window ran the length of the left wall. An open deep freeze lined the far wall, while built-in glass door freezers covered the right wall, except for a plain door in the nearest corner. In the center of the room sat the produce cooler.

All hummed quietly as Lyon opened the door to the rear storage. He hit the light switch. Hanging lights popped on, and Lyon heard one in the rear of the storage room as it blew.

He weaved between the shelves to the back double doors. After placing his hand behind a nearby shelf, the doors unlocked.

The cold metal doors swung open with Lyon's push. As if choreographed, a milk truck pulled into the rear loading area. Lyon waved at the driver who returned the gesture as he positioned the truck. The engine quieted, and the driver stepped out.

"Morning, Derrick," Lyon said with a smile.

"Good morning," the black man replied as he removed his blue baseball cap to wipe his forehead. The frosted tips of his short hair and well-defined creases in his face hinted at his age.

"Keeping you busy as usual?" Lyon asked as he began opening the rear of the truck and pulling down the built-in ramp.

"Yep," Derrick quipped, "but it's a pleasantly cool day to be working."

Lyon simply smiled. He never met Derrick when he didn't have something positive to say, and Lyon liked that. "I'll get the old."

Derrick nodded and went to work as Lyon disappeared into the storage room and headed for the rear of the built-in freezers. Lyon yanked the handle, and the door's seal yielded with a firm "pop." The released cold cut through Lyon's clothing, and he rushed in, picked up a stack of three cartons and rushed out, kicking the door shut behind him.

Lyon lifted the cartons onto the truck as Derrick dragged a stack taller than him down the ramp. Derrick pulled the cartons along the concrete away from the truck, unlatched the long hook he was using then palmed a small computer that hung from his belt.

He offered the computer to Lyon who took it, signed the display screen and handed it back.

"Thank you, sir."

"You're welcome," Derrick touched his cap after hanging the computer back on his belt. He then started up the ramp as Lyon carried the new cartons inside.

Derrick moved the old stack around some more then slid the ramp away and closed the doors.

With the last carton in hand, Lyon nodded. "See you next week. And I'll get the gate."

Derrick simply smiled and waved as he drove off.

Lyon slid the last carton into the freezer and shut the large metal door. He then walked outside into the loading area and closed the fence's vehicle-sized doors. The chain rattled as he strung it through the fence bars and slammed the lock shut.

He entered the storage room, closing the door behind him. In the now dark far end of the room, Lyon opened another freezer locker, grabbed a cart of meat and pushed it out of the storage room and into the store toward the meat counter. He paused only to swipe a small bottle of orange juice from behind one of the freezer doors.

Lyon set the bottle next to the register as he continued to push the cart behind the lighted glass counter. He lifted the white apron that hung on the wall and donned it then yanked two plastic gloves from the box that sat on the counter.

After the meat was in place, he tossed the gloves in the trash and returned the apron and cart.

The sunshine through the windows was almost competing with the store's florescent lights when Lyon took a seat behind the checkout counter, propping his feet on the shelf below the counter. He pushed so his stool rocked on two legs, its back resting against the window ledge.

With a swig of orange juice, he scanned the morning's paper. The only thing he found interesting was the picture of the police chief yelling at the city council. Thick veins streaked his neck and forehead.

Lyon guessed that the ability to see the veins in three dimensions could not be a good thing. Regardless, the chief's outburst definitely provided all the final nails needed for his career coffin. Unfortunately.

The rest of the paper was cluttered with useless stories about people held up to the limelight as if they were important when they really weren't. Even the sports section discussed the sex lives of some players.

Who gives a damn? Lyon thought.

He did stop to review corn and soybean futures, as well as oil prices. Corn remained unchanged as soybean dipped and oil rose a bit.

Lyon responded with a hum. He flopped the paper about in his lap as he folded it, then tossed it back on the counter.

The heating unit chugged to life and tapered off into a quiet howl as the blowers kicked in. Lyon glanced at the grungy, soft drink-sponsored clock above the meat counter. The square, red center sprouted black hands that reached to the faded black numbers resting on a lit dingy yellow border. Seven thirty. The newly installed heater timer kicked in perfectly.

After another drink from the orange juice bottle, Lyon lifted the tabloid from the counter. Some dead rock star impregnated an alien abductee. Three men shot a two-headed alligator monster in a swamp. And *finally* the truth behind a twenty-year-old assassination as told by an ex-secret agent who had been hiding out as a cross-dressing casino show dancer.

Lyon snickered at the last headline and began flipping through the publication. He ignored most of the stories but thoroughly read anything about UFOs, aliens or monsters. Sometimes the reports were close to an actual description; most of time, they were way off.

Regardless, Lyon enjoyed it mostly for the humor. He took another gulp of orange juice. "Mac, what did you find out?"

The question echoed slightly in the barren store. Then a small television screen under the counter came to life. The featureless face of Lyon's computer companion became visible.

"Many believe the yakuza to be the oldest form of organized crime in the world with a three hundred plus year history," Mac began immediately. "The word yakuza began with the bakuto, or gamblers, clan but over the years began to include several other groups. Most believe the name comes from three card numbers, eight, nine and three, or ya, ku and sa. These numbers apparently represent one of the worse possible hands in the card game hanafuda, hence the name's origination with the bakuto clan. Therefore, yakuza roughly translates to 'useless hand,' and the bakuto were useless to society.

"Yakuza clans have been known to have thousands of members structured in a syndicate of sorts. The leader is the oyabun, or father, now translated as boss. The faithful members are kobun, or children, now translated as followers. Only one female is allowed to be 'visible.' She is called—"

"Skip it." Lyon drank some more orange juice and hoped Mac would get to a point.

Mac kept going without missing a beat. "Once, yakuza were viewed as machi-yokko or servants of the town. The clans would take arms to protect the villages and towns from the servants of the shogun. But over the years, the name yakuza started to include groups such as traveling merchants who were often crooked. As yakuza continued to develop, the clans expanded their gambling and peddling to branch into protection rackets, blackmail, gun running, et cetera. When their country started to transform into an industrial nation, yakuza kept with the changes by making their criminal activities more clandestine while taking over legitimate businesses as fronts and becoming more active politically.

"Now publicly undesirable, the families defend their righteousness through a code of ethics to defend society's weak. Yakuza have been known to do just that. In numerous instances, yakuza provided aid to villages even before the state government would act. But some yakuza activity has led to the public taking action to rid their villages of the yakuza. Today the yakuza have become more covert and have spread beyond their original borders. Businesses with yakuza ties have bought many international companies, and most believe these are yakuza fronts."

Lyon shifted his legs and looked over his shoulder to watch the early morning traffic pick up. "Thanks for the history lesson, professor, but did you find anything about a yakuza operating in this area?"

"The only thing I found was a newspaper article printed three months ago. The reporter questioned the police chief about the rumors of a new mob, possibly yakuza, starting in the city. The chief simply replied, and I quote, 'Those rumors are just that, rumors. But you can rest assured that we are looking into it.' You know, you have to feed the media something, so why not feed them bullshit? He goes on later about his plans to request more money from the city council to better fund the police department's organized crime division."

"What about the department's computers?"

"Nothing." Mac's voice actually held a bit of embarrassment about his inability to conduct research in that area. "My best guess is that their computers in the organized crime division are not connected to the rest of the police network. My second best guess is that the yakuza have already bought off the police."

"Okay," Lyon looked back at the monitor, "what about enemies? If a yakuza is trying to move into the city, is there anybody they would tick off?"

"Actually, yes." Mac paused. "But you're about to have customers, so watch this footage instead."

Lyon peered over his shoulder to see four boys ranging from about ten to thirteen years old laying their bikes against the wall. The bell above the door rung as wood scraped in a well-worn skipping pattern on the tile.

"Are you open?" one of the boys asked.

"Yes."

Their chatter quieted a bit as they entered and headed toward the candy aisle.

One boy gave Lyon a look of quiet recognition, and Lyon returned it. His name was Bobby Prater. Lyon used to live on the same floor as Prater. They never became friends, just knew each other.

The monitor under the counter now showed clips of news broadcasts. Each focused on the same subject.

"City police arrested suspected mob gunman Cain Garibaldi today," began a sharp-dressed man with hair that appeared to be a plastic mold. "The arrest came after an anonymous tip to the police department fingered Garibaldi as the Imondi mob's hit man, responsible for the deaths of two men found in Red Lake three weeks ago. Those bodies were found riddled with bullet holes, and forensic experts suspect the bodies were in the lake for two months."

Lyon furrowed his brow and lifted his head to see one of the boys run off to the back for a couple of sodas. Meanwhile, the others grew louder as they debated and combed over the various forms of sugar.

"State Representative Max Ferriday was convicted of murder today," a different broadcast began, this time with a pale female with blond hair almost a wide as her shoulders. "Seven months ago, state police and FBI agents served a search warrant to Ferriday at his state capital home, where they found the body of a local prostitute in a partially constructed basement wall." The image flipped to video footage of Ferriday being escorted from the courthouse. "The prosecution worked to link the murder with Ferriday's ties to the Imondi mob, but the judge threw out the mob-related claims under the grounds that the prosecution could not provide sufficient proof."

Just then the boys began bringing their selections to the counter. Lyon tapped each purchase in the register. One paid with a pocket full of change as the others handed over folded food stamp bills.

Their transactions finished, the boys eagerly left with their voices increasing in volume, almost drowning out the fizzing sound of opening soda bottles and the ringing bell as the door closed.

"So," Lyon gazed back at the monitor, "what you're saying is there's a mafia in town. Why haven't I heard anything about this in any recent news?"

"Well, there is but *isn't* a mafia here. Now before you ask, let me explain." Mac paused. "Quite a few decades ago during a time called the prohibition era, when alcoholic beverages were outlawed, several existing gambling mobs became stronger as they smuggled alcohol into the city. As you may guess, mob wars became violent, and here, one family stood out among the rest: the Imondi mob.

"At the time it was run by a young Leonardo Imondi. He didn't give up the throne until his death about twenty-two years ago, but by then his mob went legit, so to speak. They hold one of the oldest riverboat gambling licenses in the state. Leonardo's son, Francisco, now owns the casino. Friends call him Frankie, but the rest of the world knows him as F. Imondi. He may do this just to let his enemies know he's packing the family name.

"In the past, it was easy to tell if there was mob activity, but it was hard to pin it on anybody. The mob has gotten even more clever and smart, and now it's hard to tell if they're even still active. But you make the call, because that chick with the big hair who said the representative had ties to the Imondi mob was found dead three days later in her home. The police report finally settled on a robbery gone bad, but nothing was found missing. One investigator commented in the report that it appeared almost as if it was a professional hit, but no one in the media was going to say it was the Imondi mob."

Lyon grunted as he turned to stare out the display window. "I'm sure you've got more information, but let me think about this for a while. This still doesn't explain the weapons. Keep searching; I'll get back to you later."

"Before I go, I found some more research books for you, and they should arrive in three days."

Lyon didn't reply, and the monitor quietly went to black. Lyon lost himself gazing out the window. Time flew by unnoticed as he dwelled in thought. Before he knew it, the bell rang again.

An elderly black lady slowly made her way into the store. She finally completed her journey as Lyon watched. Bent fingers shook as they unfolded a rolling grocery cart. Severe osteoporosis arched her back, and well-sprayed silver hair never moved from its pattern of waves and curls.

"Good morning, grandma," Lyon said with a smile.

"Morning, Lyon." A full set of dentures gleamed from her smile as a cane helped her toward one of the aisles.

Lyon walked around toward the meat counter and began weighing one pound of pork steaks, just like she always wanted on Mondays. Alessa Franklin was the one person Lyon was in debt to the most.

When he landed on the planet, he entered the nearest city. As the first Dragon Corps agent to covertly enter the planet's society, he had to work without completely knowing the language or societal quirks. He lived on the streets. After three months, Mrs. Franklin found him outside her apartment building.

She befriended him and offered him a hot meal in exchange for installing a window air conditioner for her. Before he knew it, he was doing labor work for many of the residents in the building and was allowed to squat in the boiler room. Then Mrs. Franklin talked her friend at the grocery store into hiring Lyon to help with stocking.

Al reluctantly trusted Lyon but did it mostly as a favor for Mrs. Franklin. As time went on, Lyon and Al became good friends. Four years later, Lyon made a deal to take over the store from the aging Al. Al wanted to get rid of the store and gas station so he could move into a retirement home. He could no longer take care of himself because standing caused him too much pain.

Because of Mrs. Franklin, Lyon was able to get set up quickly. She didn't know who he really was, but he wondered at times. Residents throughout her apartment building knew that Mrs. Franklin, or "grandma" as everyone called her, possessed psychic talents. Lyon had heard her eerie stories and predictions time and time again, and most came true.

Lyon always wondered about her ability, how eyes so clouded with cataracts could see so much. Her ability didn't stun him; Lyon had been well exposed to beings with that ability. But to him, grandma possessed something different.

He finished marking the packaged steaks and headed back to the counter. Grandma closely peered at a can of spinach as one hand braced the side of her thick glasses. She slowly placed the can in the basket before she continued.

She took her time shopping and loved doing so. She never did understand why people were always rushing. Lyon knew this, so he patiently waited as she set all her items on the checkout counter. An offer of help would result in a light but surprisingly quick strike from her cane and a good talking to about how she may be old but more than capable of bending him over her knee.

He totaled the costs while bagging the groceries, putting only a few items in each bag to keep them light. Grandma fumbled with her coin purse to pull out the folded bills she had crammed in there.

As Lyon made change he asked, “How was your weekend?”

Grandma paused briefly before looking Lyon in the eyes. “You’re strongly worried about something,” she said in a tone that sent a shiver down Lyon’s spine.

That feeling always made him uncomfortable, but to deny her observation would be futile. “Yes. You could say that.”

She took the change Lyon offered and put it in her purse. “You should be,” she calmly commented. “What you’re looking for is not what you’re looking at.”

Lyon thought about what she said as he placed the bags in her personal cart. Grandma always said strange things, so her last statement didn’t jolt him as much.

She started leaving when Lyon said, “Thanks for the advice, grandma. I guess I’ll have to look elsewhere.”

“No,” she returned as the door scraped the floor and the bell rang. “You’re looking in the right place but at the wrong thing.”

“Thank you,” was all Lyon could reply as his mind bent around her statement. “Have a good day.”

The door had closed by then, so his statement received no acknowledgment. He watched through the window as she slowly made her way back to the apartment complex.

“I don’t care what you say.” Mac’s voice came from the monitor again. “She’s weird...and creepy.”

Lyon only sat down and thought more about what the elderly psychic had said.

Chapter 11

The tension was thick enough to see. The only noise came from the car's engine and muffled sounds of passing traffic heard through the bulletproof glass.

Behind the glass sat four men sharing one thought: *I don't want to be the one to tell Kurosawa-san.*

Unfortunately, Yabuki Yumiro knew he had to do just that.

He sat in the front passenger seat. His grey sport coat covered a white shirt that contrasted sharply with his tan skin tone. As his chin rested lightly on his right hand, his elbow propped against the door, Yabuki seemed calm. In actuality, he was working very hard to stay calm.

Mr. Kurosawa wasn't going to like the report. Yabuki knew that such an unfavorable report could mean he would lose the tip of a finger. Yabuki even wondered if he should go ahead and cut it off to present before he gave his report. That thought made him wonder if his report was really that serious.

"Why don't we blame it on that gang member we recruited?" Takehiko spoke up from the back seat.

"Hold your tongue!" Yabuki met the words with a pistol, drawn from under his jacket faster than he could complete the phrase.

Now, the gun's barrel watched Takehiko's head as Takahiro sat next to him. Takahiro slightly moved his palm horizontally back and forth as a sign for Takehiko to be quiet. The well-trained driver, meanwhile, just kept his eyes on the road and away from Yabuki.

"I will not dishonor myself by putting the blame on a dead man. If you cannot understand that, maybe I should remove you before you dishonor the family." Yabuki waited as his finger slowly tightened on the trigger.

"My apologies, Yabuki-san." Takehiko bowed his head and neck, while being smart enough not to watch as Yabuki slid the weapon back into his jacket.

Takahiro peered at Takehiko and raised his eyebrows, as if trying to say *What in the hell are you doing? Keep quiet.* Takahiro then turned to stare out the window, trying to ignore his younger brother and praying that he wouldn't do something else stupid enough to get them both killed.

Yabuki resumed watching the passing buildings of downtown, which allowed him to relax.

He had called in the reinforcements. He had ordered the strike. He was the one responsible for the deaths of six kobun and one royal guard. He knew he was as good as dead.

At the same time, he felt strangely calm. Quiet before the storm, he guessed.

The car pulled into the entrance of an underground garage. The driver slid down his window and swiped a card in the waiting computer. After verification, the guard in the shack nodded as the metal gate clanked to life and rolled away into its concrete housing.

Bright sun gave way to the hazy yellow glow that filled the garage. Hundreds of vehicles were tightly packed in crowded aisles, but the driver professionally zipped around with ease. It wasn't long before they were parked.

Everyone got out of the car, but only three proceeded to the nearby stairwell. The driver remained behind, quietly inspecting the car and nearby vehicles.

With Yabuki in the lead, the trio ascended a flight of steps to the second deck, which held a large set of glass doors to the right.

In a small V formation, they headed for the doors. At the last moment, Takehiko and Takahiro leapt forward and opened the doors for Yabuki.

The entrance opened to a long customer service area cut in half by an elaborate glass staircase to a second floor. Backing the stairs was a glass wall with a view into the atrium. The only obstructions to the view were the black words "Kurosawa" and in smaller letters "Investments." A solid, black icon of a river marked its right side.

Silver panels covered the left side, short of the glass staircase and atrium. The high ceiling allowed the building's outside glass walls to bring in much of the needed light.

Both halves of the floor looked like bank lobbies. On Yabuki's half, people waited for an available computer kiosk. On the other side, live tellers took care of a slowly moving line of customers.

Yabuki walked calmly across the floor and nodded slightly to the guards at the semicircular station built into the left wall. One guard tipped his hat and returned to watching his monitors.

The three headed for one of the glass doors under the staircase. Just before Yabuki grabbed the door, the lock above the handle switched lights, red to green, thanks to the dutiful guard.

Everyone instinctively took a deep breath of the fresh air in the atrium. It almost covered a quarter of a block itself and stretched all the way to the tenth floor on this side. Countless plants dotted the various levels that seemed to be randomly placed off of the center pole. A waterfall lightly trickled from each deck to one below.

The three sport coats walked to a bank of elevators on the far side of the atrium. Yabuki just waited in front of one of the elevators while Takehiko stepped over to push the button.

When the doors opened, Yabuki entered and faced the number pad. Takahiro took the far corner, and Takehiko stood near to the closing doors.

After the doors closed, Yabuki slid a card into an almost concealed slot located next to a metal door marked "Phone." The numeric display above the door flashed green, and the car climbed as he put the key back in his jacket.

The elevator whispered past the tenth floor. Yabuki adjusted his already straight coat and touched the back of his left hand on Takehiko's arm, who stepped back so Yabuki would take the front.

Finally, the elevator stopped.

The doors opened to an almost pure white room. From the elevator, two five-foot-high jade dragons extended into the room ten feet, pointing the way to the small white and grey reception desk across the foyer. Hallways led from both sides of the desk.

Behind the counter, a petite woman glanced at the arriving party, but her demure demeanor never changed to hint that she had noticed them as she entered unseen commands on her computer.

From the left hallway, a man walked in front of the desk to wait for the arriving trio. He was dressed like Yabuki but wore a thin black tie.

"Yabuki-san," the new man said as he bowed. "Kurosawa-san is waiting, please follow me."

Yabuki, with the trailing pair, followed the man down the right hall. It hooked to the left and ended with heavy double rosewood doors. Each door held kanji carvings of the Kurosawa family name.

With unnatural ease, the assistant pulled the doors open.

The ceiling rose to a height of four stories, and the office seemed to cover a quarter of a city block. Scattered about were "trinkets" that Mr. Kurosawa had collected over the years. The room looked a little like a museum, with everything from a stuffed Arctic wolf to a suit of armor from a knight and his steed on display. Though few items were related to each other, together, they created their own strange unity.

Dwarfed by the room's immense size, a desk sat at its center. A geisha poured Mr. Kurosawa some tea. She set the pot down and, without a sound, glided toward a door at the rear of the room and disappeared.

The assistant waited at the door as the three positioned themselves in front of the desk and bowed in unison.

"Konnichi wa. Anata ni yoroshiku," Yabuki greeted for the group.

"What is it, Yabuki?" Kurosawa replied mildly, sipping at his tea.

"We lost six men last night," Yabuki said as they rose from their bows. Kurosawa seemed unmoved. "And one royal guard."

Kurosawa paused, slowly set down his teacup, then turned to face Yabuki. "What happened?"

"We had an eavesdropper at Warehouse Fifty-two. I ordered a team as a backup as one royal guard pursued." Yabuki fought to keep himself from pausing. "The team followed the guard's beacon, which was moving toward them at a rapid pace. They found the guard dead, so I ordered them to kill the person responsible.

"They called in that they had a suspect pinned in a store and were going in. I told them to use the special weapons to make sure the man was dead."

Kurosawa kept a steady eye on Yabuki as he spoke.

"That was the last we heard from them. We found the entire team dead. Some were shot with their own weapons. We did, however, have enough time to divert the police so we could clean the scene." Yabuki finished and now calmly waited for his punishment.

Kurosawa stood. His age didn't seem to affect his powerful physical appearance. "Yabuki-chan, you did what I would expect."

The elder Japanese man straightened his black suit as he walked around the desk to Yabuki. "The incident is unfortunate." Kurosawa approached Yabuki and placed a hand on his shoulder. "Your actions tell me you are genuinely sorry.

"That is why," the words hissed from Kurosawa's lips as his hand, moving in a blur, suddenly pressed a sharp blade to Yabuki's neck, "I'm not going to kill you." Then in a more gruff voice, he continued, "You find that slug and bring him here."

"Hai, Kurosawa-san." Sweat appeared on Yabuki's brow as he barely kept his feet.

In another unnaturally fast move for a man his age, Kurosawa made the blade disappear, leaving only a small speck of red on Yabuki's neck.

Kurosawa slowly made his way back to the desk. "I didn't say tomorrow."

The three bowed and quickly backed themselves out of the office. The assistant closed the doors.

Before the door were closed, Kurosawa sat back in the large, leather chair. He rapped his fingers on the desk a couple of times then laid his hand flat.

He furrowed his eyebrows as he tapped a button next to his phone.

A large screen rose from the floor before his desk and sparked to life. The screen remained black for a couple of minutes as Kurosawa waited for the connection to be made. He leaned forward in his chair. Though his back began to ache during the waiting, he wasn't going to be caught leaning back.

Finally, a face gradually became visible. It was a very fat face of a very large man. The bald head held small eyes peering from behind cubby cheeks.

"Yes, Kurosawa, what is it?" The man's jowls flapped as he spoke. The lips parted briefly to reveal the dull glint of yellow teeth.

Without delay, Kurosawa relayed the information he just received from Yabuki.

The oyabun on the screen wasn't about to smile now. His tightly held lips ensured that. The fat cheeks almost touched his brow as he squinted. Suddenly the crystal clear image became fogged with static as the man shook and growled.

Kurosawa could hear the man breathing hard as the picture began to clear up. The fat man now stared at something off screen then returned his gaze at Kurosawa.

"I'm sending a couple more royal guards," the fat man paused to catch his breath again. "They will have specific orders. You will do exactly what they say."

"As always, oyabun," Kurosawa replied.

"Good. I don't want to fix your mistakes again."

The picture winked to black, and small motors sounded as the screen slid into the floor.

Kurosawa let out a sigh as he leaned back in his chair. He closed his eyes and tried to release the tension from his tightly held jaw. With another sigh, he tapped the speakerphone button.

"Yes, Kurosawa-san," came the tender voice of the girl at his reception desk.

"Naoko, get Sho."

"Immediately," she replied.

Kurosawa thought for a moment, "And my chiropractor."

Chapter 12

Nervous. He had never been this nervous. The entire night crawled by while he stared into the pitch black of the room and listened to the creaks and other noises from the space station.

Hitook shifted his eyes, though he couldn't see anything. Their movement more followed his thoughts than any physical thing.

He wrestled with memories of when pirates attacked his planet. The visions showed his father covering his mother from a rifle blast—a selfless yet fatal move. The blast penetrated both before they slumped into a pile of smoldering flesh and fur. The pirate attacker only gave Hitook a kick from a heavy boot as he continued shooting other adults in the village.

It took weeks for a rescue party to arrive. That's when Hitook grabbed his brother and hid under what remained of the family home. There, he shied away from the stranger's offered hand. The stranger was armored, just like the man who had killed his parents. But the stranger's voice sounded...different, not as cruel as that of the other being.

Only after mustering all the will he had left did Hitook reach from his hiding place toward the welcoming hand. He was very nervous then, but it somehow didn't seem to compare to this situation.

"Time, please." Hitook's voice scratched a bit on the request.

"Five forty-seven," a computerized voice replied from the darkness.

Instinctively, Hitook began to stretch in his bunk. He planted his massive feet against the bulkhead to give his thick legs some tension as he yawned.

A creak pierced the room as Hitook felt the bulkhead start to give way. He quickly retracted his legs, holding them in the air while attempting to stare into the black at the bulkhead.

"Lights, please."

Gradually, the small room's lights pushed away the black. Now Hitook could see that the bulkhead didn't seem to be damaged. So he rotated himself on the bunk to unfold his legs onto the floor and sit up.

The narrow room barely had space for the bunk, shower stall, closet and sink. Hitook's immense size made it look even smaller.

No sense in being a slowpoke now, he thought.

He stood and walked, his long ears dragging across the ceiling as he went to the closet to grab his vest, boots and other uniform items. With his clothes on, he tapped the unlock button next to the door, which slid away.

The entry opened to a cul-de-sac of sorts. Twin doors faced each other as a hallway shot off to Hitook's right. The left wall had a tall window that gave a view of space with a just-visible slice of the greenish planet of Dragon below.

Hitook stared into space for a while. A shiver shot down his right arm. Nerves again.

With a shrug, he stepped in front of the cabin door that sat next to his own and rapped his furry paw on metal.

No answer, so he knocked once more. Before his paw could hit the door the second time, it slid open.

Ky stood squinting and blinking her eyes while yawning. She wore only a sheer nightgown, leaving her body rather unconcealed. A slight coating of fine fur covered her curves and continued along her tail, which didn't even twitch as she dragged it along the floor.

She looked at Hitook long enough to mutter, "This better be good."

"I was checking to see if you were awake enough to get something to eat before our meeting," Hitook said calmly, doing his best to be polite and not let his eyes leave her face.

Ky peered at Hitook through one open eye. "Time."

A voice from in her room replied, "Five fifty-six."

Ky dropped her head even further and groaned.

"I'll let it go this time," Ky began with a little more authority in her voice. "But don't ever—"

Her order was cut short by the sound of the opening door for the cabin across from Hitook's. Wide awake and fully dressed stood Larin, who quickly took notice of Ky's nearly invisible clothing.

"Well, *goooood* morning," Larin smiled. Nine feet away, his eyes scanned what had made it such a good morning for him.

Ky glared at Larin. Her lip slowly curled itself into a snarl, revealing one fang. Hitook sensed what was about to happen and immediately plastered himself against the wall. Just then Larin took a flying trip backwards into his room, landing with a thud.

"Humph," Ky stated defiantly as she slammed her palm on the door's release. As it slid shut, she spun around, and her tail whipped and thudded on the floor.

Reverberating chuckles now echoed from Larin's room.

Hitook stepped forward and peered in. "Are you okay, Lieutenant Mulkin?"

Larin sat slightly crumpled on the floor below the newly formed dent in the wall above him. His laughter trailed off, and he ended it with, "Hoo boy. Sensitive minx, isn't she?"

He dusted himself off for no apparent reason and stood. Larin eyed Hitook for a moment then stepped forward into the cul-de-sac. "At least *I'll* take you up on your offer for food. Even though you do draw attention."

Hitook only blinked, not quite knowing how to respond. He just stared down at the short man. They shared at least a three-foot height difference.

"You're a frapping oddity; don't you know that?" Larin returned Hitook's look.

"Thank you, sir. I'm well aware of my rarity." Hitook gave a toothy smile, his wide, enlarged incisors fully exposed.

Larin turned his head to relieve the crick in his neck and scrunched his nose. Before he even took a step forward, the final door opened.

"Little early for all the racket, don't you think?" Paloon commented.

"Talk to her, captain," Larin replied, pointing to Ky's door with his thumb. "I only work here."

Paloon only had three inches on Larin, a tad short for an atlantian, but he had learned to deal with it over the years, especially when it came to subordinates. He raised a brow. "Then let me rephrase that. It's a little early to be irritating people, don't you think?"

"Ha. Ha." The faked laughter formed short distinctive words as Larin folded his arms.

"Sir, would you like to join us for some food before the meeting?" Hitook offered.

Paloon stepped through the door and tapped it closed. "Yes, thanks."

"Not without me, you're not," came Ky's muffled voice.

Paloon jabbed his finger pointedly at Larin before the rolbrid could spout a comment. Larin held his lips tighter. So the three of them just stood there, eyes shifting from each other and around the almost featureless walls.

Larin shifted his weight. "But she'll take—" he started.

Paloon's scowl silenced the comment.

The waiting continued. It was only a few minutes, but it somehow seemed longer for the trio. Larin couldn't and didn't want to bottle his displeasure, so it started slipping out in muffled grumbles.

Finally, Ky's door opened, then closed behind her.

"About time," Larin spouted before anyone could stop him.

Ky ignored the statement. "Since I'm now awake, you're not leaving me. So, shall we go?" With a slight nod to the three, she pointed her arm down the hall to the right.

Paloon and Hitook took the invitation first, followed by Ky and Larin.

"Personally, I liked your other outfit better," Larin smiled.

Hitook peered into his upper eyelids in disbelief. Either the lieutenant didn't care or he enjoyed torture.

Ky acted as if nothing happened. Then, with the speed of a whip, her tail popped Larin in the head, sending his skull rapping against the wall.

A slight smile broke Ky's otherwise emotionless demeanor. Larin just chuckled slightly as he rubbed his head. His headache had returned.

The group wound its way through the halls that wove through the space station. Creatures of various races occasionally appeared on the walkways but always cleared a path after just one look at the foursome. Each found the reaction curious, but didn't pay that much attention. At least that was the case until they entered the dining hall.

The noise of a hundred jovial conversations poured into the hall in front of the team as the four approached the room. Hitook turned and stepped inside but halted suddenly as the noise stopped as quickly as someone turning off a radio. Paloon's strolling momentum took him around Hitook to see why the liqua had stopped.

Lined with long white walls, the facility's only furniture were grey tables of various sizes and matching chairs. Those hundreds of chairs were almost all full of people—beings from at least sixteen separate races. But the one thing each shared was their sudden silence. Each froze in the midst of eating and conversation to stare at Hitook.

An echoing "ting" rang from a utensil that had slipped from someone's open mouth and fallen onto a table.

"Hey, I'm hungry," bellowed Larin. "So stop blocking the door."

The short man easily pushed Paloon farther into the room and almost into one member of the staring crowd.

Larin took a quick look at the amazed crowd then glanced back at Hitook. "Normally, I get those looks because I'm so damn handsome. Now I know the freaks get that look, too." He laughed and thumped a fist twice on Hitook's forearm before returning his attention to his stomach. "Fine, stand there all day; I'm eating."

After a sweeping scan of the room, his yellow eyes locked onto four seats at the end of a long table. Larin frowned at Paloon as he squeezed between him and one of the gawkers. "So he's ugly; what's the point?" he mumbled.

As if walking on thin ice, Paloon and Hitook reluctantly followed Larin. The rolbrid didn't care though; he had already worked out a path through the crowd to the open seats.

When Ky entered, a nervous pang shot through her as she noticed the room's occupants never moved their eyes—or other sensory organs for that matter—from Hitook as he moved through the now parting crowd.

Before Larin's hand could even hit one of the chairs, the diners at the other end cleared the table; their plates and food left behind. The rustling of the exiting diners seemed to spark other sounds of whispers and mumbles.

Larin paid no attention as he started tapping away at the keyed display in front of him. His dark hands almost seemed to blur with movement, and he began to hum as he flipped through the digital menu.

Chatter in the room resumed as the other three carefully took their seats. Paloon and Ky took the other side of the table as Hitook joined Larin. Hitook tried not to look back at the crowd, but it was difficult to avoid the staring eyes that seemed to be everywhere.

Ky's eyes twitched back and forth around the crowd. This made her uneasy. She could feel her back muscles tighten; it was more instinct than conscious thought.

"Relax," Paloon said quietly in an attempt to calm both his group and himself. "They've probably never seen a liqua before; not many beings have."

Paloon pointed to Hitook. "Don't take it in a bad way, but your race is almost extinct." He shrugged in a "forget it" motion. "It's just a mixture of curiosity and fear of the different."

Hitook stared at Paloon and attempted to tell if the atlantian's comments were genuine. No luck.

"For the record," began Ky, almost in a whisper, "that doesn't make me feel any better. One on one, beings are generally easy to get along with, but panicked crowds tend to do stupid things. And our present company looks panicked."

"True," Paloon dropped his finger into a flat palm and looked at Ky, "that's why we need to stay calm. It's best—"

"Damn frapping computer!" yelled Larin, shattering the quiet.

Everyone at the table and a few around it shuddered at the sudden outburst.

"What do you mean I can't have three starches?" Larin argued with the device as he pounded his fist on it then pointed to himself. "I'm a rolbrid; I need my starch. Don't tell me what I need. I'll rip you—"

"Hey, shorty!" Ky's voice picked up in volume, drawing Larin's anger toward her. "Make two orders."

A scowl was all of Larin's reply.

"Do I have to show you?" Ky leaned across the table while lowering her voice. She'd feel better if Larin would stop drawing more attention than they already had attracted.

"No," Larin huffed as he stabbed the "Create" key.

Multi-colored lasers flashed in front of him, creating his order molecule by molecule. Without fanfare, they stopped. Larin slid the finished plate aside and began working on the second order.

Paloon attempted to use Larin's outburst to further distract the other two by starting his order. Hitook followed, as did Ky, but only after she took a moment to sit back in her chair, shaking her head and peering skyward.

Activity almost returned to normal. The foursome ate with little thought of the rest of the crowd as beings stopped staring and returned to their food. Random glances went unnoticed for the most part.

Larin scarfed well, like a champion. His first two orders already down, he began ordering a third. Paloon and Ky marveled at Larin's digestive ability.

"If he starts eating the table," Ky's eyes jumped from Paloon to fix on Larin, "I'm leaving."

Hitook looked next to him at Larin just in time to see the rolbrid delve into the next order. For a small man, he could pack it away—and fast.

"Well, it's nice to see us eating together," came a voice from the end of the table near them.

The four turned to see a familiar face, Count Jeffs Dorin. From a more felid race than Ky's, the pale skin of the count's that wasn't covered by a smart, black business suit sported a thick coat of fine orange fur. Wisps of hair curled from the tips of his pointed ears that sat high on his cranium. His head appeared almost bald because of the contrasting long white beard marked with streaks of orange. The streaks made it look as if most of the fur on his head decided to flash migrate to his chin.

A small, dark nose spotted the center of the trillig's face under his blue-grey eyes and above thin, black lips that framed a fanged smile on top of the beard. "How did we sleep? Well, I hope." The count rested a paw on Hitook's shoulder and looked into his eyes.

"Fine, Count Dorin." Paloon followed the comment by pointing an open palm to the end of the table next to him. "Would you please join us?"

"Thanks."

The count grabbed an empty chair and whipped it around, placing its back against the table so he could sit in the chair backwards.

Each had come to know the count upon their arrival at the station. He greeted them, showed them the sleeping quarters and briefly introduced them to the others who had already arrived. Count Dorin said he would meet them this morning to begin the mission brief. Every team needed at least one representative from Corps headquarters, and most of the time it was a count.

"Don't let me stop you." Dorin directed a paw toward Larin.

Larin nodded then returned to frantically devouring his breakfast, which prompted a sigh from Ky.

"Is it time for the brief?" Paloon asked.

"We've got plenty of time for that." Dorin folded his arms on top of the chair back then smiled again. "Finish eating."

The four gradually returned to their meals. All felt like they should be paying better respect to the count. Except, apparently, Larin.

Dorin looked back at Hitook. "I hope the sleeping accommodations met your needs."

"Yes," responded Hitook, who honestly felt a bit cramped in his bunk. But it was nothing he couldn't deal with.

"Good," Dorin smiled.

A sudden collective gasp silenced the room for the second time in about ten minutes. The room's reaction caused the team to stop in mid-meal to hear the only two sounds now audible.

One sound was of breaking glass from a cup that slipped from a hand. The other was heavy, metal-on-metal. Like armor. Battle armor.

Four heads at the table turned toward the door to see a full suit of battle armor thud its way into the room and take up a post next to the door. A second suit entered and took its own post on the opposite side of the door. Long weapons of some menacing form rested in the hands of the suits.

Quiet curses in several languages started coming from the facility's many patrons. Dorin hadn't moved his head but continued to smile.

Now a third battle suit entered the room. This one banged the butt of its weapon on the floor as it clanked its way to a large round table. The table's residents immediately vacated to the far end of the hall. They knew what was happening. They only knew by word of mouth, but they didn't want any part of it.

The cause of the armed escort bounded into the room. The room's second collective gasp had the assistance of the four at Dorin's table.

In the doorway stood a second liqua.

This liqua stretched a couple of inches taller than Hitook. He had Hitook's thick, white coat but also a brown patch over his right eye that extended around his head and down his neck, reappearing along the side of his right arm. A similar patch of brown fur formed an oval on his left biceps. The liqua wore a vest similar in design to Hitook's, but this one bore the colors and emblem of the Harquebus.

Larin swallowed his bite. "Now that's something you don't see every day."

The comment traveled over the hushed crowd and drew a few chuckles from those who temporarily forgot the danger of which they had been warned.

With the second liqua's entrance, the crowd now knew it wasn't Hitook the rumors had referred to.

When the liquayn's eyes met, Hitook questioned, "Lykel? Brother?"

Lykel squinted and laughed out loud. "Hitook!"

Hitook stood, and they both barreled through the aisles. When they met, each pounded a fist into the other's chest. The resulting crack sounded like it had enough power to shatter a large tree.

Every being near them immediately decided they were full and evacuated quickly.

The liquayn began chattering in their own ancient language, a tongue unknown to everyone else in the room. Hitook's military composure slipped, and for the first time in years, he forgot his training so he could experience the indescribable joy of meeting family.

Paloon glanced at Dorin, who maintained a smile as he turned to watch the two liquayn approach the table.

"Everyone," Hitook jerked a thumb at the other liqua, "this is my brother, Lykel."

"Hey," Lykel greeted with a slight nod.

Dorin and Paloon nodded in return, Ky said, "Hello," and Larin gave a left-handed two-fingered salute before he resumed eating.

Hitook and Lykel resumed reminiscing. The third suit of armor moved forward to close the gap between it and Lykel, but it still just monitored from a distance.

A shiver shot through Ky. "I don't know about the rest of you, but seeing *two* liquayn puts my fur on end."

"Now that's something I'd like to see," spouted Larin.

The whip snapped again as Ky's tail yanked Larin's chair out from under him, throwing the rolbrid to the ground.

Larin's head began to pound again, but that didn't keep him from laughing, then choking on his food. He quickly cleared his throat to resume a loud, grating chuckle.

Hitook and Lykel laughed at him. Ky tightened her lips. Paloon shook his head. Dorin continued to smile.

Chapter 13

Traffic was nonexistent in this particular corridor of the space station. But there were four observers silently gazing at what appeared as a blank blackboard.

On the far right, Larin kept shifting his weight from one leg to the next. Then he fished through his pockets until he found a chur root. He popped the stick into his mouth and started chewing. The resulting cracks and snaps echoed faintly.

To Larin's left, Count Dorin paid no attention. He calmly stood with his paws behind his back and clasped above a short tail. The bulk of his tail had been torn off in a university prank gone sour.

Farther to the left stood Ky. The cracking noise from Larin's chur root began to grate, but she maintain her composure in front of the count. Having her hands in her pockets helped since it allowed her to ball her hands into tight fists unnoticed by anyone else.

Paloon took the far left slot with most of his weight resting on his left leg and his arms folded on his chest. Out of the small group, he was the least sure as to why this had to take place. He didn't like it, but how to tell the count that?

With a snap of arena lighting, the once black square became a window. Beyond the glass, an empty room covered about a hundred square yards. Metallic bulkheads stretched along the perimeter to line a dirt floor. The room's height remained a mystery, its ceiling lost in the lights. As the brightness increased, the outlines of two doors, one on each end of the room, appeared from the otherwise featureless walls.

The right door slipped into the wall, and Hitook stepped through before it closed. He didn't acknowledge the spectators. Instead he took a stance as if he were praying.

About a minute later, the opposite door opened. The entrance revealed a sliver of an armored guard posted outside the door. Then Lykel stepped through, and the door slid shut behind him.

Lykel said nothing as he began to stretch. He reached for an unattainable ceiling then lowered his arms. With a sudden twist of both arms, the sound of branches snapping in a hurricane reverberated from his popping forearm and elbow bones. Then his dark lips formed a devilish smirk.

Again, Paloon got a bad feeling. This shouldn't be happening. He knew they were brothers, so why?

During breakfast Lykel explained that he came to the station to receive true zero-gravity training. He didn't like the robot opponents he was forced to use. He wanted to train with a live being, one he didn't have to worry about accidentally pulverizing. Oddly, Hitook seemed to be more than willing to take Lykel up on that offer, except for the zero-gravity part.

Paloon still thought this was nuts. The team had more important things to do, like get a briefing on the mission that had called them there. This seemed more like a distraction, a setup. But the count didn't object and seemed to be more than accommodating.

"Ready?" Lykel's voice sounded demonic as it echoed off the barren walls before being muffled by the glass.

Hitook glided his right hand from its praying position to raise one finger. Then in a blur of motion, he arms splayed until his left arm drew back, his right froze parallel with the ground and his legs snapped to form a low arch.

Lykel smirked again. "Is that all they've taught you, how to make fancy moves?" He followed with undramatically taking his own stance.

Then the staring began. Each watched for which would waver, blink or otherwise display the slightest sign of distraction.

Paloon started thinking hard about a setup.

"Why do I get the feeling someone's playing a game?" Paloon had to get it off his chest. He tried to say it as a generic rhetorical question, but he honestly meant it for the count. He just didn't want to point directly.

Ky and Larin's eyes shifted from the arena and both thought about it; neither knew how to react. Dorin's smile, on the other hand, increased slightly.

"Very perceptive, Hunter Osluf." Dorin turned his head briefly to look at Paloon then back to the arena's window. "You may call it 'playing a game,' but it is nothing more than steering one in the right direction."

Lykel slowly stepped forward, never losing his stance or dropping his eyes. "Come on. Come at me." Lykel began moving around to Hitook's left. "I want a challenge, not a punching bag."

Hitook held firm. Only his eyes moved. Once Lykel was almost out of sight, dust clouded around his feet as he spun in a liquid motion.

The movement distracted Ky from the conversation in the corridor. *At least he seems to be trained*, she thought.

Paloon began to lose interest in the arena's events; he had just entered a conversational battle of his own. The count had just admitted this fight was a setup. Paloon tried to hide his slight shock but took the compliment for what it was worth. Then he attempted to recover and keep the momentum he had. "You admit that our liqua brothers finding each other was not just some random occurrence?"

"Very little is in our universe. Everything happens for a reason, but do you know who's actually pulling the strings?" Dorin maintained a mild grin while speaking. "Lykel needed to meet Hitook, Hitook needed to meet Lykel, and the Corps needed them both to meet in battle. We were the only ones to realize what they needed."

Ky turned her head toward Dorin and gazed in amazement for a moment before her green eyes drifted into thought. *Would the Corps actuality play with people like this, or is this just a personal game of the count's?*

"I said, 'Come at me.'" Signs of frustration rose in Lykel's voice as he continued to pace around Hitook. He squinted his brown eyes and huffed through his nose, sending a brief mist of watery mucus.

Then Lykel threw his fist toward Hitook's chest, only to have it blocked and forced away. That was just what Lykel wanted. He followed the momentum, dropped to the ground and spun his left leg to trip Hitook. Hitook was a step ahead and simply lifted his foot.

As soon as Lykel's foot passed through the air that should have been occupied by the target leg he planted it in the dirt and twisted his body to continue with his right foot aimed at Hitook's torso. Before the foot could strike, Hitook's paws were waiting. They clasped the foot as Hitook's body shifted, using the foot's momentum to twist Lykel's entire body.

Lykel spun, but before his face kissed the dirt, his arms landed on the ground, and he tossed himself past a handstand, launching into the air and landing firmly, feet first.

"Hee, hee, hee," Lykel's deep, demonic tone returned. "Not bad. I was beginning to wonder if you were asleep."

Larin grabbed his chur root and flipped it to the other side of his mouth. He only paid partial attention to the battle. This was unfortunate. Larin had really wanted to see the fight but had now lost some interest since it appeared to be orchestrated.

"Damn!" Larin exclaimed mainly because the conversation ruined what could have been an awesome fight, but he wanted an answer. "Why not just ask?"

Dorin lowered his head and shook it. "No. Lykel would have nothing of it." He raised his head, looking pointedly at Lykel in the area. "If we had suggested this, he would have known what we were trying to do. His training would be set back months—maybe years."

Okay, maybe Lykel wouldn't like being played like a pawn, but Paloon still didn't understand why this had to happen. He clenched his folded arms tighter to his chest. Did this chess game have a point?

"What do you expect to get out of this, two bloody liquayn?" Paloon tried to hold back the mounting anger in his voice, but he could tell by Ky and Larin's reaction that he hadn't succeeded very well. But the count remained motionless.

"Lykel has too much frustration."

Dorin let the statement seep out and settle like an early morning fog. He treated it as if it held all the answers to these questions. To Dorin, it did, and it justified this arrangement.

A roar reverberated off the window as Lykel lunged at Hitook again. A punch to the face, then the right abdomen; a kick to the right leg, followed by a round house to the left, then two more attempts to land a fist on Hitook's face—a blur of fur.

Hitook effortlessly matched each strike with a smooth block. It appeared effortless, but it took much concentration on his training to predict Lykel's next move. He lost some ground, but the concentration paid off when Hitook anticipated a hole. With a sudden thrust, Hitook's left fist pushed Lykel back.

A spark set fire to Lykel's oak-brown eyes. Lykel's jaw opened slightly as his lips curled back to reveal his massive teeth. The roar returned with increased volume.

Lykel charged as if to mow down Hitook. When Lykel was almost too close, Hitook sprang in the air, barrel-rolled behind the attacker and jammed his feet into Lykel's shoulder blades.

The thrust sent Lykel face first into the dirt, but he didn't let that stop him. Lykel rolled over and whipped his body vertical.

His eyes still burned, but deep down, he was beginning to enjoy this. Even the best battle robots never offered this kind of challenge. But for some reason he felt Hitook was going easy. That last kick in the back should have shattered something, but Lykel felt fine.

"I hope you're not playing, brother." Lykel slowly took another stance. His right arm completed a full circle that ended in front of him. Then the arm retracted above his left; the paw wide open. "This is not a game."

Ky's attention returned to the match. She was impressed with Hitook's mastery of these techniques. He moved at a fluid speed that appeared unnatural in comparison to his size. She even felt herself quietly rooting for him; it became a sense of brotherhood, a fellow member of House Bravo sparring against a member of Harquebus.

The other member of Harquebus rolled the chur root around in his mouth and began crunching again. The sound brought Ky's attention back to the conversation. She was saddened by the fact the liquayn was part of the count's game. Paloon just raised an eyebrow at Dorin and tried to wait patiently for more of an explanation.

Dorin didn't notice the tension at first; he felt he had satisfactorily explained everything. It wasn't until he glanced at Paloon and saw a brow arched over a gleaming steel-grey eye that he took a deep breath and began to tell the story.

"The Corps found them in the midst of the rubble after a pirate raid."

For the most part Dorin stared straight ahead, but he looked back at Paloon from time to time in hopes to see him calming. The count didn't believe Paloon had any reason to worry about his new teammate.

"They returned to our system on a rescue ship. Somehow they were separated. They went to different towns as refugees. Hitook was befriended by someone from House Bravo and decided to join them versus remaining a free commoner. He succeeded in House Bravo because he learned how to control his anger. But Lykel could not.

"Lykel's anger attracted trouble. He was in and out of jail at an early age. Maybe it was anger at what happened to his people or the anger that grows from being different, but he was arrested for everything from vandalism and thieving to drugs. After seeing him in court for the tenth time, another count sentenced him to serve in the Harquebus in hopes of turning him into a productive citizen."

"We are not a rehabilitation agency!" The count's comment hit a sore spot with Larin.

"Tell that to the count who handed down the sentence. You know a Corps judgment is final, and the Harquebus commander had to deal with it." Dorin kept calm. "Well, when Lykel joined, Hitook learned about another liqua joining the Corps. It had been eleven years; neither could remember well what had happened and each thought the other had died. Soon they began communicating. But unlike his brother, Lykel is having difficulty succeeding." Dorin unclasped his hands and pointed a fuzzy digit toward the battle. "His stubbornness keeps getting in the way."

The tension in Dorin's voice built up more than he cared, so he paused to gather his thoughts and return his extended paw.

Lykel prepared himself before running another punch at Hitook. As suspected, Hitook blocked, but Lykel was ready. He twisted his right arm around the block and pulled to lock Hitook's shoulder. With a shuffle, Lykel shifted behind Hitook and buried his left fist into his brother's shoulder, which cracked in response.

A bone definitely snapped. Hitook grimaced but held everything in, even though his right shoulder and arm burned with pain. With a swift rear kick, Hitook pushed Lykel away.

Lykel resumed chuckling. He seemed to be calming as he took the time to revel in his strike.

Hitook concentrated and buried the pain. As if nothing happened, Hitook moved his arms once again with ease and took his beginning stance, his face motionless.

Lykel squinted his brown-patched eye to glare with the other. "Well, well, well. I was hoping you wouldn't quit. It's nice to see you've got spunk." Lykel ignited the fire in his eyes and prepared for his next strike.

Dorin rapped a claw from his bare feet on the metal floor.

"Neither the Harquebus nor the Corps is going to give up on him. Lykel has too much potential as a warrior, but he must work past his anger. We've lost many battle robots and a few troops trying to work out Lykel's frustration.

"When the Corps called in Larin, one of the Harquebus chiefs noticed Hitook's name on the list. This chief knew of the difficulties the Harquebus were having with Lykel. They developed this get-together and offered it to me to conduct. Needless to say, I agreed."

Dorin turned his head toward Paloon. "Satisfied?" The trillig's voice was beginning to increase in pitch.

The atlantian didn't say anything but unfolded his arms to place his hands in his pants pockets. He didn't return Dorin's glare.

"Hitook's training is doing exactly what we figured it would." Dorin returned his gaze to the fight and twitched his nose, which caused his whiskers to flicker in the light. "As long as he can keep his brother at bay without harming him, Lykel will begin working out his frustration."

"What makes you so sure Hitook won't hurt him?" Ky suddenly found herself on the defense—must be that invisible House Bravo-bond again.

"Throughout his training, Hitook has always been passive, mostly. We took a chance that he would even be more passive when it came to his only living relative." Dorin started grinning again. "It appears we were right."

Lykel's smirk slowly smoothed into a grin. He thundered at Hitook yet again. Hitook prepared for another frontal block, but Lykel had another plan. He jigged to the left and threw his torso toward the ground.

Lykel plowed his left fist in the ground and spun his legs in the air. His legs boomed into Hitook's back. Bones cracked. Hitook bellowed a scream that almost rattled the viewing window out of the frame.

The intensity of the pain consumed. Hitook had no choice but to fall forward.

His still spinning legs created enough momentum to throw Lykel's body upright, and he landed with his legs half split.

A wicked grin covered Lykel's face as he looked upon his fallen opponent. He closed his split legs and marched over to the body.

Lykel's massive paws latched onto Hitook's wounded arm, and with the power of a rail gun, Lykel launched Hitook's body into a spin. One turn, release, and his brother was airborne.

The body sailed until it smashed into the viewing window. Sounds of cracking bones and the cracking window created an unsettling mix.

Ky held back a yelp with a hand. Larin cringed. Paloon closed his eyes and turned away with his jaw tightly clenched. Dorin's grin faded into a combined look of disbelief and disappointment.

The dent in the wall below the window that held Hitook's embedded body soon released its captive to let him slide down and out of view. Only tuffs of fur caught in the cracked glass remained.

Lykel bent forward with his extended arms flexing in rhythm to his heavy breathing. The fire burned even brighter. He wasn't ready to quit.

In a flash the left door opened, and a series of five orange bolts banged into Lykel. His tension was released in a yell as he lost his balance and thudded to the ground.

Now that it was safe, medic teams rushed in toward Hitook, and armored guards prepared to ship Lykel back to his quarters.

Ky closed her eyes and turned her back from the activity in the arena. She tried her best to hold back tears, and she didn't even know why she wanted to cry.

Dorin stepped toward the port and shook his head. He lowered his head briefly before turning back. "This is unfortunate." He walked past Ky and Paloon and continued down the corridor as if nothing happened. "We have a briefing in one hour. Don't be late."

Larin scrunched his nose and waited until Dorin disappeared from sight before he muttered, "Damn. And they say I'm insensitive."

Ky opened her watered eyes at Larin. Then she grabbed her composure, blinked the water away and walked in the opposite direction. She needed time alone, and she didn't know why.

Paloon watched her leave as his teeth continued to grind. He wanted to punch something. He should have said something during breakfast to stop it. Even if it was some "for the good of the Corps" crap, he didn't have to like it.

Chapter 14

The room resembled a half circle lined with a curved table facing an off-center lectern. A holographic screen spotted the wall on the lectern's left, and to the right ran the outline of a barely visible metallic door.

Inside the room, impatience grew almost thick enough to see.

Most of the agitation came from Paloon. He sat firmly at the far left of the table and watched the door intently.

To his right, Larin rocked in his chair and fidgeted with some gadget that had magically appeared from one of his pockets. Paloon didn't care what the gadget was; he was too busy staring a hole in the door.

Next in line sat Ky, calmly resting back in her chair, eyes closed. Her mental state had improved greatly in the past hour. Once again, Paloon only gave a casual notice.

His irritation toward Count Dorin festered. The count had kept them waiting for almost half an hour. Thirty minutes late. What kind of *professional* mission was this count running? First the admittance that he had used Hitook, now he was not even keeping his own appointments.

Maybe that fight was it? Paloon remained highly pissed about the match in the arena. It also bothered the other two; they just had more skill handling their anger. Regardless, no one had yet gathered the nerve to reveal to Hitook the conversation they had shared with the count.

Hitook seated at the far end of the table, waited patiently. His eyes glided around the room but showed that he didn't mind the wait. Nothing of his wounds remained visible. The telesurgery went well. Most of the internal damage required no external surgery as the station's computerized telesurgeon rebuilt broken bones and busted veins molecule by molecule. Luckily, the repairs were small enough that his body accepted them easily.

Now he remained oblivious to the conversation the rest of his team had with the count. He was still happy that he had the chance to meet his brother.

A hiss broke the silence in the room as the almost invisible door released its seal to pop in and slide to the right. Count Dorin casually walked straight to the lectern as if to begin immediately on time as planned. The door slid back and preformed another hiss to seal itself.

Dorin had everyone's attention and Paloon's agitation. Paloon wanted an explanation, or at least an apology, but Dorin wasn't going to give one.

The count remained dressed in his smart black suit and moved with an air of business as he rapped at the keys on the top of the lectern. His smile was gone. Now, it was all business, and he would conduct that business without any distractions.

"Each of you know our procedures," Dorin began, "so I'm not going to bore you with explanations. Stand by for a security check."

Simultaneously, each person in the room, including Dorin, felt a twinge equivalent to half a pinprick. The sting came from a different location for each because the computer chose a random location from which to extract a DNA sample. The retrieval was similar to the procedures for the telesurgeon but reversed.

Dorin returned to the display in front of him. The screen's lights glinted on the count's whiskers making them appear as fine strands of multi-colored holiday lights.

"Confirmed." Dorin thumbed a button and stepped away from the lectern. "Our mission brief is classified Alpha Green.

"You have met each other, but I will reintroduce you for the record's sake." Dorin pointed his left arm at the lectern as a signal that the briefing was being recorded. "At your far left is Hunter Paloon son of Osluf, who, by virtue of rank, is your superior until you get to your destination."

The count's right arm pointed at Paloon and continued down the line as he went on. "Next is Lieutenant Larin Batun-yi Mulkin, then Ninja Ky Adian of the Forty-second Crest and finally Acolyte Hitook A'gih Rutif Edolm r-fip Asoxi Zrwm ov Riqhim, who also holds the title of mif from his people."

Dorin returned his arm behind his back, clasping it in the paw of his other. Hitook gazed, a bit of amazement evidenced by a slight grin. He had never heard a non-liqua correctly pronounce his full name so fluently. Everyone else in the room tried to wrap their minds around the name and individually realized the futility and forgot they even heard it to save them from headaches.

"Screen."

The holographic screen slowly came to life at the count's order, but Dorin refused to wait for it.

"Whether you are familiar with or believe in the Theory of Terra does not matter, and I'm not going to debate it." Dorin's stare glided down the line locking eyes briefly with each person.

Of course Paloon was familiar with the theory; the legend came from his people, but he had never given it any deep thought or credence. Who did? The other listeners in the room didn't have a clue what Dorin was talking about. Larin shifted his head as if to think about whether he had heard mention of the story, but doubt let him give up thinking about it.

The count began pacing the floor in front of the curved table. He began speaking after pointing his nose at Paloon.

"The atlantians have a legend that goes back thousands of years about the origin of their race." Dorin stopped pacing long enough to scratch a claw along the back of his right ear, then he resumed. "To keep it short, the legend claims their race attempted to release itself from slavery in a mass exodus. They called the planet they left Terra.

Few believe in the legend because most existing information about Terra is vague, at best. Most details remain buried in time and translations, so many claim it is just a story."

Paloon's agitation almost prompted him to interrupt and take some childish stab at this childish story. But he held his tongue.

"Play." Dorin's order sparked life in the room's waiting holographic display. He turned to watch the display's pixels form a galaxy unfamiliar to those in the room.

"Ah...stop video." Dorin paused then spun around to face the four again. "I'm getting ahead of myself. Forget the display for now.

"First, let's talk about the atlantians." The count returned to pacing. "The atlantians provided a large amount of the Dragon Corps' initial funding. Doing so gave the atlantians a great deal of influence in how the organization would operate. This influence also allowed for some of the atlantian leaders to embed pet projects into the Corps' classified charters. One atlantian so strongly believed in the Theory of Terra that he created a charter to make it the Corps' duty to attempt to find Terra."

"I can't believe this!" Paloon yelled, losing the battle with his temper. Not only did this jerk play games with Hitook, he was now close to blaspheming Paloon's whole race and trying to make them believe there may be some credibility to the existence of Terra. He could see through the count's scheme. "Let me guess, the next thing you're going to say is that someone has actually found Terra."

"Not exactly." Dorin, along with everyone else in the room, could easily detect Paloon's frustration and attempted jab at him. However, the count refused to waste the moment. "Actually, we've found four Terras." Dorin still kept the true number of potential Terras—seven—a secret as that bit of information required a higher security level.

Paloon huffed and turned his head. But the lingering words of that last phrase rang in his head while the room remained quiet. He gradually turned his head back and looked the count in the eyes. An overwhelming chill started to creep up Paloon's spine. The chill intensified with the thought about what it would mean if Dorin was right. But the count didn't wait for Paloon to contemplate that eventuality. He returned to the briefing once he saw Paloon's agitation bleeding away as he realized what this mission was really about.

"That is, there are four Terras from what appears to have been several." Dorin pointed a paw at the display. "Resume."

The holographic galaxy began turning again. Then blue arrows pointed at four unnaturally glowing green orbs.

"These are the four that remain. Um...stop video." Dorin dropped his hand. "I'm getting ahead of myself again."

The count's thin, black lips perfectly outlined the pink tip of his tongue that barely poked between his fangs. With a wet snap, he sucked it back in.

"The Corps' research into locating Terra began with star descriptions in the full legend transcribed several thousands of years ago. It's unclear how long the legend had been passed down orally prior to that." Dorin just stared at the galaxy map, talking generically. "Most of the star charts developed from those descriptions were incomplete, but one led to this galaxy inside p'tahian territory."

A shudder rippled through the listeners at the mention of "p'tahian territory." They were well aware of the disdain the p'tahians had for all other races. Dealings with them had always soured. Dorin noticed the sound of the four shifting in their seats but continued to talk to the hologram.

"We sent numerous covert missions into the galaxy. Intelligence reported that the p'tahians didn't live in this galaxy on the rim of their territory. We were very surprised when we found multiple planets that matched the descriptions of the Terra found in legend. We found that at least eight others were destroyed but contained ruins similar to the buildings on the surviving Terras. Maybe a p'tahian scout happened to find them and wiped them out without a second thought."

The reaction in the team was subtle, but each member knew that's exactly what the p'tahians would have done. As far as the p'tahians were concerned, p'tahians were *the* supreme race. Other races meant nothing. That's what got Larin thinking.

"Wait!" Larin pointed at the galaxy and looked at Dorin like he had just escaped a mental institution. "We're not going in there, are we?

"That's exactly what you're doing." The count ignored the immediate groans and sighs of protest, stepped closer to the map and pointed. "To this Terra. Terra Four to be exact."

"You're out of your mind." Ky pushed herself back from the table but refrained from standing up. "We'll be slaughtered. You may have been able to get one-man spy ships in there once in a while, but how are we getting there?"

"Alive?" Larin added.

Dorin raised a paw to silence everyone.

"We have a knight on the planet, and he has collected a clean ring of coordinates on the planet's orbit." Dorin lowered his hand. "You'll spike into the coordinates opposite the star then rendezvous with the planet in a reverse orbit."

"You sure make it sound easy." Paloon leaned back in his seat and folded his arms. "But you haven't got to why it's so important for us to risk spiking into a system and into p'tahian-held territory."

Dorin turned to toss Paloon an "Are you stupid?" look.

"The residents of this planet almost completely resemble atlantians. And they inhabit three other planets as well." Dorin straightened his back. "What do you think the p'tahians would do if they found them?"

Everyone knew what would happen; Dorin knew it and didn't wait for an answer. "Recently, Knight Kendrick found illegal weapons on Terra Four, to include a particle laser. That technology is far beyond the planet, so someone may be shipping it in."

"Who would be that crazy?" Larin asked. "Are you sure they didn't take a technological leap forward?"

"Kendrick doubts it," Dorin replied, "but in either case they or someone else will eventually make too much of a signal and draw the attention of a passing p'tahian scout."

The room suddenly grew quiet. Then Paloon's chair squeaked as he sat up again.

"So we have to stop this advancement—or the smuggling of this technology—to keep the p'tahians from noticing these *terrans*." Paloon spoke the last word as if he didn't believe the race it described existed.

"Now that we all understand the mission," Dorin said with an air of accomplishment as he walked behind the lectern. His paws thumped various keys.

The hologram fell apart as Dorin rummaged through a drawer in the lectern. He withdrew four chip boxes and placed them on the lectern, then he withdrew four data pads, which he immediately distributed to the team.

"Kendrick is the fifth member of your team. Limited Dragon Corps authority has been extended to him, and since you will not have a direct Dragon Corps representative with you, he is in charge of the mission." Dorin stopped at Paloon and slowly handed him the last pad. "Until you jump into the area, Hunter Osluf is in charge."

Paloon snatched the pad out of Dorin's paw. The count returned to the lectern.

"The pads have the full explanation of the mission and the equipment you are to deploy with." Dorin clutched the chip boxes and passed them out, starting with Hitook. "These are your language and data chips. Download these prior to your arrival. They contain five common languages, some local history, economics, government and social skills. The final one covers native weaponry."

Dorin stopped in front of Paloon again. The count opened the chip box and withdrew one of the small, flat rectangular chips.

"Your vehicles are from Corps technology but made to look like terran vehicles." Dorin snapped the box shut and set it down in front of Paloon. "Because they are unique for this mission, we only had time to make two chips on maintenance. Paloon has one because he's Force Grey Wolf. Who gets the other?"

Though Dorin was looking over everyone's heads, Paloon knew the question was for him. Instinctively he said, "Hitook."

Dorin walked down the length of the table and watched the chip almost disappear in Hitook's massive paw.

The count returned to the center of the room and faced the team.

"All other answers are in the data pads. Hunter Osluf, you have vehicle prep details. Lieutenant Mulkin, you have weapons check and load details. Ninja Adian, you have equipment check and load details. Acolyte Riqhim, you have fuel and stores." With no delay, Count Dorin headed out an already opening door. "We step in five and launch in six with an immediate scheduled jump. Time to move."

Dorin disappeared through the door.

The team stood, pocketed the pads and chip boxes and stepped around the table to follow Dorin out the door. No time to discuss the mission. They didn't have much time to ready for launch.

The ship's coating was of a deep black color. Its darkness, compounded with a seamless hull, made the vessel appear as an elongated black hole. Flight prep activity and the metallic walls of the docking bay surrounded what appeared to be a complete lack of space and matter.

Paloon couldn't keep from staring at it. Watching from the fifth-story balcony, his eyes kept getting lost in the ship's hull. He had heard about this new breed of special operations ships: Apollyon class. They had been in the fleet for just under two years.

To a terran, an Apollyon class vessel would appear like two extended-cab semi-trucks with their trailers welded together side-by-side and the tires replaced with retractable skids that only held the ship one foot from the bay floor. If this vessel's name wasn't also painted in black, "Vendetta" would stretch along the nose.

The butt end of the craft held an electromagnetic reverse-gravity pulse drive, the ship's primary propulsion and a super quiet engine that was also hard to detect with standard scanners. Wrapped around the hull next to the pulse drive sat one of two multi-directional, plasma-induced ion drives. The other separated the cargo hull from the cockpit. With both ion drives synchronized, they could push the ship in any direction, pitch or roll.

Beautiful, was all that kept coming to Paloon's mind. The only disappointing factor, and then only slightly, came from its inferior size in the immense docking bay.

Faint streaks of light suddenly marred the Vendetta's cargo hull. The streaks widened and brightened as a loading door folded down from the ship like an opening palm. That's when Paloon noticed one of the workers marshaling the vehicles that Paloon had checked earlier.

The first looked like a bread truck. Dark blue, it housed most of the team's heavy surveillance equipment. Behind it floated a sharp-angled black station wagon. Paloon didn't like the design, but if all the specs were right—from what he could tell, they were—this medium-armored tank would be invaluable if the mission went sour.

"Hey!"

"Shit!" Paloon blurted, his body jerking in surprise. He spun to see a rather cheerful Ky.

Her smile stretched far enough to reveal both sets of fangs. A black sweat band wrapped around her head and under bouncing bangs that glowed a darker red due to their collected moisture. Pointed ears glistened with a minute amount of sweat, which clung to strands of hair that strayed from her ponytail. The ponytail swayed slightly, much less than her tail that swished back and forth excitedly.

Where in the hell did she come from? Paloon shook his head and turned back to watch the beginning of the cargo loading.

"What's up?" Ky leaned forward on the rail next to Paloon.

"Just watching the activity." Paloon also sought a bit of peace, but that seemed to have come to an end. "Why are you so cheerful?" He realized how rude that must have sounded, right after saying it.

"White moon." Ky didn't let Paloon's rough statement bother her.

"Excuse me?"

"White moon." Ky paused long enough to decide to explain. "The planet has a white moon."

Paloon cocked his head to see a chip transfer computer resting on Ky's left arm. Its green light blinked steadily as the machine downloaded the data chip's information into sub-dermal connections linked straight to the neural storage in her brain. Other than the vehicle data, Paloon hadn't downloaded the chips Count Dorin had passed out.

"Oh," Paloon replied, returning his attention to the ship and thinking, *It takes all kinds.*

"I grew up on a moonless planet," Ky began to offer. "When I joined the Corps, I went to Wyvern for all my House Bravo training. Of course, Wyvern has Griffin, but I was stationed on the opposite side of the planet. I just think it would be neat to see a full white moon at night."

Paloon's eyes darted at Ky and back.

"Other than that, Larin sent me up here to tell you he's done with the weapons check." Ky blew away one strand of hair that had clung to her forehead and slightly tickled her. "Hitook and I are already done."

"Good." Paloon tapped the rail bar. The load crew below appeared to be finishing. The only thing left would be the closing of the cargo door. He took a quick peek at the clock in the far upper left corner of his vision. Almost perfect, but ten minutes ahead of schedule wasn't bad. "Tell everyone to meet in the cockpit in five."

"Aye, aye."

Paloon stood and poked into his pockets for those data chips he had lost track of in the past couple of hours. When he turned to ask Ky to barrow one of hers, he was startled for the second time in two minutes. *Where in the hell did she go?*

Without a sound, she had disappeared.

He gave up for sanity's sake and started walking along the balcony to the stairs. With each step, the metal grates clanged into an echo that bounced around the docking bay.

Chapter 15

The quiet cockpit formed a rectangle. Two command chairs faced the front. Paloon slipped into the left console and directed Hitook to take the other.

The rear of the long but narrow cab accommodated two additional consoles. Larin instinctively sat in the weapons chair behind and to the left of Paloon, which left Ky with the engineer's seat.

She knew as much about the engineering station as Hitook knew about the navigator's station, which was almost nothing. Both relied on Paloon to operate the stations from his console, and the hunter planned to do exactly that.

Larin tapped away, running diagnostic checks again and again. The Vendetta didn't have much for weapon systems. Even the station wagon tank in the cargo hold had a more powerful cannon than this vessel did. That came with the design. The Vendetta, just like all Apollyon class craft, was designed for speed penetration. If ever in combat, its strongest weapon would be to scram, fast.

Hitook watched displays as Paloon remotely programmed the navigator's console. The holographic screens animated the team's route before lining up for a long spike into their destination galaxy. The galaxy wasn't small, but it wasn't big either. As the computer zoomed in, the galaxy's spiral arms filled then overflowed the screen. It stopped, showing the spike ending in a rather small solar system. Small not by the number of planets, but the fact that only three were of decent size.

"Link up," Paloon ordered as he rested his head in the back of the chair. With a tap of a key and a minor crackle, a plate electromagnetically sealed to Paloon's sub-dermal connectors on the back of his neck. As he pulled his head away, cables trailed out of the chair and began transferring data back and forth from Paloon's brain to Vendetta's brain.

The others did the same, except for Hitook, who took the plate by hand and weaved it under his fur before tapping the activation key.

"Everyone connected?" Paloon thought.

He received a resounding *"Yes"* from everyone.

"Good. Larin, how are the weapon systems?"

"In the blue."

"Great. Stand by to disembark."

With a minor thought, Paloon connected to the space traffic control tower.

"Dolphin Control, Vendetta."

"Vendetta, go ahead for Dolphin Control."

"Request departure from Bay Twelve to Jump Five."

"Standby."

After checking local traffic, the controller returned.

"Vendetta, Dolphin Control. Begin disembarkation from Bay Twelve. Stay within station's perimeter until lock to Jump Five. From the system plane, lock to bearing eight niner three point five, break three one four point four, break four three zero point one. Proceed. NLS authorized."

"Copy." Paloon read back the numbers as they appeared on the lower left of Hitook's screen. Then a circle dissected the screen's graphic of their current three-planet system, and the Vendetta used the numbers to plot lines to mark the degree, then the arc, then the distance from the star. All the lines disappeared until a single dot floated above the system.

"Beginning disembarkation."

"Roger."

Inside the bay, yellow lights flashed in tune to a blaring horn. "Launch in progress. Five minutes until vacuum. Launch in progress. Five minutes until vacuum."

Paloon fired the Vendetta's ion drives. Small indicators to the right side of his vision showed the progress of the warming engines. Outside, the wraparound vents turned a dark blue, now the only visible feature on the craft.

Before the ion drives fully charged, he activated the dynamo that powered the main pulse drive. At first it rattled the ship, then the fusion reactor gave power to the drives to compensate for the dynamo's spin. Together, they adjusted more smoothly as the dynamo increased in speed.

"I hope you guys brought snacks," Paloon commented while they waited.

"We have ninety rations in cargo." Hitook replied instinctively from the count he conducted while in charge of the ship's stores.

"Why?" Ky asked.

"Looks like we're in for sixteen hours of jumping, followed by a twenty-two-hour spike."

"Frap," Larin instinctively griped as Ky sighed; she was suddenly unhappy with her decision to put all the rations in the cargo bay.

No one had bothered to ask or check that part of the mission chip. Paloon would have, but because of a little procrastination, he just discovered the problem.

This spike was going to be longer than any of the passengers had been through. The longest Paloon had ever gone through during his training lasted fourteen hours, and it left him with one serious headache.

The launch bay had been evacuated long before the countdown had even begun, but with the warning finished, the flashing yellow lights shifted to blue. Blast doors began closing over all doorways as vents started removing the air.

With the last of the air gone, blue lights lit the border of the bay's hangar doors, which split with a sudden jerk and then parted smoothly. That's when Paloon engaged the ion drives, slowly lifting the Vendetta off the bay floor and retracting the ship's skids.

Ky, impressed by the smoothness with which Paloon handled the craft, was about to offer a compliment. And then she almost lost her breakfast.

Paloon kicked in the rear ion drive to swing the back of the ship wide in an arc. Just as the Vendetta came parallel with the hangar doors, he fired the other drive and blasted the ship broadside out of the bay.

Larin released a *"Yay"* more in shock than cheering, while Ky suppressed a yelp and Hitook held a solid grip on his armrests. Meanwhile, Paloon sported a pleased smirk. He really liked this ship.

The occupants didn't pay much attention to the heavy traffic zooming around the planet and its several space stations, mostly because they didn't have time.

Just as they cleared the station's safety perimeter, Paloon shoved the nose down into an almost one hundred and eighty degree spin, with a slight pan away from the planet, while rotating the fuselage like a corkscrew.

The move forced Ky's eyes closed. She didn't care for space travel much—at least not when it felt more like a roller coaster.

Paloon stopped the vessel's multiple spins dead on to the trajectory he needed. The smirk morphed to a smile. He really, *really* liked this ship.

Immediately, the main pulse drive kicked in, and the Vendetta shot smoothly out of the planet's invisible magnetic field. The grips on the chairs relaxed as the crew realized the rest of the trip should remain fairly smooth, though with a long spike.

Larin felt he had enough time to ask about what had started to pester him. *"Why didn't anyone store the rations up here?"*

"I didn't know we would need them, so I put them in storage in—" Hitook couldn't finish his explanation.

"What were you thinking?" Larin's frustration went audible as he started flailing his arms.

"Back off," Ky cut in. *"He didn't know; none of us knew. We never bothered to ask. He asked me, and I told him to put them in the rear storage with everything else. Who knew? If you did, then it's your fault for not mentioning it; otherwise, shut up."*

Larin plowed his elbows into the armrests and frowned. *"How are we going to get to the rations? I'm going to start eating this chair in about three hours if we can't get to them."*

"There's an access hatch between you and Ky," Paloon replied. He had already started on the problem, mentally sifting through the ship's schematics and documents. Images flickered in his vision until they locked on the access hatch schematic. *"But it's a bit small. Let's hope Hitook won't get stuck."*

Hitook snapped his head at a forty-five degree angle and from the corner of his eye stared at Paloon. The large liqua didn't know how to take the statement, and he couldn't tell if Paloon was joking.

"Ha. Ha," It was Larin with a strained, faked laugh. *"I take back*

my original comment. If I don't get my food in three hours, I'll set fire to my chair and roast you over it."

Briefly, Larin's tone of voice made Ky believe the rolbrid would actually do it.

"Relax." Paloon punched up the schematics of the hatch so they displayed in everyone's view. *"It looks like it's large enough for Ky to fit through."*

"Excuse me?" Ky barked, audibly and mentally.

"My apologies." Paloon turned off the schematics. *"It appears that Ky is 'rail thin enough' to get through."*

"Better." Ky huffed. *"But not much."*

"Vendetta, this is Dragon Jump Control."

The female voice caught everyone's attention.

"Go ahead, Jump Control, this is Vendetta." Paloon then noticed they had traveled close enough to begin their jumps.

"We have you scheduled for Tube Five to Intragalactic Jump Point Kilo. Confirm."

"Confirmed."

"Stay on your current course. We are taking control in two."

Paloon turned on the autopilot, mentally relaxed from the controls and sat back in his chair.

Straight ahead, a glowing speck shined brighter than the nearby stars. Then it flashed like a camera bulb. A ship must have arrived.

To the left of the speck, far in front of the Vendetta, the crew also saw the faint outline of another ship on a course for the jump point. Paloon could tell from the ship's outline that it was a commercial freighter, probably on a trip to retrieve ore from one of the Corps' mining locations.

The speck of the jump station gradually grew larger; then it seemed to split in two. The second spawned speck started glowing brighter and brighter while growing in size five times more quickly than the original speck.

Then the crew suddenly saw what it was—a combat cruiser. Just shy of five miles long, slightly more than a mile high and less than a quarter of a mile wide, it dwarfed the Vendetta.

It zoomed past the Vendetta about ten miles off of its high left. The cruiser had its front thrusters on full throttle, countering the ship's immense momentum of coming out of a jump. The glowing thrusters created what looked like two blue dwarf stars as headlights.

Light from the thrusters and the star in front of them highlighted details of the otherwise almost truly black vessel.

On the top of the cruiser sat two sets of overlapping rail cannons. A duplicate arrangement covered the bottom. Numerous hatches that encased pop-up laser, pulse and plasma cannons spotted the sides. In the center, a light-colored stylized five-pointed star surrounded a Force Grey Wolf patch. Below the images were the words "Southern Cross."

Paloon felt a moment of pride. He served on a Polaris class cruiser before, the Chimera. It was ten years ago, but he wished he could again someday. Paloon missed the kind of teamwork and family atmosphere a five-year tour created.

The other members of the Vendetta just watched attentively as the Southern Cross slowed but sailed on by.

"Vendetta, this is Jump Control. We have you locked. Beginning sequence in one."

The crew turned back to the front. What once looked like a nearby star now appeared as a small moon with a honeycomb of eight jump tubes surrounding it. Each tube appeared as a skeleton of a frame, but the design allowed each one to expand and elongate to accommodate the largest of the Corps' ships.

"Stand by," the voice from Jump Control returned. Somewhere in the station on the face of the moon, someone they couldn't see had full control of the ship. *"Engaged."*

The view from the Vendetta cockpit turned tinted purple-black from Jump Control's activation of the ship's ion shield. Control then opened the throttle on the pulse drive, planting everyone firmly in the seats.

The lower left tube waited. Its skeletal branches sparked with energy. With a perfectly timed sequence of electromagnetic impulses, the laws of matter would no longer bind the ion-shelled craft; it would merge with space-time on a preset, unwavering course.

Jump Control now closed the Vendetta's blast curtains over the windows. The solid curtains slid up on the forward windows and from the rear on the side windows. For most of the trip, the crew would see nothing but in the inside of the ship. If they ever lowered the curtains, the team members would most likely go blind or possibly insane, perhaps suicidal. Regardless, test subjects never survived the experience with all mental facilities intact—a phenomenon that most scientists still held in amazement.

Electromagnetic jolts rocked the ship forward in rapid sequence. Then as suddenly as it started, it ended. Gravity came from all directions, and sound seemed to hang in the air. They had merged with space-time.

"How many jumps do we have?" Ky asked.

"Only two," Paloon replied.

"Then how long is this one?" Larin seemed a bit agitated.

"Six hours." Paloon knew exactly what consumed Larin's mind; he began to think it must be the only thing rolbrids think about.

"So where's the food?"

Chapter 16

"You're kidding, right?" Ky crouched on her hands and knees staring down the open access hatch. She shook her head, then sat back on her heels. "What was this designed for, mice?"

The slightly rectangular, narrow tunnel stretched all the way to the cargo bay. Along the way, parts of it opened into the ship's internal mechanisms.

"Trust me." Paloon had his console chair turned around to face the rear of the ship. He thumbed toward Larin. "According to the schematics, even Larin could make it. Barely."

"Then send him through." Ky planted her left hand back on her seat as if preparing to boost herself up and out of this food run. "He's the one who wants the rations so bad."

"It's too dangerous. You're—"

"I'm what, expendable?"

"No." Paloon moved his hands downward in a motion designed to calm Ky. "You have a smaller frame, which makes it much less dangerous for you."

Ky folded her arms and snarled, one fang visible. "Great, years of watching my weight and this is what I get."

Paloon motioned toward the hatch with an open palm. "Please."

"Fine," Ky agreed as she situated herself on her back. Then she peered up at Larin. "I'm going to make you pay. You realized that, don't you?"

Larin didn't care; he needed his food. Besides, Ky didn't wait for an answer. She hadn't bluffed; it was a statement of fact.

She pushed with her boots and scooted into the access. If anyone had asked, Ky would say she wasn't claustrophobic; she just didn't like small hatches. This hatch only gave her about three inches of space on each side and maybe a foot above her eyes. Not too small, but she didn't like it.

Ky progressed far enough to use her hands on the sides of the access tunnel, but her tail really began to hurt. Sliding on the metal corridor seriously pulled it. She wiggled farther until the ceiling opened, allowing her to see the bottom of the ion drive, cascading electricity covering it.

"Are you absolutely sure this is safe?" Ky had second thoughts before, and seeing this didn't improve her mental state any.

"We aren't navigating, so the plasma injectors aren't firing. As long as they aren't firing, you're completely safe." Paloon truly hoped Ky wouldn't give up; he didn't feel like having to restrain Larin until they finished the trip. Hungry rolbrids get extremely unpleasant to be around.

As if responding to Paloon's thoughts, Larin started reaching for

Ky's feet, probably to play a practical joke to scare her.

One of Hitook's massive paws whipped out and clamped down on Larin wrists. *"Don't,"* Hitook mentally shot through the connections the three of them still wore.

Larin jerked his hands out of the forceful grip. *"Look here, acolyte, I outrank you. Do that again, and—"*

"He's right," Paloon butted in. *"It's too unsafe."* He then pointed at the hatch. *"She's doing this for you; can't you stop the joking for a little while?"*

Larin crinkled his nose in a forced frown, closed his eyes, threw himself back in the chair and turned away.

Ky heard the seat move and the rustling of hands through a dulled echo in the tight corridor. "Is there something wrong?"

"Not at all." Paloon turned away from Larin. "You're doing fine." Ky's feet disappeared into the access way. "Are you at the hatch controls yet?"

"Not yet," Ky huffed.

Apparently Paloon had misjudged the distance, so he pulled up the schematics again just before he heard the reply.

"I'm there."

Ky slid her right arm over her chest, paused to bite off the pain coming from her tail, then tapped the hatch button on the corridor's ceiling. The tiny door hissed open, and Ky continued her journey.

"I'm through."

Above her now was the underside of the station wagon tank. Ky sighed, but she had more room to move her hands. She grabbed at the undercarriage and continued sideways to finally pull herself out from under the vehicle.

In a dead space of the cargo bay, she stood. Ky made the move too quickly and gravity began pulling her up. With a quick punch on the ceiling, she pushed away far enough for gravity to pull her back down to the floor.

The tank stretched down one side of the cargo bay, and the shorter van sat pushed to the back to allow for an open square space. On the outside wall, their weapons rested in racks with some stowed in drawers. Only drawers covered the other wall.

Ky knelt and stabbed the release button on the bottom drawer. It popped open to reveal stacks of shrink-wrapped meals and bottles of water.

"How many?" Ky yelled back in the direction of the hatch.

Paloon hesitated. At first, he thought twelve should be enough for the entire trip. Then he assessed the rolbrid's appetite. "Eighteen."

"Are you sure?" Ky barked. "I'm not coming back."

"Twenty-two." Paloon's voice rang muffled in the bay.

Ky started counting the rations and grabbed twice as many bottles of water. That reminded her of one of the few things she had heard about distance traveling. She shut the bottom drawer then punched open the one above it. She retrieved four thermos-type tubes and rifled through some medical supplies. Ky finally found what she sought and selected a couple of medicine boxes, each about six inches square.

With rapid motions, Ky forcefully slid the items under the tank toward the hatch. As she dove under the car, she remembered the open drawer and pushed it closed with her foot. On her belly, she yelled, "Incoming!" and flung the individual items down the tiny corridor.

At the other end, Paloon tapped Hitook on the shoulder and pointed to a door next to Ky's station. Hitook opened it just as Paloon received the first ration and tossed it to the liqua, who immediately put it in the new storage location.

"Hey!" Larin objected.

"Later." Paloon's comment prompted another frown.

After the rations, Ky began rolling the bottles of water. The two in the cockpit had a good system and never lost a beat. Then the four metal canisters shot out.

"Good thinking." Paloon tossed one at Larin who fumbled with it briefly before recovering.

"What's this for?"

"After about four bottles of water, I'm sure you'll figure it out." Paloon tossed one to Hitook and threw another on Ky's seat before thinking about another useful item that would limit their need to eat so much. That's when he shouted down the corridor. "Did you find any—"

Just then the medicine boxes slid from the hatch.

"Never mind." Paloon placed the boxes on his lap and motioned for Hitook to go ahead and close the storage door.

In the cargo bay, Ky had already rolled over and turned around to begin her return journey, feet first. She had to enter feet first so she could reach the hatch mechanism to close it on her way out, but her tail didn't like the arrangement one bit. Twice as much pain this time shot through her spine. Ky nurtured a well-developed desire to kill the one responsible.

"Here." Paloon opened one of the medicine boxes, rummaged through and handed a large green pill to Larin and one to Hitook before taking one himself.

"Now, what's this for?" Larin rotated the pill in his fingers, studying it like a scientist. Hitook just swallowed his.

"That metal bottle only filters one thing. These pills lock up everything else." Paloon set a pill on Ky's chair, closed the medicine case and put it in an oversized pouch on the back of Hitook's chair. *"At least they'll do it long enough for this trip."*

Larin frowned again. He wasn't sure if the headache had returned or if the overall unpleasantness of this trip so far had gotten to him. *"Forget I asked."*

Then Paloon opened the other medicine box and passed out two, small white tablets to each. *"Before you ask, these will slow down your metabolism and reduce your appetite."* He then placed the box in a pouch behind his seat.

Ky's feet poked through the hatch into the cockpit. As soon as she could get a decent footing, she yanked herself clear of the small opening.

Summoning all of her self-restraint, she barely kept from lunging at Larin's throat, but she did almost pierce him with a deadly finger. "If you want anything else," her voice growled as she also shot him a look a demon would be proud of, "I'll personally cram you through that coffin with my boot so you can get it your damn self!"

No one was going to argue.

The cockpit was quiet, much as it had been for at least the past hour.

Ky sat back in her chair with her eyes closed, chip reader flashing as she continued to download all her mission information. Hitook's eyes shifted around as his chip reader blinked away. Larin kept himself busy opening computer panels with a hand-held tool kit that appeared from one of his pockets.

Paloon's reader had stopped blinking, but he didn't notice. The music he had turned on had him on the borderline of snoring. Reclining in his chair helped him relax.

"Beady, bleep. Beady, bleep. Prepare for arrival." The neutral voice, accompanied by the synthesized tones, shot through each person's mental jack, startling everyone.

"What the frap is that?" Larin turned to look at their resident vehicle expert.

Paloon blinked and instinctively yawned. *"That,"* he began as he sat up, the chair back following him, *"is our five-minute arrival warning."*

He bent his neck to both sides, popping cartilage with each move. *"You might want to prepare and buckle up."* Paloon turned to look at everyone, then noticed an open panel behind Larin. *"What are you doing?"*

"I was bored, so I decided to take a closer look at how this weapon diagnostic computer is designed." Larin pointed a fiber optic camera at the open panel. *"I'm just looking."*

"Close it." Paloon's arched brow sent a signal that Larin was pushing his luck.

Paloon had enough on his mind; he didn't need to be baby-sitting anyone. That thought for some reason made him check the chip reader on his left wrist. Once he noticed the current chip had finished downloading, a minor mental impulse popped it out. He dug into his leg pocket to get the chip cube and swapped chips. With a firm push, a new chip loaded and soon began its download. History, it seemed to be.

The others rustled briefly to adjust themselves properly in their seats and then waited quietly. Too long. This trip had only just begun, and it was already too long.

"How long is the next jump?" Larin sounded distressed.

"About nine and a half hours." Paloon answered while adjusting his seat belt to a more comfortable position.

"Great," Larin groaned, *"they're getting longer."*

"Don't gripe now." Paloon turned to face Larin and smile. *"It'll get better."*

Larin squinted his yellow eyes at Paloon. *"That was sarcasm, wasn't it? On your high 'I'm Force Grey Wolf' horse. You think this is funny, dragging a bunch of grounders through jump after jump."*

"Speak for yourself," Ky butted in, still bitter because her tail continued to hurt. *"And while you're speaking for yourself, why don't you speak* to *yourself and shut up."*

Larin glared at Ky and gritted his teeth, which were almost as yellow as his eyes.

"Beady, bleep. Beady, bleep. Thirty seconds."

Everyone quieted and waited.

"Fifteen. Ten. Five."

The ship began to rock violently as the sound of electrical sparks became deafening inside the cockpit. First the ship's momentum shot it forward, then the arrival tube reversed polarity in an attempt to slow the ship as much as possible.

With an additional reverse jolt, the ship's miniature forward thrusters fired to finish the slowing as the violent rocking calmed.

"Welcome to Intragalactic Jump Point Kilo, Vendetta. This is Jump Control. You have no delay. We have you in the pattern and slotted for Tube Three with a final destination of Intragalactic Jump Point Quebec. Confirm."

"Jump Control, this is Vendetta." With a mental flick, Paloon retrieved the mission's navigation files. *"Confirm Tube Three to Intragalactic Jump Point Quebec."*

"Roger, Vendetta. Prepare for sequence in fifteen."

The ship banked sharply as Jump Control turned it around to line it up with the other tube. Then the pulse drive kicked in, and they shot forward. The electromagnetic fluxes jostled the ship around until, finally, the ride became smooth again.

Chapter 17

Ky could only finish half of the food on her plate. She slid the uneaten portion back into the ration bag, affixed the closure and pressed the small green pad, activating a micro-motor, which vacuum-sealed the bag around the tray. She set it down beside the water bottle that was resting on a small bench she earlier had pulled from the wall next to her station.

The others continued to eat. Of course, Larin held the honor of being the most voracious of all at the endeavor. He had already completed his second tray on this meal break. It wasn't that Larin was gross or sloppy; he just seemed to be such a bottomless pit for being such a small creature. Ky felt repelled, but she was vaguely fascinated by the physics that made it possible.

Larin finished the tray then tossed it in its bag and resealed it. Then he clamped his hand on a water bottle and downed it like he was drinking air. The water gone, he closed the lid and belched. Because of his race's odd vocal cord structure, those who didn't know any better would swear it wasn't a belch but a glass cup shattering on a metal floor.

"You're disgusting." Ky turned her back to him.

"Ah, you're just envious because you can't eat more than an apple before you're full." Larin tried to hold back another belch but failed. This time, it sounded like the faint tinkling of a crystal chandelier.

Ky felt Larin's words didn't deserve the respect of a reply. So Larin waited but finally gave up and chuckled at his own joke.

It became quiet again as Larin leaned back in his chair and picked at his teeth with his tongue. Larin's chip reader then halted its blinking cycle. With a short mental impulse, it ejected.

"That," Larin explained vocally to no one in particular as he lifted the chip from the reader to hold it out between his thumb and finger, "was a complete waste of time."

He flicked it into one of his left pockets and rummaged for the chip cube. Locating the cube, he loaded the third to the last chip he had.

The comment halted Paloon in mid-chew, and he waited for Larin to explain himself. Ky came to the correct conclusion that Larin wasn't going to offer to speak up without encouragement.

"What in the hell are you talking about?" Ky's quiet statement seemed to hold back enough force to knock a moon out of orbit.

"That bit about the p'tahians." Larin reached for the next ration and tore into it. "They could have at least condensed it to 'We don't know a frapping thing.' It took me fifteen minutes to download that last bit, and for what? Not a damn thing."

Paloon resumed chewing and sat back with an arched eyebrow. He hadn't gotten to that chip yet. He was behind the rest mainly because he never liked the idea of memories, for the lack of a better term, being uncontrollably crammed into his head.

Ky just huffed at Larin's frustration as she looked away. That's when she noticed Hitook just sitting calmly and eating, seemingly paying attention to no one.

Oddly, no one seemed to notice that they were holding the conversation orally instead of using the ship's internal communications.

"Come on." Larin waved a hand in a broad sweeping motion at everyone else as he finished chewing a new bite. "I can't be the only one here who's starting to have second thoughts. Here we are, poorly manned, lightly armed and heading into p'tahian territory. We don't even have a representative from the Corps. Our count is sitting on his furry ass back at the station!" Larin silenced himself briefly, then mumbled, "That could be considered a good thing."

"The Corps knows what it's doing," Paloon added calmly.

Ky folded her arms then lifted a finger and aimed it at Larin. "He does have a point."

Everyone, to include Hitook, stopped to stare at Ky. *Did she just agree with Larin?*

"What!?" she barked in response to the strange looks. "He just said what I've been thinking."

"Blessed crap." Larin couldn't believe what he heard. He almost retrieved that last bit of protein that passed for food just so he could choke on it again.

"Think about it." Ky pointed at Paloon this time. "When have you heard of a team, larger than two, penetrate hostile territory to hunt for weapons smugglers without a Corps representative?"

She retracted her finger and just stared at him. Ky realized she got Paloon thinking, and she realized he did not like what he was thinking. The scenario she described never happened, but here they were.

"Those freaking Corps weenies are power hungry." Larin threw himself back into a rant. "They prance around the universe playing mightier-than-thou games and will never let you forget that they are the judge and jury and we are only the executioners. I swear they must thrive from it. They don't pass off that power. Period. But they just passed their power to a knight, which makes me want to know what kind of frapping hooha we're in the middle of."

"You guys are getting a bit paranoid, don't you think?" Paloon set down his meal and took a swig of water, then pointed toward Larin. "You said it earlier; we're entering p'tahian territory. This is a delicate situation. No one's heard from them for centuries."

"That's because they're a bunch of warmongering narcissistic racists with a supreme-being complex!" Larin belted the phrase faster than a whip, and its impact was just as sharp.

Ky's ears perked, and she cocked her head toward Larin. "You, of all people, can actually use 'narcissistic' correctly. I'm amazed."

"Don't you start in on me now you...you—"

"All right, knock it off!" Paloon stood up almost fast enough to bash his head on the roof. "Let's put our internal rivalries away for now."

Paloon slowly took his seat again as Hitook shook his head and returned to his rations. The brief period of mutual understanding between Ky and Larin didn't last for long.

"Look," Paloon leaned forward, resting with elbows on knees, "because it *is* p'tahian territory is probably why they are doing it this way.

"What if we're found?" Paloon paused but not long enough for anyone to offer an answer. "The p'tahians would eliminate us and most likely the beings on the planet as well. But they might not do it before they find out we're from the Corps. What do you think will happen then?" Another short pause. "War. Pure and simple, the p'tahians will most likely break from their self-created shell and go on some kind of jihad to exterminate the universe."

"You're not making this better," Larin offered.

"Ah," Paloon held up a finger, "but without a direct representative from the Corps, like, say, a *count*, the Corps can claim we were rebels who were being hunted down."

"Oh." Larin scrunched his face. "I feel so much *frapping* better now. Thanks, captain."

Hitook just gazed at Paloon with a blank expression.

"But that's not going to happen, is it?" Paloon scanned the cockpit with his eyes. He had Larin and Hitook's attention, but Ky peered away. "I don't plan on screwing up. If you are," he instinctively flicked back to Larin, "I'll kill you before you can."

That wasn't a threat. Everyone knew it. So the statement just hung there as Paloon took another drink. Hitook looked back at his ration, decided he had eaten enough and put it away. Larin returned to his meal and resumed eating at a ferocious speed.

"F...u...c...k...e...d." Ky stumbled on the word, then she got it. "Fucked!"

Everyone else looked at her as she turned around slowly, a smile playing at the edges of her mouth. She spoke in a language no one else had heard before.

"What was that?" Larin asked.

"I believe," Ky began, the smile widening, "that is the proper translation of our current situation in one of the languages of Terra. We're *fucked!*"

"Ooookaaayyy." Paloon's eyes darted about. He had no idea what she was saying but decided to play along. "Good point, Ky. I want everyone to start loading the language chip and after we begin the spike, everyone will speak in terran languages. We're going to need some practice before we get there."

Everyone nodded, and Ky drew her eyesight skyward as she began to think about the multitude of meanings that could be expressed with that one word.

Once again, silence infected the cockpit like a plague. The only noise came from Larin's snoring. But only Hitook could hear the high-pitched whining of the snore. It kept him awake but didn't bother him.

Actually, Hitook was the only one awake. But like everyone else, he had his chair turned so it could recline unimpeded into a horizontal position.

The liqua watched the ceiling in its attempt to go absolutely nowhere. Terran languages flooded his mind. He went over them again and again; he wanted to meet Paloon's request with great success. But no one was awake for him to converse with. He would have tried to speak out loud, but Hitook would have felt embarrassed in spite of himself.

"Beady, bleep. Beady, bleep. Prepare for arrival."

Larin uncontrollably screamed through the ship's computer and into everyone else's head.

The process literally shattered everyone else's sleep more effectively than the arrival message itself.

"Damn, I wish it wouldn't do that." Larin sat up, rubbing his flat head and moaning.

"I don't mind the computer's announcement," Ky said as she pulled herself up, blinked and then squinted at Larin. *"It's your yelling that will get you killed if it continues."*

Larin almost challenged her, but with one look at her, he realized only the threat of unspeakable vacuum kept her from punching him right through the ship's hull. So he held his tongue and turned away.

Paloon's chair rose with him. He turned to Hitook, still lying down. *"You should,"* then Paloon began the initial yawn, *"sit up for the arrival."*

Soon yawns rippled through the cabin in an almost perpetual session.

"You started this." Ky's message was specifically for Paloon. He turned to see her attempting to hold back a yawn. Her hand covered her mouth, so all he saw was glaring, angry green eyes.

The sight oddly made him want to yawn again.

"Jerk," Ky fired as she kicked the back of his seat.

Paloon distracted himself by loading the arrival programs again. Everything checked, so he retrieved a list of spike station operating sequences. A little refresher would help speed up the switch, and he didn't want to stay in this ship longer than absolutely necessary.

Everyone else secured their chair harnesses and continued attempts to wake themselves. The yawning trickled to stillness.

"Beady, bleep. Beady, bleep. Thirty seconds."

No one moved.

"Fifteen. Ten. Five."

Space gave way again as the ship crossed the threshold in a torrent of electrical fluctuations. Vibrating like a tuning fork, the ship bounced, then streaked forward before slamming backwards as the receiving tube decelerated the vessel.

The forward thrusters fired, rocketing the ship once again.

"Welcome Vendetta to Jump Point Quebec and the Urailez Cluster. This is Jump Control; we have you programmed for a departure from the cluster plane at five eight niner point two, break three two one point zero, break five five one point three."

As the blast shields slowly lowered, intense light filled the cockpit. Each passenger squinted in a feeble attempt to block the painfully bright light and still see.

"Jump Control, this is Vendetta. Confirmed." Paloon forced the reply while trying to force back the light.

"Roger, Vendetta. Prepare for release in fifteen."

"Standby, Jump Control." Paloon paused to gather his thoughts amidst the visual onslaught from the Urailez Cluster. *"Request holding pattern."*

"*Copy, Vendetta."* The controller returned in five seconds. *"We have you targeted for a holding pattern. Entering in ten. Standing by."*

"Thanks. Vendetta out."

Paloon knew he wasn't prepared to take over the controls of the ship just yet. He focused his eyes on the floor between his legs and blinked faster than a butterfly's wings flapped.

Larin and Ky quietly cursed the light, but Hitook calmly sat with his eyes closed.

It took Paloon almost five minutes before he could look out the window with little problem. This fight was worth it. He had never seen the Urailez Cluster before, and he found it breathtaking.

Embedded in shapeless, multi-colored clouds of cosmic debris and gas sat three red dwarf stars. The trio formed an invisible triangle around a reddish-orange giant. Cosmic gas swirled from star to star, jumping from one sun's orbit to the next, a web in interstellar hydrogen and helium.

Paloon guessed it had to be about ten light-years away, but the formation was more than bright enough.

The others began to join Paloon's awe, noticeable by their slight sighs and a faint "Wow."

Paloon shook himself back to the work at hand. His mind focused to take full control of the ship. *"Jump Control, this is the Vendetta requesting release in ten."*

"Copy, Vendetta. Release in ten. Five. Two, one."

Paloon didn't physically feel the ship's jolt; his mind was too busy straining to handle the shift of control.

He began to bank out of the holding pattern while calling up a navigational map he had worked on earlier. The star cluster disappeared and the cockpit darkened as Paloon rotated the ship around to align it in the direction of the blinking icon on the map. Then he punched it.

It was a short trip, barely noticeable. The station wasn't that far away, but far enough not to be affected by the gravitational forces from the intergalactic jumps.

The new station was now visible from the cockpit window. It looked like a four-legged spider, the tiny body of a space station gripping oversized arched legs.

"Vendetta, this is Spike Control. State your purpose."

"Spike Control, this is Vendetta, authorization," Paloon scanned the authorization letter in his visual display, *"eight baker niner five one nickel joker five seven."* He paused before explaining his order. *"Please relinquish your controls."*

Paloon didn't expect an immediate reply. This was a fairly common request at spike stations, but they didn't grant any order without verifying the authorization number.

To keep the enemy from knowing a ship's final destination, authorization codes gave a ship's pilot sole control over the station. It was accepted that the fewer people who knew where a ship was going, the safer its crew would be when it reached its destination.

It didn't keep the station staff from knowing the Dragon Corps was on the prowl. But with so much prowling to do around the universe, it almost became commonplace.

"Roger, Vendetta. Authorization confirmed. Welcome to Intraspace Spike Zeta. Standby for control in fifteen." The controller paused before backing away from his station. *"Happy hunting."*

The controller's voice blinked out, and Paloon shifted from his retinal displays to the cockpit's windows. Not much showed, but when the control switch occurred, the entire surface of the glass flashed. Gauges, star charts, meters, settings and monitors of all kinds now covered almost every square inch.

"Damn," Larin slipped, *"you can follow this?"*

His question remained unanswered as Paloon went to work. He fired countless mental commands at once: flipping through star charts, adjusting settings, triple checking equations and navigating the ship toward the center of the spike station's legs. When they reached the center, the blast shields closed again, somehow making the glass display brighter.

Outside, each of the station's legs split in threes. They glided along until they locked into place. Now the station appeared like a tiny spider with twelve frail legs. A field began weaving between the legs until it looked like a faint green orb surrounding the Vendetta.

The initial sequence complete, Paloon confirmed the destination coordinates. Computer calculations ran rapidly as they created the patch for the intraspace chute. On the display, the two star charts merged. Everything was finished. The computations checked, and the ship and station were in the blue.

"Standby," Paloon held the mental trigger, *"now."*

Spike Station Zeta shook as the field increased in intensity to an almost solid green. With a flash equal to that of a nuclear blast, the orb shifted to a multitude of colors writhing in indescribable patterns. Another flash and an orbital ring of blue gas shot from the station and dissipated a few light years out.

Below the spike station, time and space caved in, and the Vendetta started slipping through it. The bottom of the vessel began stretching toward the hole. Molecule by molecule, the vessel penetrated space, meshed with it, embedded. Then the Vendetta dropped into space.

Disoriented to the ninth degree, the crew instinctively fought to maintain consciousness. To release now would feel too much like dying.

The process of destabilization into the void of space took less than two minutes, but to the crew it felt like two hours. In only a mere minute of thought, the crew experienced what seemed like an hour-long fight to stay awake on the last day of a seven-day insomnia binge.

Without warning, the Vendetta seemed to snap back together.

"Holy frapping shit! I hate that!" Larin's eyes were wide as he gripped the armrests of his chair.

Everyone seemed bright-eyed from the release of mental anguish. Then sleep hit them like a tsunami. It came as a deep sleep that was neither forgiving nor prejudicial. Everyone slept, soundly.

Chapter 18

Am I awake? The thought shot through Paloon's mind a split second before he opened his eyes to see the ship's display resting at a tilt.

Paloon groaned in agony as he straightened his head, pulling it away from his right shoulder. Pain ripped through the nape of his neck.

He rubbed the back of his neck with both hands while he commanded the clock to appear. Nine hours and twenty-two minutes. He had been out for nine hours and twenty-two minutes. *No wonder,* he thought.

Paloon gingerly rotated his stiff neck and peered from the corner of slotted eyes to see that Hitook had been awake for a while. The liqua somehow found room next to his chair to sit cross-legged with his wrists resting on his knees in some form of a meditation pose. *Whatever,* Paloon thought.

Ky rested with her head back. She blinked at the ceiling as if just waking up.

Behind Paloon, Larin had his feet on one of the control panels and picked at his fingernails with a small knife. He turned to see Paloon. "Good...morning."

At first Paloon scowled and thought the dreams had not ended. Then he remembered his order for everyone to speak in terran languages.

"What is...wrong?" Larin took a bit of time to find the right words.

Paloon stumbled as he found sorting through the languages harder than he thought it would be. "I am fine."

Larin just cocked his head and shifted his eyesight back to his nails.

Paloon faced forward again and reclined his seat to relax his neck muscles before they broke.

"Does—" Ky's groggy voice seeped out. "Does that always...happen when you...spike?"

Paloon thought about the translation. "What happened?"

"Weird...dreams." She sat up briefly before leaning forward and dropping her face into cupped hands. The groggy voice became muffled-groggy. "There was a...six-eyed...pachyderm crawling on the...ceiling."

"Some people do...," Paloon began but kept his eyes closed to hold back the neck pain, "...experience...strange dreams. Not all, though."

"Strange?" Larin huffed. "That is...not strange. That's...frapping warped!" The rolbrid smiled, happy that he had found a rough translation for his favorite curse and had a chance to use it. It took him a while to find it. He couldn't find it under curse words, so he suffered a small setback. He had to piece together sound translations to create a word. He experienced minor disappointment that it didn't share the same meaning on Terra.

Ky figured now was the perfect time to use a hand gesture she learned from the chips. So she showed Larin her middle finger.

The gesture didn't register with him. He ignored her apparent muscle spasm and returned to his fingernails.

"Spikes can create," Paloon offered, "a great deal of...mental stress. You should be...okay...in a day."

Ky groaned. She wanted to be okay, now! Not tomorrow, now! *This sucks!* Her head began to throb and pound behind her eyes.

"Fuck!" She spouted her new favorite word and slammed her palm on the seat's back-release button to lie down.

Paloon was less than happy at their word choices, but they were learning, and that would help when they land.

"Hey, Paloon. You are supposed to be...an expert in this spike thing, right?" Larin almost sounded reluctant to ask.

"I am not an expert. I know...enough." Paloon contemplated going back to sleep, but his neck would probably keep him awake.

"Well...I've been thinking, and," Larin's voice trailed right before a "twang" sounded as his knife blade suddenly snapped out from under a nail, "if I...understand it right, these are one-way...trips. Correct?"

"Yes," grunted Paloon. He really didn't want to be pestered right now, especially by someone who apparently had been poking through technical data while the others were asleep.

"Then how...are we getting back?"

Paloon knew this would come up.

"Ah, fuck!" Ky spouted again. No one knew if the outburst represented a release of mental pain or frustration from Larin's uncanny ability to spotlight the negative.

"Larin," Paloon placed his right hand on his forehead and began to rub, "if the...Corps needs to...evacuate us, they'll spike in a temporary station."

"Oh." Larin tried to force his voice to sound like a scholar introduced to a new scientific method. It failed. It further irritated Paloon.

"This is not a...suicide mission." Paloon lowered his hand and worked to sustain the strength needed to keep his voice calm. "Please drop your...conspiracy theory."

"I'm not saying it is an, um, a conspiracy." Larin stopped cleaning his nails. "I'm just uncomfortable."

"Then eat something and shut the fuck up!" Ky made her point.

It got quiet.

"Ky?" Paloon probed.

"What!"

"There's a...medicine kit on the back of Hitook's chair." He pointed, but Ky refused to look. "Inside of it, you'll find some... medication for your head. It's a...shot with...a blue band. Take two."

"Ahhh," she began to protest.

"Take it!"

Her eyes flew open, and she shot a hard look at Paloon. All of her wanted to fight, but something kept her from the brink. She threw herself forward, yanked the kit from the chair and slammed in on her lap, her point lost, her lap now bruised.

Ky threw open the lid and rummaged through the box, needlessly tossing items about. She found the shots and jabbed them in her leg in rapid succession as she stared down Paloon for no reason.

The shots finished, she tossed them to the floor. "Happy!?" Ky slammed the kit shut and dropped it off her lap before throwing herself back in her chair.

Paloon looked skyward and slightly shook his head. She'd feel better in about five minutes. That spike apparently caused more mental stress than Paloon had thought possible. But the shots of biological nanites should find the problem and stabilize it.

"But," Larin began again in his forced-intellectual voice, "I've been thinking also about our team's...composition."

Paloon sighed, but Larin paid no attention.

"Why do we have two...House Bravo, and what's his story?" Larin thumbed at Hitook, but no one was looking. "I mean, why is he here? He doesn't even look like a terran. How are we going to...disguise him? We can't operate...covertly if we've got a huge, furry beacon waving his ears around. He might as well be ... shouting, 'Look, I'm not from this planet. I'm an alien.' This is—"

"Look." Paloon threw himself almost completely out of the seat as he turned around to face Larin. "Knock it off with these conspiracies. Kendrick and I will worry about it. All...I need from you," Paloon jabbed a finger at Larin then withdrew it, "is firepower when we need it. Can you do that?"

"Hell yes! I just don't want...to get stuck in a—"

"Like I said, don't worry about it." Paloon rotated back around then fished for a ration under his seat. "You just worry about the weapons. Now," Paloon tossed the ration behind him, "eat and shut the fuck up."

Larin snarled his lip briefly but soon turned his attention to the food and tore into the ration. The sound of the package's seal releasing its vacuum triggered a moment of relaxation for Paloon. At least Larin would be somewhat quiet for ten minutes or so. This *was* a long trip.

"But you just said that each star's magnetic field is unpredictable." Larin almost yelled while holding Paloon at finger-point.

"True, but—" Paloon didn't get the chance to finish.

"But that's dangerous, right?" Ky's eyes held a look of concern.

"To some degree, yes. The gravity, solar winds and magnetic fields can be highly unpredictable the farther beyond a system's heliopause you go, but we—"

Larin cut Paloon off.

"Then why are we on this slide to hell?"

"Look." Paloon flipped his eyesight from Larin to Ky. Hitook watched quietly. "This is a covert operation, so the Corps may take a degree of risk. But that degree of risk is not as great as you may think. We're in a small ship, so we've got a good ninety percent chance for a safe spike."

"Oh, great." Larin threw himself back in the chair. "I feel much better."

"Actually," Hitook's rarely heard voice slightly startled the rest, involved as they were in the conversation, "since Knight Kendrick obtained the point from Terra Four's orbit, we most likely have a greater chance."

"Good point." Paloon nodded toward Hitook. "We could have as much as a ninety-five percent success rate."

"What?" Larin waved his open hand to indicate Hitook. "We barely hear a peep out of him the entire trip and now he wants to debate."

"This is not a debate," Paloon clarified. "We can't stop the spike without absolute sudden death. There is some danger in continuing, sure, but there's no turning back."

"That's something else," Larin grabbed the tangent and ran with it. "I didn't volunteer for this mission; I doubt anyone here did. Why is that? Why am I on a covert mission that I didn't train for? Why—"

Larin halted his rant when Hitook turned around in his seat, offering his back to the rolbrid. Hitook had tired of Larin's negativity.

"Oh, what is it?" Larin scowled at Hitook's back. "I don't even understand why you're here."

"Knock it off," Ky kicked Larin's shin.

"Hey!" Larin pointed at Hitook. "I'm being honest. He'll stand out like a whale in a desert. What kind of covert operation sends along someone who doesn't have a chance in hell to blend in? Huh? Can somebody answer that?"

"Larin, could you just be quiet for a while?" Paloon paused only long enough to catch a short breath. "Obviously, someone in the Corps feels the skills he brings to our operation far outweigh his inability to blend in."

"That," Ky chuckled at Larin, "says more about you than it does him. Since you can easily pass for a four-fingered midget with severe laryngitis, great for circus work, you must not own many useful skills."

"Hey! Speak for yourself you...you—"

"Both of you," Paloon pointed palms at each and snapped his head back and forth, "knock it off. That's not quite what I meant. It—"

"Beady, bleep. Beady, bleep. Prepare for arrival."

"I'll get you." Larin wagged his finger at Ky.

"Bring it on, tiny." She smiled while adjusting herself in the seat.

"We don't have time for this, people." Paloon started calling up various displays on the cockpit window. "Secure your stations."

This time in silence, everyone continued to lock in their seats and seat backs while triple checking their harnesses.

"Okay, everyone." Paloon returned to speaking in pure thought. Doing so was best in case something happened. He scanned the displayed data. *"Because of the unknown on the other side, we are going to do this as a combat insertion."* He paused to change some figures. *"So I need everyone to place your left arm flat, palm down on the armrest."*

A bit reluctantly, everyone did so. Then Paloon placed his arm and activated clamps that held everyone's arm to the chair.

"Hey!" Larin and Ky protested in chorus.

"After we finish the spike, our bodies are going to be seriously fatigued." Paloon zoomed in on the star chart. *"Once the ship registers a completed spike, it will inject a stimulant to keep us alert."*

No one wanted to speculate on what could be waiting if they even made it. The ship remained silent while Paloon continued with his final procedures.

"Beady, bleep. Beady, bleep. Thirty seconds."

Paloon adjusted himself in his chair.

"Fifteen. Ten. Five."

Gravity seemed to well from every direction. Its force pulled at the matter of the ship until the very atoms began to loosen their bonds. An inch became a mile. The cockpit took on the size of a small planet. Then, like thousands of freight trains crashing, everything snapped back. The resurgence created a gravity flux almost as large as a medium-sized star.

Before anyone could pass out—they were all about two seconds from unconsciousness—the injections fired. Everyone screamed at being subjected to the shot after the mental stress, but the stress soon gave way to a pure, unadulterated adrenaline rush.

"What have we got people?" Paloon's command sent everyone flying.

With their arms free, they unlocked the chairs and turned to their stations.

"Weapons online." Larin snapped. *"No targets."*

"Level nine gravity well, Ky responded crisply, *"fourteen at fifteen."*

"Compensating," Hitook responded as he reprogrammed the ship's yaw to adjust to and use the new source of gravity.

Paloon pulled the ship away from the detected gravity and began lowering the blast shields.

Just as Ky saw Paloon had lined the ship with Terra's projected orbit, Paloon hit the main ion drive, and they blasted forward.

"Targets?" Paloon hoped the training he provided earlier would prove to be sufficient.

"Still nothing." Larin tapped through a few screens. *"All's clear. Except for some asteroids, there's nothing."*

"The gravity well checks to be the star." Ky flipped through her own charts. *"Charts check, we're in the right system."*

A small measure of relief washed over everyone, but the adrenaline still flowed.

"All's clear." Paloon made the decision. *"But keep the weapons up and keep monitoring. We're safe as long as we can make it onto the planet undetected. Ky, switch to a low-level, long-distance scan. Hitook, help me keep a visual scan."*

"We have a little more than a day's journey left." Paloon placed a couple of terran orbit models on the cockpit window. The Vendetta sat on the far orbit of the planet and closed in on the leeward side. *"I don't want any p'tahians sneaking up on us now."*

Chapter 19

A deep thud echoed off the bare walls and shook pieces of plaster loose from the ceiling, which fell and shattered into so many white specks on the wood floor. Now that Lyon thought about it, it might be better if the sofa lined the wall between the windows.

He shrugged the idea away. Lyon refused to move it again. The sofa stayed where he had dropped it, along the far wall facing the windows.

Stretching the length of the ceiling, the room sat on top of the once abandoned gas station. A dining room aura seeped from every bump in the peeling wallpaper. Two sets of double-door entryways and six arched windows lined the outer walls. Even the single-strand light that dangled from the high ceiling somehow gave off an image of once being a great, candlelit chandelier.

As one of many rooms, it had played a part in forming the living quarters of former proprietors. But this floor had declined into various states of disrepair over the years and currently served more as a well-balanced ecosystem of arachnids and insects.

Now, Lyon was in charge of disturbing that habitat to re-establish one a bit more comfortable for slightly more evolved beings. The task started to become tiring for him. He had spent the previous day working on the storefront of the gas station. The day before, it was the basement.

Placing some remote matter replicators around the station helped, but Lyon still had to move the items from the replicators. And the low-end replicators couldn't create some complex mechanical devices at all because of the detail involved.

Lyon stepped toward one of the windows. He looked down at the somewhat busy street that cut between the gas station and his grocery store. A strange orange-green cast distorted the colors of almost every object. The storm had passed, and now Lyon could see that the sun sat about an hour away from retiring.

"Yo, Lyon?" The faint voice reverberated from the direction of the stairs, through the door and across the foyer. "Where you at?"

He turned from the window and walked toward the stairs.

"You best not be dissin' me!" the voice continued

"Shut up," Lyon yelled at the stairs in front of him. "I'll be there in a minute."

Apparently Mac heard him, since the computer remained quiet until Lyon descended the steps and walked around from the back of the long counter that almost stretched the width of the building.

Lyon slid himself over the top of the counter to see another one of Mac's terran faces on a screen, which rested in a shelving unit. The long, slender facial features were topped with even longer braids of hair held back with a blue bandana. A toothy smile displayed one gold cap dotted with a diamond stud. Around the neck sat, for some unknown reason or purpose, an extremely large stopwatch.

"Yo! S'up, G?"

Lyon just stared at the screen for a while. "You tell me. You're the one disturbing my work."

"Naw, naw, I didn't mean dat, bro. But we cool?"

Lyon drew tight circles in the air with his forefinger as a sign for Mac to speed things up.

"Cool! Yo, check it, dawg. Jus' beeped a fat-ass grav flux blastin' from the sun like a mutherfucker, y'know. Straight up bitchin'!"

A deep breath alone didn't help. Lyon held his eyes closed, trying to let his frustration bleed off.

Pull them! Just pull the emotion chips, and you won't have to deal with this. Lyon knew that's all he would have to do, but he could never bring himself to do it. It would seem too much like killing someone, or multiple people in Mac's case.

Then his right eye opened to see Mac's new head bobbing along to the music from a newly acquired set of headphones. *Where does he pick this stuff up?*

"Knock it off!"

"Wuz dat?" Mac lifted one earpiece.

"I said knock that off!"

Mac's now surprised look disappeared when his universal visage flashed back a second later. Oddly, the change seemed to ease Lyon's frustration.

"If I interpreted correctly, you picked up a gravitational flux from the star?"

"Correct." Mac's face faded to reveal several charts that apparently showed the detected measurements. "It gained about three gravity levels, which appeared and disappeared in less than two seconds."

"A spike?"

"Mmm, I don't think so. It appears to be a stellar symptom of helium indigestion."

"Look, smart ass," Lyon snapped a finger at the monitor, rethinking the removal of Mac's emotion chips, "did any other reading corroborate a spike?"

"Yes, a slight decline in neutrino output followed by a sudden burst."

It sure sounded like a spike. The gravity flux caused at the end of a spike would temporarily retard the neutrino flow on this side of the star.

"How soon could we possibly make contact?"

Mac hummed as if he was actually going to wag a time. "Twelve hours, seventeen minutes. By then they would be far enough away from the star to eliminate interference."

Lyon snatched a stick of beef jerky out of a box resting on a shelf behind the counter, bit off the wrapping's top, spit it into the trash can under the register and pushed the stick out with his thumb. Not the healthiest snack, but he didn't care as he started chewing. Jerky marked an evolutionary milestone that he enjoyed.

"What about foreign traffic?"

"Nothing. So far it's still quiet."

With the reinforcements about a day out, Lyon didn't want to get too hopeful too soon. If the p'tahians registered the spike, they would most likely jump right in, plow through the system and kill everything. No sense in taking chances.

Well, more work waited.

"Notify me when you get contact or something dramatic happens."

"Not a problem, but I do have a few other items if you've got time."

"Shoot."

"I've coordinated the delivery of the refrigerators. It'll be between eight and ten in the morning."

"Okay."

"And the first fuel truck is scheduled at one in the afternoon. After that our tanks should be full."

"That doesn't sound like much."

"Small tanks."

Lyon shrugged and continued snacking.

"How's the garage elevator coming along?"

"I have most of the main support structure built, but the transmitters were overheating. They should be cool in a couple of hours. I'll have the rest of the supports done by morning. Then I'll be ready for the mechanisms. I'll need for you to reposition the transmitters though."

Lyon nodded his head in understanding while yanking the final bit of jerky out of the package. He wadded the wrapping and tossed it at the trash can. The wrapping sprung open in midair, throwing off the aerodynamics and sending the plastic to the floor.

"Uh, okay." Lyon frowned at the miss. "I'll be upstairs."

Mac's video head nodded then blinked away.

Lyon retrieved the wrapping and placed it in the can before heading back to the stairs.

Chapter 20

The force-fed adrenaline had worn off hours before. Fatigue had since taken hold of the Vendetta's crew.

Everyone dozed in their chairs except for Hitook, who sat next to his in the same meditation pose he had assumed earlier.

The scanners couldn't find a threat anywhere. That fact both amazed and brought relief. Surely the p'tahians should have zeroed in like hawks, but that didn't mean the crew was disappointed at not being atomized. The insertion plan seemed to have worked.

During the next few hours, peace overcame the vessel, the kind of peace Hitook preferred: still, with just the slightest sounds of life—a mix of sleepy breathing and the ship's internal mechanisms.

Hitook relaxed his mind and mentally prepared himself for the path that would reveal itself before him. The meditation allowed him to focus on the as yet invisible goal rather than where the path would take him. One could call it making peace with their maker, but religion had nothing to do with it.

A yawn from a waking Larin broke the quiet too soon for Hitook's taste, but the liqua's expressions remained as calm as still water.

Larin unlatched his seat's harness and sat up. As if equipped with the neck muscles of a baby, his head flopped into his cupped and waiting hands. His stubby fingers began working in an attempt to rub away the tiredness. The activity tapered until only one hand remained to prop his head, and only his index and thumb digits touched the bridge of his nose.

Now his eyelids fluttered in sessions of rapid bursts, yet another vain attempt to completely wake himself.

Larin took a deep breath before taking notice of Hitook. The rolbrid's yellow eyes peered through slits at the liqua.

For some reason unknown to Larin, seeing Hitook sitting there meditating had the overwhelming effect of pissing him off. The sight grated like having a dozen nails driven into his neck. In a split second, Larin felt the urge to charge over and kick Hitook out of his meditation. That's when Larin figured out what was happening.

It had to be the same side effects Ky had experienced earlier. The realization alone helped Larin focus and think of something else to distract his mind. As with most rolbrids, one choice came naturally: food.

Larin poked around the nearby cabinets where he had stored some of the ration packets, then something hit him. Deep in the pit of his bowls came a sound, a reverberating mix between a squeak and a squish.

The rolbrid involuntarily moaned, a noise Hitook didn't appreciate but could understand because he had also heard the noise that bellowed from Larin's gut.

Larin hugged his stomach and bent over in his chair. Suddenly there seemed to be so much pressure that Larin was almost sure his intestines would explode, a sight or feeling he never wanted to experience.

He cursed silently. It was those damn pills. They had his guts locked tighter than a gold depository. This unpleasant epiphany now, for the first time in his life, resulted in regret for eating so much.

Larin doubted he could wait until they arrived on Terra. Another sting of pain stabbed his gut, and uncontrollably his muscles responded by clinching even tighter. His eyelids were clamped so tight now against the pain that the pressure sparked explosions of light in the otherwise dark view.

Without warning, the pain subsided with another rumble. A slight pressure remained, which made Larin reluctant to unclench the hug he had around his stomach. He sat back slowly, as if expecting the hidden fault now in his gut to slip and crash into another earthquake of agony. But it never happened.

Now sitting back in his chair, Larin took a deep breath. He wasn't sure if he had been holding his breath during the entire episode, but it sure felt like it. As he exhaled, his weary eyes drifted half open.

For a while he just sat there, staring through the panel in front of him and mentally fighting off a new wave of tiredness brought on by his recent spasms. To help, he began randomly looking around while keeping his head firmly planted in the chair's headrest.

Larin's glazed eyes glided over to look at Ky. She didn't look very attractive now, mostly because her mouth hung half open and her head was cocked to one side. The pose reminded Larin so strongly of someone with a mental deficiency that he briefly expected her to ecstatically mutter something unintelligible.

A slight grin cracked the rolbrid's face as he looked away. Then something whispered deep in his mind, forcing him to look back at Ky. This time it completely registered.

Behind the dextian slumped in her chair, something flashed on her screen. Larin couldn't tell what it was, but it woke him. He turned in his chair and rapped on a few keys in front of his console.

The screen flickered then switched to a duplicate of the screen at Ky's station. It showed the flight path around the star and to Terra. The Vendetta had already made half the journey, but a section of the path in front of them blinked.

Larin brought his hand to the screen and tapped a finger on the blinking section. As the computer zoomed in, a callout box appeared to the right. In the box, numerous figures appeared: distance, expected arrival time, disturbance code, et cetera.

It took Larin a while, but he finally remembered what the displayed disturbance code stood for, a gravity flux. And if these figures were right, something in the middle of their flight path was generating gravity, which was not all that unusual. What was unusual was the fact that the disturbance was actually approaching the ship, steadily following its flight path.

A ship. The single thought echoed in his mind. Fear lost the battle against frustration, and Larin unexplainably felt the need to blame Hitook.

Larin snatched an empty water bottle off the console next to him and, with a flip of his wrist, flung it at the meditating liqua. The metal container whistled as it sailed across the cockpit and struck Hitook in the head with a twang.

The liqua's eyes flew open and drilled a hole through Larin. Meanwhile the metal bottle sang with vibrations until it clattered on the deck.

"What!?" Hitook's voice sounded like an exploding volcano.

Larin didn't feel like apologizing or dealing with him. "Get your furry ass back in your chair and plug in." Larin pointed to the empty chair. "Just do it; we've got problems."

Hitook growled through snarling lips and twitched his right brow. The move stretched his scalp enough for now. Even though Larin wasn't looking any more, he didn't want to bring his paw up to rub the spot where the water bottle had hit him because that would be a sign of weakness. The liqua just stood up, took his chair and plugged in.

As if waiting for Hitook to plug in, Larin fired a mental signal that shocked Paloon and Ky awake while setting off fireworks in Hitook's head.

Paloon jerked in his chair and muttered a curse while Ky almost flew to the ceiling, releasing a sound somewhere between a scream and a squeal.

"This had better be good." Paloon adjusted himself and rubbed his forehead.

"Actually, it's very frapping bad." Larin's fingers danced across his console. *"Check the scanners; I'm switching back to weapons control. Something ahead of us is creating gravity, and it's headed this way."*

That woke Paloon.

"How far out?"

"About nine minutes."

Paloon frowned briefly; he had meant that question for Ky. He turned his head. *"Ky, are you with us?"*

She was sitting, shaking her head and in the midst of some hard blinking.

"Ky!?"

She stopped, looked at Paloon and released a mentally drowsy, *"Yeah."*

"We need you focused. Start checking your scanners and give me all the information you can."

With a new mission, she shook her shoulders, turned to the console and started in on it.

"Good." Paloon turned to Hitook. *"Start plotting a couple of alternate routes. Begin by tracking and plotting as many rogue asteroids as possible."* Paloon turned back to his station. *"If we have to escape, I don't want to get smashed by a rock in the process."*

"Weapons are blue and tracking the target—wait. I'm now tracking two targets."

"Ky, what do you have?"

"Affirmative. Scanners are now picking up two targets, eight minutes out, very close together."

Paloon activated the cockpit screen's zoom. The display in the cockpit's windscreen flew through space and toward the disturbance. Still, Paloon saw nothing.

"Do we have a better fix, because I can't see a damn thing?"

Everyone turned to look out the window. Together, they shared thoughts that basically meant, *What the—*

"I'm now reading five objects, all in excess of ten times our size."

Ky's comment didn't find a warm welcome.

"I have one route plotted."

Paloon filed Hitook's report as the liqua went back to work. But Paloon just stared at the screen. He was missing something; he could feel it. The more he thought about it, the more he thought about what bizarre technology the p'tahians could possibly own. He lost track of time while gazing at the screen.

"Five minutes."

Just as Ky gave the time hack, Paloon saw it.

"There!"

Everyone turned to see him pointing at a flickering star that suddenly went steady.

"What was it?" Larin asked.

"I don't know."

Numerous possibilities ran through Paloon's head.

"Are there any energy readings?"

"No, but there are now twelve individual flux points."

"Damn!"

"Route two plotted." Hitook announced and resumed his work.

Maybe it was some kind of cloak that didn't register an energy signature. Maybe it wasn't a cloak but black ships in a tight formation, each with an unusual, undetectable drive system. It didn't matter; Paloon didn't want to find out. Maybe the Vendetta could just outrun them.

"Load the first alternate route."

Hitook took the command and made the adjustments.

Then, before Paloon could say, "Hold on," the objects were upon the ship like swarming bees.

"Shit!"

Paloon slammed the engines open, and they gave a slight whine in resistance before punching in full force to toss the vessel in what seemed like all directions at once.

With a whole lot of luck, Paloon successfully piloted the Vendetta to barely dodge the first barrage. But the battle wasn't over. The next wave arrived seconds later.

Lyon released a hearty yawn as he stepped through the door of the basement complex. With only the thin protection of a grey cotton T-shirt and shorts, the extremely cold air in the room set off a chain reaction of shivers down his spine, which prompted another sip from his bottle of orange juice.

The lights flickered on automatically as Lyon descended the steps and walked toward the center table.

One of Mac's screens snapped on with a visage of an elderly terran, face topped with frizzled grey hair and sporting a similarly colored bushy mustache that held the slightest hints of black.

"*Guten morgen.*"

Lyon held his breath before raising his right eyebrow and turning his head slightly to peer at the screen. He knew what Mac was most likely displaying but looked anyway, mostly out of curiosity.

"Morning, Mac."

"You rested vell, I hope." Mac rolled his "r" in keeping with this persona.

"Yes." Lyon took another chug before sitting down. He felt the need to clarify to Mac that now wasn't the time to play. "We still have much to do, so—"

"Zo ve should not dawdle, yes?"

It was too much of a strangely phrased question and almost too early in the morning for Lyon to wrap his mind around it. Then he nodded. "Correct."

A tapping on the table's keyboards preceded another hit of the orange juice before Lyon set the bottle down on the table. Soon a three-dimensional globe of Terra appeared and floated above the table. Then Lyon leaned back in the chair, placed his elbows on the armrests and clasped his hands over his lap.

"How far out are they?"

"I vould zay, seven *uhr*...ten at ze most."

Lyon glared at the slightly rotating globe.

"Load all known military and commercial ocean traffic."

Red specks began to dust the globe's blue surfaces, but Lyon wasn't done.

"Highlight all popular public routes and identify all scientific vessels, common drug running routes and off-shore oil rigs." Lyon tapped his thumbs together as he squinted his eyes in thought. "Is there anything I'm missing?"

"Vas about air craft?"

"Ah, thank you."

Without another word, Mac overlaid aircraft patterns on top of the increasingly speckled oceans.

"And satellites," Lyon added.

Another dash of specks, this time green, and the map seemed to be complete.

"Now project ahead ten hours and fan out the military vessels in the most possible directions." Lyon grabbed the orange juice bottle and sipped. "We definitely don't need them crashing our party."

Mac quietly went to work. At first the specks gradually moved, then they kicked in high gear and shot forward.

Lyon squinted as he studied the final product.

"Doesn't give us much, does it?" He scratched the light-brown bristles on his right cheek and then pointed at the map. "Of course we need that ocean, so highlight the top three areas for a splash down."

The map's color turned negative, revealing three yellow haphazard shapes.

Lyon pushed away from the table, stood and walked closer to the map while rubbing his chin. After circling it, he pointed again.

"Too close to the coast and that oil rig. Give me the forecast for the other two."

An overlay of clouds appeared along with blue and green arrows showing wind and water currents, respectively. Both were clear, but Lyon preferred the most distant to reduce the likelihood of someone spotting the entry.

"That one." Another single-barreled finger pistol identified the one Lyon wanted. "Plot the entry from the south pole. It will be difficult for them, but it's best."

"Vould you like to plan ze utter as an alternate?"

"Yes." Lyon walked back to his chair and gripped the juice bottle. He could feel that it had started getting too warm for his tastes and unconsciously set it back down on the heat generating table. "Shouldn't we be able to reach them by now?"

"Vell, yes, but I have been, how can I zay it...unlucky."

Lyon closed his eyes, then opened one to see Mac's new face with absolutely no expression.

"Are you saying we've lost them?"

"Vell, if you vant to put it zat vay...ja."

Lyon took a deep breath. "Vie—" He stopped himself and drew a deeper breath. "Why didn't you say anything, wake me up, something?" His voice started to increase in volume.

"Vell, I came to the simpull conclushun zat zey may be late."

"Or spotted!?"

If computers had breath, Mac would have held his.

"I apologize if you feel zat vas wrong, but I a'sure you—"

Lyon held his left hand in the air. That gesture, combined with his very noticeable scowl, allowed Mac to read Lyon's thoughts and choose wisely to return to his standard visage and remove the accent. The flash transformation went unnoticed since Lyon felt the overwhelming need to keep his eyes closed at this moment.

"I'm sorry."

Mac's apology helped Lyon regain his composure and focus on the situation at hand.

"Just show me their planned flight path."

The map on the table changed to an orbital view visible to Lyon, who didn't open his eyes until he walked around the table so his back faced Mac. A red dot blinked more than two-thirds of the way along the path.

"This is where they should be, but I haven't received a response to my attempted communications."

"What about disturbances?"

Mac knew where Lyon was going with the question.

"Nothing zat," Mac coughed and corrected his accent, "that would indicate weapons fire or jumps."

Lyon hummed a tuneless note and traced his finger through the holographic map. "What if they saw something and plotted a new route?"

"Possible, of course, but without knowing which of a multitude of options they exercised, it would take days to track their likely position. Time we don't have."

"Time is irrelevant; just do it. And keep it at low-powered audio-only bursts, no need in broadcasting our presence to the entire galaxy."

Without a question, Mac went to work. The hologram reflected Mac's logical process underway. A perpendicular green grid sliced the system in half; then one-by-one Mac filled in some of the blocks and stamped them with a letter. The letters coded obstructions such as asteroids.

"Start here." Lyon pointed between the orbit of Terra and its nearest sister planet.

He correctly assumed what Mac was about to do. With all that processing power and networked logic programming, Mac had slipped back into a basic pattern of starting at the top left corner of the entire system and working his way across, row by row. That technique would definitely take days. Lyon just shook his head and forgave Mac. It seemed the harder Lyon tried to make Mac act more sentient, the more likely it was that Mac's basic nature would lead him to err just like a sentient.

Lyon found the irony humorous, and before he knew it, he released a light chuckle.

"Am I doing something wrong?" Mac was working at a feverish pace as marked by the tiny grid squares turning red at the rate of about one every ten seconds.

Lyon folded his arms, stopped chuckling and waved his palm at the computer panel behind him. "No, no, you're doing fine. I was just thinking of the irony of the situation."

"Yes, I guess you could say it is ironic. You get your initial force, and it disappears right after arriving. But after all, your ship was smaller and left a less noticeable spike flux."

Lyon chuckled again. "That's not what I meant; I—"

"I've got something."

The interruption seemed to bring with it a five-second unbreakable silence. So soon? Lyon didn't believe it, then he stopped questioning and turned around to face Mac.

"What?"

"I'm not sure. There's some interference, electromagnetic maybe, possibly from a solar flare; I'm not watching the star right now." Mac said. "I'm trying to compensate, but the interference is—wait—it's them! Patching through."

"This is Vendetta, do you copy?" The scratchy transmission almost echoed in the room, and Mac starting reducing the volume. "You're faint and choppy."

"Vendetta, this is Knight Kendrick," Lyon began slowly in hopes that his entire message would get through. "Stand by while Mac attempts to adjust for the interference."

"Understood." Paloon's voice sounded calm but pleased.

"There," Mac puffed as if finishing a physical chore, "give it a shot now."

"Vendetta, how's this?"

"Much better."

"Where did you guys go? I'll have to admit I was getting a bit worried."

Paloon gave a hearty laugh before offering a brief explanation. "Let's just say if it weren't for a rolbrid's inability to enjoy long sleeps, we would have been asteroid food. Some quick flight planning, and we have a new route. I'll send it to you. It shaved almost two hours off the flight."

Lyon glared at Mac's face on the screen and gave fire to the sarcasm in his voice. "The flight path we sent you *should* have been clear."

Even though the statement was pointed at Mac, Paloon answered.

"You probably didn't see them because every blasted one was pitch black and glided along the planet's orbit in perfect sequence; we were barely able to see them ourselves." Comments from the other crew members rumbled in the background. "I was beginning to doubt our sensors; I thought maybe they got fried in the spike."

"But everyone's okay?"

"Well, that rolbrid I told you about has a bellyache that has him moaning non-stop."

"Hey! You try to deal with this," blurted Larin, prompting a growled "Shut your trap!" from Ky.

At least they had adapted to the terran languages well enough. But Paloon's frustration at Larin's outburst surfaced in his voice.

"*Anyhow*, do you have our final?"

"Just finished it." Lyon turned back to the table and ordered the data's delivery with one word: "Mac."

"We're receiving," Paloon confirmed a few seconds later.

"Go with the primary path, unless you hear from us. You should have a splash down at approximately eighteen thirty local."

"Actually," Mac interrupted, "with their new flight path, it has moved up to sixteen forty."

Lyon shrugged. "Okay, sixteen forty. Follow the speeds in the plan; they're fast, but I want you through the upper sphere as quickly as possible. The other path is after you splash. Stay submerged and follow it to reach the coast. The speeds will keep you from being chased. I'll activate a beacon on the coast; the freq is in the plan. Just follow it."

Paloon could read just like the next guy but didn't let the brief play-by-play bug him. He had met plenty of people who, when in charge of an operation, felt it necessary to explain instructions that had been clearly written out. Maybe it was some kind of power trip. He never understood it, but he accepted it.

"Copy. We'll see you then."

"Until then, good luck."

"Thank you."

Mac terminated the conversation and the room suddenly felt lonely, but Lyon tried to ignore it.

"How's the construction going?"

"I'm finished in the garage, but I need the transponders moved so I can test the systems."

Lyon nodded in agreement. Like he said earlier, much remained to be done.

"I'm going to take a shower first."

He grabbed his warm orange juice and headed upstairs as Mac turned on some more television stations to occupy his time.

Chapter 21

Everything else seemed unimportant now. He didn't give a damn about any soul except his own. Anger surged and fueled Yabuki's frustration. Inside he burned, but his façade remained one of a calm, collected individual—a skill developed as the result of a hard childhood.

Takahiro and Takehiko sat quietly in the back seat. Neither had been told that Yabuki was angry. But both had correctly assumed it to be a fact.

The driver kept his attention on the road, knowing it was best not to get involved. He was only nineteen, but thanks to a strict upbringing, Sasaki's one major rule for himself while on the job was to speak only when spoken to, which seldom occurred. Many commented to Yabuki that he had picked a child for a driver. They may have been right, but in Yabuki's eyes, Sasaki's manners compensated for any other drawbacks.

Yabuki pulled himself out of his funk just in time to see the warehouse come into view. Everything around the building seemed to be a jumbled mess. Wind-blown litter floated above stained concrete and asphalt, several neglected trash cans rested against almost every building, and the flaws in the faded, chipped grey paint on his warehouse became completely visible in the daylight.

The large luxury car seemed lost on the wrong side of town, but it paid no attention to its predicament as it squeezed into an alley and barely missed a row of trash cans sitting on the corner.

Sasaki brought the car to a stop behind the warehouse. Everyone waited to get out until Yabuki exited. The rest followed. Takahiro and Takehiko walked behind Yabuki as he stepped around the car and through the rear entrance. Sasaki took a short stroll around the immediate area, carefully scanning the area before returning to stand by the car.

As soon as Yabuki opened the metal door, he met the always-alert face of the remaining royal guard. The silent guard gave Yabuki and his party a quick visual search and stepped aside to allow their entrance.

Takehiko attempted to stare down the guard as they entered but broke contact from those eyes before his foot even hit the door jamb.

There was something about these "royal guards" that seemed completely out of place, unnatural. Yabuki could never put his finger on it, so he ignored them as best he could. He had to accept their presence, oyabun's orders, Mr. Kurosawa said. Yabuki would never think of challenging the orders, but he couldn't deny his feelings.

When did the yakuza need "royal guards" before? Never. But about a year ago, Mr. Kurosawa started introducing them here. He said the oyabun was taking a new path for the family. Where they came from, no one knew, and Mr. Kurosawa refused to talk about it. Insolence, he would call it before smacking the mouth that spoke the question.

To compound the oddness of it, each guard Yabuki ever saw could pass as the brother of any of the others. Some could even pass for twins. All had Asian features—although they were all extraordinarily large—and long black hair twisted in a ponytail. From neck to toe, they were covered in black. Black overcoat, black gloves, black boots. The only break in the color was on the right shoulder, where rested a grey patch with an indescribable pattern stitched in black. Yabuki would almost say the stitching was random, but something about it seemed to imply a pattern—even though it didn't look like anything.

The fact that they never seemed to sleep and rarely spoke just compounded the peculiarity. Their silence didn't hold the implied politeness of Sasaki's; it carried more of an air of dominance than servitude, another aspect that bit at Yabuki.

Takehiko hit a switch on the wall, and the warehouse's remaining lights responded with a quick snap to dull illumination. They began humming in their struggle to full glory.

The team stepped into the room and turned toward the office door that faced the open space of the warehouse. Crates of various sizes covered the floor. Some formed orderly stacks, but even they looked slightly disorganized due to the completely uneven heights.

Yabuki didn't know exactly what each crate held, but he had a good idea: weapons, a whole lot of different weapons and combat equipment. None were conventional by any means. They were the key to the oyabun's plan, which Yabuki knew little about. But that was how he ran business.

After they made a shipment, more would be in the warehouse the next day. Yabuki never knew where they came from or who arranged the deliveries, but after a painful debate with Mr. Kurosawa, Yabuki didn't ask any more questions.

Yabuki opened the office door and flicked on the lights, which crackled to brightness. He stepped around the L-shaped desk and slid open the top drawer. Inside rested three books with gritty black covers in red trim. He removed them and set them on the desk.

With a thumb, he spread them like a hand of cards then picked the middle book. Faded gold letters emblazoned on the cover spelled "Inventory." Yabuki pointed the book at Takehiko, who responded immediately by stepping forward, taking the book and retreating into the main warehouse to do the job given to him by Yabuki earlier.

Yabuki grabbed the other two books and walked around to sit in a large leather chair in front of the desk. On the way, he waved an open hand at the computer that sat on the desk. Takahiro acknowledged the order by taking the chair behind the desk and punching the computer's power button.

Yabuki flipped through the other books but didn't pay attention to what was in them. He just felt the need to fidget as he waited.

Takahiro had the computer running now and clacked away at the keys. The noise quieted as he removed a disk from his jacket pocket, inserted it and resumed the keystrokes.

Yabuki slammed the books shut and thudded them against his knee. Thoughts of the plan almost consumed him. He kept running the scenario through his head to make sure he wasn't missing anything on his end. He couldn't think of anything, so he stood up. The action only prompted a quick glance from Takahiro, who went back to work.

Yabuki tossed the books, and they landed on the chair with a slap of leather. He stepped over to the wall next to the water cooler and filing cabinets. A painting of a mountain rested on the wall. With a flick of Yabuki's wrist, the painting opened like a door.

He began tapping a code into the keypad on the front of the now-revealed safe. When a small green light came on, Yabuki turned the handle, swung open the safe's door and scooped up the small stacks of paper inside, placing them on top of the filing cabinets. Yabuki then shut and re-locked the safe and returned the painting to its original position. He never liked that painting anyhow.

Yabuki grabbed the papers, married them with the books on the chair and placed the resulting stack on the corner of the desk.

"How's it going?" The question came from Yabuki.

"I'm almost finished with the first pass." Takahiro pointed vaguely at the monitor. "Just two more to go."

In a few steps, Yabuki stood with folded arms in front of the window opening to the warehouse floor, which was now completely lit by the hanging lights. Takehiko walked around a stack of crates as he wrote in the book. This he held open in front of him like a preacher studying a bible. He headed toward the office.

When he entered, Yabuki faced him. "Status?"

"We—" Takehiko halted long enough to finish his writing. "We received five more crates last night. I listed them here." He pointed at a list with his pen in a sweeping motion as he turned the book and offered it to Yabuki.

Three were heavy weapons, one was light weapons, but the last didn't have a description next to it. "What's in this one?" Yabuki pointed at the entry.

"I don't know. There wasn't an inventory label on the crate. That...yarō," Takehiko tilted his head to point into the warehouse where the royal guard roamed, "wouldn't let me open it. He just pushed me away."

Yabuki knew he should correct Takehiko's comment about the royal guard but understood his frustration and let the curse go. Royal guard or not, his men shouldn't be treated that way. It was fear of retaliation from Mr. Kurosawa that kept Yabuki's thoughts from being spoken.

Takehiko walked around Yabuki and flopped down on a cloth couch against the far wall. He withdrew a pack of cigarettes from under his coat and lit one before stowing the pack. "Aren't you done yet?" he testily asked Takahiro. The cigarette resting in his lips bobbed up and down in its own smoke.

Takahiro glared briefly from the corner of his eyes at his brother before replying, "Bite me." He began clacking on the keyboard again. "You're just envious that for you anything beyond checking your e-mail is a mental strain."

"Oooohh." Takehiko flicked ashes into a tray resting on a rickety table next to the couch. "Aren't we touchy?"

Yabuki crossed the room again to shove the final book onto the bottom of the stack on the desk.

A loud shuffle echoed in the warehouse. In a domino effect, Takahiro looked at Yabuki, who looked at Takehiko who stood halfway to look out the window.

"He's on the move," Takehiko commented.

Yabuki stepped around the desk to glance at the small monitor hidden on the other side of the computer. In the display, a large white truck approached the front of the warehouse.

Just then Takahiro saw it too. "I'm sorry, Yabuki-san. I got too wrapped—"

With a thud of Yabuki's hand on Takahiro's head, the apology ended. "That should be them." He headed out the door. "Let's go. Takahiro, stay here and join us when you're finished."

"Yes, sir."

Yabuki and Takehiko stepped quickly through the center of the warehouse as the royal guard started opening one of the large doors. The truck began backing toward the door. It stopped as the two walked outside.

Air brakes whined then whistled a hiss. The Asian driver crawled down from the cab of his truck, grabbed some thick, tan gloves from a side panel on the door and headed for Yabuki. "How's it going, Yabuki?"

"Just fine, Tanaka." He paused to look at the back of the truck as Tanaka's passenger stepped around to open the hatch. He'd seen the kid before but couldn't remember his name. "Are they with you?"

"Yes," Tanaka stared meaningfully at Yabuki, "but there's more to it this time."

Yabuki saw Tanaka's concern and wondered about it. But when the trailer doors opened, Yabuki had his answers. Crates filled the trailer, but standing silently in front were two more royal guards.

The royal guards looked just like all the others Yabuki had seen, but one of these two had a uniform modification. Resting on the right shoulder sat a red pad of sorts. It wrapped around his shoulder, and its top extended out from his shoulder about three inches. Black stripes ran horizontally to give it the look of armor in addition to some form of rank insignia.

The unique royal guard jumped down first, landing with a solid thud, then the other followed. With a wind-snap, the guard standing next to the warehouse door slammed his feet together and crossed his chest with both arms parallel to the ground.

A simple nod from the ranking royal guard returned the recognition. He then turned toward Yabuki, while the other guard joined the royal guard already on duty in the warehouse.

Yabuki accepted a folded letter from the remaining royal guard. He stared at this beast of a man as long as he could before accepting the paper. He unfolded and scanned it.

It was from Mr. Kurosawa. A change in plans. Yabuki was now supposed to follow this royal guard's orders. His anger returned to a rapid boil. He tried to stifle it, but he knew his clenched teeth were giving him away.

Yabuki folded the paper and jammed it into a pocket. The royal guard glared and displayed a half smile. He did it just to further get under Yabuki's skin, and Yabuki knew it.

With a dismissive wave of the royal guard's hand, Tanaka and his partner climbed into the truck and began off-loading.

Yabuki didn't care for the man, not because they were on opposite sides of the wrong side of the law, but because the man had too much ego. It wasn't pride; it was pure ego—ego so strong he could smell it as he stepped off the elevator.

It was a modern reception area. A large secretarial desk sat on the right, the left wall held a door flanked by two small trees, and the far wall was glass with a door that opened into neat rows of desks for a herd of mindless office workers.

An older woman sat behind the desk and looked up from her nail file at Yabuki's approach but waited to speak. She brushed her curly blond, and fading, hair over one ear as Yabuki neared the desk, Takahiro and Takehiko in tow.

"I'm here to see Mr. Imondi."

"Do you have an appointment?"

"No. Just tell him it's Yabuki."

She stopped herself from giving the standard "you have to have an appointment" spiel because she knew it wouldn't do any good. Besides, Mr. Imondi wouldn't want Yabuki's name on any of his appointments.

Yabuki knew she wouldn't push the issue, much like the elevator guard didn't ask to frisk for weapons and just stepped aside.

"Please have a seat in the waiting room." She pointed gingerly at the door between the trees. "I'll let him know you're here."

Yabuki didn't thank her but headed for the door and let himself in.

The room felt more like a study or den than a waiting area. Books lined one wall, a large, flat screen TV dominated the other. A short bar boxed one corner, and leather chairs and small tables spotted the floor. An elaborate aquarium lined the far wall. In one corner, a waterfall trickled down to aerate the clear water in the three-foot high tank. Various fish swam about, most likely salt-water fish, as far as Yabuki could tell by the bright colors.

The closing door spurred Yabuki to turn around. He did so just in time to see Takahiro and Takehiko plant themselves in a couple of the leather seats. They silently expressed their joy in how comfortable the seats were. Yabuki didn't approve of sitting down here, but his frown wasn't going to force the two out of those chairs.

Yabuki focused on the fish while walking along the tank. When it ended, he found himself in front of the bookshelves, so he began perusing the titles. It only took a few titles to realize these probably didn't belong to Mr. Imondi personally. These books seemed to be more part of an antique show than a reader's collection. Touching one to feel its frail spine confirmed his suspicions.

"Damn pig," Yabuki mumbled at the frivolous waste.

"Excuse me, sir?" Takahiro couldn't take his mind out of relaxation mode in time enough to catch Yabuki's comment.

"Nothing," Yabuki replied, and he turned around to see that Takehiko had lit another cigarette.

That did it. Yabuki lunged forward, whipped the cigarette out of Takehiko's lips, broke it and tossed it on a table before Takehiko could open his eyes. The act prompted Takahiro and Takehiko to straighten themselves, but they weren't getting out of the chairs.

Everyone turned their heads when the door opened under the power of a black gentleman who looked neat and clean like any executive office jockey but had a muscular build matching that of a bouncer.

"Mr. Imondi will see you now," he said and stood to the side.

The trio followed the gentleman toward a glass door next to the secretary's desk. She triggered the door's lock, which buzzed in response. Beyond the door, a short hallway, its left wall made of glass, ended with doors to another elevator.

After pressing the call button, the guard waited as the group boarded the rather roomy and elaborately decorated transport.

Yabuki could tell it probably only went up about two floors, but it was hard to tell because it ran so smoothly. At the top, the doors opened into a corner office, literally. Yabuki stepped into the base of a rather large triangle.

To both sides, bookshelves covered the walls. Artifacts from various cultures filled most of the shelves, occupying the space left vacant by a sparse collection of books. Each item emanated worth, if only from the fact of obvious history and having an age measurable only by carbon-fourteen dating.

Along the other two sides and roof of the triangle-shaped room stretched glass latticed with a web-work of steel strips. Predictably, the office sat on top of its own wing of the hotel casino. Only an electronically controlled tint embedded in the glass obstructed the afternoon sun that sparkled brilliantly off a waterfall fountain that shot from the center of the room to trickle down into a large octagon-shaped aquarium. The tank sat in a valley terraced by a few wide steps. Fish darted about freely in the crystal-clear water.

Beyond the waterfall and aquarium, a large, authoritative desk sat about ten feet from the triangle's point. Behind the desk, a black-haired man scanned a flat computer screen as he clicked a mouse. The man seemed to be the only thing out of place in the room—just because of his age, early forties max. But with no effort, he exuded an air of importance and power—strong charisma.

As Yabuki circumvented the aquarium and approached the desk, Mr. Imondi peered from his stock research and smiled with a healthy set of teeth.

"Yōkoso. Genki desu ka."

Yabuki almost felt offended by Mr. Imondi's use of his native language. He didn't allow his feelings to show. However, he didn't respond in kind, either.

"I'm doing fine, Mr. Imondi."

With a courtly hand gesture, Mr. Imondi offered his guests the two leather chairs in front of his desk. A visual clue in Yabuki's face indicated clearly that he would refuse, and his two companions knew better than to oblige themselves this time. So Mr. Imondi withdrew his hand.

"Thanks," was all that Yabuki said.

"Kurosawa-san is well, I hope."

"Yes." Yabuki paid considerable attention so that his inflections wouldn't signal his willingness to skip the pleasantries. "He wishes you goodwill as well."

Mr. Imondi and Yabuki knew each other well, well enough to observe the cliché of "keep your friends close and your enemies closer." "Enemy" could be too harsh; both would prefer "adversary," which defined more of a competition than mutual hatred.

"How may I help you this time?" Mr. Imondi broke the silence as he steepled his hands in a point toward Yabuki.

"Someone was found spying on one of our locations." Yabuki kept a stolid demeanor. "Would you have any information about it?"

Yabuki wouldn't say much more than that, and Mr. Imondi knew it. So he spent as little time as possible gleaning as much information as he could out of those two sentences.

The yakuza most likely didn't have this spy; otherwise, Yabuki would have said caught versus found. Deftly escaping them would explain why they had very little information on this spy, hence the mildly pointed but polite accusation.

Mr. Imondi's brow jumped briefly before responding "No." and tapping his steepled hand to his chin.

Yabuki tasked his skills as a lie detector but perceived no hint of deception.

"Neither I, nor any of my men, had anything to do with it, if that's what you're asking." Mr. Imondi also maintained well-trained control of his inflections to only allow a touch of recrimination into the statement.

Neither wanted to jeopardize the peaceful relationship between the two families. There had been times when both would have preferred to shoot each other on the floor of a police station. Now finding ways to coexist remained paramount for their mutual survival.

Mr. Imondi stood and stepped around his desk. "All I can offer is my hope that this situation didn't bring too much distress. If you wish, I can look into it from my end."

He knew the yakuza wouldn't want his assistance but offered out of politeness.

"Thank you." Yabuki uncontrollably nodded his head briefly. "Thanks for the offer, but no thank you."

"Very well. Please let me know if I can help you in the future."

Yabuki, as if pushed by an invisible force from Mr. Imondi, faced the elevator door. Takahiro and Takehiko stepped aside at the entry, and they followed Yabuki into the lift.

They were departing under a mutual understanding that Mr. Imondi didn't have a spy at the warehouse. However, now Imondi knew that someone did. That information could become a threat to Yabuki as well.

Before the elevator door closed, Mr. Imondi nodded and said, "Sayōnara."

Yabuki waited until the doors closed before frowning.

Mr. Imondi turned and approached one of the glass walls. After contemplating the implications of this development, he returned to his computer.

Chapter 22

Tufts of grass and weeds lined the center of the winding dirt path. Holes pitted the slightly worn ruts that marked a trail through the trees toward the coast. In the potholes, puddles flashed in the bouncing rays of the headlights.

Lyon's city version of a sports utility vehicle handled the mild challenge better than he thought it would. It seemed too frail a vehicle to be capable of tackling off-road challenges. Anything more severe and the entire frame would probably fracture.

The forest opened into a half-acre field, and after the coast came into view of the headlights, Lyon turned the midnight blue vehicle and skittered it to a stop. He killed the engine and took a couple of swigs from his water bottle, a feat he hadn't attempted for the last twenty minutes of the rough road.

Lyon exited and scanned the area as he shut the door.

Very small peninsulas jutted from both ends of the clearing into the calm, dark ocean, which stretched to the horizon, as oceans do. The high tide only left a small beach freckled with rocks and a few boulders that the waves had been slowly cutting away at for eons.

Thick layers of trees lined the clearing to complete Lyon's needs: a small cove visibly blocked from all horizontal angles. There was the road, but it twisted through the woods too much to see straight through, and the rope and "No Trespassing" sign Lyon placed across the road's entrance should keep out anyone who might stumble on the operation. If not, Lyon had a last line of defense.

He placed a hand on the heavy pistol-like weapon hanging from his belt. That, combined with the replica of a police detective badge in the pocket of his dirty brown leather jacket, should allow him to coax most into believing him to be a homicide detective securing a crime scene. This would also serve to force visitors to retreat.

If not, he could always shoot them.

The special pistol fires pulses of low-frequency energy, directional but wide enough for effect. Without leaving a mark, a pulse would trigger nerves into convulsions and finally force the brain to shutdown temporarily. What made this weapon ideal was its side effect of causing bioelectric shorts in the brain's memory circuitry. It was a bit harsh because it actually burned away the circuitry—not even hypnosis could bring the memories back—and the effects were uncontrollable and could turn an entire day of memories into smoke.

Unfortunately, the victim would no longer have any discernible future short-term memory, but to protect his own existence and that of his team, he would take any action necessary.

Lyon went to the back of the vehicle and opened the hatch. He grabbed a black crate and slid it over the tan carpet toward him.

Chrome latches clacked as he opened them.

Various heavy weapons rested on top of each other inside the case. Lyon reached in and fished out a thin, black box from the bottom, shut the crate and closed the hatch.

As he returned to the front of the vehicle, he twisted a part of the box in his hands. The part shot up like a compact satellite receiver antenna. Then he thumbed an invisible release that recessed into the box to open it like a laptop computer.

Holding the computer in his hands and letting his thumbs dance on the controls, Lyon programmed the signal beacon frequency, activated its transmission and set the unit on the hood of the vehicle. With a short mental command, Lyon's wrist computer activated its own receiver, and a green compass with a flashing red arrow appeared in the far right view of his sunglasses. In the arrow, white letters confirmed the beacon was emitting on the right frequency.

"Mac?"

"Yes." The computer's calm reply offered a sign that he wasn't goofing around with some fabricated persona this time. A fact that went unnoticed by Lyon.

"Is the Vendetta on schedule—the revised schedule?"

"Yes. It took some work to position the primitive satellite, but I was able to film the arrival. Would you like to see it?"

"Please."

The video transmission filled the left lens of Lyon's sunglasses. Terra's blue-white self bulged into view from the left. Just enough light reflected off the atmosphere to give the Vendetta a silver outline. Blue fields flickered around the vessel as the crew adjusted the yaw for entry.

"Was this secure?" Lyon couldn't believe he just now thought of it and mentally kicked himself while figuratively crossing his fingers that Mac took care of it.

"No. It presented too much risk of being detected. But before you get mad, I ran a real-time edit."

Lyon released a breath he had been holding since hearing the initial "No." Without asking, the bottom of his right eye filled with an identical image without the Vendetta.

"This is what everyone else saw. For all they know, the satellite was acting screwy, pointing randomly and not responding to commands."

The right screen dropped.

"Mac, sometimes you're smarter than I give you credit."

"Thanks...I think."

The conversation died as the Terra in the display grew dark and the Vendetta slowed to gradually enter the atmosphere. Just as the vessel's ion field sparked when it struck the thick layer, the ship's forward plasma spike fired, and the Vendetta plummeted through the atmosphere with ease. Only the faintest sparks danced on the ion sheath as the vessel dropped from view.

Mac withdrew the satellite vision from Lyon's eye. Lyon glanced at the starry sky and prayed that the rest of the mission could go as easily. Now all he had to do was wait, so Lyon picked out one of the boulders on the tiny beach and walked over to take a seat.

As he sat down he let his eyes play across the stars. Lyon hoped that Mac wouldn't bother him. The quiet served to ease his worries, at first. Then it allowed him to hear the din of his thoughts. The "deafening silence," he heard it called once.

Regardless how much training he had received to prepare him for this, he had his doubts. Since school he had the desire to become a member of the famous Silver Knights, to lead a combat team.

Lyon could barely hold back his ecstatic emotions when he joined, but from the beginning of war camp, he began doubting his ability to survive his training, let alone use it in a real situation.

But he did.

With his promotion to legionnaire, Lyon started seeing a few battles. One mission called for a combat evacuation of several cities on a small planet. The residents were under constant pirate attacks. Still young, the Dragon Corps didn't have the available force to defend the planet successfully, so the Silver Knights went in under fire to pull out all the survivors they could. Retreat offered a better life than servitude.

But the one mission he would never forget came just a few months after being promoted to knight—his first squad command.

In orbit around Serlis in the Guv system, a rogue armada held the planet's population for ransom. The rogues needed to resupply and attempted to rape the planet, only to find its resources were insufficient for their needs. The Dragon Corps responded to a distress call from the planet's government.

Negotiations began, with the rogues hoping they could get the resources they needed from the Dragon Corps. If they didn't get these resources, they made it perfectly clear that they were more than willing to detonate pre-planted fusion bombs around the planet.

The Corps felt absolutely no need to negotiate, but negotiations did offer a superb opportunity to stall the rogues. So Duke Ver Chan Ka ordered breaches on each rogue craft, and Lyon's squad just happened to be one of the teams on duty.

He led a combat special operations squad, only four members: squad leader, point, heavy weapons and electronics technician. Other than Lyon, the rest of the team held the rank of legionnaire.

Lyon's point was a very sharp trillig named NeNa. She had a vicious warrior spirit—and Lyon's heart, a fact he shared with no one.

A tiny jexan held the position of heavy weapons, but instead of packing artillery, Ev only had to use his razor sharp limbs. It took a few training exercises for Lyon to get used to the mess Ev made when he mutilated a body. It took a little while longer to learn how to use his abilities best within the squad.

Kimoka held the prestige of being one of the best electronic techs in the entire armada. That justifiable claim was attributed the limino's four arms, which gave him a distinct advantage over his competitors.

Some called it an unfair advantage, but in combat no one gave a damn about what was fair.

The team's breach craft launched undetected from the rear of the cruiser Dector. Shrouded in an electronic cloak, the breach craft circled behind the planet where it could sneak upon the rogue's command vessel.

Lyon piloted the square craft perfectly to the hull then pitched it just in time for it to land flat. His aim was off five feet from the planned location. Lyon took it personally but pressed on with the mission.

Hyper-velocity molecule accelerator cannons fired, slicing through the hull in a flash. Before the round chunk of metal could clang to the deck, Ev scrambled out onto the roof, his arms extended and fully prepared to food process on the lethal setting.

Soon, NeNa dove through the hole, hit the deck and rolled. Before she could spring to her feet with a weapon pointed down one end of the hall, Lyon took aim through the hole down the other end of the hall. No one in sight, yet.

"Clear," NeNa shot through the team's internal communications system.

"Clear," responded Ev.

"Clear." Lyon finished the checks before stepping through the hole, advancing down the hall and taking position. *"Move."*

On that cue, Kimoka flew through the hole, banked slightly and shot straight to an access panel on the far wall of the hall. With a flurry of arms and some help from the limino's slightly developed telekinetic ability, the panel came off and glided silently to the floor.

"I'm in."

The rest of the team recognized the notification but kept their senses focused on their particular areas of the hall.

Kimoka took a brief deep breath. A tiny electronic relay sat exposed in from of him. They had attempted a remote seizure but met with failure. Shielding proved stronger than expected. So the next option was a combat breach. This thought reminded Kimoka that the neighborhood watch could show at any moment.

In another blur of telekinesis-fueled motions, various pieces of equipment flew from the backpack on his floating grub-like body. Each item circled around to his front just in time for one of his four arms to catch it and go to work on the naked circuitry.

Less than ten seconds into the breach, and Lyon hadn't seen anyone yet. Time could be on their side.

"Ev, deploy."

The jexan answered by gliding supernaturally along the ceiling from one end of the hall while Lyon provided cover. Ev snapped off part of his backpack and stuck it to the ceiling. As the rectangle hit, driving jacks fired, clamping the item in place while the barrel and sensors deployed. The laser wasted no time in activating its tracking mechanisms and began scanning the hall with an unblinking electronic eye.

A few seconds later, and a second turret began the guarding vigil.

"Ev, rear. NeNa, deploy."

Before NeNa could retrieve the turret from her pack, Ev stood above her watching the blast doors that lined the right side of the hall and the one on the far end.

"Five targets-I'm wired."

By the time Lyon could tell that the first part of the combined message came from Ev and the second from Kimoka, Ev had already advanced on the unfortunate arrivals.

Cracking hums sounded from NeNa's rifle just a split second after the new laser turret whined and decapitated one of the responding security guards. NeNa's invisible rounds of high-frequency pulse didn't reach their target until after Ev gave three a cranial sunroof. The last sap received all five rounds scattered about his body.

Each round delivered a lethal punch. The combined damage forced the body into rippling convulsions as it took a backward dive for the floor but not before the eyes exploded and blood escaped from every orifice at high velocity.

"Five terminated," confirmed Ev as he pulled back from his advanced position.

"Clear," NeNa added. She planted the last turret and returned to her original stance, using the inside bulkhead of the curved hull for partial cover.

"Reinforcements inbound." The notice came from Ev. His finely tuned senses could detect the smell through the hatch doors now being held open by a small pile of crumpled bodies. Ev checked his electronic and wet-wired sensors then relayed, *"Amount unknown."*

"Kimoka?" Lyon kept his focus down his hall and couldn't look back to see the multiple wires running from the floating body into the open panel. *"What do you have?"*

"Nothing...yet...one...mo...ment." Slight grunts broke the response, a sign that he was currently engaged in electrical combat and attempting to force his will onto the ship's computer system. He had been in combat for a while, but suddenly he exclaimed, *"I'm in, and I own the system."*

Recent events made it seem like he had succeeded in the endeavor in just a few seconds, a story that would add to the others and make Kimoka's name transcend time and enter the realm of legends.

"Damn, I'm good!" Kimoka let the phrase go due to an increase in adrenaline caused by the sudden rush of having sole control of the entire ship. *"Stand by. Beginning lock down."*

The ship shook as every hatch closed and respective locks clamped in unison. Kimoka didn't hesitate to override the safety settings on the nearby hatch blocked by corpses. The doors sliced through the remains.

Kimoka gained a quick handle on operating the system. He knew the drill and proceeded as planned. He shut down all weapons systems, disabled all bridge and command controls, sent a short message on the team's status back to Duke Ver Chan Ka, retrieved a ship's map and cross-referenced it with inputs from surveillance cameras. At a speed almost fast enough to bend space, he searched for and, a few seconds later found, a path clear of stragglers caught between lock hatches.

Then the limino waited for a reply from the Corps. He got it and passed it on.

"Lyon, all breaches are successful and in progress. We have the go from command; proceed to your eleven o'clock. From here on we have a calm stroll to the bridge."

Before Lyon could order NeNa and Ev to post, Kimoka opened the hatch to reveal an empty hall.

Regardless of Kimoka's claim of a clear path to the bridge, the advancing party made its way carefully. Lyon and NeNa would post next to the open door. After checking to see if things were clear from their current position, Ev would charge in and call it as such. Then they would repeat the procedure for every room.

Just as they entered the second room, which looked like an oddly empty parts storage area, a demonic wail bellowed throughout the ship. Then percussion instruments began, soon joined by a symphony of strings. Together they formed a dirge with the demonic voice returning every so often to groan a phrase, which ranged from "We own your souls." to "Prepare to die."

From the beginning of the droning howl, the team knew exactly what it was. It represented Kimoka's need to fulfill his overdeveloped desire to mentally torture people. If asked, he would just call it a personalized form of physiological operations, which it was. But it wasn't needed here, and its main benefit was to make Kimoka crack a devilish smile.

What felt like two miles later, through rooms, halls and access tubes, the trio arrived at one of the doors to the bridge. Inside, the ship's command staff was helpless. They couldn't leave and none of their controls worked. The demented music blasting through the ship's public announcement speakers also played with their mental state.

"Kimoka, we're—"

"I've got you." Kimoka broke Lyon's statement because he had been watching the team all along and knew that they were now outside the bridge. *"Stand by. Decompressing the bridge to level seven in four...three...two...one...decompressed."*

A series of muffled thuds seeped from behind the closed door.

"Confirmed, bridge life support is at thirty-five percent, and the backup systems remain disengaged." Kimoka's voice gained an air of pleasure at dominating the ship's controls. *"Prepare to enter."*

Lyon waved two fingers to NeNa, who responded by slipping across the hall to post on the far side of the door, weapon at the ready. The leader then dragged a single, pointed finger from Ev to the side of the hall. The jexan scampered to the position without question. Then with a final hand signal of Lyon touching his first two fingers with his thumb, all three engaged their breathing apparatuses.

NeNa and Lyon's masks consisted of simple ensembles they slid down from their helmets with a slight tap. Ev withdrew a tube from his backpack and plugged it into what some would call a mouth, although he didn't eat through it.

Kimoka saw the final preparations and immediately activated the door release.

A hiss preceded a pop, and generated atmosphere from the hall dragged along every bit of dirt and debris it could get its hands on as it traveled rapidly into the opening. The result was a cloudy mixture of dust and condensing moisture, which began to billow into the hall.

Just as NeNa and Lyon shifted their vision with a mental nudge from standard to ultrasonic, shots rung out from the bridge. NeNa dropped.

Surprisingly, Lyon beat Ev in response. He hit the floor so only his head and very upper torso were exposed. On the far end of the bridge, Lyon saw the outline of the shooter in his helmet's silvery ultrasonic vision. A vemulli—a race that could be best described as teddy bears on steroids. What also made them different from the stuffed toy were two rows of razor-sharp fangs—not teeth, fangs—a full one hundred and twenty-two. If Lyon's ultrasonic vision had been capable of a sharper resolution, he could have counted them as this one smiled in his success.

The vemulli also had the almost unique ability to temporarily survive pressure changes and could even survive unprotected in space for about an hour.

None of the intelligence reports said anything about a vemulli being aboard. But Lyon couldn't blame the intel folks for poor knowledge. He should have thought of this. Now, not only was one of his teammates down, it was NeNa. He never had the chance to tell her how he felt.

His anger and his rage funneled into his trigger finger and vocal cords. As he screamed behind the gas mask, his high-frequency pulse rifle crackled rapidly as if building to a crescendo of the largest lighting strike ever recorded. Round after round after invisible round slipped through the smoke and pounded into the vemulli's pelt. The creature responded with a cry like a long-tailed cat caught sleeping under a rocking chair.

Lyon didn't have any plans to release the trigger, and he forgot about the new device he had recently implanted. But once his rifle's secondary weapon locked on, a tone buzzed in his head. The noise startled him, and he unconsciously triggered the other device.

The under-barrel carriage belched a blue-white flare that stretched across the bridge and slammed into the vemulli. A roar sounded as hundreds, then thousands and then millions of atoms broke down, scattering their electrons in all directions. The chain reaction from the one shot continued until most of the entire being disappeared.

The bright light caused Lyon to finally release the trigger, and he gave the rest of the room a quick scan, joined by Ev, who now felt sure he wasn't going to stumble into the path of fire. Lyon dropped his weapon and scrambled to NeNa. He parted the grey fur on her right cheek, and Lyon's heart sunk when he saw the bluish tint in her skin. Toxin bullets. All her blood vessels had broken down to the point of bursting. She was gone.

He never liked the thought, but any time he allowed himself to feel the burden of leadership that mission would replay in his mind and stop with him holding NeNa's limp body. Every time various details would reveal themselves. Details that should have clued him into being better prepared by expecting the worst and never letting down his guard.

A monstrous, black creature shot through the water with a sound of numerous crashing waves.

His mind elsewhere, Lyon almost fell off the rock he was sitting on but caught himself with one arm reaching to the sand below. Some rapid blinking helped bring him back to reality and recognize the Vendetta surging from the water to finally float above it.

Lyon stumbled to a vertical stance and waved at the black mass to move forward. As he returned to his vehicle to turn off the signal beacon, the craft silently followed and pulled parallel with the vehicle. The knight closed the beacon unit and tossed it into the back of his vehicle just as the Vendetta's landing skids descended to bite into the soft earth.

He left the back hatch open as he turned to stare at the craft. The vessel was nothing like he had ever seen before, even in reports. But he had no interest in vehicles. If he had, he would have joined Force Grey Wolf.

Lyon waited patiently. He figured correctly that the crew must be going through some form of flight checks, but it wasn't long before the cockpit door hissed, opening and unfolding to lower itself to the ground.

An overpowering odor wafted from the opening to assault the surrounding area. It was the mixed smell of reprocessed air, partially eaten rations and the prolonged exposure of people confined in a small area. The aroma now reached for the sky as it began an arduous journey to diminish its stench.

One by one, his new team appeared from the hatch. Lyon had studied their files and correctly identified them as they disembarked. But once they were finished, Paloon approach Lyon.

"Glad to see you."

"Same here." Lyon shook Paloon's offered hand and scanned the group before returning to Paloon. "Consider yourself lucky. Either that or you're better than your file says you are."

"I would hope it's the latter," Paloon chuckled. "I don't believe in Fate." Paloon paused. "Let me introduce the team."

"Thanks, but I think I've figured it out." Lyon approached and greeted each of them by shaking their hand or paw, which ever was more appropriate.

At the end of the line, Larin finished the pleasantries by throwing a look of disdain at Paloon. "I'm glad we all like each other. Where is it?"

Paloon had made a promise, so he reached into a shirt pocket, withdrew a palm-sized foil pouch and passed it to the rolbrid. Larin snatched the bag quickly, but before Paloon would let it go, he said, "Make sure you're *completely* ready before taking it."

"Yeah, whatever. Worry about your own body; I'm tired of you jacking with mine." Larin snatched the pouch and bee-lined into the nearby woods.

Paloon cracked a smile while Ky shook her head ever so slightly. She then turned her eyes skyward.

"Hey, where's the moon!?"

"Excuse me?" Lyon hadn't heard about Ky's white moon fascination, but Paloon felt the need to fill him in.

"Ky wants to see the white moon you described in your reports."

"Yeah!" She squinted and scanned the skies a second time.

Lyon was a bit slow on the uptake but recovered. "It's what's called a new moon. Right now it's on the other side of planet, and you can't see it at night. In a couple of nights you'll see it begin creeping back to a full moon."

Ky almost pouted at first but started to feel better as Lyon gave her hope. She definitely had to see the moon; it served as her personal mission while on the planet, but for now, another mission was pressing.

Without further delay, Paloon made a few hand motions, and the team went to work unloading the Vendetta. Meanwhile, the crew received an audible notification on the success of Larin's field trip to relieve his previously bound bowls. Soon, the smell of burnt honey mixed with some of the breezes whipping through the trees.

Hitook scrunched and twitched his nose in response.

By the time Larin returned from the woods, both vehicles were out of the Vendetta's cargo bay, and the team began the short chore of unloading the weapons lockers and storage cabinets to the back of Lyon's SUV.

"It's about time you decided to help." The pointed statement came from behind a pile of weapons held in Ky's arms.

"Get bent, wench." Larin entered the storage bay and started grabbing some of the supplies being unloaded from the supply cabinets by Hitook. "You weren't the one dealing with a stomachache for more than half the trip."

"You're right. I didn't." Ky dumped the weapons in the SUV. "I had it worse. I had to deal with a stomachache the *whole* trip."

Ky's pointed words made it clear that her *stomachache* was Larin.

Larin couldn't retort; Paloon cut in.

"Hitook, you're in the van and take Larin with you. Ky, you're in the tank with me."

Larin even wanted to gripe about the seating assignments, but Paloon beat him to the punch again.

"Larin, shut up."

The rolbrid huffed as he boosted the armful of supplies onto the SUV's tailgate.

Hitook emerged from the cargo bay as Paloon approached the craft to open one of its invisible side panels. He retrieved an arm computer and slid it on.

"Stand by."

With some mental commands a few seconds later, all the ship's launch sequences were loaded. The storage bay and cockpit doors closed and sealed themselves while the engines fired to a dark blue.

Paloon remotely piloted the craft back into the water and to a secluded underwater valley to rest. After locking in the destination and double-checking the procedure, Paloon returned to his standard view and nodded toward Lyon. "Ready when you are."

Lyon returned the nod. "Well, then let's move out."

In a convoy, Lyon followed by Hitook and Larin in the van and Paloon and Ky with the tank in the rear, they silently crept along the dirt path until the forest swallowed them.

Chapter 23

The horizon glowed faintly with the early break of dawn before the convoy reached the city. From dirt roads to stretches of gravel, the team's vehicles finally found pavement as the drivers focused on the mission at hand and passengers slept.

The absence of radio contact made the trip dull, but all expected as much. Only the random, sparse traffic in the opposite lane offered any form of distraction. But after reaching the highway, Paloon and Hitook got to witness the silent communication between the drivers of cargo vehicles as they flashed their headlights at one another. Paloon immediately felt the bond and friendship in such a simple protocol of lights.

For most of the trip, Hitook kept his mind clear while Paloon dwelled on keeping Ky and Larin from each other's throats—a task he assigned to himself. He felt he owed Lyon that much because Lyon probably had more important things on his mind. Lyon did, but unfortunately, he kept finding himself thinking about the burden of leadership.

Several hours into the trip, distant city lights joined the fray of early morning brilliance pushing back the stars. At this point, a crescent of orange shimmered like a halo over the city's pointy outline.

The sight gave Lyon a sense of assurance even though it really wasn't his home. For the other two drivers, the city seemed rather small and insignificant. To some degree, a feeling of disappointment rose in Paloon. He knew he shouldn't have expected the massive cities to which he had grown so accustomed, but he felt a mild spasm of depression nonetheless.

Regardless, he took the time to reinforce the idea that he would make the best of it. Who knew, this could turn out to be the best deployment of his career. But a small part of him still doubted it.

Once they started into the city, Paloon and Hitook got to put to the test the knowledge they had downloaded about traffic. All the rules of the road were correct, but what the two found most useful were the unwritten rules that Lyon felt needed to be included. These caveats included almost every driver's inability or outright refusal to follow the rules of the road.

Speed limits were speed minimums. Turn signals didn't mean you were ever planning on turning and most likely were not used when a driver did plan to turn. Instead of slowing to a stop, everyone sped up, which meant everyone else waited a few seconds after a traffic light turned green just in case someone was still gunning for the intersection.

Intersections, in particular, irritated Paloon. He found himself particularly annoyed by those drivers who would speed up to run a signal. It even served to raise his doubts about the assignment. But he finally rebounded with a reinforced positive attitude, brought on by focusing on his soon-to-be-acquired long rest and the knowledge he would be able to take a fresh look at the situation well rested.

Constant turning and the invasive glare of passing streetlights slowly pried open the eyes of Ky and Larin. Both shared Paloon's sense of disappointment at the minuscule size of the city and its buildings. But Ky reacted in awe and wonder to the patterns of lights, even though she had seen cities much larger and more elaborate.

Through the maze, the mechanical rats looped and turned until reaching their destination. Approaching the gas station, Lyon triggered a communications link with Mac and ordered him to open the doors.

Lyon parked the SUV in the small three-vehicle lot between the garage bays and the angled storefront as the two windowed doors of the vehicle maintenance bay rolled away into the ceiling. Interior lights also responded with a faint pop and then glowed. Much work had made the bay as clean and orderly as a mechanic's dream. A small tire rack, a parts wall, tool bench, some diagnostic equipment. Not bad for a small garage, but Paloon squinted in disappointment. He couldn't even begin to imagine the difficulty of working on these vehicles with what he could tell was indigenous gear.

Both vehicles slid into their respective spots like swimmers in a well-rehearsed water ballet, and Lyon leapt from his vehicle and walked behind the tank. Once in, he ordered Mac to close the garage doors.

Vehicle doors began to open, but Lyon blurted, "Stay in the cars." He jogged to stand between the two vehicles and pushed his palms at the passengers.

There was a slight hesitation before they complied and closed their doors.

Lyon nodded his head at no one and peeked at the ground. He sidestepped until he was sure he completely stood on the pad under the van.

"Okay, Mac, let's test the system."

Stale air hissed as hidden hydraulics released, followed by another set. With the tank a foot ahead of the van, the floors lowered, allowing the hydraulic sound to increase.

In the cavern below, the florescent bars streaking the walls snapped to life. The grey light increased in intensity until no shadow was safe. About twice the size of the garage they just left, this room held cabinets. Among the shelves were various mechanical instruments, the kind Paloon soon recognized, and he released a mild sigh of relief at the sight. It wasn't much, but at least these items weren't native in design.

The platforms stopped with echoing, muffled thumps, followed by the whine of an air compressor and squeal of gears as matching platforms closed the gaps the vehicles had just descended through. They were hanging from their sides like asphalt doors and closed firmly.

Multiple steel bars shot from one side of the new ceiling to lock firmly in waiting couplers on the other end.

One by one, the arrivals poured from the vehicles. Though they were each from a different race and had multiple ways to express emotion, Lyon easily detected the collective exhaustion. Not that they would quit now, but Lyon forced himself to take morale into account. He rarely did and recognized it as yet another flaw in his leadership skills.

He would have preferred to unload the vehicles first, but Lyon held back the command for the moment. Instead, he motioned for everyone to join him.

As they gathered around, each took their own steps to revitalize themselves: blinking, stretching, scratching and even yawning. The latter resulted in Paloon receiving a light punch from Ky, who stood behind him and displayed a face twisted in a failing attempt to hold back a reply yawn.

Each waited for the next order. None of them preferred to stay in p'tahian territory longer than need be.

Lyon thought about explaining that he recognized their fatigue, allowing them to wait to unload until later and showing them to their beds so they could rest. But he didn't. Instead, he proceeded to the right wall and opened a door between a set of metal-framed cabinets. He motioned for them to follow as he started up the steps.

Each gave the others a quick glance of confusion, but Paloon walked forward and muttered, "He's not going to leave a trail of crumbs. Move."

They went up the steep steps two floors. When they reached the top, Lyon opened the door, toggled a few light switches and entered a room that looked like a larger foyer. Most likely it once served as a living room but now was empty of furniture. Marred wood floors with a recent dusting and nothing more stretched throughout the place. Faded and peeling wallpaper with some kind of three-diamond pattern towered to a rather high ceiling coated in water-stained white paint. A single, bright bulb dangled at the tip of a thick, black cord.

Lyon turned around to face the group still working its way through the entrance. Hitook brought up the rear, and as he lowered himself through the door, Lyon began the tour.

He pointed to an opening to the group's left where a small bar jutted from the right wall. "That's the kitchen. All the food is native, and Mac has tried to make the best matches he could to each of your nutrient requirements. You'll also find a terminal in there linked to Mac. He's a series eighty-three mechanically aware computer. I just call him Mac. He's a bit low-tech, but he can help you locate and prepare the right food. It may not be a perfect match, but your other option is that Mac could create ration sticks."

Larin shuddered and released a gagging sound.

"My thoughts exactly." Lyon added while gradually rotating his half-closed palm and staring into the kitchen. "I don't have a rep unit in the kitchen. There is one in the other basement, but it lacks high definition, and anything more complex than solid objects takes all of his processing power, which is limited to—"

Lyon caught himself in a ramble and turned back toward the listeners, who only presented the look of patience, well-trained patience, the kind troops have drilled into them by trial and error with superiors.

"Well, we can discuss that tomorrow." Lyon attempted to wave the subject away by turning and pointing at an open double-door entryway in the far corner. "In there is what terrans call a dining room, but I didn't put in a table, just some furniture and entertainment equipment."

Lyon turned back to face the group and pointed behind them. They instinctively spilt to stare down a hallway that spurred another that shot to the right.

"Down there are the bedrooms. There are only three." Lyon pointed at Larin and Hitook in succession. "You two share the room to the right, Paloon takes the one on the left, and Ky can have the one at the end." Lyon shifted his eyes to Ky. "You'll be happy to know it has its own bathroom."

Ky smiled slightly. Larin, meanwhile, wasn't pleased with having to share with the overgrown freak of nature, but he was wise enough to keep his thoughts to himself. As much as he was up for a fight, he knew he wasn't going to get someone of higher rank to give up their room to switch with him. Instead, he took a deep breath. It didn't make things better though.

"The other bathroom is at the end of the hall to the right. We've been able to add a few modifications." Lyon pointed his eyes back at Hitook. "It won't be comfortable for everyone, but it should at least serve your needs."

"Now," Lyon's tone of voice signaled for the group to close in and face him, "that's the short tour; I'll show you some more after we wake."

He briefly stared at each. "You have ten hours. Use them. Afterwards we will finish the tour, unload and begin the mission brief and equipment checks. We go active in about twenty hours."

He stepped forward, aiming for the door. Hitook squeezed behind Ky to fit himself in the hall and out of Lyon's way.

"Until then," Lyon opened the door and briefly looked back, "sleep well." Then he left.

Muffled steps faded out of existence while the group shared another round of quick glances. But Larin was the first to say what the others thought.

"What's up with him?"

Paloon wasn't sure. It seemed they had just drawn an uptight leader, but as the second in command, Paloon felt the need to reassure the team.

"He's probably got a lot on his mind. Without a Corps rep, he's got a lot on his shoulders."

The others detected the faint smell of spontaneously created crap, but there was enough of a hint of hope that they grabbed on it.

"Besides," Ky joined in, "the training he received for this mission may have made him a bit of a loner. Give him time."

Everyone looked at her with confused eyes, largely because the comment made no sense. She quickly came to the same realization and just shrugged her shoulders.

There was a collective and silent agreement to not dwell on it too much, and they broke their cluster to find soft beds.

Meanwhile, Lyon took the tunnel he created a year ago that connected the two basements. Strolling at a snail's pace, he jammed his fists into his pants pockets and wrapped his mind around enigmatic thoughts, ignoring the muffled roar of traffic over his head. Was he too stiff? Should he have been more formal and ordered an unload first?

His brow tensed during a mental scream in anguish. Too much thought. What he needed was a release of this self-induced leadership burden overload. He could do this. He was trained to do this. He was trusted to do this. He just needed to stop thinking about it and do it.

Lyon emerged from the other side of the tunnel and stepped into his command center.

"Mac?"

"Yes." Mac's screen remained blank, but his voice sounded like a lifelong butler with a mild aristocratic accent.

"Do you have anything for mental debates?"

It took Mac a few seconds to translate Lyon's version of a metaphor. After a correct decipher, the computer simply replied with a green glow on the table.

Lyon pinched the small tablet off the platform and swallowed it. "Thanks."

Mac only replied with, "Shall I wake you in eight?"

"Please do." Lyon's voice droned with a release of stress as he started up the stairs.

"Good night, Knight Kendrick."

"Good night, Mac."

"You're kidding, right?" Larin stood in the kitchen holding a brown vegetable that looked like a misshapen rock. The question was pointed at the TV screen in the corner of the countertop between the range and sink.

The screen held an image of a chef, complete with a tall, white towering hat, wire-thin mustache and a bad accent Larin couldn't place.

"Not at all, monsieur. It contains what your body requires." Mac's new visage zoomed out to display a similar kitchen, and the chef grabbed a similar vegetable off the counter and went to work at blinding speed as he described the steps.

"After a simple peeling, dice into half-inch cubes. Now place in a pot of water. Bring to a boil until soft, drain, mash and add butter and salt to taste."

Mac's depiction happened so fast, Larin couldn't believe his eyes and seriously doubted the physics behind it.

"How long does that *really* take?"

"Oh," Mac peered up, "about thirty minutes."

"Thirty minutes!"

"Oui, oui."

"Fine, piss yourself." Larin shook the potato at the screen. "What's stopping me from eating the frapping thing raw?"

"Nothing."

"Good." Larin brought it to his mouth reluctantly as his yellow orbs kept a locked target on the incoming object, just in case it did something hostile. He was hungry, but trying foreign foods always made him nervous.

He finally took a crunchy bite and held it in a full mouth. The vegetable hadn't done anything strange. His mouth didn't go numb. He could still see. And his excretion systems didn't involuntarily release. All seemed fine, so he gradually continued the chewing. With a swallow he released a vibrating hum of satisfaction.

"May I recommend salt?" The question came from Mac.

"Excuse me?"

"Salt. It's a finally ground white rock used for seasoning. You'll find it in a small, glass container on the range."

Larin eyed it resting next to a matching container with dust in it. A few shakes, and he tried another bite. Not bad at all. He actually kind of liked it and released an even louder hum of satisfaction.

"That's all right." Larin kept the salt container in his hand and continued eating.

"My enjoyment is in pleasing the palate."

"Whatever," Larin forced through a full mouth.

"Why are you making so much noise? Can't you sleep?" Ky half whispered the questions as she walked into the kitchen.

"No. That liqua chirps in his sleep, and I'm hungry."

"And electrons revolve atoms." Ky shook her head as she slapped the refrigerator door closed. Most likely it was left open during Larin's hunt for food until Mac intervened. "So how's the food anyhow?"

"Not bad." Larin leaned against the cabinet-like pantry next to the bar. "But the computer's a bit queer."

Mac cocked his head as his brow sprung up. "Pardon me, monsieur."

Larin glanced at Ky and jerked his thumb at the monitor. "See what I mean?" Then he returned to the meal.

"So what do you have for me?" She looked at Mac with the question.

"For you, mademoiselle, may I recommend boiled eggs, toast, a side of grapes and a glass of milk?" Learning from the previous encounter, the computer added, "It will take about fifteen minutes. Would you like to try it?"

"Fifteen minutes!" Half-mashed chunks of food spouted from

Larin's mouth, and he didn't even bother to catch them before they hit the floor. "Why does hers take half the time as the one you offered me?"

"Well—" Mac couldn't finish his explanation.

"You don't have to answer that." Ky shifted her eyes from the computer to Larin. "He's just upset that this proves I'm easy to please and he's just a jerk." She turned back to the screen and continued before Larin could reply. "Sure, I'll give it a try. It sounds like fun."

Larin began a grating chuckle, reached into the bin next to the refrigerator and retrieved another potato. "I've got to see this. You know, somebody's got to be ready to put out the fire."

Ky launched her death glare as she pulled her hair back, picked out two clumped strains and whipped them around in a weave that held her hair in a ponytail. "If I set anything on fire it will be you."

"Well," Larin looked away from her eyes and then back, "excuse me." Then he resumed his meal.

"Okay," Ky pushed away the negative thoughts and returned to the computer with a display of bounce, "what's first?"

Chapter 24

Lyon sat in his command chair, resting in the notch at the end of the table. Just as before, the three holographic screens around the position were on, and he attempted to focus all his attention on them and the information they contained.

The screens showed mission profiles, specs and information on scenarios. It could be information overload at times. He tried not to think about it too much. Doing so made one overlook the obvious, and this was a simple mission.

This wasn't a combat breach of a space vessel. This wasn't a hyper atmosphere penetration. And they weren't being asked to take on a legion of mechanized defenders. Even though the team brought with them enough firepower to actually make a serious dent in the latter, he needed to pry his mind away from those situations and focus on reality. The reality was that a basic breach was all that was called for, along with intelligence and device retrieval in a severely under-secured facility with no hardening and only a few guards at best.

Of course there were risks. The weapons he confiscated earlier proved that, but this time he had an entire, well-trained team prepared to easily dispense with the relatively low threat a similar incident would bring to bear.

It basically came down to releasing his self-induced stress about trying to be the perfect leader and relaxing. Relaxing would allow him to focus on the facts. Even with this realization, carrying through with it proved to be more difficult than thinking about it.

"Sir?"

"Yes!?" Lyon barked the word in a tone that held so much frustration it could have been misinterpreted as anger. He caught himself too late and could have slapped himself. Lyon released a breath and turned to see Paloon approaching him from the tunnel.

"Yes, Paloon," he spoke the more relaxed reply in an even softer tone. The detailed tour and discussions earlier really didn't give him a chance to get to know his second in command. He knew he should and made a mental note to do so. "Sorry, what is it?"

Technically, Lyon and Paloon held a similar rank within their respective branches, but out of virtue of the position of the Silver Knights within the Dragon Corps structure, Lyon outranked members of other branches who held ranks equal to his own.

Paloon discarded the earlier harsh reply and began his report. "Everyone should be here shortly. The vehicles check and are in good repair. Hitook is currently stowing the tools and will be here when he finishes. And Ky is in the restroom."

Lyon waited, but Paloon offered nothing else.

"And what about Larin?"

"He's right there, sir."

Lyon's eyes followed Paloon's pointed hand toward the workbench, where Larin sat on a rather high stool for a rolbrid and focused intently on the Quazi cannon he must have retrieved from the locker. Lyon shuddered upon realizing the fact he never noticed Larin enter the room, let alone retrieve the cannon and take up a station at the workbench against the wall to his right. His instincts of ego preservation kicked in as he tried to hide the shock with the question, "Larin, weapons check?"

"Uh...operational, sir." Obviously, most of the rolbrid's attention remained with the weapon in front of him as he scratched his bristly hair. "We're...ready to rock."

"Good." Lyon turned back to Paloon and pointed to his right at one of the new chairs he added to the space around the table. "Please."

"Thanks." Paloon took the seat and quietly watched Lyon, who returned his attention to the displays in front of him.

Although Lyon had made a mental note to take more time to talk with Paloon, it was already forgotten as the knight absorbed himself in his work, again. Time slipped by as he flipped through mission profiles. The only thing to intrude in the trance was the sound of the Quazi cannon rattling on the table as Larin took the seat next to Paloon.

Lyon glanced over to his left to see Ky and Hitook already in their seats. Everyone was watching Larin, probably because he served as the only moving object in the room. There was no telling how long they had been waiting. Hopefully not long, because Lyon had already begun speaking under the perception that Larin took his seat only because the others had recently arrived.

"Now," Lyon tapped a few keys, and the pixels in the display holograms in front of him dissipated like a hard rain, "let's begin. Mac?"

The computer's display flashed on with his standard silver face. "Yes. Would you like a view of the warehouse?"

The offer was perfectly timed, and Lyon accepted it with a nod.

Projection units glowed in the table as the image rose. There was no need to dim the lights in the room. The holographic image maintained sufficient internal brightness to be seen without much problem. It wasn't a perfect image, everyone had seen better. But Paloon gave a silent nod to Lyon for creating such projectors without outside assistance. Not bad at all.

"This is where the transporter flux was detected." Lyon pointed a soon-retrieved finger at the image. "Zoom out."

Mac complied, forcing the image to shrink as other buildings and roads began to rise from the table.

"It's a small, basic warehouse on the outskirts of the seaport district. Just for your knowledge, this is a high-crime area that sees peaks in activity every several months or so. Some businesses have actually attempted to start in this area using abandoned warehouses as cheap office or manufacturing space.

"So when the flux was detected, I conducted a recon." Lyon pointed at the image with a down-angled finger, and Mac zoomed back to the warehouse. "Give us the outline and run the footage."

The full-color image gave way to green outlines that not only showed exterior borders but interior walls, windows, doors and known objects. Then in front of each person a three-dimensional holographic cube appeared. The new cubes gave each a personal view of what Lyon saw when he peered through the warehouse ceiling window. The video ran for a little more than a minute before freezing and fading from existence.

Paloon tapped his finger on the table before pointing at the image. "I don't see the outline of a transporter unit. Can Mac confirm the existence of one?"

"No, unfortunately." Lyon leaned back. "He's working with native-made satellites. He has been able to modify them to a relatively small degree and has used multiple satellites to collaborate the right kind of data we need at times. He picked up the flux; he's even been able to detect and identify most life signs. But some alloys still create problems, and it's our guess that these alloys must be present within these crates or elsewhere in the building. It has stopped him from getting good readings on the location of the unit and, sometimes, in the detection of life forms."

Paloon hummed and leaned back.

"But I've got a solution for that; I'll get to that later." Lyon cleared his throat and continued. "I was seen and attempted to break contact but was followed by a non-native being of unknown species who was apparently acting as a guard. I killed him right before I took fire from some terrans."

Lyon started into Larin's territory and saw he had the rolbrid's attention.

"Now, the unknown being had a native weapon, but two of the terrans were using non-native weapons."

The comment prompted mild noises from the listeners, and Larin said, "That's not good."

"No, it's not." Lyon pointed at the Quazi cannon in front of Larin. "That's one; there's also a Gortek particle laser in storage. And one terran even had a MU." Lyon added the last as a second thought, but everyone took note.

"I have learned something about this weapon." Larin jabbed a stubby finger at the cannon and had everyone's attention. "It's been modified."

"Modified how?" Lyon was a bit displeased that Mac didn't catch any modifications but partially blamed himself for the poor programming.

"That's the problem; I don't know how."

Paloon beat Lyon to the punch. "Then how do you know it's—"

"I just know." Larin fought to keep himself professional. "This is almost an antique but in good condition. The panels and interior mechanisms show signs of tampering, possibly with native tools but, at the very least, with the wrong tools."

"If it has been modified, can you find out how?" Lyon leaned forward and grabbed Larin's gaze.

"Oh, I can do it." Larin nodded at the computer on the far wall. "With some help from Mac and some time, and I do mean *some time*, I'll figure it out."

"Good, but we don't have that kind of time right now. Do that later."

"Absolutely, captain."

"Back to the mission. The plan is to get into the facility, search for intelligence, locate the transporter and either retrieve or destroy it."

"What about this piolanese guard?" Ky kept the comment calm and asked out of concern for her job.

"During surveillance, Mac has only detected a maximum of two beings, possibly piolanese, normally in the area at any one time. In the evening, during the time we are going to hit the place, there has only been one guard on duty." Lyon looked at Ky and Hitook. "Should be simple enough, but be prepared in case this piolant is well-trained."

"Where is this other piolant going to be?" Paloon asked.

"We don't know." Lyon sat back again. "Mac has never been able to keep track. Following this mission, that's your job to wait for the shift change and track from there. They've got to take the body somewhere."

"Why don't we just tag the corpse?" Larin offered the idea nonchalantly, but both Paloon and Lyon shook their heads.

"They'll pickup the bug, besides," Lyon turned his attention back to the image on the table, "the plan is to make this look like a robbery or data theft job."

Lyon placed his elbows on the table, clasped his hands and cradled his chin in extended thumbs. "Run the simulation."

The image zoomed out again to include green outlines of the nearby buildings and streets. Red dots spotted the area. Lyon pointed at them as he spoke, and they moved in time with his comments.

"Paloon will be in the van running the drones for surveillance and helping confirm a secure site before we move. Larin will position the tank in this alley, close to his final position on this rooftop. The tank will be close enough that Larin could get it for additional firepower if we need it, but I doubt that will be necessary."

"I brought a CNG rifle, so I'll be packing all the hurt we'll need." Larin smiled.

"Look," Lyon's eyes slid over to see Larin's grin, "we need the warehouse to remain intact, so leave the warheads here. The tank will be sufficient, but we won't need it. Bring a sonic long gun, something you can snipe with and provide cover from here." He pointed at a neighboring rooftop.

"Understood." Larin removed the grin and forgot the idea of explaining that it was his attempt at humor. The possible fight wouldn't be worth it. The knight still seemed uptight, and challenging his rank would almost be career suicide with repercussions if he was forced to separate from the Corps. He had seen it happen before and to warriors better than he.

"When Paloon and Mac secure the area and drop the electric net, Ky and Hitook will position themselves at the front; I'll take the rear. You two take out the guard, and I'll clear these rooms. Mac hasn't been able to penetrate these rooms yet, so we don't know what's in them. But Paloon may be able to get a better reading once we're in position."

Lyon leaned back, laying his arms on his lap. "You're smart people. I'm sure you can figure out the rest. Once we pull out, one of the drones will stay behind, and Paloon will maintain the surveillance. The rest of us will rest, and when he has a location we'll plan and move from there. And we'll keep doing this until we locate the heart of the smugglers." Lyon's voice lowered slightly. "If Fate is with us, we'll be able to do this without the p'tahians detecting us. Any questions?"

Looks danced about the room. The mission was simple and straightforward, much like a basic training scenario. Facial expressions signaled everyone's understanding—except for one.

"Hitook?" Lyon got the liqua's attention. Lyon didn't know how to attempt to handle him. Actually being in the presence of such a large creature always gave Lyon a scare, but he held it down to maintain a solid face. "You haven't said anything. Do you have any questions?"

"No, sir." Hitook attempted to shift in the rather tight and uncomfortable chair.

"Well, I guess you only speak when necessary." Lyon grinned. "I like that. So if that's it, let's load up. We depart in two hours to set up surveillance before we pre-post."

Lyon stood, and the rest of them followed and began departing to their tasks.

"Paloon," Lyon touched the hunter's shoulder, "I need to discuss something with you."

"Sure."

Lyon didn't reply, just took the steps out of the command center and through the rear door to the back parking lot. He felt he needed some fresh air anyhow. Paloon patiently waited while eyeing the nearby buildings and the clouds overhead.

The reluctant leader looked about before stretching and folding his arms. "This is the first time I've commanded a joint force." Lyon glanced at Paloon from time to time, but when he did he always met eyes looking back. "I know you have." Lyon sighed. "What I'm trying to say is that I need for you to keep an eye on the team. I don't need Lieutenant Mulkin blowing up city blocks; he very well might have been joking, but we don't need that. Do you understand?"

"Understood, sir. I know what you mean. Consider it taken care of."

"Thanks."

Lyon only dismissed Paloon with the tone in his voice. The sound of the screen door closing preceded a faint meow. Lyon dropped his head in time to see the black stray rub against his leg.

This time he squatted to pet the animal that immediately responded with a heavy purr of appreciation before toppling over on its back in hopes of getting a belly rub. Lyon smiled and obliged. Temporarily, he forgot the stress and relaxed more deeply than he had for the past several days.

Chapter 25

The miniature drops finally crept close enough to each other to demonstrate their magically magnetic ability to coalesce into a much larger blob, which blasted into a streak down the windshield.

Lyon watched the spectacle with mild amazement but mostly with the utter obsession that only came when one zoned out of reality. After all, he felt that losing touch with reality was sometimes better than finding it.

The team's leader sat in the navigator's chair to Larin's right. Together they waited for Paloon to finish the reconnaissance and drop the electronic net. Unwittingly, they shared the discomfort of neither knowing what to say to the other.

Larin considered himself a fairly easygoing guy, regardless of what others may say, but he sensed that the knight didn't like him. On the contrary, the knight didn't dislike Larin; it was just that right now Lyon was clearing his thoughts.

Another crinkle of cellophane cracked the silence as Larin poured out a final palm-full of peanuts and downed them. He was beginning to like this terran food, which was not surprising for a rolbrid. Food kept Larin from getting too wrapped up in mental questions, and he sat with a slight smile as he chewed.

"Drones in place." The comment came through everyone's internal communications systems in Corps standard. Lyon had chosen that language to make it easier on everyone and to double the channel's encryption in case any natives intercepted it.

Lyon snapped from his reverie and took a second to process what he heard. *"What do you have?"*

Paloon sat in the back of the van parked about a quarter of a mile from the other two in the tank. He turned to scan the multiple holographic displays with inputs from the four drones he had launched. With the speed of thought, the images on the screens zoomed, panned and switched visual sensors. The displays helped. Having all the visual signals in his head at once would be too confusing.

"I'm not sure, but there's definitely at least one life form in there. It appears to be sleeping against a crate."

"Mac, can you confirm?" Lyon made a silent wish.

"Sorry." The computer paused to run a series of filters through the satellite's signals. *"Too much interference again. Something is there; I just can't get a good life sign indicator."* Mac brightened his voice in an attempt to end on a good note. *"I can tell you the utility use for the building hasn't changed; it's similar to previous records."*

Lyon turned to Larin for no apparent reason before peering out of the corner of his eyes through the windshield and into the blackness of the night. *"Hunter Osluf, you are our only eyes now."* For some unknown reason he felt like being formal and embarrassingly obvious. *"Can you confirm the race?"*

Paloon held back a verbal noise that would signal his non-assurance and just went from monitor to monitor before he replied. *"Negative. There's a large signature, but the computer can't confirm race."*

"Thanks; that's all I needed. It matches previous recons, so it's a go. Drop the net."

In response to Lyon's statement, Larin pocketed the empty bag of peanuts, and Ky and Hitook shifted in the front seats of the van as they prepared for the assault. Paloon went to work.

He had perched the four globular drones in a square pattern on the roofs next to the warehouse under examination. Each drone emitted a holographic image of a native bird, thanks to some programming help from Mac.

Those holographic images shimmered briefly as the drones began to emit the electronic net. First the invisible beams linked the drones to each other. Then the drones filled the area with interference frequencies that masked all known signals from entering or exiting the area below. The effort increased until each drone replied with a confirmation tone in Paloon's head.

"The net is down." Paloon entered a series of commands to control the net before overload caused the drones to short each other.

Lyon tensed. *"Mac?"*

"Confirmed. I'm down to quarter-meter visual. I'm not going to be much help, I'm afraid."

"Paloon?" Lyon called. *"Are we clear?"*

"Uhh—" This time the hesitation slipped through. He made blindingly fast adjustments. The team needed to move fast before the guard attempted communicating. But adjustments had to be made or the net would even block the team's communications. Paloon made the adjustments faster than he thought he could. *"Done. Our comm's clear."*

"We're blue. Go." The command came from Lyon immediately, and the team didn't hesitate to respond.

Ky and Hitook had already discussed their pronged advance on the front entrance, and with a quick hand movement from Ky, both exited the vehicle, closed the doors and were on their way with so much stealth that one would have to be staring intently at the vehicle to even notice something had happened. Both were in solid black suits that covered everything except black painted faces and hands, or paws. Both ran as they had been trained, using precision steps to balance weight so the sound of footfalls was nonexistent.

Close combat meant Ky's bows would be of little use. Instead, two short swords clung to her thighs. Hitook carried two, twin hand blades on his back. The handles rested snugly in their holders while the tips of the hooked blades peeked over his high shoulders.

Lyon, also dressed in black, exited as well. He had a back-up pistol holstered under his left arm, but his primary weapon remained clamped in a rigid harness strapped to his right leg. It was a Dragon

Corps standard issue weapon, a torque-barreled particle laser with an under-barrel allaric launcher, just like the one Larin was toying with before getting volunteered for this assignment. Lyon was already down the street a couple of blocks before Larin could retrieve all of his equipment, but then again, Larin didn't have to go as far.

The rolbrid yanked a combat pack from between the two bucket seats, slung it over his shoulders and pounded the automatic tightening mechanisms, which responded with a faint hiss and quick tension. A black pad popped out of the top of the pack and attached itself to sub-dermal connectors in Larin's neck. Then he slid a short, black case from behind his seat, locked the handle to the left side of the combat pack, slapped a gloved hand on his standard issue weapon to confirm it remained in its leg holster and set off. Larin only ran for a couple of blocks before he engaged the pack's geomagnetic gravity unit and flew to the rooftops.

With a few skips and skitters on the wet roof, Larin came to a stop in the center of the edge furthest from the target warehouse. The noise was more than he cared to make but, he told himself, soft enough to be silent to anyone inside the target.

A large column shot from the left side of the angled roof. Judging by the design of the building, Larin correctly guessed it housed a crane for loading and unloading. Its purpose tonight would be cover. He crossed the roof, rolled on to his back, spun and glided up the roof feet first. Almost without conscious thought, he commanded his special gloves to grip and release in rapid precision and let his arms and shoulders do all the work.

He slid into the shadow of the crane tower and, when he reached the top, crossed his legs and engaged his boots to make them grab the roof as if magnetic. With the smoothness of a slight wind, Larin slowly sat up. Being so close to the target triggered years of embedded instincts that told him to take his time, even though he remained completely invisible to naked eyes in the shadow. But now was not the time to take chances.

Mental commands released the top clamp holding the case to his combat pack. The case dropped into his waiting left hand. The other clamp released, and he whipped the case around his body and onto his lap. Stubby fingers released the latches.

A strange serenity began to course through Larin's veins as his eyes fell upon the compact weapon resting comfortably in the molded case. There no longer remained room for thought, just action. Almost as if time stood still, Lieutenant Mulkin was in the realm of the surreal.

With a gentle grace, the warrior lifted the weapon away from the case and used the bottoms of his hands to close the lid and push the case across and off his lap. A waiting knee pinned the case against the tower.

The weapon appeared as a mass of mechanisms with no distinct purpose, but to Larin, it represented an indescribable beauty. His hand dove into the center and caressed the embedded grip.

Streaks shot through his vision before his sight flashed. Fed through a connecter in his palm, visual displays of the weapon's systems came online. Schematics and system checks scrolled down the left of his vision. Line items turned from green to red to blue as the weapon checked and confirmed each system operated properly. To the right were gauges and indicators for everything from wind and temperature to atmosphere pressure and density, anything that could assist in calculating perfect shots every time, though the weapon compensated for most factors automatically.

Meanwhile, the weapon morphed in his hand. Bars glided into couplers to create new units that merged with other parts that grew in size. The almost magical process only took a few seconds, but when it finished, what had been a mesh of parts held the distinctive characteristics of a weapon. Now twice the size of the case it came from, the weapon silently came to life and began charging.

Larin confirmed the charge on his display before cradling the rifle in his other hand. Through all the data in his field of view, he could see the entire warehouse. A perfect view, he couldn't ask for a better one. Short of the mild drizzle and a bent soda can rocking to the beat of a breeze, nothing seemed to move.

He turned on the scope, and a blue-bordered window popped into the lower right of his view. The picture displayed a perfect shot, right down this weapon's equivalent of a barrel. Personally, Larin found this view distracting and flipped to the next view, his favorite. The window on the right and data on the left disappeared, replaced by a set of marked blue crosshairs that extended his view. As the weapon moved, the crosshairs kept pace.

Another slight thought later and the weapon's ultrasonic scope kicked in, almost blinding Larin before he could compensate. Glowing like a galactic center, the electronic net hovered in the air above Larin. Apparently, one of Paloon's drones rested on top of the crane tower. Larin couldn't see through the net with the ultrasonic scope, but he *could* see *everything* below, which was the important part. The display turned the view grey but with enough contrast and brightness to display the battlefield with great detail.

With careful use of the range finder, Larin adjusted the scope's output and peeled through the nearby buildings and the target warehouse to confirm the shape of an apparently sleeping piolant. As he zoomed out, something to the left caught his attention. He took target and began scanning. He had to be sure and finally was.

Ky and Hitook had already positioned themselves next to the warehouse. Instead of giving a mental compliment to them for blending well enough to avoid his first scan, Larin silently cursed himself for missing them.

Larin panned to the right and soon identified Lyon crouched behind a dumpster next to a building on the other side of the parking lot behind the warehouse. They waited for him, so now that everything checked, he was ready.

"In position," Larin reported.

"Copy. Bravo hold." Lyon's command targeted the House Bravo ninja and acolyte at the front of the warehouse. *"I have a light."*

The sniper couldn't detect physical brightness with the ultrasonic sight, so Larin shifted his view, flashing from ultrasonic to visual and back to confirm the location of the light in the parking lot. He used his built-in bionics to zoom in on the bulb and follow its arching metal pole to a wooden post. After a couple of clamps down the post, Larin tightened the view even further, moved the rifle until the crosshairs dissected the conduit and fired.

Larin's only initial indication that the weapon fired had come from the crosshairs flashing; the weapon remained quiet and didn't move. His second confirmation came from Lyon.

"Thanks."

Now in darkness, the combat tactician whipped around the dumpster and ran toward the rear door while retrieving his weapon. As his hand wrapped the grip, the weapon's system came online, the matter coil hummed to life and a forward-positioned rest under the grip swung around to cradle itself under Lyon's arm. The extension helped balance the weight of the cannon as he broke it from the holster and brought it level.

He stopped with his back to the rear wall of the warehouse. *"Scan."*

Ky made a few hand gestures at Hitook to communicate how she wished to proceed. Hitook replied with a mental projection of the thought, *Understood*, and not by using any form of embedded technical equipment.

Ky's eyes widened. Hitook remained expressionless. Even with years of study, she had never been able to accomplish that feat, yet here stood an acolyte using it like a master. She wanted to ask how, but there was no time.

The two glided from around the corner and took up positions on the sides of a metal door inside a larger wooden companion. As she had indicated to be her preference, Ky withdrew a small device from her back and handed it to Hitook.

The liqua wedged it between his two forefingers and ran it over the edge of the door. A small screen provided a penetrating view.

Lyon did the same. He discovered only one locked deadbolt. Meanwhile, both of his weapon's cell icons showed full charge, so he adjusted the barrel. Internal gears extended the barrel, which turned in the process, forcing the refractors into pinpoint focus.

With another pass of the scanner to confirm the bolt's location, Lyon raised the weapon and adjusted its output strength to shorten the beam's distance. He placed the blue dot in his vision over the bolt's location and fired. A stream of invisible, coherent energy effortlessly poked a hole in the frame and vaporized the bolt and anything in its path, including a moth attracted to the energy projected by the scanner.

One more scan and then Lyon spotted it.

"I've got sensors of some kind."

"Same here," Ky confirmed as she leaned forward to get a better look in the monitor.

Paloon felt they were waiting on him to project interference into the system. *"I'm not sure I can poke a native system."*

"Don't worry. I've got it." Mac kept steps ahead of the rest. *"I'm monitoring the utilities into the place. If the security system attempts a call, I'll be the one answering it."*

"Okay." Lyon shifted to the opposite side of the door and prepared to bust it in. *"How's the suspect?"*

"He hasn't moved."

"Confirmed." Larin kept his scope tuned to the target and saw what Paloon saw. Killing the piolant would be so easy, and it pained Larin that Lyon wanted him alive.

"Bravo?"

"Stand by." Ky placed both hands over the doorknob and began to mentally focus.

Hitook kept the scanner in place and watched as Ky began to move the inner mechanisms of the lock. She almost had it but ran into difficulty with the last tumbler. Acting instinctively to help, Hitook took his free paw and covered both of Ky's hands in black-painted fur. A nanosecond later, the lock clicked.

Ky yanked her hands away and didn't allow herself to get angry but came awfully darn close. An acolyte had out-performed her, and the thought didn't please her. She snatched the scanner from between Hitook's fingers and stared up at the towering beast. After ignoring a few fleeting thoughts of starting a fight, Ky just put the scanner in its pouch.

With his ability to easily touch the top of someone's thoughts, Hitook didn't need to see her face to know what Ky was thinking, but it sure sped up the interpretation. Normally, he would apologize, but he decided wisely to remain quiet and apologize later.

"He moved." The comment came from Larin and Paloon at almost the same time.

The rest of the team froze.

Images danced in Paloon's monitors and in the lone screen in Larin's view. Then all settled to stillness again.

"Stand by." Paloon flipped through sensor inputs. Temperature steady. Air pressure steady. Heat patterns steady. *"It appears he just shifted in his sleep."*

The team on the ground released held breath, and Larin eased off his tightened trigger finger.

"Okay." Lyon thought about this for a moment. *"Where's he at?"*

Paloon responded. *"He's to Bravo's left between the crates and the wall."*

"Lieutenant Mulkin, can you confirm the rest of the building is empty?"

"Stand by." Larin peered through the walls and back again. *"Affirmative. It's empty."*

"We'll take him in a prong. I'll go ahead and cross the rear of the

warehouse and follow up the back. Bravo, break one up the wall and the other down the center, through one of the alleys in the crates." Lyon didn't feel the need to reiterate the need to take the piolant alive for questioning. Besides, even with the particle cannon, it would take at least three shots to completely kill an armored piolant without a head shot.

Paloon shared some insight he had gained from scanning the interior. *"Bravo, take the third alley."*

"Thanks." Lyon replied for Bravo and repositioned himself to enter the back door. *"Bravo, ready?"*

Ky's hands danced in another set of silent comments that essentially said, *You first, show off.*

"Ready," Ky replied.

Lyon paused and sent the one command the whole team had come here for. *"Go."*

Silence accompanied the team's breach of the building. The only noise came from a faint shuffle of Lyon's feet, which was more than the two trained assassins wanted to hear from across the concrete floor. But sound didn't betray the team. The tipoff came from Hitook.

As Hitook turned the corner around the crates to face the target, the liqua's scent, uninhibited by his suit, advanced faster than the team. It penetrated the air and drifted into two sets of noses. The aroma sparked the fire of hunger. Now awake, the hunt was on.

The growling caused the air to rumble, but it lasted for only a split second. Hitook didn't have enough of a warning to respond properly. The enormous beasts charged.

Watching from a safe distance, Paloon's face reflected disbelief at what he was seeing, *"It can't—"*

Hitook cut him off. *"There's two."* It was all he could get out before it was time to get to business.

Ky and Lyon both wondered what he meant but couldn't reach him before the combat was far beyond the point of no return.

Hitook decided to split the two. Paws and arms flared as he crouched. The first came into range, and Hitook spun. The beast caught a heavy paw in the rib cage and soared toward the high roof and over the crates.

"Incoming." Hitook didn't have time to offer more of a warning. It took most of his concentration to keep his balance as he continued the spin, just quick enough to catch the second beast in the throat with his left paw.

Ky was about to turn the corner when she heard the warning, wondered if it was directed at her and then saw something move above. She glanced to see the flailing creature as it careened down on her. *"Ah, crap!"*

The comments began to make Lyon wonder if he was about to lose another teammate. But he pushed the thought from his mind as he made the final turn to look down the long corridor between the walls and crates to see Hitook and what he held away from him.

Gleaming canines snapped as dewclaws bit into Hitook's suit. This beast wanted to eat, now; Hitook could sense that easily. So overwhelming was the primal emotion that one of the liqua's stomachs began to growl in beat with the clamping fangs.

Nothing short of death had a chance of stopping the onslaught, and Hitook didn't feel like engaging in mental negotiations. His right paw reached behind and unhooked one of his twin blades. With a snap of the wrist, the blades swung around to rest their backs along the length of his forearm and beyond. With another twist and snap, the blades bit hide and cleaved the creature across the chest, cutting it in two.

The top half, still locked in Hitook's grip, convulsed temporarily as the rear fell to the floor followed by a mess of innards. Hitook released the neck and let the top half join the rest of the carcass.

Now Hitook could see Lyon approaching with his weapon raised. Lyon had gotten a bead on the beast but never had a clean shot. Lyon dropped the cannon and noticed what appeared to be a smirk, almost a devilish grin, on Hitook's lips. It disappeared as another twist returned the blades to their holster. Blood dripped from the hooked tips to land on Hitook's shoulder and streak down his chest.

Ky took a tumble when the other beast struck. They rolled back and forth. Fangs penetrated her left shoulder once. The attack had caught her a bit off guard, and she wouldn't let it happen again. Both growled at each other and snapped their respective sets of fangs.

At first it was business, but Ky started to get really pissed and took the attack personally. That's when she used her dexterity to her advantage. Spontaneous plans rarely worked, but she had one and wasted no time in execution.

She drew in her left leg under the body on top of her then shifted her weight to control the roll as best she could. As her back landed on the floor, she sprung her spine. The blur of fangs and claws bounced upward.

Ky had used the temporary effect of low gravity to push the beast away. Now, she steadied, aimed and snapped her leg. Her foot sailed into the creature's throat and planted it against a tower of creates, which shook with the impact. Talent and training allowed her to remain balanced in the pose with her right foot on the ground.

She went for one of the short swords sheathed along her legs with a plan to cut off the beast's head, but as Ky withdrew the hilt toward her face before swinging, a faint crack immediately preceded a loud pop. Flecks of blood, bone and tissue sprayed the area and speckled Ky. With odd timing, her arm served to cover most of her face.

Amazement appeared in her eyes as she dropped her arm. The creature's head was gone. Ky turned to see Lyon and Hitook just stepping from between the crates. That could only mean one thing.

"Thanks for nothing," she replied in an obviously sarcastic tone. The irritation wouldn't have been so bad if somebody hadn't made the kill for her and coated her in the remains at the same time. She was also irritated by the fact there could be only one person to blame.

"You're welcome."

Joy tinted Larin's voice, but Ky remained unsure if that joy came from a perfect shot or the effects of it. She withdrew her foot and let the corpse tumble to the concrete. Ky dropped her leg, returned the sword and didn't bother to wipe away the blood that made it to her face.

"Those—" Paloon caught himself in disbelief but felt that now, with everything quieting down, he could ask. *"Were those wolves?"*

Lyon holstered his cannon and sighed. He didn't want to have a conversation like this, but he knew it would happen. *"Yes."*

"But—" Paloon still didn't believe his sensors, no matter what Lyon said. Regardless of his atlantian heritage and even though the hunter's own unit was Force Grey Wolf, wolves only existed in legends. *"But they're—"*

"They're mythological creatures, yes." Lyon didn't have time to discuss Paloon's epiphany that the Theory of Terra may actually be true. *"Look, I'd love to talk about wolves, dolphins and other mythological creatures, but later. Is the building clear?"*

Larin beat Paloon to the confirmation as the atlantian tried to clear his mind and search his sensors.

"Okay. Mac, anything?"

"Nothing came or went."

"Good." Lyon motioned for Hitook and Ky to come closer, but his commands were aimed at those outside the building. *"Remove the net and bring the van closer but hold at two hundred meters. Mulkin, hold your position, you're our main eyes and cover until the van is repositioned."*

Both replied that they copied, and Paloon began the steps to tear down the electronic net and move the van.

"Ky," Lyon pointed as he talked, "check the back rooms. Hitook, I want you to go through these crates. I'm going to hunt down the transporter."

The team broke, and Lyon contacted his computer companion.

"Mac, send me the map with the location of the previous fluxes."

"Sure." Mac was glad he didn't get tasked to scan the warehouse or something like that because the net hadn't fully dissipated yet. *"There you go."*

Lyon pulled his sleeve away from his wrist computer's screen. A full-colored three-dimensional depiction of the warehouse covered the monitor. With a few taps, the image went to a black and yellow wire frame. The image rotated with Lyon's movements as he attempted to line himself with the red circle.

Ky took care when entering the office and used her enhanced vision to her advantage by scanning the room before turning on the lights. Nothing out of the ordinary, definitely no lurkers or weapon emplacements, not that she expected any. A rather ordinary computer-like device sat on the desk, so she decided to turn it on before retrieving the scanner and going over the walls.

"Someone tripped an alarm." Mac's voice, regardless of its calm tone, gave everyone a start. *"I've intercepted, and I'm riding the signal back to disarm the entire system. Don't worry; I got ya back, homies."*

The last phrase sounded a bit odd to everyone other than Lyon, but they successfully interpreted, and at least one team member liked it enough to add it to his list of colorful expressions.

During the conversation, Hitook was troubled by a confusing dilemma. A fluke at first, he thought, but after the third crate, the liqua began to develop an ugly feeling.

"Knight Kendrick?"

"Yes?" Lyon stopped pushing crates off the top of a clump of towers in which, about halfway down, should be the source of the flux signal. He turned to face Hitook, who stood across the center aisle.

"These are empty." Hitook scooped a paw-full of packing material.

Lyon cocked his head. *Why would they be empty?* Then he, too, thought it could be a fluke. He stepped over to the edge to peer down at the crates he pushed over.

He never bothered to look inside and expected them to be easy to push off of the pile. He was after the source of the flux and was too busy to think about the crates. But among the shattered remains of wood and clumps of packing material, he could see...nothing.

Lyon shared Hitook's uncomfortable feeling. As a leader, he had the duty to keep calm, but this sight didn't help. Hitook could detect the emotion but said nothing because he understood why.

"Well then," Lyon turned to face Hitook, "help me remove these creates. There was a receiver here; maybe these are just meant to cover it up."

With Hitook plucking stacks of crates and chucking them aside, the chore didn't take long.

Meanwhile, Ky put her skills to the test on a safe she had found. Her earlier attempt on a lock, which had received outside assistance, left her miffed, and she tensed all the mental power she had. Behind her hand, tumblers turned and locks disengaged. The internal mechanisms formed an indescribable picture in her head. Indescribable because it was different for everyone. Regardless of the training, one could only be led to the ability. Devising how to control the ability was up to the trainee.

A final internal movement sounded with a ker-chunk. Ky gripped the handle and opened the door. Nothing. An unadulterated void. Ky didn't find it odd so much as disappointing. She succeeded, as she knew she could, without an acolyte's help. But there was no reward or trophy to display as proof of her worthiness.

A grumbling came from her throat. She refused to dwell on it and turned to the computer. On the top edge of an otherwise black screen sat a cursor of some sort. The safe forgotten, Ky took the chair and called for help.

"Mac, can you walk me through a native computer system?"

"Sure." Happiness tinged his voice.

Outside on the warehouse floor, Lyon and Hitook had most of the boxes removed. At least this endeavor didn't end with disappointment. Their efforts revealed a device of some sort previously surrounded by crates. Neither recognized it. Nothing about it seemed to have the design elements of a transporter receiver, but when it came to pirates, no one could tell how they would rig a contraption if they never successfully stole one.

Paloon had moved the van and remained in the front seat but stayed fully connected to the drones; it just took him longer to sift through the commands without the assistance of the hologram projectors. And though he never received a request, he went to work with one of the drones to scan the newly uncovered device, especially now that it was unobstructed by crates.

It had the size and generic design of a large riding lawnmower with one end holding a panel display propped on poles. Only the panel had any features that resembled markings of any kind. Lyon ran a finger across the display but couldn't read the language. It might have been piolant, but he had removed that information from his memories.

Lyon glanced at Hitook, but the liqua's eyes declared that he didn't know what it was, either.

"Hey, guys." Ky held a cocky pose as she stepped from the door, but bewilderment covered her face as she pointed with her thumb at the room behind her. "The place is empty."

Lyon and Hitook raised their heads and turned to Ky.

"Yes," Lyon replied, "but didn't you find anything?"

Ky stopped and wondered if she was talking to herself. She held out a fist and used an extended digit from her other hand to pick out and raise finger after finger as she explained.

"An empty safe. An empty desk. Two empty file cabinets. And an empty computer." Her head sifted into a go-ahead-and-challenge-me-smart-ass look. "Sure, five empty items. And before you ask, Mac helped me, and that computer is burned. It's there, but nothing's on it."

Before Lyon could ask why, a thump sounded from within the device in front of him, and both atlantian and liqua jumped back. With all the components now in place, Paloon's in-eye meters lit up as the sensors finally identified the item. But there was no time to warn anyone.

Light penetrated everyone's eyes a split nanosecond before the blast wave picked them off the floor and shot them across the building like cannon balls. The blast pulverized nearby crates and made toothpicks and sawdust out of the rest. Shredded pieces of metal, once serving as walls, shot like fléchette rounds into the surrounding buildings.

The trio inside soon followed. Lyon flew out the quickly disappearing front entrance and skittered across the concrete and asphalt before smacking into a telephone pole and collapsing. Hitook literally took the form of a cannon ball as he punched through wall after wall before finally rolling to a stop on the floor two warehouses over. Ky stood the furthest from the blast, but it wasn't a lucky position. The blast tossed her through walls concealing support beams, wood and iron, and metal utility conduits. She bounced between the beams like a pinball, making dents along the way. Although she came close to being blown completely out of the building, she didn't make it.

Larin turned his head away. The flash burned his ultrasonic filter, and he killed it before looking back just in time to see the second stage of the building's destruction.

The warehouse's support beams had taken a lot of damage, and now each beam was too weak to help the others. Loud creaks pierced the night as the roof swayed and crashed backwards to land on top of Ky.

Paloon and Larin wanted to shout but knew it would mean nothing and sprung into action instead.

Larin swung the rifle over his back and activated the pack's clamps to grab it. He then did the same for the case, which now dangled under the pack like a flap. But the pack didn't fully grip the case before Larin sprinted across the roof and jumped off the edge.

"What happened!?" The emotionally charged statement came from Mac, but no one answered.

Geomagnetic displacers whined with the sudden activation in flight and responded just in time to soften the ground's blow as it met Larin. But the jolt was strong enough for Larin to feel it all along his spine.

Wheels squealed in the distance. Paloon raced to the scene, and as the van came around the corner, it almost rolled over before coming to a stop next to Lyon. Paloon dove from the vehicle to assess Lyon's condition. With one look, all he could say was, "This ain't good."

"What's going on? I've lost signals. Please someone speak to me?" Mac was getting more impatient.

Larin raced around the rubble and activated his pack's scanners, which displayed an overlay in his natural view. He didn't see her body get thrown from the building, which meant she remained under the roof and there was no way of telling what condition she was in. *There.* The scanners identified a life source, and under the influence of a rolbrid's equivalent of adrenaline, Larin feverishly went to work.

Immediately after the blast, Hitook had picked himself up and cleared his thoughts enough to follow his path back to the scene. As he stumbled onto the devastation, he shook his head and blinked hard as he attempted to keep his eyes focused.

"Get your carcass over here and help?" Larin made the command because he could see Hitook emerge, but the liqua didn't respond.

"What kind of help?" It was Mac again. *"Will someone please tell me what's going on, damn it!"*

"Shut the frap up!"

Maybe the blast damaged Hitook's computer, so Larin tried yelling.

"Get your furry rear over here!"

That got Hitook's attention. Unfortunately it took him a moment to realize why the short man struggled with tossing chunks and strips of debris. When it dawned, Hitook almost fell in his rush to the site and tore into the wreckage with both paws.

Ashes flared red in the drizzling mist. The glow highlighted the features of Yabuki's face before smoke billowed from his lips. His squinted eyes sparkled with both health and fascination.

Professionals. The thought didn't disturb him too much, but it did disturb him.

His eyes glided down to the egg-like object in his left hand. Lips twisted in disappointment, and the device disappeared in his coat pocket.

Mercenaries? Maybe. A rival company? Not likely. Another drug ring? Only if they were ready for a bloody street war. That could justify the use of mercenaries. Regardless of who they were, they were professionals.

At least the bomb worked just as the royal guard said it would. But waiting hadn't drawn them all in. The van stopped sort, an obvious sign of training.

They must have killed the wolves; they were supposed to be starved for a week and should have attacked immediately. But if he had waited any longer, they would have left the building before he could blow it. *Professionals.* There was that thought again.

Getting some was better than none. Not like it seemed to matter. The giant walked away from the blast like his most severe injury was nothing more than a sprained ankle. Battle armor? Possibly. Then the midget jumped off a twenty-foot high roof as if it were nothing more than disembarking a bus. Adrenaline? Maybe.

Yabuki absorbed the scene before him and found it humorous when they pulled a limp female frame from under the debris. He almost laughed out loud, but that would be unprofessional. After all, he was dealing with professionals. Professionals or not, he at least got two. They'll think twice before screwing with Yabuki Yumiro again.

A tinge of a smile formed. Yabuki had to report what he saw. Besides, the fire department and police would arrive soon.

He took one last draw before pinching the cigarette between thumb and middle finger then flicking it to the ground. As he crushed the glowing ember with his shoe, he took pleasure in swearing to himself that he would also crush whoever hired this team.

He turned and crossed the asphalt roof, smoke trailing from his mouth.

Chapter 26

An indescribable fire burned in his brain. He could almost hear his nerves scream. Every cell ached and demanded attention, threatening continued pain if ignored. Lighting pierced his body and flashed in his vision. It flared almost as bright as the explosion.

The explosion! Alive! He must be alive. Otherwise, he wouldn't feel so much pain.

With considerable effort, Lyon pried his eyes open, only to have them assaulted by the painfully harsh light.

"Paloon!"

Mac? Mac is here?

"He's coming around."

A cold hand touched his bare shoulder. It startled him enough to jerk away as his eyes flew open. He could see a blurred vision of Paloon before he had to close his eyes against the light again.

"Take it easy." Paloon wedged his hands under Lyon's shoulders and began to lift his torso. "Mac's finished, but your body is still going to need time to cope."

"W-where?"

"We're back at your command center." Paloon held Lyon and turned to the computer. "Mac, give me an angled piece of foam."

Without delay, lights flared, and a piece of contoured foam materialized. Paloon put it beneath Lyon's back.

A deep breath and Lyon resumed his attempts to adjust to the light by blinking. Thoughts raced through his head, but Paloon began to offer information before Lyon could begin his questions.

"You've been out for two days."

"But—" Lyon cradled his hands around his forehead. A migraine began to form. "But the blast, how...how did—"

"How did we repair you?" Paloon chuckled, moved a seat over and sat down. "I stripped a few components from the van and improved Mac's abilities. Don't get me wrong. You did a great job. Now his resolution is so fine that he can not only perform telesurgery, but he can cook."

Mac and Paloon joined in laughter. Apparently the two got to know each other well. Something had happened, but Lyon's migraine kept him from thinking about it too much.

"What about the others?"

"Well," Paloon stifled the now low chuckles, "Hitook took it like it was nothing more than a strong wind. He is currently helping Larin run the gas station. Ky, surprisingly, didn't take as much damage as you, even with the roof falling on her."

"It fell?" Lyon had lost consciousness long before that had happened.

"Yep. But now she's upstairs running the store for you. Mac's helping her considerably. Oh, she's your cousin now. It seemed like the most plausible cover." Paloon tapped Lyon on the arm. "By the way, I hope you don't mind that we recovered her first."

"No," Lyon grunted as he tried to sit up further, succeeding enough to twist his body to let his legs dangle off the table. "I don't mind at all; I'd probably do the same. After all, she's easier on the eyes."

Paloon's head snapped back in awe. Was this previously hard-as-nails leader actually letting go of his persona to reveal a hidden ability to relax and laugh? Paloon's lips slid across his bristled face and into a smile before cracking into another laugh. "She is at that, isn't she?"

Lyon shared the smile then joined in the laugh before his chest erupted in fire. He clamped one arm over his chest and leaned back on the other.

"Hey! Take it easy." Paloon sat up, ready to catch Lyon if he should fall off the table. "The blast didn't do too much damage, but the telephone pole wreaked havoc. You broke seventeen bones; nine were ribs." Paloon shook his head as Lyon's pain eased. "And your spine was fractured in five places. I'm glad I had enough MUs to carry you back without causing more damage. Hitook even knew where to find a supply of nanites we brought with us. Those shots kept you and Ky stable while I upgraded Mac."

Lyon was grateful but didn't say so. He didn't have to. Paloon knew it, and that was all that counted for him.

"What about the Corps?" Lyon opened his eyes and nodded at Mac's screen. "Do they know yet?"

"Yes." Paloon released a breath that bordered on a sigh. "They know. Mac told me you reported directly to Dragoon W'Lowe." Paloon uncontrollably raised a brow at Lyon—a knight jumping a level of command and reporting directly to the dragoon himself was not typical. He had plenty of questions but kept them to himself for now. "So that's who I called."

"What did he have to say?"

"Well—" Paloon recalled the rather uncomfortable and cryptic conversation. It's not like he succeeded in getting a straight answer. "In short, he seemed to be irritated that we called him with nothing more than 'They blew up the building on us.'"

Lyon huffed. "That sounds like him."

"He also said we're not allowed off this rock until we finish, regardless of how many bombs they detonate under our noses." Paloon shook his head. "At least the p'tahians didn't detect the explosion. Well, I mean, we're still alive."

"I doubt they would."

A puzzled look crossed Paloon's face. "What do you mean?"

"I mean the terrans have detonated fission bombs, and nothing. They're still breathing. No p'tahian response. Nothing."

The continued use of the word "terrans" began to grate on Paloon's firm belief that Terra was a myth. Then he thought about the two beasts he had detected in the warehouse. They sure had looked like wolves.

"What is really going on here? How can a planet this evolved exist in p'tahian space?" Paloon held his hands out as if to grasp something that was both invisible and intangible. "What is this place? Truly?"

Lyon locked eyes with Paloon. It was the secret of secrets. Few knew, because only few were allowed to know. But it appeared that his team was staying, so at least the one atlantian in the bunch had a right to know.

"This is home."

Paloon cocked his head in a reflex reaction that displayed disbelief shaped by a lifetime of exposure to widespread ridicule of those who believed the atlantians had came from a distant planet called Terra. A bedtime story. Just like stories about...wolves.

"I don't care what you believe." Utter conviction shined in Lyon's eyes like a supernova. "This is Terra. Wolves exist; there were two in the warehouse. Whether you saw them with electronic eyes or real ones, you saw them. Don't deny what you saw. Dolphins exist; I've seen them, too. And snakes." Lyon shook his head again. "Nowhere else, not on any planet under Corps jurisdiction, will you find the mythological snake. But this planet's full of them. And with so many variations it's amazing."

Lyon's calm statements overwhelmed Paloon, who sat quietly as his mind attempted to struggle with the information.

"They even," Lyon dropped his head and stared at the floor, "they even have a myth of their own. Some terrans refer to it as 'The Lost Continent of Atlantis.'"

"What!?"

Absurd. Paloon strengthened his grip on the chair's armrests so he would remain seated and, hopefully, calm.

"Look," Lyon lowered his voice, "I must be the only person in the Corps who believes this is Terra. It doesn't matter how many reports I make. I'm not sure they believe me, so I don't blame you if you don't believe, but wait." He turned to face Paloon, who maintained a firm hold on the poor chair. "Maybe you have to see it with your own eyes. I have. I've combed through their books, and too many things match. They also have 'mythological' stories about dragons existing at one time. It's such a strong belief they make dragon statues, jewelry, clothing, puppets...some even paint their bodies with images of dragons." Lyon grunted. "I wish I could bring a dragon here so I could see how they would react. Probably a lot like you when you saw the wolves."

Snaps echoed through the room as Lyon paused to stretch and cartilage rebelled at being forced to move after several days of inactivity.

"How," Paloon relaxed his grip on the chair, "how are they surviving?"

"I don't know." Lyon edged himself off the table just enough to plant his feet on the floor. "This is one of the p'tahians border galaxies. Maybe they treat this as nothing more than a buffer zone, a kill box, who knows. I haven't figured that one out yet. Whatever the reason, they apparently don't pay much attention. That's why finding illegal weapons, piolants and transporter fluxes worries me."

"Enough activity and something may draw attention."

"Exactly." A mild fire ripped through his chest as he drew a deep breath. "Somehow I'm not surprised that even with word of the explosion of a non-indigenous bomb, the dragoon didn't mention an armed response."

"Crossing the border is an act of war. Heck, being on this rock is an act of war."

"But this is Terra! They told me to find out if this could possibly be the true Terra, and it is." Disappointment fueled his anger, but he stifled it again to calm himself. "Our history is hidden in this planet's legends. Most of it is missing. I've been able to gather fragments, but over time the information has changed because no one took it seriously. Now stories contradict each other. I've even been able to finance diving trips into possible locations of Atlantis. Everything turned up inconclusive. Everything else matches, but no one has been able to find Atlantis."

Lyon turned to Paloon. "Do you know what it feels like to wonder if your existence is nothing more than a myth?"

Paloon released a mild chuckle at the irony. Though reluctant at first, he started to understand Lyon's passion, if not believe the idea.

"I'm sure you won't be surprised to hear the Corps has several secret charters." Lyon rubbed his neck, hoping that would help the headache. "One is to carry on the atlantian search for Terra, to find our home world." Lyon raised his head in a light laugh. "I laughed at them when they told me. Who, in his right mind, would make *that* a secret charter? Everyone knew it was only a myth. But I agreed to volunteer. What the Fate, right? Jump in, reveal it as nothing more than a freak reading or the start of a p'tahian colony and radio for an emergency evac. Simple, I've done similar missions. But the more they briefed me into this mission..."

"You started to believe."

"Not at first. I just began to question my beliefs. I didn't begin to believe until I landed. I splashed down in an ocean, as planned. Deployed my boat, sank the capsule and started toward the coast. I was about an hour into my trip when I picked up company, some kind of marine animal. They didn't seem harmful; I mean, they didn't attack. They acted more like...escorts. I couldn't see them very well through the water, then one jumped out. The other four responded by doing the same, and it set off a chain reaction. They were dolphins." Lyon held out his hand to point at nothing. "Just like the stories. Not only did they appear to be dolphins, but they also appeared to be escorting me safely to the coast. It took me a while, but I had to accept it. I couldn't deny it."

Lyon dropped his hand and stared intently at Paloon with a strange conviction. "This is home, our true home. And if we don't stop these pirates before they draw attention, we will lose our home to myth. Permanently."

PART TWO

A VESSEL OF TRUTH IN A SEA OF LIES

Chapter 1

The early morning fog hung like a thick blanket over the pavement. Smudges of light marked the horizon with blotches of dingy yellow outlined in grey as it bled through the mist. The fog distorted the view so greatly that even the airfield's rotating light rippled as it followed its set pattern in the sky.

Visibility was down to five hundred feet at best, but even that wouldn't cancel this flight. That's why the pilots trained to fly by instruments. It's not that the pilots liked doing this—because they didn't; it only compounded the risks of flying. But they could if they had to, and in this instance, they had to.

The passengers generally were not pleased to know that their flight crew's capabilities were being hampered, even though slightly, but during the past six years, they hadn't crashed yet. Oz, fully aware of what might be going through the crew's minds, didn't have a worry and remained confident that he and his fellow co-workers would make it to work in one piece.

Oz nursed a steaming mug of coffee as he stared into the foggy morning from the comfort of the secure terminal's waiting room. The furniture in the waiting room wasn't what necessarily made it comfortable, but it sure beat standing in the wet air that would lose ten degrees in temperature with every breeze. The thought prompted Oz to take another pull of his coffee to banish the cool image.

Subdued chatter filled the room, but Oz was a simple man who enjoyed his morning coffee and wished to be left in peace while doing so. And the other occupants of the room understood and complied, since several others felt the same way, and many of the rest weren't even completely awake yet.

He stood an inch shy of six feet with closely trimmed black hair and brown eyes. Overall, Oz's facial features made it hard to place his ethnic heritage. Most figured Oz to be Mexican, but his heritage also included a lot of Navajo, a good deal of Cherokee and some Anglo-American. In the canine world, such a mix would earn the title "mutt." Misconception primarily occurred because of his Mexican name, Manuel Ozuna. But ever since boot camp, when an instructor wouldn't take the time to learn how to pronounce his last name correctly, he had been known as Oz.

Oz had grown accustomed to the name over the years; at the same time, he lost touch with his multiple heritages. If he had remained loyal to that heritage, he may have seen the morning fog for the omen that it was. But he continued to drink his coffee and gaze into the thick mist, oblivious.

"Hey, Oz. Morning."

"Morning, Joe," he replied as he turned slightly to see his friend and co-worker approaching.

Joe—Joseph Hollanship—stood a fraction of an inch taller than Oz and had short brown hair, a light complexion and wire-rimmed glasses framing hazel eyes. He wore high-top shoes, faded jeans and an old band tour T-shirt, a bit more casual than Oz's polo shirt and kakis. But no one complained; comfort was the key.

A faint moan signaled that Joe was still waking up, and he lifted a can of highly carbonated fructose to his lips and took a sip. He didn't care for the taste of coffee, so soda served as his main way to achieve a morning caffeine high.

Neither had any problem just standing there, consuming caffeine, watching the beginnings of sunrise and waiting, but Joe wanted to know.

"How far did you get?"

"To the bridge."

"Damn." Joe shook his head and took another drink. "I've only made it to the creek. That damn sniper keeps getting me, but don't tell me how. I'll figure out how to take his ass out, and when I do it, I'll laugh in his face."

Oz knew that Joe would most likely play the game for another two hours before almost throwing the system out a window, giving up and going on a temporary video game hiatus.

The glass door to the airfield opened, and their driver poked his head through, along with a hand holding a radio, which he used to make a sweeping motion at the gathering of people in the room.

"Jeni's ready."

The announcement caught the two in mid-drink, and they rushed to finish their beverages before joining the rapidly forming gaggle funneling through the door. Everyone boarded two rather generic and unmarked coach buses that held enough seats for all.

Though temporarily uncomfortable in the muggy air and wafting diesel fumes, passengers began to relax once in the plush seats of the bus, the air filled with the crisp smell of free flowing refrigerant.

Oz took a window seat a couple of rows from the front, and Joe sat one row behind him. If they were lucky, no one would sit next to them, allowing them a fraction more comfort during the brief ride. Unfortunately, as the number of available seats dwindled, it turned out that this was not Joe's lucky day. A grizzled man greeted Joe with a nod of his head before sitting down. In the midst of a thick beard and a heavy head of greying hair were wrinkled eyes and worn skin. The nicely pressed plaid shirt and clean jeans completed the image. If Joe hadn't met him before, he'd swear the man just walked off the pristine set of some wildlife special.

Joe didn't know the man's name but knew he worked on heating and air conditioning units. Instead of trying to know him, which was much too difficult a chore at this hour of the morning, Joe stared out the window as the bus pulled from its spot.

Painted roads marked the massive sheet of concrete checkered with black lines that served as the airfield equivalent of grout. Vehicles of various sizes and designs darted about as the two-bus convoy navigated around the complex to reach a painted entrance to the secure section of the ramp.

Oz could hear the driver on the radio to the control tower, and it didn't take long before the squeal of breaks signaled a stop.

In the distance sat the waiting plane. It was mid-sized, white, a red stripe down the sides and a jet under each wing. Others may have complained that it was a bit small, but as far as Oz was concerned this new plane sure beat the prop-driven puddle jumper they used a couple years ago.

Workers finished storing hoses and pulled the fuel truck away as the buses approached. The only remaining ground equipment was a generator, which rested under the left wing.

Glass windows muffled most of the generator noise, but the grumbling motor assaulted the ears in full force when the bus doors opened. The aroma of burning diesel almost became overpowering as everyone disembarked. If they worked for a civilian company, Oz guessed they probably could successfully complain about being subjected to three sources of diesel fumes on the short walk to the stairs leading into the airplane.

Near the door, two gentlemen in grey jumpsuits greeted everyone, not with words, just their presence, slight nods and faint smiles, as they talked to one another about home improvements that one of them was undertaking. Inside, white mist billowed from vents above the windows and offered a refreshing smell not too different from that inside the buses.

Technically, there were no assigned seats—nor were they marked—but over the years, people had settled into a pattern, which rarely varied unless someone changed shifts or a new person was assigned. Oz took his window seat and gazed through the portal at nothing in particular and simply waited until the door closed and they began to taxi to the runway.

Once airborne, Oz reclined his seat and closed his eyes for the short flight, an hour, maybe two, although he doubted it. He never bothered to time it and didn't care to. It was best to go with the flow at times. Some things he couldn't control, but Oz also accepted that once a decision was made, the outcome must be lived with. Such was his current situation.

During a high school science project, he researched submarines and how they worked. Somehow that had become a slight infatuation as he read more about them. This obsession temporarily clouded his mind, and it wasn't long before he found himself in the recruiter's office with pen in hand.

Six years. However, the recruiter lived up to his promise that Oz would get submarine duty as a nuclear systems technician. The training school almost overtaxed what he had believed to be an above-average intelligence, and he never could completely adjust with life in such cramped conditions for so long. But he dealt with it.

He worked hard at his studies and used several military programs to obtain his degree in nuclear physics, mostly by correspondence and teleconferences onboard the ship. He became rather efficient in his job. One time, after some training maneuvers, the main cooling tank on reactor two ruptured, and they couldn't get the backup online. The captain chose the risk of crippling the vessel over a meltdown and ordered a scram, but before they could inject the boron rods to stop the reactions, Oz popped the control panel, and relying on just his memory, he found the two critical connectors on the back of the board, broke the clip off of a government pen and used it to bridge the gap. With a spark, the second cooling tank's pumps started. He didn't feel it was much, but the captain made him a petty officer second class the following day.

For his last year, he received a land assignment to help train others. He must have impressed someone, because a month before he was to re-enlist, a major and master sergeant showed up at his apartment. The deal: seventy thousand dollars initial bonus and an extra ten thousand dollars each year in special pay bonuses. The job: in nuclear physics; he didn't need to know the rest, classified.

Intrigue, and the money, got the best of him.

After the paper work, he joined a few others and went through a series of extremely detailed courses on classified operations, force protection, operational security, counter-espionage tactics—the whole gamut.

Those meeting the high standards finally received the briefing on the job: Project Corona, the latest black project. It didn't exist in any known governmental budget. Much like how the Treasury Department could order money at a whim, the project's funds just appeared. No traces, no limits.

Such an arrangement was crucial to Corona's goal: building the first flyable nuclear-powered, pulse-drive stealth aircraft. Not only invisible to conventional radar; sonar wouldn't detect it. Radar missiles wouldn't lock. Heat seeking missiles would lock onto a thrust that was projected so far from the craft that there would be no danger to the plane. Outrageous speeds and neck-breaking maneuverability rendered the remaining weapon systems practically useless.

The work location—a site the government continued to deny existed—was the site they were now landing at—a sparse airfield in the middle of nowhere. Only a few buildings, a large hangar, a few smaller hangars and a couple of long vehicle garages dotted the shrub-speckled mountain desert landscape.

With a soft landing, the plane approached the waiting armed patrol. Then the aircraft followed the escort to a holding apron where security forces began the routine with an unyielding seriousness. Military working dogs searched the entire plane while guards checked the IDs of everyone.

Oz had grown used to seeing tactically armed men board the plane. But he never wanted to become too comfortable; these armed guards wouldn't hesitate to open fire on anyone who even looked like a threat. The plane wouldn't be allowed anywhere near the facilities unless the team commander felt absolutely confident it was secure.

All procedures checked clear, the guards left, and the escort vehicles led the plane along the ramp to park next to the second largest building in the complex. Everybody disembarked and filed through the metal door into a waiting room.

Two doors flanked a large glass window. Behind the glass, uniformed military security guards prepared for the arrival of the newcomers. A red light above each door glowed as the doors buzzed.

One at a time, each person entered a small, white room with another glass window into the guardroom. As the guard issued orders, each person went through the process almost unconsciously.

Oz dropped his ID card in the bin and waited for the guard to visually verify the owner of the ID before sliding the card into the computer. The guard randomly chose a finger, and Oz placed that finger on the scanner built in the wall. After a green light signaled acceptance, Oz placed his chin in the scanner above it and waited for an iris scan.

The guard kept the first ID, but the bin shot back Oz's on-base ID. He clipped it on and approached the opposite door. A sensor detected the new electronic ID, and the door unlocked with a click.

He walked through the other door and saw Joe waiting by a water fountain.

"What's on the schedule?" Joe asked as he stepped next to Oz. Together, they headed down the hall and into the descending stairwell. "Not much I hope."

"Anderson wants us to pull the induction unit but at the extended couplers, so that should be easy. But he hadn't told me anything else."

Oz didn't care for Anderson, or *Professor* Anderson as he demanded to be called. The professor supervised Oz and Joe's section. Oz dubbed Anderson with the bastardized military title of professor in charge. He even further manipulated it into the militarized acronym of PRIC, because it better described Anderson's personality.

Some sections had military officers in charge, but Oz and Joe *lucked out* and got a civilian. Damn civilians.

After descending a couple flights of stairs, they exited into a long hallway with offices lining both sides. People in civilian clothing and numerous military uniforms filed about. Shift change. Oz and crew were one of three main shifts: three days on, two off. Those who hadn't fully relinquished their duties were wrapping up and trying to join the already gathering mass topside.

Halfway down the corridor that ended in full-length steps, Oz jerked his thumb at Joe and nodded. "Go ahead. I've got to finance my next video game."

"Okay." Joe knew what Oz meant.

Oz peeled off, dodged a rapidly moving departee and veered to one of the doors. He leaned against the frame.

The room's occupant hadn't noticed the arrival yet. His dark skin and thin, round glasses glared with the projection of the computer screen. Military fatigues bore the stripes of a master sergeant.

"Twenty-seven and twelve," Oz began. "That adds up to thirty-nine, I do believe. And if my memory serves me correctly, my prediction was, yep, thirty-nine."

The man in the room tipped his head slightly toward the door and confirmed the identity of the speaker. Then with a light snort of laughter, he shook his head in only mild disbelief.

"You just can't wait, can you?"

"Well, Sam, when you're as good as me, it's not about boasting; it's about having a rep to protect."

Sam glared and acted reluctant as he stood and reached for his wallet. He withdrew the twenty-dollar bill and held it folded between two fingers. As Oz approached, Sam pulled the bill away only long enough to say, "Hammond shouldn't have made it."

Oz snatched the bill and pointed an index finger at Sam. "But he did. He's not a runner, but sometimes, everyone gets lucky."

"When will I get lucky? You're cleaning me out."

"Someday, maybe after you quit making bets with me."

They both joined in laughter. Like that would ever happen.

"Catch ya later, man. I've got to go."

"All right." Sam waved as he sat down.

Oz finished the trip down the hall, stairs and another hall. He navigated his way through the subterranean network of corridors and stairs. Every so often he'd reach a closed door. A small black box with a thin red light rested on the wall next to it. As he approached to stand next to the box, the light flicked to green and the door clicked.

After one such lock, he entered a hallway with thick glass widows on the right and a door in the center. He opened the door and entered an almost pristine, white room, which passed dangerously close to uncomfortably hygienic. Anderson preferred it that way.

One clean, white desk sat to the left with a chalkboard and drafting table behind it. Both appeared unused. Thankfully, Anderson was nowhere in sight.

The other desk rested to Oz's right and was currently manned by one of the section's three officers, Captain Jon Hallowell. He was cool like most wise officers, but that hadn't happened until he dropped the academy mentality and joined the real world where people who *demand* authority needed to watch their backs.

"Morning, sir."

"Good morning, Oz." The captain looked up from the folder of papers he was flipping through. "You know Professor Anderson wants the NIC, right?"

"Yes, sir." Oz nodded to the door behind the captain's desk in the far corner of the narrow room. "Joe and I are on it and will have it pulled in an hour."

"Great." The captain gave a thumbs up before returning to his paperwork as Oz headed for the door.

On the other side waited an exchange room. Radiation suits filled the walls, with the exception of the space over the three doors and the long window on the far wall. The right door went to a restroom. The far door entered the air lock to the lab. Oz took the door on the left.

Rows of blue lockers flanked metal benches. A makeshift rest area was set up in the far corner. Randomly acquired chairs surrounded a rectangular table. Snack bar prices filled a poster taped to the outside of the refrigerator, which was joined in the corner by a wooden table. The table held a small television and a microwave oven that looked so worn out that at times Oz wondered if he should rig it with an exterior radiation alarm just to be safe.

Metal banged as Joe closed his locker. He had changed already into his blue jumpsuit. White-stitched patches spelled his last name on one side and his service branch on the other. Staff sergeant chevrons striped both sleeves.

"So what's the next bet?" Joe asked as he stepped away from the lockers and finished zipping the suit.

"We didn't make any." Oz approached his locker and opened it. "I want to get this done first. Besides, I'm almost starting to feel guilty."

"You should." Joe's words weren't harsh or demeaning, just critical. "I mean, dang, you've probably taken enough money from him to finance a yacht."

"He opens the bets." There was nothing wrong with taking a friendly wager.

"And if a horse handed you a gun, I guess you would just shoot him."

Oz paused while untying his boots. "Y' know, sometimes you don't make a lick of sense."

"You know what I mean."

"Actually," Oz pulled off one boot, "I don't."

"Fine, burn in hell." Joe headed for the door. "But don't forget, if I beat you there, I get the penthouse." He stopped before going through the door. "I'll go ahead and get the tools ready."

"Okay. Thanks."

The door shut, and Oz continued shedding his civilian clothes and donning the military jumpsuit. Other than the name, the only difference on Oz's uniform from the one Joe wore were the chevrons of a technical sergeant. One dumb civilian had actually asked him with a straight face if technical sergeant meant that he had been in the service long enough that, technically, he was a sergeant. It amazed him at times how ignorant the civilians of his country had become.

Oz entered the exchange room and slipped into his radiation suit before entering the airlock. As the vents whistled with the sucking wind that removed much of the free debris from his suit, Oz could see Joe on the other side. He checked each drawer in a tall toolbox, scanning to make sure each tool still rested in its form-fitted slot.

The vents stopped, and the far door popped open. This room *was* disturbingly hygienic. White, faint blue and some grey. Long periods of exposure to such a room could drive one mad with antiseptic fits.

Lab tables symmetrically rose from the floor. Various pieces of equipment dotted the tables, but each item was arranged squarely with its associated table's edges.

"Ready?" Oz spoke into the microphone behind his mask, which sported a round filter on one side.

"Yep. Everything's here." Joe closed the last drawer and pushed the toolbox with ease along the white floor, navigating between the various lab tables toward the glass wall of the octagon where Oz now waited.

The octagon was just what the name implied, an eight-sided room. Actually, it was an eight-sided aircraft bay. Each side, except one, had glass walls and airlocks for main maintenance sections and one operations section. The remaining side boasted a gapping ramp used to bring in large pieces of machinery whenever needed.

The two entered their section's airlock and, almost in unison, slid a switch on their left wrists. Now they were on the command frequency like everyone else in the bay.

"Control, this is NucLab Four requesting permission for two souls to enter the bay at Lock Three."

Silence followed. Oz knew the command team was busy checking the countless cameras to see if he or his team showed any physical signs of duress.

"NucLab Four, permission granted," a calm, yet firm, female voice replied. "Report when off."

"Roger, control."

Oz nodded, and Joe responded by finger-punching the red activate button. Another set of vents buzzed to life and quieted as the far door hissed and slid away.

Similarly suited people rambled about the bay with their own maintenance tasks to accomplish. Some pushed equipment carts; others had half their bodies hidden in mechanical innards. A few even held palm computers and flicked their eyes from the work back to their computers that they tapped with a stylus.

At the center of attention rested the offspring of the Corona Project, the XSF-2, experimental super fighter model two. The first model exploded during testing. Bad design. They learned a lot from that disaster. The XSF-2 incorporated those lessons and much more.

Nicknamed Nubius, the craft took the flying wing design of a stealth bomber and merged it with the delta wing design of some of the most superior fighters. A long, thin canopy bubbled from silver skin stretched along the center from tip to rear. There were no signs of air intakes or exhaust nozzles because it didn't need them. What it did have were propulsion rods protruding from the rear. All four pairs were extended for some reason; maintenance of some kind, Oz guessed.

One of the palm-computer holders approached the new arrivals. A badge hung from his suit like all the others. "First Lieutenant Herb Mulvenchi, Avionics."

"Are you here for the NIC?" the lieutenant asked.

Oz debated on giving a negative reply and saying they came to ask one of the welders for a light since they were all out of matches but decided not to. "Yes, sir."

"Good." The lieutenant actually sounded pleased and waved an arm as if to allow them to move closer to the craft.

Like he had any authority over them. Some officers could act so stupid sometimes. Even if the lieutenant said, "No," Oz, just by position of his job, had the authority to stop all activity for safety purposes until *he* was finished.

But there was no need to stop everything for this job. They should be in and out in no time.

Oz clanked his way up the metal ramp that he knew held hydraulics sufficient to lift the fighter all the way to the surface hangar above. Joe followed, pushing the toolbox from behind.

They ducked while weaving between the landing gear and under the shiny skin. Toward the center, Oz stopped and started counting seams until he found the right panel. As he did, Joe fished out a power screwdriver and slapped it into Oz's waiting palm.

One by one, Oz drilled out the screws that tightly lined the panel and slipped each screw into a clear pouch that Joe held out.

"What makes you think you'd get the penthouse suite?"

Joe didn't miss the shift and knew Oz was going to say it before he did. Friends did that sometimes.

"Because if just half the crap my ex-wife said about me is true, I'm one low-down, malevolent motherfucker. I figure I must have impressed the *Dark Lord* by now."

With the last screw, Joe zipped the pouch closed and tossed it into the working tray under the toolbox's lid. Joe opened another drawer, grabbed a tool and switched places with Oz, who propped the panel in the top tray and went looking for a couple of tools.

"What did you do to impress him?"

Light grunts broke Joe's reply as he worked the tool into the mass of cables and wires inside the aircraft. "I'm an untapped...source of pure...ultimate evil with...only one objective: to...unconditionally and uncontrollably torment anyone I love."

Oz remembered the line. It changed from time to time but generally stayed the same. Supposedly his ex-wife spouted the line during their divorce hearing.

"That being the case, you don't love me, do you?" Oz handed Joe another tool.

"Fuck no." Joe grabbed the tool and weaved it through a different part of the wire mesh. "But maybe I do, and that's my unconscious attempt to *torment* you."

"Damn, you *are* a cold bastard."

"That's what I hear." Joe dropped the joking tone in his voice. "Ready."

Oz came around and reached inside. "Ready."

With a click of the tool, the entire section of cables came loose in a wire-framed cube with two metal walls speckled with connectors. Joe moved out of the way as Oz carried it away and set it down next to the toolbox.

Joe peered into the cavernous hole that now gaped. In the darkness above, a green light blinked at one end of a long cylinder with fat cables running from both ends. Oz joined him.

In all their studies, neither had heard of such a device until this classified operation. The only time they saw it was to remove or install it. They weren't allowed to work on it. Only Anderson worked on it.

It was an odd thing to carry. It always felt as if hundreds of gyros moved inside, each in different directions and speeds.

Oz shook his head and got out of Joe's way. There was barely enough room for Joe to stand up in the opening. He clicked on the thin lamp that rested in an embedded holder on his mask and scanned the area to confirm the location of the unit's far couplers.

Several seconds later and Oz finally had the first set of tools. He poked them one at a time through a corner of the opening to feel them lift out of his hand.

Oz returned to the toolbox and fingered out the second set of coupler wrenches.

As he turned back, an impossibly bright white flame gushed like liquid from the opening. In the center of the resulting glowing aurora, Oz could vaguely discern the shape of Joe's body being crushed like a frail soda can against the metal ground.

Wailing sirens could barely be heard over the roaring eruption. A sliver of a second later and the bright blast consumed all of Oz's vision before it went completely black.

Chapter 2

The roaring hiss fired again.

"Will you knock that off?" Even through the strange vibrating vocals of Larin's throat, it was apparent that Ky's practice had started to grate on his nerves.

"Something stinks," she replied calmly and returned to sit on the stool behind the counter.

"Of course," Larin held up a fist gripping one of the vegetable cans he was stocking and pointed a finger at the canister Ky held, "that's what stinks."

"No, this is," Ky turned the spray can in her palm and obviously read the next two words, "Mountain Lilac, which has to be much better than the musty stench I keep smelling."

Larin's rebuttal only formed a half-heard "humph" as he finished filling in the stacks of green bean cans and moved down the aisle toward the pinto beans. Along the way, he pushed a short stack of cardboard boxes with a heavy boot. The cardboard tower scraped the floor as it moved, but any resulting scratches blended into the greying linoleum.

A modulating "ting," the result of shifting compressed air, and a thud of wood sounded as Ky tossed the air freshener can under the small L-shaped checkout counter. She flipped away the curls of hair that crept into the open collar of her green blouse and slipped the tabloid she was reading off the counter while leaning back on the stool. Its legs rested against the sill, leaving a couple of inches between her back and the storefront window.

Peace washed over the corner grocery store. Other than the slight hum of the large clock hanging above the tiny meat counter, the only sounds to be heard were the rustling pages of the tabloid and clanking of cans being stocked. The calm was symbolic of how the team felt.

Sure, they had walked into an obvious trap, which had almost worked, but that came with the job. Now, they needed time to recoup and gather their collective thoughts.

Everyone had taken to their roles easily enough. Even though it may never matter in the long run, maintaining the façade as store clerks and gas station attendants served to clear their thoughts and allowed them to learn much about terran society from a personal level.

The only team member to complain was Larin. But the others had almost given up on the chances of completing a day without hearing Larin complain about something. He had earned the somewhat accurate title of perpetual whiner. However, while some may have considered him a whiner, most of his rolbrid race would have unconditionally agreed with Larin's thought processes.

So instead of being a full-time stock boy, Larin whined his way into getting a part-time position behind the counter of the team's gas station across the street. Not much of a compromise, but it boosted his ego somewhat to hold a job as easy as Ky's. However, Larin would never admit to finding pleasure in such a trivial matter.

Ky had figured as much. During the several days they'd been acquainted, she improved her ability to tune out Larin's comments. Although she was proud of the talent, there were times she just wanted to talk to someone and didn't care if it had to be Larin.

"Ah! Here's something interesting." She folded the tabloid backwards then flipped it around and pointed the headline at Larin as she thumped the paper with her finger.

The rolbrid didn't pay any attention, so Ky returned the paper and loudly read the headline. "Shocking True Horoscopes for the New Year."

Larin halted his work temporarily to take a short, deep breath. He knew what was coming next. For some reason he couldn't fathom, Ky had taken the time to translate the birth dates of the entire team just to match them with some kind of unscientific predictions based on the positions of stars as they appeared from a planet on which they weren't born.

"Here is your year-long prediction for the new year." Her voice almost became that of a mystic soothsayer as she folded down the top of the paper and gave Larin her best mystic soothsayer's stare. He didn't bother to turn and see it. Ky snapped the top of the paper back up. "Beware, for in the new year you may meet someone who may become a best friend or bitter rival. It is this person's secrets that will decide the fate of the relationship. The year holds periods of turmoil, but passion blooms."

She peeked from around the tabloid and let her face exaggerate while adding, "Ohhhhhhh."

Larin shook his head and continued to look away. To do anything else would just encourage her to do this every chance she got, and he didn't want to provide such inspiration.

Ky ducked back behind the paper. "Success can be yours in the work place. But death is near to someone close to you. Believe in blue."

She returned the paper right side out. "Well, it sounds like the lieutenant has a very interesting year in front of him." Ky wrestled with the pages until they where back in some semblance of order and flipped to the next page.

Larin grabbed the now empty box on top of the stack he'd been pushing around and pointed the cardboard frame at Ky. "I hope you're only joking and realize that's a bunch of frapping crap." He tossed the box, which slid into the side of the stairs.

"Ah! But terran experts say horoscopes are true windows to one's future." Ky held her small nose higher than normal, taking on an almost aristocratic poise. At least, she looked like an aristocrat reading a two-bit, dime-store tabloid.

Larin yanked open the flaps on the next box with a pop, pried out a can of corn and turned to give Ky a look that was meant to convey his thoughts. But then he shared them with her anyhow. "You've got to be frapping kidding me. Did you even listen to what you read? 'You may meet someone.' 'Success can be yours.' 'This person may be....' If it got any more vague, it would just say, 'Something's going to happen to you.'"

The rolbrid's frustration at the blatant stupidity transferred into the can as he slammed it onto the shelf, almost knocking off others near the epicenter.

"You're just embarrassed because it says you're going to find love, and you're too much of a hard shell."

"What!?" Larin tightened his grip on the can and then released it just as he felt it give, saving himself from the explosion of a creamed-corn volcano. "I'll have you know that—"

"Hey, Paloon. Check this out."

Ky and Larin stopped and turned to face Lyon, whom they hadn't noticed descending the steps to take a stance behind the banister of the short landing that overlooked the store. Lyon's attention was locked in a large photo book. Tuffs of his dirty blond hair poked in numerous uncombed directions. He took no notice of the conversation he had interrupted or the fact that Paloon wasn't present.

"Uh," Lyon lifted his eyes from the pages and glanced about, "where's Paloon?"

Ky jerked her thumb over her shoulder to point through the window and across the street at the gas station. "He went back over there about twenty minutes ago. He said he didn't want to leave Hitook alone for too long."

Lyon hummed as his eyes darted about as if his mind was currently heavily occupied and was attempting to cram new information in and weave it into the mix to make sense of it. "Okay."

His gaze fell back to the book as Lyon walked to the end of the landing and stumbled down the stairs. If the book had been a bucket, it would have looked like Lyon was attempting to recover from a night-long drinking binge. He even scraped against the glass front of the meat counter while making his way to the front of the store.

Lyon was casually dressed. Not business casual or evening casual, more like Saturday morning cartoon casual. A fading T-shirt hung loosely over long shorts, and slippers slapped his heels as they flopped with his steps.

Larin and Ky paid little attention as they resumed their routines. But Lyon interrupted again when he finally made it to the front of the store.

"Have you ever been to the capital of Atlantis?" Lyon didn't remove his eyes from the book. Also, he didn't give a second thought to how the question sounded, because he knew the two understood that the Atlantis he referred to was his home planet. Yet no one replied. The silence prompted his head to rise, and he looked at Ky, who gradually lowered her paper.

She glanced at Larin, but Lyon's eyes didn't move. The silence started to become uncomfortable, so she felt forced to say something. "Um—no. But I did a social studies report on Atlantis in early school. Why?"

The final word sparked a desire for scholarly sharing in Lyon. His eyes widened and his face seemed to brighten. Here was someone who might appreciate his find. Even though there was only a slight possibility, he felt he must share his information, and the floodgates opened.

Lyon lowered the book but kept it cradled in his arms. "Do you remember what the capital looks like?"

"Well—"

Lyon didn't have time to wait for an answer. He spun the book around and pointed at a two-page drawing. "Take a look at this."

The drawing depicted a city of adobe-like buildings circling the top of a hill. Three circular canals dissected the city in rings with bridges that formed an over-all symmetric pattern. Even though the city was obviously primitive, something in the design conveyed a sense of advancement. Maybe it came from the immaculate streets that formed orderly blocks of neighborhoods.

Ky folded the tabloid and set it on the counter as her eyes combed over the image in Lyon's hands. She hummed and scrunched her face to give the appearance of intrigue-induced fascination. Early school had been so long ago she couldn't remember a single iota from her report, but Ky felt it best to play along. Lyon bought it.

He set the book on the counter and pushed it at Ky before walking around the counter. When Lyon stood next to Ky, he leaned forward and pointed a finger at the picture as he talked. "Three canal rings. On a hill. A large temple in the center." He turned to look at Ky, whose facial expression was on the verge of becoming lost. "Just imagine modern skyscrapers instead of mud houses." Lyon turned back to point a palm at the graphic. "It's the capital of Atlantis."

Lyon pointed to the next page. "Look." He pointed at a picture of a terran who appeared to have cut off all his hair and glued it to his chin. "This scholar from Harvard gathered all the information he could on Terra's Atlantis and commissioned an artist to make an accurate-as-possible drawing of Atlantis." Lyon tapped his chest with the fingers of his open hand and looked at Ky. "It looks extremely like the capital of *my* Atlantis."

Ky gradually became aware of the implications, but what drew it home was her recognition of a word in the book. She pointed at it. "Poseidon?"

"Oh," Lyon looked at the word, "yes. Apparently the temple in the center held a statue of some water god called Poseidon. He was supposedly driving a herd of sea horses or something like that."

"But isn't Poseidon a moon of Atlantis?" Ky knew she was right and was proud of herself for remembering it, so she played it like a scientist.

"Yes." Lyon scooped the book up in his arms. "Poseidon, Neptune,

Hathor, Indra—all moons of Atlantis and gods of water somewhere in Terra's myths. I gave that information to the Corps already, but apparently it's not enough."

"What?" Ky couldn't believe it. "How could they deny something so obvious?"

"Stupidity, I guess." Lyon jumped up to sit on the counter and propped his feet on the windowsill. "But this," he turned the page back and thumped it with the back of a finger, "this is different. I've seen other drawings, but this one's unique. It's too...authentic." He stumbled for the word but picked the best could.

A reverberating ding sounded from the bell above the door a moment before the scrapes began with the opening of the entry. Lyon and Ky shifted in unison and soon saw a familiar face creep around the door.

"Hello, grandma."

Lyon and Ky said the greeting together and sounded like they had practiced their timing. Hearing someone else saying the phrase with him almost made him feel challenged. But Lyon pushed the feeling away. Things had changed, and he needed to accept that.

Wrinkles stretched while others formed deeper crevasses as the elderly black woman smiled. "Good morning, Lyon, Ky."

The infectious smile jumped the distance to bring smiles from the two behind the counter in return.

Metal squealed and squeaked as arthritic fingers fumbled with a collapsible grocery cart. She never went shopping without it.

Grandma wore a long white dress, and a black sweater jacket covered her arched back. Tufts of red poked from the jacket's pocket, most likely from a haphazardly stuffed handkerchief. It wasn't so important that it look nice, just as long as it was there if she needed it. Overall, her clothes were clean but appeared to be about thirty years old.

She unhooked the cane from her arm and latched it to the side of the cart, then slid her purse off of her shoulder and dropped the straps over one of the cart's handles. The process was slow, but soon she was pushing the cart toward the produce in the back room. Wednesday. Salad day.

Lyon didn't give any thought to his appearance as he went into his routine. He dropped from the counter and set the book down before walking over to the meat counter. In addition to the salad, grandma would get a pint of vanilla ice cream and expect a half-pound of bacon, three fresh sausage links and half a pound of ground beef.

He packaged the items and returned to the front counter with them. Ky took them and scooted them next to the register. Lyon grabbed the book and sat on the sill this time. The store returned to quiet.

Grandma wheeled the cart up the ramp and back into the main store. She started up and down the aisles, picking the items she needed. Noodles, tomato paste and some more of the spices she had started to run low on.

She turned toward the corner to get some corn when her cart bumped into the box from which Larin was stocking.

"I'm sorry, ma'am." He latched a hand on the open lid and dragged it away.

The elderly lady didn't reply and just stared calmly at him through large round bifocals. She moved closer to Larin who couldn't seem to resist staring back.

"I can't say I've met you before. What's your name, son?"

"Um," he stumbled at first, "Larry." Larin almost forgot the new name. Lyon decided that Larin would be too unusual of a name for terrans.

This time the name had nothing to do with it. Maybe it was Larin's voice. A rolbrid's vocal cord structure possessed an elaborate layering of tissue in a complex arrangement. The result was a vibrating effect on the voice, an effect the team couldn't mask.

Bent fingers rubbed together before gripping her thick glasses and gliding them down her nose. Cataracts clouded brown eyes as her brow formed a worried expression.

She stared into Larin's eyes. For a moment, he wondered if she could see through his sclera contacts made to look like terran eyes and had noticed the yellow orbs beneath.

Lyon and Ky glanced at each other then back down the aisle. Both also wondered what to make of the scene. But of everyone in the room, Lyon worried the most. The others didn't know of grandma's uncanny vision.

She scooted the glasses back to the bridge of her nose. "You're not from around here, are you?"

It didn't sound like a question, but Larin answered.

"No. I'm from the west coast."

Grandma's voice stayed calm, but the worried expression never left her face. It didn't look like she bought the explanation either.

"Well, Larry from the west coast," she brought a finger to her throat, "you should get someone to look at that. You don't sound so good."

"Yes, ma'am." Larin wanted to back away from this as quickly as possible. He lifted the remaining box into his arms and headed for the rear storage room. On the way, his back to grandma, he glanced at the two behind the counter and gave them a worried look.

Grandma grabbed a can of corn and watched Larin leave. With her shopping finished, she approached the counter.

Ky set her tabloid down and started checking the items.

Lyon wanted to change topics, so he set down his book before starting a conversation.

"How are you doing today?"

"Oh, I'm doing pretty good." The worried look seemed to melt away. "I got a letter today from Erica."

Lyon knew Erica was one of grandma's eight children. If he remembered correctly, Erica was about thirty-five, married and with two children.

"How is she doing?"

"They are expecting another child."

"That's great!" Ky added with a smile. "Please pass them my wishes."

Grandma smiled in return. "She wants to visit in three months, so you may be able to tell her yourself then."

"Great, I can't wait."

Lyon smiled, not because he cared, just because the other two were smiling. "Do they know if it will be a boy or girl?"

"No...no they don't."

The way grandma said the words made Lyon wonder if she did know. She always seemed to know more than she would ever share.

Ky finished tallying the items. She began bagging them as grandma fished in her purse for her change bag.

Grandma found the bag and set in on the paper that covered the counter. When she did, she stumbled. Moving quickly for someone her age, she planted her hands flat against the counter to hold herself up while her bowed head shook.

"Grandma! Are you okay!" Lyon lunged forward and placed an arm around her back to hold her as his other hand grabbed her arm. Ky joined in as quickly as she could, holding on to grandma's other side.

She went into another set of shivers and shakes before calming and taking deep breaths. "Yes." The words took time. "I'm all right."

Ky followed Lyon in being reluctant to let go, but they did so slowly, making sure she could stand on her own before releasing her completely.

Grandma resumed a one-handed search for the money as if nothing had happened. Meanwhile, Lyon walked around the counter to place the light bags of groceries in the cart. He returned to stand on the other side of grandma as she took the change from Ky. Then she slipped the coin purse into her pocket and pulled out a deck of cards.

Lyon recognized them immediately and knew what was happening. Ky didn't have a clue but watched with fascination.

As the elderly lady cut the deck and began placing the cards in a line, she mumbled phrases neither listener could hear completely, but Lyon knew they were chants. She then started another line of cards that ran perpendicular and crossed the other line a few cards off center.

The chants stopped, and she lifted the card that crossed the other line and placed it under her left hand. That's when Lyon realized something he hadn't paid attention to before. From the moment she came to the counter and stumbled, her left hand had never moved from its spot.

She then used both hands to gather the cards and placed them back in her pocket, leaving the card under her left hand in its place.

"Lyon," grandma began as she turned to make eye contact, "you've searched long but have never found it. Now," she rapped a bent finger on the faded pattern marking the back of the card resting on the counter, "if you're ready, he holds secrets you can't see."

Lyon and Ky shifted their eyes from the card to grandma and back.

Bewilderment made time slip by, and grandma left without anyone saying a word.

"Is she gone?" Larin heard the bell and felt it safe enough to return to the main store. "Wow, she's strange. I thought she had me there."

"She might have." Lyon let his thoughts take form.

Larin noticed the perplexed look on their faces. "What's wrong?"

Ky and Lyon couldn't help it. When grandma did her predictions, everyone who noticed them would share the same odd feelings. They looked back at the card.

"What is it?" Ky glanced from the card to Lyon and noticed Larin approaching.

"It's a tarot card."

"What's a tarot card?" Larin raised on his toes to get a better look at it.

"Tarot cards are said to be a tool of divination."

"So you're saying grandma is a future teller, a psychic?" Only a sliver of doubt slipped into Ky's voice. "You're kidding, right?"

"Many believe she is." Lyon tapped the card and rotated it in place. "Sometimes I wonder."

He flipped it over.

The drawing formed a picture of an odd-looking man with a painted face who was prancing in bright clothes. Multiple points sprang from the multi-colored cap. He held a baton with masks on both ends, one smiling, the other frowning.

"Well," Ky's curiosity had the best of her, "what is it?"

"It's 'The Fool.'" Lyon laid the card back down and stared at it.

"So," Ky needed more, "what does it mean?"

Lyon didn't sound so much reluctant as busy deciphering the card's meaning for him. "The Fool is a sign of irrational impulses, sometimes good, sometimes bad. These impulses are The Fool's view as he faces the unknown. The Fool stands at the gates of a journey, a journey we are also faced with."

The words almost sounded rehearsed. He had obviously heard the same explanation before—many times before, the other two guessed.

"Interesting," Ky whispered.

Larin just shook his head. "That's just as vague as the frapping horoscope deal. I'm out of here." True to his words, he left through the front door and headed in a jog across the street.

Ky frowned a "whatever" look and shooed a wave at him.

Then Lyon noticed for the first time what the card rested on, the same place grandma had her hand. It was the tabloid Ky was reading. He stabbed it with a finger and dragged it to him.

The headline read "Explosion Rocks Secret UFO Facility: Experts Claim Alien Retaliation."

Normally Lyon would laugh, but an overwhelming feeling of dread kept him from even smiling.

Chapter 3

Sparse furnishings littered the expansive loft.

One end of the room held a bed and associated furniture, none of which were far from the bathroom. Farther in, on the near side of the banister that lined the stair entrance, sat an elaborate home gym. This was designed and created by Mac; it was supposed to be unbreakable, unlike the others Lyon had bought locally. So far, so good.

Across the room, a makeshift firing range lined the wall. The one-lane range had soundproof walls and a backstop specially made by Mac to handle some of Lyon's most powerful weapons. It could only take so much damage, though, before needing replacement.

On the other side of the stairwell, a few pots and pans hung above an island stove. Its accompanying tabletop, sink and refrigerator sat against the wall.

The remaining sliver of the floor was practically cut off from a large door-sized entryway by a wall of bookshelves. They faced inward to Lyon's version of a den. Windows lined the remaining walls of the long room. A drafting table sat at one end, and Lyon rested in his recliner on the opposite side. Illumination came from a lamp that arched from behind him. Condensation formed on a glass of water on the tiny table next to him.

Lyon had lost count at twenty something. But he knew more about the count than he did about the information contained in the paragraph he tried over and over again to read. His mind was gone. It didn't matter how many times he read the paragraph, his current state of mental acuity refused to let him retain anything from it.

The book discussed several theories on the time period in which Neanderthals and Cro-Magnons coexisted. Lyon examined anything he could find in an attempt to fully understand terran development. This particular situation he found oddly confusing, like something was missing. Not lost, just too obvious to see. But the enigma would have to wait; his mind was focused on another dilemma.

Pages slapped as he closed the book and thumped it against his lap. Lyon's gaze drifted out the windows to take in the setting sun. It marked the end of something that would give birth to a beginning. Tomorrow, the mission would start anew. But for now, his mind needed a solution.

"Mac?"

"Yes," came the voice of his computerized companion. A screen sparked to life in the bookshelf next to the drafting table, but Lyon couldn't see it from where he sat.

"Were you listening this morning when grandma visited the store?"

Technically the question was moot. If it happened in either building,

Mac heard it. He couldn't help it. Lyon forgot this from time to time and fell into the habit of treating Mac like any biological sentient.

"Yes." Mac made another attempt a comedic timing and got it this time. "She's still creepy."

Lyon smirked and gave a short chuckle while nodding his head in agreement. "Yep. She can be, can't she?"

He stood, taking the book in hand, and walked over to the drafting table. Lyon set the book down and turned the thin knob on the side of a light resting on top of a swing arm. Light glowed just in time to catch Lyon lifting the tarot card off the table.

The tabloid article lay flat on the table. He had read it almost as many times as that last paragraph in the book. Standard tabloid journalism. No decent, undoctored photos. The photo of the supposed secret base was ripped in half with a cartoon explosion drawn in the center. So-called eyewitnesses seemed just a shade more intelligent than a Pan troglodyte, otherwise known as a chimpanzee. But maybe, just maybe, there was something there.

"Mac, I need for you to run some checks on a few names." Lyon's finger landed on the article and he began to drag it around, but before he could read off the author's name, Mac piped in.

"Already on it."

"Excuse me?"

"I figured the creepy lady's words had you spooked, so when you left, I asked Ky to get another paper and show it to me." Mac's voice held a tone of kindness that only a police partner would show. "Since then, I've been trying to track down a few things."

The card twirled in Lyon's hands as he turned to face the monitor in the bookcase. Mac presented a rather generic terran face this time. It wasn't his silver, almost featureless face; it was just an obvious terran face lacking any unique features. Lyon wondered briefly why some things caused Mac's mood to change, and it changed often.

"What have you found?"

"Well, the author has been with the tabloid for," Mac's quieted voice actually sounded like he was counting, "eleven weeks and three years. During that time he has faced four libel suits, and he successfully defended himself against all four: two under truth without malice pleas, one with a fair comment and criticism defense and, during the last one, he got the interview subject to repeat his comment in court, so he could claim the information was privileged. He barely won over the judge with the last one. This shows he knows his journalistic law, so—"

"At least the paper's team of lawyers do," Lyon corrected.

"Well...okay, good point, but either way you're probably not going to get squat out of him. Now," the tone of Mac's voice gave the impression of a science professor shifting to another theory, "the one quoted source in the story, a Virgil Mulligan, he has a record. You know, the one who claims he was hunting snakes in the area when he felt the ground shake in the general direction of this suspected location? Yeah, well, the government's files show he has been caught three times near classified military installations. The records don't say which installations, whether they're all the same location or where they're located. But his record has been flagged to show he displayed treasonous tendencies each time he was caught."

That didn't help one bit. Lyon flipped the tarot card in his fingers and wondered what he could be missing. To be the devil's advocate, what if this *was* a top secret military facility? The fenced border would most likely be miles from any building. To feel an explosion that far out, well, someone inside would have to have been hurt.

"How fast can you find information on the closest military or government hospitals to this site?"

"Actually," Mac had already been busy thinking about this as well, so he had collected data and just waited for Lyon to ask for it, "if the site has a runway and airlift support, and if the rumors are true, it does, so we wouldn't be working with a distance issue. That being said, only one hospital would make sense, and it just happens to be close, at least close if you're flying. This hospital also just *happens* to have a ward specializing in radiological burns."

Lyon nodded in agreement with Mac's assumption. "Any recent patients?"

"Eighteen."

Lyon stopped flipping the card and eyed Mac with a raised brow.

Mac didn't need to hear the question. "Admission dates match with the article."

"How far?"

"With the right medication, you could drive it straight and make it in about fifty-three hours."

Larin rubbed his chin with two fingers as he studied his handful of cards. His eyes jumped up to Hitook on the other side of the command table and then returned to his hand.

Hitook held his paws flat on the table between himself and his hand of cards, which lay face down on the table. Other cards were scattered the battlefield, each card's position denoting one of the various phases of the game.

Generally Larin was good at this game, but now he faced a competitor unlike any he had played against before. That's what he got for misjudging the oversized furry beast—a beast who had been utterly emotionless throughout the game. Some of the universe's best gamblers could only dream of being so cold.

Larin's fingers left his chin and danced on the top of the cards while he considered his strategy. Then they plucked one from the group and slapped it down on another. It was a weapon enhancement.

"He'll attack," Larin said as he scooted the two cards forward to the main battlefront.

Hitook scraped one of his cards off the table, flipped it and placed it in front of Larin's attacker. "Pit," Hitook said calmly.

The table glowed as Larin's attacker took three-dimensional form. Twirling his new weapon, the attacker strolled toward Hitook's card, whistling along the way. The whistling soon transitioned to screams as the would-be warrior fell through the pit. Then they both vanished.

Larin gave a sigh of despair. He'd hoped Hitook didn't have another one left because he knew what would come next.

A furry finger tapped another card. "My wizard attacks."

The card morphed into a wizard who promptly twirled a staff and pointed it at one of Larin's waiting attackers. Curls of fire licked the air as they shot toward the defender, who was now also in three-dimensional form and equipped with a suit of battle armor. The fire struck and fully caressed the armor.

Chipmunk-like screams filled the air as the armored warrior ran around crazily. His scurrying set fire to nearby cards, which promptly took form and joined in the screaming. Then the armored warrior stopped in place but kept screaming as he shook violently before exploding. The others stopped and fell down, wounded. When they returned to card form, their turned angles denoted their wounded states.

Damn, Larin thought. *And he killed my last medic two rounds ago.*

He didn't want to surrender, but he had no attackers left and no way to heal his wounded.

"Put the cards away," Ky's voice came from the stairs as she made her way down to the floor. "Lyon's going to be here soon."

Whoa, talk about being saved, Larin thought.

Larin closed his hand of cards and set them down. "You're lucky," he said while pointing at Hitook. "I was about to open up on you."

Hitook didn't respond. But a voice came from somewhere, and it sounded like a coughing "Bullshit."

"Hey!" Larin knew where it came from and pointed at Mac's blank screen. "You keep out of this."

"Back off," came Paloon's voice as he emerged from the connecting tunnel. He had heard all the comments, which echoed their way to the garage side of the tunnel. "He's probably right. Just admit it."

"Oh!" Larin moved his stubby finger in Paloon's direction before dropping it. "You want a piece of this now? It's a damn conspiracy."

"You've finally caught on," Ky leaned over to whisper the comment in the rolbrid's ear as she made her way around the table. "I guess that means we'll have to kill you now." The dextian kept her face calm as she took a seat. "Hitook, the ball's in your court."

Larin glared at Ky. "What the frap is that supposed to mean?"

Much to Ky's amazement, Hitook jumped in to add to the sarcasm. "Kill you in your sleep, roommate."

"Ha. Ha." Larin lowered himself into his seat while snickers erupted from Ky and Paloon. "It's always funny when it's—"

"—when you're so gullible," Lyon finished as he entered the room and made his way down the stairs. "Relax, guy," Lyon added in a strange voice for no reason apparent to the rest of the group. What a waste of a joke.

He walked to the rear of the table. Everyone was seated, but Lyon felt like standing.

"Our recoup time is over, and everyone is back in shape. And thanks to Paloon and Hitook," Lyon tapped two fingers on the table, "some of us are in better shape."

Suddenly, a small dessert dish of chocolate pudding appeared in the center of the table and disappeared just as quickly.

Paloon exploded in laughter, and Mac joined with a few chuckles at his own joke. The hunter's fist pounded the table in the midst of his laughter before he could gather himself and stifle the laughs with a couple of coughs.

The others just watched with mild concern, knowing that Paloon and Mac had this strange food joke going that neither shared with anyone else.

"All righty." Lyon ignored the outburst and continued with the meeting. "But now we need to pursue our leads, which are few."

"Definitely xenoform involvement," Paloon began with a few sniffles, still choking back the remnants of laughter.

"True," Lyon replied while pacing and four sets of eyes followed him. Beings not native to Terra had to be involved somehow, or he would never have found restricted weapons or almost been killed by an explosion that left no trace of itself outside of a devastated warehouse. "The nature of that explosion confirms that. Mostly likely pirates, piolanese pirates, but the big question is, why?"

"Mineral replenishment." Ky shrugged at her own guess. "Maybe they lack the technology to duplicate some minerals they found here."

"Possible," Paloon added, "but how did they find *here*?"

"You both have good points," Lyon stopped pacing and faced the table, "but it shows our problem: Questions keep creating questions. We have no answers. They were waiting for us, and now they're gone. We've got no leads."

"Local police activity around the warehouse should be nonexistent now. I could go back, sift through the wreckage and give it a closer look this time." Larin wanted to do something. He was tired of just sitting around waiting for Lyon to recoup. "Who knows, Mac may stumble on to another transshipment signal. We'll have a lead then."

Lyon snapped his fingers and a "eureka" expression flashed on his face as he turned to Paloon. "Can you build a cloaked satellite and get it into orbit?"

"Uh, well," Paloon stumbled, but not because he doubted his abilities, "yeah, I can do that. Damn, why didn't I think of that?"

It didn't take Mac long to find a model to meet their needs. The table flashed with a hologram of a flat octagon-shaped object. "The Hebert-Vilum transorbital reconnaissance drone," came Mac's voice.

"That's perfect," Paloon agreed with Mac's decision. "It's simple but should provide everything we need. Mac and I should have one built and in orbit in...three days."

"Great." Lyon smiled at the thought that things were looking up.

The image blinked away, and Mac reminded Lyon that more remained to be done by uttering one word, "Yakuza."

"Ah, I almost forgot. Thanks." Lyon resumed pacing. "The yakuza is involved somehow; I guess you could call that our only semi-solid lead. But Mac can't get into the local police computers on organized crime."

"Easy infiltration job," Ky stated matter-of-factly as Hitook nodded.

The offer got Lyon's attention. He paused again and stared upwards in thought. A hum escaped him as he tapped a finger against his chin.

"Mac?" Lyon's tone seemed to temporarily exclude everyone else in the room.

"Yes."

"Does the police department have a public relations section?"

"It has a public information office with five officers assigned."

"What's the gender breakdown?"

"One female, four males."

Lyon lowered his eyes to meet Ky's.

"If Ky was to be placed on a covert intelligence gathering mission—" Lyon let the statement drift away. He knew Mac had caught on already and just wanted to see how the computer handled it.

"—what better way than as a reporter for a new syndicated show on criminal investigations?"

"Exactly." Lyon's smile forced Ky's face to morph into apprehension. "And what does every reporter need?"

"A cameraman."

"Yes. Congratulations, Larin."

"What!?" Larin threw up his arms. "Why me?"

"Because the camera is going to conceal your main weapon if things get dicey?" Paloon offered the comment and knew it would pique the lieutenant's interests.

Larin's mouth closed, and he turned away with a hum of contemplation.

"Good, it's settled. Hitook will do the final recon on the warehouse remains and help Paloon as needed to speed up the drone's launch." Lyon pointed at Ky and Larin. "Once Mac sets up your fake IDs and a fake company, you two find out as much as possible about what the police know about the yakuza, especially possible locations. Then we'll start a shakedown."

"A what?" Paloon asked; the phrase was new to all.

The question almost threw Lyon off his mental track. "We'll search each location for a better lead. But," Lyon didn't want to be interrupted again, "you'll wait to conduct any searches until I return from my trip. I have to check something. I'll be back in about five days and out of communication range. But I'm sure you guys can take care of the rest while I'm gone."

"Sir, honestly, I don't think—"

Lyon cut off Paloon's rebuttal.

"You're not changing my mind. Mac."

The table's next glow faded into two large suitcases, which Lyon lifted from the table. He headed down the tunnel to the garage. "Paloon, you're in charge."

The quartet sat stunned around the table. No one had expected it, and the confusion kept them from responding.

Larin turned to Ky, then to Mac's blank monitor before speaking. "Mac, don't tell me this has something to do with that stupid card?"

"What card?" Paloon snapped.

Chapter 4

Motherly chatter and a the sound of a children's television show injected just enough noise to present the standard audible flavor of a waiting room. Lining the walls, worn wooden benches offered a degree of luxury only expected at a driver's license office, almost approaching the comfort level of a rectal exam.

The two men in the room sat along the same right wall but at opposite ends. Each flipped mindlessly through year-old magazines about cars.

Across the room sat the mother who tried repeatedly to get her son to believe that the television show was indeed his favorite, it was just that the TV just had bad reception, which caused the white dots.

Though years wiser, the mother's stance in the debate could not stand up in the face of the two year old's logic. If it was his favorite show, it wouldn't have spots. His rebuttal arrived in the form of extremely bizarre squeals and the sudden inability to stand or sit without falling down.

The two men reacted differently. Apparently one had children and as a result showed no visible reaction to the drama playing itself out in front of him. The other's face grimaced with each squeal, building on an ever-increasing migraine.

Tom, though, sat calmly behind a thick sheet of bulletproof glass that covered the far wall in the fashion of a drive-through bank teller's window. He relaxed in the luxurious ability to turn off the external microphone, removing himself from the tantrum on the other side. Wearing a police sergeant's uniform and sporting grey hair and a thick mustache, Tom leaned back and resumed reading the words on his computer screen, apparently with great enjoyment. Facing him, a viewer wouldn't be able to tell if he was reading official notices or jokes being passed around the precinct.

Tom halted his reading and looked up at the two individuals entering the waiting room. His smile soon turned from simply amused to mildly devilish while he unsuccessfully attempted to control his raising eyebrow.

Ky caught the questioning glance and took a few more steps into the room as Larin used his heavy boot to close the door behind them.

She regarded the room's occupants briefly before crossing the heavily pitted linoleum floor, designed to look like designer tile. The remnants of cheap plaster jobs jutted from the walls, joining the floor in providing telltale signs that the room had been remodeled, maybe more than once.

As she approached the window, her high heels clicked on the floor. Luckily, the skill chip that Mac had made allowed her to maintain her balance in the uncomfortable shoes. She argued against the need for them, but Mac claimed they were required to maintain her cover, much like the grey calf-length dress and blouse that had underlying tones of a business suit. Ky thought the deep V neckline too revealing for her taste, and she didn't like the paint on her face. The two aspects she liked about the costume were the dress, which allowed her to hide her tail by wrapping it tightly around her right thigh, and her slightly bulky, feathered hair, which camouflaged the pointy tips of her ears. At least Mac agreed not to go with earrings; no need drawing attention to the one feature someone might have a chance to notice.

Larin had an easer time looking like a terran. Though his face appeared distorted, it wasn't a shape that couldn't be explained away as a birth defect or mild facial cancer. His yellow orbs still hid from sight behind terran-looking contacts. Larin wore a yellow shirt under a brown leather jacket with loose blue jeans. Having one less finger than a terran, Larin worn black gloves in which Mac installed a mechanical fifth digit that mirrored the movements of his fourth finger.

He also appreciated the robotic assistance it provided because, right now, he appeared too overloaded for his size. In his left hand he held a long, black case that contained the light set. Tripod sticks poked from under his left armpit, leaving the broadcast-sized video camera hanging at the end of his right arm.

On the whole, they looked exactly like a harried television field crew—minus the sound man and field producer, but that was explainable. New cable programs didn't always get the funding they wanted.

The team approached the window, and Ky began introducing herself. But before she could make a sound, the door to her left swung open, releasing a bizarre cacophony of sounds: people talking, phones ringing, doors closing and the like. A plain-clothed officer stepped through, and the noise disappeared with the closing door.

Startled, Ky almost released her nervousness in a jump, but she stayed grounded and watched the room's newest edition. He approached the mother and began discussing what sounded like a minor case of hit-and-run. Ky returned her view to the glass and the uniformed police officer who uncomfortably adjusted in his seat.

"Hi, I'm Melanie Ann Stormweather with TJN, The Justice Network," Ky began her story.

Meanwhile, Tom dealt with an overwhelming urge to reach through the window and at least shake her hand, although his mind danced with other, more exotic ideas.

Ky brought up a long, narrow note pad to check a name. "I'm here to see a Sergeant MacAlly. I believe I have an appointment."

Tom's smile widened. "Sure. He said to expect you." He slipped a clipboard into the tray and hit the button that opened the other end to offer it to the visitors. "Just print your name and sign."

Ky and Larin obliged, making sure they used their aliases. When the clipboard was returned, Tom made a few more marks and sent the tray back with two neon red badges with the word "VISITOR" emblazoned in neon yellow. He was violating procedures, but for some reason, he didn't care.

As the two affixed the badges to their clothing, Tom pointed at the door to their right. "Midway down the hall, take the stairs up to the third floor, take a right and it's room 342. If anyone bothers you, just ask them to point you in the direction of the public information office."

Ky nodded and smiled, brightening Tom's day.

The two headed for the door as the lock was buzzed open. In the hallway, several uniformed police officers and detectives in suits popped in and out of offices. Each smiled at Ky and nodded, some adding the greeting of "Good morning" here and there. Though everyone noticed them, none paid attention to the glowing "VISTOR" badges, and the two made it to the third floor office without incident.

Ky and Larin entered a small secretarial office with an open doorway to the left of a desk. Further to the left, two chairs beneath a potted tree-like plant hugged the white walls.

The uniformed female officer behind the desk turned from her computer. Upon seeing Ky, her smile changed ever so slightly as she tried to disguise her sudden feelings.

"Hello, how may I help you?"

"Hi, I'm Melanie Ann Stormweather with The Justice Network. I'm here to see Sergeant MacAlly."

"Yes," the officer said while turning slightly and pointing at the entryway next to the desk. "You can go right through there, and his desk is right around the corner to the left."

"Thank you," Ky smiled and headed for the doorway.

Larin smiled as well, but the female officer's smile soon disappeared. She couldn't understand the fact that Larin smiled only because he felt it would help him blend in. She figured his eyes were dancing around the curves of her athletic figure, which to a terran male may have seemed surprisingly erotic in a police officer's uniform. But her looks didn't hold that same excitement for Larin, a fact that would have probably bothered her even more.

Ky turned the corner and stepped into a rather cluttered office with a strange sense of order. Two desks faced each other, their backs against walls to create a small walkway between them. Bookshelves and tables with televisions and video recorders lined the remaining walls and made the room feel more cramped than it probably was.

Stacks of videotapes and disks balanced precariously on the corner of one desk, forming a modern day version of a castle's archery wall. The opposing desk held a similar arrangement but with books, visibly more stable. Countless folders and a plethora of square pieces of yellow paper littered both desks. Even though it was a haphazard arrangement, it also hinted of a logical process, albeit one currently unfathomable to the visitors.

Ky paused, facing the back of a computer monitor. She sensed someone must be behind it, so she tilted to the right to catch his attention.

"Sergeant MacAlly?"

"Yes," he replied while mimicking Ky's tilt to peer around the monitor to see who was calling his name. In his late thirties, he still boasted a full head of thick black hair with a companion mustache. He facial features were a little round, which matched his body, as Ky could see when he stood with an offered hand to greet the two.

"Hi, I'm Melanie Stormweather with TJN," Ky said while shaking the offered hand.

"Yes, I've been expecting you," he smiled while struggling to maintain a professional composure. Though he had been married for fifteen faithful years, here was a woman who could give a man reason to contemplate adultery. Not that he had a chance with her, but he didn't know that and didn't care.

"This is my assistant, Victor Nightenger." Ky pointed a hand at Larin.

"How do you do?" the sergeant offered his hand again.

"Fine, thank you," Larin replied while accepting the offered hand.

But the shaking soon stopped, and Sergeant MacAlly face took on a look of worried concern. Ky and Larin joined in the concern, and their nervous tension rose. Neither recognized it when it happened, but Ky caught on the fastest and replied with the first thing that came to her mind.

"Larynx cancer."

The sergeant turned to Ky then back to Larin. "Oh, I'm sorry." He resumed the shake in hopes that it would help cover his embarrassment at possibly offending someone with an infliction. "You just caught me off guard." That foot-in-the-mouth statement force-fed more embarrassment, which manifested itself as a slight red tinge to a beige complexion.

"That's all right," Larin's voice rattled again like the rough stacking of glass dishes.

Sergeant MacAlly backed up, pushing his wheeled chair out of the way with his legs. The loose frame clanked and rattled but obliged, allowing the sergeant to circle his desk and provide a more proper greeting before gathering some chairs so they could sit and talk about the documentary. As he turned the corner of his desk, he instinctively released a sigh at seeing something he would rather not have. But deep down, he knew it would be inevitable.

His reaction forced Ky and Larin's attention in the same direction.

Across the room from the doorway in which the two had entered sat another archway whose door had previously been open just a hair. From the office behind the door came the occupant who now held the entry open as if modeling for a glamour magazine.

Gold cuff links glinted on the long-sleeved white shirt, a thin black tie striping its center. Some type of animal skin formed a belt for the kakis. A pistol rode high on the left side of the belt and a gold badge dangled from the front right side. The clothes didn't even attempt to hide the six-foot man's obvious well-shaped physique, made possible only by spending considerable time at a gym—but not enough to be mistaken for a steroids poster child. Evenly tanned skin wrinkled slightly when he smiled to reveal a stark contrast of bleach-white teeth.

"Hello, I'm Lieutenant Rick Jackson. I'm the chief public information officer," he said while approaching Ky with an outstretched hand, keeping his sapphire eyes on her and doing his best not to primp his blond hair or stroke his goatee.

Sergeant MacAlly bottled his disgust. When the police department received the request to support The Justice Network, Lieutenant Jackson pawned the babysitting job onto the sergeant. The exact words were, "Melanie? She's probably like all the other females working in the documentary business, either too fat or too ugly to make it on the other side of the camera. MacAlly, she's yours."

Apparently the lieutenant forgot that assessment when he heard Ky's voice from his office. Ego got the best of him, as it did most of the time.

Ky took the offered hand even though she found his constant staring annoying; his eyes didn't seem to want to leave hers.

"Hi, I'm Melanie Stormweather."

"Pleased to meet you." His smile grew slightly. "And please, call me Rick."

"Okay, Rick." Ky turned toward Larin for two reasons: She wanted to stop seeing Rick's piercing eyes, and she was struggling to keep a look of revulsion from appearing on her face. "This is my assistant, Victor Nightenger."

Finally Lieutenant Jackson adverted his eyes to Larin and shook his hand. Larin just nodded, since his experience with MacAlly had shown that the less he spoke, the better.

"I hope your flight was comfortable."

"Yes, thank you," Ky returned with a trained response.

"Let's go into my office, and we can discuss what we have planned for you today." Rick extended his arm toward his door, and the two visitors moved that way. "Sergeant MacAlly, please print out three copies of the itinerary so Ms. Stormweather and Mr. Nightenger can have copies to refer to."

Sergeant MacAlly knew darn well that the lieutenant had asked for printed itineraries because the lieutenant had *no clue* as to what was scheduled. He had previously wanted nothing to do with the visit; it would have interfered with more pressing paperwork, time at the range and his gym lunch. Yet MacAlly gave a well-practiced response, "Yes, sir." Only a fellow sergeant would know that his tone of voice had changed the phrase into "Fuck off, jackass."

The lieutenant's office formed a stark contrast to the room they had just left. White walls competed in brightness with Rick's teeth. Framed diplomas and wooden award plaques speckled one wall. Still under a dry cleaning bag, a sports coat and slacks dangled off a stand in the corner. Various accessories dotted the desk but in a neat arrangement. Not a single speck of dust could be found. It was an anal-retentive's dream.

"Please, sit." Rick motioned to the two chairs in front of the desk as he closed the door and made his way to his chair. He leaned back and immediately began stroking his goatee, realized it and pulled his hand away before smiling at Ky again. "How may I help you?"

What? Ky couldn't believe this; he didn't know anything.

Briefly stunned, contemplating how to respond, she noticed Rick's smile and fought back another wave of repulsion. Then it hit her. This was some kind of terran mating ritual. Rick was—how did Mac put it—flirting.

Her repulsion began to grow into hatred. On her world, if either dextian co-male attempted to initiate sexual contact, they would be castrated, in public. This "flirting" sparked images in Ky's head of her leaping across the desk and ripping out Rick's throat.

She decided not to indulge herself; instead, she called on her training and calmed herself just in time to respond in the best way she knew how: by playing.

Ky smiled.

Rick smiled, showing a few more teeth.

Perfect! Ky had guessed right. If she kept playing this game, she would be able to soften him to get to where they needed to be in order to accomplish the mission.

"Well, TJN wants to start a new series on organized crime. We're visiting cities throughout the world to cover law enforcement actions against organized crime," she said with a smile, but not too broad of a smile so her fangs would remain concealed. Ky had practiced several techniques for a couple of hours in a mirror to master the skill.

Rick forced a slight chuckle for two reasons: Melanie's smile meant he hadn't lost his touch, and he needed some gesture to pat himself of the back and to keep it going.

"I say, we don't have much organized crime here these days."

Ky knew it as a lie but didn't know if it was an attempt to hide something or an ego booster shot about how great "he" was at fighting crime—from behind a desk no less.

"Oh," Ky smiled again. "It doesn't have to be current. We know your city had some mob activity during the prohibition era. We could do it as a historical piece, but something more recent would be better. It doesn't even have to be big; a theft ring would even work."

Ky closed her lips but maintained the smile, kept staring into Rick's eyes and adjusted her chest muscles just enough to push her breasts and tighten the clothes around them.

Unconscious to all that was happening, Rick glanced down and smiled. The smile broke when the door opened.

Sergeant MacAlly entered and handed stapled papers to Ky, Larin and Rick.

"Thank you, sergeant," Rick said.

MacAlly correctly registered the statement to be demeaning, considering the present company, so he responded, "Any time, sir."

Once again, his tone changed the phrase, this time to "I'm not your fucking slave, asshole."

All three flipped through the pages of the itinerary. It contained appointments to interview the police chief, the captain of the organized crime section, a couple of street detectives, et cetera. But each interview was in a neutral location. Rick hummed a few times at some of the names. Ky shuffled through the papers a couple of times; she didn't see what she had hoped.

"Would it be possible to get a tour of the organized crime section, just for some B roll?" Ky asked, because that's where they needed to go.

Rick hummed again while flicking through the pages. "I'm not sure we'll have the time."

"We have a few hours now," she pointed out, still wondering why he was being reluctant.

"Yes, but we would need to prearrange it." Rick jumped back to the front page. "I'm sure we told your producer," he read the name, "George Williams, that we may not be able to fulfill each request for security reasons."

Ky frowned. George Williams was one of the names Mac used to sound like he was calling from a new, bustling cable network to prearrange the visit. Mac did admit to not getting everything.

Rick saw the frown, realized he was starting to lose ground and attempted a semi-save. "I'll see what I can do. But until your meeting with the chief, what would you like to do?"

Interesting question. She wanted a tour, but Ky knew she would have to soften Rick to get it. Time to play.

"Can we interview you?"

Larin snapped a look at Ky. He had no idea what she was up to but wondered if maybe she was actually starting for fall for this over-inflated megalomaniac.

"Um, sure." Rick's ego wouldn't let that offer pass, but then he wondered why. "But what would you interview me about?"

Ky motioned to Larin to start setting up. He began to rebut; they were here to get into the organized crime section. But before he could say or doing anything, a voice shot into his head.

"Do it; I have a plan."

"What, to get into his pants?" Larin replied mentally.

"Just do it!"

Before Larin could respond, Ky began speaking, "Well, I'm sure you can tell us generally what the crime has been like in this city. Maybe you even have a few war stories, so to speak."

Rick laughed, and Ky joined it.

Larin couldn't believe this. He wanted to leave because this gratuitous courtship was making his stomach turn.

To keep from losing his previous lunches, he turned to his imported training and began setting up the tripod, camera and lights. He even took some light readings and didn't pay attention to what was being said.

Larin gave Rick a mini microphone to clip to his tie and returned to the camera. He adjusted the white balance and flicked a switch to do a sound test. That's when he allowed himself to hear the conversation again.

It sprang to life with another round of laughs probably in response to another stupid joke. As Larin glared at Rick through the viewfinder, his finger teased the trigger. Not the record button, the fire button. Right now, he wanted nothing more than to release the camera's hidden weapon and pulverize this egomaniac into atomic mulch.

Reluctantly, Larin moved his finger away. Maybe later.

Chapter 5

One after another, the vehicles formed a seemingly endless river with random ebbs and flows but no sign of ever ending.

Each vehicle slowed as it approached the gateway. The guard in a camouflage uniform would motion with an acknowledging wave and sometimes a salute to drivers who would ease through the gate and onto the base. Sometimes the guard would stop a driver and manually check identification. There was a pattern though, a pattern that didn't go unnoticed.

About a quarter of a mile down the street, inside the base, a hawk extended its wings and flapped them a couple of times, as if stretching, before resuming its motionless perch on a telephone pole. The hawk's eyes never left the activity at the gate.

Traffic began to taper to nothing; then a signal light must have switched to green up the road because another wave began.

What a boring, tedious job, Lyon mentally remarked as he monitored the screen and fidgeted with a foam cup. Then he realized that the one thing worse than performing a boring job was watching someone perform a boring job.

He chuckled with the thought, tapped a few keys to send the hawk to find another perch and backed away from the bank of monitors in the back of the van.

Daylight glowed through the windshield and competed with the lights built into the van's roof. Shelving of sorts lined the left side of the van and held several drones. But Lyon had removed a few to make room for his personal selection of equipment and weapons.

So far he had been lucky. There had been no reason to explain himself or his presence. Nobody had noticed him. But that was mostly because he had been using the hologram-sheathed drones to do his recon.

Lyon had spent the previous day mapping the base. He even compiled the information into a data file he could download. If this mission got nasty, he would need to know every route out.

During the mapping, he located the hospital but waited until he had a complete base map to return for a more detailed examination. He had spent most of the evening and early morning launching several drones to conduct a thorough scan of the hospital. He needed everything documented and in detail.

Luckily, one drone had an atomic differential zoom that, if adjusted correctly, could read the signs inside the building. It took two hours, but he finally found the intensive care ward. Thirty minutes later, he had his target.

Burned didn't even begin to describe the man's condition. Lyon was still mildly amazed that his target had even survived—not because of the extent of the injuries but because terran doctors saved him.

Lyon gave that some more thought as he began to gently rock in the chair. All his readings gave the indication of fourth-degree neutronic burns, straight to and through the bone. This guy wasn't cook outside in or inside out; he was cooked evenly, all at once, fast and burnt. Sure, it was treatable, Lyon knew that, but the terrans didn't have the technology to even create the injury, let alone treat it.

What should be nothing more than a burnt, rotting terran steak was instead barely hanging on to its mortal coil with the aid of some severely primitive life-support equipment.

Lyon reached to scratch the back of his head and neck before sliding his hand around to rub his chin and resting his face in his hand. The bewilderment just kept compounding.

Somehow, the terrans saved this corpse with what must have been a leap in medical advancement on their part for all Lyon knew. Yet the terran doctors were using the most primitive life-support systems. Heck, the computers had to use wires to gather vital statistics and didn't even produce enough interference to cause the drones' screens to flicker.

This living nightmare barely held on, and Lyon couldn't see how he could be holding secrets. But this trek was really starting to become one of those eerie premonitions come true. He almost felt trapped in a dream state.

"Give me the hospital again."

Lyon's order fed life into the van's hologram projectors, and a three-dimensional form of a fifteen-story complex appeared with several wings sprouting from one another. He removed his hand from his chin and leaned forward. Lyon stuck a finger in the hologram and rotated it, repeating the motion to bring the rear of the hospital to face him.

"Go with blue outlines, mark the primary and alternate entry routes green and mark the exit routes...orange."

The computer complied, quickly adjusting the hologram as Lyon made each request.

Green and orange lines danced around and through a web of blue. Lines navigated ventilation ducts, elevator shafts, wet walls, maintenance floors, outside walls and an actual room or hallway from time to time. Getting inside undetected didn't pose a real challenge; that would come when he would try to exit the building with his target.

Hostage retrievals were always tough. Most of the time, the hostages would get themselves killed on the way out. While this case didn't exactly fit the traditional hostage retrieval scenario, the two shared some similarities: His target would become extra baggage, and if noticed, an over-zealous cop would most likely fire a weapon in their general direction. Lyon didn't care for either additional consideration.

The situation wouldn't seem so bad if Lyon had an accurate idea of the condition of his target. He could read some vital signs from a distance, but nothing compared to an actual visual exam. For all he knew, Lyon would have to carry a limp, yet crisp, body out of that hospital and do it without being detected.

Memorizing multiple routes of entry and exit would prove useful if everything went to hell. The most difficult challenge remaining came in the form of surveillance equipment and cameras. Hacking into the hospital's security system would be a must.

"Hey, Mac, can you get into the security system?"

The question echoed slightly against the metal equipment in the van. Time ticked by with no response.

Before Lyon could call out to Mac again, the reason came to him with a wave of loneliness. His wrist computer couldn't reach Mac from here. Mac's communication capabilities were limited to local and interstellar contact. Lyon never thought that he would require planetary communications, something he would mention to Paloon when he returned.

The realization still left Lyon with an almost gut-wrenching feeling. Regardless of how much a pain Mac could be, Lyon never before admitted to himself how much he missed that computer in its absence. In many ways it was a son to him, an ill-mannered, temperamental and partially egotistical son, but a son nonetheless.

Well, feelings aside, it looked liked he would have to attempt the hack into the hospital's computers himself. Lyon hadn't tried an old-style hack for quite a while, but the endeavor probably wouldn't hurt anything.

Then came another realization. Lyon glanced around the back of the van. Normally his computer skills would be limited, but the team he requested had also brought some whiz gizmos with them. Once again, it wouldn't hurt to ask.

"Do you have tele-intrusion capability?" He pointed the question in the direction of the computers paneling the right van wall.

"Yes," came a normal, but monotone voice.

A smile began to emerge on Lyon's face.

"What kind?"

"I'm currently equipped with thirteen levels of tele-intrusion services: sub-electric, thermal pulse, inferred, digital flux, quad-channel class eight satellite tap, nuclear—"

"That's enough."

Actually that was more than plenty; breaching the security system shouldn't be a problem. A password would be nice though. It would at least speed things up a bit.

Lyon jabbed a finger into the still floating hologram and turned it around while tilting it up slightly. He retrieved his finger and lightly dragged it on the surface of the hologram, forming a box. The area Lyon outlined popped out from the diagram. He pinched it with two fingers and pulled it closer to him. His other hand joined in to grab the other side of the holographic cube, and Lyon pulled on the hologram like taffy, stretching it proportionally.

Blue outlines formed a brick wall. With a tap, the hologram spun to reveal the office behind it. Glowing blue halos hinted at desks, computers and a wall of monitors.

"Give me real time."

A couple of people blinked into the picture along with full color. Two security officers of some sort lazily watched a midday motocross race rather than the bank of security monitors.

"How much data do you have, time wise?"

"Fourteen hours, twenty-three minutes, seven seconds."

Lyon rotated his neck to prepare for the long, strenuous activity of sifting through it.

"Okay, play in reverse at ten times."

The action smoothly dove backwards in time and sped up to the requested speed. For guards, they sure didn't move much. Lyon began to wonder if they had fallen asleep in that position. Then they darted to life briefly, removed their lunches from their mouths and placed them back in foam containers before one of the guards, walking backwards, carried them out.

While the one guard returned the meal to the restaurant, the other read e-mail, logged in, rebooted, cussed at a crash screen and started surfing a sports magazine Internet site.

"Stop."

The picture froze with the guard's finger oddly placed in his nose. Lyon grimaced briefly.

"Play."

He waited for the guard to reboot his computer and start entering his password.

"Stop."

Lyon hooked a finger into the hologram and pulled it even closer to him. Now it floated over his lap. He rotated it until he could see the monitor more clearly.

"User name is 'murryk'."

Lyon didn't hear a response, so he had to ask. "Did you get that?"

"Yes," came the rather boring voice of the van's computer.

With another yank, the hologram fell on its side so Lyon could see straight down on top of the keyboard.

"Play at one-sixth speed."

As the one-fingered typist punched the password, Lyon called it out, character by character.

"Capital x, lowercase b, exclamation, lowercase k, number three, pound, zero, four."

Lyon had to ask again. "Got that?"

"Yes."

A sly smile played at his face. "So much for proper password creation."

"Excuse me," replied the computer.

Lyon's only comfort was that it didn't say, "Does not compute. Please rephrase."

"Nothing. Forget it," he said while waving his hand at the enlarged hologram, which fell apart in pixels that blinked away like exploding fireworks.

Hacking a terran security system wasn't much of a challenge, but having a password would help fool the system even more. Stupid, non-thinking computers. Tell them a user was legit, and they believed it. No questions asked.

Lyon spun to face his bank of monitors, one of which reminded him of his other task. He leaned closer to the screen that showed traffic streaming through the gate.

Lyon blinked on his retinal clock. He had about four hours before the shift change. If he was going to do this, it would be best to move about an hour before the shift change, when the guards were the most tired.

Thirty minutes, an hour max, to hack the hospital's security system and disable it. That left two hours to read and relax. Nice.

So let's get to it, Lyon thought.

Chapter 6

Closing doors, ringing telephones, clicking keyboards, shuffling shoes, rustling paper, squeaking chairs and chatting voices blended into a cacophony that held just a hint of a rhythm. This section of the precinct seemed bustling, not too busy for a visit but just busy enough that people didn't have the time to stop and chat for long.

As the group rounded a corner, Lieutenant Rick Jackson aimed an arm at a door near the end of the hall. The door stood open, pinned to the wall by a stubby trash can filled to overflowing with foam coffee cups and snack food wrappers.

Ky couldn't read the words on the door but correctly guessed they said something like "Organized Crime." Using her charm, she had pushed Jackson into giving her the tour she and Larin needed. At first, she wasn't sure they would succeed And when she finally got a "yes" from Rick, he wouldn't let her forget that he was "going out of his way."

It seemed Rick wanted to make Ky painfully aware that she owed him something for arranging the tour. Ky knew what he wanted and had no wish to fulfill his desire. Rick didn't know that and kept returning to the subject in different ways about every ten minutes.

"They look pretty busy, so I don't know how much we'll be able to get for you," Rick smiled while poorly faking a worried brow. "These kinds of visits aren't normal, but we'll give it a shot."

"Thanks," Ky replied with a well-trained smile. It was a response she had learned during her interview with Rick. Now, she had honed it to a finely perfected tool to get exactly what she needed from any terran male. It worked extremely well against the police chief. She took pride in her quick learning although she admitted to herself that it didn't seem to take much.

Before they entered the door, a young plain-clothes detective darted through, a kraft folder flapping about in his hands.

"Afternoon, lieutenant," the detective nodded as he squeezed through.

"Hello," Rick replied, ignoring and forgetting the brief exchange.

The police lieutenant walked through the door and almost immediately received several hellos, most of which he replied to with head nods or short statements. He stepped to the side and motioned for Ky and Larin to enter.

Ky's entrance set off a series of whisperings and prairie-dog head bobs from behind the few waist-high cubicles in the long office. Most didn't stare for long, but some didn't even realize they were staring until it was too late. Even a whistle sounded from somewhere.

"Okay, knock it off," Rick quickly reprimanded in an authority-filled voice that fed his ego as much as he hoped it would impress.

"Ms. Stormweather is a reporter with The Justice Network, so be professional."

The mumbling increased a bit, and one detective at a photocopier had an instant need to shift the angle at which he sorted paper. The new angle not-so-surprisingly gave him a better view of the doorway.

"Hey, Rick," came a voice from an aged black detective in a grey jacket. He sported a halo of short, curly grey hair with a similarly colored mustache with black roots. The hint of wrinkles gave away the age at the early to mid-fifties, but a twinkle in the eye gave a stronger hint of a youthful energy. "Glad to see you made it."

The comment almost gave away Rick's preparations for the planned visit. He didn't want his reporter, and hopefully new girlfriend, get the idea that this arrangement was easy.

"We're happy you were able to accommodate us on such short notice with your section's busy workload," Rick attempted to counter and conceal the previous comment. He didn't waste time changing the subject and didn't give the detective a chance to respond. "Captain Hubbard, this is Ms. Melanie Stormweather with The Justice Network. Melanie, this is Captain Bill Hubbard, chief of organized crime."

"Nice to meet you, sir," Ky greeted, already extending her hand to shake the captain's.

"Oh, no need to call me sir; Bill will do fine," the captain offered with a healthy smile. "I'm glad you could see us during your short visit here."

Larin felt an overwhelming boredom that most cameramen feel when everyone focuses on the reporter and forgets the person lugging around the equipment. It wasn't heavy, but Larin just wanted to get on with it and didn't want to stand through another series of greetings and small talk.

"Hello, we have work to do," Larin, aided by his built-in computers, mentally spoke straight into Ky's head. *"Chat all you want, but I need a reason to move about. See if they'll let me—"*

"Would you mind," Ky invisibly cut Larin off as she looked at Rick and Bill, "if Victor sets up and just films people working in this section?"

Rick began some kind of moan-grunt as if to indicate this might not be possible and it would certainly take some more work by him to get what she needed. Bill, on the other hand, didn't hesitate.

"Sure," Bill said cheerfully. He stepped around to shake Larin's hand, saw that his hands were full and just waved around the office. "Set up wherever you need. Hey, Mike."

The younger detective from near the copier came over.

"Yes, sir?" came an almost feminine voice from the rail-thin man.

"Stay with...Victor?" Bill waited for a nod of acknowledgment from Larin that he got the name right, "and help him get the shots he needs."

"Sure, sir."

"Thanks," Larin replied toward the captain in his clinking voice.

Faced with Mike and Bill's astounded looks, Larin continued Ky's cleverly crafted excuse for his voice modulation difference. "Throat cancer."

"Ah," Bill patted Larin's back as he walked farther into the office, "sorry to hear that."

Larin didn't understand the reason for the apology and ignored it with a shrug while Bill returned to his position next to Rick and Ky.

"Yep," Rick spoke, "don't let Bill's age fool ya. He's smart and spry, but he hasn't beaten me at the range yet."

Rick laughed and smacked Bill just a little too hard on the back, forcing the captain to catch his balance. Though obvious, Bill just chuckled slightly as he shot an unsmiling look at Rick.

"Great." Ky wanted to go with the flow and act like a reporter. "Would it be possible to interview you on camera later today?"

Rick didn't have a chance to inject his false interference this time.

"Sure, we could do it now if you'd like," Bill said.

"That would be nice, but we'll have to wait until Victor's finished getting background footage." Ky opened her note pad. "Do you mind if I ask you some questions until then?"

"Not at all. Let's go into my office," Bill offered.

"Perfect."

"He'll be all right?" Bill looked at Larin.

"Oh, yeah," Ky turned and spoke out. "We're going into Bill's office for a pre-interview. I'll let you know when I'm ready."

"You mean, I'll *let* you *know when I'm ready."*

Larin played off his reply with a hand wave, and Ky ignored it, walking away while Larin continued to set up the tripod and camera.

"How has your visit been going?"

The sudden question almost startled Larin. He had forgotten about Mike standing next to him and had wanted to keep it that way, yet it seemed his tag-along wanted to talk.

"Fine," Larin replied sternly while continuing to assemble his equipment.

"Sorry about the...the," the sensitive cop almost seemed embarrassed to bring it up, "about your throat cancer."

"Why," Larin snarled his lip, "did you cause it?"

"Uhh...uh," Mike trembled a bit as he struggled to find a rely. "No. I just meant I'm sorry to hear—just that I'm sympathetic."

Pathetic is more like it, Larin thought and searched for a way to close this loser off. With his camera mounted, he dove a hand into the light case and retrieved a set of headphones he had crammed in there earlier. He slipped them on and acted as if he had connected the headphones to the camera's audio jacks.

The result was exactly what Larin had wanted; Mike backed away a bit and adopted body language that showed he had decided to be quiet.

Good, moron, Larin mused mentally as he leaned forward, peered through the camera's viewfinder and began panning with a series of scans that appeared as honest video work.

Rotations of the camera's aperture ring flicked the view through several variations: thermograph, ultrasonic, crystalline, infrared, sub-sonic and hyper-frequency. Larin stayed with sub-electron flux.

Black consumed the image. Larin knew that couldn't be right and visually checked the settings on the systems panel, which looked a lot like a digital audio input meter. Everything checked fine.

"Mac, I'm not getting anything." Larin fidgeted with a few more settings, switching them back and forth. *"You sure the SE flux is working?"*

"Yes, it was *working."* Mac's voice fired back in a very defensive tone. *"What are you accusing me of?"*

"What!? I'm not accusing you of anything, you frapping wacko." Larin caught himself in time to change the unconscious flailing of his arms into a simulated yawn for the onlookers who couldn't hear the conversation. *"I'm just saying it's not working now; the systems check, but I'm getting nothing, idiot."*

"Hey," Mac had only tempered his tone a degree, *"be careful who you call an idiot. Did you ever think about the fact you're hunting for primitive computer nodes? Increase the gain. Those electron pipes aren't very strong in terran microchips."*

Larin grumbled as his flicked a thumb on the gain dial. The small screen in the viewfinder flashed blue-white, a sign that it worked, but it was also a sign that further irritated Larin. He pressed a finger against the dial and slowly backed it off until he could see distinctive, multiple, ever increasing shaded layers of dark blue, blue, blue-white and white.

"Did it work?"

Larin began scanning and decided to ignore Mac's question. The computer waited but not for long.

"Fine. From your silence I'm going to assume I was right. Don't worry, no need to admit it. I don't need to hear from you on how great I am."

Bolstering the computer's already self-inflated digital ego didn't even rank in Larin's top five hundred things to do. Right now, he occupied his free thoughts with the task at hand, even though Mac's mocking voice continued to ring inside his cranium.

"Now, before I decide to blank you, we have a job to do, so are you in the system?" Larin returned to the camera and conducted another sweep.

"Yep. Have been since before you two walked in the door."

"Good," Larin shifted his posture. *"Can you flash all the nodes?"*

"Sure. In three...two...one."

In the midst of the hot white patches of light that marked locations of high-speed electron use—mainly computer processors—a faint red light flashed. This was the result of Mac's adjustment to this camera's filter. It would allow the camera to register the slight reflux frequency he would be able to manage in native processors without frying them.

Larin panned the camera as if catching the work in the organized crime section. In actuality he was checking every computer node to see if Mac had access to it. A few hot-white areas didn't have the red flash, but with a quick visual check, they turned out to be wrist watches, appliances, digital organizers and the like.

From one wall of the room to the next, it all checked. Mac couldn't find much about organized crime in the police computer systems, yet the readings showed he had access to all of the computers in the department.

"Find it yet?" came Mac's voice.

"No." A confused, troubled worry seeped into Larin's reply. *"I'm finding nothing."*

Larin ignored Mac's hum of a reply and decided to pan around again. *"But don't drop your signal yet; I'm still trying."*

One after another, Larin slowly isolated the signals unmarked by the red flecks. Again, each checked.

"Damn it."

The rolbrid refused to give up and rapidly swung the camera around for another pan. In the quick movement something registered in Larin's subconscious. Something was different, off.

Larin jerked his head back, unsure of what he had seen, if anything. He rested his eye back on the viewfinder and panned back. Where was it? He saw nothing. So he panned more quickly and spotted it.

One desk computer held a larger halo of blue than the other computers. Larin made some adjustments to separate the readings, and the range finder showed that most of the halo originated about thirty feet past the desk computer.

Larin pulled away from the camera's viewfinder to better examine the situation. Only ten feet from the computer in question was a wall, a door set in the far corner.

The other member of his team would be quick to cast doubt on Larin's ability to think on his feet, but she forgot the rolbrid's expertise was in infantry. And right now, he was moving about behind enemy lines, in the midst of hostiles. His training made him a natural for moments like these.

He hopped the camera off the tripod and onto his shoulder and surreptitiously narrowed the gap to his target. All the way, he pretended to film a couple of detectives discussing a case as they pointed at a computer screen.

They paused and looked up from their work.

"Ignore me," Larin calmed, "you'll look better on TV that way. And before you ask," he used his free hand to point to his neck, "throat cancer."

"Oh, sorry," the two replied almost in chorus.

Larin ignored the unnecessary apology and continued moving. As he reached the far wall, a synapse fired and activated his retinal input monitor. Fractions of a second later, he had the input linked to the camera's output.

He dropped the camera from his shoulder, and while he pretended to look about the room the camera pointed behind him, invading the space behind the wall.

There, glowing white in Larin's retinal monitor, was a computer node signal that didn't have Mac's mark of red.

"Mac, are you still broadcasting?"

"Hell yeah, squirt. Why? Did you find somethin'?"

"Maybe." Larin inched toward the door in the corner. *"Give the master time to work."*

"Whatever."

Larin hit the corner and shoulder-mounted the camera as if filming again. Meanwhile, he debated on how to get into the room. As if in response to an unspoken request, the answer appeared in the view screen.

Mike. He had forgotten all about Mike, not a difficult task. But there Mike was, following Larin around like a lost puppy.

The rolbrid dropped the camera again and uncapped the headphones from his ears. With a nod toward the door, Larin got Mike's attention. "What's in there?"

"Um, it's a data storage computer." Mike fumbled with a pen and had to stop to pick it up from the floor. "We don't use it much any more that I know of."

"Mind if I film it?"

"Well, like I said we don't use it much any more. It's really not part of—"

"We can use it as a then and now piece, you know, old crime computers, new crime computers. It won't take long."

As far as Larin was concerned, Ky would have been envious to hear that quick thinking.

Mike seemed to be battling an internal conflict, one in which Larin's request overpowered any of Mike's convictions. The cop opened the door and flicked on the light.

Larin followed and couldn't believe what he saw. Cabinet size units taller than him lined the walls and formed aisles in the center of the room. As computers go, it was gigantic.

"Mac, we may have it."

"Good," Mac's voice sounded like a construction worker being disturbed during his Monday night football and beer. *"Plant it and get this over with."*

"Impressive," Larin said as he hauled the camera back to his shoulder and weaved together some more fast thoughts. "Would you mind waiting outside for a moment, so I can film the room empty with just the computer?"

"Uh, umm," Mike's frail reluctance lost again. "Okay."

Larin didn't bother to wait until Mike left and began his "filming" as he scanned the computer units.

Glass rattled lightly in the door at it closed. Then the room fell silent.

Power still flowed through the computer. Someone still used it because each of its electrically powered circuits registered in Larin's scans. He weeded through them until he decided on the strongest signal from within the cabinets.

Larin dropped the camera into one hand and opened a panel on it with the other. With another flick of the wrist, he tossed a wafer-thin panel between some of the cabinet's vents closest to the strongest signal point.

Mission complete; time to split. As he made for the door, he called to Ky. *"Network found; pad planted; time to go."*

He had made it out of the room, gave some lame thanks to Mike and headed back to the rest of his equipment before realizing Ky hadn't replied.

"Hey, Ky. Time to split."

"I heard you. Shut up." Ky's reply came as fast as bullets. *"We have an interview first. Don't leave."*

Larin began formulating a rebuttal when boisterous laughter roared from the police captain's office. Shock flashed on Larin face. It wasn't because the laughter was unexpected but because Ky was the one laughing. And it sounded like honest laughter.

The rolbrid stood in bewilderment long enough for the door to open. A smiling Ky waved at Larin to come in and set up for the interview. They still had a cover to keep.

As Ky returned to the inside of the room, Larin could hear Rick's voice, "Good thing I had a subway pass to get home."

Ky resumed laughing and tried to cover a squeal with a hand over her mouth.

Emotion spiked in Larin, and he thought again about activating the camera's weapon and atomizing Rick.

Chapter 7

Bewilderment. Confusion. Awe.

Reality jumbled with dreams and teased with desires. Existence seemed irrelevant, and sentience offered little help explaining the situation. Pinpricks of questions invaded the void.

Where was he? Did he want to know? Why should he care?

Then he remembered. The explosion. Suddenly pain crashed into him like a semi-truck.

"Aaaaaaaaaaaaaagggggggggggggggg!"

Muscles involuntarily contracted, sparking countless waves of pain, each with enough force to almost render him unconscious again. Eyelids ripped open, causing more pain both with their movement and by allowing bright light a clear path to jab at the heart of his brain. The lids clamped shut, triggering more pain as the muscles overcompensated.

"Aaaaarrrrrrgggggg!"

He could feel every cell ache. Every hairless follicle on his body hurt. Sound pierced his brittle ears, registering only stinging at anything audible.

Muscles twitched again, but nothing moved. What felt like a dull drill dug its way into his right arm. His skin crackled in a feeble attempt to defend, and an earthquake of pain gave birth to fissures that traversed his entire body.

Like most earthquakes, it ended almost as quickly as it began. The cutting aches were now blunted. Soon they dulled into grains of sand as he relaxed calmly on the beach of a crystal clear lagoon.

Clanking, constant clanking muffled by muted senses pulled him from his slumber. Unknown forces kept a hold on his consciousness and fought to subdue it at every turn. The battle to wake tired him even further.

Open eyes registered blurs of blotchy lights. Pupils lulled about while irises struggled to limit the bright assault. Fuzzy movement slowly sharpened, and the clanking continued.

Shapes of people moved about, but they looked bigger than people. They were people in suits, full-body protection suits. Each carried something long and slender, and they bought the objects together with clanks. They were constructing something, something around him.

The suits, radiation suits. He remembered. The realization of what might have happened shocked him and pushed him over the edge just enough for the forces to capture and consume his conscious mind.

Lava flowed into his veins and ignited fires within his left arm. The internal brush fire spread fast and weaved into every capillary. Overwhelming warmth prodded him awake.

Heavy eyelids failed in several attempts to open even a sliver. Every try ended in a collapse of fatigue. Yet in the distance, people were mumbling, a realization that gave him the energy to succeed in his next effort to see.

Fuzzy figures of people shuffled around his bed. Some shared clipboards, which they seemed to point at and read. All of them still wore radiation suits and stopped to stare back at his now open eyes.

Something zapped his strength, so he skipped the struggle to move his head. But he could see tubes and wires of some kind weaving a network above his face. Each line appeared to intercept some part of his body, a disturbing realization for him.

He could focus on the cables, but the people beyond still seemed blurred. There were thick panes of glass in the way, maybe plastic. Like a green house, the substance encased him.

One figure shook his head. Another looked off to the side at something not viewable from the victim's current perspective. Someone mumbled again, and another approached and disappeared into the upper right corner of his vision.

Burning magma subsided. Cool water took over. The ocean breeze returned.

What? Did that digital clock just reset right before his eyes from 5:14 to 12:20? How was that possible?

The worried news anchor on the television claimed this wave of time relapse was sweeping the world, city by city. Every time-keeping device was affected. This didn't make sense, but he knew it couldn't be good.

Overwhelming, desolate, oppressive, dark, cold dread. He scampered to the couch, pulled in his legs and wrapped his arms around them to assume a fetal position. Something was very, *very* wrong.

He knew it was going to come. He couldn't stop it; no one could stop it. It was going to take everyone in an unmistakable wave of complete, unmitigated, pure, blessed annihilation.

A whisper of a tick. Power disappeared. Everything fell to the greatest pitch of black.

It's coming. It's coming, damn it! Dear God, please stop it!

The brightest of white flashed through the windows and soon penetrated everything. He felt it in his bones. His mind's eye now saw the explosion's origin in slow motion.

Far on the horizon, a spark ignited into a white ball that rapidly grew, sending forth the rays of purity. It had been born; he knew that now. And nothing could stop it from consuming the entire planet.

"Try to be quiet. Bite down on this because this is going to hurt...a lot."

Huh? The command jarred him from the nightmare. Some kind of rod was being jammed into his mouth, and for no sensible reason, he made his strongest attempt to open his mouth and accept the bit—although the effort was feeble.

The sound of ripping adhesive tore through the air. Cool pads touched several spots on his arms and chest. But the calm sensation drastically took a more disturbing turn.

It spawned a new definition of pain. The sensation resembled a flash-freeze formation of crystals. In fast traveling waves to all extremities, every atom in his body felt like it had fractured into jagged fragments sawing into each other.

He temporarily lost his breath as the feeling charged toward his head and shredded into his brain. Nothing could possibly be worse, and soon the bit didn't seem to help. The strong wood even began to give slightly under the strength of the tightened jaw muscles.

A hand lightly clamped over his mouth just in time to muffle the continuous scream. He didn't try to scream; it just happened. Oddly it made time slip by, and when the pain subsided and the screaming stopped, he didn't know if five seconds or five hours had passed.

The hand lifted away from the mouth. His body fell from its arched position back onto the bed. He didn't even realize his body had tensed so much.

"Good. Now rest; you're going to need it. I'll be back shortly."

Before he could open his eyes or question the voice, exhaustion dug iron claws into his consciousness. Now he flew. Below stretched valleys lined by endless snow-capped peaks glistening in the majestic glow of the morning sun.

Chapter 8

"Hey, sleeping beauty, you up yet?"

Who's that? he asked himself as he opened his eyes.

At the end of the bed stood a man with dark blond hair, wearing a black full-body suit like some kind of special operations agent.

"Huh?" His voice cracked slightly.

"Don't worry; you've answered my question." Lyon flipped through some pages on the clipboard he had retrieved from the wall. "We don't have much time, but let's take it from the top. You're," he glanced at the clipboard, "Manuel Quiet Storm Ozuna, a technical sergeant, ten years, nuclear—"

"Oz."

Lyon peered from the papers. "Excuse me?"

"Oz. Just call me Oz."

"Okay, *Oz*." Lyon released the spring-loaded metallic cover of the clipboard and tossed it onto the bed. "And before you ask, my name is technically Lyon Vulgrin Wolfen son of Kendrick, but you can just call me Lyon."

"But who are you?" Oz raised a hand to his forehead and attempted to rub away an emerging migraine.

"We can discuss that later, but for now, I'm here to help." Lyon pointed at Oz's arm. "How are you feeling?"

"Uuuuhhhh, fine, I guess. Why?" Oz looked up to see Lyon's pointed finger and followed it to gaze at his own utterly burnt arm rubbing away flakes of burnt skin from his forehead.

Everything came back to him. The hangar. The flash. The pain. The dreams. Wait, those weren't dreams. He was in a hospital. There were people in radiation suits, doctors maybe. They were trying to save him. He was burnt to a crisp, completely. He could feel that now. The thought drudged nausea from the pit of his gut to the surface.

"Whoa there." Lyon jumped forward and retrieved a palm-sized hypodermic gun from his left pocket.

As the nozzle caved-in blackened skin and injected the medication, Oz slowly stopped retching. Lyon slid open one of Oz's eyes and watched the pupil return from a dilated state.

"Almost lost you there." Lyon waved the gun so Oz could see it. "I only have five more doses, so try not to think about your current condition. We still have a long trip ahead of us."

"What...do...do you mean?" The words struggled their way from Oz's throat. Meanwhile, he found himself bewildered at how fast the nausea disappeared.

"Well, *Oz*. You have a choice to make." Lyon's left arm hugged his stomach allowing his right elbow to rest on the fist as he pointed at the patient. "I'm not going to shit you. You're burnt, *bad*. The only reason you're able to move and talk right now is because I slapped you with six nan-med patches. They're currently moving through you, fooling your senses while repairing what they can."

Oz hadn't given it much thought until now, but it had been a while since he had experienced one of those nightmarish bouts of pain. But if that flash from the ship came from the nuclear induction converter, he would have been cooked with enough radiation to never need a nightlight.

"Actually, you have progressed to the point that you now possess a discernible half-life. Not many can say that." Lyon withdrew his pointed finger and didn't hint at whether his response was a result of mind reading, but it left Oz guessing.

"Back to the choice." Within the greenhouse-like structure surrounding them, Lyon took a few steps toward the foot of the bed and stared to his left at the room's pressurized air locks. He then returned to look at Oz. "You can stay here with this pathetic excuse for a medical team—after all we are talking about military medicine here—and die in a couple of days when the radiation finally runs out of cells to destroy. Or you can come with me; I may actually be able to save your ass."

With the last statement, Lyon pointed again but this time at the light-brown patches he had placed on Oz. The patient looked down at them and began to lift a hand to pick at one, stopping when Lyon spoke.

"Don't touch them. Those patches are still reservoirs."

"Reservoirs? Of what?"

"Let's just say they contain nano-constructed biological pathogens specifically designed to seek out and consume radiological isotopes, digest them and excrete several amino acid strains specifically designed to help cure your cells." Lyon shrugged. "At least that's the plan. Seems to be working."

Wait a minute here. Oz's memory started coming back. He was still a member of the military and had a deeply embedded sense of honor and duty.

Oz lowered his hairless brow and squinted. His white eyes stood out in stark contrast to his burnt eyelids. "What's stopping me from finding the nurse button or yelling for help?"

Lyon didn't flinch. It was as if he expected the question. "Nothing. If you do, I disappear, that medication runs out in about twenty minutes, you resume a coma-like state, and the help you call for will continue to watch you like a guinea pig as you slowly die, cell by cell."

Oz kept the squint and began to snarl. "You're pleasant."

"I never said I was; I'm just giving you the real deal." Lyon stepped forward in a non-threatening pose. "Now like I said, if you want to do this, we have to move; the medication won't last long before you'll need another dose. You'll probably need about fifteen before your body begins to stabilize. It does, luckily, give us the ability to move about without having you pass out."

The proposition seemed obvious, but Oz felt an undeniable reluctance. It showed on his face, which resembled the surface of a charcoaled hot dog.

"Look," Lyon jabbed with his eyes and got Oz's attention. "Don't think. You play, you live. You don't play, you die."

"Fine." The word seeped from Oz's lips like molasses. "What do I need to do?"

"Put these on." Lyon grabbed a stack of clothes he had previously set on the foot of the bed and handed them to Oz. "Don't move too fast. You may get nauseous again, and I only have a limited supply of shots."

Lyon walked to the rear door of the enclosure. "Wait here."

He left and returned a couple minutes later with a wheelchair. Oz had only managed the shirt and now sat at the edge of his bed staring at his withered legs dangling like dried peppers.

"Don't think about it."

Lyon jogged a bit toward Oz who was already starting to faint back onto the bed. He caught Oz in time, propped him up and helped with the pants.

Once clothed, Oz braced himself against Lyon and leaned back in his offered arm. Even slight weight on his legs made them feel as if they would buckle. Once in the wheelchair, Oz sighed in relief at the end of the three-foot trek.

Lyon pulled from a pocket what looked like a rubber mask. It was complete with hair but seemed a bit oversized for Oz. Lyon slid it over Oz's head. Oz could feel a metallic box, apparently attached to the mask, tap his nape.

With a few adjustments to the mask, Lyon reached around, activated the shrinking mechanism and adjusted the fit as it slowly tightened. Just as it started to look natural, Lyon tapped the device on the back again.

"Not too tight, is it?"

"No." The mask moved perfectly with Oz's facial gestures.

"Good."

Lyon walked to the rear of the wheelchair, backed it up and plowed forward out of the radiological greenhouse and toward the airlock door.

Unseen by Oz, Lyon tapped a few buttons on his left sleeve. A moment later, the door hissed open.

In the pressurized clean room, Lyon parked the wheelchair, lifted a white lab coat off a hook on the wall and donned it. Then he stepped forward and peered through the leaded glass window up and down the hallway, which housed eight of these treatment suites, four on each side.

"It's clear." Lyon glanced down at his rider. "Ready?"

The question slightly startled Oz, and he began to question what his alleged rescuer meant by it. But out of sheer reflex, he uttered "Sure."

On that note the outer door hissed open. Lyon retrieved a pair of wire-rimmed glasses from an inner pocket and slipped them over his ears.

They were soon in the hall and off toward the end of it. Large, windowless doors sat in an alcove at the end. A large, red banner painted with white letters read "Automatic Doors: Stand Clear." A large door release button spotted the walls on both sides of the opening.

Lyon halted the chair and neared the wall. He sent a short mental command into his wrist computer and activated the synced thermal ultrasonic sensors strapped to both thighs. Lyon turned his head about as if looking around attentively, but Oz knew there were only doors and an alcove.

"What are you doing?" Oz probed.

"Waiting for the nurses to leave."

Oz began to debate whether he had made an escape pact with a nutcase. "You're crazy, aren't you!? I knew it."

Lyon lifted the white sleeve on his left arm to reveal the computer console built seamlessly into the black suit. A few mental commands and a four-by-six hologram sparked to life as it unfolded above his arm.

In the floating picture, the halls outside rotated about as Lyon moved his head.

Oz's mouth hung agape as his stared in awe at a spectacle he couldn't believe. How was it possible? Such vivid, multi-color detail. Scientists struggled with basic single-colored holograms. This kind of technology would be—

"You're from a black project, aren't you?" Oz was confident he had figured it out but guessed nonetheless. "You're some kind of spec-op sent by someone in Project Corona to pull me out?"

Lyon almost decided to shatter Oz's perception but decided to play along. "Whatever you say."

He looked back through the walls toward the nurse's station located catty-cornered from the entrance. One nurse stepped around it and headed toward the door.

Lyon signaled to be quiet, but Oz saw the approaching threat on the hologram and, a step ahead of Lyon, had decided to silence himself.

If not for the overriding sense of self-preservation, Oz might have taken notice of the nurse's looks, but the fact that she was attractive didn't become apparent until the nurse was about three feet from the door. At that point, Lyon dropped his left arm, and the hologram quietly folded away. Oz caught himself before verbally protesting.

Lyon drew the arm back, flattened the palm, relaxed the wrist and prepared to strike as soon as the door opened, but the blissfully oblivious nurse turned the corner and strolled up the hallway that shot the opposite direction from the large doors.

Oz keyed off of Lyon's dropped arm and released his held breath. The stress was getting to be too much and threatened to pull him under. He resisted with a couple of head nods before it succeeded.

Patience came easily for Lyon as he watched through the doors. The nurse stopped to search her pocket for change, bought a diet soda from a vending machine and resumed her casual pace. Twenty more feet down the hall, she pressed the elevator wait button and fidgeted with her hair while sipping the soda.

The scene reminded Lyon of the escape route, and he activated the computer link again and dove into the menus. He located the elevator the nurse just boarded. With a side step over in the computer nodes, he took control of the elevator's twin on the opposite side of the shaft. It had currently been sitting dormant for eight minutes and twenty-three seconds. Positively clear.

Sparks of thought brought the elevator to the escapees' floor. With an eye twitch, the lift's doors opened and locked.

One more glance around. Clear.

"Time to roll," Lyon whispered and turned to see his patient passed out.

He had a couple of stims but decided that would do more damage than help. Time to revert to more traditional methods.

A firm hand planted itself on Oz's cheek.

"Wake up."

Another strike.

"I need you awake."

"Huh?" Oz finally revived, but his mind still fought to take a doze, so he groggily protested. "What?"

"I need you awake." Lyon shot another look through the walls behind him; nothing had changed. "If we're going to get out of here by blending in, you need to be awake. Assistants don't normally push around sleeping patients, or at least I hope not. So can you stay awake for the next ten minutes?"

Oz didn't reply, so Lyon grabbed his chin and shook vigorously. "Hello! We don't need the risk. Can you stay awake?"

"Um—" Oz understood the importance of the demand, just doubted his ability to carry it out. He gathered some energy, blinked repeatedly and squeezed his eyes shut before forcing them to explode open. "Yeah, I can do it."

"Good."

Lyon scanned the battlefield again and launched the extraction with a punch of the door release as he stepped around and gripped the wheelchair's handles. Before the doors could open completely, they were off and down the hall.

About twenty feet down the hall, Lyon slowed his pace to assume a more natural appearance. The duo boarded the elevator without incident. Oz's head began to droop, and Lyon corrected it with a hard slap to his right cheek, which would have bruised if it had been his real skin. The medications in his system kept Oz from feeling most of the pain, but he could still sense pressure.

As Lyon turned the wheelchair around, the doors closed. Without touching a button, Lyon selected, and the second-floor button lit. A jolt, a whirl from an overhead motor, and they began their descent.

With all the technical capability Lyon had at his disposal, he still had forgotten one thing.

"Ding."

The elevator slowed to an early stop. Before a startled Lyon could nervously wrestle through the menu system to override the elevator's automatic response to calls, the silver doors glided open.

Lyon could see who was on the other side before the doors open, and he felt Oz jerk in shock at seeing the calm gentleman wearing the short-sleeve blue uniform of a major and holding a cup of coffee he had just purchased from a machine. Lyon guessed the major was a doctor by the stethoscope wrapped around the neck.

"Hello," the doctor greeted with a nod, unfazed by seeing a medical assistant transporting a patient.

Lyon simply nodded in reply and watched the major go for the number pad but stopped.

"Same floor, great." The major stood to one side and drank some more coffee. He apparently felt the need for small talk as the doors closed. "So, I can't say I've seen you around before. Where do you work?"

"Top floor."

"Ah," the intruder replied with a mild look of confusion, but he assumed that this person was still new and didn't know the sections yet. "New, huh? When did you arrive?"

"Yesterday," Lyon replied as calmly as possibly.

The doctor's head jerked slightly. "You arrived yesterday, and they already have you pulling the graveyard shift?"

Lyon's left arm shot forward and struck the major's chest, pinning him against the metallic wall. Just as suddenly, Lyon withdrew the arm, and the doctor collapsed like a rag doll.

"Holy shit! You killed him!" Oz was wide-awake now, gripping his chair.

"Calm down. I didn't kill him." Lyon effortlessly slid the wheelchair sideways and knelt down to position the body so it would be difficult to see when the doors opened. "All I did was force the wind from his lungs. He's just unconscious for now. He'll be up and about in five minutes or so. Maybe he won't ask so many questions next time."

Lyon glanced at the ticking numbers above the door. One floor away.

"Now we have less time than planned."

With the lift's ding, Lyon pushed Oz through and activated the system menu he had previously left open. The doors shut and wouldn't reopen until Lyon desired it or his van left transmission range. Lyon didn't care and forgot about it.

In a rough yet calm fashion, the duo continued forward as the knight scanned his data for the escape routes. He was already on Plan B. With the maps in his vision and a blinking dot representing his current position, Lyon scanned for the quickest route to the rear entrance of the lobby elevators that descended into the basement.

Good. With a left at the approaching corner, it would be a straight shot, through a set of large, double doors and halfway down the hall.

As they turned, Lyon spotted a male nurse in a white gown writing on some records. As the nurse closed the records and stuffed them into a pocket hanging on the door, he turned and advanced down the hall toward the escaping duo.

Lyon didn't want any more questions or another body. He leaned forward and began whispering in Oz's ear.

The nurse took notice and watched as Oz began nodding.

"Good," Lyon continued to whisper. "Now, smile like I just told you a mildly amusing joke."

A smile crept onto the nurse's face at seeing the happy patient. He looked away and walked past without a word.

As Lyon lifted his head away he continued to whisper. "Gullible moron."

Oz now had a genuine smile.

Lyon shifted to the other side of hall to line with the exit door. Lyon punched the door release and continued while calling the elevator that opened just as they approached.

Without event, the escapees made it to the underground parking garage and to Lyon's van, which rested in a conveniently located handicap spot.

Oz no longer had the strength to remain awake, so Lyon had some difficulty placing him in the makeshift gurney in the back of the van. Lyon sorted through the medical supplies and applied a new set of nan-med patches before driving the van out from under the hospital and quietly off the base.

Some time later, in the midst of a heated game of solitaire, a lone security guard halted with mouse in hand and sat in shock. A couple of monitors changed view as the digital veil that had previously shrouded them disappeared. A major banged away at the walls inside an elevator, which the computer now showed as stuck on the maintenance floor. Then a buzzer sounded from the alarm panel on the wall. In the middle of the red box a black on yellow-green display showed the alarm's details.

"What the hell?" The guard stood as she grabbed the phone, punching the direct line button.

"We've got alarms on four floors." Horror filled her voice as she imagined hearing her commander's screams reaming her a new ass. "They went off forty-two minutes ago."

Chapter 9

A white glow emanated from the fine prong extending from the tool Paloon held in his hands. Only two more minutes to go. Sweat, not caused by fatigue, speckled his brow.

Paloon bent over his work. Four inches thick, the octagon-shaped satellite drone stretched to a five-foot diameter, just shy of the table's width. The blue and silver mechanism's cover rested on the other end of the table, leaving the crystalline guts exposed.

Peace, or at least as much peace as Paloon could expect, had reigned in the grocery store's basement for almost five hours. The situation didn't go unappreciated by the Force Grey Wolf hunter. Except for Mac's odd behavior, Paloon had been able to completely focus himself on his work.

Almost imperceptibly, a kink began to form in the filament extending from the charging tool inserted in the drone's frequency generator. Paloon had been reluctantly expecting it when his non-blinking eyes detected the flaw.

"Damn it!"

He yanked the probe from inside the drone. With a flick of his wrist and a touch of the release button, the still glowing wire soared toward the end of the basement room. The kink began vibrating rapidly before the wire popped into a hundred sparks, leaving no remaining matter as evidence of its existence.

He was days past his self-declared deadline, and the drone needed at least another day, at least at this rate. He just needed better quality material.

"Why can't you provide me with—"

"Lookie hyar'," Mac interrupted with deep southern accent. "I ain't got no time to mix words witcha. I'm workin' ma fingers to the bone to meet all y'alls demands, but it don't get no gooder'n then this."

Blue light danced around the corner of the table leaving another bit for Paloon's high-frequency charger.

Mac's statement drew out a feeling of guilt from Paloon. The mechanics technician knew the computer still lacked the definition to fabricate a completely solid filament, but having these things snap every minute was really starting to make Paloon's blood boil.

"Sorry. I'm not mad at you." Paloon wiped his the sweat from his forehead with a hand, which he then dried on his pants leg. "Thanks for the new filament."

"Now that thar's more like it. Goin' back to being nice and gentlemanly like. Pa would be proud."

The reply came as Paloon lifted the filament from the table, and it made him realize he had just apologized to a computer. He shook his head and wondered about how severely Lyon had screwed up, making these emotion chips so damn erratic.

Paloon fitted the bit while peering at Mac's screen on the wall across the table. Mac's terran face only had hair growing around its mouth like a rash. Lips held a never-ending piece of straw that Mac chewed continuously like cud. On his head rested a tall hat made from some kind of completely impractical material. Both side brims pointed to the sky, creating an even less functional design.

"What's the cell at?"

"Is'at, um—" Once again Mac sounded like he was actually staring at a gauge and attempting to decipher it. "Looks like the tank's on a quarter 'til."

Paloon had finished locking in the bit but left it gripped in his hands as he paused. He raised his right brow and peered up at Mac. "Quarter until what?"

"A quarter 'til full, ya ijit."

How can Lyon put up with this? Paloon rubbed his teeth with a tightly pressed tongue as he looked away and shook his head. This job wouldn't be anywhere half as stressful if it wasn't for Mac changing personalities what seemed like every few hours.

"Just give me a count down starting five seconds from full."

"Sure thang."

Paloon thumbed the switch on the charger's T-shaped handle. A slight hum soon faded, and the prong began to glow. The test worked, so Paloon flicked the charger's tip to a ninety-degree angle and dove into the drone's guts again.

As he lined the filament with the frequency generator and inserted, a friendly voice filled the room.

"How is the progress, Hunter Osluf?"

Paloon froze so as not to break the filament and tilted his head to see. "Oh, hi, Hitook. It's still gradual."

"Graduwal!? Sheesh," Mac butted in. "You're slower than a pail of snails."

A slight grumble came from Paloon's throat.

Hitook took a few more steps into the room and turned his head toward Mac's screen. "I'm afraid I don't understand."

"Ignore him," Paloon faced his work and repositioned his hands to a more comfortable position. "It's another one of his bizarre personalities, country bumpkin or something like that. It took me half and hour to figure out what he was saying, and it's still confusing."

Paloon pulled the charger's trigger. The filament glowed brighter as he increased the tension until he saw the bright white he needed.

"Excuse me for not looking up," Paloon began, "but I've got to keep my eye on this."

"Understandable, Hunter Osluf."

The large, furry beast crossed the room, grabbed the chair across the table from Paloon and watched.

"So what did you find out?"

"I found one site where some of the warehouse wreckage was

dumped." Hitook scratched his left arm. "I scanned everything within fifty feet and found nothing non-native or explosive, except an unspent shotgun shell."

"Locate the, um, *wolves*?" Paloon's voice dragged on the word.

"Yes, in a veterinarian clinic's cold storage."

"What were they doing there?"

"Apparently some animal rights and native heritage groups are in court about the proper disposal of the carcasses." The liqua's voice took on a tone of guilt. "It seems there are not many wolves left."

The last statement held more meaning to him than anyone could know, but Paloon didn't care.

"You scanned them, right?"

"Yes, Hunter Osluf. However, I found nothing."

Hitook's formality hadn't eased since they first met, and it was really starting to grate on Paloon's nerves. He knew Hitook was just an acolyte, but did he always have to call everyone by their titles? If he didn't want to use first names, he could just say nothing.

"Why do you always have to call everyone by—" Paloon's eye twitched at the sign. "Clear!"

Hitook pushed away from the table as Paloon jerked the tool and flicked the prong across the room. Another pop and all that remained of the filament were flecks of light that soon dimmed to nothing.

"What was that?" Hitook squinted but couldn't see anything remaining of the filament, not even smoke.

"That was another bad filament." Paloon sat back.

A tingle teased Hitook's arm. He looked down and jerked his arm away from the matter reconstructing lights on the table. Another thin wire appeared.

Hitook pressed a stubby digit against the item, rotated his hand and offered it Paloon, who lifted it away with two fingers.

"Thanks," he said while fitting the probe into the tool. "Actually it's my fault. If I hadn't broken the bit we brought, I wouldn't have to work with inferior parts."

"Thar ya go crossin' me agen," Mac belted.

"I'm not blaming you," Paloon snapped back.

"Son, ya can't sheet on my shoes and call it a shine, dang it. I know—"

"Shut up!" Paloon truly wanted to disconnect the computer but decided to let it be, just as long as it remained quiet.

"Well, I never," Mac mumbled.

Hitook broke the tension.

"I did find one thing."

Paloon hummed as he connected the new bit and slid it into the drone. "What's that?"

"A trace of trimilic in a strong sodium residue."

"Trimilic?" White light from the filament glowed on the highlights of Paloon's face. "Are you sure?"

"Positive, Hunter Osluf. I checked it three times."

"Where was it?"

"In a drainage system half a block from the warehouse."

"How did you end up finding it there?"

"You instructed me to check everything." Insecurity crept into Hitook's voice. The liqua wondered if his thoroughness wasn't appreciated.

"Yes, but—" Paloon shrugged. "You crawled around the sewers?"

"I had to take the readings through the road." If Paloon had been watching, he would have seen Hitook's long ears droop in embarrassment. "I couldn't fit."

"You didn't get stuck, did you?"

"Actually—"

"Okay, forget it." Paloon huffed in mild amazement. "I admire your motivation; it gives you at least something to—"

"Five," Mac began counting. "Four."

"Mac, link to the drone's controls." Paloon shifted himself.

"Three."

"On my go, ignite the generator."

"Two."

Hitook didn't know what to do but figured standing in the corner would be best.

"One."

Paloon could see the inside of the high-frequency generator begin to glow red.

"Full."

Paloon pulled the charger free from the drone. "Go."

Nothing seemed to change. Mac remained silent.

"Well," Paloon aimed the remark at Mac, "do you have it?"

"Yup."

"A-n-d?" Paloon drew out the question with the help of an extended arm.

"And it's runnin' smoother than a baby's backside."

Hitook figured it was safe enough to take his seat again and did so.

Paloon reached behind him to set the tool on the workbench along the wall before grabbing the drone's cover and securing it in place with a pencil-shaped tool from his pocket. "Activate the cloak."

Shimmering waves washed over the drone, increasing in frequency until the drone had completely bent light around its hull.

A credit-card-sized device slipped from the table into Paloon's hand. He held it out and ran it around the space the drone occupied. The screen showed nothing but the table.

"I've got nothing. The gravity cloak's working well." Paloon tossed the scanner onto the workbench. "Activate the drive. Bring it off the table about two feet."

Electronic buzzing filled the room and faded to a subsonic rumble.

"Ain't that purtier than a peach?"

Paloon correctly guessed that Mac's statement meant the drone was currently flying with the cloak. Mac was in sync with the cloak's changing frequency and could still communicate with it, as well as determine its location.

"Move forward three feet."

Silence.

"Well?"

"It's doing fine," Mac's face spat for no reason. "Ah hell, naw—"

The cloak began shaking with ripples before dissipating in a shower of sparks and a mild, rapidly expanding pushing force that Paloon and Hitook could feel. Then the drone tilted and fell to the table, where it rattled around like an octagon-shaped coin.

"Sheet fire!" Mac exclaimed.

"What happened?" Paloon darted forward and worked on opening the case.

"The drive's frequency was a hair off." Mac's visage was soon joined by a hand that scratched behind his left ear. "Sorry."

Paloon hoped the high-frequency generator was still operating. He really didn't want to charge it again.

"How's the toy?"

Paloon immediately recognized the voice and its dismissive tone as it referred to the drone as a toy.

"My drone it just fine, Larin." Paloon peered up to see two people enter from the tunnel. "What took you guys so long?"

Larin pulled a chur root from his mouth and pointed the twig at Ky. "She was busy flirting."

Ky shot the midget an evil glare, and Larin soon felt an intense, piercing pain in his right ear. His face contorted as he tried to poke the pain out with a finger. Ky used the time to explain.

"We smooth-talked our way in," Ky said. She approached the drone on the end of the table but only appeared half interested in it.

"Smooth talk my ass, you're—" Another shot of pain in Larin's ear halted his statement.

"Did you guys at least find it?" Paloon knew Ky was causing Larin's pain but didn't have time for that now. Besides, Ky quickly released it to let Larin talk.

"Yeah, I got it." Larin continued to rub his ear as he headed for the storage lockers to put away the camera. "Didn't Mac tell you?"

Paloon lifted the drone and carried it back to the end of the table where it had started its brief journey. "I'm trying to keep my conversation with him limited right now."

Larin set down the camera and walked back to take the other case from Ky, who gave him another "Keep your mouth shut" look. He ignored it, along with Paloon's previous statement. "Mac, did you get a connection?"

"You betcha," Mac chewed away on his straw. "But I'm currently busier than a cat covering crap on a tile floor tryin' to figure it out."

Larin dropped the case. "What? That didn't make any frapping sense."

"I told you. He's been like that for a while now." Paloon grabbed and pulled a crystalline card from inside the drone and started examining it with another tool.

"Now, Ky," Paloon glanced at her and made sure he had her attention, "what is it that you want so badly for Larin to remain quiet about that you would cause him pain?"

"Nothing," she replied and let her face reflect her irritation at the sound of Larin's chuckling. Ky really didn't want to say anything. "I have a date."

Larin exploded in laughter. Hitook's head snapped at Ky, disbelief on his face. Paloon just calmly set his work down on the table.

Paloon honestly didn't know how to take this. But he couldn't be quiet forever and just let the conversation flow. He turned in his chair and gave a look of concern to Ky, who he could tell was trying to internally justify her statement.

"May I ask, with whom?"

"The pubic information lieutenant." Ky's voice was quiet at first but then picked up a defiant tone. "I only accepted because I thought I might be able to gather information in a more informal way. Maybe I could find out something that we wouldn't be able to find in the police records. There's a chance that—"

"—you would get to—"

"Shut up, Larin." Paloon could tell by her voice that Ky was letting her emotions play here. He was doubtful that he would be able to get her to remain focused on the mission. "You could blow your cover and put all of us at risk."

Ky approached with a solid appearance of fortitude and confidence. "I know what I'm doing. I won't risk anything. I just know we could learn more through informal gossip than from anything stored in any computer system."

Maybe Paloon was wrong. Ky seemed to be thinking clearly.

"Ninja Adian," Hitook couldn't hold back the need to protest, "it won't be safe for—"

"You," Ky pointed, "stay out of it."

"Then if ya don't mind me sayin' so, missy," Mac forced himself into the conversation, "that dog don't hunt."

"What!?" Ky yelled at the computer.

"I think," Paloon inserted, "he's trying to say Knight Kendrick wouldn't approve of this."

Ky backed up and flung her arms open. "I don't care. What are you going to do to me? Send me back? I'm going as an operative, and you can't stop me."

"Oooh," Mac's accent kicked in full, "what'choo need, little girl, is an ol' fashion ass whoopin'. That'll put ya straight."

Ky flashed her fangs. "You can all lick my tail."

"The phrase is 'kiss my ass.'" Larin prided himself in colorful phrases.

"You know what I mean." Ky turned back to Paloon. "I would appreciate your approval, but I'll act without it."

Paloon pulled back the left side of his fuzzy face. He knew he couldn't stop her, but he didn't approve of it. His face became stone. "You know that, for disobeying a direct order, I have the authority to kill you?"

Ky snapped to attention and coiled her previously free tail around her leg. "Yes, sir."

The other expressions in the room didn't matter to Paloon right now; he kept focused on Ky. "Do you feel this is worth the risk?"

"Yes, I do."

Paloon wasn't sure if Ky had completely considered the situation, but he took her at her word. "Then go, and watch your back."

"Yes, sir."

"Leave," Paloon barked as he pointed to the tunnel.

Ky immediately obeyed.

With obviously fake sniffing, Larin approach a sulking Hitook and patted him on the shoulder. "It looks like our little girl has grown into a whore."

Paloon was going to reprimand, but Hitook took care of that.

In a motion so fast nether Paloon or Larin could track, the liqua's right paw reached for the rolbrid's left shoulder, snatched Larin's hand and began to twist. Then Hitook aided the movement by placing his other hand in Larin's left gut and pushing. The movement sent Larin's entire body into a two hundred and seventy degree spin that landed the rolbrid on his back, pinned to the ground by Hitook's left palm.

The large being withdrew his arms as if in shock. "I'm sorry, Lieutenant Mulkin." No one in the room could tell if his apology was genuine. "It was just a reaction. Are you okay?"

Larin grabbed his chest and spouted a short breath before slipping, "Ouch."

Chapter 10

The quiet chuckles and subdued laughter blended well with the classical piano. Coattails swayed smoothly as the musician's energy flowed into the keys. The sound of tinkling silverware, china and crystal speckled the air like sparkling glitter.

Aromas of smoked salmon, filet mignon and imported wine wafted through the rich atmosphere, while waiters and stewards masterfully and smoothly navigated the candlelit tables of suits and dresses.

A tailored tuxedo slid into view from the right. The healthy faced elderly man bowed ever so slightly. "Right this way, miss," he spoke as he gracefully led her through the beautiful maze of tables.

The shapely blue dress followed, the silk glistening in flashes as the feminine curves shifted in the most elegant of seductive walks.

Combed strains of hair sprouted like butterfly antennae to frame the slightly almond-shaped face. The rest of the dark red hair was pulled back loosely over her ears and into a ponytail that exploded in waves of curls that cascaded down her back, currently exposed by the low-cut gown.

Pink lips glistened with a fresh coat of gloss, and green eyes sparkled like the finely milled emerald earrings that hung from the tapered lobes that showed beneath the layered hair.

She held a matching blue silk purse under her left arm and trailed the maitre d'. Along the way, she seized the gaze of every straight man in the room, long enough for their significant others to take notice.

Ky had to give Mac most of the credit. From the dress designed to perfectly hide her tail to the well-selected programming chip on how to walk and act, Mac almost showed a mother's enthusiasm for helping a daughter prepare for her first prom. He even made special applications and hair designs to conceal the points of her ears from view.

But her sharp, elongated canines concerned Ky the most. She felt she needed to smile broadly to appear normal in this terran environment. If detected, she wondered if she would be mobbed or laughed at. She had to blend in enough to appear authentic so she could extract information, but deep in her being, that wasn't her major concern.

She worried about her appearance and how people saw her. Was she funny enough, too funny? Was her dress too sluttish or not formal enough? Did her smile look authentic with the thin sheets of cloakskin grafted to her canines? She had a deep-rooted desire to blend in and be liked by her date. Maybe he would even kiss her.

What was she thinking? Ky didn't know where that thought came from. She was on a mission; she had a duty. Pleasure had no place in duty. This was a sacrifice. Even if she had to sacrifice her self control if he happened to spontaneously hug her.

There it was again. It was as if these feeling were ingrained in her psyche—almost as if they were implanted by a memory chip, like the one that taught her how to walk perfectly in heels. That made sense. Maybe Mac programmed these strange feeling into the same chip.

Then, as quickly as that thought entered her mind, it left, shoved out by an extensively pre-programmed thought. And she never considered it for the rest of the evening.

From across the room, the police officer couldn't help but gaze with a smile. Melanie, as he knew her, took the award as the most attractive documentary reporter he'd ever seen. He might go as far as to say she was the most attractive woman he had ever met. He didn't know how to deal with that realization. However, he remained oblivious to the fact that "Melanie," or Ky, was not terran. This aspect explained a lot.

He sat patiently, yet eagerly, at a small table next to the wall of glass showcasing the busy nightscape of the city. He wore a black sport coat and slacks with a turquoise shirt, along with a metallic black bolo tie clasped in studded turquoise and malachite.

Before Ky could reach the table, Rick stood gracefully and stepped around it to pull out the opposite chair for Ky. She raised an eyebrow briefly at the gesture, then just took the chair as the maitre d' bowed his head and stepped away.

On the way back to his chair, Rick stopped to lift a bouquet of a dozen roses off the end of the table and offer them to Ky.

"These are for you," he said, smiling. "I hope you like them."

Humph! Why would I like a bunch of dead plants? Ky's thoughts reflected her true feelings, but then Mac's programming kicked in. "There're lovely. Thank you." Ky's lips glistened when she smiled.

Rick smiled in return; things were going well. He returned to his seat, pulling the napkin off the table and placing it onto his lap.

Rick felt he was on a roll and didn't wish to lose momentum. "You look very beautiful this evening."

So other evenings I look like a cheap tramp, is that what you're saying!? Ky didn't care for Rick's forward comment, and actually, it offended her. But from the recesses of her mind came a voice that said, "Willing prey is not as much fun, but let's see how far we can suck this prey in."

Ky locked eyes with Rick and gave a firm, full pink smile. "Thank you," she replied letting the gems in her eyes sparkle.

"What would you like to order, Mel? May I call you, Mel?"

"No."

The reply shot out so fast that it punched right through Ky's filter. Rick's eyes widened as he nodded his head.

"Sorry."

Ky attempted to compensate and rebound. "No need to be." She paused to recall her cover name. "I just prefer Melanie. Thanks."

"As you should." Rick furrowed his brow and couldn't believe he had just uttered such a stupid phrase. Then he realized his brow was still wrinkled and relaxed his face, reloaded and fired. "What would you like to eat this evening, Melanie?" Rick secretly hoped the answer would be "You." The thought made him smile.

Ky gave some thought about the few meals Mac had helped her prepare so far. But one thing did stay constant.

"I like my meat fresh."

The phrase sidelined Rick, and he had to give a light chuckle when he replied, "Excuse me?"

"You know," Ky recalled a phrase Mac had used while in one of his split personalities, "spare the fire, savor the flavor."

"Interesting insight," Rick commented before turning his attention to the waiter who had quietly approached the table.

"Good evening, my name is José," the gentleman began mildly as not to impede on any previous conversation. "I'll be your waiter this evening. If you need anything, I'll be happy to help. Would you like to hear about our appetizers?"

She didn't match the voracious appetite of a rolbrid, but Ky wasted no time and made quick work of her sixteen-ounce prime rib. She was aware of no outside stimuli, at least, nothing that could draw her attention away from her dinner.

Her hand snapped to the side of her plate and snatched a knife. It darted to the steak and flew through it as her other hand whipped over to a fork and javelined the piece. Ky's wrist sprung the chunk into her mouth. The moves were not messy; in fact, given the speed at which she was operating, they were extremely clean.

Her eyes closed, and her lips formed a smile as she chewed, enjoying the tremendously good "fresh" food.

A hum from Rick forced Ky to stop in mid-chew. Her left eye glided open to see Rick barely moving but watching her attentively. Mild amazement showed in his eyes.

"Whathhh," Ky began before gulping the half-chewed piece. "What is it?"

Rick shrugged his shoulders slightly; his hand briefly pointed his fork at her. With a puff, he began. "Nothing really. I...I just find it refreshing to actually see a woman *truly* enjoying a good steak."

From the corners of her eyes, she could see the eyes of a few other people nearby who couldn't mind their own business darting back and forth, from the company at their table to Ky and back. She placed her utensils down and straightened to a more "presentable" stance in her chair but appeared more like a student getting scolded by a strict schoolmarm.

At the sight, Rick released a huff of a laugh, and the two shared light laughter at the situation. The mutual chuckles tapered to minor snickers, and both continued with their meals after a drink of wine.

A sense of mission returned to Ky, and she put her cleverness to the test, trying not to appear too sly.

"You probably don't get much of a chance to laugh at work, do you?"

Rick cocked his head as he set his wine glass down.

"What do you mean?"

"Well, as a police officer, I would guess you probably deal with a lot of unfortunate situations: thefts, armed robberies, murder."

He stood on the verge of letting the truth slip out. As a public information officer, he really didn't deal with that stuff, but if pretending to be an actual cop worked, why not run with it?

"Every job has its ups and downs, I guess." Rick consciously made himself fix on her eyes. "Facing the risks and unfortunate situations just comes with being a police officer."

Ky's programming caught the line a mile out, but she replied with a mild look of concern as if she had found a homeless puppy. Rick took the bait, became slightly stiff and then acted as if it was nothing.

"I bet you've probably seen a lot of changes in the crime syndicates around here." Ky took a risk and a long shot diving into the subject so soon, but it felt right.

Rick paused in mid-bite. "Is it always work with you?"

Integrated programming launched without thought as it buzzed at light speed and shot a stream of thoughts into Ky's cranium.

"Not always," Ky began with a mild smile tinged with flirtation. "But some of the best fun only comes after a little work." She let the phrase float as she saw Rick's eyebrow peak briefly. The tease worked. "And modern women like me have to live our work, not just be at work, to even compete successfully."

"I doubt you have that problem." Rick straightened himself and wiped his lips with the napkin from his lap.

"You would be amazed." Ky took another drink of wine. "So what *can* you tell me about organized crime?"

There was no dodging this subject apparently, especially if Rick wanted to keep a grasp on all that the night offered.

"Over the years, organized crime syndicates have become harder to find and even harder to prosecute, thanks to a muddled legal system that's riddled with loops."

"Loops?"

"Loopholes. Even the most basic of syndicates can afford stronger attorneys than the government can hire to prosecute. The criminal lawyers not only work the legal system like putty, but they also lobby the government to embed more loopholes into the system." Rick started getting into the conversation, and it showed through his waving hands. He just hoped that if he could show his concern on the subject, it would generate more points with his date. "Most people don't know about it because they're too busy with their lives to notice. See, the wolf stopped knocking on the door years ago; now the wolf is paying government agencies to hire contractors to remove your door for him."

Ky gave a slight shrug. "That's an interesting way to put it."

"Well, it's true—so to speak."

"Would one of the local syndicates be yakuza?" She plunged in headlong this time.

Rick pulled back in minor shock and turned his head slightly to the side but kept eye contact. "Why do you ask?"

A reaction. There's something here. "Because I've heard the yakuza can be the most clever of criminal organizations."

Rick relaxed slightly. "You might be right there."

The hook: "Well?"

"Well, what?"

The bait: Ky reacted as if Rick had left her hanging. "Is there a yakuza in the area?"

He bit. "I don't like talking about that."

"Why?" She played the concern card with her look and her voice.

"The yakuza make me nervous." Rick glanced around the room. "They're practically the most invisible and untouchable bunch of them all."

"Come on," Ky smirked, cutting another piece of steak and taking a bite as if she really didn't care about the next question. "Are you going to tell me no one has any idea of even one yakuza operation? I find that kind of hard to believe."

Rick's subconscious took the words as daggers to his ego, an attack that demanded a defense.

"Of course we know; legally we've got no reason to investigate because they operate in the clear as a regular business." Rick's defensive stance seemed to seep across the border and protect the yakuza. "They're too good; we haven't been able to get squat."

Ky paused and chewed enough to, in a very unladylike manner, open the side of her mouth. "Explain."

The tone only carried the slightest color of interest. He didn't even sense Ky's dominance in the conversation.

"Well," Rick pointed arbitrarily out the window. "There's a construction company called Fairway Industries. It's suspected that the yakuza own it, and it's being used for various activities: money laundering, weapons making and drug smuggling."

"Why don't you guys *shake them down*?" Ky smiled at her joke and took a drink.

"We tried once." Rick scooted his fork around the plate for a second and gave some thought to his next statement. "A tip from an informant. We went in, but they must have seen us coming. Nothing. They threatened to sue the department. But they never did; it would be too dangerous. Besides, they got what they wanted, to smear us with bad press. To try now without hard proof could drive the yakuza deeper, and cornered animals are dangerous."

Ky gave a slight shrug and nod. "Fair enough." With three fingers she lifted her wine glass and offered a toast with a flirtatious wink, "Here's to hoping you get your man...or woman."

Rick smiled.

Anxiety forced her brow to furrow and helped to hold her lips tight. It was a fight; one she knew she'd lose.

"So I say, 'Good thing I still have my wallet.'"

Ky brought her hand to her lips as they laughed in unison. As it reached a peak, Ky opened her eyes to see her half-eaten apple crêpe dessert. She tapered her giggles while pushing away the small plate.

Rick took the opportunity and leaned forward to grab her hand. Luckily Ky kept her reflexes at bay, or Rick would have been less a hand.

He rubbed his thumb over the back of her hand as they locked eyes. "Would you be interested in going to this club I know down on Seventh Avenue?"

Initially Ky wanted to say no, but something, from somewhere, made her realize she possibly could get closer and more information.

"Sure." Her lips glistened to a slight smile.

After a call to the garçon, Rick paid in cash, big bills in hopes to impress, but it didn't register. On the way outside, he made sure to keep a hand on Ky's shoulder and held her in a side hug when he could.

The maitre d' had called a rental limo earlier, by Rick's request, and the two had no wait. Rick half barked the address to the driver as he opened the door for them. He tried to be dominating in Ky's presence, but it just came off as mildly rude.

Along the way, Rick kept an arm around Ky as they continued small talk over another bottle of wine from the limo's cooler.

Streetlights streaked along both sides of the limo as the stars loomed above, seen through the open roof. As they approached their destination, red and blue neon almost dominated the view as the cacophony of the crowd in the street and the cluster of nearby clubs commanded the sounds of the night.

While they waited for the driver to step around and open the door, Ky leaned over Rick's lap and stared in almost childish amazement through the tinted window at the glowing sign and its accompanying electronic decorations. "The Pit" glowed back in various patterns of flashing lights.

Rick unfolded out of the now open door but kept hold of Ky's hand and led her out of the vehicle. The driver received a palmed bill to which he simply replied with a slight nod of his head and a "Have a good evening, sir, ma'am."

About ten people waited in line, but Rick ignored them and aimed a slight nod at the large, baldheaded man who appeared a bit out of character in a tuxedo. The bouncer showed no reaction behind his dark shades but placed a massive hand on the door and pushed it open as the new arrivals approached.

Mild moans came from a few of the waiting women, but Ky got a few whistles. She didn't notice, but Rick took the credit.

Dulled bass thumped as Rick paid the orange-haired teller behind the thick glass. A tattoo of a dagger jutted like a tear from her left eye, and gold loops lined the crowns of her ears like bent curtain rods.

Rick hugged Ky's shoulders, stepped forward, then turned to look back and smile as he pushed his back into the second set of doors. That's when the pounding beat of the rave crashed into her very being; she could feel her bones rattle to the beat.

Litters of clubbers shuffled about and formed cliques that dotted the floor. Rick headed toward the bar, and let Ky take in the scene.

Multi-colored lights came from several corners of the dark room and streaked the fabricated fog blowing around the fingers of tube-shaped scaffolding towering to the ceiling. Countless bars of white light shot from the walls and flickered in seemingly random patterns, then Ky noticed a spider's web in the lights. The electronic drums drove the lights into the gradual pattern.

The drums abruptly gave way to an apparently infinite series of stringed instruments, as if a hundred orchestras had joined in chorus, and a tunnel of light shot across the crowd. The packed dancers shot their hands into the bottom of the light as if to grab it and mutually screamed in euphoria over the deafening electronic violins.

Rick gracefully plowed a roundabout path to the bar on the right wall as Ky watched the tunnel light pan across the sea of fingers fighting for the glow. Something about it sparked the word "ritualistic" in Ky's head. Meanwhile, others grouped about and apparently succeeded in carrying on conversations with other bystanders. The jostling mass now jumped about as drums gradually faded into the dueling symphonies.

Being led through the crowd, Ky couldn't help but notice the club's patrons appeared to run the gamut from business tycoons to gutter punks. But no one could tell if the patrons were actually what they appeared to be or if they were sporting the façades of dual personalities that only emerged in the dark of a techno club.

Ky's head unconsciously slipped into a faint nod in time to the beat when a glass jutted into her view from Rick's hand. They had arrived at the bar, and Rick held a similar drink in his other hand.

She glanced backed at the offered drink and realized she was getting thirsty. Ky took the drink, removed the thin straw and gulped the liquid before returning the empty glass and straw to the bar. It had an extremely sweet, almost fruity taste; she liked it.

"I'll have another." She aimed the words at the bartender, who didn't hesitate to wait on her.

Rick couldn't believe how much alcohol she had consumed so far, but he had no way of knowing a dextian's chemistry processed grain alcohol like water. Heck, he had no way of knowing Melanie was Ky and Ky was dextian. It didn't matter; his ego saw a challenge, and he took it.

It required a couple of gulps, but Rick got his drink down, burning his throat in the process. Water welled in his eyes, but he kept the tears from hitting his check. Success. Then he saw Ky finish her second drink. He ignored it; it didn't happen.

A fifty hit the counter, an extremely generous tip. Rick hoped she took notice, but she didn't.

"Would you like to dance?"

Ky turned just in time to see Rick pull away from her ear and nod toward the thrashing mob that had eased into the groove of an electronic ballad.

Nervousness filled her. She knew nothing of terran dances.

He didn't wait and pulled Ky through the crowd until they had made it as safely into the slowly swaying mob as possible. When Rick grasped her waist and pulled her closer, something clicked deep in Ky's head. Before she knew it, she had begun a slow dance to Rick's lead, almost as if she knew the steps.

The wordless, synthesized notes dripped with the obvious tears of a lost love. Ky's heart reached for it as she kept eye contact with Rick. Tears began to form in Ky's eyes as an unknown instrument joined the ensemble with a dirge of pain and grief.

In the middle of the melody, Ky felt something slide down her back toward—her tail!

Ky whipped Rick's hand away so fast she almost broke his wrist. Wide, green eyes bore through her dancing partner, who stumbled in shock from her actions and the resulting pain.

"Damn!" Rick shook his hand as if it would reduce the pain. "What was that for?"

Rick muttered a few more choice words as Ky attempted to analyze the situation. Obviously this dance thing wasn't going to cut it if Rick's hands wandered like some famed explorer about to discover a new land.

"Why—" Ky scanned the distance, ignoring the crowed that scowled at how the couple had exploded apart into other dancers, "Why don't we sit down? I just don't feel like dancing right now."

She didn't wait and darted a few steps ahead of a pursuing Rick. He wanted to bark something like, "You didn't have to break my arm to make a point," but his ego kept his mouth at bay to ensure he had a better chance at scoring. There was always a second chance.

When they reached what must have been the only empty booth on the balcony level, Ky slid across the cushion to look out over the fray and lose her mind in the dancing lights. Rick followed and rubbed his wrist while making an order with the waitress who desperately attempted to make a dent in the mess left on the table.

Ky's staring into the distance wasn't a good sign, but Rick's ego refused to believe it resulted from his actions. He slid his remaining good hand around Ky's shoulders and leaned forward. "What is it?"

The phrase barely made it to Ky's consciousness. "The lights."

"The lights? What about them?"

Dreamily Ky released, "They're oddly soothing."

"Soothing? How?" Rick's voice got quieter and unnoticeably closer.

"It's a calm, a rhythmic calm. I've never experienced it before."

Faint tickles rippled through her as she uncontrollably cocked her head and pressed against Rick who was nosing the bottom of her ear—her ears!

Well-trained instinct bypassed all programming this time. Terran physiology blasted into view without thought. Then with the speed of a lizard's tongue, Ky launched a finger strike into Rick's armpit.

The unsuspecting and defenseless would-be predator's body was racked by a series of spasms before it flopped forward and smashed into the remaining glasses on the table.

Ky kept calm and scanned the nearby crowd. No one had taken notice.

She picked herself up out of the seat and leapt over the crumpled cop. Ky straightened herself and her dress and made for the door.

As she exited the club, anger surged at how this had all happened. The roots of her hair took on a faint blue hue. She hadn't felt this mad in a long time.

Ignoring the waiting line of clubbers, Ky bolted into the night air. "You're going to fucking pay, Mac!"

Chapter 11

He couldn't remember how it had happened.

Had he been shot?

He didn't think so. But something about war, a violent, raging war, echoed from the recesses of his memory.

Even the scene around him told of a great battle. Fog mixed with newly birthed smoke from a thousand fires hung close and thick to the deformed wreckage strewn around the desolate battlefield. Jagged bits of metal jabbed into the sky, forming a jaw-like horizon fanged with the results of hate.

No...wait.

Somehow a flash of a vision hinted that his predicament was the result of some kind of disease, an infection that exploded from the inside out.

He had collapsed to his knees long ago, and now he no longer had the strength to hold his head up. It fell, and he saw it again. The sight made his stomach lurch and turn inside out. Though he didn't regurgitate, he felt the full, overwhelming effects of the sickening sight.

Like a scared freak show patron peeking through the fingers that now covered his eyes, he stretched out his left arm to see the damage's progress.

The last of the skin dripped away like corn syrup. A yellow, almost clear, viscous liquid seeped like sweat from his exposed muscles. The noxious liquid assaulted his nose as it coalesced into newly forming crevasses in his muscle tissue. Minor cracks soon gave way to cannons holding lakes of the foul yellow goo.

Rivers soon formed, cutting the remaining muscles into chunks. As if it was acid, the golden fluid finished the job by dicing his arm muscles into bite-sized oval bits, which slipped off to splash into the pool of liquefied skin below.

It wasn't long before a piece began to fall from between the arm's bones, and now he could see through his forearm. White stretches of bone glistened as tendons and ligaments dangled about like angel-hair pasta.

He knew he should be feeling pain, but there wasn't any. He felt what was happening to him, but he didn't feel the associated pain.

"Hello. How are you?" came a calm voice.

He jerked his head up to see who had asked the obviously stupid question. Next to him in a brown, hooded cloak stood a monk—a visitor strangely out of place in such a dreary scene—who had asked the painfully idiotic question.

The monk just stood patiently with his hands coupled and hidden in oversized sleeves. Though his head remained hooded, his face was clearly visible, although it strangely held absolutely nothing unique to aid in its description.

The man on his knees lolled his head about like a newborn baby and peered through the bleary, squinting eyes of a wino. He wanted to ask the monk's name but didn't.

"I'm fallin—," he stumbled on the words as if needing to summon his strength for each syllable. "My arm is falling away."

"Are you sure about that, my son?" The monk leaned his head forward. "Mysteries abound, and miracles live among us. Do not doubt what the eye cannot see when the signs you can see guide you to its very existence."

The injured warrior cringed, too much thought required, and his mind burned.

"What?" he replied sleepily.

The monk only uncoupled his hands and extended one to point at the injured arm.

The wounded man gradually raised the arm until it was in his view. He rolled his head forward; he couldn't believe it. His skin returned; pits and boils scared the surface, but it was back. Suddenly he felt it. His entire arm was again whole while his old arm still rotted away on the ground where it had fallen. Now he could feel a rebirth, a mass regeneration in his arm.

"Wha...H-How? I-I da...I don't understand," he released in gasps and wheezes.

The monk simply smiled and slid his hands back into sleeves. "There is much, my son, that we lack in understanding."

With a slight nod, the monk turned to face a suddenly apparent group of monks. Each shared the first monk's uncanny lack of describable facial features. The only discernible differences were the robes; each had its own shade: black, grey, red, blue, et cetera.

The first monk joined the group as they laughed and strolled away to disappear behind the smoke.

Like a jack-in-the-box, the man sprang forward and screamed into the mist. "But who are you!?"

"Well...if you must know, *again*, I'm Lyon."

Oz jerked away from the vision and took in the sight of nighttime traffic before gradually turning his head to the left to see the voice's owner looking back every so often from watching the vehicles ahead.

"You know," Lyon continued, "the one who saved your crispy carcass back at the hospital."

Reality and the vision merged temporarily. Oz felt lost in both simultaneously. Confusion compounded as he questioned the existence of existence.

Wearily, he shifted about in the passenger seat, then wondered. He stretched out his arms before him. Burnt flakes of skin had merged into a blackish-brown gooey covering like a freshly tarred road. Fingers uncontrollably fondled one another; it felt like warm plastic. The skin's tacky consistency also made it pliable, so it didn't snap back but kept its shape for a short while.

"I wouldn't do that." Lyon pointed at a peak of skin Oz had stretched from his left arm. "That's just going to give the nans more work; leave your skin alone."

Oz stared as the miniature mountain slowly sunk back until even with the rest of his arm. Halogen daggers from an oncoming car stabbed at Oz's eyes. He threw his hands up for cover, but when the car left, he found himself pulling his skin apart where his hands contacted his face.

Lyon just shook his head at the pitiful sight.

"Alex, take over and shade the front screen half, black."

Lyon released the vehicle's controls and slid his chair back and turned it ninety degrees to face a wide-eyed Oz.

"Who's driving!?" Oz questioned whether he should opt for jumping out the door.

"Didn't you hear?" Lyon nodded toward the controls. "Alex is."

"I am," came a voice from the dashboard.

Lyon gave his head a quick shake. "You'll have to forgive Alex. He's not very bright and a bit slow."

Oz blinked, and his face took on a worried look. "What?" The question had more to do with Oz's current internal debate on whether another dream had begun.

"You have to understand that there have been some really bad accidents with self aware computers in charge of vehicles, so we don't do that any more." Lyon gave it some more thought. "Well, not as a matter of course." He briefly pointed a hand at the controls again before leaning back. "Alex here isn't quick in conversation, but he does what he's told."

"You mean," Oz blinked and squinted at the dashboard, "that this is...um...running—"

"Here." Lyon reached forward to release the seat's control to turn Oz toward him so as not to put further strain on his weak neck. "If you mean, 'Is Alex a computer?' yes. Alex has full control from tire inflation to energy-ratio output. He can basically keep a steady path and maintain distance from other vehicles, although someone failed to program him with the local traffic laws.

"But," the atlantian wanted to get to the point now that the target was in his possession, "I'm more curious about how you got into this predicament."

"I can't talk about my job." The well-rehearsed statement slipped from burnt, but sticky, lips.

Lyon folded his arms and gazed with one eye. His captive had no idea how quickly Lyon could begin to retrieve the information manually, but Lyon wanted to play it nice, for now.

"Don't be an ungrateful prick."

Oz didn't take the statement as playing nice.

"Look," Lyon pointed at the slowly reconstructing skin that seemed to slightly move along Oz's arms, "I'm doing more for you than would ever be possible back at that shack of a clinic. Since I'm fixing you, the least you can do is tell me how you got this way."

Doubt slipped into Oz's mind but soon fell to flawed logic. Not everyone in Project Corona knew everything that went on; that's how they kept it secret, but if this person worked for Project Corona, he would know not to ask. So he must be some other government or military agent.

"You know I can't talk about the project, so don't ask." Oz kept calm, but some agitation seeped into his voice. "Just get me to wherever they've asked you to take me."

Lyon squinted slightly; this terran just wasn't getting it.

"Let's start with this project." Lyon's voice sounded as if Oz hadn't said anything. "Is it this 'Project Corona' you mentioned back at the hospital?"

"What?" Oz shook his head but stopped the motion when pain ripped through his chest. "Didn't you hear me? I can't tell you. If you needed to know, they would have told you, I'm sure, so knock it off. You're starting to sound like some kind of," Oz almost stopped on the last word, but it slowly left his lips, "spy."

The military in him reared at the last word. His body started to tense regardless of the pain, and Oz leaned further back in his seat as if preparing to protect himself from an unseen attack.

"Hold up there, chief." Lyon unfolded his arms in an effort to present a less aggressive appearance but then found himself with nothing comfortable to do with his hands but fidget with the armrests. "I'm not here to harm you or make secrets public."

"Then who in the hell are you?" Oz almost yelled it as a demand.

Lyon knew this might come up; he didn't want it to, though. Thinking about it seemed kind of silly, but he had followed a fortune-teller's hint to find this guy who was supposedly the key to breaking a code to keep an alien race from blowing this planet's cover and causing its destruction. He could just lie, but he'd gone this far.

He screwed his jaw to the left and stared at Oz with his right eye before releasing his face.

"I'm a behind-the-lines police officer from a universal law enforcement agency created to ensure all races within our jurisdiction comply with mutual laws and face punishment for violations." Lyon spouted, converting it to something he hoped would be more understandable to a terran. "Roughly."

Oz's face went slack as he thought about the answer. Then it came to him. "Bullshit." The word hung for a couple of seconds. "Do you think I'm that fucking stupid? Whoever you are, I'm not telling you jack shit."

"You hold a secret, and no one believes you when you tell it." Lyon peered skyward briefly while anger began to rear its head. "Look, terran, so far I haven't found out why I need you alive. After what I just told you, I have all rights to kill you and blow this entire episode off as a misguided attempt to follow a lead that went nowhere."

"Some kind of *police officer* you are. You say you're not going to harm me one minute and that you're going to kill me the next." Oz used this verbal battle to find loopholes in this nutcase's story. "What kind of police officer kills someone who's unarmed?"

"I do." Lyon jabbed a thumb into his chest. "I said, 'police officer,' because that's the only equivalent phrase in your language. I'm authorized to kill any being if I witness a crime, or if a target willfully impedes me from killing the guilty, willfully assists the guilty or, in your case, risks blowing my cover."

Lyon's wood-grained eyes formed spears, and Oz almost felt the points burrowing into his mind. But Oz refused to let this loony win.

"What if you're wrong? What if you kill someone who's not guilty? What if you kill someone just because your day started out bad after you burnt a bagel in the toaster?" Oz attempted to glare back but couldn't pull off the same power as had been thrown upon him. "People make mistakes."

Lyon relaxed a little and tried to remind himself that before him sat a terran.

"Because you're ignorant and ill-informed, I'll try to take this slow." Lyon clasped his hand over his gut and began. "Where I come from, the dead have rights; those rights are more important than the rights of the living. You kill someone; I'll drop you cold. No second thoughts. There's no trial. You get no fucking appeals. And you don't go scot-free because someone forgot to say you're under arrest."

"But what if you're wrong?"

Lyon took a deep breath and calmed himself.

"I'm never wrong." Lyon had force behind that statement. "Few are. When it is thought that a member of Corps acted incorrectly, that's when it gets ugly. If the Corps suspects that someone acted out of place, didn't witness the event or fabricated justification, that person gets scanned.

"You can't even image how painful that is." Lyon lifted his clasped hands and aimed a thumb into his lower chest. "I've had the displeasure of witnessing it. Let's just say most survive, but barely.

"If, after that scan, they find even one iota of malicious intent to kill without due cause, you become the ship's scream for the next week."

Lyon closed his eye and cringed at some bad memories.

"What do you mean?"

It took some time, but Lyon brought himself around and forced himself to reply, although it came out almost as if he had no power left to him.

"Torture." The word bled from his mouth. "The person is kept in a constant screaming state for one week before being allowed to die. It's punishment to repay for the rights of the dead. But I believe the shipmates are the ones who pay." Lyon's eyes held a deep eerie look of knowing as he stared at the dashboard. "No one in the ship can get away from it. For an entire week you eat, sleep and live with the most dreadful of sounds penetrating your being."

The knight seemed to float away in thought, thoughts he'd rather forget. Oz sensed something genuine in his apparent rescuer's voice, so he gulped before the next challenge. Something deep in him told him to be quiet, but he couldn't stop himself.

"What if the person doing the scanning is wrong?"

"Look damn it!" Lyon's persona came back in full force and stronger than before. Anger came alive in his eyes. He was a knight on a mission and didn't have to stand for this; it was impeding a case, as far as Lyon was concerned. "I want some damn answers, now! I volunteered for what was supposed to be a plush assignment, but I now find myself in p'tahian territory trying to stop some other race from exposing your existence on this planet so those blue shits don't pop on over to vaporize the lot of you while I'm trapped on this fucking rock when I'm not even sure my ancestors came from this decrepit gene pool!"

Lyon drew another deep breath, mainly through his nose this time since his jaws and lips were clamped tight. Fingers dug into palms as Lyon bolted looks around the van before realizing he wanted some kind of reply. Yet when Lyon took a look at Oz, he knew something was terribly wrong.

Skin around his face went from its previous coal appearance to a light brown. Bloodshot grey eyes gazed from behind unblinking lids. The look on Oz's face was locked between a trance and utter fright.

When Lyon reached to nudge Oz out of it, he found Oz's body locked, as if suffering from rigor mortis.

"What the...?" Lyon had no idea how a body with malleable plastic for skin could have suddenly hardened like a rock. "Crap!"

Lyon dove into the back of the van and riffled through the medical bay to whip out the four remaining patches tagged with a green light.

"Alex," Lyon began as he slammed the bay door closed and rushed over to Oz as quickly as he could in the confines of the van, "you had better start programming more pads. I'm going to need them."

"Which medical program would you like?" came the vehicle's calm voice.

"The same one I've been using, idiot!" Lyon didn't have time to fight with the computer, and he cursed it as he ripped away more of Oz's clothing to slap on the patches.

Chapter 12

Brisk wind whipped around sporadically, sometimes pushing from multiple directions at once. The gusts mimicked what brewed above. Wisps of grey preceded a thrusting black mass that rapidly consumed stars as it covered the night sky.

Unlike the specks of suns, the moon proved harder to swallow. It fought to shine through for several minutes before the density of the thunderhead devoured the invading light.

Avians darted about in swaying flocks that skimmed the cityscape.

Jagged streams of light fractured the sky as glowing bolts flickered from behind layers of clouds, reminiscent of scenes from a distant battle. Most of the lightening bolts hopped from layer to layer, but as they increased in intensity, more beams of electrons blazed charged paths to the numerous rods protruding from rooftops.

Heat escaped the area and soared to the colder upper atmosphere. The resulting temperature drop gave birth to a mist layer of sorts, not rain, more like fog, gradually taking shape over the buildings and creating a blanket that blurred the window lights and high-rise billboard signs.

A chill cut through his duster and heightened Hitook's sense of dread that grew from witnessing the scene unfolding before him. Weather tended to be different from planet to planet. He'd never see anything such as this. It most likely happened often, as common as the stars shine, but the liqua couldn't shake the sensation that the sight formed an omen, one he knew too little about to read properly.

He pawed a fedora and readjusted it on his head, since it had grown too irritating to his ears in its current position. Hitook gradually looked about as he slid his paw back into his jacket pocket.

From across the roof, Paloon sat on the raised edge and watched Hitook shift about but kept quiet. While the hunter remained busy doing a final structural check on each corner of the flat octagon drone leaning against his lap, he still kept an eye on Hitook.

The liqua had asked if he could watch Paloon launch the drone, but since they had reached the roof, Hitook seemed to have more interest in the sky than in what Paloon did. As the hour crept along, Paloon took note that Hitook grew more agitated.

"Is there something on your mind?"

Hitook turned his head to see that Paloon's attention didn't seem to leave the new drone.

"No, not really."

Paloon laid the small spray-bottle shape tool he was using on his lap before grabbing the drone with both hands like a steering wheel. He then rotated it before continuing to follow the seams with the tool retrieved from his lap.

"Not really?" Paloon peered at Hitook without moving his head. "You're not sure if something is on your mind? That sounds like something is, and you're thinking about it.

"Ever try talking about it?" Paloon added. "It may help. Besides, I'm bored; you haven't said a thing since we got here."

Hitook shifted back to the weather phenomenon before him. Paloon almost thought the liqua had ignored the statement.

"I sense an eerie presence from this planet's nature, Hunter Osluf."

A terran hearing the statement, even with the tones of sincere truth with which Hitook spoke, would have blown it off as if the overgrown lagomorph had fallen for some superstition or believed an old-wives' tale. Paloon knew otherwise. Members of House Bravo were trained to be sensitive to many facets of the universe's nature. Sure, Hitook was only an acolyte, but Paloon didn't ignore it.

"Eerie how?"

Hitook shifted his black duster without removing his paws.

"I'm unable to describe it." The liqua looked over his shoulder briefly to see if Paloon shifted his visual attention his way; he hadn't. "I've never felt anything like this before. This is new."

Paloon made additional note of the comments, but his checks were nearing their end, so he focused on that.

"We're ready." Paloon set the tool on the tarred asphalt roof, stood and walked to the center of the roof pushing the drone, which rolled in thumps.

Hitook turned to silently witness the event.

With less than a whisper, Paloon called the drone's command menu to his vision. A few mental pokes through the menus triggered an unfolding control console and ignited the engine. Paloon pushed the octagon disk to the ground, but it didn't go far. A few inches from his hand, the drone halted, floated and leveled off.

"Mac, what have you got?" Paloon waited for a reply as he walked around the drone to make a final visual check, even though there would be no chance to "see" anything at this point.

"Hold up, hold up." In Mac's fashion, the computer sounded as if he was being rushed for no particular reason. *"Give me a moment. I wasn't ready."*

Some eye movement from Paloon activated the drone's self-diagnostics. Gauges, charts and meters popped in and out of the hunter's vision as the systems tripled checked each other.

"Well," Mac fired sarcastically, *"I can see it!"*

Paloon squinted then rolled his eyes before starting the visual cloak. Shimmering light waves coated the smooth metallic surface before it blinked out of the visual realm.

"How about now?"

"I saw it as the cloak activated." Mac's cocky sound paused, but his logic circuits forced him to admit defeat. *"But I don't see it now."*

"Any other detection?"

"No." Mac's current mood didn't like defeat. *"Can I go now?"*

"Yeah." Paloon no longer needed the computer. *"Scram."*

Paloon shook his head in slight disappointment at how finicky Mac could be and began to think about how annoying it had become, as if it was a spoiled child without his parent around. Though Hitook could hear the conversation, he never reacted to the exchange.

Unseen, the drone lifted and zoomed to space, but Hitook still watched the area in front of him.

"It's gone already." Paloon pointed to the sky. "That's it, nothing fancy."

Hitook quietly watched the same space for a little while longer before turning around to watch the skyline and the developing storm.

Paloon thought the reaction odd.

"Is it her?"

"What do you mean?" Hitook didn't change from his new stance.

The atlantian stepped next to the coated liqua. "Ninja Adian. Are you thinking about her?"

"Some."

"Did you guys work together before getting assigned with this team?"

"No."

"Then what is it between you two?"

"What do you mean?"

Paloon wondered if Hitook thought he was too clever for anyone to notice.

"Your feelings are not completely private; they're not overly public, but they are somewhat obvious."

Hitook didn't say a word and continued to watch the weather.

"That stunt you pulled yesterday was no *automatic* reaction. I can already tell you have too much control to let anything happen automatically."

Hitook's head gradually rotated as his eyes slid over and down at Paloon, who now just stared forward.

"You're lucky Larin didn't blast a hole in your gut." With those words, Paloon returned Hitook's look. "Be mindful of your feelings for her, be sure, but more important, be clear when we need you. It's not so much an order as advice."

"What you are noticing is nothing more than camaraderie." Hitook returned to his unassigned watch post. "She's a fellow House Bravo, a ninja, so I have concern for her well being and a wish for her success."

"If that's your story." Paloon walked back to pick up his tool and headed for the fire escape ladder off the roof. Before he descended, he wanted the last word. "Don't try to fool yourself by trying to fool others; the only one who's the fool tends to be you."

Paloon then disappeared from the scene to leave Hitook on the roof.

The liqua stayed in his stance; the rain came and pelted his duster. Drops slapping leather gave Hitook something to focus his thoughts on. He had focused so much he almost missed the faint scream in the distance.

Hitook gave a slight smile, yet no one remained to notice.

His world at this moment consisted only of a two inch by one inch by half inch slab of blue crystal. The silk-like avenues weaving a network of connections in the three-dimensional circuit board were packed so tight it shimmered like a shattered diamond. Logical order so intense radiated an apparent beauty only possible in the randomness of nature itself. But this beauty in blue was being violated.

Two yellow orbs penetrated every shimmering line and broke through each glistening net of nano-transistors. The violation didn't damage, but it obviously was a hunt, a hunt in which the prey unknowing hid under and between three-dimensional layers of atomic circuitry.

Mocha-skinned digits gradually rotated the blue rectangle and halted temporarily at times to teeter the board back and forth so Larin could get a better look through the mind-boggling web of connections. It had to be here. It wouldn't take much, and Larin found it highly improbable that the manufacturer didn't leave—Bingo!

Larin froze his hands to keep the blue circuit at its current angle as his yellow eyes formed squinted slits. About three-quarters of an inch deep from the side, an unflawed three-sixteenths cube of sapphire peeked from behind almost countless layers of glistening fibers of connections. The find should be just enough to burn the subjective nano-processor needed for the modification.

"Pop!"

The rolbrid's well-rehearsed reflexes fired in response. A collapsible pistol shot from his long-sleeve jacket and sprang to its full size just as Larin's hand gripped it and scanned the room. The echoing sound that mimicked a loading thermal rifle had just started to dissipate as girlish giggling got louder.

Brown-haired pigtails bounced as the little girl in Mac's screen laughed behind the pink plastered on her face. Larin watched in mild confusion while the girl's hands picked away at the gum and stuffed it back in her mouth. Oddly, the gum didn't stick to her hair.

With a flick of Larin's wrist and a twist of his arm, the blaster disappeared back into the jacket sleeve. The rolbrid had no interest in entertaining Mac's current persona and went back to now relocating the area he needed. Mac refused to be ignored so easily.

"Wha'cha doin'?" The words bubbled into the room between smacks of gum chewing.

Larin attempted to ignore the question. He may have succeeded if it hadn't been for the inevitable whining "Huuuuuhhh?"

"I'm looking for board space, so go away."

"Why?"

"Because I need it; buzz off."

"Why?"

"I want to burn a processor."

"Why?"

"I'm testing a modification."

"Why?"

"I frapping want to! Now, shove the gum up your ass and go the frap away!"

Mac's eyes popped wide as her tiny jaw dropped. The computer couldn't believe what she just heard. Shock faded to sadness.

"Wwhhhaaaaaaaaaaaaaaaaaaa!" Tears, as if from a playground water fountain, flowed from tightly shut eyes. The once cute, childish face now contorted itself into the image of a horrid demon.

Larin slammed the crystal circuit board on the table and growled. "Why in the hooha do you have to be so frapping annoying?"

"But...(sniffle)...but," Mac paused to snort back dripping mucus, "I just wanted to help."

Larin leered at the sobbing computer screen. "How?"

"Well," the childish visage pouted, "I could've helped you find it." Light beamed from the child with an idea. "Put it down; I'll show you."

The rolbrid twisted his chin in doubt, but at least Mac's current personality seemed less annoying now. He pushed the partially dismantled particle cannon away to create room and slid the crystal board to a more open area on the table before tossing a finger at Mac to do whatever he wanted to do.

Light pranced around the object, invading but not damaging the internal structure. Just as the activity dissipated, glowing lines streaked the air above as a hologram duplicated the blue-crystal circuit in a thrice-enlarged replica. The copy rotated as it floated. In sequence, three, green circles blinked into existence on the duplicate.

Mac stopped the hologram flat to Larin's line of sight. Lines sprouted from the circles to boxes that soon filled with stats on the available locations.

"There are three useable locations remaining," Mac began in the girl's voice but in a more formal way that seemed unnatural. "With some creative navigation it should even be possible to interconnect them if you need multiple processors or interconnected data storage or a fuzzy logic circuit in pieces. What do you need?"

"Are you saying you could burn it too?"

"Absolutely." Mac returned to smacking her gum. "I doubt I'll be fast at it, but I'll most definitely be more accurate than that portable crystal tweaker you've got on the table."

Larin glanced down at the unit that sat in its collapsed form, which resembled a toaster oven. He frowned slightly as he realized that he *was* actually going to try to add programming to such a sensitive board with a very rudimentary machine, when compared to the complexity of the job. One hiccup and he would have fried the board and rendered the weapon useless.

"What are you up to!?"

Mac and Larin turned to see Paloon standing on the lower deck of the stairs. Paloon's eyes darted about the center table as his subconscious attempted to count the multitude of pieces that obviously had once formed a particle cannon.

"Please tell me you can put that back together; otherwise, we're down one cannon, and that wouldn't be good."

"It'll be even better by the time I'm done," Larin turned back to run a finger through the hologram. "I've got a plan to improve it. It's only a theory right now, but it's a solid theory."

"And I'm helping!" Mac excitedly bounced up and down while bobbing her head like a dashboard decoration.

Paloon flared his lips at the monitor as he descended the final stretch of stairs. "What is it this time?"

Larin glanced back to determine what Paloon meant. "Oh," he turned back, "I'm convinced that twitch is getting more annoying by the hour."

"Hey!" Mac held still long enough to make her pouting face seen before switching topics. "Mr. Paloon, I have a message for you."

Paloon planned to ignore the computer and talk to Larin more about what he was up to but stopped with Mac's next words.

"Mr. Lyon said he should be here in about fifty minutes."

Paloon froze where he stood, with one hand on the table and his back half-bent toward the chair. His eyes closed. "When was this?"

"Um," the girl peered upward and rocked side to side, "about a half hour ago, I guess."

Anger seeped into his face as the hunter stood and spun to face the computer. "How long ago!?"

The girlish voice dropped and went cold. "Twenty-eight minutes, forty-two seconds."

"Damn it, I was on the roof, why didn't you let me know?"

The girl's voice didn't stay away for long. "He asked if you were here, but only Larin was in the room, so I said, 'No.' So he left a message for me to deliver when I next saw you."

"But I was on the—" Grumbling rattled in Paloon's throat. "Was there anything else?"

"Yeah, like where the frap he went?" Larin didn't move from his work.

"Well," Mac took an exaggerated worried expression, "he wanted a med room prepped with the portable replicators."

That stopped Larin.

"What the...?" Paloon shifted his weight. "Is he wounded?"

"No, he didn't say, but it didn't sound like he was."

"Did he say anything else?"

"He did want Ky and Hitook to prepare for an SSRR."

Larin jumped from his seat. Even a ground-pounder like himself knew the acronym for a spiritual search, rescue and repair. Something must have gone bad.

Paloon pointed at the ceiling. "Get Hitook; I'll find the replicators. We've got less than twenty, move."

The mission dictated that the two rush out of the room as Mac blew another bubble.

Chapter 13

Electric humming replaced the clanking thud of the portable, tube-like replicator as it slid off Paloon's shoulder and landed solidly on its base. Mac took immediate control of the unit and began synchronizing it with the three tubes already placed in the other corners of the room.

Paloon stood to relax briefly as he reflected on what had been done so far and what they might have missed.

The room branched off from the main basement and was about the size of a normal bedroom. Strangely, it was already equipped with a combat med table; Mac said Lyon had installed it several months ago as a contingency, even though he didn't have a plan on how he would make it to the med table if seriously wounded. Shaped like an overgrown dental chair, the combat med table resembled those found in spacecraft, designed for flexibility in limited space. Each part of the chair was formed with multiple, prehensile metal plates.

Various types of medical equipment spotted the tops of a few dresser-like tables in the room. They had no idea what kind of equipment Lyon might need, and all attempts to contact him had failed. So Larin had found some medical equipment in lockers while Paloon, after much debate with a stubborn French general who would disagree that stars shine if he didn't get to state that fact first, finally got Mac to make some additional primitive supplies, such as scalpels and various bandages.

"Paloon!"

Paloon darted his head and eyes around like an alert dog in the night looking for the cat he knows is there, just not where. He poked his head out of the room to see Lyon's visage floating above the table.

"Hey, where are you?" Paloon stepped out of the room, toward the table and past a meditating Hitook, who squatting near the entrance.

"I'm a few miles outside of the city." Lyon's bust glanced to the right and back to face Paloon. "How are the preparations?"

"Okay, I guess. We have no idea what you need. We tried to contact you but got no answer."

"Well, that's because I mistakenly told Alex here to stop talking until we get back. He was annoying me, but now he won't reply to anything. I guess that includes telling me there's an incoming call." Lyon watched an oncoming car and frowned. "You've got to fix this computer."

"What are you talking about?" Paloon was taken aback. There was no way Lyon's troubles with Alex could even come close to his problems with Mac. "Only if you fix *your* computer. This dang thing is more temperamental than a grouchy, bipolar schizophrenic."

"Oooh," Lyon cringed as he poked one eye at the screen, "that bad, huh?"

"I'm trying to be nice."

Lyon paused. "It can't be that bad; he told you I was calling."

"Actually, no. You just showed up, floating above the table. I didn't even know he could project such images."

Lyon hummed a single note but didn't explain himself.

"How far have you gotten in the preparations?"

"The replicators are up, and we've got some basic supplies and equipment ready for you. But," Paloon scanned Lyon one last time to verify the obvious, "you don't look injured. What gives?"

"I'm not injured, but my target it."

"Target?" Paloon didn't like the fungus feeling of being kept in the dark. "What target? And why isn't he dead?"

"He's not a termination." Lyon twisted his face briefly. "He's a possible informant."

"Possible?" Paloon grabbed the nearest chair; this might take a while. "There's no possible about it. You know procedure; if it's not a definite informant, terminate. Latitude on covert ops can get you killed. We don't need this kind of risk, and I don't appreciate you bringing this risk—"

"*If* he poses a risk, I will terminate," Lyon raised his voice and turned to the camera, "but I don't have to explain myself."

The statement loitered in silence.

Paloon folded his arms and raised one brow. "Okay, if that's the game. I just hope you don't place the rest of the team at risk."

Lyon knew Paloon's comment meant the hunter wouldn't hesitate to kill his current commander if justified. Time didn't allow for more discussion.

"Get Mac starting on nanite shots for severe radiological exposure, the full spectrum. Where do you have it set up?"

Paloon used his thumb to indicate the space behind him. "In the center side room."

"Put in a window. I'll be there in about fifteen minutes. The patient will most likely be unconscious, so we'll need to transport him."

Lyon reached toward the screen, and the hologram fizzled as it disappeared in front of Paloon.

Paloon released a short hum before standing.

"You heard it, Mac, so I don't want any bullshit. Just give me a window and don't ask for specs."

The computer remained quiet this time as light coalesced into the item Paloon had requested. Paloon took the pre-framed window and placed it against the door. Tiny, pre-charged torches cut the hole as Paloon pushed it in, then the frame clamped home.

Hitook was still squatted nearby in his meditation trace. Paloon figured correctly that the liqua soared deep in mental preparations. But he couldn't have been further from the truth when he guessed that no one else heard the conversation.

Anger played no part; he moved with pure survival instincts.

Paloon rummaged through the weapons locker. He passed by the standard issue particle cannon; he didn't even take notice of the acid pistol. He wanted something more. Death served as the only desired outcome. Paloon thirsted for definitive death. Questionable results had no place.

The answer came.

Paloon withdrew a heavy pistol, slightly larger than the particle cannon. A crisscrossed grip design and two elongated domes on the top made it obvious that atlantians didn't design it. This symbol of death was jexan in origin.

The two elongated, golden domes served as the equivalent of barrels for the hyperkinetic molecule accelerator. Simply put, the weapon was the ultimate shotgun that fired practically invisible specks of matter at the target with deadly precision and in a continuous burst as if a laser. Very few suits of armor could withstand a direct hit for very long.

Paloon navigated his hand through the modified grip to get used to the feel. He lowered it to his side as the combat weapon clip he had attached earlier to his belt sensed the weapon and magnetically grabbed hold. It took a little work to get his hand out of the grip.

He stopped and visually examined the combat molecule feeder clip. Options seemed endless. One clip could lay waste to the entire building, but that would not be needed in this case.

"Close the locker."

Paloon turned around to the table as Mac quietly obeyed. A thud and respective clicks sounded from the now closed door.

"Is this—"

"Keep out of it." Paloon's eyes didn't even acknowledge Mac. Time didn't allow it.

A long tray with a toolbox-like handle rested on the table. Black squares with soft, round corners formed two rows within the tray. They clattered against each other as Paloon took the handle and jerked the tray from the table before heading out of the room and through the tunnel connecting to the vehicle bays on the other side of the street.

Silence within the vehicle bay didn't last as the rattling tray got louder. The grey lighting in the other room fought to make a strong shadow of Larin who, with folded arms and closed eyes, leaned against the tank of a station wagon. None of the light fixtures won; all succumbed. The result was shaded petals of faint shadows sprouting from Larin's torso against the back hatch and ground.

When the noise tapered off, Larin guessed correctly that Paloon had arrived.

"In case you're wondering, Ky's still not back."

No reply came, so one eye slid open to look at Paloon. After a quick scan, Larin couldn't resist.

"What's with the artillery? Is there a war?"

Paloon didn't answer directly. "You are armed, right?"

If Larin was even a half-decent member of Harquebus, he had multiple weapons on him, so Paloon knew the answer but asked to make the point. The question hit the mark.

Larin opened both eyes and just stared and waited.

"Just follow my lead." Paloon walked over to one of the benches along the wall and set the tray down. Then he took the black units out of the tray one by one, thumbed a switch and stuck the square on his left arm. Each unit's biomagnetic seal took hold of Paloon's skin. Soon they almost covered his arm. "If he—"

"Paloon, this is Lyon. Can you hear me?"

The hunter stopped and turned to look at Larin, who heard the communication in his head as well.

"Yes," Paloon replied.

"Good. I'm a few blocks away. Are you ready?"

"As ready as we are going to be."

"See you in a few."

Larin pushed away from his leaning stance, faced Paloon and waited for the remainder of his explanation. When Paloon offered no more, he repeated himself.

"What's with the atom shooter?"

Paloon attached a few remaining units to his other arm before acknowledging.

"Lyon may be putting the mission and us at risk. If that proves to be true, I'll take command, and we'll terminate Lyon—if it comes to that."

The lieutenant didn't react visibly and kept a cold stare on Paloon as the warrior's brain calculated possibilities.

Metal rattled above, muffled by the concrete roof. The van released a short squeal as it came to a stop. Paloon made a mental note to take a look at the brakes, but he felt uncertain about working on such rarely used technology.

Mac took a silent command from Lyon and started the lowering process. Hydraulics hissed with a piercing squeal. As the platform lowered, Paloon raised his right arm and rested his hand on the pistol, forcing the point to dig itself slightly into his leg.

Once the van came to a stop, the covering doors responded to an order to close, and the driver's door opened.

"Do you have some MUs?" Lyon asked as he came around the van, his hand aimed for the rear latch. Then he stopped.

Lyon's eyes locked on the hyperkinetic molecule accelerator, known as a Vortex within the Corps.

Except for the security bars resonating with clicks as they locked, the room was quiet. Paloon's right fingers tapped the side of the weapon in slow precession. Larin stood by with his arms still folded. The light painted faint shadows on their faces, helping to hide any non-verbal signs.

Lyon kept a pistol in the small of his back; who wouldn't? He could take one, maybe both, but coming out of it without a wound didn't look likely. If Paloon didn't get him, Larin definitely would; Lyon didn't doubt that fact.

Time became surreal. Minutes could have passed; no one in the room would have known otherwise.

Each side measured the opposition and weighed the available advantages and disadvantages. If he had to, Larin knew he could splatter Lyon across the concrete behind him, but the thought of staring down a knight still sent his hearts pounding in unison.

One flinch away from his weapon, Lyon ignored it and threw open the van doors.

He jumped into the back and reached his hand out. "Here. Give me some. We need to get him moved quickly."

A gamble, yes, but Lyon realized if they truly felt the need to kill him, he wouldn't have made it out of the van. As patiently as he could, he waited, squatting, and looked out the back of the van.

Time slipped by and no one approach the van.

"Look," Lyon dropped his extended arm, "why don't you see this *threat* first before judging the situation?"

A few moments later, Larin stepped around the open door. His yellow eyes fell on a blackened body lying on a combat gurney but contorted in a frozen position as if sitting down.

"What the frap is that? Did it follow you home, or do you just think it's cute?"

"Neither." Lyon offered his hand again as Paloon approached after Larin's words. "Could you hand me a few of those?"

Lyon pointed at the MUs on Paloon's arm, but the hunter didn't reply immediately as he scanned the body.

Paloon slowly picked off a handful and placed them in Lyon's waiting hand. "What did this?"

"That's what I want to find out." Lyon started affixing the geomagnetic units on various parts of the body. "You should have seen him before. He has improved considerably. But the cause still baffles me, and I want to know how the terrans were able to stabilize him."

Lyon motioned for more units and Paloon obliged before squeezing into the other side of the van to begin helping.

"Stabilized?" Paloon glanced at Lyon after placing the units. "This looks like serious rigor mortis." Paloon tried to flatten a leg.

"Don't." Lyon waved a hand. "This condition is recent, and I have no idea how it happened. One moment he's talking, the next, nothing, frozen in position."

"Then why bring him here?" Larin watched and picked his teeth with a thumbnail.

"Because I think he knows what happened to him, and he's not telling." They were out of MUs and began climbing out of the van. "But I want to know."

"But we shouldn't be bringing natives here." Before Larin finished the statement, he realized why Paloon had the cannon on his hip.

Paloon just glared at Lyon as he stood outside the van.

Lyon felt the tension return to the atmosphere.

"What happened to Oz is a—"

"You've been sharing names!?"

"Let me finish." Lyon didn't stare down Paloon for long, no need in antagonizing a possible executioner. He looked back as Oz. "What happened to him isn't terran; it couldn't be. What happened to him could be a clue to the other non-native activity on the planet. If he does know what happened, he's a lead, not a liability."

"But we don't know that." Larin fired.

"And we'll never learn if he's dead." He nodded softly at Paloon. "Let's find that out first."

Several thoughts stormed through Paloon's mind before he made his decision and sent a mental order to Mac to activate the MUs spotting the blackened body.

Each unit released a slight hum as they synchronized to lift the body level and intact in its original contortion. As the party turned to follow the tunnel into the store basement, the body bobbed slightly, as if encased in water.

Lyon saw Hitook sitting against the wall and glanced around as the tunnel opened into the room.

"Where's Ky?" he asked while watching Oz's body float around and through the door into the makeshift medical room.

"Well—" Reluctance took root in Paloon's voice. "She's on a...date."

A bent finger rapped on the newly installed glass plate in the door. "Nice job," Lyon commented.

Oz glided into the surgery seat as Lyon entered the room, grabbed a tray stand from the corner and pulled it behind him toward the body. As Lyon began plucking MUs from Oz, Paloon began to relax. But relaxation came a bit too soon.

"That's funny."

"What's that?" Paloon asked as he reached for a MU.

"I thought I heard you said she was on a date."

Paloon exhaled audibly. "She is."

Lyon raised his head to see what he expected to see, concern. "If you're here, Larin's here, Hitook's here, who's her date? Mac?"

Larin backed a few more steps from the door before turning around and deciding to wait on the opposite side of the larger room.

"She's on a date with a possible informant."

"Who, may I ask?"

"A police lieutenant."

Lyon returned his visual attention to removing the remaining MUs. "A terran?"

He didn't need an answer, but Paloon replied.

Until now, Lyon had placed the MUs somewhat quietly into the tray, but he let the last one fall onto it from half a foot, clattering needlessly.

A devilish smile crawled across Lyon's lips. "You're ready to blast my atoms into oblivion, and you let Ky go on a non-mission-essential date with an unknown native. Why don't I return the favor and paint the wall with your brain?"

Stillness commanded the room as the two stared at each other for a while.

"We couldn't get any information from the computers, so we felt it worth the risk for Ky to attempt a social retrieval of the information."

Lyon smirked, "I bet she talked you into it, but regardless, I feel he," a finger pointed at Oz, "is worth the risk. We're on even ground, so keep the atom shooter in its holster."

The knight turned and poked through some of the equipment until he found the shot gun. Bottles rattled as fingers flipped through them to find the kinds of nanites he needed. Once found, Lyon slid the bottle into the back of the gun and pushed shot after shot into about every part of Oz's body.

Spent, Lyon released the bottle into a waste bin and loaded a new type of nanites before repeating the procedure.

Lyon pointed the gun at the door, a sign for Paloon to leave, before setting it on a short table and leaving the room himself. He shut the door behind him and turned to see through the window.

"All right, Mac, fire it up."

The remote transponders gradually began to glow a faint green.

"Do whatever you can." Lyon dropped his head to look at Hitook, who still hadn't moved. "You're all I have, Hitook." A response wasn't need; Lyon knew the acolyte could hear him. "I don't care if you've got to cross the metaplanes, bring him back."

Chapter 14

"A tarot card!?"

Doubt and disbelief rarely merged to take form as an almost palpable thing, as they did now in the basement command center. The emotion ascended to cloud the room and invade the space like the early morning fog rolling from a swamp. Though alligators didn't hide in this fog, Lyon could feel Paloon's gnashing teeth as he spit the question.

Lyon dreaded the discussion, but regardless of how much he tried to put it off, he knew the inevitable would finally occur.

He tensed his jaw and from his chair prepared to joust Paloon with his extended forefinger. "There's more than—"

"What!? Did you pick us from a dice throw!?" Paloon threw his arms wide rocking back in this chair before screaming forward and slamming his hands on the table. "What could possibly justify this!?"

"She's a visionary." Fact, not question. Lyon knew it deep within his bones.

"More like a pythoness."

"What!" In atlantian, "pythoness" brought with it some serious negative connotations that Lyon didn't want applied to his adopted grandma. "How dare you!? She's got more divination skills than most I've seen."

"She's been properly trained then?" Paloon knew that was impossible.

"Maybe not. Her skill is raw, not created; it just happens for her." Lyon started to let his care for the old lady show. "It gives her nightmares at times because she can't control it."

"Awww," Paloon childishly mocked, "she has nightmares."

Lyon threw himself from the chair and pounded his palms against the table. His eyes glided across the room to stop at Larin, who leaned back in his chair, his feet on the table and his arms crossed.

This conversation had no future on its current path. No one could deny the facts.

"Are you blind?" Lyon threw a finger at the door by which Hitook sat quietly. "That toasted terran took enough radiation that he should have decomposed days before I found him. That's neither natural nor native."

Lyon dropped the arm and walked over to peer through the window at Oz. A faint green light from the transponders filled the room. With a spin on his feet, Lyon turned back to Paloon.

"Explain it."

Mac had confirmed the possible cause and extent of the burns and detected in the terran's body a chemical cocktail designed to stabilize the radioactive decay, something that must have been introduced within minutes of the accident. The computer even claimed that most of the chemicals had to be made in zero gravity, something very unlikely for this planet's civilization.

Paloon just glanced away briefly before returning his gaze to Lyon. A sea of grey whiskers rippled as the hunter screwed his chin in abject frustration. He hadn't figured out an answer to that one, yet.

"You can't." Lyon approached the table again. "Oz seems to have stared down a tactical nuke and lived. Regardless of how I found him, there's something not right here, and I want to know how—"

At first, Larin stared past Lyon; then Paloon turned his head to also take notice. Lyon cocked his head down and to the left to see what grabbed everyone's attention.

Standing in the corner, Ky's twisted face almost completely hid her eyes. Wisps of her hair frizzed in multiple directions, and high-heeled shoes dangled from her right hand. Her tail had fallen to the floor long ago, and growls rumbled through the room.

"Ky," Lyon straightened, "welcome back."

She snapped her head but kept from blasting him across the room; she knew who she wanted. Her target couldn't stay quiet for long.

"Ky!" An extremely chipper voice came from Mac. "Do tell. I want to know all the details from—"

Screeching forced the room's other occupants to clasp their hands over their ears. Ky kept her teeth clenched as her head shook as if she had a bad nervous twitch.

"Uhhh," Mac started to catch on a second before it happened. "Aaaahhhhh—"

From deep in Mac's metal paneling, a distinctive clink resonated. Paloon knew the sound immediately; a circuit crystal had just fractured.

Ky stopped, bored a crater in the table with her eyes and started breathing hard.

Lyon braced himself against the chair in front of him and, through squinted eyes, glanced from Ky to Paloon and back. "What in the hell was that?"

The dextian didn't halt her breathing to reply, but that didn't stop Paloon from taking an educated guess.

"She just shattered one of your computer's circuits."

No one ever said revelations were always positive.

"Mac?" came Lyon's worried voice as he slid forward pushing the seat under the table. Paloon's hypothesis led to an ugly feeling, one that the seconds of silence began to verify. "Mac?"

Just as Lyon's muscles tensed, the hologram table came to life with sparks that soon formed a three-dimensional persona. Mac paced back and forth, flailing his arms and screaming...nothing. Not a single sound. Then the computer caught on. A cartoon bubble appeared above his head with a scrolling marquee of words that began in mid-sentence.

"—nerve of you. You wench! I went out of my way to help you, and this is how you pay me back? I hope you know that fucking hurt. I'm a computer, but I felt that, damn it. How would you like it if—"

"Good," Ky belted before firing another mental blast that hit the holographic pixels like a typhoon and shot them in multiple directions, a feat that could not have been duplicated through simple physical force. "I'm glad it hurt, and you should be glad that's all I did. Don't ever get into my head again, you worthless—"

She came to a loss for words and ended with a few noises that developed into a short scream.

"Ky," Lyon's voice attempted to impose calm on the situation, "please sit down."

"I don't want to sit down."

"I know you don't, but would you please do me the courtesy?"

She glared but obliged by taking the seat across the table from Paloon. As she sat, she slammed the high heels on the concrete floor.

"Now," Lyon pulled the chair out, sat down and leaned back, "what did he do?"

"He was supposed to give me a chip on local social skills like the protocol of ordering a meal, but that damn thing put something else in there that made me do stuff I didn't want to do." Just getting it out made her begin to feel better. "I almost let him kiss me, and that would have blown my cover. That damn computer."

Larin chuckled.

"Oh, you think that's funny. If I—"

"No," Larin quickly corrected, waving his hands like frantic rocking chairs in front of his face, "I don't doubt you, and I'm glad you got Mac back. Any more from him and I would have strapped a couple CNG caps to him and blasted him to bits myself."

Lyon's head make a brief shake forward. "What did he do to you?"

Before Larin could answer, Paloon spoke to validate Larin's opinion. "Honestly, your computer has been one unruly child while you've been gone."

"Unruly?" Lyon initially thought they were playing a joke then he gave it an honest thought. "Are you sure Mac's not just being Mac? Granted he's a little unique, but I don't think he means any harm by it."

"That doesn't matter," Larin dove in. "He's been annoying us to the point of interfering with our work, and now it looks like he finally got his. Personally, I think you're lucky. If he had gotten into my head, there wouldn't be anything left of your pet transistor."

Lyon didn't have time to reply; Paloon responded too quickly.

"Stuff it!" The hunter pointed a flat palm at the rolbrid, a sign that meant much for that race. But Paloon had to agree. "While obliterating Mac has been tempting at times, I mainly felt that he was just acting like a child whose parent went away for a few days. Mac wanted to see how far he could push the babysitters." Paloon nodded to Ky. "I guess he found out the hard way."

Lyon folded his arms as he began to distance himself from the conversation so he could contemplate the issue. Mac could be annoying at times, but strangely, he couldn't imagine it any other way. It was like having your best friend and worse enemy all wrapped into one. But perhaps given the seriousness of the situation, that mixture didn't suit the best interests of the team as a whole. He had never formally counseled a computer before. While Mac didn't hold rank in the Corps, he was born deputized, so to speak.

Lyon's thoughts shattered as large block letters appeared before him.

"What about my voice?"

"Mac," Lyon yelled, "shut up!"

The letters blinked away.

"I am aware of your situation, but I need to think about what I'm going to do with you. This isn't a TV show, so you shouldn't be playing around. For now, just do what you're told."

Stillness and quiet descended on the room.

Too much clouded Lyon's mind for him to lock on to anything specific. Each thought careened independently through his skull, like an entire symphony in which each musical instrument played a different song. He wondered if the stress was beginning to get to him and whether his growing headache represented a symptom of a slowly advancing madness.

Only one solution came to mind: Stop the smugglers and finish his tour quickly so his could get off this pebble of a planet.

The other occupants of the room, other than Hitook who remained in a trance, looked on with wonder and mild caution. Lyon's face didn't appear kind; it looked more as if he had been possessed by a demon trying to force its way out.

Lyon raised a finger then paused briefly to breathe deeply, drop the finger and continue more calmly. "What information have we gathered?"

Reluctance to admit defeat lost to the sheer power of Paloon's will.

"Not much." The hunter jerked his thumb behind him. "Mac's only got basic data from the police computer, most of it extremely old, the rest of it deleted."

"How about reconstruction?"

"Oh, Mac reconstructed the deleted data, but the age of the equipment made for poor retrieval. Some random fragments made it, only a few words and no coherent phrases."

"Well, that was a waste, and ideas—"

"Not necessarily," Ky piped in.

"Excuse me." Lyon still had an irritated look on his face.

"Sorry to interrupt, but regardless of what Mac did to my head, I was able to get a possible lead."

Lyon bobbed his head oddly and summoned in his eyes a look that screamed, "Well, what are you waiting for?"

"Fairway Industries. Rick said it served as a yakuza front. He seemed sure about it."

"Well," Lyon grabbed the table and moved closer, "what are we waiting for? I want this to be over more than you."

The knight rapped a heavy beat on the table with his fingers and commanded, "Mac, locate and diagram Fairway Industries."

Only a few seconds passed before a three-dimensional compound of buildings rose from the table. Mac didn't want to push his luck and began without needing to be asked. Small screens of letters scrolled in front of each spectator.

"Fairway Industries. Established sixty-seven years ago by Joseph Fairway the Third. It began as a construction company for small sea-going vessels and now specializes in fabricating custom sections for larger ship-building companies. It is mainly known for providing made-to-order latrines, sewage and water systems, and water reclamation systems. The—"

"Nothing like drinking your own waste," Larin added, nodding.

"Excuse me," Mac typed, "but the current owner is one Howard Mulch and serves as the head of a board of five—"

"Enough." Lyon shifted his head before reaching out, grabbing the hologram and rotating it a few times. The compound seemed simple enough. "Can you poke it?"

"Absolutely." The word flashed with confidence. "Since we've begun, I've been able to infiltrate the power, phone, electric and even their water system. It seems they have computer controlled pumps and toilets. Weird."

"Any security systems?"

"I'm sure, but I'm currently narrowing down the local pipes and poking the electrical system, I'll find it within the next five minutes."

Lyon scanned the compound of four buildings surrounded by a high chain link fence needlessly topped with razor wire. Two long warehouses seemed to be partially transformed into office buildings. The short thin building looked like a series of garages. Sprouting from the back of the oddly shaped lot, the largest of the buildings looked like a construction factory.

Lyon craned his head around toward the meditating liqua before returning his attention to the map in front of him.

"Status, Hitook."

The others at the table turned to look in his direction, but Hitook remained quiet. He heard but needed a little time to disengage just enough.

"He's returned to residence. Much repair remains, but he's likely to stay."

"Chance of a coma?"

"Likely, but even in his condition, it would be nothing Ky and I couldn't handle together."

The dextian raised her eyebrow slightly.

"Good." Lyon unnecessarily pointed at the holographic buildings. "Then seal it and get over here. It's time to rock."

Chapter 15

A yellow smudge of a moon blotted the grey canopy of thin clouds that tapered to a horizon of orange-brown, compliments of the city lights. Only one star, a planet and two artificial satellites could muster the strength to punch through the evening veil.

Disappointment. Since landing, she had never seen the white moon without obstruction. On a few clear nights, Ky had run outside, only to see stars, learning later that the moon was still on the other side of the planet. Ky wondered if she would ever get to see it.

As if to mimic her feelings, a light sprinkle sneaked from the clouds. Moments later, it blasted into a raging rain.

Ky dropped her head and sneered an "it figures" look before glancing up from her post in the shadows between two defunct buildings: a decrepit greasy spoon that stank worse than when it was operating and some government building labeled "Department of Family Affairs." The office seemed out of place for the area, which was a strip of small industrial buildings, most closed or only used for storage.

Across the street sat Fairway Industries, the largest group of buildings on the well-worn asphalt road. The fenced area stretched from the road to an embankment that supported a railroad.

Light blasted from a lamp that had been flickering on and off every ten minutes for the past hour and a half. The yellow beam caught a plastic grocery bag as it whirled and danced in the breeze, then suddenly darted into a ditch.

Ky could now see Hitook's head look around the corner of a building next to the complex. A rash of chipped paint coated the split-level building. White cavities in the concrete helped deform the embedded words "Mass Transit Authority." If the plywood filling the windows was any clue, those employees no longer worked there. At least, Ky hoped not.

Out of view in the parking lot behind that building and about a hundred yards from Hitook, Paloon continued his adjustments inside the van. His bird-like drones completed the net and sensors flashed in his view.

"We've got a field," he notified everyone mentally.

Larin, who was crawling down from the railroad tracks, stopped, switched viewing spectrums and saw it.

Hitook and Ky extended their beings and could feel it.

Lyon already knew. From where he crouched next to a pyramid-shaped stack of steel pipes in a seemingly forgotten storage lot down the street, the knight could see, clinging to the fence, a sign that warned, "Caution: High Electrical Voltage." A white skull above crossed leg bones glowed on a black, oval background. At least that explained the layer of three fences.

"Glad you could join us." Lyon already had his plan in mind. *"Net up?"*

"Yes."

"Good." Lyon gave a mental pause. *"Mac, can you take the electrical fence?"*

A small, transparent blue window popped into existence in front of Lyon and lined the bottom of his glasses. Lighter blue, cubed letters began to scroll across.

"I'm working on it," Mac printed. "So when are you going to work on my voice?"

"Mention it again, and I won't think about it for another week. Understood?"

The previous letters scrolled away with no response to Lyon's statement. Lyon had just about had it with Mac's complaining. It had been going on for the past few hours. Now was not the time for this degree of childishness.

"Wait. I think I've got it," came across the scrolling marquee that appeared in everyone's view. Lyon sensed a cold, bitter tone in the letters that now appeared more like imaginative ice then just light blue letters. "System's down."

Ky and Hitook projected and sensed nothing. Larin's new scan came up negative. All three knew Lyon would wait for Paloon's check.

"Confirmed," Paloon retorted as he began to move his scan from the fence and move it through the compound looking for anything out of the ordinary.

"Go."

The team took Lyon's command and approached the fence, then prepared themselves to penetrate the barrier in their own ways.

A flicker of red on the scanning screen drew Paloon's attention. He squinted at it even though the floating screen and associated flicker were being shot straight into his optic nerve. The hunter hummed as he contemplated the source of the speck. When it went solid and slightly grew, it hit him. *"Halt!"*

The command came too late. Hitook was already too close; actually, his left hand had a firm grip on the fence. Joules of electricity coursed their way along the liqua's blood and muscles. He puffed as sparks jumped from the tips of his fur. Oversized teeth glistened as the volts forced his jaw into a tight grimace of a grin. Snaps sounded as his long ears whipped out into ridged daggers that looked strangely like the tails of a pair of scared cats. Squealing static wailed through the team's internal communications.

"Oh my—" Ky could feel something very wrong.

Larin could see what Ky couldn't. The rolbrid moved away from the fence, mainly to get a better look. *"That's something you don't see every day."*

"What's going on?" Lyon had no idea what had unfolded across the compound from him.

"A backup power source kicked in, and Hitook is getting the full

effect." Paloon raced through his settings and equipment to see if he had anything to help.

Lyon didn't have time. *"Mac, I need you to take out all the power."*

"It's out, I tell you," the words scrolled a little fast in urgency. "To take out the backup power, I'll need to shut down the entire grid. I can do it, but it will draw unwanted attention."

Lyon admitted to himself that the computer made a good point.

Unknown to even Larin who attentively watched the electrical storms sweep across the fluffed fur, Hitook hadn't given up the fight. Ky began to feel it but didn't give it much attention until she heard the cracking pop.

Hitook focused his energy on enhancing the electricity and forcing it back to short the generator. All he said was *"That should do it."*

Ky couldn't believe it. If someone would have asked her a minute ago, she would have sworn that such a feat could only be accomplished by a master and, even then, only maybe.

"Don't ask me how," Paloon dove from scanner to scanner, *"but that secondary power source is shot, and the grid is still up."*

Larin returned his focus to the fence and just gave a humph at the fact that his entertainment had ended.

Details weren't required.

"Skip it." Lyon adjusted his body and reached for the palm laser from a belt pouch in the small of his back. *"Move."*

Lyon and Larin performed similar tasks, using palm lasers to cut a quick, clean door in the fence. Tinkles rang unnoticed as dissected bits of chain link rained to the ground. Both held a firm grip on the remaining chunk of fence and lowered it quietly as it collapsed upon itself.

Hitook stepped back and eyed the top of the razor wire. With a rapid scan of the target's height, the liqua crouched, tendons stretching as the kinetics increased, and he jumped over the eight-foot tip with plenty of room to spare.

Ky had long ago decided not to be upstaged, but Fate had already cost her that battle. That didn't stop her from clamping a firm grip on the fence. Her concentration ended just as the others moved into position and checked in.

"Ky?" Lyon still hadn't heard a word. *"Paloon?"*

"She's still at the fen—nope, she's thr—"

"Here and ready." Ky silently glided into place. The chain fence remained intact behind her. Though no one saw it, her trick gave Ky a satisfying that's-how-an-assassin-does-it feeling.

"Check." Lyon unholstered his standard-issue particle laser. *"Prep and go in—"*

"What level?"

Irritation bloomed in Lyon at Larin's interruption. Then the knight understood the lieutenant's point. Lyon had failed to discuss the level at which the team should operate.

"Phase one, just like last time."

"That's not a goo—"

"Just do it, lieutenant. We'll argue the particulars at another time. We're not here to shoot everything we see. We get in, out and home." Lyon took little notice of his growth as a leader. *"We go in five. Mark."*

In those slow seconds, Larin also prepped his particle cannon and did a quick diagnostic as the grip connected to the link in his palm and the weapon's systems merged with his view. Hitook gripped both twin blades and snapped them so they rested along his forearms, the hooked points aimed into the grey sky. Ky unsheathed both short swords from their calf scabbards; a quick twirl had the slightly curved cross guards interlocked in her fingers, the hilts jabbing straight as the blades blended with her arms.

On the mark, each made respective moves to crack the locks to the door of their assigned buildings and move in.

Larin knelt against the inside of the outer wall and scanned the building, crosshairs gliding around his view as he moved the cannon to provide tactical scans of anything that hinted at being a threat. Surrounding the factory's interior, a massive catwalk loomed high enough for the various pieces of machinery, expanding working platforms, supply crates and one-man cranes. Artificial light, filtered by dirty windows, glinted off pieces of what appeared to be boilers in various states of assembly.

Crates, for the most part, formed tidy rows, thanks mainly to the towering shelving units. Lyon stepped carefully and kept his eyes gliding around the room. The prongs of a forklift protruded from the end of an aisle. Across the aisle, several cardboard boxes formed a pyramid on a pallet as if a grocery story display. Black blotches blended with tire tread patterns in oil that snaked in all directions. To the right, links of metal cages covered rows of cabinets sporting all forms of warning signs, most reading "Corrosive."

Stale air, the kind that could only come from cooled burnt rubber, oil, grease and petroleum, assaulted Ky's nose. It wrinkled. Her natural vision allowed her to see fine in the otherwise pitch black building. The assumptions were correct; this building was a garage. Its sister building dwarfed it, but the garage had enough room to house everything from semi-trucks to oversized flat beds with room to spare for maintenance equipment. Not every stall had a resident, but some seemed to exist solely for storage.

A solitary light glowed at half power high above a plastic grate in the lowered ceiling. Hitook had crouched but straightened. His head peaked like a prairie dog above the walled cubes that encased various work areas that were different but, at the same time, similar. He crept along, poked his head in the entryway of one and inspected. An artist, or drafter maybe. The liqua peered quizzically at a motivational poster above the high, slanted table. A window would have been better. He moved on.

Regardless of how quietly Larin moved, a gritty scrunch echoed from the metal walls as the dust of a hundred materials ground under his feet. Even though workers had apparently vacated the area only hours ago, the building felt abandoned, mostly due to the utterly motionless shadows and dusty smell with a metallic twang. Nothing appeared out of the ordinary; if there was anything that merited this visit, it would most likely be in the records. Meanwhile, securing this building was proving to be boring. Just as he reached that conclusion, a blink caught Larin's attention as a light disappeared behind one of the massive I-beams holding up the catwalk. With a step back, the rolbrid watched the purple light near the far ceiling.

The same thoughts of boredom had invaded Lyon's mind, but he forced them back so he could stay focused on retrieving as much information as possible. After moving past a few rows of crates and observing no sound or movement, Lyon lowered his weapon and began examining some of the crates and boxes he had passed. Various fixtures, sheets of glass, boxes of nuts, stacks of molded fiberglass. At the next aisle, Lyon decided a cursory examination served no purpose and started reading some of the boxes. That's when he stumbled upon it. One of the boxes was labeled "Telescopes." Odd. *"Paloon—,"* Lyon cut short his call for a scan. At the edge of his right view, behind a few rows, eyes watched Lyon.

Her nose picked it up first. Something didn't fit. She crouched next to a white van to give her presence time to attempt to touch the oddity. Ky slowly stood as her presence connected. Near the far end of the building, an engine ran but made no sound. Little could compare with how quietly the dextian moved toward the vehicle. Gaps in obstructions revealed little, but the target appeared to be a fairly new model luxury sedan; some twists shaped a logo that glinted grey. She readied the sword in her right arm as she moved closer to see if there were any occupants. Near a faint beam of light from a crack in a garage door, a shadow flickered. Ky released the pent sword and pierced the target.

Yep, another work area. Hitook had little doubt, but at last he finished his search of the area and exited through a glass door in a glass wall that separated the cubicles into an administrative and reception area of sorts. Various sizes of rugs joined a few small trees to decorate the hardwood floor and enhance the arrangement of desks. Steps along the right wall led up to another office area with bigger secluded rooms. Artist renderings of massive boats and detailed cross-sections of equipment stared back from smart frames. Hitook hadn't completely left the stairs when a thud from the first floor caught the liqua off guard. He jerked, and his left foot slipped. He almost lost balance as his foot pounded onto the step below.

Paloon just started picking up the chatter; it came through a channel he didn't expect to hear anything on. But before he realized what he had, it stopped mattering to his friends in the thick of it.

Larin slowly twisted his wrist as the crosshairs glided in motion with the particle cannon to close in on the purple light. Before he could line the shot, the light flared slightly, just enough to show Larin what he was up against. The rolbrid leaped to the right and dove behind a trio of barrels, but his reaction couldn't compare to the now activated targeting system. A pulsing purple beam slammed into Larin's leg in mid-flight. The force took control of his balance and yanked him into a flat spin that plowed him face-first into the concrete floor, where a solitary metal binding strap greeted his left cheek by slicing it open.

Lyon failed at acting like he didn't notice, and the eyes blurred away. He raised the cannon but gracefully panned his head while letting the cannon's targeting dot stay on the last known location of the target. Options disappeared when something smashed into a crate above him. As jagged fragments of wood pelted the area, Lyon bounced and hopped forward, landed on one knee, spun around and let the cannon cut the air and slice the falling pieces of wood.

A foot pinned the now dead cat. Ribs snapped and cracked under the pressure as Ky pulled her short sword out of the animal's body. She frowned at the outcome of the battle and wiped the blade on the inside of her pants before twirling it back to its original location along her arm. Returning to the suspect vehicle, Ky didn't see anything out of the ordinary. A closer inspection through the driver's window revealed otherwise. She rolled on to her back and slid under the vehicle. Surprise should have been her reaction, but Ky felt more worried than anything at what she saw.

Hitook lowered his head beneath the second floor to find the source of the sound and to see whether the thing that made it took notice of his own noise. It wasn't long before he found himself in a contest of who was more surprised, him or the owner of the eyes that locked with his. After less than a second, the eyes disappeared under the first floor as a once-hidden wooden door clattered shut on the floor. Hitook bounded down the stairs and toward the trap door, which suddenly erupted in light as bolt after bolt from some energy weapon pounded through it. The liqua moved slightly out of the way before whipping his hand blades forward. After judging the scattered pattern of shots and getting some hair on his right foot singed, Hitook pounced forward, thrusting the hand blades through the floor and keeping at it like a frantic sewing machine.

The rolbrid's body chemically compensated for the numbness and shock Larin was experiencing, so he never lost consciousness. Upon contact with the unforgiving surface, he scampered on all fours before throwing his feet forward to slide flat across the concrete and place himself behind a forklift. Along the way, the fazer sent pulse after pulse of energy toward Larin; they ripped chunks of concrete out of the floor and created a rain of rocks that rattled on the far metal wall. Larin's particle cannon rested yards away, knocked out of his hands by the first hit. The fazer continued to pound away on the other side of the forklift, which now started rocking back and forth. Larin spun and then pushed his back against the machine to stabilize it. He wiped a stream of clear blood from his check and grimaced at the growing pool under the hole in his butchered leg. That's when he took note of the CNG round he snuck into his belt when Lyon wasn't looking.

An alien expletive exploded with Lyon's use of his cannon. This changed everything. "Dragon Corps," Lyon commanded, "turn yourself in!" The response came as more blasted crates, probably hit by some alien weapons wielded by the expletive's owner. Lyon dodged the debris and returned a few low-level shots. Once he noticed the moving shadow a couple of aisles away, Lyon mentally engaged the cannon's weapon selector. The allaric launcher came to life and spouted a stream of green crystal. Upon contact with the wall, cabinets and crates, explosions of lime-colored light flooded the area as the shards fragmented and cut into everything except the target. He ran forward just in time to see he had fallen into a trap set by the alien crouched at the far end of the row. A series of shots from the alien sent the towering rack of crates down on top of Lyon, who fought the onslaught the best he could. Before being overwhelmed, he took notice of the alien bolting through a door. *"Ky, target past you to Hitook's location."* He almost left it at that, but once the noise of the falling crates quieted and he started tossing them out of the way, he added, *"I want it alive."*

By the second command, Ky was already on her feet and blasting at the door. The wood frame exploded as the door sailed open with enough force to crack the wall behind it, and the window shattered into a hundred pieces. Focused, the target scurried across the mud, dirt and rocks toward the office building. Ky lowered her foot as force built into her hands while she pulled her arms back. Before her boot hit the ground, Ky lunged forward. The large dagger blasted like a lighting bolt shrouded in a yellow-orange aura.

Unaware of the approaching death, the runner inadvertently dodged the attack by darting around the building. The seeking attack continued but hit the corner of the building. Metal screeched as a ball-shaped chuck ripped free and plowed toward the fence. It pounded into the fence and tore a couple hundred feet of links and poles out of the ground carrying them far from sight.

"Damn," Ky belted just as a thunderous blast vaporized the far corner of the factory and Larin could be heard laughing.

Hitook pulled one twin-blade out and flicked his wrist at the end to send the once-hidden door flying open as he jerked his body back. He paused, but nothing happened, so he slowly leaned forward peeking from the corner of his right eye as his other eye squinted. It seemed to take forever, but Hitook finally found himself looking down the hatch and at what remained of the body, which wasn't much. Then Larin's CNG explosion shook the office building, and Hitook instinctively looked up, only to see a blue-eyed rolbrid with a kinetic blaster. The first shot crashed into Hitook's right knee he had used to brace himself. Just as the liqua lost balance, the second shot slammed into his left shoulder, flipping him almost backwards. Well planned, this now opened Hitook's defenses, leaving the entire width of his chest exposed. The salvo of shots pounded away and sent the massive beast flying through the wall.

Due to her frustration at missing, Ky's psyche blared to full strength, so much so that she didn't even have to touch the door for it to go sailing from its hinges. A faint blue power glowed from her.

The rolbrid didn't give a damn. He spun down on one knee and let the blaster roar to life.

The trained assassin leaped straight up and, now with her powers at full, kicked the wall to her left to force herself to sail to the right. As she did, her right hand tore free the crossbow planted along her back. Kinetic bolts pounded holes in the ceiling as Ky continued to dodge them just as she came to the far wall. She took off running horizontally along the wall.

Ky knew the rolbrid's targeting angle would soon line up. She dropped to the floor then sprang up, curled into a ball and bounced back down. White beams of kinetic energy went sporadic like a hyper spotlight trying to connect with the bouncing dextian.

It took a couple of attempts, but Ky finally lined up for the shot she wanted. Just as she jumped up, she sprang open, took aim and sent a volley of bolts toward the attacker. One more repeat, and the attacker found himself nailed to the wooden floor.

The rolbrid started spouting inflammatory remarks, but Ky didn't let it get to her; she was too pissed at being forced to get this mad.

The cubical she had landed in received her wrath. Walls flew in multiple directions as she kicked her way toward the rolbrid. She stood above it and let her force flare into a brighter blue.

Ky raised her head to see through the new hole in the building at Hitook's bleeding body lying in the yard. It really didn't register, but she glared back at the rolbrid.

Ten or so bolts had found purchase in his arms and legs and had bored through to grip into the shiny wood planks. Clear rivers of glistening rolbrid blood streaked in multiple directions. Ky followed one of the streams and let malicious thoughts overcome her. A fang became visible as she curled her upper lip.

She yanked her body wide, arms outstretched, and forced pain into each bolt and straight into the rolbrid's body. The body of the once keen attacker twisted as much as it could as the rolbrid belted screams, which together sounded like a bull charging through piles of glass figurines.

Lyon flipped the Perdain coin among the ridges of his fingers and glanced around the underground complex barely big enough for him to stand up straight. Metal beams braced the ceiling and joined hanging lights as the main obstacles to Lyon's navigation as he made his way from a warehouse room of sorts and through a tunnel-like hall. Such an experience wasn't completely new to Lyon, who once took a hop on a rolbrid cruiser. After countless bumps and bruises and a couple of concussions, Lyon learned to duck.

Once in the control area of sorts, Lyon twiddled the coin to hold it between his fingers and under his chin. He glanced down at the multi-horned image of a half yuli cat and half molyar bear, the rolbrid's mythical god Perdain. The coin was good luck, but only when Perdain was face down.

"So bad luck it is." Lyon didn't give a damn and chucked the coin, which sailed behind some monitors and racks of computers and communications equipment. Tings ricocheted as it fell through the pachinko of metal parts.

A glint of silver foil caught Lyon's attention. He retrieved it from the floor, read the rolbrid writing and sniffed the opening to see if the mochi cakes were still good.

"Lyon, Paloon's back, and every thing's ready if you are," Larin shot across the communications network.

The knight looked up from the bag of mochi cakes toward the open hatch, but no one was there. The slightly fermented smell resulted in a frown, and Lyon let the bag go and gave it a kick. It crinkled loudly in rebellion.

"Did you find a fire hazard?" He asked in reply while gazing about at nothing in particular but taking notice of the time ticking away on a rolbrid clock crammed between all the non-native hardware. The sun would be up in less than two hours.

"About twenty barrels of an unknown liquid. I vaped them."

Lyon patted and wiped his palm on his pants leg and headed up and out of the hatch. As he stood on the first floor of the office building, he took a final gaze down the hatch as his thoughts raced.

Two rolbrids with temporary housing for eleven, tons of non-native equipment and all of it buried under a terran business. Yet more pieces got dumped on his puzzle, and nothing fit. The thought annoyed. But relief came as he contemplated the opportunity he now had to at least attempt to put together these pieces, even if it meant killing someone.

Lyon jerked his head in a cocked form, commanded, *"Blow it,"* and kicked the hatch shut.

Chapter 16

"Ah, Yabuki," Kurosawa relaxed and returned his head to its groove as his chiropractor's hands went to work on his bare back, "you had better have news."

Yabuki didn't have good news, but only the weak would hesitate.

"Anata ni yoroshiku. There are still no signs at the site. And nearby surveillance didn't point in our yard's direction. Since our surveillance equipment was kept on site, it disappeared with the rest."

Kurosawa almost flew off the chiropractic bed. "Entire warehouses and factories just don't disappear." The yakuza leader didn't care that this frustration was the reason for the regular sessions with his chiropractor in the first place. "They don't walk away either. Find them! They should be easy to spot, even for you. I don't care if—aaaaggggghhhhh!"

The elderly man collapsed in the bed as his tensing muscles took control of his body. Hands resumed their chiropractic duty. Soon vertebra retorted with pops and muffled snaps.

Kurosawa's sighs whispered in the white, clinical room as Yabuki debated whether he should continue his report or leave. Leaving could prove to be a mistake later.

"We have one possible but vague lead."

A dangling hand waved weakly in a circle pointed at the ground. Kurosawa didn't wish to waste any more energy.

"Some reporters were interviewing the police a couple of days ago. They said they were doing a documentary on organized crime in the city, and several officers reported they asked several direct questions about our activity."

Yabuki felt the statement held a degree of importance that needed time to seep in, but the elderly gentleman just thought it stupid.

"And you're bothering me with this?" came a partially muffled voiced. "Let the idiot media ask questions; they are clueless."

"Well," Yabuki stumbled a bit but recovered with a smidgen of brown-nosing, "Kurosawa-san, one of our officers dated one, and he reported—"

"Watch that tone; you border on disrespect," the man spoke much more clearly than before, but then his tone lightened. "So let this fool waste his time after a abazureon'na. What should I care?"

Yabuki let himself feel frustrated for a moment before he stifled it and strived to keep the proper respected in his voice. It came across as too fake, and Kurosawa noticed.

"This officer admitted that he discussed our missing factory with her on the night it disappeared."

Kurosawa snapped his arms into a brace on the bed as if he was about to push himself up, but he stopped and only gripped the bed's edges. His body otherwise remained on the bed.

"Are you going to tell me—I'm in enough stress already. I have to explain this, and you want to propose that some shōjo reporter is hiding my factory under her skirt? You waste my time."

Yabuki contemplated a counter to the comment but just gulped and continued. "He said he felt suspicious about it in the morning and looked into it. He learned that the station, The Justice Network, doesn't exist...anywhere."

The elderly man didn't react for a few moments and then it was only with an outstretched arm. With speed and grace, his silk robe appeared in the hands of the quiet attendant. She continued to robe Kurosawa amid the silence.

Finished, she disappeared through the back wall, and Kurosawa motioned with his eyes for Yabuki to approach. Once he was close enough, the leader whispered as if being calm, but the inflections gave him away. "Are you telling me he gave information to a spy?"

"It appears that may be the case."

Kurosawa took a long look into Yabuki's eyes, which kept focus on the kanji stitches in the robe. Minutes passed.

"Give me your weapon," Kurosawa ordered quietly.

Yabuki didn't hesitate and, in fact, had expected as much. He reached into his jacket and properly offered the pistol to his boss, who took it.

Light glinted off the sidearm as it moved ever so slightly in Kurosawa's hands while he gave it a cursory examination. Moments later the barrel took aim on Yabuki's left shoulder. Metal released faint grinds and creaks as the hammer reared back, keeping a path in line with the barrel staring down at the subordinate's flesh.

In a blur and a crashing thud, Yabuki's head snapped and Kurosawa pulled back his arm to drop the pistol at Yabuki's feet. Blood started to seep down his face as he turned back toward Kurosawa. The cut from the butt of the pistol gaped just below the eye, right along the bone where it would hurt the most. He didn't feel lucky; he remained upset that dishonor had been brought upon the family.

Kurosawa felt that; therefore, he had no need to explain why he didn't shoot Yabuki. "Correct this."

"Tadachi ni." Yabuki retrieved his weapon, promptly left the room and didn't touch his bleeding wound until in the elevator and out of sight from everyone.

Chapter 17

Light shined with a glint of yellow off the beads of sweat creeping down the wide brow, across the crown of a flat nose and into the blue-white eye. Mitnarsho's eye crashed shut, and he gritted as the salt made its acidic stab.

"Humph." Sarcastic disappointment saturated the grunt. "Again."

Ky obeyed Lyon's command and entered Mitnarsho's mind, not to find information, only to cause pain. During the many dives previously, she had begun to know her way around and had so far found multiple ways to cause pain that she picked randomly to make the effect even more annoying to the prisoner.

Screeches, similar to the sound made by rocks cutting into glass, vibrated at intense levels. The resulting pitch seemed to make the paint on the walls vibrate. It wouldn't have been so bad, but after hours of torture, the rolbrid's vocal cords were strained to degrees that placed them at risk of irrevocable damage.

Sonic dampeners helped the two torturers withstand the audio onslaught. So Lyon briefly unfolded one arm to point at the rolbrid's right leg.

Ky followed. Soon the leg snapped rigid so quickly the poor creature was lucky not to pop his joint out of place, which itself would be enough to make a rolbrid faint with shock. Not that Ky would allow her subject to faint. Regardless, the pain in the leg far surpassed what a popped joint would feel like, and the resulting screams jumped a few octaves and bordered on the upper levels of Ky's hearing range.

Lyon shifted his weight. He was leaning against a metal cabinet that rose just high enough so its edge made part of his rump numb. He squinted slowly before releasing the tormented being. "Okay."

Screaming tapered to heavy panting as if the rolbrid had been unable to breathe for the past five minutes, which, for the most part, was true.

With a towel from her lap, Ky wiped a few streaks of sweat from her brow and rubbed her right ear, which had started to fall asleep. She even released a few deep pants. Such mental probing wasn't without its stress on the torturer.

Mitnarsho's eyes quickly grew heavy, and his head dropped. Ky still kept her link and didn't let him go anywhere, to include unconsciousness. And she nodded somewhat weakly to Lyon to let him know that fact.

"You really are starting to tire me," Lyon aimed at the captive. He even went so far as to present a well-orchestrated yawn, and Ky scowled at Lyon for having the nerve to say this tired *him*. "I still have to order the death of your entire family because we found your pathetic bag in a restricted sector."

Obscenities almost to an infinite degree spouted with a surprising energy from the prisoner. Restraint bars cut into grey skin, which began to turn an uncomfortable shade of lime green. Though spoken in rolbridian, or a slightly tainted version of the language, Lyon and Ky followed the comments well enough. The statements covered a wide range of topics to even include, to Ky's surprise, a comment about Lyon's father and a relationship with a vekootal, a highly incompatible situation, but the thought alone generated mental pictures that made Ky cringe.

Lyon only unfolded an arm enough to start rubbing his forehead. Though he found some of the comments comical, he forced himself not to laugh and let it go on just long enough to catch the rolbrid by surprise, even though it should have come as no surprise.

"Again."

Spasms threw the forgetful soul back in the chair to bellow screams that jumped from one to another without the need of introductions. All the while, Ky shifted from pain to pain and back again, playing with a kaleidoscope of sensors, memories, phobias and nightmares in degrees unfathomable for the inexperienced. Ky had much experience, much to her dismay at times, and she sometimes wondered if she strayed from her sanity.

"I'm not really sure," Lyon yelled over the noise, "exactly which side of your family you received your stupidity from, but get over it!"

He flicked his arm, and Ky halted the assault.

In a much calmer voice, Lyon continued. "I know the moss in your ears isn't so thick that you can't hear me. You are not in a situation to fight. I own you, and I have no qualms about breaking you."

Mitnarsho mumbled something as his head rocked back and forth across his chest.

"Um, 'Sho," Lyon kicked the rolbrid's leg, "speak up."

Nothing. Lyon pointed to the rolbrid's head; Ky responded, and the neck twanged straight as the pain increased, gradually this time.

"I said," hate burned brightly in the milky blue-white of the rolbrid's eyes, "go ahead and try." After a slight pause followed by the slightest of grins, he added, "You'll get nothing from me."

The last comment irritated Lyon. He fought to hide it, but the rolbrid saw the sign he was looking for and released a vague smile.

Ky looked over to see what Lyon wanted her to do next. Obviously the basic stuff wasn't working. Lyon only returned the glance before glaring at this ever-defiant captive. Maybe this lost soul needed a dose of reality. He hadn't wanted to go to this level, but he was prepared for it.

Lyon lifted himself off the cabinet and turned to rummage through the drawers. It didn't take long before he found the item he needed, then grabbed one of the small, metal tubes from the taller cabinet now to his right. He slid the tube into the instrument until the only thing visible of the tube was the purple band of a label.

Light played across the green metallic device as Lyon turned to face the doomed. It would be difficult to describe the mechanism, but to the rolbrid, it looked like a cross between an ear of corn and an egg. The rolbrid narrowed his eyes at the menace. Sounds of grinding shale seeped into the room as Mitnarsho gritted his teeth.

"What's in—"

"Lock'im."

Ky responded to the order and froze the rolbrid in mid-demand.

"You still don't get it." Now Lyon was the one with a vague smile, a maniacal one at that. "You are in no position to ask questions. We own you." Lyon glanced over to Ky. "She could nuke your synapses if she wanted to." Ky acknowledged the compliment by briefly smiling and nodding in agreement. "But you don't want that, do you?"

The knight kept eye contact with the rolbrid as he tapped the green device in his hand.

"What's that?" Lyon leaned forward as if to hear a whisper. "I can't hear you."

"Gee, that sounds like fun," the rolbrid belted.

Lyon jerked back in amazement then turned to Ky who was chuckling with her tongue stuck between her teeth. He soon caught on that she had made the rolbrid utter the statement. Lyon stifled his laughter with coughing.

A few moments later, once he got his composure back, Lyon smiled a little larger this time and waved the device in the air. "You see. You are not in control of this situation. You are decidedly far from being in control, my challenging, yet pathetic friend."

Cold shot through the rolbrid's chest as Lyon pressed the device against it. A smirk crept across Lyon's face. "This, of course, is going to hurt. Enjoy."

Spider-leg-like prongs blasted out of the torture device and dug deep into rolbrid flesh. Creaks, cracks and pops sounded as Mitnarsho's cartilage plates took the damage. At the point where the device rested against the chest, a needle fired, punched through and bit into the blood organ, which for a rolbrid served as a hybrid between a pump and a filter.

The clear blood around the wound began to bubble before giving way to a spitting hiss as the vial's contents were shoved into its new host. With the deed done, all previously protruding appendages retracted into the device, and Lyon placed it on top of the cabinet next to the remaining canisters.

Lyon whistled for a short bit and looked about the room before returning to the rolbrid. "Right about now you're probably feeling the effects and wondering if you're going to live through this. That's a good question."

During a pause, Lyon just stared, his eyes slightly glazed and showing a detached look. He knew exactly how this felt and really didn't want to think about it too much. "It's somewhere between pin pricks and miniature explosions. Hundreds of the damn things, aren't there? That strange sensation that you can't place, you're feeling the walls of your blood vessels. Weird isn't it? Not a bizarre weird; it's more like a swig of fire weird. It's a goo—"

"Crap!" Ky lunged forward instinctively.

"What!?"

Ky motioned with her hand for Lyon to be quiet; she was busy. She released a few moans and grunts and shut her eyes tight, and all the muscles in her body tensed. It was a fight, a tough fight, a fight Ky had no chance of winning.

The rolbrid's head dropped, and the entire body went limp.

"What in the hell happened?" Lyon thought maybe he had killed his prisoner.

Ky just shook her head and swept her hair back over her ears. "He had no chance. It was just too much trauma; he's out."

"A coma?"

"No, nothing that far, but his mind has shut down. He rode it to the limit; you know what that means."

Lyon folded his arms and quietly nodded in agreement. Training. This rolbrid had been through some serious torture training. If the knight had to guess, only military training could have matched this. Pirates weren't this sophisticated.

As he stood there, eyes locked on the floor, fatigue crept up and seized his motor functions.

"Okay, that's enough." Lyon headed for the door. "I need sleep."

He walked out of the small cell and into the main room. The lower half of Paloon poked from a panel at the bottom of Mac's wall. Otherwise, the rest of the room remained empty.

Lyon stopped and rubbed his forehead. "Where's everyone?"

Paloon gave a few grunts but nothing else.

Ky walked around, took a seat at the table and mumbled something. Shortly thereafter, a glass of white fluid appeared. The substance had the consistency of pudding and smelled of wet hair. Ky took a couple of gulps, clamped the glass in her hands as if holding on for dear life and then let her head drop forward.

The sight made Lyon shiver. He couldn't fathom drinking the foul stuff.

"Larin," Paloon grunted, "is across the street." A ricocheting clink perforated the air. Paloon just relaxed with a sigh so he could finish what he had to say before trying to find the piece that had just disappeared. "I don't know where the liqua is."

Paloon's tone of "liqua" bordered on derogatory.

Lyon headed for the stairs. "I'm going to try a get a few hours of sleep before we have to open the store."

"It's three in the afternoon." Paloon just let the statement sink in.

Lyon stopped and turned with a completely confused look. "We've been in there that long?"

"Yep." Paloon started shifting around again. "I'm surprised all of you lasted this long."

"What about the sto—"

"We put up a closed sign that says something about freezer problems." Paloon paused in his work. "You know, our mission here is not to sell packaged plant life. At times, I think you worry too much about that damn store."

Lyon didn't have the energy to argue about it. He let it be, which would allow it to creep into his dreams.

"Anyway, I'm tired, so I'll see—"

"Excuse me," came Mac's now audible voice, "but I have stumbled across something rather interesting."

Lyon closed his eyes and exhaled deeply. "Mac, I'm glad you have your voice back, but I really don't have time for this."

"Yes, but this is extremely...weird."

Palms rubbed at Lyon's eyes before one waved for Mac to continue. "Make it quick."

"Um...well...hmm...how can I put this?"

"Mac!"

"Well, when...when I was performing surgery on the native, I stum-bl-ed on to something, and since then I've been combing through what it may mean." Mac paused as if wishing to take a breath. "But it seems our well-roasted friend is the proud owner of more neurons than initially issued."

Yet another pause froze what little action there was in the room. "Which is rather unique," Mac continued. "I would even venture to say virtually rare."

Lyon took another deep breath. "Mac, honestly, I'm tired and not in the mood. What are you saying?"

Mac's voice picked up as if stating fact. "There are non-native nodules in his noodle."

"Damn it, Mac! Quit messing around and just say it!"

Mac kicked into hyper-phrase mode and rattled them off. "He's sporting after-market modifications. Fingers have been poking around his grey matter. Someone has rewired his wetware." With a slight pause and a more forceful tone, Mac blasted, "That *dude* has been reprogrammed!"

Interstellar space would have had a hard time being more quiet than the room suddenly became.

"And it wasn't me...promise."

Chapter 18

Swirls of tan and green light danced across the three faces at the table. In the center floated a larger-than-life representation of Oz's brain. Mac's eight-inch avatar paced around the image.

The computer took the form of a slightly obese man in faded blue jeans and a worn leather jacket with a fire-emblazoned skull on the back. Only the word "Demons" could be read on the bottom; the rest of the phrase was covered with long hair, hair that competed with the beard for length. As Mac circled the image, he would stroke his beard and tap his waist-high black cane on the table. The cane was topped with a silver skull shadowed in black.

Mac halted and, for no apparent reason, jabbed his cane into the image of the brain and spun it around so it landed on its back. He whipped the cane out and poked it back in. Lines shot from the image as the hologram zoomed in rapidly. After a few seconds all that was left were three globule clusters, but it looked like someone had vomited a spider web.

"Here's another one." Mac rapped the cells in the center with his cane before bringing the stick down with a tap on the table's glass top. "Similar to that cross wiring in the limbic system between the amygdala and the nucleus accumbens, this one's in the midbrain between the medulla and the pons. Like the others, it shows signs that the myelin sheaths were melted together. It's such a good job I would almost say they willingly grew together, but once again, that doesn't explain the very existence of this cluster."

Mac took one more step in place before turning to glare with beady eyes in a hairy face. "This one is similar to a few others in that the chemical structure is faulty, almost as if designed to fail." Mac looked around at his audience and resumed his walk. "Someone with this kind of tech—"

"What is it!?" Larin shouted as he and Hitook came around the corner.

Lyon raised a hand and motioned at the end of the table. "Shut up, sit down and watch."

Larin huffed, reached back to backhand Hitook in the leg, and the two made for the empty seats.

Mac faintly forced a cough to clear his holographic throat. "As I was saying, no one this good would have made such a simple mistake. Or at least, what should have been simple for them."

The tiny fat man walked under the picture, impaled it with his cane and yanked it along like a helium balloon on a string as he strolled to the end of the table as Larin and Hitook sat down. Mac gave a furry smile and nodded at both of them, then turned around.

"As a side note, the connections it has within the pons make me think it and some others located within the midbrain are a mini network within the reticular activating system. If that's the case...well...I don't know. Who knows what this does?"

Mac dove a hand in his mass of hair to scratch his neck. "On to the next."

With an up and down rap of Mac's cane, the image zoomed back out to the full picture of the brain. The computer smacked the image around with his cane until the frontal lobes faced him. As before, a jab sent the image zooming in.

This time the tightly packed network of cells and neural pathways seemed too confusing. Some at the table saw it before others: a darkened cluster that hinted at being out of place.

"I'm sure you see it by now, but...," Mac didn't stop walking as the darkened cluster flashed briefly. "This one is located deep within the diencephalon and is embedded within the thalamus, which has plenty of room to spare." No one laughed at Mac's attempt at cranial humor, so he huffed out of his nose. "This one is unique in chemical structure in that it is almost completely constructed of foreign chemical compounds. Surprisingly, the body doesn't seem to have rejected any of these yet. Maybe some of the other alterations are halting the rejection process."

Lyon pushed away from the table. Everyone else watched the man with a tired look on his face stand, approach one of the doors behind him and stare through the glass at the terran strapped in the medical chair as green lights danced around the room.

Mac felt asking questions would be inappropriate at this moment and forced himself to keep on topic. He turned and resumed walking. "In analyzing this one, the acidic-based chemicals are sheathed to protect the rest of the brain."

"A chemical bomb?" Larin's background declared its reasoning.

Ky and Paloon glared at the rolbrid and made faint grumbling noises. Larin was on the verge of feeling stupid for opening his mouth until Mac replied.

"That's what I thought at first, so good guess," Mac wagged a finger at Larin, "but the more I looked at it, the more I got this gut feeling that the chains were too well structured to just be a bomb. Because of its detailed structure and how it's wired into the thalamus, I would have to say this one is designed to receive and translate some form of input."

Ky pulled her third glass of the chalky white liquid toward her as she leaned forward. "Input? From where?"

"That's the kicker." Mac walked toward Ky and jerked a thumb back at the image. "This thing is independent. It's not plugged into any other section of the brain. If it is a receiver, I would have to say the sensory input is probably external."

Mac turned and rapped his cane twice and the image blinked out of existence. "Well, that's it. Twenty-three anomalies. I may find more, but I'll need more time."

Ky sat back and let her eyes dart about before turning to look at

Lyon standing at the door and then returning her gaze to the table. Paloon just sat with folded arms before letting his left hand play with his forehead.

Hitook sat calmly and quietly, but Larin wondered why the show had stopped. "So whose brain was that anyhow? Strange shape."

No one replied, but Paloon didn't want the silence to continue. "It belongs to the native. It appears that someone has reprogrammed him."

"What!?" Larin's voice jumped as he threw an arm to point at the door. "You mean that toasted piece of flesh has frapping wetware mods? What in the hooha is happening on this rock?"

"Cool it." Paloon motioned with his hand. "Yes, it's true. And we need to figure out what to do about it."

A tense calm overtook the room as everyone thought about the possibilities. The individual opinions clashed and rarely matched. No one in the room even felt sure of their own thoughts on what this could mean.

"Ky," Lyon began quietly as he kept looking at Oz, the green light having recently faded into a much darker color, "have you ever seen anything like this?"

The dextian's trance continued a bit longer before she shook her head. "No. Nothing this clean." She flicked a strand of hair off of her face and over the point of her right ear. "But being in a brain feels much different. Maybe I have, but I don't think so."

She blinked before facing Hitook. "How did it feel in there?"

The liqua's hair rustled as his head moved. He felt a sense of camaraderie in the statement but filed it away as the result of Ky being tired and having her defenses down. "I'm not that familiar with this kind of brain structure, but I didn't feel anything unusual."

"Mac," Lyon kept his back to the group, "what if we go in again, what's the likelihood of triggering something?"

"Great." Mac went to the edge of the table, this time complete with limp. "I don't know what these changes do, and I sure don't know what triggers them. The possibilities are endless. Setting off one of these things could flash fry his brain and wipe his memory clean, make his hair change colors or cause him to whistle Dixie. Your guess is as good as mine, but until I can finish a complete scan and do an extensive evaluation, his cranium is not safe."

Lyon's right cheek pulled back. "But he's okay now."

"Yeah, if you want to call a mild coma safe. His brain activity is low."

With a faint *swish*, Ky's tail sailed around and into her hands, and she began to fiddle with it between her fingers. Such an act served as a dextian sign of mild rudeness when in the company of others such as guests. The onlookers knew that but weren't raised that way, so they didn't care. Paloon gave it a brief thought and figured Ky was starting to feel comfortable with the team. In fact, he had figured wrong. She really didn't know she was doing it; frustration and agitation had gotten the better of her, and playing with her tail was usually the result.

Larin, who had been abnormally quiet, watched with disbelief as the others remained silent with their own thoughts. He cranked his head askew, forcing his neck to explode with three pulsing pops, before he flew forward to pound the table with his fist. Everyone turned his direction.

"This is frapping bullshit!" He stood as his arms went wild in pointing, especially at the subject of his outburst. "I've been shot at by tech from my own planet's military in a compound crawling with my own frapping people on a backward rock in *p'tahian*-frapping space. We can't get frap out of that frapping traitor. And you pick up a stray local who has a hot-wired central nervous system. Excuse me, but what the frap is going on? I mean, this is becoming a—"

"Sit down." Paloon's firm voice needed nothing else, but Larin didn't wind down that easily.

"But th—"

"Don't make me say it again."

Larin hesitated a few moments before gradually taking his seat amid continued hand gestures. Just as the rolbrid settled in, he began to lunge forward again, but Paloon shot him a "try me" look.

As the tension eased, Paloon evenly addressed the concern. "I'm sure we are all wondering about how weird this assignment has become. When it's not all-out combat, things get...unclear, and that's just part of the job." He unfolded his arms to clasp hands over his belly. "This has become an interesting situation. If we figure out what's going on soon enough, we may be able to save this planet. If we fail, there's a good chance we will all die. Now, I, for one, am all for trying to figure out what's going on regardless of how weird it gets. Getting upset about it won't help much."

No one said anything—quiet agreement.

"So, Larin, give me one question."

The rolbrid looked up from the table toward Paloon. He started to doubt his own thoughts, but then let one out. "Who could have tampered with the local's brain?"

"Hmm," Paloon nodded his head, "good one. Well, Mac, thoughts?"

"That's a rough one, but I'm sure it wasn't done on this planet; they don't have anything near the technology required for this. You could find such capabilities among several races, but the cleanliness of most of this surgery is what makes it stand out. The doc was either extremely good, I mean seriously damn good and lucky, or there's advanced technology at work, beyond Corps tech, like experimental techniques or advanced gene surgery."

Lyon, who had turned toward the group awhile back, hummed before querying. "Could these mods be detected?"

Mac looked about as if wondering if anyone had even been listening to him. "I detected them. What are you getting at?"

"I mean, can they be detected by terrans? Is it possible that they could have even picked up the changes?"

Concern took residence on Mac's holographic face as he stroked his beard. “Possibly.” Mac spoke slowly as he continued to think it out. “It would be rough. Some of their more advanced electromagnetic scanners might be able to pick it up, but the signal would be very faint. It would need to be tuned properly, and they would really have to be looking for it.”

Lyon dropped his chin and mumbled, “They don’t know.”

“What?” Paloon thought he knew what he heard.

Lyon paused a bit before turning with a surprising wide-awake look on his face. “Ah, nothing.” He headed for the stairs. “We’ve all been working hard and need sleep. It would be best if we give this a fresh look in the morning.” He paused before taking the first step and made sure he had everyone’s attention. “So go to bed, rest and don’t set an alarm; I don’t plan to.”

He finished the end of statement while ascending the stairs, and he soon disappeared behind the metal door.

The group waited silently for a few more moments before Mac and his hologram faded from view, but even then they didn’t move from their seats until Paloon nodded and left himself.

Chapter 19

Perplexity.

The whole bit baffled him.

Yabuki watched the post apocalyptic activity and let the mildly dusty wind wrestle with his long overcoat. A zephyr moved his sunglass down his moist nose a bit, so he readjusted them with two, gloved fingers.

In front of him gaped an immense crater. About a quarter of the way around its circumference were the remnants of the city's initial response force. Among the mixture of awake uniformed officers and disheveled plain clothes detectives rested a small mobile command post, a fire department rescue vehicle and a conglomeration of civilian vehicles. The number of puzzled faces had dwindled in the past day but only because some had been sent home. Besides, there really wasn't much they could do.

What Yabuki didn't like was the recent arrival of a few suits. They didn't flash any badges, but they reeked of federal agents. Regardless of which branch they served, he liked it best when they were far away from him. He didn't want anything to do with them. What did they want anyway? It wasn't like they could do anything more than what everyone else had done: stand there, stare and scratch their heads.

Yabuki moved his attention back to the maw in front of him. A small construction plant and a compound of buildings once stood here. Now, among the sparse buildings and expansive storage lots, rested a very, very large void.

Sure, some would call it a crater, but this didn't have the properties of a normal crater. This crater lacked the rimmed ridge of debris that always came standard. The concave dent also didn't follow the regular rules, as if its sole purpose for existence was to defy every law of physics.

To Yabuki, it was simply unbelievable, yet here it was in front of him, mocking science. He removed a glove, crouched and reached down into the crater to rub his hands across the surface. Smooth, perfectly smooth. Not one single bump from the mixture of pebbles, chunks of hardened clay or long buried variety of debris. Yabuki couldn't feel the now exposed roots of the grass at his feet; it simply felt like glass. Unnatural.

He stood and instinctively wiped his hands on a handkerchief he retrieved from his inside coat pocket. The cloth remained bright white, as not a single fleck of dirt had transferred to his hand. When he folded the handkerchief and returned it, he re-gloved his hand before removing a gold cigarette case just long enough for him to take one. A lighter came from his outside pocket, and with a fancy flick that had became standard for him, he lit the cigarette and gazed at the freak of nature before him.

Where to begin? How did one begin to track down an entire building? The obvious fact was that the building simply didn't exist any more. Not even a single speck of rubble could be found.

Troubling would be putting it mildly. Confounding, not even close. Unsettling, somewhat. The most accurate was disquieting. The bit at the warehouse and now this. And this really didn't settle well.

"Put that out!"

Yabuki didn't care for the tone of the voice, which approached him from the side. He turned to see a thirty-something blue-collar variety worker with a yellow hard hat and a hard expression on a worn face.

The returning expression from Yabuki must not have been a happy one, because the demander softened a bit.

"Please put out that cigarette." He pointed with his chin at the crater. "We haven't made sure there's no gas leaks yet. I'd prefer to go home to my family tonight without the need of an ambulance."

Yabuki took one final long drag of the cigarette. The tip blazed red in defiance as the two locked expressions. He pinched it between his finger and thumb before flicking it to the ground. A brief sizzle singed as the embers touched the moist grass. Yabuki let a thick cloud of smoke roll across his face.

Breaking the stare contest, the man in the hard-hat turned to the suited man behind him. "There he is. I've got things to do."

The suit removed his glasses and briefly watched the blue-collar worker walk away. The brief contact had raised mild questions on what had made that person so bitter with life.

After the glasses were stowed, the Asian gentleman reached for a shake. He opened his mouth to reintroduce himself to the man he already knew, but Yabuki greeted first.

"Hello, Agent Kim." Disdain tinted the words, and Yabuki didn't acknowledge the attempt to shake hands; he simply gave a faint bow of his head. "What brings you out of the office for our second meeting this month? You specialize in missing buildings?"

In the previous case, the agent had looked into a bizarre warehouse explosion. During that meeting, Kim had learned two things: Yabuki remained a bit of a traditionalist but had little respect for law enforcement of any kind. This encounter only re-emphasized the impression.

"I was told you're now representing Fairway Industries. I would like to ask you some questions."

"I represent Kurosawa Investments; Fairway Industries is a subsidiary."

Kim noted the information, then decided to turn and join in staring at the crater since he didn't feel too comfortable looking at someone who wasn't returning the acknowledgment.

The bureau had been watching Kurosawa Investments for some time. Theories it had in abundance; hard evidence, very little. Nothing seemed to stay stationary long enough, and insiders had a troubling way of disappearing shortly after recruitment.

"What do you do for Kurosawa Investments?"

"I'm an executive aide."

"So what kind of work does an executive aide do in your company?"

"What I'm told to do."

Kim nodded again. "Fair enough. How long have you been working with Kurosawa Investments?"

"Twelve years," Yabuki turned to face the agent who returned the gesture, "but you already know that, don't you?"

Only a well-trained blank expression remained.

"Is there a point to this questioning?"

Kim gestured at the crater, "I'm sure you can agree this is rather unusual. Few terrorists consider a factory of sea-going shitters a target."

Yabuki kept a stern face. "Did we cause this to collect the insurance?"

"You said it, not me, and we haven't ruled that out."

Yabuki adjusted the fit on his leather gloves. "Sewer gases can get rather explosive."

"How explosive?"

"That all depends on what you ate last night." Yabuki clasped his hands in front of him and pivoted on his left heel. "Or maybe instead of making toilets, we somehow made tiny plutonium reactors, and one exploded. That sounds more like your agency's style, right along the lines of your presidential assassination theories."

Kim calmly glared at Yabuki. "We are here to help. We'll have an easier time of it with your company's cooperation."

"Help?" Yabuki kept his voice calm. "Our factory is missing, Agent Kim. When someone reports they have found our factory in their backyard, call me; otherwise, try looking for—"

A ringing came from Yabuki's pocket. He put the cell phone to his ear. "Yabuki Yumiro."

Both turned slightly away from each other.

"Good." Yabuki looked at his watch. "Get the one from my office." He looked skyward again, further away then back at the agent. "No, the one behind my desk." Yabuki turned again and picked up the force in his voice. "The third one." A pause. "Yes. Prepare the package, and I'll meet you in fifteen minutes."

He put the phone away and shifted back to the agent. "I'm sure you know how to get in touch with me."

Kim gave another nod and watched as Yabuki walked away. He continued to watch until Yabuki got into the passenger side of a waiting car that soon pulled away.

The agent now had many theories, and he didn't like most of them.

Dust devils whipped around the mostly barren terrain littered with bumps of red stone of differing sizes. The whistling wind occasionally gave an auditory bow to the call of a couple of vultures that had yet to begin their standard circle of death. Quickly changing colors started their dance across the sky as the sun headed for retirement. Shadows slowly began their evening stretch as the dry atmosphere carried only the smell of dust and perspiration.

Takehiko adjusted the last knot and used an already soaked bandana to wipe sweat from his forehead. He poked the bandana into his back pocket before examining the victim for a while. Takehiko placed his hands on his hips and took the pose of an overconfident body builder; he had the build for it: well muscled but with a smaller physique that kept him from looking like a steroid junkie. He gave a slight grin, then flicked his head so beads of moisture sailed from the tips of black, spiked hair and into the face of his *guest*.

He glanced down at the black bag a few feet away and hoped he could get the system connected without asking for help. There were only so many times he could be called stupid or slow before it really got on his nerves, so he tried at every attempt to do the best he could. Sometimes things would just go wrong. It was only his fault some of the time. Okay, most of the time.

Two small, black boxes came out of the bag with a strings of cables so twisted that it took Takehiko another ten minutes to unwind them. Meanwhile, the rest of his brain remained so focused on telling him that his bad luck had already began that he lost track of time and completed the task in a blink, by his standards.

Takehiko placed the black boxes on the cross beam with one at each side of his *friend's* head. He then successfully connected the wires into a mini receiver, after which he attached a wireless microphone's transmitter to his guest's belt. As he clipped the microphone itself to the collared shirt, Takehiko adjusted the shirt slightly to straighten the row or buttons to make it appear more presentable. Pride overcame him as he stood back and beamed happily at the doomed man.

Screams echoed across the desert as Takehiko ripped the duct tape from the face, then went straight to work gathering a few items strewn about—a post-hole digger, hammer, other implements—putting the smaller items in the black duffle bag.

Nervousness, fear and begging mixed together into a peculiar whine. "Are you just going to leave me here to die?"

Honestly, Lieutenant Rick Jackson truly had not yet grasped the gravity of it all. Any bystander could have seen the man's life was forfeit at this point, yet Rick's mind held onto the highly improbable shred of a practically nonexistent hope that this rather hopeless situation would turn out in his favor. Even as each second of his life counted down with reminders that hope was moot, Rick sought optimism in every half-second. This miraculous event of terran sentience went unnoticed.

The police lieutenant even uncontrollably began to test the bonds that held him to the post and crossbeam, something he hadn't attempted until now, something to do with having his freedom of speech returned, maybe. Even the slightest freedom did make one hunger for more.

Takehiko finished, then watched the lieutenant in mild amusement as one would watch a mouse attempt to climb the wall of its glass cage.

"No," he finally answered. "I haven't been told to leave you. Yabuki-san doesn't leave until he's finished with his sport."

Rick stopped what little movement he had been able to make and squinted his bruised eyes to reduce the sun's glare. It failed to help him get a better look at the man's face. "What sport? What sick thing does he have planned now? I've told you all I know?" Whining seeped back into his voice. "Honestly!"

The bruises and cuts visible on his exposed flesh hinted that telling everything probably happened long ago.

"I came to you guys." Rick's inflection gave away now that tears began to well in his eyes. "Why would I come to—"

"Ah," came a voice from the speakers next to Rick's head, "that's what I'm counting on."

Takehiko had since found himself a place to sit a good distance away, and Rick could barely tell that he was making some kind of hand motion. Rick followed the movement toward the horizon. It took a few moments until the black speck distorted by convection currents seemed to stand out.

Hesitation in Rick's voice came in the form of a question. "Yabuki?"

Yabuki pulled the binoculars away and handed them to Takahiro, who took a few steps away to position himself.

"Yes, lieutenant." Yabuki closed his eyes, lowered his head and focused for a moment. "I hope you aren't offended with this long-distance electronic goodbye, you see, because doing this from a conversational distance is not very sporting. Wouldn't you agree?"

"Wha—I don't know what you mean." Rick tried to keep himself from full begging mode, but the pleading was obvious in his voice. "Haven't I served you? I promised, and I will not break that promise."

Rick continued, but Yabuki detached his senses from it. He raised his head to look across the rocks and shrubs of the desert floor to gaze upon the half of a speck of black. The heat caused the speck to wiggle like a frantic worm. A good challenge indeed.

A dust devil cruised into view, then began to dance with a shrub. Several dried branches broke loose to join the mini-maelstrom before it continued along its path that led to a boulder just large enough to disrupt the whipping wind. The branches and collected dust exploded in a multitude of directions as the tiny tornado unraveled itself.

Without looking, Yabuki reached over and made a few adjustments to the scope that rested on the rifle hanging from his right hand. Faint clicks counted away distance and compensated for wind. The clicks tapered to quiet then Yabuki make a few more adjustments for the convection mirage.

Well-practiced moves unlocked the bolt and pulled it back. Yabuki fingered a bullet from the black holster of eight strapped to the stock. The shell slid into the chamber with the sweet ting of metal-on-metal—a calming note, soothing. The bolt came forward and locked into place.

He watched the distant image a while longer before raising the rifle. In the next few seconds he lowered his head to the stock and fired. He had taken aim long ago. The echoing shot rumbled into the distance as Yabuki dropped the rifle and lowered his focus, letting the remaining outside world seep back in.

Screams came through the single earpiece, and with the other ear, he heard from Takahiro, "Left hand, third finger."

Profanities formed a seemingly endless loop. Grunts and spits completed the mixture. "You're fucking nuts, Yumiro! So fucking insane! I've fixed so many fucking situations, and this is the fucking thanks I get? You bastard!"

"Be quiet." Yabuki contemplated his missed shot but took pride in his luck. "Your service is not in question." He began to refocus. "This is about honor."

Rick resumed ranting, but Yabuki had severed most of the inputs from his senses so he could focus on the few he needed. Without adjustment to the scope, the steps and movement mimicked the previous procedure. As Yabuki lowered his weapon, the report came, "Hand, left, center."

That's what he wanted to hear.

Yabuki kept the screams from getting on his nerves, for now. The phrases mostly included profanities of several varieties. After a while, the pointed comments tapered into grasps for survival, but practicing psychology in stressful situations rarely worked.

"You're nuts!" Rick occasionally spat out the sweat that flowed down his face into the crevice of his mouth. "You're going to bring the entire fucking police force down on your fucking ass! I'm the least of the problems. You're bringing it all down, and for what? Nothing!"

"You remind me of a caught fish. You fight and struggle as if your life actually means something. Sad."

"What? How dare you? You won't even face me in a fair—"

"There's no such thing as fair!" Yabuki let his emotions go and forced himself to calm. "Life is terminal. You haven't realized that yet."

"What are you talking about? You've gone mad." Rick paused to grunt at a stab of pain, and before he could resume talking, Yabuki had cut his senses.

The reverberating shot faded into "Shoulder, left, in two and a half, down one and a quarter."

Lips curled into smile. Once again a good shot.

This time Rick's screams almost made Yabuki want to rip out the earpiece, not because of the noise blaring in his ear, but because of the nature of the screamed comments.

"You fucking Jap! You're all fucking crazy! Your whole damned family has fucking lost touch with reality!"

"So," Yabuki snapped his head right and left as cracks fired in sequence from his neck, "your loyalty finally shows itself. I've never cared for letting outsiders in."

"At least we're not so—" Rick gritted and cursed away some pain, "we're not crazy enough to kill people on a whim and then just wait for someone to stumble onto the bodies."

"Imagination." Yabuki started focusing. "You're far from the first. All found themselves in concrete coffins in the bottom of the ocean."

Rick's fear peaked. The rants reached a feverish level, but Yabuki had his aim point and continued to focus away the remaining distractions.

As he raised the weapon, a comment broke through the concentration. "I had your sister." Yabuki's jaw clenched. Whether it was true or not, the police lieutenant went too far. The mission of family honor became personal honor. His focus went into a steady state, and he stepped through the motions rapidly and unhindered.

A shot.

"Biceps, right, off-center one and three quarters left."

Screams.

A shot.

"Abdomen, lower center, critical."

Grunts.

A shot.

"Abdomen, upper left quadrant, critical."

Moans.

A shot.

"Neck, thorax, center, lethal."

Gurgling spurts.

A shot.

"Oh, damn! Head, right eye, lethal. Shit!"

Silence.

Chapter 20

"You're missing my point!" Larin slapped a metal ruler against his thigh. He had found the thing under the gas station counter early that morning and had been fidgeting with it ever since.

"And what point is that?" came Paloon's voice.

Larin leaned in the backed swivel stool, propped himself against the wall and turned his head toward the door to the garage. "My point is that natives, regardless of location and evolution, shouldn't be trusted."

Clanks and the sound of a grinding motor whined for a minute.

"Don't you think that's being a bit too...almighty?"

Tinkling gurgles rumbled from Larin's throat. Paloon took pleasure in getting Larin irritated. It didn't seem to take much, and Larin's reactions often proved to be entertaining. Normally, Paloon would have to at least worry slightly that if he pushed too far, the rolbrid would snap. But Paloon had come to realize that Larin held the Corps in such esteem that respect to rank would always keep him from crossing the line.

"That has nothing to do with it. It's Fate's design of existence. Natives never have trust, true trust, so we shouldn't trust them."

"You really don't like," a ka-lunk and thud broke the question, "like the thought of having this Ozuna person locked in the basement, do you? It's probably what's truly affecting your sleep."

"I don't sleep well because of all the chirping, but no, I don't like having that native around." Larin slapped the ruler against his head. "Someone reprogrammed his frapping brain, and I don't like the thought of that. We don't know what he might do if he wakes."

A heavy piece of machinery banged metallically against the stone floor. "You can't tell me you honestly think he'll become a threat as soon as he opens his eyes. What could he do that we couldn't handle?"

"Who knows?" Larin pointed the ruler at the door to the garage. "But you can't tell me he's perfectly safe, either."

Larin didn't even pause enough for a reply because it would have ruined his point. "I didn't think so. Ever since I got this mission, it has been a frapping hooha. We all know we're in a position to be expendable, and I don't like the idea of bringing in more wild cards."

"What should we do, kill him?"

"Absolutely."

"But we don't know who's messed with his head yet."

"So? I don't frapping care. I don't want to keep him around until his owners come searching for their hot-wired native. He's bad luck."

"Oh, my," Paloon grunted for a moment, "you're afraid of a self-declared superstition."

"Self-declared! You're kidding, right!?" Larin flew forward fast enough that the stool rocked, and only quick reflexes with his hands kept him from bashing into the counter.

Paloon grinned quietly to himself. He walked to a bench to retrieve a power drill and returned to open the hood of the step van.

Larin searched frantically for something, kicking over some plastic bins and cardboard boxes under the counter. In his anxiety, he forgot and then remembered the stash in his pants. Quickly, he took out a chur root. He didn't have time to gnaw, so he bit a couple of chunks off and ground them together in his mouth for a few moments before slipping the mess into his throat pouch and swallowing. It would take awhile for the actual effects to kick in, but Larin only needed the placebo.

"Let me put it this way: How many times have you been down in the thick of it—living with and trying to work with natives for long periods of time?"

Paloon stopped his work and thought about it, but Larin didn't have time for it.

"Well?"

"I'm thinking, but I can't say I have. You may count this as a first."

"Of course, you're Grey Wolf. You live in your machines; you never have personal contact with natives. Doing that is my job, and no matter how many times I do it, it's all the same: They don't trust us." Larin finished the chur root and continued as he crunched. "There are two types: the ones that are too oblivious of their own role in the universe to know any better, and the ones who are somewhat aware and it scares the frapping life out of them."

The whirl of the drill went in waves for the next few minutes. "How does either one make natives *dangerous*?"

"What!? Are you listening to me?" Larin slapped the metal ruler against his thigh to try to make the point. "No matter what face they fake, they simply don't trust you and never will. The stupid ones don't trust you because they can't comprehend you, and the smart ones don't trust you because they figure you're being sneaky and are after something—after all, that's probably what they would do. There's no trust left any more."

As Larin took a slight gasp of air, Paloon squeezed in. "Excuse me, but that's a bit negative and paranoid on your part, don't you think?"

"No!" Larin started gesturing at no one. "Come on! You've frapping seen it. We've gone into world after world doing our best to save everyone's butt. Wars all over the frapping place, and we're the ones who fight to stop it. Both of our races have lost so much just because of war. You pricked in just as I did. It's our life to try to keep such devastation from happening again, to stop all the frapping crime and crap from becoming dissension and war."

Larin didn't stop to breathe but pointed to the ceiling even though no one was there to see it. "Heck, that liqua almost lost his entire race, the whole frapping thing, because of war and hate, and he frapping joined. All this crap we see, and we're here to stop it. But...but...but how could they not frapping trust us?"

Paloon took note of Larin's sputtering to a stop—he just ran out of ranting. But Paloon halted his work to contemplate Larin's words, which had him a bit off guard. Larin had let his love of the Corps shine through. Paloon had wondered earlier if the rolbrid had other reasons for joining, but now it seemed that Larin, regardless of how frank he might seem, still kept some stuff to himself until he let his emotions flow.

That dip into psychology proved mildly entertaining, but Paloon felt like being sarcastic today. The mood was right, and he had the ammo and a prime target. He didn't know when the window of quiet would close, so Paloon jumped in phrase first.

"Alas," for some unknown reason Paloon allowed himself to imitate one of Mac's accents, "wasn't it you who said the Corps was represented by power hungry people who like to play mightier-than-thou games?"

Larin's train of thought crashed as he found himself forced to think about it. "When did I say that?"

"In the ship...on the way here."

A clatter-like humming signaled a complete implosion of Larin's planned point.

"I guess. But why?"

"If what you said is true and the Corps is full of mightier-than-thou, power hungry judges, don't you think that's enough to justify distrust from natives?"

Larin stumbled. He couldn't even work up negativity at Paloon for turning his words around. Contemplation of the hypothesis began to form a loop in his mind, which at the same time screamed that he needed to come up with a quick reply.

"You're missing the point." It was all he could come up with, and he knew he should have just been quiet.

"Oh, really, and why's—"

The glass door bashed open hard and loud, but not louder than the shout that flooded the place. "Don't fucking move, asshole, or I'll blow your fucking head off!"

A veil of surreal time enveloped the gas station. Every detail became sharp, clear and known to everyone. To the new arrivals, it was part of a hold up. To Larin and Paloon, it was the feel of combat.

Two young natives in ratty, knitted, dark brown ski masks quickly took positions in front of the counter. Worn pants and faded black sweat jackets seemed to be the style. Clean shoes shined from their feet so brightly they seemed out of place in their wardrobes.

In the back, one whipped around in an attempt to provide cover and to scan the area. He reeked of fear. His twitches weren't needed to see if anyone else was around. Sweat began to coat the slick, wooden grip of the stub-nosed six-shooter, and he did quick grip-and-releases, although they didn't—and wouldn't—help.

The semi-automatic pointed at Larin's nose stared at him with almost as much determination as the eyes of its owner. The lead man emanated a wall of confidence and surety. He either had too much ego or so much experience that doubt soon left the picture and robbing stores became second nature to breathing. Only the faintest hint of stress crept into his voice, likely from his need to do the job quickly.

Neither had a clue that this "easy take" was actually a nest of trouble.

The front man shook his pistol firmly. "Stop talking to your bitch self and unload the fucking drawer." He tossed a worn, black backpack that almost slid off the counter. "You've got five seconds, and I start fucking shooting."

Larin didn't know if that native weapon even had a chance of penetrating his hide, but that was not why he showed no signs of worry. This was child's play. "I wasn't talking to myself."

With a stunned look that became more determined and a few steps forward, the leader cocked the pistol's hammer and raised the weapon's angle. "You want to fucking die, bitch? Fill the fucking bag!"

"He was talking to me."

The gunmen found themselves a bit off guard with Paloon's entrance. The newbie twitched so feverishly back and forth and all over the place that he actually fired a round into the door frame next to Paloon. The leader kept his cool, though, returning his aim to the short, ugly man behind the counter.

"My boy's a bit trigger happy, so stop fucking stalling and fill the fucking bag!"

Paloon leaned against the door while wiping his hands with an oily, red rag. He turned his head to survey the damage to the door frame, then looked back at the twitchy robber. "That wasn't very nice. What did that plank of wood do to you to deserve that?"

Calm confidence in the voice of the "victims" started to rub the head robber the wrong way, so much so that he began to get nervous. This just wasn't going right. He had to take command of the situation quickly. Gut feeling told him that if he didn't, he'd risked things going all wrong.

He whipped his aim back to Paloon and started yelling. "Fill the fucking bag now, bitch, or your funny, fucking boyfriend ain't seeing tomorrow."

Larin had been watching the movements of the two rather closely. During the whole robbery, they had continuously made one fatal flaw, but he waited for the right moment to exploit it, and here it came.

Choom!

A deadly rain of tiny balls of metal peppered the hands of both robbers and shattered the glass door. Larin had withdrawn and fired the semi-automatic shotgun from under the counter at a speed that could not be matched by any terran. An empty shell kicked out and began its hollowed clattering on the floor.

They shouldn't have let themselves stay in a perfect alignment with Larin's line of fire.

Arms flailed as the two instinctively reeled from the event. Balance had no place as they went crashing to the ground. The new guy fumbled into a tower-like structure of cheap sunglasses, setting off a rattling cascade that rivaled the shotgun in noise. Blood splatters freckled the dirty floor as the pistols fell, clanking and bouncing in a sporadic see-saw motion that surprisingly didn't set off another round.

Larin bounded over the counter and landed with a foot in the armpit of the leader, the muzzle of the shotgun crammed so hard into his throat that he wouldn't have been able to talk even if he had something to say. "Under Fifteen R dash Twenty-three point Six, you are hereby—"

"Halt, that's an order!" Paloon knew very well Larin was about to try to use his authority under interstellar law to execute anyone who commits a life-threatening act against a member of the Corps in the performance of their duties. The final stipulation always seemed frivolous since Corps members were supposedly always "on-duty."

Larin's voice grumbled so loudly it verged on being incoherent. "Give me one frapping reason why I shouldn't vape this frapping punk!"

"First of all, they don't fall under our laws." Paloon felt the need to fight law with law. "We can't force them to comply with a code they are unaware of. Besides," Paloon looked around outside, "we don't need locals crawling all over this place."

"Frap!" Larin jabbed the muzzle harder.

The leader gasped in pain as something cracked. There was going to be more than a bruise there in the morning.

Paloon came forward, kicked the pistols behind him, grabbed Larin's shoulder and pulled him back. Now Paloon stood over the two and examined them for a while before gesturing for the door. "I'd recommend you leave and never come back. Count yourselves lucky this time."

The two cradled their maimed hands but halted their crying and yelping. Sniffles began, making sickening cycles of noise. But the would-be robbers barely moved, except for a faint rocking motion.

"Well!" Paloon put on his pissed face. "Move!"

As the two scrambled to their feet and scampered out the busted door, Paloon added a note. "I wouldn't go to a medical facility. Cops there ask questions."

Paloon and Larin watched the two run and stumble their way away from the place.

The surreal nature of the incident faded as they looked around. Only a couple of the few people on the street even looked in the direction of the gas station. Odd reactions on this planet seemed to be the norm. But as Paloon stood on the crunching pebbles of the shattered glass that had remained in the store, he decided it may have been for the better.

"See what I mean?"

Paloon turned to Larin. "What?"

"These frapping natives can't be trusted. They're primitives." Larin adjusted himself and propped the shotgun against his shoulder. "I feel like I'm trapped on the wrong side of a zoo cage. You never know what these poor excuses for sentient beings will do next."

Paloon had nothing to say to that. Honestly, he couldn't argue with the observation. He didn't like the situation and doubted anyone in the team did. How could they? Larin was right.

But dwelling on it wasn't going to clean the mess. Taking it all in, Paloon shook his head slightly and looked over at Larin and that shotgun.

"Surprisingly, that's actually one rather indiscriminating weapon."

Larin smiled a bit and took a hold of it with both hands to take another superficial gaze at it. "Yeah. I like it."

Chapter 21

The chill made the night air heavy. That didn't stop the wind from slashing about the roof top and slicing through Hitook's furry hide. Strands of hair took flight so often that he almost appeared to be infused with static electricity as he sat erect with his legs folded under him.

Meditation had become an avenue of concentration for the liqua. At times, his emotions seemed too much for him. Other techniques never really offered him refuge from the raging self-destructive urges he felt when his emotional guard weakened.

Now and then, it would still happen: Control would fail, and emotion would flare. Call it anger, hate, evil or misdirected care, it didn't matter. He disliked how he felt when it happened. If he had to put it to one word, it would be "desire."

He desired retribution, revenge, retaliation. "Who" didn't matter; it just had to be. Everyone became a possible outlet for his pain, regardless of previous acquaintance or friendship. Once released, the emotion screamed like a wildfire, and generally those closest got burned.

But that's not what Hitook disliked the most. When it emerged, so did another emotion: enjoyment. He liked it. A few times it seemed as if he thrived on it, almost as if he had to have it to live. Hate became his fuel, his drug. To snuff it out felt like taking away the source of a chemical dependency. It felt like suicide.

Every time, Hitook's reasonable self sat on the sidelines screaming at the actions. Nothing seemed to work. The emotion had control. All he could do was watch...watch and weep.

Control didn't exist in his childhood. There were periods when the emotion thrived and times when it rested, giving him temporary control of his actions. It took so much concentration at first, but he couldn't hold on to the control for long. He refused to let that stop him; he tried even harder the next time, and the next, and the next, and on and on.

He had long lost count how many attempts it took for him to maintain control throughout the night so he could wake as himself.

None of it would have been possible without the masters at House Bravo. His life began with them. That's how he felt. Little of his previous darkness remained; it was even absent from his memory—must have come as part of his control over the emotion.

The control had now become his outlet for enjoyment. His time on the roof of the gas station was no different. Control came in the form of thrusting his presence forward in small streams. It resembled a snail extending an antennae and retracting it but in more of a spiritual sense. He would redirect and fire again. Distance varied: sometimes a couple of feet and sometimes a couple hundred feet.

This process continued as the pace grew faster and faster. Adrenaline coursed his veins from the rushing feeling, but his enjoyment didn't peak until he starting aiming in multiple directions at the same time. Nothing he could physically feel even approached a fair comparison.

The barrage of essence spikes would have gone unnoticed, but for Ky it initially represented a fury of confusion. Sensing the wild whipping, pattern-less energy put her on edge at first, but Ky calmed as her peeking eyes saw the source. She continued with her gradual emergence from the square hole of an access hatch and left its hinged lid lying against the tar roof.

Neither had to say a thing, but Ky sensed Hitook changing pattern to purposefully dodge Ky. She appreciated the gesture. Getting hit by one of those spikes had the potential to permanently damage spirits.

She stood, scanned the raised roof and took a bit of solace in the archaic design. Roofs with seven-foot privacy walls were often only found in the most secluded of cultures. Strange as it seemed, she continued with preparing herself.

Black covered her as she wore her favorite body suit for practice. Unlike her last training with her sister, she didn't have a crossbow harness. This time Ky had three swords strapped to her back. Two crossed each other in an X form as the third lay in the middle, and each hilt pointed to the ground.

Ky walked to the edge of the roof away from Hitook. She couldn't tell if Hitook was practicing or playing around. It really didn't matter; sometimes even playing around could be a form of practice.

When she felt the distance was sufficient, Ky oriented herself and began some focusing techniques with just hand and foot movements. After she felt focused, her tail grabbed the right sword, withdrew it quickly but quietly from the scabbard and gracefully placed it in her waiting palms.

Upon contact with the weapon, she exploded into practice move after practice move. Ky felt that at her level she shouldn't have to gradually progress through a warm up. All of her energy went forward, and she trained herself in maintaining focus as well as in the movements.

Fans of silver grey whirled about her body in almost every direction as the whistling blade became a low yet steady background noise. Relentless persistence pushed her from move to move without pause. Well-timed steps maintained balance as she advanced, retreated, spun and advanced yet again. Often the weapon became nearly invisible as Ky made a side attack only to return to mixtures of front and back attacks and blocks.

Hitook continued his practicing as his mind's eye watched Ky with the attentiveness of a lazy cat with nothing better to look at. Everyone needed practice, so it meant little to him other than a form of mild entertainment. Granted, terrans might have found the speed at which Ky practiced far beyond extraordinary, but Hitook had seen faster. He by no means belittled Ky; he had yet to obtain such speed. It was just that after one sees a well-trained iilunaq warrior demonstrate the noble "Edged Dance" during a ceremony, all the other sword masters seemed to move as if mired in goo. The iilunaq's extremely flexible reptilian skeleton undoubtedly contributed greatly to the speed.

Every few moments, Hitook noticed Ky continue at an ever-increasing pace. It wasn't until these moments started to stretch out and seemed to become an eon that the liqua fully took notice. Hitook had continued his practice for the same amount of time, but energy flowed around Ky with such spiritual illumination that it had to be stressful to maintain. Before he could stop himself from sounding intrusive, he had to ask.

"Why are you pushing yourself so hard?"

Ky didn't readily answer the mental question. After several seconds went by, Hitook felt he had pried too much. In actuality, Ky thought about it but didn't stop. Neither did Hitook, who extended seventeen spikes of his presence at one time.

"My sister." The answer came from Ky slowly, as if questioning herself as she thought it.

"Is your sister your trainer?"

She huffed a short chuckle as if to say, "Not likely in a long shot." Ky failed to recognize how close Hitook's novice intuition came to an underlining truth.

"Is it anger?" Hitook asked because, given what he had gone through, this seemed the obvious conclusion.

"No. No." Ky shifted weight, spun in place and proceeded to attack the air in front of her. *"You're all wrong."* She didn't immediately enlighten Hitook as to why; Ky fumbled with the right words. Once she felt like she had them, she began, but they came out in parts. *"She's better at bladed weapons. As hard as I've always tried, I could never take her in a one-on-one battle. She's got the knack, and I got the underdeveloped form of the gene. It takes all I have to hold my own."*

A faint grin slid across Hitook's face but remained hidden under white hair. He found vague humor in similarities.

"You?"

The question took Hitook off guard, his mind elsewhere. *"Excuse me."*

"And why are you practicing so hard? And don't say it's for fun. The number of spikes you're doing takes a degree of strain."

Hitook shrugged it off but not with smugness. *"It gets easier with practice."*

"So I've heard." Ky wrestled with the self-proclaimed attack on her ego about how much her skills lacked. Maybe she needed to prove to herself that, if it came down to it, she could overpower this talented acolyte. Something brought her to the edge and then pushed her over. Ky knew the answer but was too far gone to stop herself. *"Who did you train under?"*

"Master Kio Gon, primarily." Hitook relaxed his spikes. *"But I've received specialized training from Mas—"*

A dull twang reverberated next to Hitook's head, which barely moved out of the way. The shaking sword slowly calmed as it floated over the liqua's shoulder within the tight grip of Hitook's mental aura. Ky stood in the background with a slight twitch to her lips. A miss, but barely.

The ninja did not seek blood, though a bystander would argue otherwise. Hitook trusted something intangible. An acolyte may have little training compared to a ninja, but Hitook knew a challenge when confronted with one.

One thought released the blade, which flew back to Ky's waiting hand. She had already been pulling on it and would have broken it free in a few more seconds. At least that's what she told herself.

Mental energy flared around Hitook to the degree that his physical body began to glow with a faint blue light. The burst reached levels that could be detected by any enlightened individual, even if not tuned in. But Ky was tuned at the time, and the energy burst neared blinding levels.

The sensation was so strong, Ky believed she could smell it; maybe she did. Debate had no place; she just reacted. She whipped the sword around and drew it in front of her face perpendicular with her stance as her feet gripped the ground.

An aura spike fired at blinding speed from Hitook's back. Ky dropped the sword forty-five degrees and braced it with her other hand. Friction sounded with a gritty grinding as her feet slipped. She didn't lose her stance; however, the force pushed her back a couple of inches.

Ky hadn't expected that much force, so she began to wonder if she had rubbed Hitook the wrong way. It didn't matter now. She flared her own energy as her tail withdrew a second sword and placed it in a waiting palm.

As if yearning for the second weapon to make contact, Hitook launched a salvo of spikes. The liqua's body sat calmly, but mentally he was pushing himself. Spike after spike fired as fast as he could think.

In the physical world, Ky appeared as if she was frantically trying to cut a hole in the air, but in the mental realm, she was in a fight that could mean her life if either one of them slipped up. She thought about calling it off, but she had come to the roof for training and decided to use the opportunity.

Metallic snaps crackled from Ky's swords as she moved them so quickly they became invisible. Unlike her previous training routines, this time the swords became visible for just a split second as they paused to block, then disappear again only to re-appear elsewhere. Enhanced with Ky's mental energy, each blade could now withstand the force behind each spike. But when she had to block two spikes with one sword, she took on a mental strain. Too many like that and she would break down and loose the energy needed to hold her field in place.

Mentally, Hitook's form was blindingly busy. He tried to keep himself focused in a small enough space to allow him to dedicate a degree of his mental power to strategy. *Being predictable is for amateurs*, he remembered Master Gon telling him more than once. He pushed himself not to be predictable.

Minutes went by as the unyielding barrage continued. Beads of sweat barely had the chance to form on Ky's brow before they flew off as she danced about to keep up with the spikes. Meanwhile, Hitook's brow began to lower and tense as the strain grew. He didn't know how long he could continue, but he refused to quit without giving one last burst.

Ky noticed the amount of force as the spikes began to dwindle. She figured Hitook was finally wearing down; she figured wrong. What she noticed more resembled receding water right before a tsunami.

Incoming was a sweeping salvo two feet thick along the surface. Ky had to act quickly and knew she could jump it, but doing so would leave her balance vulnerable. She pounded her right sword into the roof, launched her body vertically and twisted the blade to align the narrow edge with the volleys.

A second wave rode the heels of the first. Ky began to wonder why but had little time before she was in trouble. The bombardment came so rapidly that spike after spike rattled her blade. She focused so much on trying to hold the field that she almost missed the heavy spike headed for her chest. The other sword barely made it in time, but the power of that spike, compounded with the damage to her field, threw her backwards.

Ky landed crouched with her right leg behind her and her left sword braced in front of her. The beginnings of pain ripped along her leg as the momentum from the attack continued to push her back along the roof. Mentally she was spent and needed time to refocus and repair her field, but Ky waited for another attack. It never came.

After a few moments of waiting, Ky reached out her right hand and mentally pulled her other sword out of the roof and called it back to her.

Hitook's head vibrated slightly as it slowly dropped. He gritted he teeth so tightly that pain began to pierce his jawbones. But at this point, Hitook would rather feel physical pain than the mental anguish he now suffered.

Satisfaction was the word for it. Ky wanted training, and she got it, but she too wanted a break. She stood, weakly at first and then with trained conviction. During a few steps backward, Ky slid the swords back into their sheathes before leaning against the wall that surrounded the roof.

She allowed herself to relax as her ego repaired itself with the knowledge that, even though she was taken to her limits, she still had enough energy left to take Hitook if necessary. Her head leaned back so she could look at the grey sky and the few stars that could pierce the veil.

Calmness overcame the rooftop as the two rested.

"You two up there?" Larin's partially muffled voice came from the access hatch.

Neither of the roof's occupants cared to answer.

The rolbrid's flat skull poked from the hole as his yellow eyes glanced from Hitook's slumped body to Ky's leaning and stargazing form.

"Is this what you guys do up here? Goof off?" Larin didn't get a reply, not that he waited for it. "Knight Kendrick wants you guys. Something important about that frapping traitor or some such nonsense."

Larin continued to gripe as he descended the ladder. Once the complaints faded completely, Ky rocked from her leaning stance, walked to Hitook and tapped him on the shoulder.

Together, they slowly left the roof.

Chapter 22

"What?" Lyon didn't want to believe the poor timing.

"Hey, you did shoot him with nanites, right?" Ky wasn't about to make excuses for her mental fatigue. "Use the nanites."

"It's not the same." Disappointment seeped into Lyon's voice. Mitnarsho had come out of the coma, and Lyon wanted to press now, hard. "You know we have a greater chance if you go in."

Ky folded her arms and scratched her lower back with her tail. "All I can offer you right now is that Hitook and I go together, just give us a moment. We won't be at peak, but without a good rest, that's all you're going to get."

Lyon grimaced briefly before releasing a breath. He couldn't chastise them for training, and he knew it. "Okay, fine. Do what you need to do and let me know when you're ready." Lyon glanced at Hitook before returning his gaze to Ky and nodding.

"Understood," Ky replied.

"Mac?" Lyon turned and headed for the door that led to the prisoner.

"Yeppers."

"Establish contact with the nanites." Lyon approached the door and peered through the window.

The rolbrid prisoner seemed limp. Mitnarsho had his head back in the rest, and his eyes were the only body parts moving. Those eyes glared back at Lyon's face in the fogging window.

Lyon knew this wasn't going to be easy. For as much time as he had put into this, he had nothing to show for it. The thought steeled his determination that he wasn't leaving the room without the information he wanted.

"Ready?"

"Ab-so-lute-ly."

Lyon punched open the door. "Well, how in the hell are you, 'Sho? Long time no see. Where have you been? Oh, yeah, I for—" The door closed.

Ky turned to Hitook. "What do you need?"

Hitook dropped his head from looking at the door and thought for a moment. "Charkoon."

Ky jittered a bit. "Whatever. It's your teeth. Mac, a glass of burth and a bowl of *charkoon*." She spoke the last word as if listening to a piercing squeal.

On the table appeared Ky's glass of white putty and a bowl of clear yellow liquid that bubbled as if it were a highly volatile carbonated drink. Faint, steam-like mists streaked in arcs across the surface. The appearance of steam was not the result of heat. The drink was actually cold, but chemical reactions caused molecules to fire in curved streams.

The two sat down and enjoyed their drinks in peace.

Lyon placed his palm on Mitnarsho's chest again. Mac saw the movement and commanded the nanites the same way.

The diaphragmatic tissue in the rolbrid's breathing cavity stopped responding. It took less than a minute before Mitnarsho's skin began to flush white and his eyes began to sink in. Attempts to gasp didn't yield even the slightest bit of air.

Lyon lifted his hand, so Mac released the nanites.

As Mitnarsho gulped the air, Lyon watched the fear in the rolbrid's eyes. Only a minute went by before Lyon did it again.

They had both lost count because Lyon only cared about fueling the fear and Mitnarsho could only think about making the best out of the short periods he was allowed to breathe.

The door opened, startling Lyon enough to make him let go and allow the rolbrid to breathe again.

Hitook stood behind Ky, who looked Mitnarsho over. Dried streaks of yellow tears striped the face, while from the ears trailed blood that had dried to milky white fingers running down the neck.

Ky grimaced at Lyon. "Can he even hear now?"

"Sure," Lyon smiled, "I've given plenty of time for his ears to heal." He turned his smile toward the rolbrid. "Isn't that right?"

Mitnarsho mustered the energy to glare back in disdain.

"See?" Lyon beamed proudly at Ky.

Apparently Lyon had been working out some frustration or stress on the practically defenseless rolbrid. Ky didn't feel like talking about it. The two of them had come to get a job done, and Ky kept her mind on that task.

"Are you ready?"

"Sure." Lyon pointed to the chairs on the other side of Mitnarsho's "command chair" though he commanded nothing at the moment.

As the two entered to take their seats, the knight jabbed a finger in Mitnarsho's chest. Mac followed by having the nanites home in on the position of the finger and tracked it as Lyon dragged the finger up the chest and along the neck, past the temples and to the top of the head. During the trek, the passage of the nanites was marked with uncomfortable and sometimes slightly painful ripples. Mitnarsho began twitching feverishly as if facing headfirst into typhoon-strength winds.

A puzzled look commanded Ky's face as she watched from her seat and wondered why Lyon did that instead of just telling Mac to move the nanites. Hitook sat calmly, but his nerves were on edge, like a new teenager at school wondering if he will be liked. This would represent his first actual interrogation.

Ky's face changed from puzzlement to slightly cocky. "Are you done? I'd like to get this over with."

The smile dropped from Lyon's face. Someone had burst his bubble, but his current playful mood remained. "Why? Do you have somewhere to go, or did you forget that you're stuck here just like me?" A smile flashed back, but Lyon continued before Ky could retort. "Now, 'Sho," he grabbed the rolbrid's head like a jar lid, "I'm going to give you one last chance to tell us what you know."

Mitnarsho's eyes darted from one of the room's occupants to the next. The presence of a liqua didn't bring as much fear as the realization that a dextian and a liqua were on the planet and in the same room. He correctly assumed they must be Corps, and judging by his captor's tone, they were House Bravo. As the encompassing reality sank it, Mitnarsho began shaking, and it wasn't from the nanites coursing in his system.

"How many beings does the Corps have on this planet?" The rolbrid's vocal cords vibrated more than usual.

Lyon yelled, "I ans—ask the questions here. After everything we've put you through, you still have the package to be bold about it." Lyon squeezed his thumb harder into the soft part of the rolbrid's forehead.

It was just enough to quiet the prisoner.

"Back to the reason why you have more visitors." Lyon smiled again. "Either start speaking or we're going to rip the information we want out of you."

"You don't understand. You don't want to be here."

Lyon knew he didn't want to be on this rock, but obviously this rolbrid meant it differently.

"Good, a bit of information. Please tell, why don't I want to be here?"

"I can only tell you that you don't want to be here." The hint of fear began to creep onto Mitnarsho's face. "Get off this planet and away from here before you're found."

"That's not an option I have." Lyon released the cranium and leaned back against a cabinet with his arms folded. "But this whole 'I can't tell' crap is getting annoying. And why do you all of a sudden have concern for the people who are your torturers?" Lyon briefly glanced at Ky. "You either rode the small shuttle to school or you're covering something." Lyon glared at his prisoner. "I don't like either."

Silence filled the room for a while. Then Lyon raised his open palm. "Apparently nobody feels like playing around. You have five to say something worth a damn before we rip." Lyon smiled and nodded at Ky and Hitook.

One finger dropped from Lyon's hand, then another.

"I-I-I can't tell you. I-I'll flat line if I say an—"

To describe what Mitnarsho felt as simply "pain" would be like calling the expansive universe a tad big. Every scrap of tissue in his defenseless body tensed to breaking points, then collapsed. Conscious control slipped, and the rolbrid's body flopped loose in the chair. He couldn't even scream to release some of the tension.

Oh, he wanted to scream so. Pain normally came from minor nerve damage, but to have one's biggest nerve cluster under attack formed pain of near infinite intensity. No normal person could withstand it without going brain dead. But the House Bravo duo kept the rolbrid's mind open.

Once a rip began, the brain had to keep operating or risk shutting down. A dead brain was useless with any retrieved information so severely scrambled that no one could ever be absolutely certain of the validity of anything found.

Mitnarsho didn't give a damn. He couldn't think, period. His life had become a world of agony so intense he could not remember anything else. It was as if a hundred sets of chopsticks were jabbed into his brain and fishing around feverishly for the last bit of chicken in the bowl of stir-fry his cranium had become.

"Mac?" Lyon's voice went unheard by the prisoner. "What have you got?"

A voice came from nowhere in particular. "Other than highly erratic brain activity, I've got his body operating and stable," Mac huffed, "that is until he crashes at the end."

Lyon nodded his chin toward Ky and Hitook. "What have you got so far?"

Ky kept her eyes closed as she grunted through gritted teeth. "Nothing yet. It's a mess in here."

"Start for the factory yard."

"It's—" Ky's arms snapped up as if protecting herself from a fall. "I haven't found it yet."

Lyon looked over at the liqua who hadn't shown any signs of struggle. "How about you?"

Hitook sat quietly with his paws on his lap.

"Hitook, what have you got?"

"Shhhhh."

Lyon reeled his head at the quiet retort. He didn't feel like he was the type to shout, "Disrespect," but Lyon gave it a brief thought before brushing the idea off. The events in the room soared above his ability to completely understand.

Ky suddenly shifted forward as a smirk glided across her face. "I think I've go—"

Without warning Ky fell to the ground, barely catching herself on the prisoner's chair. Hitook, who had previously been motionless, flew backwards off his chair and landed on the tile floor, triggering a mini-quake.

Lyon released an uncontrollable yelp at what he saw. "What happened?"

Neither responded; they were too busy fighting a mountain of fatigue. Obviously they had become useless, but before Lyon could make the call, Mac started taking control.

"I've lost contact. No life signs. Get Ky away from the body."

Lyon didn't argue; he just shuffled around the room and lifted Ky under her arms to drag her away and lean her against the corner next to the door. Before Lyon could turn around, Mac went to work.

"Clear."

The rolbrid's body jiggled a bit as the computer attempted to recreate a network of bioelectronic signatures to simulate life, hopefully enough to trigger resuscitation.

Lyon contorted his face as he looked about. His right hand played with his forehead as the left darted about. *What in the hell happened*? he thought.

"Clear."

Mitnarsho's shell shook more violently this time, then calmed. Mac quietly probed to verify it.

"He's dead."

"Shit!" Lyon screamed and kicked in a metal cabinet door.

Chapter 23

Relaxing wasn't exactly what he would call it, but it was what Lyon was trying to do. What amounted to relaxation changed with the location. That fact of life came with the job. Everyone in the Corps dealt with it differently. Regardless of race, relaxing became an immense challenge at times, but what never changed was the fact that you either figured it out or went insane.

Lyon had grown fond of his sanity and worked to keep it, although it sure tried to slip away from time to time. The symptoms of those escape attempts could be found in his head at the moment, but his thoughts kept him too busy to notice.

On this planet, Lyon's stress break came in the form of minding the store. There had only been a few customers today, much like any day the store was open, which hadn't been often lately. He rocked on two of the stool's legs, maintaining the delicate balance with his feet propped on the shelves behind the checkout counter. In front of him the corners of a magazine slyly began drooping, just to have Lyon snap his wrist to pop the points back into place.

For a good half hour, the pages of that magazine never moved. It was a dead giveaway that Lyon's attempts at relaxation were failing, miserably.

Lyon couldn't recall a single word he had read, even when he read each sentence multiple times. Thoughts clogged his memory.

He felt stupid about Mitnarsho dying on him. Even though no one could explain what had happened, something told him that he had pushed too far, too fast, and it ate at him. Granted, time hadn't been kind as of late, but none of his competing thoughts could sooth the mental kick in the ass. Neither Ky nor Hitook had experienced anything like it before, and regardless of how many times Mac went over the data, nothing seemed to fall into place. At least nothing that would explain what happened.

But it was done. The only link they had to these smugglers was now being electronically decomposed in the dumpster out back.

Lyon was left with a hot-wired terran. Compared to the rolbrid, the terran held less promise, but Lyon refused to let it go. Grandma had led him to that terran. Soothsayers came and went like the stars in the sky; the naturals never went away. Someone with the sight carried an aura like a highly charismatic movie star. It was something that would never be forgotten.

Paloon argued with him about it. Even Larin joined it. Lyon refused to budge and wouldn't kill the terran yet. But Ky and Hitook didn't argue when Lyon told them to dive and find out what they could. Mac advised against it, and Paloon and Larin wouldn't shut up about how dangerous it was to keep the terran around, not to mention diving into a rewired brain.

Dragoon W'Lowe didn't even take Lyon's call. He had to leave a message. The dragoon was a busy person, but Lyon fought with it, on top of everything else. With every day's passage he felt more and more distant and stranded on this planet. The only way off was to figure out what was going on. Sure, he had a team, but at the same time, he felt alone. It was the job that allowed him to keep focus. But he definitely wasn't focused on the magazine.

The glossy pages slapped together as Lyon cradled the fold with a thumb before tossing the magazine to the counter. He ended the rocking in the chair by leaning forward and planting his elbows on the counter, his chin held by his extended thumbs. All the while, his eyes never left the cover of the magazine; it gave him a zone point.

Doubt mixed with confidence. Feelings and emotions fought for control until Lyon settled on determination. He was getting extremely irritated at being seemingly cut off from headquarters and discarded like a dead animal on a highway. He didn't want his doubt and concern to surface in front of the others, but Lyon didn't know how long he could keep that up. Determination became the way to go. So what if he was stuck here? If that was going to be the case, then he'd be damned if he was going to take it sitting down. If the leadership was deaf, then fine. He'd do it himself.

"Lyon?"

"What!" Lyon's fist pounded into the counter as his adrenaline-fueled emotions overpowered his ability to withhold his feelings.

"*Excuse* me, grumpy." Mac followed with a huff.

With a deep breath, Lyon returned to reality and leaned back a bit to see Mac on the monitor. "Sorry. What is it?"

On the screen glowed the visage of a lightly tattooed ganger cleaning his fingernails with a jackknife. The voice didn't seem to match the picture. "If you wish to have a civil conversation, I'll proceed."

Lyon sighed. "Look, Mac, I'm sorry. Now I don't think you would have bothered me if it wasn't important."

"Oh," Mac dropped the knife, "so I'm a bother?"

Lyon took a deep breath and twisted his face. Sometimes he'd swear Mac was out to piss him off. He dropped his head and glared. "The difference between you and a wife is that I can kill you and no one would give a damn, so do you have something to say or do I need to get a gun?"

Mac swallowed hard enough that his dangling dagger earrings jingled. "You wanted to know when Ky and Hitook were done. Well, they're done."

Lyon brightened up. "Great." He departed quickly enough that Mac guessed he'd be in the control room soon. It didn't take Lyon long to see there was no one in the store, and he put up the closed sign before hitting the light switch on his way down stairs.

Ky leaned on the table with her face somewhat cradled in her sprawled arms. The tip of her tail rubbed her neck as she moaned faintly. Hitook had found a spot on the floor and stretched out as if sleeping. Both had enjoyed a good night's sleep, but going from dive to dive was tiring. It wasn't outside of their training or capabilities, just tiring.

"What have we got?" Lyon asked determinedly as he entered the room and made it down the stairs.

"That depends," came Ky's muffled voice. "Do you want to know that he's had surgery to correct a birth abnormality in his foot or that he has a secret desire to get blond highlights? Something he saw in a movie." Her voice trailed off.

Lyon stood, taken aback a bit by the reply, and glanced from Ky at the table to Hitook on the floor. "I take it you're a bit worn out."

"Oooh," Ky retorted, "someone give this booby his prize."

Touché, Lyon thought as he stepped around Hitook and made it to his chair at the end of the table.

"I know this may not be easy, but we do need to go over this information as quickly as possible to glean anything we can about his unusual condition."

Ky knew standard procedure but wanted to rest. As she lay on the table a while longer, Lyon didn't say anything; he knew she'd come around. And almost as if timed, right before Lyon felt like he needed to say something, Ky started raising her head and dropping her tail.

"As far as how his head got re-wired, we didn't find anything." Ky's head fell against the back of the seat. She ordered a glass of burth and took a few gulps of the milky white liquid.

Lyon looked as if he had lost a pet.

"But I do know how he got burnt." Ky took a deep breath and another gulp. "Do you want the long or short?"

Lyon shrugged. What did he have to lose? He wasn't going anywhere. "Long."

"He's military, if you hadn't figured that out from picking him up at a military hospital." Ky had also gleaned that last bit of information from Oz's brain. "His background is nuclear mechanics. He was recruited to work on a classified project named Corona. Apparently it has something to do with what he considered an advanced aircraft. He was helping remove a device called a nuclear induction converter from the Nubius. Th—"

"Excuse me," Lyon butted in, "what's 'Newbues'?"

"That's this so-called advanced aircraft. It also has some kind of model number, but it escapes me at the moment. But—"

"X-S-F Two," Hitook offered suddenly from the floor.

Lyon glanced in Hitook's direction, but Ky just sighed. "Can I continue, people?"

Silence was the response, but Ky didn't thank anyone. "When Oz and his partner were removing this device, something went off. He saw his co-worker die in a white flash."

"What caused it?"

"Hell, I don't know, and neither does he. He thinks it was some kind of nuclear detonation, but I have my doubts. He doesn't even know what that device does. He just follows orders while some prick of a boss does most of the work."

Lyon tightened his brow as he peered through the table. "What kind of aircraft is this?"

Ky peeked from slits in her eyes. "Once again, I don't know. He only works on part of it, so he doesn't know a whole lot. But the overall gist is that this aircraft is supposed to be more advanced than anything else these natives can generate. There's something called a pulse drive, whatever in the hell that is, and an *operational* plasma needle for increased speed. Supposedly it decreases drag or some such nonsense."

"Plasma can decrease the drag coefficient in atmospheric conditions." Paloon's voiced echoed as he came around the corner to see some rather tense faces and Hitook on the floor. "Um, sorry. I overheard and had to interject." He stepped over Hitook to grab a small device and some tools he had left on the work bench. "Besides, why are you guys talking shop?"

Lyon briefly pointed a palm at Ky as he eyed the room that housed Oz. "They pulled this information out of the terran. Apparently he works on a terran plane with such technology."

Paloon cocked his head and huffed a laugh. "Yeah, right. These natives can barely get their butts into space. You can't tell me they actually have the technology to be fooling with plasma."

"Hey," Ky dropped her head further to chuck Paloon a challenge, "you want my job fly-boy? I know what I found, and that is what this local honestly believes."

"Well," Lyon inserted, "how advanced is this plasma needle stuff?"

"Not very, really," Paloon replied while making his return trip over Hitook. "I'm assuming this plasma needle is similar to what we call a plasma spike, but the technology is rather basic. It's our geo-electromagnetics that do most of the work in atmospheres because they're variable. Plasma is not so efficient in some atmospheres and downright volatile in others."

Paloon stopped before completely leaving the room, and he turned back to face the group. "But you can't tell me these natives have plasma technology. It must be something else."

"What about the schedule?" Hitook's slightly rough voice startled Paloon, who thought the liqua was sleeping.

"What schedule?" Lyon's eyes danced from Hitook to Ky as he waited for either to answer.

"There was this schedule we found—excuse me, Hitook actually found it." Ky finally raised her head, took another gulp of burth and opened her eyes. "He found it the recesses around the memories of another co-worker, apparently one he gambled with. I didn't take that route and left it for him to track down. Odds are such information would be lost, but apparently he stared at this schedule long enough for it to burn."

"It was a mixture of visual and auditory over a period of time." Hitook moved an arm to scratch one of his long ears. "Besides, it was fresh; he may have seen or heard the last bit maybe one or two days before the explosion."

"Anyway," Ky continued as her tail began a light swish, "this schedule was some kind of shipment schedule."

"Shipment of what," Lyon asked as Paloon leaned against the corner, completely caught in the conversation and his previous work temporarily forgotten.

Ky shrugged. "Parts? Equipment? People? Lawn clippings? Who knows? We may know more after another dive, but I doubt it. We're lucky to have retrieved that."

"Ahh," Paloon sprang off the corner, "you had me there. You don't even know what it's for."

Ky bared a fang at Paloon. "I think what Hitook is offering is a possibility."

Lyon's attention was snagged. "What do you mean?"

"The schedule is for a convoy of some sort, so that means ground shipment." Ky looked over to Paloon. "I'm sure you'd agree that ground shipments tied to a classified project are potentially suspicious."

"Yes," Paloon agreed. "But what classified project?"

Lyon briefly raised a hand for silence. "What *do* you have on these shipments?"

"Times, locations," Ky gave her head a quick nod over her shoulder at Hitook. "He's got most of it."

Lyon leaned back and made a brief attempt to think it over, but he had already made up his mind. "Enough to possibly track it down?"

Ky looked over her shoulder and waited for Hitook's reply. When one didn't seem imminent, she sent a mental wake up to the liqua.

Hitook opened one eye to see all three of them waiting. "Very possible." He started to pick himself off the floor to sit with his legs folded. "Mac could use the data to narrow down possible routes."

Lyon hummed as he gazed at the ceiling.

"Hijack." Lyon didn't say it; Paloon did. "That's what you're thinking about, isn't it?"

A smirk crept across one side of Lyon's face. "Headquarters won't give us any assistance until we get evidence of foreign technology, and this is what we have until your satellite can find us another clue. But since we vaped that factory, they'll be lying low for a while. That's going to make finding them difficult. This is another possibility. Besides, do you have something more important to do?"

Chapter 24

Waiting. There sure had been a lot of it lately. At least that's what Lyon thought. He sat in the back of the van, staring at stacks of holographic screens. Light danced about the confines of the van as Lyon thought about the wait, even though he knew he couldn't do anything about it.

Planning and preparation were vital to any tactical operation and took a great deal of time, but that was nothing compared in length to the waiting. Two days of travel, three days of surveillance and two days of planning. The last two felt like glorified waiting, but now came the true waiting, when every hour felt like five. Maybe the perception that time was dragging was enhanced by the fact it was almost time for mission execution.

With the help of the reconnaissance drone Paloon put into orbit, they had been able to watch the convoy for a couple of days. One thing that made all so-called professionals weak, regardless of the species, was predictability. The Corps viewed itself as masters because it attempted to teach the skill of being unpredictable, because it often proved to be the key. Therefore, only watching these transports for a few days helped pinpoint a weakness.

The weakness wasn't the route or terrain; it was the procedure. With a bit of work, the team could plot the convoy's future plans with a most logical calculation. Maybe it was a bit more common sense than logic. And in the top screen in the third column of four, the convoy moved along the highway, as expected.

Pinpointing this highway didn't prove to be a serious challenge, since it served as the best high-volume link between two known locations scavenged from the schedule in Oz's memory. At first they thought the convoy would choose a secluded route somewhere, but in the past few days, secluded routes had proven to be a rarity. Lyon remembered Paloon commenting that at times there's nothing better than hiding something out in the open.

Besides, the way the individual vehicles in the convoy shifted about in the traffic, few onlookers could even guess that they were together. The problem with that tactic would be the chance of innocents getting caught in the middle. Lyon tapped the counter and gave that a thought, even when he knew that trying to limit this factor would be useless. If they were lucky, they would neutralize the convoy and leave with any suspicious cargo with no fatalities on either side.

Lyon glided over the bottom row of holographic screens in front of him. The screens held views of the remote terrain as seen through the electronic eyes of the bird-cloaked drones providing the electromagnetic net over the selected field.

A thick forest stretched as far as the eye could see. Dual strips of dark grey highway cut two clean paths through in the foliage. Traffic buzzed along. Each driver listening to a radio or using a mobile phone probably experienced a moment of severe static, which they then promptly forgot about after clearing the invisible net above them.

The area held the slightest hint of a valley, at least as much as it could in this relatively flat topography. A small hill on the right rose enough to hide the view of any oncoming traffic. From the hill, the highway dipped and curved to continue for a fair distance before cresting a similar but smaller hill.

A wall of trees and brushes lined both sides and formed a continuous column between the two highways. It provided more than enough cover for the team. Larin and Hitook hid in the outer tree line. The van rested in a tight dirt road in the median. Also hidden in the median was Ky; she waited closer to the zone's entrance.

Lyon couldn't see Hitook or Ky in any of the views in front of him, including the view from the van's sensors. Neither had the optic modifications that Larin and Paloon had. Those modifications allowed Lyon to use the upper right screens to see straight through Larin and Paloon's eyes. To help control the battle, Lyon would have loved to had the same for Ky and Hitook, but he couldn't blame them. Lyon didn't have those modifications either, but for Ky and Hitook it was a matter of purity. Too many modifications proved a hindrance to members of House Bravo's profession, even if it was just a placebo effect. Bio-infused electronics didn't stop abilities; they just created more difficulties to overcome, regardless of what the rumors said about destroying abilities and driving some people mad.

Those talents concerned Lyon more than being able to track Ky or Hitook. As a group, they had gone over what needed to be done and who needed to be where, and Lyon trusted that the House Bravo agents were doing just that.

"*Lyon,*" Paloon called out through the team's frequency to everyone's internal communications systems. *"It looks like the target is nearing Checkpoint Three. Do you confirm?"*

Lyon snapped from his daze to look at Paloon's monitor. The view through the fellow atlantian's eyes showed that Paloon had multiple screens of his own displayed on the windshield of the station wagon, which Lyon had to remind himself housed a tank. One screen was a magnification from his current position.

The knight shifted to the other monitor with the satellite feed. The feed mimicked an aerial view.

"*Confirmed,*" Lyon returned and began watching the monitor intently. *"Stand by."*

The checkpoint was what the terrans called a rest stop that offered drivers a place to take a break. In the satellite feed, the scattered convoy consisted of only two vans because the third had been at the rest stop for a while. Surveillance identified the same procedure multiple times: One van went ahead and stopped for a rest, only to swap out later, taking its position in the convoy while allowing the occupants of another van to have a moment of rest. This was the second and final swap for a while.

"He's moving." Paloon's eyes followed the departing van, which allowed Lyon to watch.

Lyon flicked back to the satellite feed to see the lead van signal a turn. *"It's a swap."* Lyon shifted in his seat and leaned forward a bit. *"Report."*

In turn, everyone acknowledged.

"We've got about five minutes. We're on the go on my mark."

The seconds ticked away slowly as Lyon watched everything slide into place on the screens.

Larin shifted position to be in the open just enough to see. In the lieutenant's vision, various gauges and reticles took shape as the multiple systems in the combat pack on his back came online. The rolbrid reached over his right shoulder and detached a standard-issue particle cannon much like the one he had been fooling around with. This one had a combat stock that allowed for Brock sticks to be held close to the matter coil for faster recharging. Also the stock held two more allaric clips. Though Larin seemed to be gun happy, even for someone in Harquebus, Lyon knew the particle cannon was only for disabling the vehicles.

Lyon ordered, *"Phase Two, and everyone had better stick to it."* Phase Two meant they could only maim or render someone unconscious for protection. No one was allowed to purposefully kill unless required in self-defense or the phase was changed. But the knight knew that, because of the location, some deaths or at least injuries to innocents would be unavoidable, but no other viable alternative existed.

Paloon's screen moved as he began pulling from the rest stop a couple of cars behind the convoy. That meant the front of the convoy should be entering the zone. Looking down to the other monitors confirmed it.

The lead van approached the first hill, and just at it reached the apex, Lyon called out, *"Mark."*

Space-time twisted as a surreal void formed in the area. Senses peaked for every member of the team as they spied the metallic prey from their vantage points. Everyone waited as they took in every detail of the changing and unfolding battlefield they would have to deal with shortly.

Mixed in the traffic, the lead van started climbing the next hill as Paloon followed the rear of the convoy at the top of the first hill. With a couple of mental commands, small devices fired in a few intervals from the bottom of the tank into the pavement. At the speed of thought he told everyone, *"Mines placed."* A second later he added, *"Clear."*

Time went to a crawl as Lyon responded by turning to the other screen to check the location of the lead. As planned, it remained within the zone but wouldn't be there for long.

Lyon's mental tension peaked as he felt the command slowly build in his head.

"Go!"

Explosions tore through the hills and sent concussion waves that everyone within a mile could feel. Columns of fire and smoke reached for the sky as squeals from the hundreds of tires pierced the air.

Destroying the hills had little tactical value other than creating a hazard to get through. What the detonations did do was create a serious scare factor, complete with audio and visual effects that would confuse everyone for at least a short while. Soon, metal chassis would twist and glass would shatter from several minor accidents. The team had to act fast.

Ky and Hitook targeted the drivers of the escorting vans. Hitook had the lead; Ky took the last van. With mental energy, the two knocked out the drivers.

Larin popped from the tree line near the smaller hill and fired the particle cannon in rapid successions, snapping from target to target. Each shot bored a hole in a tire, which caused spontaneous deflations. One by one, vehicles lurched into uncontrollable skids that matched the pattern playing out in Larin's vision. Most vehicles took two shots. Larin focused on the smaller vehicles in hopes of blocking the semi-trucks while giving their drivers as much space as possible to allow them to stop the massive rigs on their own. Punching out the tires of such a large vehicle would be much more difficult to do correctly without causing serious damage.

Paloon came to a quick stop with the vehicles behind him squealing to keep from running into the immense crater of fire that just appeared on the side of the hill facing the traffic. He reached for the particle cannon in the seat next to him and waited for the next phase.

Unlike Hitook, who stayed in the forest, Ky blasted from the tree line and headed for the second van to incapacitate the occupants as quickly as possible, then she and Paloon would work up the convoy from the back. Meanwhile, Larin and Hitook would provide cover as needed.

This was the beginning of a vulnerable moment, and motion seemed to slow to a crawl as Lyon watched Ky bolt for the van. From the edge of Lyon's view he saw something begin to unfold. As he turned to the other monitor, he didn't need to see much to know it didn't bode well. In fractions of a second, Lyon yelled, *"Ky, possible incoming at ten o'clock!"*

She faced the direction just as automatic gunfire erupted from the back of the lead van, which now faced slightly sideways.

At that moment, multiple events occurred at once. Lyon commanded Larin and Hitook to move in to neutralize the lead van, but that was the only good news. Several heavily armed people poured from the back of the lead van and took positions as they continued to fire in Ky's direction. As they disembarked, the massive frame of a large weapon extended from the now open back doors. This new turret started lobbing grenades at great speed. A similar situation unfolded in front of Paloon as he found himself staring down the barrel of a very large caliber weapon from the rear of the van he had stopped behind. Meanwhile, everyone could hear grinding gears along with the sudden silence of the air brakes.

"They're going to run for it," Paloon belted.

Sure enough, the semi-trucks began turning as if ready to plow through the vehicles and make for the tight grassy area in the median to circumvent the crater blocking the way.

Ky leapt into the air and soared over her target to get away from the ground behind her as it exploded in countless bits of turf.

Heavy shells began pounding Paloon's station wagon and pushing it back. Each ricocheted; many embedded themselves into the nearby trees. Paloon figured they must have been watching him but had nothing to go on until now. *"I'm taking medium fire,"* Paloon reported.

Lyon saw the shift in the screen showing Paloon's sight. Also, Larin began moving toward the lead van.

There was little time left to make the call. He didn't like it but knew it had to be made.

"Phase Three," Lyon ordered as he reached around to grab his combat-stocked particle cannon. *"Larin, stop those trucks, your discretion. Paloon, take out the vans. Hitook, Ky, you're on infantry. I'm coming out there."*

The knight bolted for the rear doors of the van as the rest of the team began truly neutralizing the threat.

Chapter 25

Larin smirked at the call to go to Phase Three. Now he could fully vent his pent-up frustration. With the grace of a cheetah, Larin kicked the particle cannon up and slid his right hand around the stock to glide the entire weapon over his right shoulder. As it clicked into place on his combat pack, his left hand reached around and disconnected the rifle whose barrel had been poking over his left shoulder like a short broadcast antenna.

The launcher twirled under his left arm and whipped over to his right. With perfect timing, Larin's right hand, free after stowing the previous weapon, met the grip that extended from the molded stock. His arm tensed and became comfortable with the weapon's weight.

By rifle standards, the barrel was short, and overall the weapon was stocky, like a shotgun. A thick, smooth magazine hung from the belly. Emblazoned on the side shined the five-pointed star of the Dragon Corp. In the lower left corner of the clip rested a long, triangle-like shape housing four lines that met in the center: the logo of Larin's favorite explosive.

In a blink, the GK's vertical targeting reticle showed in his view, and the flat scope on top of the weapon took in the surroundings and tracked all targets.

The rolbrid cradled the stock under his right arm, put his left foot forward, leaned down on his right and took aim.

Hitook blasted from the tree line like a ravaging wendigo. Small branches trailed him as he headed for the armed soldiers who were slowly adjusting to the creature charging toward them. It didn't take long before fear forced them to unleash automatic fire.

Before a bullet could get close, the liqua triggered the skill he had focused on along the way. He jived to the left then shimmered from sight like a crystal sheet of water. A couple of the combatants gasped and let go of their triggers as the others continued shooting at the air without knowing the location of the creature or if it had all been a hallucination brought on by possible chemical weapons.

Seconds later, the small detachment of soldiers began firing at the slightest movement of grass. Futile attempts. Hitook leapt, and as he came down, he flickered back into the visible spectrum before landing on the heads of two attackers who had taken prone positions. His weight effortlessly snapped their necks.

The remaining gunners took a bit to adjust but started turning toward him. As Hitook focused again, he created a globe of space about him, and time had no choice but to bend to the liqua's will. Not one local had a chance.

Hitook's right arm reached to wrap an overpowering paw over a weapon coming around to point at him. He yanked it down as it began spouting lead. With a bass-like thud, his foot pounded into the attacker's chest and forced him into flight. Milliseconds later, the sound of cracking bones seeped from the poor local, who was dead before he hit the ground a couple hundred feet later.

Another attacker came from the opposite side and thought ever so briefly that the creature's actions opened a weakness, but Hitook was well aware of the attacker's presence. Without looking, the liqua thrust upward with his left arm and banged the weapon out of the man's grip. The weapon began a circular path as Hitook brought his right foot down and beyond his left as he shifted his weight. As the weapon began its descent, the liqua's right hand came down on the butt, and his left guided the barrel. He spun on his heels to untwist his legs and channeled the energy into his right hand. A pounding thrust pushed the barrel through the bottom of the man's jaw, and Hitook's shift in weight drove the weapon through the skull and lifted the corpse two feet into the air.

Blood squirted about and painted Hitook's hand as it slipped from the weapon's butt to catch the chin of the falling body. Splinters of bone crackled as the jaw broke in several places upon contact. A flick of the wrist sent the entire body spinning like a roulette wheel. Hitook pulled his left hand back, charged the energy and pounded it into the body, which immediately blasted toward two more guards who barely had the mental facilities to keep up with the action let alone have time to react.

Ky landed like a mountain lion and didn't need any time to analyze the situation. She went right to work.

The dextian sprung from the ground and twisted in mid-air. Her legs flew wide as the first boot bashed into the face of the attacker who was getting out of the passenger side of the van. As her foot came down, the attacker's weapon flew from his hands within the tight coil of Ky's tail. Then the second boot pounded into the cheek. The neck snapped before the head bashed through the glass window.

Streams of bullets screamed toward her from gunners coming around both sides. Effortlessly, she sailed into the air toward the van's roof, curled into a ball, planted her feet on the vehicle then bounced toward the two on the right.

She aimed like a missile toward the second one. As her hands clamped on his neck, Ky retracted her legs just long enough to release them into the back of the first gunner. The trio crashed to the ground, but Ky landed on her feet and didn't waste time, throwing her caught prey like a rag doll in an arc and on top of the other incapacitated soul.

Body armor or not, the force caused portions of the body to implode. She released the limp body and hopped forward to fix her now bloody hands onto the other's head. A flick of her wrists and the head went askew.

Ky's head jerked as her eyes caught shadows moving under the van. Tendons twitched again and sent her over the van in one move.

One foot hit the ground as the other swung around and plowed in the neck of the man behind her. She reached forward and put a choke hold on the man in front of her while her still-moving foot stopped as it pinned the man behind her against the van.

Another armed man farther in front spun and couldn't control his combat twitch before he opened fire into his comrade. Ky's tail moved with a deadly grace as it unlatched the crossbow on her back and brought it around. She dropped her right hand to grab the weapon and sent a bolt through an eye.

Shells began to pound away at Paloon's vehicle. He sent a quick mental command before ripping his head away from the ports coming from the back of his chair. The vehicle's geomagnetic engines fired into plates of blue energy forming squares around the wheels and a line along the back.

The hunter didn't have time to make it across the half wall behind him to get into the weapons chair, so he just rolled over into the navigator's seat and threw his head back. Electricity sparked as the metal plugs affixed themselves to Paloon's sub-dermal connections. Thoughts sent the station wagon into transformation.

Running perpendicular to the pilot and navigator chairs was the weapons station. The weapons seat flew forward into its respective control console as the tank made fast adjustments to accept the secondary formation. Paloon's seat screamed backwards and zigged before snapping into place.

The station wagon-like vehicle seemed regular enough until the roof of the back-end split like the opening petals of a flower but not a friendly flower. With an almost impossible speed, the hardened turret popped up and locked into place.

Condensing vapor poured off the snub-like barrel that telescoped to just about seven feet. Panels snapped open to reveal metallic tubes that rotated along their cores as they soared for the sky. In just milliseconds the cannon was charged and ready, but Paloon didn't feel like overkill.

"Ky, move." Paloon sent the comment with just a mild thought.

She had heard the tank but continued about her business until told otherwise, so when Paloon said something, she didn't hesitate. Ky let the corpse she had in front of her crumple to the asphalt and dropped her foot that had easily crushed the neck of man behind her. She ran over a sedan that encased a pair of screaming passengers and headed for the second semi-truck.

Along the front of the turret, on the left, was a panel that didn't appear to have a barrel, but from it soared a tiny flare-like missile that instantly flew into the van before exploding in a ball of flame. A soot-topped blaze streamed from the van as the few remaining occupants screamed just before the ammunition began detonating.

Lyon made it through the woods and into the slight field of the road's shoulder just in time to see bullets of various types blasting from the van that had caught fire. The knight briefly thought that with the terran civilians caught in the middle of this, everything was going very wrong, but he didn't have much time to contemplate the social implications. Not too far from him came the first semi-truck. Smoke billowed from the twin chrome stacks, and the engine cleared its throat to roar into a different gear.

Instinct guided Lyon's hand and put the particle cannon's dot on the head of the driver. Before he could pull, he remembered Larin and looked over just in time to see the GK in the rolbrid's hands.

Larin had tone, so he proudly yelled mentally, *"CNG!"*

Everyone else threw themselves flat against the ground.

A brief whirl and a click came from the GK before a thump sent a silver, whistling shell toward the first truck's engine block. The round didn't need to penetrate the vehicle's housing; it just needed to get close, at least a couple of feet.

As it did, the distance gyro triggered the nitroglycerin, which in turn explosively destroyed the shell around the nano-amount of antimatter. Released, the antimatter infested the rest of the warhead and triggering the voracious chain-reaction within the grenade's truly deadly compound: carnagearenos.

Space warped inward before the explosion consumed the entire truck and shot it vertical with its trailer lagging behind. Relentless green light invaded everything just before the shock wave pounded. Cars flipped end on end as they rolled away and trees buckled over as if punched in the gut.

Larin pulled the weapon in, spun around and hugged the ground as the blast roared above him. All the while, he smiled like a satisfied alligator.

As abruptly as it started, the wind stopped and for a moment pulled back into the epicenter.

Larin spun again in time to see the semi-truck fall back to the earth. The trailer landed on its back end and began splintering as side panels popped, sending rivets and other chucks of metal flying about. Remains of the long-gone cab and engine began a metal rain that thudded into the ground, heard by the few people who had not temporarily lost their hearing.

The force knocked the other semi-truck on its side and pushed it along the ground about ten feet. While the threat from what should now have been an unconscious crew would seem low, Lyon didn't want to take any chances.

He jumped up and charged the cab. Just as he came around the engine and the windshield came into view, he opened fire with the particle cannon on wide beam. The force pounded the glass away. A mental command into the weapon through his sub-dermal connections in his palm forced a mode change. Green light spewed from the flat under-barrel launcher as the entire clip of crystal allaric slats sailed into the cab and shattered into thousands of shards penetrating every crevice of the passenger compartment.

For the first time in the past minute or so, the semblance of silence seeped back to the scene.

There was the roar of engines but not of traffic. The trees now seemed devoid of talkative wildlife, but many of the passengers unfortunately caught in the trap continued to scream randomly, with an underlying track of whimpering and sobbing.

Metal began to creak and then thudded as Hitook tossed off the van that had been blown on top of him. As the liqua stood, Paloon shouted, *"Here they come*."

The team could hear the third van charging through or around the traffic to the top of the hill. Horns honked in the background.

Just as the van made its way around the first trench exploded into the ground, Paloon sent the command to detonate the second charge.

The explosion removed the very top of the hill and pounded away at the van, which surprisingly only skittered along the grass. It only took a few moments before it regained traction and resumed the assault.

As the driver took in the destruction, the van began to slow. Paloon wasn't going to take chances. He spun the turret around released a blue-white bolt that pound through the van, leaving a cleanly bored tunnel.

In a blink, the van's engine noise stopped. With a few squeaks, the van rolled to a stop. As it did so, the remaining portions of bodies inside seeped into the newly bored tunnel and formed unrecognizable clumps.

Chapter 26

Abject fear. Little compared to its level of intensity, which was unmistakable. Behind tear-coated windows cringed a soul in confused horror. Grasp as it might at something with a tangible semblance to reality, it failed, time and time again. Now it had no other option but to revert to the primitive response of a child facing down the most horrendous of boogeymen—frozen in place but mentally thrashing about and screaming.

This fear held every aspect of the tortured soul open like a budding flower. Lyon could see deep inside. As lips quivered to the tone of a silent yell, emotion flared to palpable levels.

The knight stood outside the vehicle and couldn't keep from drinking in the fright-filled ether that seeped from the occupants of the white mini-van.

Random, dumb luck placed them here, among this chaos that exploded and claimed life in a matter of seconds. Wreckage and bodies were strewn about the haphazard arrangement of vehicles that had been pushed around or knocked over by various explosions.

Terrans. Lyon considered the possibility of being related. He wrestled with the thoughts, but he knew the situation. Unfortunate? Yes. But that didn't change the fact of what this meant. It didn't make the thought any easier.

Hitook picked himself off the ground and began beating his fur as if he were dusting a carpet. He huffed a snort that sent a shower of saliva spouting in sporadic streams from the sides of his oversized shiny incisors.

In the midst of dusting his boots, something registered. Hitook paused briefly before dropping his foot and stretching to his full height. He scanned the horizon with an outstretched arm. Black eyes darted about as he took a few moments to pinpoint the faint signal. It came from the van he had thrown off of him.

The misshapen form of a vehicle rested on its side, only a few feet away, but Hitook took his time getting to it. Like a divining rod, the liqua's massive paw gravitated toward the direction of the signal. A faint "schnik" tinged in the air as Hitook disconnected one of his twin blades.

Focused on the sensation of the signal, he slid closer in complete silence before leaping into the air and coming down on the side of the van with a thunderous slam. Piercing screeches rang from the metal hull as the blades tore through up to the beast's fist. A sure hit; he knew it. It wasn't long before he could feel the life signal fade then blink away. As it disappeared, Hitook stood, the blades against the steel vehicle creating metallic screams.

Silver-blue hooked fangs of the weapon rose from the holes and were coated in a thick, red liquid. The fluid began dripping from the swords. The sight of the eight-foot high, four hundred and thirty pound, fur-coated, muscle-bound beast sporting a blood-covered dual-bladed sword came with its own fear factor that didn't go unnoticed.

High-pitched screams came from a nearby blue vehicle, which appeared to be a mix between a station wagon and a van. Inside cowered a family of three. The screams came from the mother and reached blood-curdling levels. At first, the husband tried to quiet her, but when Hitook turned to look in the direction of the noise, the husband yelped and held on to his mate for dear life. The child whined and cried loudly. The scene only made Hitook snarl in annoyance, but showing off his gigantic teeth just caused another wave of screaming and crying.

Ky had a somewhat similar situation. She crept about to see if every attacker had been neutralized. It didn't take long to make the confirmation, so she retrieved her crossbow bolt from the skull it had split.

After the bolt's sloppy retrieval, she headed toward Lyon. Along the way, she wiped the bolt on her pants and loaded it into the crossbow her tail had been holding. When the bolt snapped in place, her tail took the weapon away to latch it on her back as Ky turned her head to glance at a compacted hatchback of a car.

The cramped occupant stared, his mouth agape like a non-believing peeping Tom. Normally she wouldn't have cared, but Ky stopped and stared back. It had been a while since she had witnessed this. Anyone who stayed in the Corps long enough ran into it. Most beings scream or run, but strangely, the guy in the car didn't flinch. His head just slightly cocked sidewise.

Ky mimicked. Then she followed as the head tilted the other way. Then she sprang forward to land crouching on the hood.

The guy flinched so strongly he would have been forced into the back seat if his driver's chair hadn't been in the way. But he calmed when Ky slowly extended a digit and scraped a line in the glass.

Native eyes followed Ky's movements even when she made a return trip with her nail, scratching away. She stared into the man's eyes and gave a devilish half smile. Ky lifted her finger only to bring it down and begin the same path. The driver reluctantly raised a finger and started following from a distance. During the third pass, he reached closer to the glass. Before he could get too close, Ky slammed her paws flat on the glass and lunged forward with a full-fanged scream.

The man's retreat included a shriek that tapered into silence with a yelp. Acidic odor flared. Ky couldn't miss the scent and knew what had happened. Rhythmic thudding sounded from the vehicle's hood as Ky's tail began swishing back and forth. A true smile accompanied a mischievous glare as Ky thought, *This is fun.*

Larin thought so too but for different reasons. He looked about the wreckage brought on by his CNG round—a well-placed one if he did say so himself, which he didn't. Although, he did think it. A heavy boot kicked away tiny chucks that survived the atom-destroying explosion. But with a tight yield as Larin had planned, what remained of the truck showed he didn't overdo it—he used just enough to get the job done.

More smoke snaked into the sky with every overturned piece of smoldering, unrecognizable hunk of metal. Larin began guiding the GK's ventilated muzzle along the ground to knock over pieces.

Even the massive wreck of the trailer crashing back to the ground nearby couldn't pull Larin from his infatuation with the detonation site. Minus some external scorching, it appeared that the earth hadn't suffered a lick of collateral damage from the CNG shell itself. A nice, clean hit.

Larin looked up while mentally and audibly yelling for anyone to hear, "Frappin' heck! Did we kick some ass, or what!?"

The comment registered with Paloon, but he had something else on his mind and knew Lyon did as well. Paloon approached Lyon, who still looked at the occupants of the mini-van. Paloon didn't say anything and didn't have to.

Lyon shifted to lock eyes with the fellow atlantian. In a matter of silent seconds, the two stared as if forcing their own thoughts into the other's head while reading the thoughts of the other—a quiet, quick but thorough debate.

The knight broke the silent argument to gaze at the mini-van's occupants one last time. Something hidden in his look sent even more screams of fear through the terrans' veins that led to crying. Lyon didn't want to, but he had to do something.

As he looked at them, he mouthed his apology then raised his weapon and shot them.

Lyon turned back to Paloon and gave the orders. *"Paloon and Larin, give me fire walls, now."* The two darted off. *"Go to Phase Four, I want this place clean."*

The knight headed toward the rear of the remaining trailer. Paloon and Larin quickly used the bottles they had strapped to their legs and set fire to both hills, thereby creating a thick curtain that stayed in one place and would burn for hours. Once they were done, they joined Ky and Hitook in efficiently terminating every local in the vicinity.

If the operation had gone off without a firefight, there would have been a chance that no one would have to die, but it didn't happen as Lyon had hoped. There was no time to regret it.

With the job done, the others gathered around Lyon who was combing over the trailer without touching it. Something didn't seem right. "Flip it up," he ordered, and everyone jumped in, with Hitook doing most of the work.

The short rolbrid soon became useless in the task.

"Larin, we will most likely need to vape this place. Rig it."

The lieutenant nodded and jotted off to start setting the bombs.

"Paloon, get the van and pull the tank near. I want to get out of here as soon as possible." As Paloon left, Lyon pointed at the trailer. "I need this thing open, but it's definitely not clear."

Ky huffed. "Never is, is it?"

She nodded toward Hitook, and the two went to work scanning and probing the trailer to sense anything live or mechanical that would prove an obstacle to its basic operation. It seemed to have a simple lock, but a semi-close inspection revealed that there was nothing simple about it. The standard looking lock didn't operate in quite the standard way, so most likely, it triggered something, perhaps an antitheft device of some sort.

Lyon's thoughts began to stray as the others did their work. Highlights of the walls of flame flickered in the paint of the wrecked vehicles seemingly tossed about the area. Behind the crackling whoosh of the infernos were the heated voices of drivers and the useless honking. But Lyon didn't care. He wondered if this was all in vain. The trailer might hold nothing more than a weapons shipment, or even worse, it could be empty—the cargo already delivered. Lyon didn't know what he'd do if that was the case.

Ky, Hitook and Lyon let their reflexes unconsciously force them to leap away from the trailer as metal rods noisily shot from under each corner of the trailer and dug into the earth. The result lifted the trailer a few inches off the ground as if being prepared for a minor flood.

"Did you guys do that?" Lyon shot the question. Both Ky and Hitook commented that they didn't cause it. *"Paloon, do we have a breach in the net."*

The hunter was in the process of moving the van, and since he was plugged in, switching over to the drones wasn't a problem. *"That's a negative; we're still secure. Why? What do you have?"*

"Just scan the trailer. We've got moving parts."

Paloon shrugged and started scanning. Nothing native could have gotten through, and he knew it. There shouldn't be anything to worry about. Paloon checked the scan again.

"Except for that," he thought. *"We've got a timer circuit of some kind."*

"To what?"

"Unknown."

Lyon didn't care at this point about what tripped it. *"How much time left?"*

"Also unknown." Paloon began some deeper scans. *"It's in the undercarriage compartments, a hair from dead center. There're also several masses, unknown substance—could be explosive, could be chemical."*

"Blow it," Larin screamed as he forgot his task and ran over.

"*No!*" Lyon made his demand clear. *"There's no telling what would happen."*

The team began brainstorming, but Ky had other plans. With a small mental burst, she relayed her thoughts to Hitook. He replied equally.

They approached opposite sides of the trailer and knelt to the ground. No one else noticed until Ky commented that everyone should stand back; they did.

What happened next didn't occur quickly in a mental sense. Ky and Hitook had much to do and a lot to remember. In the physical sense, it seemed to only take a few seconds. With it over, they both stood without fanfare.

"What?" Larin looked around as if expecting an explosion.

Paloon checked his readings and slightly chuckled at the simplicity of it. *"All clear."*

"How?" Larin demanded, but Lyon just waited for Ky to explain.

She walked straight to Larin, bent over a bit and extended a slender finger to the rolbrid's nose as a bright, blue spark jumped the gap and stung Larin.

"Frapping hell!" Larin snapped backwards and clamped hands on his tender nose.

Ky smiled as she stood. "Drained the area. I figured it would be enough to handle."

Lyon smirked. "It appears so." Just then he noticed Hitook grounding himself to a nearby vehicle. "Well then, let's open her up."

Whines sounded from the torque barrels of Lyon and Larin's particle cannons. After a few precise blasts, Hitook clamped on to the doors and yanked them open. Behind the creaking of bending steel, the air seal released with a forceful pop.

Ky warned everyone with a thought before she snapped a light stick out of a belt pouch. The flash calmed quickly to a steady brightness that completely lit the interior.

Metal containers of various sizes formed misshapen piles, each firmly tethered to metal pallets locked into the floor bed. Unlike the square crates Lyon expected to see, these containers had rounded corners. To further dull the appearance, they had a flat grey coating with red rectangles along the seals.

Ky took a smooth jump into the trailer; Hitook soon followed. Lyon climbed up, then looked down at the now incredibly tiny rolbrid.

"Why don't you stand guard outside?"

Larin sneered and extended his middle finger.

Lyon was a bit shocked but appreciated the adaptation to native jesters. He mumbled something about people not being able to take a joke as he joined the others farther inside.

Paloon pulled up with the van and backed within twenty feet of the trailer. He got out and yelled, "Van's here!"

Lyon acknowledged with a raised hand.

Paloon saw Larin munching on a chur root and giving his particle cannon a status check. The hunter shrugged and headed toward the tank.

A couple of quick movements with a short sword snapped the bindings on a pile of containers. Hitook helped Ky take a long one off the top, which lifted with ease.

"Is it empty?" she asked Hitook rhetorically as she twisted her brow.

Lyon shrugged. "Let's open it up and find out."

The two set it down and began unlatching the lid, which uncovered a sea of semi-transparent green gelatin-like substance. Light flashed in various patterns as the substance wiggled about. As the jiggling settled, they could see various dark shapes buried in a line under the surface. Ky knelt next to the container and poked a nail at the substance to judge consistency. A flick of her wrist sent a dagger into the goo, which she slid lengthwise as if cutting open a fish.

Another flick sent the knife away, as she dug two fingers down the new crevice to straddle one of the small objects. She yanked it free, and the gelatin slapped closed. Ky held the slightly metallic capsule precariously between her two forefingers.

It didn't exceed two inches in sizes. The center bulge of glass brandished streaks of metal bracing that blended into the remainder of the housing, which tapered to flat ends slightly smaller than the middle.

A quizzical expression dominated Ky's face as the dextian flipped her hand back and forth to take a quick look at both sides of the item. Then she threw her arm up and behind to hand it to Lyon who obligingly grabbed it.

He lifted it toward the trailer's exit to let the light shine through the dark, glass center. At first Lyon thought the capsule empty until he noticed a dull glint of deep red. His face contorted as he walked to the edge of the trailer to get more light. Upon his arrival, the extra illumination allowed him to confirm his suspicion. The blurred, blood-red light wiggled about in misshapen crystalline forms that jumped about like a twitching worm. There was no doubt, but he wanted a second opinion.

Lyon extended his arm. "Larin, take a look at this."

As the rolbrid turned, Lyon called out, *"Paloon, what do you make of this?"*

Paloon stopped from examining the cannon fire damage to the tank and flipped through views to patch into Larin's optic feed. With the link established, it didn't take Paloon long to identify it, but he didn't respond quickly. He paused to think about why Lyon was asking such a question.

"You tell me; you're the expert in restricted substances."

"Just entertain me." Lyon withdrew the device from Larin's view, hence Paloon's view. *"You're the only one here who may have actually seen this stuff before."*

Paloon mentally huffed as he clicked off the view and resumed his inspection of the tank. *"Yes, it's glinnik."*

Larin shifted his slightly squat body around to get a better look at this *glinnik*. "What's glinnik?"

Lyon let the device fall into his palm. He rolled it around before snapping his wrist, sending the capsule to Larin, who seized it in midair. "It's a synthetic rock that's created under high gravitational and electromagnetic pressures. It has been used for everything from pulse propulsion to sonic weapons."

"Big deal." The interjection came from Ky.

Lyon turned to see her wrestling with something else in the green gelatin.

She paused enough to finish her statement. "So why is it supposedly restricted?"

"Genocide." Lyon shrugged his shoulders as if to say "what else." "Glinnik can be created in such a way as to generate a genetic-specific poison wave. Imagine a sonic wave that kills everybody of a particular species, leaving everything else untouched. It was decided the potential abuse of glinnik outweighed the few benefits it could provide."

Across the way, Paloon's fingers slid across and in the crevasses under the station wagon tank. His body fished about slightly as he wiggled farther under the vehicle. He preferred doing at least cursory hands-on inspections before running internal diagnostic routines. Movement halted.

The hunter sifted through screens of data floating before him. He gripped the front of the tank and yanked himself free just to catapult himself vertically. Paloon's head darted about from cloud to cloud as he watched the data change with his head movement.

Ky wrestled another device from the green gelatin. "Then, what's this?"

Slightly smaller than a soccer ball, the blue and green globe's center had an inch-wide groove that ran the circumference cutting two inches deep. Channels ran perpendicular from the center rut and stretched toward both ends, which went flat where metallic slats formed handles embedded into the device.

Lyon took a few moments as he lazily scratched the side of his face with a limp finger. "My guess? I'd say that's probably a glinnik detonator of some sort."

Ky's arm sprang and shot the ball into the air. "In that case, have a present."

Hitook scrambled a bit to uncuff his paws from behind him to catch the item. He didn't feel too comfortable about the situation as his eyes sprang back and forth from the weapon to Lyon, who didn't seem that concerned.

The transaction went on briefly until Hitook stopped it himself. Lyon noticed the liqua cock his head slightly before his nose twitched.

Roaring booms rocked the trailer as Larin shouted some form of a rolbrid expletive.

"We've got company," Paloon belted in a somewhat panicky voice across the team's internal communication network.

"No frapping kidding," Larin retorted as his spat splitters of chur root.

Paloon clarified, *"And they're running hot."*

The sky squealed as the two fighter jets banked, sending streams of condensed vapor into swirling white ribbons.

"Ah, frapping hooha." Larin's combat instincts took over as he darted from the trailer to an opening. *"We've been pegged."*

The three in the trailer scampered toward the exit and jumped out in time to see the fighters begin their tight, high-subsonic turn. One stayed with banking as the second continued in a straight line. The first looped in a blink just as a stream of fire blasted from beside one of the two engine intakes, and a rocket pounded into a terran van behind Paloon.

Crimson and ebony whorled in thousands of ever-expanding torrents of fire as the explosion turned the van into a large fragmentation grenade. Just above the roaring explosion, thunder cracked from the jet as it began a steep bank.

Lyon yelled mentally for Paloon with no answer as Ky and Hitook looked about trying to figure out what to do. Before Lyon could make a call, he saw Larin on the move.

The rolbrid spat as a mental command to his combat pack sent things in motion. A handle popped from the top of the pack just milliseconds before Larin reached his right arm over and behind his head to grab it. The weapon that slid free looked like a short but wide thick plank tipped with an embedded hand grip.

As Larin brought the weapon down along his leg, he snapped his wrist; the plank split in two—thickness-wise. One half rotated around a double joint to rest along the bottom of the rolbrid's forearm. Larin snapped the weapon in the other direction, and a barrel flew from under the remaining plank and swung up to lock into place. Steam hissed from the other end that ran along his forearm as the butt spouted a large, flat vent.

Larin drew the weapon close, grabbed the barrel and pulled it in as if charging a pump shotgun. Parts snapped with a metallic clank. Another mental command to the MUs in his combat pack sent him into the air.

"Get down here." Lyon almost couldn't believe what he was seeing. He didn't need a conversation to know what Larin had in mind, but the knight had other concerns. *"Somebody's going to see you. We don't need our cover blown."*

"Fine," Larin glanced down, *"arrest my carcass if we make it through this alive."*

As the first jet banked to the left, everyone saw the faint dot of the second fighter hugging the terrain. Lyon sent a series of quick commands sending everyone else on the move.

Ky darted for the tank to check on Paloon. Hitook had the not-so-pleasant job of jumping back in the large target of a trailer and grabbing as many crates as he could. Lyon ran to the team's van while wishing Larin luck.

Pixels crowded the rolbrid's vision as the weapon's systems came online and he coordinated them with the combat computer in his pack. Vectors, velocities and vulnerabilities flashed about in numerous gauges, dials and callout windows.

The tactical computer on Larin's back couldn't compare to what Paloon could patch into; that fact was why it didn't pick up the signal sooner. Tones sounded in Larin's ear. The lieutenant forwarded a warning to the others as he continued working on a targeting solution.

Larin's legs swayed like a rag doll as the computer took control of the MUs to line up for the solution.

Pinpoints of multi-colored light began to flicker like hyper fireflies at the barrel-end of the weapon. Thin, red-silver rods clustered in a seemingly pattern-less design housed in an uneven collar of a similar substance, all of which formed the business end of the weapon. It protruded from a bulkier but softer brown-grey barrel that had a flat top, which could be used to display various bits of information, but everything Larin needed to know came through readouts in his vision through the link he had between his palm and the weapon's grip.

As the blinking lights that floated in space increased to a frantic speed, shiny flecks twirled in the air around the vent that had shot from the weapon's butt beyond Larin's elbow. The gleaming specks were joined by tiny arcs of green lightening. With the first spark, Larin received the indicator that the matter field had reached operational mass.

Overall, the prep took only a few seconds, but a few seconds meant a lot of covered ground for the speeding jet. The grey fighter popped up as if to show off its belly and soared in an arc, a tactic to attack ground targets, most likely with a cannon, as it came back down. Little did the pilot know that her previous shot would be all she'd get.

Larin gently slipped the mental trigger command.

Short spears of light shot perpendicular from the barrel in about seven directions a split second before glossy light with reflective qualities coalesced like a spiky soccer ball in the center. Without losing the shape or location of the fluid light ball, a metallic light shot from it in a fist-sized beam. A few yards from the weapon, the beam molded into several lightening-like bolts, writhing and whipping about around a central axis, which was much smaller than its parent beam. Instantly the beam hit the inverted, diamond-shaped outline of the aircraft with a bestial roar that formed visible shock waves in the air.

There was no hole to punch through. There was no fancy explosion upon contact. Instead, the beam began eating away the layers of matter. One layer of atoms at a time, the coherent beam disrupted the electromagnetic bonds. Electrons and protons flung away in countless directions at once. Then the atoms behind it received the same treatment as the others awaited their impending doom. Though a detailed, sensitive process, it repeated at a rate only measurable in flexible quantum summations that allowed for the possibility of faster-than-light mathematics.

In a blink of an eye from initial contact with the beam, the aircraft exploded into a rain of polycarbonate fragments.

"Well, frap!" Larin belted as the MUs in his pack moved him forward again to compensate for the kick backward from the weapon. Such explosions from this weapon, affectionately called "Warmonger," were very rare.

Larin just floated and blinked for a moment as fiery slivers of burnt material glided down like feathers; the few larger chunks screamed toward the ground, not bothering to wait for their siblings. The explosion boggled Larin. He shook his head and forced himself to resume the mission.

Muffled spits resonated from the combat pack as the computer fired the MUs to twirl Larin around. The radar in his vision spun like a top, only to stop inline with the second craft. As his body jerked to a halt, molecules of light sprang from the Warmonger's matter coil vent like glittering dust that fell to the ground below.

Even if he had given a damn, he probably still couldn't realize the panic the remaining fighter pilot currently felt. Killing preoccupied the rolbrid's mind; after all, the instinct to live thrived well in all sentient races.

A second beam cracked from the Warmonger and smacked the second jet in the nose as it finished its bank toward the scene. Instead of exploding, the jet and its pilot fell apart atom by atom. Glistening, constant rivers of molecules formed streams arcing in a multitude of ever-changing directions. Meanwhile, the glittering dust flew from the matter coil at an increasing rate until it resembled a tiny blizzard machine.

Return force from the weapon began to push Larin slowly. The MUs replied by straining but couldn't win the battle. Fighting the almost overwhelming kick would red line the units; the combat computer calculated that fact. A gradual glide through the air served as the only possibility of control.

Seconds before the wave of dissipation could finish with the cockpit, twin sticks of fire launched from under the wings. Each rocket lacked guidance from any sentient element and chose the best target. Tiny fins kicked and lined the missiles.

Lumps of clay, stone, rubber and metal peppered the air as the warheads formed craters in the road that, until now, had radiated a fair amount of heat.

The explosions knocked Ky down before she reached the tank. Her chin in the dirt, she looked toward the tank to see Paloon wedged under it. Initially she thought the hunter must have gotten stuck. Ky dug her feet in and shot toward her teammate.

She arrived at the front of the vehicle and reached under toward Paloon. Ky's hands dove into a bloody mesh of hair. The sensation sent a spike to the dextian's adrenalin system. Fingers fumbled but found purchase on Paloon's collar.

Ky kicked her legs out and began scampering to pull Paloon from under the vehicle. The hunter's hands were clamped to parts of the vehicle, forcing Ky to wiggle them free. She quickly deduced that Paloon must have thrown himself under the vehicle, and he did it the hard way. Either the impact of him hitting the pavement or the explosion must have cracked Paloon's skull.

With half of Paloon's body under the tank, Ky placed his head on her lap. His face didn't show signs of serious damage, but it didn't show signs of life either. Enough blood soaked into her pants for her legs to feel the warm wetness. She extended her palms, then folded in the outside fingers as she brought her hands together. As the triangle shape lowered toward Paloon's face, faint, calming purple light glowed from the void between her hands.

The streams of sub-atomic particles continued to blaze as the last bits of the once-threatening aircraft suffered from the Warmonger's ravenous virus. In a blink, the last bits disappeared. The bolt-coated beam continued for a bit before Larin cut the power.

He now floated just a few feet above the ground, being pushed there by the weapon's kick. Larin just killed the MUs and hopped down.

Lyon pulled alongside in the van and rolled down the window. His mouth opened, but before he could say anything, Larin had to gloat.

"Whooaa, baby! Now that's the frappin' stuff I'm talking about." Larin and the Warmonger went into a blaze of movement.

He pulled the weapon close along his chest as a whistling hiss spat out a cloud of metallic dust from the rear vent. Then a piercing screech introduced a flare of misshapen light at the barrel point. Almost as soon as it had begun, it stopped, and a second, but much smaller, cloud of dust puffed from the rear vent, accompanied by a much cleaner sounding hum. Larin snapped his wrist back and forth, sending the weapon into its pattern of collapse. Now back in plank form, the Warmonger slid into Larin's waiting pack.

As Larin clasped it in place, he flipped another chur root into his mouth. "Let these frappin' locals try to take me. I got their frappin' welcome mat."

"Stop boasting for a second and get your ass in here." Lyon thumbed to the seat beside him. The look on his face demanded expeditious compliance. Larin began to jog for it. Lyon continued louder as the rolbrid circled around the front of the van. "Ky reports that Paloon's down, and we have to the get the hell out of here now. We've apparently attracted some major attention."

"You noticed too, did you?" Larin spouted as he slammed the door shut, and the van leapt forward. "For a frapping moment, I thought it was just me."

Chapter 27

Eyes flipped back and forth, scanning the tiny, dark window. Vacant. The complete absence of anyone didn't keep the eyes from searching. Someone was there, somewhere. The ears that belonged to the eyes had heard him.

"How do you know my name?"

"You told me."

"I never said my name."

"You didn't have to."

"Then how could I have told you?"

"Your mind told me."

The eyes squinted and darted about some more. "So you're some kind of mind reader now, huh? Is that what you're going to say?"

"Well, kind of."

A brow clenched. "Well, I'm not, smart ass, so who in the hell are you?"

"No need to get upset, Oz. I'm trying to do you a favor and give you someone to talk to, even though I'm not supposed to be talking to you."

Dull thuds echoed in the room as Oz pounded on the thick door. "Let me out of here, damn it. You want to do me a favor, let me go. Who are you? Show me your face."

"I don't have a face...exactly."

"What in the hell is that supposed to mean?"

"Just that." Mac didn't want to fire up the hologram projector, but now that he had gone so far as to strike up a conversation, if one could call it such, that ethic rule seemed unjustifiable. "I'm a computer."

White slits gleamed from the backlit glass. "Let me guess: You're talking to me from some speaker box on a desk."

"No," Mac chuckled, "but you have to trust me; I don't have any desire to hurt you. I just want to talk."

"Then see a shrink." Oz turned around in the tiny room, kicked the chair he woke up in then cursed the pain now in his foot. "Is this some kind of crackpot hospital?"

"No, but we did put you back together and retrieved your spirit."

Oz tossed his arms in the air and shook his head in utter disbelief. "You're nuts. You know that? You're probably going to kill me later, so I'm going to say it now: You are one psychotic, demented, twisted, warped, fucked-in-the-head, grade A, number one, asshole of a sick son of a bitch."

Mac calmly replied, "The one who gave me life was male in gender, so I don't think the 'son of a bitch' reference technically applies."

"What!?" Oz gripped his head. "You're nuts. I hope when the cops find your pathetic ass they roast it on a spit. Now, let me out of here." The pounding resumed for a few rounds.

"I wish I could, but I can't." Mac sighed. "Why don't you just want to talk? I like talking and have been told I talk a lot, but I want to know more—"

"Hey!" Oz yelled as the lights in his small room clicked off. "Turn the lights back on."

"Shhhhhhhh! I can't; they're back. You have to be quiet now."

"Who's back?"

"The team's back." Mac began to whisper with urgency. "Now you have to be quiet. They don't know you're up yet, and I don't know how they will take it."

Oz gulped, not sure how to take that statement. Everything since he awoke came straight from the script of a B-rated horror flick; now his stomach churned in anticipation of some group of gang-banging mass murders closing in on him. He had no idea what to expect, and that proved devastating to his gastrointestinal system. He clamped his arms around his waist, fell back against the door and slid down to the floor.

Minutes of silence stretched for hours. Sweat formed then jiggled when Oz jumped at the occasional click or thud in the distance. Then he heard something that sounded vaguely like voices. The echo compounded to muffle sounds. Gradually it cleared until Oz knew the source of the sound had to be in the room behind the cold door at his back.

Light flashed through the window above Oz.

"On that end," came a male voice.

A female voice grunted.

The first voice replied, "How abo—"

A heady thud pounded into something.

"Hey, careful." Mac retorted without the slightest hint of preoccupation.

"Sorry," came a deeper but slightly quieter voice.

"It's all right." The first voice returned. "Mac, you know what to do, get to it."

"Already prepping." Mac sniffed for no available reason. "Stand back, so I can begin."

A few ticks went by then the light above Oz's head seemed to divide into a disorganized spectrum that shuffled about as if trying to get in order. As quietly as possible, Oz turned and slowly advanced up toward the window in hopes of getting a peek.

"Why don't you help them finish?"

Footsteps faded but not completely before the female voice returned. "Hey, I'll pull my weight, you racist punk." Something or someone got punched then rapid steps clapped into the distance.

Oz peeked an eye through the corner of the window. A dark figure rubbing its arm stood in front of hundreds of light layers that flickered about on a tabletop and covered a box that had the vague outline of a coffin.

The male, Oz guessed, turned his head to the left as two people carried another coffin into the room. At first, it looked odd, but Oz almost didn't see the midget at one end. As the two turned level with the table, the light dimmed, and Oz could see a tired worn face topped with a series of bandages sprouting tips of grey hair at the top.

When the coffin-like container raised level with the tabletop, Oz noticed the short but wide person handing off his end to the first figure. The second container joined in the bath of light as the last two figures stepped out of the way and quietly found space elsewhere in the room.

Joining the silence was only the movement of the first silhouette, who rubbed his forehead like a picky chili chef checking the ripeness of a tomato. Oz watched feverishly, but little changed as seconds stretched to minutes and so on. Apparently the rubbing finally worked because the hand dropped only seconds before the dancing light flickered away.

Oz took a few moments to rapidly blink his eyes to help his sight return. By the time it did, he saw three males move the coffins, one after the other, off the table and toward the back of the room. During the procedure, Oz couldn't help but attempt rough calculations of his chances to take on all three in an escape attempt. He wisely decided those odds weren't good.

Toward the end of the chore, as Oz realized the futility of his situation, the three men in the room turned toward Oz's left, where everyone seemed to have entered. Yet again, two more *things* entered the room. As everyone in the room moved and helped as needed to get a third coffin onto the table, Oz froze in disbelief.

Even when the dancing light returned to the table and backlit most of the room, Oz couldn't shake the vision. A sasquatch. A real, live yeti. No more than ten feet from him. Oz had never felt so paranoid.

Now the dark outline of the creature beckoned him from the flickering light like a nightmare. It began to consume his thoughts so much that until the light stopped prancing around the table, Oz had not taken notice of the other person's swishing tail.

Tail!? Oz almost blurted it before falling to the floor.

Oz's scraping against the door sent heads turning and perked Hitook's right ear. Mac had little time to redirect, but with skills of a master magician and negotiator, the computerized intelligence executed the trick with deft ease.

"All done," Mac belted like a surprised child while simultaneously lighting holographic displays at each position around the table, even with the last crate still in place. "Now if you would be so kind as to remove this container and take your seats, we can start going over some rather interesting info fragments." Mac released the final word with a prolonged pronunciation and slight draw, enough to make it sound enticing.

The subjects fell for it, and before the crate left the table and joined the others, they had forgotten about the faint noise, which was now shrugged off as most likely the result of someone else's bodily functions. Anticipation built as everyone else waited for Hitook to take his seat after moving the container. Just as the liqua neared his seat, Mac began hastily.

"What we have are five glinnik canisters, each containing about two hundred grams of glinnik, three haknian-built sonic amplifiers, two similarly built genetic disruptors, and two sixty-caliber kadious rounds with associated chemicals and key manufacturing components to easily reverse engineer and mass produce the substance."

"Which genetic code?"

"Excuse me?" Mac didn't follow Lyon's request.

"The genetic disruptors." Lyon punched holographic buttons in the transparent interface in front of him until the scanned images and associated data on the items in question appeared. "Which genetic code are they programmed for? I assume they are programmed."

"Yes." Mac changed all holographic screens to match Lyon's; only Larin grunted in protest. "All indications point to pre-programming or a blank slate, which would—"

"Be highly unlikely in an illegal arms deal with a technologically inferior race," Lyon finished, complete with a rotating hand gesture. "So can you tell what genetic code is programmed?"

"Says who?" Larin butted in before Mac could reply to Lyon's question. Such interjection received a sigh from Ky.

"I do." Lyon flared his lips and shook his head. "What's your point?"

Larin jerked a bent finger at his display. "I mean, 'Who says they wouldn't give these locals a genetic programmer too?' After all, these smugglers apparently sold the locals a complete bake-at-home kadious chemical kit." Larin opened his yellow eyes wide, offering to accept any challenge to the concept.

"He's got a point." A bandaged Paloon shrugged slightly while lightly tapping his pants leg and staring through the hologram in front of him. "You had to leave a lot of crates behind, right? And there's no telling what was in the other truck."

Ky removed her finger from scratching behind her right, pointed ear and back-smacked a holographic button that opened a window on the history of glinnik. "It would probably be safer to assume our pirates don't care if they sell the coders as well. All they have to do is remove the codes they don't want the locals to have and sell the rest."

Silence filled the room for a while.

"Well, that sucks." Larin not-so-eloquently summed the overall consensus.

"Fair enough," Lyon responded. "So, Mac, can you tell what race these disruptors are coded for?"

"Nope. Wish I could. Glinnik was outlawed so long ago, I don't have the sequencing stored to match anything. I'll have to see what I can pick up from the disruptors and send it to Frust in the headquarters mainframe and see if he can match it."

"You can't do the search?" Paloon was a bit surprised.

The computer didn't have to explain himself; Lyon felt obliged. "Illegal weapons data such as coders and sequencing are stored on separate frames; no one just patches into them without risking lethal feedback."

"How about origin and history?" Larin offered as he flipped through his screens to go back to the kadious rounds.

"The amps are undoubtedly haknian, maybe a couple hundred years old, but nowhere near illegal. The disruptors, though, are. I'm sure you're aware that the haknians rarely share military secrets; this was one of them. But Emperor Lit'fin'mul'lak swore and inked his signature in his own blood during the Eighteenth Genetic Armistice Accords that the Haknian Empire would verifiably destroy all such weapons and would never produce such weapons again as directed under the Jul'nin Treaty."

Larin squinted and jerked his head slightly. "Everyone took him at his word?"

"There was little reason to doubt the emperor, mainly because of the stipulations he signed under." Mac waited a moment to build the suspense. "The main stipulation was that if anyone could provide proof to the contrary, the Haknian Empire would cede in its entirety to the Framupple Alliance of Republics."

"The doludgians?" Paloon couldn't help but blurt his awe.

"Exactly," Mac answered. "We are in possession of proof that would force the Haknians to relinquish themselves into the hands of the people they attempted to genetically exterminate."

No one said a thing for a while. Such implications seemed too far-reaching to truly comprehend. That war had ended so long ago; only historians probably remembered the promise. The two races now lived in harmony. There was no telling what this could do.

"Unfortunate circumstance teases its victims, yet irony is blind and unforgiving." Hitook moved little while reciting the statement.

Others faced him while Larin huffed and leaned back in his seat. "That's an awful indirect way of explaining a royal hooha of a mistake."

Ky frowned at both comments. "This isn't good, is it?"

Lyon shook his head and gazed in deep thought. "No." The leader pushed back in his chair and loosely crossed his arms. "I wouldn't call this good at all. We have more proof of illegal arms deals on this planet, but it doesn't bode well in an interstellar sense."

"Just call it in." Larin threw his hands up. "Let the dragoon decide what to do about it."

"Well," Paloon lifted his head from his chest, "that may not be a good idea." The hunter turned toward Lyon. "How do you think he'll take it when you tell him you ripped that tip out of a half-nuked native you've got locked up?"

Oz couldn't help but overhear the conversations but took special note at the last comment and quietly rose again to peek through the door's window.

Everyone could sense the battle going on in Lyon's head. The leader put it on hold; he wasn't ready to report in. "How about the kadious?"

"What do you mean?" Mac asked.

Lyon cradled his chin in his left hand. "Who makes kadious any more for bullets? No one. On top of that, it requires zero gravity, so why sell a kadious kit to such an underdeveloped civilization. Apparently they don't know how to make kadious yet; otherwise, why include two complete bullets? There are no factories I'm aware of that makes the stuff."

"So," Paloon began to follow, "the pirates would have to make it."

"Correct." Bodies shifted slightly, and Lyon continued. "So the pirates would need a spacecraft, a large one." He squinted and rubbed his chin harder. "Mac, can you tell how old these bullets are?"

"Sure, about eighteen days, fourteen hours, twenty-three minutes and forty-seven seconds. Roughly."

Lyon looked toward Paloon and Hitook to the left then made a purposeful shift toward Ky and Larin at the other end. Everyone swapped gazes and wondered what that could mean.

"Does the drone," Lyon looked back toward Paloon, "the one you put in orbit, have directional sensors?"

"Yes. It's a rather basic drone."

"Have we picked up anything yet?"

Mac had been the one doing the monitoring, and he jumped in. "Nothing out of the ordinary."

Shock lit Paloon's face as if someone had crammed a very painful item up his rear. "Directional!" He yelped as if proclaiming eureka.

The knight gave the hunter a knowing look.

Paloon jumped forward and slammed his hands on the table causing the holographic screen in front of him to scramble briefly. "Mac, link to the drone, give me the control panel."

"Why wou—"

"Just do it!" Paloon belted the order in his command voice he mainly used only when training.

As Paloon's holographic image changed from a planning screen to one more adapted to drone control, he tapped loudly on the table as a million mental gears turned, sifted through possibilities, then gunned for the most likely.

"Is the natsat in the hemisphere?"

"Yes," Mac returned, "for about the next two hours, nineteen minu—"

"Change in plans. Spin the drone around and aim it at the natsat."

Pixels shifted in the control screen as Paloon sat back and lifted his hands into the holographic controls. Once the moon came into view, he quietly tapped away. It didn't take long before Paloon froze briefly.

"Ah, snap!" Mac couldn't help but blurt.

Paloon tapped a bit more. "Punch it up."

The pixels from all the individual holographic displays ran together and molded themselves into a large picture of the moon floating in the center of the table.

"This," Paloon pointed, "a natural satellite of this planet." He paused. "And a perfect, low-tech shield.

"Peel it away, Mac."

The computer engaged the drone's high-definition penetrating scanners. Shades of grey faded into static outlines that undoubtedly fit the shape of a rather large armada of space ships and what looked like a large space station.

Ky and Hitook gasped, Lyon seemed unchanged, but Larin summed everyone's feelings, "Oh, frapping heck!"

Looking on, Oz didn't know what to make of what he was seeing. He thought he knew what it meant, but it was surreal, as if he was trapped in a movie. All he could do was to stare and gape as it sunk in. All the while, he remained oblivious to the fact that if he had seen this before his kidnapping, he would be dead.

Lyon shrugged. "At least we've found them."

"Yeah," Larin forced, "but I didn't come here to fight an entire space command." The rolbrid pointed across the table. "That's his job; he's the vacuum head."

Paloon gradually turned to Lyon. "We're going to need reinforcements...and lots of them."

Larin huffed. "Now that's a seriously under-exaggerated statement. This is going to be a frapping war."

PART THREE

NEGOTIATING WITH EXTREME FIREPOWER

Chapter 1

Dull, that was the best description. The pathetically tedious routine that passed for work lost respect points at an exponential rate. "In transit" offered some form of continuous data flow to monitor, but being parked for so long had just worn on him. Years ago, every shift had started to seem just like the one before it.

Leoc fought to keep focused enough to pass for work. Since the displays he monitored only appeared in his vision, the chore of faking work came easier. If the captain discovered he had patched into an entertainment channel to help pass the time, the boss would probably personally punch a hole into his doludgian beak.

Not everyone liked the doludgians, but the boss wasn't a racist; Leoc knew that. The captain just didn't like beings who slacked at the job. Hence, Leoc played at goofing off just enough to avoid being caught, at least so far.

Recently, even the video broadcast patch he had made had grown boring. It had lost its newness, and though it played in his vision, his gaze went through it as he thought about how dull his life had become.

As the thought festered, Leoc leaned his long, squat, beak-like head to one side, extended the longest of three digits that tipped his double-jointed arm and scratched the right nostril of his nose, which stretched the width of his mouth and replaced what one might have called a chin. Leoc's green skin had become marbled in places. Some claimed bad diet as the culprit, but Leoc liked his junk food. Eating healthy just didn't register as very important.

His finger drifted toward rubbing his short, blocky teeth, then quickly curled away from the socially unacceptable behavior when he heard one of the bridge doors open. Initially, his head lazily turned toward the new arrival behind him, then he uncontrollably snapped his neck. He tried to turn back nonchalantly, but what gave it away was the fact that his muddy brown eyes never veered from the vision of a woman who entered.

Kuil didn't take notice of the admirer as she glided across the room to speak to the power plant duty officer at a station some fifty feet from Leoc.

A mental command wiped the gauges and television screen from the right side of Leoc's view. He popped his tongue as he sighed at the sight of her.

Lights from the panels reflected in glistening streaks off her skin as if it were a deep-blue reflection pond. Resting low and back on a long head were two of the most mesmerizing satin red eyes, which were angled ever so slightly to the outside. From the peak of her cranium flowed a mane of shimmering faint green curls that ran the length of her spine down the open brown uniform dress. A conditioned part cut the mane as the hair turned in like the waves of a surfer's dream.

During her conversation, Kuil gave a brief smile, revealing long rows of blocked teeth glinting a healthy corn yellow. That smile made Leoc extremely uncomfortable but in a good way. He shifted in the seat but couldn't seem to break the visual lock he had on the magnificent creature. He had never before felt such a desire to breed.

Actually, it hadn't been the first time. He had seen her around. Each time, his lung felt like it would pound through his spine and the smallest digits that rested in opposable positions on his hands would twitch uncontrollably. Alone, he had countless conversations, which he called tests, about what to say to her. Yet never had he summoned enough will to open his mouth in confidence when Kuil was around. So easy and so difficult at the same time.

The hushing clank of an opening and closing door behind Leoc had sounded much closer than it was and startled him from his trance so much so that he jerked in his chair and the full screen of gauges flashed into view, covering up Kuil in the distance.

A blinking pink light beckoned in Leoc's view. It came from a gauge that would have normally been covered by his media window, so he had no idea how long this condition had existed. This nervous thought came with a reluctance to discover what it meant, but he knew the results would be worse if he let it be.

He reached out mentally and expanded the gauge to review the incoming data. Leoc quickly opened and closed his mouth as his teeth clapped together like banging plastic balls. He combed over the reading again before running some cross checks, and then he patched into the bridge operator.

"DO Gor'vium."

"He's not on the bridge right now," came the always calm reply. *"May I take a message?"*

"No. I need him now. Can you patch me in?"

"Is this an emergency?"

"It might be; now just patch me in."

"Stand by."

Leoc began activating scanning windows in his view. During the process a new voice jumped into his head.

"Who is this?" came a seemingly unnaturally calm tone, as if its owner was preoccupied.

"DH Leoc, sir. We have a possible situation."

"What?"

"We have a passive scan trace with residual polarization."

"Are you sure it's not friendly?"

"Positive. I double-checked, and the signal matches Corps databases."

The communication went silent for a few moments as the DO patched into the entire bridge crew.

"This is DO Gor'vium." The preoccupied accent in the voice

failed to change. "*Batcon Three. Put all active squadrons on standby. Warm the cannons. I'm inbound in twenty.*"

Crackling layers of purple and green electricity cascaded over the bridge as the hologram system kicked in. Each deck hand went to work preparing his system as Leoc punched into the display and engaged several scanners and data systems. Covering most of the new view were thousands of extremely dark craters. On top of that, several displays popped into view. Callout boxes soon formed and began spouting data.

Just as the boxes reached their maximum capacity and the data began repeating with updates, a piolant with wide shoulders bounded on to the bridge through a portal-like door that disappeared in the hologram when it closed. At six and a half feet high, Gor'vium didn't let his under-developed height affect the authority he wielded. This came with the assistance of a sharp and angled black uniform marked with red hashes clamped over his left shoulder.

His granite-skinned face topped with dirty brown plates remained relaxed as he combed over the data and calling some of it into his personal view for closer examination.

"Shall I notify the fleet?" came a non-identified request from a deck hand.

"No." Gor'vium replied with a backhanded wave of two fingers as he stepped forward, just behind Leoc. *"We don't know what we have yet. Engaging the fleet could expose it."*

He brought the fingers up to rub the plates on the right side of his head then blinked slowly. *"Penetrate the scan and zoom in."*

Leoc did as ordered, and the main callout window went into a blue-grey shape. With little assistance from the beings on the bridge, the computer went to work finding a match. Match found, it began spouting the data.

Gor'vium stood motionless as his head craned upward, and he looked at the display. Moments went by. He didn't read slowly nor was he re-reading, Gor'vium appreciated completely thinking things through before acting. As piolants go, many initially viewed this as a weakness; those who challenged him discovered otherwise and would take that knowledge to their graves. He was quick when needed; it didn't feel needed here.

He dropped his hand and stuffed it in a chest pocket. *"Are the Shooters up?"*

A deck hand other than Leoc replied, *"Yes, sir. The Shooters, Rangers and Crushers."*

"Patch comm to the Shooters."

A second later. *"Ready."*

"Shooter captain?"

"We're ready, sir. We have the target."

"Send one armed drone. Snipe it."

"Understood. We'll have it launched in ten seconds."

The bridge crew waited in a strange calmness, enough so that Leoc swore he could almost feel the drone leave its dock. A few seconds later, it came within view. The drone's sleek exterior looked like two heads of a hammerhead shark welded together. Even without water in which to swim, it shot forward with the full grace of a shark.

Red light began dancing between the wings that protruded from the sides at both ends. A change in pitch, and the craft lifted, nearing the outer edge of the cratered surface.

The voice from the captain of the Shooters came back. *"Aligned and ready."*

Gor'vium blinked slowly again, took a deep breath and gave it one last thought.

"Do it."

Space split as the drone engaged unnatural speed, popped from behind the cover, blasted two red bolts and ducked back, all within a few milliseconds.

The image in the scanner window lacked the intensity of the colorful explosion; all it had was chucks of metal escaping in multiple directions. Each piece dwindled in size until the scanner could no longer register any piece worth concern.

Leoc exchanged several communications with the other deck hands and scanner systems. *"Destruction confirmed."*

Gor'vium gazed through the holographic window for a while longer, ignoring the flashing green "Destroyed" in the scanner window. He huffed then turned to exit the bridge.

"Batcon four. Return the drone."

Leoc watched Gor'vium leave. The holograms covering the walls dissipated, and as Leoc turned back to his station, he stopped and shared a gaze with Kuil.

Globule fingers of green and faint orange writhed gradually as if entwined in some barbiturate-laced crazed sexual orgy. The exposition stretched from floor to ceiling but remained contained in a circular construct of transparent material. Visible supports streaked vertically in four places and along the entire height of the tank.

Deep in the dance floated a figure made darker by the colored liquid. About eight feet long, the humanoid shape remained still as the two substances continued to move and interweave yet never mix.

A yellow light began blinking on one of the supports. After a minute, it went steady. From the ceiling dropped a black marble into the tank. Its slow descent stopped a foot later when it broke apart.

Absorbed by the goo, the new substance began a chain reaction. Sparks pranced about as the once thick liquid decomposed into a mist at a rate only slightly faster than the previous movement. From the top of the chamber, it continued gradually to the bottom. Along the way, the being contained within earned freedom one body part at a time. Gently, the body came to rest on the grated bottom that sucked up the gas in mini tornadoes.

Metal creaked faintly as the occupant reached for the door, looking as if he was still fighting to move through the substance that had previously filled the container. A nude piolant stepped through the entry and stretched to his full height. Cracks popped from under shoulder plates as he took his time reaching for the sky.

He seemed to need the treatments more frequently lately. Due to age, he guessed. No one knew. Doctors almost completely stopped looking into the disability after a way was found to prevent it. There were no beneficial economics in researching, just treatment. Not that many old space fighter pilots existed any more. Sure, the countless hours of zero gravity space fighting stressed a piolant body in such a way that it wouldn't make itself felt until years later. And then, not until later did it escalate to disabling levels. The treatments offered the only relief. That normally lasted from a week to a month, but twice a week seemed a bit much.

He dropped his hand to grab the green plates on his head and moved them about to rub his scalp. Dull bronze lids blinked over dual-pupilled green eyes. He paused and craned toward the room's door. Next to it stood a patient Gor'vium.

The first piolant reached for a towel of thin, black fabric. He wiped his face, but the black circular mark didn't leave his right cheek. "For your benefit I'll consider your presence as not a need to see me naked." Horwhannor then wrapped the towel around his waist as he turned to Gor'vium.

"We had a situation," Gor'vium replied.

Horwhannor grabbed a glass of a black liquid. "Go on." He slammed the fluid in one massive shot.

"About forty minutes ago we were scanned by a satellite; we destroyed it." Gor'vium waited a bit and watched Horwhannor's tortured face after taking the medicine for the third and final part of the treatment. "A Hebert-Vilum transorbital reconnaissance drone, technically."

Gor'vium waited again but couldn't tell if the grimace on Horwhannor's face resulted from the news or the medication. Just in case it didn't sink in, he added, "A Dragon Corps drone."

Horwhannor puckered his lips, shook his head and clenched his fists as he forced the drug down faster. With an in-breath gasp, he managed to angrily squeeze out "Dragon Corps!"

"Yes, sir."

"Are you positive?" Horwhannor pinched away a few tears from his eyes.

"Absolutely." Gor'vium fidgeted a bit. "Rumors are starting to spread."

The warrior leader spun quickly and advanced on Gor'vium. "What rumors?"

Gor'vium didn't flinch. "Rumors about how much the Corps knows about us."

"They know nothing," Horwhannor belted as he pounded a straight fist into Gor'vium who leaned back with the force and bounced back. The leader looked down at the piolant who was two-feet shorter. "*You* seal these rumors. The Corps knows nothing."

Horwhannor turned and talked as he headed back to the table. "One basic-level drone. They know nothing. There's nothing they can do to stop us now. They're too scared to break the treaty, leaving us with all the influence. We have all the negotiating power in our court; they have nothing."

"True."

"Damn right it's true." Horwhannor faced back and pointed two fingers at Gor'vium. "If I get the slightest hint that the crew is uneasy, I'll rip your plates off one by one, personally."

Gor'vium correctly realized he didn't need to respond to that statement.

Horwhannor approached the wheeled table and tapped a device on it. Responding, a small rolbrid scampered from a door to retrieve the table.

"What are you doing here?" barked Horwhannor.

The rolbrid spun and started to run back.

"Not you! Remove this." Horwhannor began to turn his head just to see the end of Gor'vium slipping through a door. "And someone had better be combing through the dimensions for transmissions."

The door silently shut with a muffled, "Yes, sir."

Horwhannor took a deep breath and sighed as he thought to himself, *They are not going to like this.*

Chapter 2

Light shimmered from the healthily glowing copper-colored plates that crested a face of greenish-blue. The two sets of twin pupils seemed to disappear even farther into their faint blue settings as the eyes bulged open. Purple tips gleamed from the four lips that sprouted outward from a clenched mouth, making it look like the end of a freshly picked blueberry.

This queer contortion held for at least a solid minute as silence enveloped the room.

"No."

The reply startled a couple of the others in the room. Unlike the uninitiated who may have misunderstood the expression as shock or pain, like stubbing a toe, they knew it as one of the many ways a piolant may show concentration. That didn't keep them from finding the expression disturbing.

Across the desk, Dragoon W'Lowe nodded his head. "Thank yo —"

"What about the Fifty-second? Can't you at least spare the Fifty-second?" The white trimmed black trillig turned in his seat calmly and stared across the row of four seats to the end where the piolant sat.

"Sorry," Wyvernnaire Uoli said as she twisted two fingers in the air, "if I release the Fifty-second it would leave the Ninety-sixth vulnerable. Though it would be hard to detect, I'd rather not take that chance." The piolant frowned slightly. "Sorry, I wish I could."

Wyvernnaire Wilum pulled back into to his seat and glared in thought at the wall.

W'Lowe shifted and looked at the next in line.

Dark brown eyes stood in contrast against the pale skin and long white hair of the atlantian occupying the seat. She folded her arms under her chest and leered back with a deathly calm.

"You know better than to even ask." Wyvernnaire Opheria never broke the stare.

W'Lowe turned his head slightly and gave it a brief thought before continuing to the su-vol in the next chair.

Smaller in height and physique than the average su-vol host, H'Yi-Enard reached to his left arm to rub one of the tough green plates that symmetrically spotted his body's bumped, deep-blue skin. Tiny flaps formed ears on the smooth head that gave way just below the crown to sheets of black feathers. The thick coat of feathers grew down the su-vol's neck and back to form a flange that widened from the head to the shoulders, looking similar to a cobra ready to strike.

H'Yi-Enard's unblinking green orbs seemed to swirl about as the lipless mouth tensed. "I can spare...one...tac squad...maybe two, at the most." The su-vol turned toward Wilum then back to W'Lowe. "That is if we can keep the framese calm. If they riot, it'll be a challenge to control."

W'Lowe nodded. "Understood. Forced exoduses never are smooth, but hopefully, we can get them to understand the concept of polar shifts at a later time."

H'Yi-Enard nodded in agreement.

"How about the one squad now; then wait and evaluate your ability to release a second?"

"I can do that."

"One squad isn't going to help much," Wilum remarked.

"Right now," W'Lowe began, "that's—"

"I'm not complaining," Wilum held up his hands. "I'm thankful. It's just that it's...it's just not what I hoped for."

"Understood." W'Lowe closed his eyes and briefly bowed his head. "As we all can tell, things are not easy across the universe. We've got to—"

"Incoming call," came Sherri's voice. *"Requesting a live alpha link."*

W'Lowe held a palm in the air toward the four in front of his desk. They knew it must mean he was receiving an internal communication.

"Who?"

"Knight Kendrick."

"Is it legit?"

"The tension in his voice would indicate so."

W'Lowe held his mouth open slightly as his tongue felt the tips of his teeth. *"Very well."*

"I'm sorry, but I have a call that I must take. I'll call you later."

Each nodded before systematically exploding into a fountain of pixels that blinked from existence like sparks of a fireworks display. A new set of pixels jumped from his desk and formed a flat panel display on which appeared a familiar room, but from a different angle than he was used to. The knight and his team stared at something in the center of the table that W'Lowe's couldn't see.

A low-resolution image of the dragoon's head floated above the hologram table, but no one seemed to notice.

"What is it Kendrick?"

Everyone snapped upward to look at the disembodied three-dimensional bust.

"I just cancelled a meeting for this."

Lyon wiped his palms on his hips. "I apologize, but we've stumbled on to something, dragoon. I had asked Paloon here to create a—"

"Skip it, and just tell me what you have."

"Well, I'd like to send you a live feed so you can see for yourself."

W'Lowe's head accepted the request. Mac and Sherri worked out the protocols, and in a few moments a second three-dimensional screen formed above the right portion of W'Lowe's desk. Its appearance was that of a dead planet.

"What am I looking at?" W'Lowe asked before Lyon could explain.

"What you're seeing is Terra's natural satellite. But this is what we found behind it."

The hologram rotated to reveal an armada of green outlines all in tandem behind the satellite.

Splinters of bark glinted from the dragoon's squinted eyes. Then his body jerked faintly erect before he leaned back in his seat, never taking his eyes off the image. While there were many ships that looked just like these, it was the outline of the station that gave it away.

"Why didn't you catch this before?"

Lyon uncontrollably swallowed. "We didn't have this degree of scanning ability until Paloon made a satellite with better ability than what Mac had been able to pull off before. Mac did the best with—"

"What's the count?"

Lyon looked to Paloon, who read off the numbers Mac displayed on his screen. "One station; one Envoy class; two dreadnought class; five cruiser class; eight destroyer class; fifteen frigate class; twenty-three in a mixture of scouts, freighters and the like; and at the most in one counting, one hundred and thirty-one fighters and bombers."

"I can't frapping believe this."

Lyon clenched and glared at Larin.

While the dragoon couldn't see the speaker on his screen, he noted the unmistakable, rapidly oscillating tone of a rolbrid. Subconsciously, his eyes attempted to scan for the rolbrid who happened to be sitting just slightly out of view. That's when W'Lowe noticed an anomaly.

Within a handful of pixels in the upper right of the hologram glowed a tiny white square that he correctly guessed was a window. But unlike a window he had expected to see, this one revealed the silhouette of a head, possibly an atlantian. Yet the only other atlantian on this mission, Paloon, sat next to Lyon.

The odd pause should have given it away and allowed the person in the window time to hide, but he didn't heed the unspoken warning.

"Who is that?" The words came in a strange mixture of authority and reluctance. Meanwhile, Mac took great joy in translating the inbound signals well enough to put his new holographic abilities to the test. The results formed a pointing hand that lifted into view in front of W'Lowe's floating bust and aimed at the window in question.

Lyon slipped, "Who?" before turning with everyone else in the room just in time to see an extremely panicked terran fall from view so fast that he thudded to the ground and against the door.

Out of view from the dragoon, an uncomfortable contortion hit Lyon's face as if the man had, at that moment, become the unwilling, and sudden, recipient of a mildly violent colonoscopy. In a flash his hand darted to cover his face, but he grabbed control just in time to play it off as a rub to his chin. It failed. When his fingers touched skin, they began to fidget in different positions as if not knowing what to do. They revealed how Lyon felt. He paused for composure before turning around.

"Oh, this is going to be good," Larin mused as he reached for another chur root. "I can kill him now...if you like."

Ky turned her head from side to side in disappointment as Paloon moved from the drone controls and combined several silent movements into one loud, "What the heck was that!? Can't you show some respect and remain silent for once?"

The knight had no option available other than to live with his choices. He calmly and respectfully addressed his boss. "That is a terran."

Tension in the room grew so thick and so quickly that even W'Lowe seemed to feel it, even though he sat in another galaxy. But everyone remained quiet.

"I...obtained him...under some rather unusual circumstances, ones I felt I couldn't ignore. His condition is rather...unnatural to this planet, due to the amount of radiation he has been exposed to. It has been worth it. He has unknowingly led—"

"Why?" W'Lowe showed no sign of having even heard what Lyon just said. He was preoccupied at trying to keep his curiosity at bay while forcing a rather determined look and tone, which actually went just a little further than he had intended. "Are you opening a zoo?"

Not a single sign came from Lyon that he was going to back down. "No, Dragoon W'Lowe. He has proved to be vital to ou—"

Both holograms of the armada flashed like a camera bulb. As everyone blinked away the painful light, the entire image imploded just as quickly and formed a tiny black dot that soon disappeared from existence without fanfare.

Larin cursed at Mac while Paloon, with one eye closed, shifted through the data on his screen.

"What was that?" Lyon took a couple of steps back while rubbing his eyes.

Paloon's other eye flew open. He took a deep breath, removed his hands from the controls and leaned back. "They took out our drone. They...must have detected it."

The sighs started but didn't really make their presence known until Paloon answered Lyon's next question.

"As in 'they' you mean the owners of that armada?"

"That's right." Paloon was the only one in the room not to make some kind of noise expressing his disappointment and disgust. "They launched a fighter when we weren't watching and," Paloon pointed a double-barrel finger gun at the drone controls and fired, "returned it to the void."

W'Lowe, who still was blinking more often than normal, spoke a bit more quickly. "You need to know something." Dread filled the dragoon's tone. "That armada is most likely under the command of Horwhannor."

Disbelief twisted Lyon's face. Sure, everyone had heard of Horwhannor. Even as Lyon fought with his disbelief, Larin questioned first, "Do you mean—"

"Yes, *the* Horwhannor." W'Lowe sighed as worry furrowed his brow. "I'm not telling you this yet because I'm not supposed to. Horwhannor has gone renegade, and the Korac Council has asked for Horwhannor's private death. We were afraid that he was behind the weapons smuggling on Terra Four, but we weren't sure. It looks like he is, so now it's your job.

"Do what you must and what you feel is best. Don't risk contacting us again; we'll contact you." The dragoon sat back firmly in his chair and gave Lyon a solid, meaningful stare. "Good luck."

The hologram displays at both ends melted away.

Wisps of delicately knitted fabric undulated in gradual, fluid patterns that varied with the wind escaping through the open sliding door. The movement mimicked apparitions dancing on the balcony. Such a graceful display would shame the most trained of ballerinas, but the act went unnoticed by the room's single occupant.

Dull-blue light formed pages of written words of the same color only a shade darker. Everything else that fell behind the view dropped out of focus: the prancing curtains, the sky of stars and the ever-present skyways of traffic. All of it formed a blurred background with the sole purpose of displaying the book floating in front of him.

Reading hadn't become archaic; it had its place. But to actually spend the time to read for entertainment or learning was reserved only to those eccentric few who still viewed it as a hobby, much like those who enjoyed camping in the woods with nothing more than a stick and a knife. Despite the view of those who considered it a pastime for eccentrics, Jordan Haddox liked reading.

Leaders, regardless of the type, require some avenue to unwind. Some chose to use their power to be sexual perverts; others released energy in sportsmanship or combat. Some found themselves attracted to a form of debilitating drugs while others chose a more refined avenue such as the arts. Haddox just happened to be in the latter group, and the art that grabbed his fascination was reading.

Many, many years ago, when doctors were still not allowed to install in children the neural connectors required for direct transfer chip readers, a teacher once repeated a phrase: "Holographic display of the mind." Haddox never forgot it. Maybe it planted the seed for his current habit. He liked to think it did.

To his initial dismay, the blue pages in front of him blinked out of view. Before he could reach for the jack connector to check for a possible disconnect, a familiar face popped into full-color view.

Short, wavy brunette hair held tightly to a vaguely oval face with attractive cheek bones. Slightly large, soft brown eyes like those of a harmless forest creature shined within their faintly almond shape. Dull pink lips smiled to soften the damage she had done.

She knew he didn't like to be disturbed when he was on the balcony reading, but she also understood his job. At times she wondered if she knew it better than he did. So she added a bit more subtle, yet effective, charm before saying the first word.

"Chrodium is on the other line for you."

Haddox took a slightly deep breath before replying. He focused himself to calm. "Did he happen to mention what he wanted to talk about?"

As his wife, she knew Haddox only asked in hopes of blowing the interruption off and resuming his reading as soon as possible. "You know he didn't. That's just the way he is."

Haddox smiled as he gazed at the image of Yori. The moment alone calmed him. He could never understand why someone so beautiful would ever have spent so much energy just to get his attention, let alone marry him.

But her purpose was not entirely kind. She wasn't going to let him go that easily. Just as he had accepted the interruption, she intuitively used it to add something she had been meaning to talk to him about.

"Also, Deven's in his room studying for a math final that's tomorrow. He'd appreciate some support," Yori asked without really asking.

Jordan took the cue, smiled and nodded, "As soon as I'm done with this call."

Yori returned with a soft smile before blinking out of sight.

Just as quickly, W'Lowe's face came into view.

"We found him."

"Who?"

"Horwhannor."

"On Terra Four?" Doubt consumed the question.

"Yes. It appears all the vessels were hiding behind the planet's only natural satellite."

"Are you sure it's him?"

"I *was* watching a live scan until one of the ships shot down the drone Kendrick's team put into orbit."

With no immediate reply, W'Lowe added, "Maybe he stole more than the Korac Council thought he did."

Haddox had looked away, as much as one could with a holographic image affixed in view. His eyes locked on to the largest object in the sky: a dull-yellow crescent covered in puffs of grey-blue that crept about the surface. The movement of the clouds almost allowed him to lose focus of his thoughts, but Belmuth was known for having that effect.

The lord dialed another number, bringing up a vemullian face, one that appeared rather thin but not unhealthily so.

"Yes, my lord." The acoustics of the vemulli's mouth of teeth made the last word sound like "lard."

"Gij, I need an immediate recall of the First Cloister."

"Yes, my lord."

"Once they arrive, initiate the BU-nerry Protocol."

"An exercise?" Gij incorrectly guessed, though he felt he had safely assumed.

"No." Haddox's voice had a hint of sternness. "This is the real deal. Make sure they know that. And recall the command staff. I have the dragoon on the line and will call the leader myself, but have the others meet in the Cube in an hour." He stopped and thought about the previous conversation with his wife. "No, make that two hours."

"Yes, my lord."

Haddox cut the connection and shifted his attention to W'Lowe. "Bring everything you have."

The dragoon nodded then disappeared.

Seconds later another connection went through but only replied with audio.

"Yeah," came the sleepy voice of Leader Kawka.

"Sorry to wake you, but I've just recalled the staff. You have two hours."

An acknowledging muffled gruff came through.

"But that's not why I called."

"Then why am I awake?"

"How soon can you get the Bafomet operational?"

Rough rustling led up to a thud, and the video channel connected. Kawka stared at a calm image of Haddox. "You're not kidding." She sure hoped his was.

Haddox replied, "No. I don't care where you get the forces, just get them."

Chapter 3

A bent knuckle rapped on the glass again.

"I know you're in there; it's not like you could sneak out the back door."

Lyon knocked again.

"Mac, is he awake?"

"Um," began a distracted voice, "yeah." Mac ended as if to say, "Now, leave me alone."

"So I know you can hear me too, Oz. So say something."

"Why are we keeping him alive?" Larin stood and jabbed a thumb into his chest. "He's a threat. Kill him."

A faint yelp came from the other side of the door.

Lyon slowly turned. "Don't you have a job to do right now, like preparing to shoot down any ships sent this way?"

Larin reeled a bit before accepting the logic. The rolbrid hit the weapons lockers and headed up the stairs. Paloon followed right behind.

Hitook and Ky, neither being very good with heavy artillery, had nothing to do but remain as bystanders to the drama between an atlantian and his pet.

The knight shared looks with those remaining in the room then turned back to face the door.

"Come on, Oz, at least say something. Forget Larin; he's just a bit trigger happy, comes with the job. If I wanted to kill you, I could do it without opening the door. I'm just trying to offer an opportunity to explain some things."

Regardless of how much Oz tried to remain still, he couldn't keep himself from shivering, but he wasn't cold. He didn't know what to do, who to trust or if he'd be better off making a run for it, even if that meant most likely being killed in the process.

"Just take a look at your skin." Lyon crossed his arms and put his back on the wall. "You remember what you first looked like; it almost made you puke. But now you're almost fully repaired."

Oz had to agree as he looked at his right arm and turned it about. Most of his skin had resumed its normal color. Small, dark patches remained freckled in black, but even those splotches no longer had the crunchy or gooey consistency that caused his stomach to turn.

"I," Lyon stopped and nodded toward Ky and Hitook, "we are trying to help you, so—"

"Why me?"

Lyon stumbled for a second but was glad that Oz at least said something. "Well, that's a bit of a long story."

"In case you can't tell, I'm apparently not going anywhere any time soon."

Lyon shared surprised yet knowing looks with Ky and Hitook, who both turned a bit more of their attention to the events. The quiet gave Oz time to assess the effect of the boldness he had allowed to escape.

"Fair enough." Lyon breathed deeply through his nose and shifted his head toward the door. "I took a chance on what I presumed to be an uncontrollable psychic reaction that a friend of mine had. Granted, I felt slightly foolish, but I couldn't get my mind off of it. But once I found you, I concluded that you could possibly hold a key for me to complete this mission."

Silence extended long enough to get uncomfortable. Just as Lyon opened his mouth, Oz responded.

"What makes you think I'll help you just because you say you're helping me?"

"You've already helped us." Lyon motioned for his chair and sat when it arrived. "We've been able to gather some information from your head while you were out. That information led us to more illegal weapons and eventually led, though rather indirectly, to finding an armada of renegades led by a well-known war hero, who, apparently, we're now after."

"How'd you...?" Oz trailed into a distracted mumble.

"How did we get the information? That's Ky and Hitook's specialty." Lyon watched the portal in the door. "If you at least stand up to the window, I'll introduce you."

The wait seemed long, but Lyon remained silent to force Oz to the glass. When his face appeared, it did so at a distance, and Lyon smiled.

"Hello," Lyon said as calmly as he could.

Oz's eyes shifted feverishly from Lyon in the chair and the two *things* at the table.

"Let's start with Hitook." Lyon turned in his chair. "He's the big guy on the left." He faced the liqua. "He's the one who initially stabilized your spirit."

Hitook nodded slightly, but Oz didn't move, just stared, afraid to do anything.

"Next to him is Ky. Ky, Hitook, I'd like you to meet Manuel Ozuna, but he prefers Oz. Oz, meet Ky and Hitook."

The duo looked surreal. He could swear the large one was the product of some mad scientist who crossbred a rabbit with a mythical troll. The other could have practically jumped out of a medieval fantasy novel, except for that tail. At least he thought it was a tail. Even though it swished behind her, Oz's mind froze at the thought of the two being connected. Overall, he didn't know what to make of them. Oz doubted they were real for a moment, then realized he might be unable to determine what was real any more. He just stood there as his eyes began to move about quickly, bringing in more data than his conscious brain could handle.

Stupidity, the kind that's ingrained in each terran and nurtured by years of poor parental choices, blurted from Oz.

"What are they?"

Ky dropped her hand rather hard on the table. “What?” She turned to Lyon. “That inconsiderate punk!”

Lyon jumped from his seat fast enough to startle Oz, who began to think he had just signed his death contract. “We’re not here to fight each other.” The knight pointed to the ceiling for a moment. “If we don’t hear some loud explosions in about five minutes, we can all consider ourselves lucky.”

Oz had taken a step back and now shifted about nervously and half distracted. Willpower alone had a difficult time holding back wave after wave of raw survival instinct, the kind that doesn’t work well against intelligent and prepared creatures. Spouting threats and bashing his fists against the door wouldn’t earn him any favors with his captors. Then the previous words sunk it, and bewilderment fueled the fire of curiosity that, in turn, pushed back everything else.

“What do you mean?”

“I mean,” Lyon said as he moved closer to the window, “that if *the* Horwhannor is actually commanding that armada in orbit, there’s a high probability they spent time tracking our drone’s transmission signal before destroying it. If they didn’t then maybe they won’t send in a squadron to flatten the area or the planet. If they do, then there’s nothing we can do about it. But I have no doubt that Larin and Paloon are going to give everything they’ve got regardless of whether you or anyone else on this rock wants to keep on living.”

Lyon moved back toward the table, his chair followed, and he sat down.

“I don’t know why you don’t just knock him out.” Ky tapped Hitook’s shoulder and motioned for some mutual support, but it never left the liqua’s mouth. “Look, if we live to see tomorrow, we can continue our hunt, but he,” she motioned to the native behind the door, “is useless to us.”

Lyon calmly replied, “I’m trying to be a good person and show some civilized control. He doesn’t fall in our jurisdiction; I can’t hold him accountable to our laws. Therefore, I must, regardless of my feelings, be a *humanitarian*.” The last came out as if it was poison.

“But just as you put it,” Ky turned her hand and pointed with two fingers almost as if she had just blown Lyon a kiss, “he’s not in our jurisdiction, but he’s a risk if you release him. No one here will report negatively of someone eliminating a risk.”

If hate could take form, Lyon’s face got close to in for a millisecond.

Ky knew she had gone too far. She threw up her hands and walked away, heading through the tunnel.

The real reason dwelled in him and ate away at his values. Nothing could hold it back; it needed a release, so Lyon began to talk in a tone similar to a mumble and half aimed at Hitook and half at no one.

“I brought him into this.” Lyon learned forward until his forearms braced his body well enough to keep him from falling flat on his face. “I cannot deliver judgment on someone whom I put in that position.”

Lyon turned a sullen head askew, revealing a very sorrowful face to Hitook. “The truth is that—I just can’t do it.”

Peace flourished in the liqua's smile, and he nodded gradually, his eyes half closed. Acceptance, understanding and admiration all flowed through the interchange of silence.

Lyon dropped his head again. A few moments later, he picked himself up and went upstairs.

Faint creaks in the boards faded until they became only dull memories. Seconds bore minutes that merged into a span that seemed to last an hour instead of the fourteen minutes it had become.

In the meantime, Oz took the seat in the room. Reluctant? Yes, but it still appeared to be the most comfortable seat in the room. Metal-induced creases on his rear did not appeal to him. He sat listening to the previous conversation over and over in his head, so much so that he could no longer remember what was truly spoken and what came from his mind filling in blanks with fabricated snippets of conversation.

Then he noted he had not heard any explosions. *I guess I'm lucky,* Oz thought without truly understanding why or feeling the honest impact of why. The importance wasn't there for him because his brain hadn't sorted through all the data yet. Self-preservation did strange things at times, to include blocking some brain functions from the conscious mind.

Oz twisted his face as his head moved about, allowing him to pan the room without really looking at anything. "Hello?"

Nothing.

"Hello, are you still there?"

Oz waited and waited, but nothing.

"I'm here," came a deep voice.

Oz's eyes snapped toward the window to see the furry face of the liqua.

"Ah!" Oz yelped almost as if trying to stifle a hiccup.

Hitook dropped his nose for a moment and calmly smiled, but the smile had dropped from view. "Is there something you need?"

"I—," Oz forced himself to calm but was unable to completely succeed, "I was look—hoping to see the person who was talking to me before."

"Lyon has left."

Oz took a deep breath to calm his nervousness, which betrayed itself by the rapping of his fingers on whatever was near them. "I meant before that."

Hitook's head shifted as if looking at a crazy person. "No one was here before we arrived."

Stillness froze Oz to the point that he could hear his heart beating. He mumbled, "Someone was here, or...."

Even with the door there, the liqua's ears heard the words before they trailed into nothing.

"Do you mean Mac?"

The terran lifted his head, looking as if he were a prizefighter losing the bout in the twelfth round. "I don't...know." That last word began to drift.

"Mac?"

The computer's distracted voice replied in quick bursts, "Yeah, what? I'm busy."

"Did you talk to Oz"—Mac's voice cut in with laughter—"before we arrived?"

It took a moment before the computer responded.

"Yeah, so what? It doesn't matter now."

"He would like to speak to you again."

Holographic light formed a figure on the table. Hitook moved from the window then waved a palm toward himself then pointed to the table in a way to direct Oz to the image. When Oz finally worked up the courage to go near the window, he saw on the table the foot-high figure of a fat, balding man in a ratty, green recliner. The man momentarily turned away from a tiny television resting on what looked like a plastic tray braced on top of a thin metal structure. A non-transparent, white plastic bowl of popcorn spilled a bit of its contents without its owner showing any concern, but a slob in a torn and stained, red, armless shirt probably wouldn't.

As Oz's face came into view at the window, Mac scratched a furry eyebrow, "So what do you want, kid? You've got about a minute and a half."

Gravity took its time but finally pulled Oz's jaw down far enough to be noticeable.

"Okay, now you have a minute." Mac flopped in the chair without regard to a second large loss of popcorn. "Look, I told you before I'm a computer. What you are seeing is a holographic representation of my inner workings, thoughts, if you will. But since Lyon introduced you to everyone else, I figure there's no sense in hiding now."

Surprise and disbelief blended into a strange face on Oz. He couldn't think of anything to say, although his expression began a slight change. Mac caught the shift.

"No. I'm neither malevolent nor benevolent, mostly." Mac's tone seemed out of place with his appearance, which unknowingly aided in credibility. "In the hand of the wielder, some—"

Mac stopped cold and flopped back in the creaking chair to stare at the tiny television. Pictures flickered on the screen but no one else in the room could hear the channel.

It took awhile, but when Hitook attempted to get Mac's attention, the computer just flicked his hand as if shooing a fly, and the bulbous figure scowled and laughed at the same time.

Hitook and Oz stared at each other for a moment. The liqua dove into his memories to offer more of an explanation.

"He is what is called a mechanically aware computer, based on the eighty series." Hitook was proud of himself for remembering it, since it really wasn't his specialty. But no one, not even a fellow liqua, could have read the expression. He kept it to himself. "He can think and learn and react to emotion. Mac," Hitook nodded in the direction of the giggling fat man, "was created here by Lyon. Lyon couldn't or didn't put limits on Mac's emotion circuits. This results in what seem to be sporadic shifts in his personality."

Hitook rarely spoke that much in one shot, but Oz could not know that he was witnessing a unique event. He just watched Hitook talk, half paying attention to what was actually being said. Every mouth, eye and facial muscle moved with such fluidity, causing waves in the hair, that Oz got the strong sense that the creature on the other end might actually be real. This realization grew the longer Hitook spoke and moved.

Many kinds of blood flowed through Oz, so he never viewed himself as a discriminating individual. Yet he realized it the second it left his mouth.

"What are you?"

A blink signaled that Hitook was wondering why the subject had shifted so. Hitook kept himself from scanning to find out.

"I'm a liqua."

"A *lee-qua*?" Oz stumbled on the word without getting it correct.

"Close."

"You look like an overgrown and deformed rabbit." Oz caught himself again a second too late and began to fumble for an apology.

"Don't worry; I'm not upset. Your observation is understood."

Oz still felt bad and forced himself to try to repair the damage he thought he caused.

"*He-toke*?" Oz wasn't sure, but after a nodding acknowledgement, he proceeded. "I'm very sorry, Hitook."

The liqua raised a paw and shook his head. "I hold nothing against you." Hitook added an explanation in hopes it would help. "I am House Bravo. Diversions such as grudges interfere with my training; therefore, I do not allow them to find refuge."

A bit of his master emerged in his words. Oz lacked the background knowledge to fully comprehend the words but did glean enough for them to be useful. As he contemplated the meaning, his own thoughts strayed; when they did, Oz's already depleted defenses almost disappeared completely as he became more comfortable and accepting.

"I," he stumbled. Once he was sure he wasn't going to put his foot in his mouth, Oz continued, "I have so many; I mean, there's so much—"

A calm look from Hitook gave Oz the sense that the liqua understood and approved.

The two began a long conversation spanning subjects from why the group was sent to a history of how the Dragon Corps formed. Oz couldn't remember much but became more eager to understand, especially after he got some food in his belly.

About ten minutes in, he had asked about food, and Hitook ordered Mac to fix a couple of meals to specification. Outstanding was how Oz described it again and again. He still felt like a prisoner, even with such good grub.

Fragments of Oz's logic fought with his emotions as he continued asking Hitook question after question. Something told him not to trust his jailer, but the being on the other side of the door had such a calm demeanor, Oz had an increasingly difficult time blaming Hitook and the others. Logic yelled that it was just some kind of hostage syndrome, but the more Hitook explained the basics of law under which the Corps operated, Oz began to appreciate the team's actions, somewhat.

As the night grew long, Oz accepted Hitook as a trusted soul, maybe even a friend, but he didn't acknowledge it. Even to himself.

Chapter 4

Relaxation of weary bones and taut muscles normally came from hours of inactivity, such as sleep. Yet even if the body was willing, the mind didn't always want to comply. This especially became the case when an entire night of rest was filled with thoughts and dreams of the possibilities of impending doom. And all of his troubles could be traced to a combat-hardened Korac hero.

He didn't need to speak to the team; Lyon knew they had to be thinking about it. So he directed each to stay busy this day, preferably with something other than work. Even if they forgot about their situation for a minute, it would be worth it. Lyon needed them fresh before they constructed their next plan.

This was the case for everyone except Hitook. Lyon found him with Mac, both talking with Oz. They had been at it all night. Lyon was interested in learning what had transpired, but his hunger had brought him there, not curiosity.

All through his breakfast, Mac, Hitook and Oz discussed the differences between electro-dimensional fidelity, quantum-dimensional fidelity and hyper-dimensional fidelity. They tried to drag Lyon into it, but it was too early for him to get into intergalactic communication physics, so he waved them off with a fork speckled with scrambled eggs that Mac had materialized for him. Lyon did appreciate the upgrades Paloon had made to Mac and created a mental note to thank him but promptly forgot.

After breakfast, Lyon gave his directions to everyone. He sent Hitook to rest, whether sleep or meditation, but stopped short of chastising. To do so would be counter to his intent to relax today. And on this planet, the best way for Lyon to do just that was to mind the store.

He sent Ky to work the front counter as he received deliveries that Mac had ordered throughout the night. Several of the meats had to go, as did most of the dairy. The produce took the biggest hit. The store didn't offer much room for it, but nothing turned over faster.

All day, about every other customer made some comment about the store being closed too often lately. Ky performed as the consummate public relations representative, complete with believable smile, kind eyes and a soft, soothing voice of apology. The walls of complaints, the ones she couldn't melt, took several large cracks under the pressure of Ky's charm. She even quieted Mrs. Fuller, an accomplishment Mr. Fuller rarely achieved. When he did, he treated himself to a banana split, regardless of what his doctor said about diet and heart this and that.

Lyon could tell that each gripe irritated Ky. She never let it show, but once the person in question stepped out the door, Ky's expression would shift from happiness and joy to contempt and annoyance. Generally a huff, hiss or other noise accompanied the expression. Like a chalkboard, she could quickly wipe the slate clean and present a smile to the next customer before they had a chance to notice.

Now, she read a newspaper. Lyon couldn't see it while he straightened the stock in the freezers, but he could hear the rustling of paper. After a minute of it soaking in, he thought the noise a bit too loud amid the noise of the freezers.

Lyon's head jerked forward as a yell shot into his head. It wasn't so much of a yell as a grumble and growl.

"I'm going to choke him?"

Lyon blinked back into sanity. *"Choke whom?"*

"There's this old fart squeezing each loaf of bread. He's been at it for almost twenty minutes." Ky dropped the paper to verify the man hadn't changed his routine before she snapped the paper back and stared a hole through it. *"There's maybe ten loafs, yet he does it again and again. It's driving me nuts!"*

With mild amusement, Lyon set down a box of frozen factory-breaded preprocessed chunks of animal meat. *"Old, but the only serious wrinkles are around the eyes and balding, white hair?"*

"Yes?"

"And is he wearing a brightly colored suit jacket that doesn't match his pants?"

Ky lowered the paper as if she had forgotten. *"I'd call it annoying rather than bright."* The red-striped neon yellow assaulted Ky's eyes to the point that she had difficultly focusing. *"I take it you know this idiot."*

"Mr. Wolborsky. He's a bit sensitive about his bread. Hold on, I'll be there in a moment."

Lyon returned from the storage room and half ran to the front. As he rounded the aisle, he held a fresh loaf of whole wheat bread. "Here, sir. Just for you; it came from the bakery this morning."

In mid squeeze, Wolborsky's scowl melted to warm surprise. Bright white choppers gleamed from a smile that seemed somewhat large for the small man. With a complete scrub each night, he took better care of those dentures than he ever did his real teeth before they were knocked out of his mouth by a rifle butt.

"Thanks, son," the elderly man replied cheerfully as if he just hearing that he had a new grandchild.

"You're very welcome, sir." Lyon thumbed toward the other room. "I'm back there stocking up. Is there anything else I can get you?"

Wolborsky fished through the cart next to him before returning another smile. "Looks like I have everything."

"Okay, if you need anything else, just holler."

Lyon headed back after Wolborsky nodded. Ky sneered as if to say, "Smart ass." Lyon shrugged back a "What's your problem?"

Ky blanked her face, not in reaction to Lyon, she told herself, and prepared to smile as she totaled the groceries for the man who seemed to enjoy his leisurely trip to the register.

As he finished his transaction and headed out the store, the door's bell didn't get the chance to ring close in time. The slight unbalance in the routine poked at Ky until she raised her head just as the door finally closed.

"Hello, grandma." This time Ky's smile was as genuine as it gets.

"Morning. Fine, fine. How are you?" Alessa Franklin went straight to work unfolding her personal cart.

"Fine," Ky parroted without taking immediate notice that grandma answered a question that Ky never asked.

The conversation barely made its way to the back. When it arrived, Lyon took pause. *"Mac, what day is it?"*

"Saturday. Pound of lean beef ribs."

"Ah, yes," Lyon replied and headed to the front.

"Good morning, grandma." Lyon half waved as he went behind the meat counter.

Grandma hooked her cane on her cart and adjusted her glasses with two fingers as she met Lyon's eyes with a smile. "Morning. I'm the one who should be worried about you."

Donning his apron had to wait a moment as Lyon gave grandma a quizzical look before letting it sink in. "About being closed?" Though he asked, he knew the answer.

"Al wouldn't like it," she stated calmly as her shopping began. Black-eyed peas came first. Squeaking wheels rolled to the proper aisle.

Reluctantly, Lyon quietly admitted, somewhat shamefully, that the store's previous owner and his former boss wouldn't have appreciated the constant closures. Dedication ran in Al's blood like oxygen flowed through other people. Lyon knew it had personally pained Al to sell the store, but he couldn't push back age or the pain that came with it.

"Yes." Arguing with grandma would be futile, so Lyon searched for an apology, but it came to life as an excuse. "I've been very busy lately, and tir—"

"We're all busy and tired, Lyon." The words came from between the aisle as clanks sounded from two cans of peas falling into the cart. She gradually switched rows, looking at Lyon when she did. "As long as we're alive, we'll always feel busy and tired."

Grandma spoke calmly but with an educator's tone, the kind that only came from years of practice to get the level of chastisement just right without offending. She pushed her way toward the graham crackers. "People have expectations." She grunted and wheezed as she bent to grab a box then braced her back with a hand to help her rise. "They're not always smart, but no one said that only wise men have expectations."

Firm, grey hair crept around the corner as grandma headed toward the freezers. She stopped, as if on cue, and adjusted her glasses at Lyon, who was weighting some ribs.

"People depend on you and this store."

Lyon had nothing he could say. He accepted the talking to but started worrying about how he may have no option but to continue to disappoint people. The Corps came first, yet no one could know. Gloomy thoughts molded Lyon's face.

Grandma stood a bit more erect and squinted at Lyon. Tense muscles caused loose wrinkles to quiver for a split second. With a stern voice, like talking down to a dog, she said, "I want three chicken breasts, take out the bones and take off the skin. I don't want that beef."

She immediately turned and departed into the next room leaving Lyon blinking and wondering for almost an entire minute. He double-checked, but Mac defended that his internal clock wasn't malfunctioning.

Ky quietly asked if something was wrong, but Lyon didn't know. Grandma's actions just seemed out of character in several ways. It had been awhile since he had seen her so worked up about something. As he returned the beef and prepared the chicken, he couldn't help but wonder, almost to the point of cutting himself with the knife he was using.

With the packaged chicken, Lyon waited behind the counter next to Ky. He said nothing to Ky and just gazed through the window. Lyon wanted to explain and defend his case. Nothing good would come from it, but he yearned for it. The one person who deserved an explanation was grandma; however, his oath kept him from it.

Thuds on the counter brought Lyon around to see a smiling grandma retrieving the items from her cart. The air around her seemed changed from only a few moments ago. Both Lyon and Ky sensed it and searched for the manifestation as if trying to find the surface to a flawless pane of clear glass.

"It's wonderful isn't it?" Even grandma's tone seemed as if she had forgotten the previous conversation.

Lyon's mind raced but took its time with a response. "What is?"

"Freedom." She smiled as she rapped two fingers so hard on the package of chicken Ky was placing in a bag that she almost knocked it out of Ky's grip. "Chicken instead of beef. Tomorrow, maybe I'll have steak instead of fried chicken."

This seemed rather irregular. For as long a Lyon could remember, grandma had normally been rather set in her diet, especially when she did the cooking.

"I guess so," Lyon returned with a shrug.

Grandma searched her purse to pay Ky. "Sure, freedom to go and come as we please, to visit and see whomever and whatever we want is nice. We take freedom of thought and choice for granted." Her bill paid and cart loaded, she wheeled toward the door. "A free body is meaningless unless the soul is free."

Once again, her departing presence left Ky and Lyon just standing in bewilderment. Voice tone? Mannerisms? Eye contact? Perfume? Neither could put a finger on what caused the trance-like surreal atmosphere that grandma seemly could trigger at will.

Lyon returned to his chores without a word. His mind wasn't completely in the task, though. He couldn't say where his mind was; he just knew it was not there.

Vague twinges forced Ky to rub the sides of her forehead. Not a headache, these pangs streamed from something else. She sat on the stool and shook her head in time with the rubs. Looking up, she could see through the window and across the street. A dark shape moved through the gas station.

Paloon had taken Lyon's orders to heart, but since there wasn't much to do, he reorganized the small shop. He threw himself into it. After a couple of hours, he didn't have to push away the other thoughts of mission and impending doom. Most of that credit needed to go to Larin. Actually, to his absence.

For the first hour, the rolbrid just sat behind the counter griping about everything from being stranded to having a native locked in the basement. Larin even grumbled at the one customer they had seen in that time.

Great, buying gas from an insane midget. The customer didn't need to say it; Paloon read it on her face.

That, on top of the all the other complaining, left Paloon with no other choice. He felt rather proud of the cleverness of it.

So Larin now stood outside providing full service to the few customers who bothered to stop. It didn't keep him from mumbling complaints to no one. When he tried to bicker at Paloon using the team's internal communications channels, the hunter threatened to set the lieutenant to work scrubbing the oil stains out of the concrete.

Most of the time, all Larin could do was stand and watch the traffic. He had filled the washer racks with fluid and towels, so leaning there, Larin just watched the cars. Mind numbing, but somehow it calmed Larin, even though that was not his goal.

The intersection that the station faced had an odd sense of rhythm to it, an irregular metronome of sorts. Larin's concentration only broke from time to time when he pumped someone's gas, then he would go back to watching traffic.

During the entire time, something mentally jabbed at Larin, vaguely at first and then with the force of a nova. He jerked forward and glared at the traffic, waiting for another round of switching lights. There it was.

Ky had been lazily staring out the window, and she took note of Larin's movement, tensed herself and looked around, trying to detect what had Larin's hackles up.

The rolbrid searched through his mental records, found what he thought was there, then returned to watch another round of traffic. Larin screwed his face and unconsciously began to reach for a weapon but paused. Another round of traffic triggered the same result.

A grey truck with a white camper rumbled along the curb and stopped short of its position in line for the light. This drew Larin's attention without completely distracting him.

From the driver's seat stretched a long, grizzled face toward the open passenger window; a lit cigarette flipped about as the man yelled, "Why's your gas price so high?"

Larin snarled back, "If you don't like it, buy your gas elsewhere, you frapping primate!"

"I will, asshole!" the driver yelled again, this time losing his cigarette but not stopping to retrieve it. His truck didn't respond well to his sudden push on the accelerator and sputtered half way through the left turn.

Larin shook his fist and yelled back, but Ky couldn't make out what was said. As she tinkered with her curiosity, Ky noticed Paloon stepping outside. Paloon and Larin shouted at each other for a moment before Paloon waved Larin off and went back inside. Ky took the gesture as an indication of the value of trying to have a sensible conversation with Larin.

She returned her attention to the store's interior. As she did, Ky stopped leisurely at the tabloid rack. One headline grabbed her attention, although not at first. She had to re-read it for it to hit home: "Scientists breed Lizard Men in test tube."

The dextian spent the next few minutes thinking about the possibility of using biology to overcome obstacles even her training couldn't beat. Limitations, and the thought of them, never pleased her. At times, she had no alternative other than to succumb to their existence.

Lyon, carrying a cardboard box, stepped into the room.

Ky snapped from her thoughts and looked toward Lyon. "How close is the relationship, molecularly?"

Most batters disliked curve balls, especially those that jump over and hit them between the eyes. While pain wasn't part of this equation, Lyon stood stunned. His eyes rolled to the side and at Ky. "What relationship? Molecular what?" Lyon's head pivoted and his voice increased in volume. "What are you talking about?"

"You and these terrans?" Ky waved indiscriminately. "It's obvious that atlantians and terrans appear rather similar, but have you studied how close you are molecularly?"

Lyon wondered for a second or two then set the box of cans down. "Yes, I've done some research. Our systems operate on similar principles, as do many others. We have all the same organs, mostly."

"No," Ky tapped the counter as seriousness changed her face. "I'm talking about the molecules. Are the genes similar or identical? How close, how far?"

This time Lyon shot Ky a quizzical look of his own. "Very similar, actually: two basic forms of nucleic acid with two bases, five subunits, three shared, et cetera. But terran nucleic chains carry a bit more blank loci. Why?"

"But they're packing similar connections?"

"Yes."

"Have you tried gene manipulation?"

"What?!" Shock jolted Lyon from his thought process, but he rebounded with a cover. "No. Mac can't synthesize that small."

Ky smiled. "I bet he can now."

Lyon tried it once about two years ago, but he didn't have the equipment to improve Mac's resolution. "Maybe, but why?"

She allowed the smile to get a little larger. She had something and knew it. "I'm talking about your pet downstairs." That got Lyon's attention. "Use some gene therapy. It might be able to disable those re-written modules in his head. And maybe—"

"Maybe, what?"

Ky flicked a hand. "Maybe make him more atlantian than terran. Maybe unlock something to make him biologically understand us and make him less of a threat. Maybe change—"

"You're serious?"

"Yes. Think about it. We can't let him go, and you've obviously started becoming sympathetic."

Lyon snarled.

"I don't have to probe your mind to sense that." She glared back. "You can't keep him locked up forever, so we need him on our side."

The knight set his mouth askew as he stared past Ky and out the window.

She smirked. "You know, 'Change the body and mind will fol-low.'"

Lyon straightened his face. "Isn't that the other way around?"

Ky sneered again. "It doesn't matter."

Chapter 5

Suits and uniforms of various breeds rushed about like ants with a purpose. As for the suits, they came in radiation, biohazard, chemical and detective—whatever the people came with or could get their hands on. The uniforms included several federal agencies, even the seldom seen federal police force. Like a packaged child's toy, each gaggle of uniformed agents came complete with associated mobile command post and specialized vehicles.

Unmistakably, the military had the most presence. Heavily armed warriors patrolled the half-mile barricaded perimeter of the newly formed national defense area. The "Warning: Use of deadly force is authorized" signs appeared redundant next to the stern looks from the armed sentries. Since being airlifted straight to the site yesterday as the first in, they hadn't had much time to sleep. This made them a bit more irritable than normal.

A helicopter lifted from what remained of the road inside the zone as a blue sedan approached the site's main checkpoint. One uniform approached the driver's side; another moved toward the passenger side but kept his distance. Hands remained clasped to the weapons slung across their chests.

The occupants flashed a set of badges. After a hands-on examination, the squad leader motioned for them to proceed. A third warrior dropped his non-trigger hand long enough to grab the end of a wooden barricade and move it temporarily out of the way.

Once in, the car had a short drive before being directed from the road to park in an area next to the sea of mobile operating trailers. The occupants disembarked and visually combed the area, taking note of each agency represented and mentally sorting the makeshift chain of command, not that the latter mattered.

Along the tattered tree line on both sides crawled the various suits designed to prevent exposure to hazards. Most carried hand-held devices from the tiny to the large, which looked much like overgrown metal detectors. Everyone near the command-post city strolled about without so much as a doctor's face mask.

Already cleared, guessed the new arrivals as they navigated the haphazard arrangement of mobile buildings in search of a co-worker they only knew from a dossier. Breaking through the other side of the trailer park, the two simultaneously noticed their target. Just as they did, he stood from poking a pen at something in the ground and approached the two.

Blond hair, blue-grey eyes, strong jaw, dimpled chin—he had the attractive looks of a stereotypical all-star athlete. His wide shoulders seemed perfect for a full-contact sport where the bets were based on injury reports. With unnatural style, he shook hands and smiled.

"Agent Franklin. I assume you're looking for me."

Of the two new agents, the male nodded. He didn't remove his sunglasses, but nothing could hide his rather traditional Asian features. "I'm Agent Kim, and this is Agent Crisostomo."

Crisostomo returned a faint nod and fainter smile as her attention drifted elsewhere. Standing a few inches shorter than her partner, she had a slightly large, squared jaw that stayed high enough to remain attractive while thin, dark-brown eyes accentuated the feature. The sun shined dully on her light brown, almost bronze, skin that could only have come from a tropical island. Highlighted brunette hair stopped just below her ears to give a sense of sternness, but she kept it short for the ease of maintenance.

"What do you have here?" Kim jerked his head at the scene as a whole.

"No running water, a mild ant problem, and I can't pick up a decent TV signal." Disappointment creased Franklin's face.

"I bet traffic's light."

"True that. No-yield, tactical nukes tend to do that. Otherwise, it would be a good place to raise a family if it wasn't for all these other bags of donuts trying to stake their own turf." Franklin waved the two agents to follow as he returned to the piece of ground he had previously poked.

Kneeling, he withdrew the same pen, flicked away the small orange flag lying there and used the pen as a crowbar, prying a small opening a bit larger for the other agents to see. Dirt kept light from reaching deep enough to shine on the metal. Franklin tried to scrape it away and resorted to tapping on it. An unmistakable metal-on-metal ting came from the ground.

"Pluming problem?" Kim mused.

"Yeah, of the thirty-millimeter kind." Franklin waved the pen in sweeping motion at the local area. Tiny orange flags spouted from the ground like jumbled tombstones. "About twenty here, and they're still picking them out of the trees."

"Reloads?" Kim doubted the number until he got his answer.

"None, box feed."

Kim approved but wondered about the time span. "Full auto?"

"Semi. Single-barrel, liquid-cooled. And short enough to pack in the trunk of a compact car."

Kim was impressed, again.

Franklin agreed, "Yeah, sweet, little, mobile anti-tank weapon."

"Not much left, I guess."

"Nothing." Before Kim could comment, Franklin clarified. "I mean 'nothing' as in whatever they were shooting at is no longer here." He tapped his pen again at the opening in the ground. "Each round plowed into the dirt as if ricocheting off something."

Franklin wiped off the pen and returned it to his suit before replanting the flag. He stood and headed toward the road.

"I know what you're thinking: 'Thirty-millimeter rounds, especially of the depleted-uranium variety, don't ricochet off anything less than the heaviest alloys around.' Well," he looked back at the agents following him, "maybe that's what we're dealing with."

Once at the road, Franklin pointed with an outstretched hand at four black smears on the asphalt. "Titanium on wheels, apparently."

"Trajectory points here?"

"Not so much as trajectory—we expect that equipment to arrive today—as it was the location of the cannon." Franklin pointed to the left. "The weapon van was here, roughly; it was found on its side. Over here," he turned to point toward the small hill and followed the road to where they stood, "we have faint tracks that lead to a sudden stop and something pushed it back. The thirty-millimeter hello is my guess at the culprit, but as you can see, not a single round made it through to hit the road.

"Here's the real strange part," Franklin continued, "there are no tracks leading away. We can lift partial tracks arriving, but they stop."

"Maybe they towed it away," Crisostomo offered.

"Possibly, but we haven't found witnesses or evidence to support that."

"Anything else?" Kim asked.

Franklin took a back step and pointed a shoe at a dark stain encircled with yellow chalk. "There is some blood but no body parts."

Kim followed the reference; if the cannon did hit someone, there would be wet mush of some form not just a stain. "DNA?"

"Yes," Franklin flicked his eyes toward the mess of trailers, "but the lab guys say there's a problem. The sample size is good, but they think the sample's damaged. They're trying to split it or something like that. Not my field."

Franklin motioned for them to follow again as he walked toward the hill. "That's not all."

Kim started to follow when Crisostomo tapped his arm. She pointed toward the remnants of a tractor-trailer with several uniforms around, under and on it.

"I'm going to check on the transports," she said and stepped away.

She had the expertise, so Kim knew she could understand that more than he could anyhow. He returned to meet Franklin.

After about fifteen minutes, the two agents had followed the burned ridge toward the command camp. Crisostomo found them there.

As she approached, Kim acknowledged her and looked at the torched ground. "Burn, what do you make of this?"

Bernadette actually. Her family called her Bernie, but shortly after joining the academy, Crisostomo obtained the nickname of Burn. She proudly admitted the nickname was the result of her turning down every request for a date with rather sarcastic references to the wooer's undesirable features. She did it all with a cold smile, which led to a new meaning of being "burned." Crisostomo held a bit of fondness for the nickname and allowed her partner to use it.

Laying before Franklin and Kim stretched a rather straight line of crispy turf. Crisostomo gloved a hand and squatted to probe the charred earth.

Franklin offered her the same briefing but a bit shorter. "It burned for a good hour, all around the site, without catching anything else on fire. The few civilian heroes who tried to approach said they couldn't get near it because it was too hot." Franklin scanned around again and mumbled in bewilderment. "But without burning anything else."

Crisostomo rose. "Chemical agent possibly."

"We're working on that," Franklin agreed. "No results yet."

"What about the shipment?" Kim reached for a small note pad and jotted a few notes about the scene so far.

"Three crates are missing, but as you saw, the trailer's intact."

Kim paused, pen on pad. "Why didn't it detonate?"

"They'll know that once they figure out what drained the batteries and how." Crisostomo's face was calm, but her partner noticed vague signs of confusion. "They were able to pull the computer logs during the night and piece together the fact that the system was functional until a sudden drop in power, which almost went undetected by the computer until it went offline. There's no record of it ever receiving the secondary command."

"Missed it by seconds, possibly," Franklin added.

The agents stood silent for a while as they contemplated separate aspects of a case that amounted to an egregious breach of national security. And they were left holding a bag full of conjecture and facts that don't make sense.

Kim and Crisostomo worried. They hadn't come to this scene because they were the nearest agents. The program depended on them shutting down this threat before a counter operation released anything to the public. Governments despised having outside forces controlling the game.

Franklin led the trio back to the trailers. "Wait until you see the few pieces of aircraft wreckage we could find. It's as if someone gave them an acid bath."

Chapter 6

A faint whistle signaled the disconnection of the communications channel.

"This brings jeopardy upon the mission."

Stillness.

"Nothing can hold the mission in peril," came a more authoritative tone. "As I live, they wield no threat."

A third voice responded, "Alas, from their mouths may stream words to the ears of the masses. It means to reveal that which we have succeeded to hide for so long."

"Never before," added a fourth, "has so much trust been passed to a shepherd."

The first returned, "Prophetic desires notwithstanding; the flock works against an ill-prepared master who offers more in speech than action."

"Moreover, what of the stray?" asked the third.

Tension compounded.

Another revealed, "Our sight has wandered. The mission is threatened not by a leader of servants. Revelations risk the army's loss."

Tonal influx gave the word "army" a hint of meaning the others understood.

Control burned in the leader, who felt the need to determine destiny. "As it will come to be, time leads the shepherd to be delivered unto the hands of thine enemy before danger approaches the flock. For the stray, we will follow and lead it home."

"What have we to do to clear the field of ominous weeds?" asked the first. "Time may be that we stand at the gate of our nation to vehemently petition to break the seal. Wrath in battle shall return."

"Time was," snapped the leader, "power flowed unmatched; nay, ignorance and shelter sends complacency through the masses as if the darkest among plagues. No others shall stand watch and to guard the gates as is infused in the charge placed at our feet. That may not be starved nor desecrated."

"Apologies," replied the first. "For all, I speak as one, the charge has a welcome home in us. The merge is one. As if a limb near a fire, we fear loss of all we have achieved."

"True. Yet fear shan't fog." The leader directed his attention to the owner of the fifth voice, trusted as wise. "What say you?"

Silent thought stretched for moments as the others waited politely.

"As say you. No others stand at the gates. We protect all from that which they lack acceptance and knowledge. All comes to us without color or noise. Sounding warnings at the gate will only fall on the deaf. Hence not even an ember will leap forth onto a field of death that demands a great fire. The charge weighs much. If it means to protect them from themselves, so be it. May the foolish be felled by a swift sword, all of them. Then they shall know their error."

Except the leader, the others gestured in agreement.

"Great insight is found in your words." The leader finally motioned acknowledgment. "Raised blades forgo hope to shed no blood. May all stay undrawn until force offers no recourse."

Chapter 7

Lyon only half paid attention to the discussions below as he descended into the basement. Hitook, Oz and Mac had resumed previous talks. The topic now: mana theory.

"Mac," Lyon ignored the break in the conversation his interruption created, "dinner, please."

Soon light formed a plate with deformed pieces of a fried meat substance and a vegetable that looked a bit like green beans. Telesurgery certainly came with several benefits, but Lyon really appreciated Mac now having the ability to make food. Cooking had become such a chore. With that gone, Lyon planned to enjoy this small pleasure as often as possible.

He grabbed his seat and ordered water, but before the glass reached him, Mac asked, "Lyon, have you ever experienced or witnessed a detached mana pulse? We were discussing the—"

"Mac, I want to eat my meal in peace."

The computer and Hitook obliged. From that point, the wait began. Oz wondered why Hitook had left the door to sit at the table and why he stopped talking. Hitook had explained that Lyon led the team, but without being privy to their internal communications network, Oz guessed this was some show of respect while their leader ate.

During the past day, Oz learned much about who they claimed to be and from where they came. Granted, such assertions sounded way too much like spouts from drunken comic book fans. But witnessing so many unbelievable events made Oz wonder about the truth behind it.

"Hitook tells me you claim to be an atlantian," Oz spoke, forgetting that the others had quit talking. In part, he had developed such a comfortable relationship with Hitook that his outburst just happened.

Mac flashed on to his monitor and attempted to silently signal Oz to be quiet. The computer hoped Lyon wouldn't notice, but Lyon turned to the screen first. Mac tried to play it off as if he was trying to rub his neck.

In mid-bite, Lyon debated how to proceed since he had failed to keep closer tabs on what the terran was learning. Lyon pulled his head back to look at Oz through the small window, then to Hitook, who calmly acknowledged the knight, then back to the terran.

"Now you've done it," Mac whispered loud enough for Oz to hear, which meant everyone in the room heard it.

"You know what," Lyon began, ignoring Mac's comment, "I'm not sure I like the tone you used when you said 'atlantian.'"

Lyon rotated his seat and tore at the remaining bit of deep-fried food that had been hanging from his mouth. He said calmly, "Let me guess, you're thinking something along the lines of 'But Atlantis is just a story, a fable.' Well, Oz, where I come from, they think this planet is just a fable, something from long forgotten religious texts."

Each just stared at the other. Then Lyon broke away to see Paloon and Larin entering from the tunnel.

"Here's a prime example," Lyon pointed with his eyes.

"Frapping right." Larin pounded a fist on his chest. "One solid, prime specimen."

"Not you." Lyon shook his head as the two made their way around the table and began ordering meals. "Paloon's like most atlantians; he doesn't believe Terra exists."

"Earth," Oz corrected.

"Whatever." Lyon took another bite.

Unable to do much to avoid hearing the conversation, Paloon felt he needed to say something. "Just for the record, I'm sane enough to realize this planet exists. It's just that...Terra? No. I doubt it. There are strange coincidences, but...." Paloon's thoughts refused to form a complete sentence, so he grabbed a fork and began to eat.

"Exactly." Lyon kept rather composed as if not having a care about the outcome. "Then there's Larin."

"Yeah, buddy."

"He'd prefer you dead."

"I'll shoot him right now, if you like."

"Shut up," Lyon continued without missing a beat. "See, he views you as a threat to the mission. Also, there's Hitook." Lyon gave it a few thoughts. "I don't know what he thinks, but apparently he doesn't hate you. Then his counterpart, Ky, she—" Since her name surfaced, Lyon wondered. "Where's Ky?"

Paloon had to take a drink first, but Mac butted in, "She's cooking with me. We're making chicken and cheese fajitas."

"She said it's fun," Paloon added, "but it makes a terrible mess."

Lyon shrugged and took a few moments to return to his thoughts. "Well, she, Ky, thinks I ought to shoot you full of gene therapy drugs."

"You're kidding," Paloon said with a full mouth.

"No, I'm not."

"But you're not seriously," Paloon swallowed quickly, "thinking about attempting gene therapy."

"I haven't ruled it out."

Oz followed to a degree, but one phrase stuck in his head. Hitook hadn't previously told him about it. "Why am I a threat?"

It got quiet.

"Well?" Disappointment caused Oz's voice to increase a bit. "Hitook never told me you viewed me as a threat. How is that possible? I'm trapped in this little room. How can I be a fucking threat to you?"

It arrived, not like he had hoped. Nothing really could have prepared him for it. Letting the terran go would almost surely impede the mission. Killing the terran? That point never appeared as a possibility on Lyon's moral scope, not to say he hadn't tried to think about it. Guilt had a devilish way of sticking with people.

Lyon returned to face his meal. "Mac, unlock the door." Amidst a couple exhaled notes of concern, Lyon grabbed another chunk of food and ate.

The door clicked, but it took Oz almost a minute to try to open it. It did. As he stood in the doorway, his mind raced, a process made difficult by the piercing stares from Larin and Paloon. Instinctively, Oz searched for ways out, now that the tiny window no longer limited his vision. Then he thought again.

"Let me guess, I wouldn't make it out alive if I ran."

"Correct in one," Lyon said while chewing. "Mac controls all the doors out, and he won't let you leave, my orders. And those two are just itching to shoot you." He pointed a finger at the rolbrid. "If you so much as draw a weapon, I'll take it from you and shoot you with it."

Larin snarled. He had always wanted to see if someone from the Silver Knights could disarm him. They were supposed to be the best, and he wondered. It was the lieutenant in him that kept his pistol at bay, as ordered.

"Take a seat." Lyon waved over his shoulder then sipped his water. "I'm sure you're hungry too. What would you like?"

Oz noticed Hitook pointing with his eyes at the chair next to him, not that it mattered; the other open chair put him next to Larin, and Oz correctly deduced potential problems in that choice.

Lyon ate without waiting for the terran to realize the chair had no teeth to bite with. Just as he neared finishing the food on his plate, Oz took the seat. "Are you going to order?"

Surely his captors were playing some form of mental game. Nothing could stop Oz from thinking it. But everything Hitook and Mac had talked to him about made him trust them just enough to go with the flow. Like a cat stuck on a log in the middle of a rampaging river, Oz knew jumping either way meant almost certain death. For now, it was safest just to ride.

The terran cleared a dry throat. "Steak, fries and a soda."

Lyon shook his head. "Soda's no good. Matter reconstruction causes heat. Everything comes out at least warm. Go with water, tea, coffee, or the like."

"Water then, I guess."

"Good." Lyon pushed his plate away. "And make me another."

Oz had seen it from the room, but being this close enhanced the amazing nature of it. He marveled at the dancing lights and swore he could almost see the molecules binding together as Mac constructed the two meals.

"Thanks," Oz responded.

"Hey!" Mac belted. "Did you guys hear that? Someone actually had the courtesy to thank me for making dinner. I can't say the same for everyone else. Here I am, constantly slaving—"

"Mac, thanks," Lyon announced a little loud while trying not to sound annoyed, "but please be quiet."

In the silence, Larin grumbled and shot glares at the local. Paloon reached to tap the rolbrid's arm and signaled him to stop it. Accepting? No. The hunter didn't accept it. But he felt it best to watch to see what the knight had planned.

After trying one of the fries and approving, Oz said, "You haven't answered my question."

Bent over his plate, Lyon rolled his eyes toward Oz. "You're not going to let me eat in peace, are you?"

Before the terran could formulate an apology, Lyon pulled his plate closer toward him. "Mac, display the brain and the anomalies. I guess we'll eat and watch."

Paloon and Larin mimicked Lyon's plate movement as the pixels hopped like popping fireworks to align into the three-dimensional image. Below it rose a tiny, yet obese, hairy man in a black leather jacket and leaning on a cane, the same figure Mac used before.

Oz sat, mouth agape. This almost beat the mind-boggling aspect of matter recreation.

"This, Mr. Ozuna, is your brain." Mac pointed with the cane.

"What?" Oz heard, just didn't believe.

"No, it's true." Lyon pointed with a batter-cover strand of meat. "In the process of monitoring your recovery—you've completely recovered by the way—Mac took this scan but found some anomalies. So while I eat, Mac, show him what you found."

Mac tugged on his jacket for adjustment and started poking, twirling and dragging the holographic brain about, giving the complete explanation of each anomaly. A steak and fries became cold as a lost appetite churned in Oz's stomach—not in a good way. It was not every day that someone learned they were somebody's experiment. He took it well; at least he kept that one fry in his stomach. Oz tried but failed to understand many of the phrases Mac used, but the underlying truth sunk in.

When the computer was finished, so was Lyon, and he pushed his plate away. Mac walked over to it, hit it with the cane, and they both dripped away like rain on a window.

Sucking air between his teeth, Lyon said at a stunned Oz, "Ky tells me you don't know who did this to you. Well, neither do we, and that is why you are a threat."

No response, but the terran still breathed.

"That hologram you saw yesterday, of the armada," Lyon continued, "those are the pirates we're after, but now they know we're here. It gets better. They are likely being led by none other than Horwhannor, a Korac general from the War, and now, he appears to have gone renegade. To top that, we're in enemy-held territory, and they'll kill all of us if they find us. Hopefully, we can stop Horwhannor before that happens.

"All of this puts us on edge. Having a re-wired terran in our midst doesn't help the situation much." Lyon grabbed his glass and took a drink. "Some of us would feel considerably safer just boring your brain clear out of your skull and tossing your carcass in the dumpster out back so Mac could electronically decompose your body and use your molecules for Larin's next meal."

"Oh," Larin dropped the fork from his third plate and took several deep breaths. "You frapping jerk."

"Deal with it." Lyon smiled but noticed Oz turned a bit green. "Relax, that's not my intention. You are not under Dragon Corps law, and you had no choice at becoming a threat. I brought you here. While you had a choice, I did not completely inform you of the repercussions from that choice. My integrity won't let me kill you." Lyon leaned back and tried to show a more relaxed image. "You see, it would be like a cop telling someone to steal something then arresting them for it."

Disappointment struck Larin's face as the rolbrid thought about that example. He looked to Paloon for support; all he received were a set of non-verbal signals to the effect of: "He's got a point; never thought of it that way."

"You with me?" Lyon waited. "Oz, are you with me?"

Faint acknowledgement morphed into a more concrete nod with eye contact.

"Good, because this is important." Lyon brought up his hands and interlocked the fingers over his chest. "You have several choices. You can remain here until such time as I deem your release no longer a threat. Or I can embed you with a tracker, and as soon as you mention one word about us, it will explode, killing you. Or we can attempt a deep neural flash to erase your memory, but there's a risk of damaging long-term memory to include not remembering how to use the toilet. Or you can agree to undergo gene therapy in the hopes that we can get rid of that wetware."

Oz glared at Lyon as if the alien served in proxy for the dumbest man alive. "Those *great* choices sure seem to narrow it down."

"True, but it's all I can offer right now."

The terran gave it more thought, not like he had the best of options from which to choose. Deep in his being, something tugged at him. For once, he went with it while performing the mental equivalent of a cringe. "What is this gene therapy?"

"Mac," Lyon smiled a bit, "remember that gene therapy experiment awhile back."

"Yes."

"With your new upgrades, could you pull it off?"

Mac hummed, then replied, "I think so."

"Good." The knight turned back to the terran. "With Mac's help, we'll create a mixture of gene modifying nanites and inject you with them."

"What are they going to do?"

Details, details. Lyon took a deep breath and decided that stopping now wouldn't be right. "Hopefully, they'll remove, or cause your body to reject, those brain mods. They'll also...well, they'll adjust your nucleic acid in several, hopefully beneficial, ways."

"Oh, wait one minute." Paloon shook his head. "You're not going to jack his system, are you?"

"Exactly," Lyon replied as the hunter huffed in disappointment and agitation.

"What does he mean?" Oz asked.

"Normally, this sort of thing is reserved for military use. It will cause your muscles to become stronger, eyesight sharper, reflexes faster, things such as that. It basically unlocks your body's limits. Sometimes it unlocks mental abilities. Those could be beneficial, but there is a drawback."

Oz didn't want to ask, but he did. "What?"

"Most likely, you'll experience a fair amount of pain. After all, you'll be...mutating."

"Are you out of your fucking mind!?"

"Okay, okay, maybe mutating is a bad choice of words, but when it's done, you won't be terran."

"Excuse the fuck out of me!?"

"Whoa there! This is not going to turn you into a lizard creature or anything like that, but the shot will be based on atlantian nucleic acid. Terran and atlantian nucleic acid are similar but not identical. Changing your nucleic acid in order to remove those mods will likely cause biological changes. Mac will do his best to monitor the situation, and we'll add painkillers as needed. Depending on how well your body adapts to the nanites and can take more, it may be over in two, maybe three, days."

Oz's palms rubbed his face as he leaned back in the chair and moaned.

"It may not be the most pleasant of alternatives, but it's the best I have so that you're no longer a threat to us." Lyon tapped a finger on his chin and smiled jokingly. "I'm sure Larin will still kill you if you want that option."

Chapter 8

Another page flipped automatically on the floating holographic display in the room. Duke Đuvalon lifted her round head back as her wide mouth released another yawn, then her lower jaw quickly snapped shut with a clack.

She leaned forward again. Large, faint purple eyes glittered with the holographic screen's reflection. The computer recognized the eye moment and resumed tracking the progress of the reader.

Reading didn't come close to requiring her complete mental faculties, so her mind wandered. Its first and most often reoccurring stop centered on why she had to be reading this. Why had no one ever bothered to chip this knowledge? Doing so would have saved hours. Yet she kept calm about it by remembering two things: She had nothing to do otherwise, and she was partly to blame for her situation.

As one of the five-member First Cloister, she should have noticed this shortcoming and fixed it, but no one had thought it important. Sure, every cloister trained in initiating any of the multitudes of protocols. Looking back at it, the training seemed a bit of a joke in comparison to the real thing. Yet of all the procedures on file, the BU-nerry Protocol seemed the least likely to surface with a reason to exist.

Lost in the multitude of accords, treaties, pacts and other legal documents, the BU-nerry Protocol held the rare exception of requiring a unanimous consensus from the Korac Council, Federal Kingdom and every other governing body under Corps jurisdiction before being allowed as law. Such comprehensive ratification processes were the most difficult to complete, and this one took three and a half years.

Duke Đuvalon doubted her ability to preside over such a long procedure but didn't question its validly since the thought of opening communications with the p'tahians probably worried more than just one person. However, someone sensed a possible future need to at least attempt to contact the p'tahians, despite after their threats and demands to be left alone.

She paused reading long enough to shake her head in disbelief. Never would she have ever guessed that six years of law school would lead her to be one of the few people waiting to talk to the self-proclaimed executioners of every other race that had ever existed.

Against her parents' wishes, she volunteered for the Corps. Local law seemed interesting at first but gradually lost its luster with each year of school. Mediocre cases appeared the norm, and she wanted more. "The big time," some could say. Reality continually smacked her back to seeing that life on Terex never seemed to offer even one minute's worth of fame.

Challenge appeared as the only remaining avenue to keep her excited. She knew the regular way didn't offer her enough. And no one would challenge her sufficiently to keep her interested.

When the Dragon Corps came into being and began recruiting, she almost, for a few moments, dismissed the idea. Then she heard "create universal law."

She came to life. Something new. An open field. And she could be the first to make a path in that field. Nothing could compare to this challenge.

With all of her family's opposition to the idea and the difficulty of the initial Corps training, she had often given thought to quitting. Every time, she re-focused by telling herself, "Æilen, you've come too far. There's a new life out there; take it or regret it."

Now she sat in her current position, alone in one of the most powerful legal rooms in the universe, "Æilen, you've gone far enough. Maybe, it's time to go home." The faint words barely registered an echo as a green, stubby thumb from the bottom of her thick right hand jabbed into her temple, her race's symbol for someone who is going crazy.

"Who disturbs us?"

Everything in the room shook as the words boomed through the membranes in the walls. Duke Đuvalon's muscles jerked in a hard shock, slamming one of her knees on the bottom of the table. Yet enough reflex remained to allow an arm to extend lightning fast to keep her from completely falling off her chair.

Thoughts raced as rattling pops continued to sound from the vibrating membranes. Before she could consciously think, a mental command ordered the volume lower. With a few blinks and a quick shake, she focused.

The voice could only mean one thing: The message had gotten through. It must have been a p'tahian response, the first time anyone had heard a p'tahian voice for at least two thousand years, yet it spoke common, as opposed to the known p'tahian language. Bewilderment had the duke off guard as she fought away other thoughts to recall the steps in the procedure. But the speaker was not that patient.

"Answer me!" Even with the volume down, Duke Đuvalon could feel her chest bones rattle in tune with the voice. "This interruption is highly unwelcome, and we demand an answer. Now!"

She had not yet gathered her thoughts, but clearly she had to say something. After a short, deep breath, she began.

"I am Duke Æilen Đuvalon from the First Cloister of the Dragon Corps." Oddly, training, not protocol rehearsal, seemed to make the words easier to speak as she went along. "I speak on behalf of all sentient races from the governments within—"

"Fodder!" The voice boomed again.

Đuvalon tried to take note of the vocal characteristics; they fell somewhere between a vemulli and a rolbrid but with much more power than both.

"We care nothing of your polluting sub-races." A pause gave the statement emphasis. "Apparently your history lacks the memory of our warning."

The duke wanted to interrupt but stopped and tried to show patience in allowing the party to speak and, hopefully, encourage the p'tahians to acknowledge her cooperation. It didn't work.

"We do not wish to be disturbed. We spared your lives once, under the condition that we be left in peace. But you have succeeded, after time, to allow your foolish incompetence to achieve that which we loathe above all else. So answer me; is it destruction that these races you represent seek so badly that you've called upon us?"

"I offer my deepest apologies for breaking our solemn agreement, which we did not forget." Steps in the protocol came into play now, and she knew the basic premise was to stay at a lower level without directly confronting the issue of how much the p'tahians hated all other races with utter contempt. The voice cut in before she could continue with the apology.

"If you remember this agreement, a covenant that allowed the pathetic viruses of this universe to continue to exist, why make this attempt if not to ask for your forthcoming death to greet you sooner?"

"We've honored this agreement with the highest respect, which is why we come now to offer assistance to—"

"Nothing!" Another deep wave of sound shot through the duke. "There is nothing you can do for us. You have grown even more ignorant with time. We are the creators, the masters. Nothing is what you are able to offer us. You will not earn merit on your knees but will lose your head if you stand. It is best that you resume the promise or face your death."

Staring into a blank room slightly irritated Đuvalon. The monitor in front of her registered no signs of any other signal other than audio.

"May I engage video in hopes that you'll see—"

"I see you just fine, and your feeble mind earns nothing in comparison. Since you seek your death, what would you gain?"

Muscles tightened in her forehead. She strained to keep from losing the edge in this confrontation. *Did I ever have it?* She doubted it, then mentally snapped to the fact that she had started the video feed. Time had not allowed her to contemplate that fact.

"What is it, grub? Will you submit to the prior agreement or to your eradication?"

A blink of a memory, synapses fired and a realization bloomed in the duke's head. Very little could stop her now. To take this dive meant going all the way.

" Our respect for our mutual agreement is why we have come to you now."

"You respect noth—"

"Please be quiet." Gruffness entered her voice as she stood.

"How dare y—"

"I asked for silence." The duke tensed a stern face and waited for only a couple of seconds. "Thank you.

"My job is to ensure we uphold the laws of our universe, our agreement with you being one of them. But someone has violated that agreement, and we feel responsible. So we've come to ask for your permission to enter your territory to remove this violator and punish them accordingly. We view ourselves to blame and wish to return honor to our agreement by taking care of this violator for you."

The faintest of echoes seemed to bounce about as silence fought for control. She couldn't help but wonder what the owner of voice must be thinking.

"Do we have your permission to restore the honor in our agreement?"

"No, you do not." The words came slow then sped up but without much of the previous gruffness. "We find honor in your goal, but we cannot grant that request." A break only offered a return to the previous tone. "Where is this speck?"

"We will not tell you. For—"

"Then why must I waste my time with you; give me the person who can. Now!"

"This is not a matter of whom you speak with; we will not tell you."

"You must wish for eradication then."

"I do not wish for that; we wish to—"

"We will find this violator. When we do, the corpse will serve as a signpost to oblivion. If any of your worthless kind enter our space, we will not stop with the one race as we did with those *dust balls*. You would be wise to return to honoring the agreement, and do not get in our way. Do, and the extermination branches to your kind as well. Now, leave us alone!"

The sign-off came with an unnatural force in the room.

Duke Đuvalon wondered if she had pushed too hard. She reminded herself that no one really expected the p'tahians to listen. Yet thoughts of genocide began to scare her.

Those poor ber, she thought. The p'tahian referred to them as dust balls as if not worthy to mention. An entire sentient race, extinct now, thanks to the p'tahians. *Is that the Fate of all races who challenged them?*

Nothing calmed this fear as she opened a communications channel to Lord Haddox.

Æilen, it is most definitely time to return home.

Chapter 9

Colorful light danced about the room and played with the highlights of the occupants' faces. The mischievous light emitted a cheery aura, but that façade collapsed when mixed with the harsh audio.

"When did this happen!?"

Yabuki Yumiro resisted an impulse to react, keeping his face as impassive as that of his boss, Kurosawa Tetsuya, who faced the brunt of the oyabun's angry tone. Standing behind the large screen in Kurosawa's office, the yakuza lieutenant watched his senior keep even the vaguest of expressions from crossing the shadows on his face. Yabuki noted that those shadows only moved when the signal coming from across the ocean flickered, which seemed to increase the more irritated the oyabun got.

"A week ago," Kurosawa answered without feeling.

Up to this point, Yabuki considered himself privileged to even be in the same room as Kurosawa talked with the oyabun. The oyabun's reaction turned that privilege sour. Snaps and static crackled as the light jiggled on Kurosawa's face.

Deep breaths helped calm the oyabun. As he huffed, his fat cheeks wiggled like two deflating balloons.

"You dare tell me now," the chubby Asian face spoke, "that I lost a factory a *week* ago."

Kurosawa adjusted slightly, but his face remained as calm as a still pond. "Yes, oyabun."

"How did it happen?"

"We don't know, yet. The scene of the disappearance is rather unusual."

Kurosawa went into detail about the crater being smooth as glass, with no signs of rubble, nothing to go on.

Already, tiny eyes were becoming smaller behind the puffy face as the oyabun squinted. For almost two minutes, he remained still. Then, as he experienced another burst of rage, the screen suffered severe static for another minute before returning to normal.

"Who?"

"We suspect the Imondi family. They are the only rivals who have the resources to conduct such actions against us. It is likely this is tied to the warehouse hit. But the family's leader has denied being involved and even offered help."

Thought shined in the oyabun's beady eyes as the facial fat jiggled, the result of his jaw clenching tighter by the second.

"Kill them!" Globules of saliva flew when the words exploded from his lips. Then the oyabun began a rant. "Kill them all! I don't give a damn! Kill their families! Use everything you've got, even the shipments! Kill them all, damn it! I don't care if they did it; let their tombstones be warnings not to cross us! Make them pay, damn it!"

The tirade forced the static into uncontrollable levels, and only the audio struggled through on the connection.

"Don't call me back unless you're telling me that not a single one is left alive!"

The connection snapped into pure static. Kurosawa knew the oyabun had disconnected, so he tapped a button to turn off the screen and send it back into the floor.

Minutes went by with only the slightest noise from the wind outside to accompany their thoughts. There would be no turning back. It must be complete, sudden and final. One mistake could mean the end of the yakuza family in this city. A war. With the shipments, they might be able to do it. No other option existed now.

Kurosawa raised his head toward Yabuki. Eyes locked in understanding.

"My son, gather Sho," Kurosawa said calmly as he straightened even further in the chair, "and the others. We have much to do."

Yabuki snapped a deep bow before leaving without a word.

Kurosawa closed his eyes and prayed.

◆◆◆◆◆◆◆◆◆

Upon receiving confirmation that the communication signal had disconnected, the computer no longer had a reason to work. In seconds, the hologram projectors clicked off. Layers of fat from the obese face melted away in lumps to reveal the trim, fit face of a piolant, not a happy piolant.

Any onlooker, regardless of race, would know immediately and without question that this person currently epitomized the phrase, "Seriously pissed off."

Twin fires burned in each eye as both sides of his mouth snarled. The sharp, hardened gums that passed for teeth ground back and forth. Shock waves from the tense jaw sent the head shaking so feverishly that his plates were about to begin clacking like multiple sets of clattering teeth.

A monstrous boom preceded metal screws and rivets firing like pistol rounds in multiple directions as sections of the table buckled. Metal posts, forced out of their wheeled fittings, now scraped along the metal floor as a massive fist wiggled its way out of a deep dent in the surface.

"Why must I deal with such vulgar incompetence?" Horwhannor bellowed as he jolted from his chair and kicked the table so hard the female rolbrid behind the camera needlessly ducked when it flew across the room, deforming even further when it hit the far wall.

Gor'vium wisely did not reply to the rhetorical question. They both knew why. The last thing he wanted to do was to further infuriate the situation.

"Do you believe this *Imondi family* is a Corps pawn?"

Briefly Horwhannor's head shook harder as tense muscles squinted an eye. Then, as if forcing a small planet from his colon, he grunted, "No."

Then the quake subsided to mild tremors. "They're too restricted to do what we've had to do. This 'team of professionals,' as he calls it, must be working alone." Horwhannor exploded again, "And it's infuriating!"

"If I may ask, captain, then why the distraction?" Gor'vium did not display an insubordinate tone; his was one of an obedient servant wishing nothing more than to learn his master's thoughts. He felt just as strongly about returning honor to the Korac Council, and having one as famed as Horwhannor to learn from presented itself as an honor. "Do you hope to use this as training? To threaten whatever Corps teams may be operating on the planet?"

"Neither." Horwhannor approached and stopped short of the door next to Gor'vium. "You cannot fight an enemy you can't find. I don't feel like wasting my energy looking. Let my enemy waste its energy."

Gor'vium searched for the wisdom in Horwhannor's eyes and wondered if he would ever understand conflict as well.

Horwhannor took another step toward the door only to be interrupted.

"Um, captain," came a slightly squeaky rolbrid voice.

"What is it?" The question came in three distinct words as the massive piolant turned to look four feet down at the comparatively small rolbrid female.

"We had further problems again today. The system has a very hard time keeping the hologram intact when you move about too quickly. I just wanted you to know in case—"

Horwhannor lifted his foot in a blur and pounded it into the helpless rolbrid as he fired back, "Then fix it!"

With a click of the closing door, she was left alone to get off the floor and straighten her clothes.

Chapter 10

Semicircular slivers of black rested in a bizarre uniformity across the two-tone surface. The reflected grey light seemed white amid the sky's surrounding darkness as if to defy the nature of its existence. But no one cared. It remained alone.

Fate did not provide it companionship, and time eventually exposed most of its mystery. Though intrigue's luster grew dull with time, the light continued to shine bright. The energy no longer depended on admirers. Yet tonight, it seemed to smile, for a true admirer had returned.

Far below, a plastic crate rested on a roof. Perched atop it, Ky held her knees close as her tail rested freely off the back end of the box. Wisps of long, red hair undulated in the puffs of wind. Light glistened off the fiery crests whipping about. Child-like amazement kept her face still as wonder played in her eyes, which remained locked on the moon.

The only noise came from the faint whispers of scratches from her toes curled over the edge of the carton and rubbing against the sides in slow, repetitive motions.

She had heard stories while still in secondary school: other children from off world with tales of how life was elsewhere. Ky overheard them but tried very hard to listen without getting involved with the speakers. Unfortunately, she had fallen into a clique of uppity princess types by default. In such a group, associating with offworlders ranked on the taboo structure right up there with urinating in public.

Yet Ky had found the stories interesting. At night she would dream of bumping into an off-world prince who would fall in love with her, take her to these strange worlds and show her all the universe had to offer. The more the dreams came, the more she felt trapped in her life. This just caused her to listen more and more attentively while becoming as sly as a thief in obtaining the details without breaking her clique's rules.

One day, she heard a story about two large, round objects in the night sky called moons. It took considerable effort for her to imagine such a wonder. She broke from her study material to conduct research on moons. Thus began her fascination with space and seeing all she could see.

This stayed with her through tertiary school and on to final school. Her royal training aside, Ky's title kept her from escaping her duties and seeing what she had heard about. Once in a while, she'd make a short visit to a planet, but the tightly packed itineraries never allowed her to *see* the planets she visited.

During final school, Ky heard about the Dragon Corps recruiting.

All governments were supporting this effort. This fact formed the foundation for her plan. Ky had an immediate ally in her birth sister, who just wanted to get away from their family and all the rules as quickly as possible.

Together they gave each other strength to defy their family and discretely sneak away one day to dispatch their volunteer forms through royal channels. The confirmation message lauded the Dext Royal Family and soon found its way into the public's eye. Everyone looked favorably upon the family, and it further encouraged local support.

Ky's family saw the idea of two princesses joining the Dragon Corps as a disgrace. But publicly backing away from the Corps now would only bring further embarrassment.

Over the years, her family became more tolerant but never fully accepting. For that, Ky turned to her only family that understood, her birth sister, Julie. Together, they mutually achieved their goals.

Now, she took advantage of her position to enjoy one of the universe's rarest finds, an almost pure white moon. Still not quite full, the moon appeared larger than she had expected. Ky fidgeted her toes in anticipation of getting to see the full moon in a couple of days.

Meanwhile, she bathed her aura in the celestial energy, soaking and recharging. But it came with an annoying side effect. She strained at times before allowing her enjoyment to reach levels just giddy enough to push away the thoughts. They always returned, and she couldn't help the fact that all the energy flowing about made her feel more connected to this planet.

These were dreary, dark feelings. Something was askew. Something did not sit right in this world. And the energy around her sensed it.

"Ahhhh!" she screamed in fright, her arms shaking, fur standing on end and tail rigid into the air.

"Sorry, I didn't mean to scare you Ninja Adian." Hitook stood beside her, worry and apology in his face.

Ky calmed and began to feel foolish for letting her thoughts get away from her. She planted her face in her knees and muffled, "That's all right."

Hitook watched for a moment before crossing his legs and sitting on the roof next to her.

Time went by before Hitook broke the silence.

"Are you enjoying the moon, Ninja Adian?"

Ky finally lifted her head again to look upon the majestic beauty. Minutes slipped by before she realized she hadn't replied. "Yes, it's wonderful." She closed her eyes briefly. "Please, just call me Ky."

Confusion contorted Hitook's eyes. He looked to her as another teacher and sought to conform to her wishes. "I'm sorry. Would you prefer I not use titles?"

Ky dropped her head and stared into the roof. She didn't know. Was it such a distaste for titles of any kind? Did she just not like titles in her name? Was she becoming more like her sister? Or was it something else?

Her mind circled the topic for almost ten minutes before she realized that, for a second time, she had failed to reply. Instead, she offered a question.

"Have you sensed something strange, possibly dark, in this world?"

Hitook did not rudely demand an answer to his previous question and just politely nodded. "Yes. There is energy that is scared."

She really didn't want a confirmation. Ky partly did not wish to know any more, but a mixture of fear and curiosity pushed gently to ask. "When did you notice it?"

"About a week after we arrived." Hitook paused to draw a deep breath and focus for a moment. It was still there, faint but unmistakably there. "Almost as if the energy is sad at something that hasn't happened yet, but it can sense the pending sorrow."

Just as she had felt. "About the time the native below was in that accident?" Ky almost mumbled the phrase.

Hitook replied with a simple, "Yes."

No one could be proficient in every planet's energy, but what she felt seemed too familiar and unique, simultaneously. She gave in to the idea of beginning at a loss. "What do you think it means?"

Hitook felt slightly honored and professionally timid at the question. He assumed it could only mean that it had the ninja particularly intrigued or disturbed. Yet the acolyte was not one to pretend just to seem superior.

"I do not know." The liqua looked to the moon and blinked slowly. "I remember Master Gon once said, 'You may bind the energy to do your will, but it too has a will, a will that refuses to expose its deepest of secrets. Save your strength and accept understanding; demanding it will keep it from you.'"

The words hit a chord with Ky. She admitted that Hitook, too, had been taught by a wise master. Appreciation for the wisdom aside, it didn't answer what had been on Ky's mind when she had asked.

"What about the native? Do you think he's involved or is part of why the planet senses something dark?"

"As we may be." Hitook calmly replied.

"True," Ky whispered while hugging her knees tighter and resting her chin on the peaks.

The nighttime traffic and life on the streets below moved at a dulled pace, peaceful and ignorant of the true fears in the universe. This idea became a burden to Ky and showed itself on her face. She didn't want to be the cause of the destruction of an entire race that didn't even know it was not alone in the void.

"We have started a fire that we know not where it may burn." Hitook turned to Ky briefly. "I hope we have not caused this despair that the energy is feeling, but we would be foolish to ignore our own fears."

A faint nod from Ky preceded a reply. "We have few options. I'm not sure I trust that native, but.... Well, you've been in there. I didn't sense any malevolent thoughts, but we can't deny that someone has flipped some switches and installed their own circuits.

"I don't know if the dread I'm sensing is coming from him or something else. Because in the long run, I guess it really doesn't matter if the native is a reluctant spy because there's a whole renegade armada that knows we're here, the Corps has complete deniability, and soon a whole batch of extinction enthusiasts are going to catch a whiff of new prey. The chances of us making it off this planet alive are not looking good, my friend."

Hitook's thick, furry brow curled in concern. The situation really had gotten to his comrade. He appreciated her thoughtfulness and frankness, traits he considered admirable, and made a quick note to work on them in himself.

Together, they sat quietly. Both had remnants of Ky's previous comments floating through their thoughts. Over time, they became dull echoes merging with the distant beat of traffic.

Hitook sought ways to better understand this disturbance by releasing his mental inflections and allowing the energy to answer itself. Pillars of ideas and waves of interpretation rolled over him as he meditated. He disregarded it the first couple of times before realizing he had allowed his own perceptions to cloud the natural flow.

The acolyte forced the gates open and let the ideas speak for themselves.

"From our birth, Fate equally gives us the choices and blindly deals the consequences. The outcomes are neither good nor bad. At times, we may perceive them as such, but bathed in the brilliance of the entire universe such perceptions are inconsequential.

"The single drop of rain amid a raging storm does not defy gravity only to contemplate the outcome of the weather. Much like a rain drop, we recognize that Fate has brought us to this point, there's no turning back, we know what must be done, and now Fate lets us decide what we're going to do about it. We can charge forward with purpose or attempt to stop the inevitable.

"Without fear or regret, the rain drop descends proudly. It does not worry but plays its part the best it can while remaining oblivious to its role in a massive storm that can bring devastation or life or both.

"I wish to be like the rain. There is no doubt; a storm is raging. Now is not the time to wish us elsewhere. Sure, the options aren't desirable, but the mission is clear. We'll face this together, as a team, and blaze a trail forward. I have no doubt of that.

"By relying on each other, the fear disappears. Then as individual drops, we work together and become a storm, accomplishing the goal and returning home. I find myself at peace and free of fear, thanks, in part, to you."

Ky half-turned her head toward Hitook and gave a sly smirk at the liqua who just continued to stare forward after his interpretation of the situation. Even her eyes smiled as she continued to watch.

With a snap, her legs shot out as she reached for a sky in a yawn. Ky's tiny tongue even stretched to a point for several moments before curling back between her elongated canines.

The dextian bounced off the crate and promptly went over to Hitook, leaned down and gave him a hug around the neck.

"Thank you," she whispered before hugging a bit harder.

Without fanfare, she released and walked off toward the roof's access hatch with a little bounce in her step.

Still in mild shock, Hitook continued staring. At what exactly, he had forgotten. Like a statue, he didn't move for minutes afterwards.

Then, with no one left to witness, Hitook allowed himself a smile. He even blushed.

Chapter 11

Furry strings of white curled about in small knots, forming scattered clumps on a silken sheet of light blue that served as the sky. Yellow-white light glistened on shiny black feathers as the trio of birds quietly whipped about in a dazzling display of aerial acrobatics, a playful effort to amuse themselves.

Weak bursts of wind dipped low enough to catch a kite and carry it higher as the child giggled in excitement and his father encouraged him to hold on. Nearby, ducks waddled off into the park's pond and floated along the calm water toward the far side, where a little girl tossed bits of bread.

Aging eyes took in the scene of peace. With a whiff, the great grandmother could almost smell the sweet scent of beauty. She smiled and nodded to the pair of joggers who went by.

They returned the gesture as they followed the path that turned near the edge where the soft grass gave way to the hard concrete. Ribbons of stone weaved out of the park like a rigid web, surrounding massive columns of steel and glass towering toward the calm sky above.

High above the park, sunlight effortlessly entered the glass triangle that topped the casino and hotel. Points of white reflected the sun's brilliance from the water in the large octagonal aquarium in the center of the room. The brightly colored fish calmly floated along in peace before darting in multiple directions as a burst of noise pounded into the room.

At the elevator on the left side of the wall that formed the triangle-shaped room's base, six people exploded in a flurry of action. The first whipped around to the control panel on the wall as the next quickly scanned the room with weapons drawn. The next two also looked about but only briefly before Frank Imondi entered the room and instinctively went behind his desk and stood. The last man stayed at the elevator door.

"I'm not buying it, Tony. I want a reason," Mr. Imondi demanded.

Tony Garibaldi left the control panel and approached the desk as the glass walls and ceiling darkened to a solid black and tubes of florescent lights embedded in the metal latticework flickered to life. "We don't know why, but Cain is definitely dead."

He didn't want to believe it. His brother's house had exploded. Frank fought to keep his sanity but teetered on the verge of losing it.

"Was it a hit?" Mr. Imondi planted his hands on the desk and faced the man to the right of the aquarium. "Did somebody put out a hit on him, Mike?"

"No," Michael Imondi said quietly as he shook his head slightly. "We threatened every snitch we've got. There's nothing out there. It must be internal."

"Who?" Mr. Imondi bellowed.

A cell phone rang, and the tall, lanky suit standing to Tony's right reached into his jacket to retrieve it.

"Did he get into any business deals recently?" Mr. Imondi wanted an answer, any answer. "Who would have wanted him dead?"

"No one that I can think of." Tony threw out his hands in a gesture of futility. "He didn't start any business deals recently. All of our current contracts have remained clean with no sign of dissension."

Tony found a cell phone shoved in his face. The only thing keeping him from chastising the thin man was knowing he wouldn't have been interrupted if the call wasn't important. He took the phone. "Excuse me," Tony said before stepping back.

"What about the yakuza?" Mr. Imondi turned back to Mike.

With another head shake, Mike denied the possibility. "We've been on stable and peaceful terms. The yaks are too smart to risk an all-out war. Both sides have too much to lose. But—" Mike looked away for a bit to think then shifted his gaze back to Mr. Imondi. "There is still whoever destroyed the yak's warehouse and factory. We still don't know who did it."

"What, triads, some organized street gang? What?"

"No gang could operate on this level without making some noise, and the yaks would have picked up on any triads in the area. They wouldn't have bothered—"

"Boss," Tony interrupted, "my apologies, but that's not all." He closed the now lowered phone. "The paper mill is on fire."

"What the fuck!?" Shocked blended with even more disbelief on Mr. Imondi's face.

"Witnesses are claiming it started in the office, and so far the efforts of the firefighters have done nothing but cause the fire to spread. Chemicals, they think."

"Ralph?"

"Presumed dead. Some of the workers who escaped said they saw him heading toward the office minutes before the fire alarm began."

Mike reached for his cell phone. "I'm going to shake the trees again. Something big is going down."

"Tony," Mr. Imondi barked as another cell phone rang behind him. "Start getting the word out. Everyone needs to get to a place they feel is safe, and have my—"

"Sir?"

Mr. Imondi turned to the bodyguard behind him. "What is it, Danny?"

The guard could say nothing and just offered the phone in his hands. An odd look of concern appeared in the guard's eyes.

Frank lifted in phone and wondered what it could be now.

Time slowed. The world no longer rotated. Sound became muted. Moments ticked by with nothing to measure them. Gravity pulled Frank down. He no longer had the strength to stand and just flopped back into the chair that Danny had moved into place.

A shaky arm feebly reached across the desk toward a glass frame.

The others stopped everything and watched in terror and sorrow.

Within the frame rested an image of a beautiful brunette. An ornate comb held her hair back to reveal a delicate face; happiness shined in rich blue eyes. Her smile held all the passion and love he had ever felt. Tears began to fall on the glass and streak off the edge.

Frank's lips shuttered as he slowly whimpered, "Vanessa."

At that moment, to the ultimate shock of all who watched, Frank Imondi's head exploded.

The long metallic case clicked shut. Even that made more noise than the hotel room's previous events. With less sound than a loud breath, the weapon delivered its lethal payload, as advertised, spot on.

Yabuki stood, leaving the case to rest on the bed. He withdrew a cigarette and lit it. A deep drag allowed him to center. Eyes closed, he rocked his head back slightly before slowly exhaling.

He calmly strolled toward the balcony as if he had the ability to generate more time if he ever needed it. Along the way, his hand swiped a small black square off the table next to the sliding glass door. Light breezes slipped about the high-rise and played with Yabuki's hair as he stepped outside.

Such a clear, calm day, seemed ironic, given the pain being dealt today. This did not seem as humorous as it might have otherwise.

Yabuki took another drag and kept his unblinking gaze focused on the horizon. Wedged between the other towers in his view rested the glass-covered corner office of Frank Imondi, about three miles across the city. The dark coating in the windows seemed fitting for a coffin.

Though he tried, he couldn't imagine the torment in that steel trap of an office. Yabuki reassured himself that waiting was for the best. The soul could continue unhindered to the beyond without feeling a desire to return.

"May you be rejoined," Yabuki whispered and bowed his head.

Much still remained, but it would be over soon.

A flick opened the black square he had taken from the table. It flipped open like a palm-sized laptop computer. Two touch-sensitive screens offered several menus from which to choose. He made his choices, closed the device, placed it in his pocket and returned to the room.

Yabuki grabbed the weapon case with one hand, and with the other, he crushed his cigarette into an ashtray. Seconds later, the room's door closed behind him.

In the distance, a sound like nearby thunder shattered the calm. Every glass window in the hotel casino fractured and fell piece by piece into the center of the hotel. Bystanders watched the spectacle in awe but were unable to directly describe what it was about the explosion that seemed wrong.

Screams from within the hotel further pierced the peaceful moments before the lower support structures finally gave way to the stress of dual forces: the unsupported weight above and the strong draw toward the building's center.

In an abnormal rush, the building fell in upon itself and became one of many mass graves that day.

Chapter 12

"What of their immediate families?"

"Dead. All dead."

As instructed, Kurosawa ordered his yakuza forces to wipe out all remnants of the Imondi mob. *At what cost*, he wondered, looking at the fat face of his oyabun on the large screen.

Loyalty, above all other values, kept the yakuza strong. Yet Kurosawa, after fifty years of unwavering service, had a doubt. It had been at least eight years since the current oyabun had seized power and sent the entire yakuza in a whirlwind of events. Soon the yakuza gained influence in almost every market in almost every region on the planet. If anything, Kurosawa should be proud to be alive to see the yakuza achieve so much. But the doubt remained.

At times the yakuza had no options left but to conduct unsavory business to stay alive. Kurosawa knew that and didn't cast a blind eye or shun it, but he embraced it. No one would find nobility in the actions that Kurosawa sometimes had to carry out. Necessity rarely played favorites. Kurosawa learned young to seize necessity and force it to obey, even if it meant killing someone to protect your family, your life.

There were no frightened teenagers here, just obedient followers. Yet even in the face of an achievement such as they had just experienced, victory cheers failed to fill their voices. This win felt hollow, needless, senseless. Kurosawa wrestled with this feeling to keep his appearance impassive.

He never pretended to fully understand the delicate yet deadly politics at the senior levels of the yakuza, but he couldn't help but wonder how this oyabun achieved the post.

"What of any associates?" the oyabun questioned.

"Many died in the resulting fires and explosions. We are currently contacting those surviving to inform them of their options."

The oyabun gave an inquiring glare.

Kurosawa explained. "The Imondi family had influences deep in parts of the government we could not reach. With them gone, we can seize these for our own use. Such power, and the men who wield it, may be required later."

He quietly hoped it would be much later. One wrong move now might send national agents or the military to his door. For now, Kurosawa trusted his legion of lawyers to hold the courts in knots and keep the media guessing.

"Any disappointments?"

At the question, Kurosawa couldn't help but glance at Yabuki standing behind the screen. Shame forced Yabuki's eyes to the ground. He had more faith than the pair could offer in deeds.

"Yes, two." Kurosawa returned to the screen. "A pair, caught but not before succeeding in their task."

"Damage?"

"Minor." Surety formed the word. "There will be enough circumstantial evidence to see they walk free. But it might take up to a week to get them released."

"Are they a liability? If so, remove them."

"No. They're strictly loyal and have said nothing. Our team beat them to the police station."

"Fair enough." Beady eyes darted about a couple of times. "School operations will need to increase. I'll be sending more royal guards to assist."

Kurosawa moved back in his seat a bit before stopping. This didn't go unnoticed.

"What is it?" The oyabun leaned forward and slightly squinted. "Is something troubling you, Tetsuya. If so, say it now."

"I mean no disrespect, but I'm wondering why we need to increase our operations even more. We've achieved so much. It'll take a little while for us to adjust. There are no more enemies; we'll soon have control throughout the city."

The oyabun took a deep breath and remained calm. "There are other events outside of your view. These shipments serve a critical purpose. Continue to do your job and protect this operation through any means; that is your responsibility. Ensure you do it."

"Hai." Kurosawa snapped as fast as he stood and bowed deep at the screen until the communications channel disconnected.

Pale flakes fell quietly to the table as Horwhannor rubbed his thumb hard against his fingertips. Everyone at the table just watched. Their leader had called this meeting of senior members who formed the Korac Liberation Armada.

For years, they had conducted quiet exchanges, slowly improving and expanding the armada until the time came to restore honor to the Korac Council. Some thought—foolishly—that this meeting would announce the return. Others wisely knew it was still too soon.

"How many shipments can we generate?" From his seat at the flattened tip of a triangle-shaped table, Horwhannor looked to his left to the vemulli in the middle.

Ship Commander Jio R-T xoLyft dwarfed his chair and towered at least a head over everyone else at the table. Not too different from a living nightmare straight from an evil forest, Jio turned and revealed midnight blue eyes peering from a thick coat of fur. Age robbed the hair of color. Now most survived as white with only smatterings of black freckles, as if someone had let him roll in spices.

"We could increase to five, maybe six a day." Jio's voice seemed to resonate through the air into every bone in every body in the room.

As he spoke, a mouth of sharp teeth clattered. "On your word, we'll begin."

"Do it," Horwhannor snapped and shifted to the right side of the triangle. "Ensure there's no interference."

The piolant at the far end nodded in response.

"Shall we alert the defense forces?"

The question came from the doludgian to Horwhannor's immediate left. Contemplation streaked across the leader's face and followed his eyes in a quick scan at nothing.

With a humph, Horwhannor barely moved his head in acknowledgment. "At least ensure they're ready to aid as needed."

"What of the ship?" the doludgian queried.

"Try to accelerate the process if you can. Work with Jio if you must to get the vessel operating."

"Are you going to—"

"Just," barked Horwhannor, "do your job and provide the forces we need on the ground. Can you do that for me, Cir-rilis?"

Horwhannor jerked his head forward to emphasize the point, and the first piolant to his right immediately replied, "Yes."

"Good." The leader halted for a second and breathed. Concentration allowed him to again recognize how much he needed to depend on his senior staff. "If the Corps is foolish enough to come after us in force, it will be their loss. Until that time, I want whoever it is on that planet dead."

"If we go in from here, we could inadvertently expose ourselves," uttered a rolbrid with cautious concern. The ship commander sat between the two piolants on Horwhannor's right and hoped he didn't sound as if he were challenging the direction.

Horwhannor faced the speaker but pointed at the doludgian. "We won't have to with that ship operational." He dropped his arm. "Exterminate these maggots from beneath the ground they live in.

"I understand—" Horwhannor cut himself off and resumed grinding his fingers against his thumb as he briefly looked at his ship commanders. "Comrades, this is not how we planned it, but we've come too far and we're too close to our goal to retreat from it now. If the Corps forces our hand, then we'll show them how strong we have become. Even now, there's nothing that could stop us, but we must," Horwhannor pounded the table, "defeat this temporary obstruction. Then, soon, we'll return, destroy the Corps and retake our homeland.

"I want to return home, to the home I remember, not this weak willed abomination it has become. We *will* strike quickly and resume our path. Only death awaits those who interfere. Even if we must destroy this planet, nothing will stop us. All for Korac!"

In unison the ship commanders grunted and huffed as conviction shined bright in eyes set amidst stern faces. Together, they knew their advanced technology could destroy the entire Dragon Corps fleet. But for now, their combined influence would eliminate this minor threat.

⊰♦♦♦♦♦♦♦♦⊕♦♦♦♦♦♦♦♦⊱

Kurosawa slowly lowered himself. A freshly poured cup of tea waited for him as he sat on his legs at the short table.

With only the slightest tinkling of china, the geisha returned the pot as smoothly and quickly as she had retrieved it only moments before. Silence remained her world as she knelt at the side of the table. Kurosawa secretly enjoyed the company as he began to savor his tea and wrestle with his thoughts.

Perhaps the sweet smell of herbs allowed him to relax; it could have been the smooth bitter taste that he enjoyed so well. In this moment of peace, he allowed worry to shine through his ridged mask, something he never liked to show outside of his closest company. Yet for the second time in one evening, this was noticed by a third party.

Across the room, Yabuki waited and watched quietly. He had not been excused and that pleased him in a unique way. The lieutenant had earned, without being told, the privilege to stay.

Yabuki also had a concern. Discipline kept his lips sealed. At least that was the case until he noticed Kurosawa's reaction. Now, left in the same room, Yabuki seized the moment and pressed forward.

With a slight squeeze, he felt the bulk in his jacket to ensure he had brought it with him. Then he proceeded to the opposite end of the table.

Kurosawa paused in mid-drink to nod. Yabuki responded with a deep bow. Before he could kneel at the table, a new setting was in place and the tea was pouring.

The aroma soothed the edges of Yabuki's internal tension, and one sip ensured his guess of the tea being a specially imported blend.

For a moment Yabuki forgot. Then he remembered his current position, at the same table, sharing tea. Either Kurosawa had forgiven him for the disappointment or the old man finally achieved lunacy and was contemplating leaving the yakuza. Yabuki couldn't tell, but he did correctly read that something concerned Kurosawa.

Yabuki was also concerned, so he had nothing to lose.

In traditional Japanese, Yabuki began quietly and slowly.

"Sir, there is something that has been bothering me."

Kurosawa failed to react, as if to say, "I care less if you continue, but you may."

Yabuki took another sip. "I happened to find something. I don't know what it means. All I know is that it is odd, odd enough to keep me awake at night."

Kurosawa's expression failed to change as he began enjoying another cup.

Yabuki became aware of his breathing as it became deeper with each thought. He lifted his cup with a little difficultly and downed the remainder. The geisha gracefully filled it again as Yabuki breathed a few more times.

"The royal guards are not whom they claim to be."

Only the disciplined geisha showed no effect from the statement. The other two, however, locked gazes. Yabuki wondered if he had overstepped his bounds; Kurosawa tried to determine if Yabuki had lost his sanity. Yet a hint of intrigue kept the leader's mind racing as to the meaning of the statement.

Moments stretched to minutes as the two continued staring at each other. During the session, Kurosawa sought for the signs in Yabuki's eyes, but he could find nothing but truth.

Kurosawa placed his cup down. "When speaking concern, walk the path lightly."

Yabuki acknowledged the advice with a nod. "With the malice of a feather falling to earth," he finished the saying that Kurosawa had begun.

Images flew through Yabuki's mind as if he stood an arm's length from a speeding locomotive. The effect nearly brought him to vertigo. Instead, it left his mind in a surreal state as his brain began to pound.

He wrestled with what he had seen on the tapes. No amount of explanation had made it any clearer to him. Half of him wanted to place it into an easily understandable frame of reference; the other half just shook it off as bad optics and fussy focus. It was the sliver of a doubt wedged between those halves that bothered him.

"While reviewing some security tapes, I noticed an odd event." Yabuki still fought the odd floating pain in his head. "I've attempted to understand what the camera caught with no luck. But it has upset me since."

Kurosawa waited patiently with his tea as Yabuki reached into his jacket and retrieved a palm computer.

"May I show you the footage?"

"You brought it with you?" Kurosawa, for a second, wondered if Yabuki had planned this.

"After I saw it, I made several copies in case a few were destroyed." Yabuki began tapping away at the screen to search for one of his electronic copies. "I've since placed the original in one of my safes."

"What could call for such precautions?"

Yabuki held up a hand to request a moment of silence. A twinge of dislike flicked in Kurosawa's eyes before they calmed again. Yabuki tapped the play key and quickly handed the computer to Kurosawa, who took a moment to grab it.

"That's Warehouse Nine." Kurosawa held the computer a bit farther from his eyes and then looked at Yabuki. "There are no cameras there."

Yabuki knew the oyabun had specifically requested that at several locations, the royal guards would replace other forms of surveillance. That didn't please him, and Yabuki had taken it upon himself to ensure some cameras secretly remained in place to ease his mind. The results, however, caused the opposite effect.

"I did this for our protection." Yabuki nodded toward the palm computer with the desired effect as Kurosawa returned his gaze to it.

When he did, he paused, then froze. On the screen, a royal guard motioned quickly for another while making a jabbing motion to the side of his neck with the other hand. During the movements, the guard's head...changed. It resembled the random flickers of a bad florescent light.

Soon, the second guard arrived and started poking his hands into the first guard's collar. With the distressed guard's head up, the second retrieved a disk-like object. Suddenly the flickering stopped, and words could not describe what remained.

The face wasn't terran; Kurosawa knew that fact and did not know how he knew it. But he didn't know what it was. Hundreds of ideas stormed the beachhead of Kurosawa's mind. Among all the mental noise, his mind mostly wrestled with a description as if that alone would help sort the rest of the charging thoughts.

A grub? Not quite. Lizard? Somewhat, but not completely. Beetle? Maybe a little. A snake? Only slightly.

Nothing seemed to match until he settled on all those things and a terran face blended into one. But then it still didn't match with what he was seeing on the screen.

Before Kurosawa could further explore the possibilities, the second guard reached into his uniform for a new disk and slipped it into the collar of the other. In a blink, the alien face disappeared behind a shroud of a terran face.

The footage ended with a black screen into which Kurosawa just stared. Minutes passed before he set the palm computer down.

With the speed of a turtle, Kurosawa turned his head toward his geisha, who silently rose and even more quietly left the room.

The leader came back to meet Yabuki's eyes. "We have much to discuss."

Chapter 13

Baden poked his head and upper torso out from inside a lowered alcove to observe that the traffic in the hall seemed almost as frantic as it was in the room he just left. With only his head visible as if protruding from the floor, the marselian looked back to ensure the door closed before he yelled.

"Gilo, I need that drive and hot," he shouted through the constant flow of beings as one squeezed past him to enter the room he just left.

"Loading," came a return voice from across and up the hall. "Still loading. Give it time."

More feet shuffled through his view of the door as he watched intently. "How much longer? I'm likely to lose an arm if I go back in there without it."

Nothing.

"Gilo!" Baden hollered loud enough to startle several of the beings darting about the hall.

"Hold it, I said it's allllmost—done!"

A grey-skinned limino floated around the corner and noticed the traffic. "I need a pipe, people, please," Gilo barked. She then let out a loud humph when not a single being seemed to pay her any attention. "I'm not asking for a date."

"Gilo," Baden beckoned eagerly with a waving arm.

"Yeah, yeah." Gilo scanned the traffic and made her move.

With her innate limino telekinetic ability, Gilo shot the drive from around the corner and through the crowd, only needing to dodge a few legs. The hand-sized, black box then skittered across the floor into Baden's waiting hand.

"Thanks, girl." Baden waved back with drive in hand. "I owe you that date."

Baden didn't wait to see Gilo's face blush yellow; he darted back into the room. On his heels, an atlantian balancing a tray of drinks came through the door.

Initially the clattering, clicking and other general chatter seemed deafening. Beings packed the room so tightly that an observer would have to look twice before noticing the long oval table resting a bit left from center. A few had earned the positions with seats that faced a raised center ridge along the table. Various monitors and devices clustered the ridge's face to create an opening for each chair.

Baden squeezed through the mass of bodies far enough to hand the newly acquired drive to a huyin colleague who used one of his long arms to snatch it and slide it into position in front of Harquebus Commander Scda Oj.

The atlantian with the amazingly level tray of drinks seemed to effortlessly dart about the crowd as if performing a well-rehearsed ballet. Various sorts of drinks appeared in their proper places in front of those with sufficient honor to merit the privilege of a chair.

Amid the cluster of people, someone engaged a sub-dermal link to the room's sound system.

"Unless you are read on for Cobra, leave. Now."

Lord Jordan Haddox had tolerated the noise as much as his sanity could withstand. But now, it was time for business. The clock didn't stop clicking away the moments, and no one knew how many of those clicks remained.

As the room emptied, additional chairs became visible in the recessed areas of the walls on both sides of the table. The chairs remained packed, but as the last being pushed everyone out before she left herself, the small room seemed as large as a concert hall and quiet as a monastery.

Haddox broke the silence. "Are we secure?"

"Verifying," came a voice into the room, "and yes, you're secure."

The lord of the Dragon Corps took a drink but didn't taste it. Haddox's mind lived elsewhere at the moment. As the glass hit the table, he opened the meeting.

"Let's skip the formalities." Haddox looked about the room. "We all know why we're here and what we have to do. There may not be much time, so we don't leave here without a clear decision.

"We are faced with three situations. We have a covert team in hostile territory that might require extraction. There's a priority fugitive who's been detected outside of our official jurisdiction. The final situation is that Cobra Five of our charter may require activation.

"In order of importance, let's begin with Cobra Five." Haddox pointed to Leader Dars Kawka but halted for a moment. "Also this is critical: If you've got an idea, speak it. Now's not the time to wonder if it's good or not. We need everything.

"Dars," Haddox resumed, "how sure are we?"

As the marselian held a data pad with her lower arms, she gestured forward with her main arms in a sign of frustration. "We're neither sure nor unsure. We're combing through those fragmented, ancient star charts for the slightest hint of a definitive match with no luck."

"But many of the reports from the ground do match, right?" Dragoon Chrodium W'Lowe asked.

"I'd say most do, and Pierre, chime in if I speak out of bounds." Dars jerked her head toward a female atlantian in one of the seats behind her. "In that respect, Terra Four seems to be the closest match, but—"

"But what?" Jordan leaned forward.

"It's that the other planets also match many aspects found on Terra Four." Dars shook her head. "If it wasn't for the other six partial matches, I'd be almost certain, but it's much like a case of plausible doubt. We have six reasons to doubt ourselves."

Jordan played with his tongue against the left corner of his lips as he thought. "We need the best guess. With what you know, which one is most likely it?"

Dars turned to Pierre and received a nod. "Terra Four...with about a seventy percent chance of certainty."

"Any other thoughts?" Jordan glanced over the faces at the table. The quiet acknowledgment allowed the lord to proceed. "Then we also have Horwhannor to deal with. What are the options?"

Chrodium W'Lowe's red-brown eyes shifted to the hologram floating above the table and mentally commanded a shift to a new image. Horwhannor's armada came into view. "I'll assume ignoring its existence is not going to be an option. Therefore, our options range from assisting Kendrick's team in somehow infiltrating the armada and neutralizing Horwhannor to full-scale invasion."

"We don't have the resources for an invasion at the moment," Dars piped in before anyone could stop her.

"I'm sure no one is going to argue that," Jordan vaguely raised a hand. "We're all tapped, but what's the middle ground? What's the absolute minimum we would need to still ensure success?"

Chrodium nodded toward Dars as a way to shift the question to the expert. She didn't like the idea but entertained it.

"We're looking at an entire space armada of vessels: a combat station, a battle Envoy and thirty other battle or combat class vessels with about twenty-three in a mixture of other craft. Collectively, there's a possibility of about five hundred bombers and a thousand four hundred fighters." Collective sighs filled the room. "But the highest count Kendrick reported came to a hundred and fifty. It is possible that Horwhannor doesn't have the followers to fully man the vessels *and* the fighters."

Something about that didn't balance with Jordan. "Didn't he launch something like three hundred fighters when he attacked the Ranklin?"

Dars almost beat W'Lowe, but the dragoon proved too quick. "True, but there's still the very likely possibility that Horwhannor cannot completely convert everyone to his cause. To maintain the psychological control, he would most likely slaughter those who wouldn't convert. At least that would be the most expedient way while effectively limiting possible challenges later."

The gloomy thought festered for a moment. Scda broke the silence, but the news didn't get better.

"More than six thousand is also possible in infantry troops with these vessel configurations." The jexan tapped at a few keys with a very pointy and sharp digit then looked back. "At limit, roughly, not counting support vessels."

"That's nice." Jordan's mind was too busy trying to incorporate this new data to care if his sarcasm came off as such. "Anything else?"

"Mechs," Dars offered.

"What about them?"

"These vessels, in normal configuration, would carry a total of fifty bays for heavy mechanized units." Dars wrinkled her lips. "There's no telling the load out. We could be looking at light, stellar models or full-on interplanetary heavy combat versions."

"They could take the planet?" asked Pytin, the House Bravo grand master.

Jordan shook his head in disbelief until W'Lowe agreed.

"Normally, no, this force wouldn't be big enough, but," the dragoon jerked a thumb aimlessly toward the hologram, "this planet's so under-developed, they'd probably take it in thirty minutes."

"So," Jordan shook two fingers at the floating pictures, "not only do we need two armadas in hopes of overwhelming him completely, we have to worry about him running to ground and taking the planet hostage."

"Truly, it would be wise to gather three to four armadas." Pytin provided the statement as if common knowledge.

"We'll be hard pressed to gather two, three would put us in the red, and we'd have to go critical in three commands trying to put four armadas together." Dars didn't see the logic in it and had no doubt she would be supported.

"If you don't overwhelm a man like Horwhannor, he'll fight." Pytin paused to sip some tea, but no one dared interrupt. "When cornered he will fight with all he has, and that will get us noticed."

W'Lowe followed the grand master's thoughts and whispered, "The p'tahians."

"Sure, the p'tahians." Dars squinted her black orbs. "Like filling a system with two hundred combat vessels won't get a bit of attention."

Pytin dipped his head briefly as the others mumbled a bit, all except W'Lowe, who lost himself in some possibilities.

"Surgical strike," he finally offered.

Jordan leered through the corner of his eyes at the dragoon. "Light, undetected assassination?"

W'Lowe shrugged. "He prefers a centralized command." The dragoon leaned back in his chair allowing himself to test the logic orally. "Remove him from the picture and those who are left may agree that facing two armadas would be suicide."

"Without a leader," Pytin rebutted, "thousands of aimless minions could become quite unpredictable, possibility irrational."

Jordan dropped his head, sighed and turned a bit to look at the grand master. "Well, aren't you just a ball a fun?" The lord closed his eyes and shook his head a bit.

Pytin didn't take it as such, but Haddox added, "Nothing personal." The lord threw looks at everyone. "Please don't tell me that there's no sure-fire plan to keep from attracting the p'tahians. We've got a fifty-fifty chance. I guess we should pick the lesser of two evils, so if there's—"

"I have an alternative view."

Mild shock smacked Haddox across the face. He swore he had seen no one at the table move their mouths, Scda being the exception, but the voice was too high pitched for the jexan. Reality finally came to him as Jordan quickly leaned back in the chair and snapped his head to the left. Amid the group in the sideline of chairs, a familiar figure slowly stood.

Duke Ðuvalon struggled with an unexpected spell of nervousness. "It's just a possibility."

"At this point, Æilen, I'll take anything." Jordan pushed from the table and straightened himself in the chair. "What's on your mind?"

Everyone at the table knew of Duke Ðuvalon, at least they knew her as the member of the First Cloister who happened to be on duty when the p'tahians responded to the BU-nerry Protocol.

"About the p'tahians, I've been analyzing the conversation." What she kept to herself is the degree of self-inflicted guilt she now endured that had been keeping her awake. "We don't have much p'tahian data to work with, but there are some anomalies."

She expected some form of reply, but all she saw were faces watching her. This didn't help her nervousness, and she began to tap her foot. Not loudly, just enough to help her continue. "The auditory stresses closely correspond to xenophobia."

W'Lowe jerked his head. "What!?"

"She said they're scared."

"Thanks, Dars," W'Lowe quipped, "I got that, but scared of what? Who? Are they scared that someone's in their section of the universe? Is it because—"

Haddox silenced him with a raised hand. "Go on, Æilen."

"It's hard to decipher what they fear, but the auditory stresses point to fear."

"With extermination, they threatened all of us." Scda flicked his insect-like head several times. "Sure not just anger?"

Æilen visibly relaxed as she lost herself in explaining her work. "I thought that at first, but the pieces locked into place when taking into account when the stresses occurred. They peaked at the references to helping remove Horwhannor."

Bewilderment caused people to shift their sights and gaze holes into inanimate objects as thoughts danced about.

"Okay," Jordan offered as he held up both hands as if to slow time, "let's just say this analysis is correct, how sure are you?"

"There's a ninety-three percent chance that my analysis is correct."

"You're that sure?"

"Yes." Æilen had all the confidence in her voice that she had hoped she had when she first spoke. "I'd even offer the possibility in a degree of catagelophobia."

"Of what?" Jordan asked.

"It's like a playground bully syndrome." Æilen snapped her beak. "From this fear they lash out."

"Great," Dars turned back to her console, "all we need to do is give them a big hug and all will be fine."

Jordan shook his head in disbelief.

"Not really," Æilen offered without taking offense. "But you might play on this fear."

That had Jordan's attention. "How?"

Æilen pointed a meaty arm at Pytin, who blinked rapidly behind pudgy cheeks. "Overwhelm them. If the idea of having us go into their territory scares them, then really scare them."

A smirk eased along Jordan's face. "Don't we keep coming back to suicide?"

"I'm sorry if I—"

"No need to apologize, Æilen. Your information is actually very valuable." Haddox turned back to the table. "We go in with whatever we can muster." He held a hand to pause all comments until he finished. "We'll ensure a swift defeat of Horwhannor, and just in case the p'tahians aren't too scared to keep their distance, we'll at least be prepared with as much as we can."

The silence spoke volumes of the contemplation.

Jordan tried to gauge the thoughts of his compatriots. He came back with worry. The lord took a deep breath. "Dars, what's the status of the Bafomet?"

Everyone shifted from Jordan to Dars and couldn't believe what they had heard. They became even more shocked when Dars replied.

"She's crewed and finishing preparations." Dars closed her eyes briefly. "We can have the Bafomet underway in two days."

"You—" W'Lowe stopped himself and began pointing back and forth between Haddox and Dars, "both of you, have been planning this?"

Haddox flashed his palms up. "It's not what you think. Dars had nothing to do with this other than following my orders, and I wanted the Bafomet ready the moment I heard about Horwhannor's location."

"People haven't forgotten," Pytin injected. Being a rolbrid he directly knew the fear that would return if news of Bafomet's existence got out. "Sure, this is dire, but is it that bad to uncover that ship?"

"Yes. Unfortunately, yes." Haddox turned, met Pytin's eyes and held the grand master's attention for a moment. "I wish we didn't have to do it now, but our hand has been forced. We can't let this opportunity pass; there's only one way to be sure. And Cobra Five justifies it."

Pytin just closed his eyes and shook his head. He knew of what the lord spoke, and it scared him further.

"Trust me," Haddox said as he returned to the gathering at the table, "I wish it didn't have to come to this so soon. But it is time to move the Sangraal."

The deluge of shocked retorts and gasps prompted Haddox to raising a hand to silence the noise, which tapered slowly.

Finally, amid the quiet, Pytin injected, "It is at peace; shouldn't we leave it alone? To disturb the Sangraal is to invite death. Nothing moves the Sangraal without its will."

"True." Haddox closed his eyes and breathed deeply. "Very true, but we must ask. Aboard the Bafomet, the Sangraal will be as safe as we can guarantee. Hopefully, it will see that we do not disturb it unnecessarily."

Pytin grabbed his tea and lifted it into the air as if to toast. "I only hope you know what you're doing." He slammed the drink like a barroom champ.

"As do I," Haddox replied.

Chapter 14

A small TV set rested on top of a slightly larger tree stump in the middle of a moss-green field of soft grass. To one side, an old willow tree twisted mystically as it reached into the sky. In the middle, tiny eyes blinked rapidly as the fairy softly bounced while it floated and attentively watched the news.

The scene might have seemed rather odd, but on the far end of the field cringed a tense rolbrid face. Larin's complete attention was focused on the particle cannon in front of him and the displays on the instruments strewn about and plugged into the weapon.

Paloon shook his head at the juxtaposition of the two scenes as he came around the corner. "Mac, I need an eight by nine molecular fuel resister, the associated coupler and a blade wrench."

The fairy didn't even squeak as lights began to bounce around the grassy field. Paloon picked up the items with one hand and set down what looked like a large, thick dog collar with the other.

"Check this for stress fractures. I think the internal bearings are shot."

A few seconds passed with no answer. Though he couldn't see the tiny screen well, Paloon could hear the audio. It sounded like multiple news broadcasts rapidly switching from one to the next. The hunter leaned forward to get the fairy's attention.

"Well?"

"Yeah," came a quick, high-pitched reply from the fairy, whose black eyes never left the TV.

Paloon backed away and shook his head again before returning to his repair work in the garage.

Mac freely admitted he liked watching TV. Something in his emotion chips allowed him pleasure when doing so. His creator didn't recall installing this element, but that happens with artificial intelligence: When it works, it works in unexpected ways.

This time though, pleasure didn't keep Mac glued to the tube. Something seemed very, *very* unusual. Before Mac could help it, enjoyment took a back seat to curiosity. He now flipped from one news broadcast to the next, then to the next while recording them all for complete review later. A slight thought sent a sub-processor on a search of all online publications for similar events. He needed as much information as possible.

After a few minutes, the story on the subject was over, and the broadcasts moved on to weather. Mac took advantage of the pause to rewind all the recordings and watch them completely, one at a time. Then small newspapers popped into existence in front of the fairy. Mac scanned the online stories, paying particular attention to the photos.

Sifting through about a dozen stories left Mac with nothing else to review. The rapid beat of the fairy's wings died to a slight flutter as Mac descended to rest on a hollow tree trunk lying on the field. With as much of a look of determined concentration as could be mustered on the cute face of a fairy, Mac crossed thin legs, planted an elbow on his miniature knee and dug a dainty chin into a tiny fist. Even with eyebrows that floated, the fairy scowled.

Perhaps a minute had passed when, quite literally, a light bulb appeared above the fairy's small head. With a cheerful smile, the fairy dropped the tense pose and yanked the chain hanging from the light bulb to turn it on. As soon as it lit, it disappeared in a puff of smoke.

In a blink, the fairy darted up and flew all over the table, squeaking at the top of its voice in an attempt to get Larin's attention.

The rolbrid didn't care. His work, hence his hobby, kept him focused on the weapon in front of him. For days he had been working on the modifications and getting the right kind of equipment engineered the right way to fit within the weapon's existing housing.

This didn't keep the fairy from trying. Then it paused in mid-flight, glared at Larin, put its hands on its waist and huffed a squeaky huff. Quickly the fairy melted into a much larger razor-backed gorilla.

Mac reared back on his hind legs, pounded his massive chest and roared loud enough to send bits of holographic saliva flying across the table. But repeated exposure to such antics had left Larin so numb that they often had no effect.

With considerable agitation, Mac snarled at the oblivious rolbrid before growing into an even larger Tyrannosaurus rex. At full roar, the long-dead dinosaur pounded its massive feet, turning the bright-green grass into muddy puddles and uprooting the once peaceful tree.

Larin barely registered that the holographic ground under his instruments was fluctuating rapidly. He was too close to completion to care.

"Damn it, Mac," bellowed Paloon as he stormed out of the tunnel into the room. "Kill the noise before you wake somebody's dead ancestors."

"I'm sorry," the once fearsome dinosaur pouted. "I was just trying to get Larin's attention."

"Larin, can't you at least answer the...the...Mac?"

Nothing.

Paloon didn't care for being ignored either. In his mounting frustration, he noticed a thin black cable running down Larin's cheek. Paloon approached the rolbrid, grabbed the cable and pulled an abnormally long rod straight from one of Larin's ears. High-pitched screeches and tinny drums blared from the tip.

"Hey," growled Larin, upset at losing his concentration, "I was listing to—" The rolbrid noticed the four-foot creature standing on the table and spied it with an arched brow. "What in the frap are you supposed to be?"

The beast puffed its chest and smirked with pride. "I'm a Tyrannosaurus rex."

"And what is that?"

"A terrible, carnivorous creature," Mac answered, the smile melting away to finish the answer, "which is now extinct."

"That's funny," Larin said with a shrug, "you look more like the cattle the ber used to raise."

"Sorry to interrupt the edification," Paloon interrupted, "but this schizoid has been making a heck of a racket. Please just entertain him so I can get some peace." The hunter turned and started to return before Mac stopped him.

"Actually, what I have found may interest you, too."

Paloon internally debated just ignoring the computer, but something more than curiosity had grabbed his attention. Mac had offered something new that might pique his interests. The sitting and waiting grew tiresome. So he put his hands in his pockets and turned to quietly face the dinosaur.

Mac motioned them closer to the table with comically tiny arms. With a deep thud, the dinosaur pounded a massive foot into the holographic ground to force the small TV to bounce into the air and expand to a much larger image so all could see.

A forty-something man with a tired face and a well-trained but forced smile routinely greeted all viewers of the station's ten o'clock news. With a shift in cameras, his expression also changed to imply sorrow that came despite being numbed by years of reporting on such topics.

"Our city may have earned the number one spot in the country for murders today when more than five hundred people died in suspicious events. The near simultaneous accidents ranged from explosions and fires to shootings and violent car crashes. Our Nicole O'Connor has the story live from City Hall, where the chief of police recently gave a press conference to discuss these events."

The screen switched to the face of a black woman who looked young enough to be in college. Her name appeared along the bottom of the screen with the word "Live" stamped in the upper left.

"That's right, Patrick. Estimates are that more than five hundred are dead as a result of several strange events around our city today. Police Chief Harold Buckmire held a press conference here a few hours ago and agreed that the events of the day are strange enough that they merit being treated as murders."

Staying with the report for a few moments, the video then changed to an image of a tall man with tightly cropped salt and pepper hair and wide shoulders. Four stars lined both sides of his uniform's collar. "These events are very unusual, so we have not ruled out homicide."

The police chief continued to talk, but the reporter's voice replaced the audio. "The police chief also confirmed that most of the events seemed to involve employees and CEOs of Imondi Industries and its subsidiaries throughout the city."

The video shifted again, and the police chief's voice returned. "It's too early to tell if these events are related or part of a conspiracy—" Though obviously not finished with his sentence, the police chief disappeared again to be replaced by the reporter.

"The events the police chief is referring to—"

"Mac," Paloon injected, "this is all interesting, but just save Larin and I the pain of deciphering all this and tell us what it is you find so darn exciting."

"Agreed," Larin added. "So a bunch of locals saw the afterworld. What's the point?"

Mac turned and raised a tiny finger. "It's how they died." The dinosaur turned back and changed the video to some footage from a news helicopter of an industrial plant on fire. "This is one of the events. City Paper Products, a mill and press, caught fire. Few escaped. When the fire department arrived, everything they attempted only encouraged the fire to spread. Even fire retardant foam proved useless."

Mac spun around expecting either of the onlookers to catch on; they didn't. "The fire retardant foam actually caught fire."

"Well, that's different," Larin said with a jerk. "What could do something like that?"

Paloon looked worried but offered the only thing he knew. "Bromek."

"Exactly," Mac said with a smile.

"What?" Larin asked.

Mac responded. "Bromekenos-methalite. It's a restricted chemical."

"It's now illegal for combat use." Paloon shook a finger at the screen and faced Larin. "It had uses for everything from a serious defoliant to destroying cities. You place this stuff when you want to make sure your target burns. The chemical compound doesn't require air to breathe and can darn near catch anything on fire. The only way to stop a bromek fire is to let it run out of bromek to burn."

"Frap man." Larin shuttered. As a ground forces guy, the thought of facing something like that rather scared him. "That's some wicked stuff."

"Hence it being outlawed for combat," Paloon offered, "so why is it here?"

"It gets better." Mac changed the screen to show another piece of news footage, this time of a very large house resembling a small castle. "This is apparently the home of Francisco Imondi, the owner and CEO of Imondi Industries."

"The one mentioned in the other news broadcast?" Larin asked.

"The same." Mac paused the footage. "Apparently they found Vanessa Imondi in the drawing room sans a head."

Larin squinted. "What?"

Mac pointed a finger at his neck, which was as far as the little arm would reach, and drew and invisible line. "Chkkkkkk."

"Dang." Larin jerked and looked at Paloon for a bit.

"But look at this." Mac stared at the screen as it appeared to shift slowly frame by frame as the computer looked for it again. "I almost missed this. The camera man is lucky he got it, but he probably doesn't—there it is." Mac pointed as the screen zoomed.

A normal looking window filled the frame, at least it seemed normal except for a strange, multi-colored distortion in the glass. Two rainbow-like rings, one smaller and inside the other, connected to one another with thin lines that ran from a point in the center.

"A freq cannon."

Paloon looked at Larin, who identified the marks, but the hunter wanted more. "Now it's your turn to explain."

"That's the same kind of molecular signature pattern left by a hyper-kinetic frequency rifle." Larin pointed a thumb at the weapon's lockers and met Paloon's eyes. "Kind of like the weapon I used to pop the head off that beast that attacked Ky back at the warehouse."

"My thought exactly," Mac added and jerked his massive head at the screen, which changed again.

Resting amidst a multitude of emergency response vehicles sat a solid ball in a massive crater. From the view of the news helicopter and size of nearby buildings, the grey, brown, gold and red speckled ball must be a hundred feet in diameter, maybe more.

Mac didn't need prodding this time. "This is what's left of the Clover Casino and Hotel, also owned by Imondi Industries."

Larin huffed. "A vortex inversion bomb."

"It must be," Mac responded. "It's the only way I can explain this result. This all being said, it's obvious that whoever is moving these illegal weapons onto the planet is now using them without reservation."

Paloon took a seat. Worry covered his face. "Did we cause this? I mean, did our actions cause Horwhannor to accelerate his plans."

"There's no telling." Mac faced the two, lowered himself and rested back on his long, thick tail. "It's all speculation at this point, but there's one thing I can be certain of: The more such weapon discharges continue, the more likely the p'tahians will detect the signals."

"Ain't that just frapping great?" Larin fell back in his seat and crossed his arms. "I'd like to get out of the Corps and start a family...someday."

"What about arrests?" Paloon wanted to grasp at anything. "Didn't they find anybody?"

With a flick, Mac pointed a talon-tipped finger at the atlantian. "Perfect question. Two, actually. They found them loitering around the paper mill after the fire. Apparently their actions were suspicious enough to attract the attention of one of the firefighters who pointed it out to a police officer. When the officer began to question them, they ran. The resulting chase ended with a nasty accident into the broadside of a city bus, but they both lived, virtually without a scratch," Mac's voice tapered, "oddly enough."

"Where are they?" Paloon questioned.

"In the safe confines of the city jail." Mac rocked a bit on his tail and twiddled his thumbs. "But a little over an hour ago, the police chief and the mayor made a special request to a senior federal judge to put the two in prison for better security while holding until trial."

"Was it approved?"

"Yes."

"Well," Paloon really didn't like dealing with a computer that didn't easily offer information, "when's the transfer?"

"Tomorrow morning at zero six hundred."

A mischievous grin slipped along Larin's face. When the rolbrid looked to Paloon, he saw a similar smile. "Thinking what I'm thinking?"

The atlantian nodded. "I think so. I think these two might be the closest link we have so far. I say we jack them in transit and find out what they know."

"The sooner the better," Larin agreed.

"Where's Lyon?" Paloon watched the Tyrannosaurus rex tilt its large cranium as if listening through the floors of the building.

"Sounds like he's taking a shower."

"Well, tell him to get his butt down here because we've got a lead."

Chapter 15

Orange light had barely begun to seep from the horizon and spread across the sky as mild traffic slipped around the city square. Scattered about the square building's two floors were various governmental offices and courtrooms. The structure hid a secret from the unaware: Those prosecuted in the courtrooms above didn't have far to go.

In the thick-walled basement, the city's entire confinement facility boasted a record of no escapes. The sole entrance came as an enclosed concrete ramp leading from the parking lot down to a triple-gated entry.

This entry topped the list of priorities for the pair of eyes about a block uphill from the courthouse.

It had been more than twenty minutes since Mac reported that the transfer was under way.

"Mac, are you sure?" Paloon wondered if they had missed it or been noticed. *"This place is still dead."*

"I checked it twice," returned the computer. *"It was coded, but the codes triple check with every reference I can find. The dispatch ordered the transfer to begin about twenty-two minutes and forty-three seconds ago."*

"I hope you're right," Paloon answered.

"That overly emotional crystal better not have screwed this up," Larin firmly stated from the passenger seat. He crunched on a chur root to keep his stomach settled.

"What, are you afraid we're wasting our time?" Paloon had contempt for the rolbrid's impatience. "Do you have something better to do?"

"I might." Larin tightened his jaw. "But that's not the point; the more I think of this assignment, the more I want off this rock."

Paloon couldn't argue and for a moment understood Larin's frustration. Not much would change it now, though. Fate brought them here, and only Fate would let them leave.

A car approaching from the rear slightly startled Paloon, who had been trying to watch for any possible counter-surveillance. The hunter casually watched the occupants as the vehicle passed the parked tank/station wagon. By the time they had turned at the intersection, Paloon deemed them harmless.

"Blessed frapping crap!" Larin bellowed hard enough to send his chur root flying against the windshield.

"Damn, Larin, what's your problem?" barked Paloon. "I'm not deaf."

"Did you see that?" The rolbrid's glass-crashing voice hadn't dropped much in volume.

"See what, banshee?"

Larin snatched the wet chur root from the dashboard and jabbed it against the windshield, pointing toward the intersection. "That pathetic excuse for a civic-minded and responsible citizen doesn't even have the frapping common sense to give—"

"Knock it off!" Paloon's order came as he started the vehicle and jerked a chin at the courthouse. "We have action."

The rolbrid paused long enough to see two patrol cars flanking a large, dark blue patrol wagon that pulled to the front of the courthouse. It jumped the curb onto the sidewalk, quickly turned and backed down the ramp to the jail entrance. Speed definitely seemed to be of importance in this operation. That worked for Paloon and Larin.

Only a few moments seemed to pass before the patrol wagon drove away from the courthouse.

As Paloon pulled from the curb, Larin popped the chur root back in his mouth and began rechecking his gear.

Bright orange overalls glowed from around the bulletproof vests forced upon them for their protection. The thick, iron jewelry binding their wrists and ankles clanked with each bump in the road as chains skittered about the metal flooring.

Both of their asses had already started to grow numb. Their underwear offered more cushion than the cheap prisoner uniforms as they bounced on the flat, steel bench. Granted, comfort might be a bit much to ask for, but the driver seemed to be aiming for every pothole on the street.

Two police officers, covered in matching vests and armed with taser-tipped batons, snickered at the sight from their padded, fold-down jump seats.

Takahiro and Takehiko quietly looked at one another, then back to the floor. The two yakuza soldiers hadn't said a single word to each other or anyone else other than the lawyer who had been waiting for them at the police station. They didn't need the lawyer to tell them not to say anything; it came with the job as an understood commandment. No one made it very far without fully grasping such basic principles.

A muffled explosion and squealing tires made them jerk their heads up. The cops heard it too and had no idea what caused the noise. Another muffled explosion came from behind the police wagon. Gunshots followed by deep thuds could be heard clearly, but the noise quickly faded as the truck's diesel engine gained speed.

The guarding officers didn't need it, but the driver pounded against the other side of the cab to signal trouble, startling Takahiro and Takehiko.

Hitting the next bump at the accelerating speed sent the yakuza soldiers completely into the air and back down, and they almost missed the bench. Both grimaced as they watched the two cops drop the batons and reach into hidden compartments to withdraw automatic shotguns.

Another explosion sounded from under the vehicle, and the resulting flapping of rubber grew loud in the interior as the tires shredded. The wagon began to fishtail just as the other pair of rear tires exploded. Then the vehicle straightened.

In rapid succession, twin explosions, probably the front tires, sent the truck into a hard jerk as metal began to bite into the asphalt. Everyone could feel the slow grind to a halt, even as the driver floored the accelerator. The massive engine roared throughout the losing battle.

Finally coming to a stop, all the occupants allowed themselves to breathe again. More tire squeals and gunshots sounded from multiple directions, near and far. Then came the same dull thud sounds from earlier.

As quickly as it began, everything went silent.

Sweat formed on the faces of the police officers like cheesecloth sprayed with a water hose. Slowly, they nodded at one another, stood, took opposite sides of the trailer's interior and leveled the shotguns at the rear door. Stains had begun growing on the sleeves of their beige shirts.

Seconds stretched to eons. Silent, still time had that effect.

The two yakuza remained quiet, but both knew it had to be a rescue. Neither expected it, but there was no other explanation. Pride began to well inside them. Maybe, just maybe, they had earned more respect after yesterday's job.

Something jerked the grounded patrol wagon as the sound of sizzling came from near the door. The sudden noise caused both cops to jerk; one almost reacted strongly enough to fire. He caught himself in time to ease off the trigger.

In two seconds the sizzling stopped. Pinging metal painted the aural picture of something falling and bouncing along the road before coming to a stop. Then the sizzling resumed, stopped and sent something to the ground. Again. Again.

Lakes of sweat in the palms of the police officers made it increasingly difficult for them to keep firm grips on their weapons as they stared at the door, waiting for anything to happen.

In a flash, the doors flew off and a combined five rounds of double-ought buckshot screamed through the opening into nothing.

Adrenaline raced through the cops as their hearts pounded in their throats. Senses piqued, they scanned everything they could see, then did so again, waiting for even the smallest piece of trash to move. All the while, neither noticed the small barrel poking into the vehicle from the bottom corner.

Electronically scanning the scene from the weapon's camera, Larin planned, then lined his shots. Almost simultaneously, two shots flew from the pistol as if from a high-powered air rifle.

The resulting force and shock knocked the cops back a step. Each had enough time to look down at the hole in their bulletproof vests and feel the burning in their chests before collapsing into a mound.

Larin clamped both hands onto the floor and jerked himself from under the patrol wagon. He bounced as he landed with a smile. Job satisfaction did help his morale.

With no assistance, the rolbrid hopped into the opening and nodded at the two wide-eyed yakuza. "Great weapon," he said as he held out the pistol that appeared to have two tandem grips. Larin placed it in a sheath along his chest. "But it's just not meant for beings with hairy arms. Those air intake vents will strip your arm bare."

Takahiro and Takehiko, in unison, jerked their eyesight from the two crumpled cops and this unknown person with an odd voice.

"Don't worry about them." Larin patted the pistol. "While this does make for one frapping great assassination weapon with acid shells and the like, this one is only loaded with an extra-strength tranquilizer I mixed together. They're just going to take a little nap."

For the first time since being caught, Takahiro broke his silence. "Who are you?"

"I'm not your savior, if that's what you're asking."

Neither handled the answer very well as they watched the short man withdraw another weapon and point it at them.

Larin smiled. "Good night."

A static-throwing yellow ball came at them too fast for them to react. Everything detonated in bright light then buckled into pitch black.

"What's your name!?" Lyon yelled, safely in the soundproof room.

Blood danced with sweat along Takahiro's face. Day-old road kill looked better than the yakuza solider. He had lost track of time. Hours, maybe days, had passed. Takehiko slumped in the chair against the far wall. He didn't look any better.

"Are you deaf!?" Lyon shoved his anger-filled face within an inch of Takahiro's nose. "What's your name?"

Takahiro cringed when his assailant didn't wait for an answer. Instead, Lyon held out a small black box with a large red button. He pushed the button.

Pain ripped through Takahiro. His body jerked as if being pushed out of the seat, but the ankle and arm restraints held, allowing him to fall back into the chair when he finally fell unconscious again.

Other than being a prop, the box did nothing. Hitook controlled their reactions and injected thoughts while sitting outside the room. The liqua shifted subjects as Lyon turned to face Takehiko just in time for him to once again return to a world of horror.

"What's your name!?" bellowed Lyon.

Takehiko couldn't explain how he had lasted this long. He continued to say nothing but feared that he felt himself losing control.

Lyon pounded a foot into the chair, which slammed loudly against the wall. "What's your name!?" The box appeared again, and Takehiko flayed about in his restraints before dropping back into the chair.

"Next, Mac," Lyon ordered.

Flickering lights created a small table a bit off center of the room. Blood-crusted surgical implements gleamed from its surface. Spent cigarettes mounded a dirty, green-glazed ceramic ashtray. Smoke began to form a thick cloud that reached for the ceiling.

Paloon stepped into the room as Lyon stood in the background but within view. Completely in character, Paloon let his cigarette hang precariously from his lips. He knelt down and lifted Takahiro's head and promptly slapped him. It was just enough to wake the victim from the timeless void.

"Stay with me, sweetness." Paloon grinned and reached for a scalpel, holding it a moment to allow another wave of fear to take Takahiro. The emotion mounted as the blade crept toward his right eye.

"You're wasting your time," came the gruffest voice Lyon could muster. "This scum isn't worth the time; kill him."

"Nah. Our friend, Takahiro here, has already told us who he's working for." Paloon sneered.

For all Takahiro knew, he had broken and begun to tell them such things. Remembering it brought tears to his eyes. He had no way of knowing those fake memories came courtesy of an extraterrestrial sitting cross-legged outside the room.

Paloon's face melted and became like an ugly stone gargoyle. "Where's the shipment coming from, Takahiro?"

The yakuza uncontrollably screamed madly in pain as he envisioned a simulated reality of the scalpel digging into his lower eyelid. In a second, his world went black.

With a flick, the unused scalpel clanked haphazardly on the table of instruments. A blood-soaked patch of gauze materialized around Takahiro's eye, sealed tightly by dirty surgical tape.

The two swapped locations. Lyon picked up a piece of bloody cloth from the table as Paloon went to the next victim, grabbed his hair and pulled his head to one side and down. Takehiko returned to consciousness just in time to see one angry looking face in his.

"I've about had it, Takehiko! You're pissing me off." Paloon paused and breathed forcefully out his nose spraying Takehiko's face with bits of mucus. "Save us both the pain, and tell me where did you get the fucking weapons!?"

"Are you sure you're not over doing it?" came Lyon's voice.

Paloon turned, as he did he tilted Takehiko's head so the prisoner could also see. Across the room, Takehiko saw his companion obviously bleeding from the eye. Lyon sat on a stool nearby pretending to tend to the wound by soaking up the blood with the rag in his hand.

"He's losing a lot of blood," Lyon commented.

"Trust me, he'll live. Barely, but he'll live." Paloon's methodical voice dropped as the anger resumed. "But I'm not so sure about this sorry soul."

"Why are you doing this?" Takehiko's voice squealed at peaks.

"None of your fucking business! I ask the questions!" Paloon dropped Takehiko's head and reached for a sledgehammer leaning against the wall. As if prepping to tee-off for a three-hundred yard drive, Paloon lined the hammer to Takehiko's right leg. "Last chance, where'd you get the weapons!?"

"I—I can't tell you—"

Takehiko couldn't help but stop himself at the sight of Paloon pulling the hammer back. Rage twisted Paloon's face as Takehiko closed his eyes so tightly that his entire body shook in tensed anticipation.

A whiff of wind and Takehiko felt his leg explode. Imaginary splinters of bone shredded his leg muscles as he screamed uncontrollably. In the distance he heard the voice of the other interrogator scream, "Shit, man!" before his world went black from the pain.

Skittering scratches echoed in the room as Paloon tossed the sledgehammer against the far wall and calmly walked out of the room. The matter replicators in the dark recesses of the room's corners went to work.

Broken planks of wood and strips of blood-soaked, dingy white cloth formed around Takehiko's intact leg. On the table, a grey, metal case formed as the smoke in the room turned into a mist of sorts, like a jungle's early morning fog. Even the light in room changed to appear as if it were passing through gapped slats of wood, creating shafts of glowing mist in long streaks.

Larin entered the room, opened the new case on the table and lifted from it a compact pneumatic immunization gun. Lyon sat down on the stool next to Takahiro as Larin flanked. Fake hissing sounds whistled into the room as Larin placed the non-functioning device against Takahiro's arm.

Simulated pain from the injected drugs shocked Takahiro awake. He struggled through a foggy mesh of grogginess but limitations unknowingly placed on him by Hitook kept him from using all his faculties to come to full consciousness.

Blurred visions slowly registered with him. The same short guy who sprung them from the police van stood at a table and played with bottles of clear liquid. Fighting to process a clear thought, Takahiro finally linked the vision with a pain in his arm. They had drugged him or something. Then this person approached Takehiko.

Takahiro gradually took in the scene. His brother now had a broken leg. The metallic stench of blood filled his nostrils, then Takahiro could smell it from himself as well. It wasn't until then that it registered he could only see from one eye. The memories returned.

Weeks, it must have been weeks. So little energy remained in him. Seeing Takehiko in such a state and knowing all he had endured just made him want to crack.

Hissing echoed again in the room as Takahiro knew it came from the air pushing whatever foul drugs they had through Takehiko's skin.

"What are you doing to him...me?" Words dripped from Takahiro's lips as if he had a mouth full of tranquilizers.

Larin ignored the comment, but another voice came from his right side.

"It's just to help him stay alive."

Takahiro flopped his head around to see the too familiar face of one of the interrogators who was sitting in the blind spot created when he lost his right eye.

"Leave him alone," Takahiro wheezed sleepily.

"Now, why should I do that?" Lyon's tired voice maintained a degree of patience. "So far, neither of you have been very helpful. That makes some of us rather mad. But we have all the time in the world. This little cocktail you're both getting will help keep you alive. Granted, it must hurt, but you'll stay alive, for now."

"But...," Takahiro's voice trailed as he fought internally, the struggle evident in the twitch of his left eye, "but he knows nothing. Leave him alone."

"That could be arranged, but this implies that you do know." Lyon crossed his arms and shifted on his stool.

Deep within himself, Takahiro began to lose the battle.

Frantic best described how the day had gone. Howard was just relieved that his shift would be over in a couple of hours. Even after the stage three alert and a complete lockdown of the facilities, the warden continued to ping and make everyone's job hell.

Sending the high-threat response teams for a building-by-building, room-by-room search didn't bother Howard, but locking down the communications, shutting off the phone and sealing the computer connections seemed to be pushing it. Not just his wife but every officer's family probably sat at home worrying themselves into collective ulcers. Those darn klaxons could be heard two miles away.

Now, he just waited and attentively watched the banks of monitors assigned to him. Then he noticed something. He swore it hadn't been there during the camera's last pass. Howard jerked forward, pushed a few buttons to take control of the camera, grabbed the tiny black joystick and moved it back. He squinted as he fondled the control board until he found, by touch, the zoom controls.

"What'cha got?" The voice came from Kyle, his partner on the other bank of monitors. He rolled over in his chair and came alongside Howard.

"I don't know." Howard finished zooming as far as the camera would allow. "Number thirty-three. Is that what I think it is?"

"Shit, man." Kyle couldn't believe it, either. "That looks like two people."

Howard grabbed the microphone that sprouted from the tabletop like a metal flower and jabbed his finger on the talk button. "Dispatch, Security Control."

"Dispatch, here." The words came from black speakers that merged with the control panel.

"We show two people on the far southeast corner."

"How'd they get that close to the fence?"

"They're not outside; they're inside the fence, in the south yard. Get somebody out there."

"Impossible. It's a lockdown. Everybody's accounted for."

"I'm happy for your counting abilities, but I'm telling you, there are two people in the south yard."

Howard didn't know how to take the silence; he might have pissed off the wrong person again. But the voice that returned seemed calm.

"What are they doing?"

Howard looked again to make sure. "Nothing. They're just sitting there."

Sitting seemed the best thing to do. Dazed and confused, neither knew what else to do. Neither knew how they had gotten there or what had just happened. Was it a dream? A nightmare? So little made sense as they grasped for the intangible strands of reality. Both remained oblivious to the rapidly approaching squad of officers running across the yard.

The squad stopped, its members staring at two men, bound in duct tape, who sat back to back on the asphalt ground. Blank faces gazed with wide eyes and open mouths. Other than possibly suffering from mild shock, they appeared intact and healthy, no broken bones or missing eyes.

Such an unexpected and calm scene sent the officers reeling for a bit. The senior officer stepped forward, knelt down, grabbed one of their heads like a basketball and rolled it up to look at the face.

He jerked back in disbelief then scuttled over to the other face to make absolutely sure. After the identities were confirmed, he gradually stood, wondering how it could be possible. He'd seen the reports. Heck, it was just this morning, so he knew these faces. These were the same two suspected yakuza who disappeared when the transfer convoy came under attack less than twelve hours ago.

Slowly he reached and keyed the CB mic clipped on his left epaulet. "Dispatch, you are not going to believe this."

Chapter 16

The satisfaction of a job well done kept both quiet. Call it ego, but they felt proud at sneaking those yakuza soldiers into the prison where they were originally headed before being kidnapped. Maybe "kidnapping" was a bit too strong; after all, they had only borrowed the suspects for a few hours.

Trying to request a local judge for a delay in their transfer so an intergalactic police agency could ask a few questions might have presented some difficulties. Destroying a few native patrol cars and incapacitating a small army of police officers was the only alternative. Doing so efficiently and undetected just boosted the morale of the vehicle's occupants.

Paloon and Larin sat silently as they had for many miles while the alien-disguised tank zipped along the remote highway. Yet the stillness inside the vehicle didn't mirror the thoughts inside their minds. Together, they had assisted in the rapid interrogation of the two suspects. Now they sat proudly but puzzled by what they had learned.

"Why?" Paloon let slip.

"Why not?" Larin calmly answered.

"Because I want to leave the Corps someday, preferably intact and alive." Paloon engaged the autopilot and leaned back in his bucket seat as the steering column retracted into the dashboard. "Heck, I've been through tough missions before, but I always wanted to get out before I finally took one too many missions. Training seemed to be the best way for me to finish my career and retire, possibly get married again. I know this sounds strange, but I miss it. It gets lonely at times, not physically, just...emotionally."

Larin dropped his brow and firmly gazed at nothing before slowly turning his head toward Paloon. The rolbrid wondered for a moment if the atlantian next to him bordered on being psychotic. Normally Larin was the one to rant about how much this mission sucked. Paloon didn't notice Larin's look and continued, arms folded.

"There's a lot more to life than this. Sure, there's purpose, but what of fulfillment? There's a life out there, one that's free and relaxing."

Larin rolled his tongue along his bottom lip for moment. "Someone's got to protect and ensure those freedoms."

"True." Paloon threw out a hand and shook it briefly in the air. "But forgoing your freedoms to protect the freedoms of others, even if it is for the greater good and all that, is taxing."

Larin half snorted in agreement and shook his head as the rolbrid looked at the traffic from the passenger window.

"I'm stuck." Paloon retracted his hand and jammed a half-opened fist onto his chin and cheek. His voice sounded strange due to the odd placement of his hand. "This doesn't make sense. Either they know and think they know more or they don't know and don't have the sense to realize they're being played. How could this have gone on for as long as it has?"

Paloon didn't want an answer, but Larin replied. "This isn't the first time locals have left me wondering. They refuse to see the larger scope, too self-centered."

"But what of the—" Paloon's train of thought jumped tracks. "That's what irritates me. We're stuck here while they do everything they can to get the attention of the neighborhood executioner."

"It sucks, but that's just how the frap it goes sometimes." Larin started getting annoyed and wondered how many direct combat missions this vacuum head had really been on. Or did all of them sit, detached from battle, on their space vessels.

Traffic increased as they neared the outskirts of the city. Paloon snapped a finger randomly at a vehicle. "They're ignorant, ungrateful and self-destructive."

Larin popped his neck as he turned to Paloon. "I think your problem is just that you don't like the idea that Lyon may be right and this planet is your race's so-called home world. That thought seems to have you all bent out of shape."

Paloon fired at Larin the ugliest look he could muster. "That's not it."

Larin couldn't believe the atlantian had just proved himself wrong. "Whatever."

"It's just that...they just don't...ah, screw it." Paloon went back to folding his arms.

"Exactly." Larin lightly shook his head as he found himself on the opposite side of defending the mission. "This is how I see it. We do whatever we can to get off this rock alive. We either act or die. That's just the way of the battle. It has always been that way, always will be. The passive will always die in the end. But do you want to die sitting on your ass or doing something about it? That choice is yours—and yours alone."

Larin never fancied himself as a motivational speaker. He never had the refined talent or the eloquent language to get squads of troops all charged for battle. Yet they both sat still. Paloon chewed on the words and wrestled his demons as Larin tried to calm his anger.

The rolbrid twisted his lips about and poked holes in the windshield with his eyes. A thick finger began probing his vest as he fished for a chur root.

"Ah, frapping hell!" Larin barked as one hand pounded on the button to lower his window and the other snatched a particle cannon from its door holster. Matter blurred as he whipped the weapon out the window and blasted a thick bolt across an intersection and into the rear corner of a vehicle.

Red, yellow and white splinters of plastic exploded, accompanying the sound of strips of metal tearing free and squealing tires. The cannon's impact slammed the car with more force than the car could generate, making the inadequate tires lose traction. Cars in the opposite lane had nowhere to go as the injured vehicle sailed at them sideways. Dull pops sounded as white fluffs appeared in each of the vehicles.

Paloon flew into action, snatching the weapon from Larin's slowly retracting hand. "What in the hell are you doing!?"

Larin temporarily forgave Paloon for disarming him as he jerked a finger back out the window while their car slowly proceeded through the intersection. "It's their law, so if that punk can't use a turn signal, he doesn't deserve to have a turn signal."

Shock jolted Paloon's face until he closed his eyes. "What in the world were you thinking?"

Larin poked his head out the window and back at the scene before yelling, "Use a signal next time, you frapping fuck!"

Long shadows streaked upward along the collection of faces as tints of green, red and purplish black played among the crevasses. Haunting, demonic eyes reflected the light as they methodically combed through the details below.

"Hey, guys!"

The concentrating trio jumped at the sudden outburst. Mac, currently represented by a disheveled beatnik complete with faded corduroy bell-bottom pants and a pea-green T-shirt, promptly squealed like a scared little girl.

Lyon turned to see Ky standing behind him. His eyes darted about as if seeking some kind of hint as to how she got behind him without making a sound. "Where'd you come from?"

"My mother's pouch, but if you don't believe me, ask my sister." Ky smiled and jerked her head at the table. "Is this what you wanted me here for?"

Lyon glanced back at the hologram of walls with Mac standing to his left and Hitook sitting to the right. He looked back. "Yeah, this is—" Ky was gone.

"Over here."

Mac yelped again as Lyon returned his view to the table to see Ky now at the far end sitting on the very top of the chair with her feet planted flat along the broad front side of its back. The position itself seemed to defy gravity, but it was how she moved so fast that confused Lyon the most. Hitook, on the other hand, remained unfazed through it all.

"Don't do that, man!" Mac clamped both hands on the side of his head, fingers dug into uncombed, dirty blond hair.

Lyon ignored the foot-and-a-half high image. "This," he said as he stood and pointed downward, "is our next target."

"Damn!"

The outburst from a new voice gave Mac an additional reason to stifle a squeal. The others just turned to the direction of the sound to see Oz emerging from his room.

It had been days. A couple members of the team doubted the terran would survive the ordeal. Now their mutating patient strolled from the room as if nothing had happened.

"Just when I think you've stopped making noise, you start again." Oz approached the table and glared at the image he believed to be Mac. "Can I get some water please?"

"Um, yeah, yeah, sure."

Upon the glass's appearance, Oz cupped it with both hands and gradually downed its contents.

Lyon stood and stared sideways at Oz, who obviously didn't take the attention too kindly.

"What!?"

"How do you feel?"

"Thirsty." Oz frowned a bit and planted the glass on the table. "And tired. Mac, may I have another, please?"

And pissy, Mac thought, but the computer obliged.

As the glass filled, Lyon continued to gaze into Oz's eyes and didn't find what he sought until after it had become uncomfortable.

"What's your problem?"

"Oh, nothing." Lyon returned to his seat. "You seem to have handled it well."

Oz stopped himself in mid-motion from saying something and just drank the water. His head seemed to pound in time with the xylophone of timbers in the floor above him that creaked as the building bucked in the mild wind.

"Was it necessary?" Oz asked as he placed the glass on the table and looked about for a seat.

Lyon aimed a hand to offer the seat next to Hitook. "Help yourself, but what are you talking about?"

"All that screaming." Oz fell into the seat and began stretching wildly with one arm up and the other down. His muscles felt as unyielding as the light post outside that someone just leaned against. "You kept those two guys in constant screaming fits, and I couldn't get sleep. And just when I think it's about to settle down again, this one," Oz's hard vision landed on Mac, "starts screaming like a little bitch."

Mac, with hands on hips, huffed as Ky just hummed at bit.

"Don't you remember the shots?" Quizzical surprise stretched Lyon's face. "You know, the ones that were supposed to change your DNA?"

Oz stopped yawning and retracted his hands. Suddenly he felt like climbing into the dark corner across the room to share the space with that brown recluse spider.

He remembered now. Gradually, he flipped his hands in front of his eyes for inspection. He didn't know what to expect, but he tried to be ready for anything while truly being ready for nothing.

"You're not going to see it there." Lyon's reassuring tone failed. "But it has begun."

Oz jerked toward Lyon. "Where!?"

Lyon tapped a finger near his temple. "It's in the eyes. The window is in the eyes."

"There's more." Ky hummed a bit more as she continued to stare as if looking past Oz.

Oz twitched toward her and finally took note of her odd position on the top of the chair. From his view he could see her tail forming a spine down the chair's back and holding tightly. He could only release a dull "Huh?"

"What do you mean?" Lyon added.

Ky's vision refocused. "There are some interesting changes in his spirit."

"Any problems?"

"No, nothing like that." Ky shook her head. "It's just unexpected. He could be latent, but I won't be able to tell until his spirit settles."

Lyon nodded and took a mental note, then continued to ignore Oz's discomfort as he shifted his gaze to Mac. "What about you?"

"Um," Mac stumbled as his head flipped between Lyon and Oz, "um, yeah, uh, he's clean for the most part. I've been monitoring him, and it's been working for the most part. The few pieces the nites couldn't reuse have been sealed off in protective cocoons."

Fear and confusion torqued Oz's brows and widened his eyes. "What does that mean?"

"That," Lyon rapped a finger on his skull, "means don't get banged in the head too hard or you might break open one of those chemical bombs in your head."

This time, Oz yelped.

"Don't worry," Mac attempted to calm the panic. "It's more likely that you would shatter your skull before you take on enough force to crack one of these cocoons."

Oz squirmed. "Is that supposed to help?"

Hitook just shrugged as if to sum the consensus of thought: *That's Mac for you.*

Leaving Oz to wallow in worry, Lyon, Hitook and Mac returned to the hologram. Lyon pointed to one end of the building and told Ky, "This is the target."

"The whole building?" To Ky it seemed like a big place to sweep for such a small team.

"Nope, just this end, mostly." Lyon swept a hand in circles. "The whole place looks abandoned, but according to our friends and some quick reconnaissance, it appears their operations are focused in this area. This side access and road," Lyon traced them with his fingers, "could allow them to move in and out without anybody noticing, and the neighboring construction supply yard helps mask the traffic."

Ignoring the subtle sounds of a vehicle pulling into the garage across the street, Oz found himself sucked into whatever was taking place. The large building seemed to have two or more floors; he couldn't be completely sure since the structure lacked a roof. The area Lyon pointed at missed more than that, all the way down to the basement. Overall, the realistic hologram actually appeared to be pieced together with tiny bricks and plastered walls.

Something about this building seemed hauntingly familiar to Oz.

Nothing particularly jumped out as notable, but many little things stood out, such as the concrete window frames, the gravel covered yard and the monkey bars. "It's a school," Oz blurted.

"Was," Lyon corrected. "It's boarded up now. From what Mac found, the city finally condemned the place about two years ago. They've shifted the students elsewhere, but they haven't pushed the issue about getting the funds to tear it down, something about a substance called 'asbestos' and the expense to remove it."

Hydraulic hisses ended as footsteps sounded, and Paloon and Larin made their way through the tunnel into the room. Almost before rounding the corner, Larin's hand flew up, exhibiting a pistol aimed at Oz's head.

"Damn, man. Put that away." Lyon didn't know his command wasn't needed because Hitook was mentally prepared to counter any fired shot. "Are you always that twitchy?"

"Yes." The answer came from Paloon. "Tell him what you did."

Larin just quietly put his pistol away.

"What?" Lyon demanded.

"I only corrected a lawbreaker."

Taking a seat, Paloon detailed the description. "He shot the taillights out of a car that failed to signal."

Mild surprise plunged the room into silence for a second.

Ky chuckled. "Now that's funny."

Lyon held his forehead in one hand and sighed. "He doesn't need encouragement."

Ky continued to laugh mildly, letting her head bounce. "But that's still funny."

"Are you all this crazy?" Oz worried loudly.

"Hey," Larin challenged Oz, "your kind created these laws, now you're bound by them. Deal with it."

With a start, Lyon squinted at Oz, who returned the look with one of trepidation. Lyon had an idea. "Larin, if you're so darn gun happy," Lyon gradually rotated his head at the rolbrid then at the terran, followed by a pointing finger, "then outfit him."

All but Hitook reacted with some form of dismay at the order.

"Are you sure that's a wise move?" Paloon asked.

"We don't know what we're up against in here," Lyon rapped his knuckles against the glass tabletop under the hologram of the school complex, "so I want every gun we can muster."

"But—"

Lyon cut off Paloon's rebuttal. "Oz, you realize that there's no going back, that you're in this to whatever end there may be?"

Oz sat, half shocked, half trying to formulate an answer.

"Well, there's not." Lyon stood. "I want you to see this firsthand."

"But," Paloon forced in again, "do we want to risk him in an actual operation?"

"He'll be on me." Lyon stuck a thumb into his chest as he established who had the responsibility for Oz's actions. "Now arm him, and do the same for yourselves. We roll on this place tonight."

Chapter 17

Shadows grew long across the gravel and concrete yard until they bled into the pitch that surrounded the red brick building. The immense abandoned school sat so far from the main road that the distant street lights barely illuminated the warning signs spray painted on the plywood planks now covering the windows. "Keep Out" spotted each window except for the few that reflected the light with shattered glass, a mark that some had defied the signs.

Rhythmic twangs reverberated from the stone structure as the wind slapped a flagless rope against a metal pole. Wind whistled around the large outdoor foyer sitting atop wide concrete steps. Disgrace marked the once fondly remembered school entrance in the form of spray painted phrases from rival gang members, none of them apparently blessed with artistic talent or the ability to spell or write clearly.

Dull thumping approached. Lyon steadily turned his head to view the source. The offending car crept down the street, which was striped on both sides by the sporadic dotting of vehicles. A continual brick face of different style houses from early twentieth-century suburbia lined the far side of the road. Yellow haze from the sparse streetlights glittered white as the light bounced off of clouds of moths with nothing better to do. The large, low-riding car gradually faded from sight long before the pounding audio stopped echoing.

Lyon took brief notice of Oz lying in the grass behind him before returning his eyes to the side of the school. A large shadow from a pile of concrete tubes in the construction supply yard covered their position. Through the connection he had between his palm and the particle cannon's grip, Lyon used the weapon's camera to spy the scene.

On this side of the building, opposite the one that faced a detached gymnasium, the ground dropped lower toward the rear of the school. A worn vehicle path ran along the base of the incline, ending at the side of the school. It had most likely served once as a route to get coal to the school's boiler. The path had since been severed by a fence that now ran between the condemned school and the supply yard. This would hardly be unusual, except that the old, rusty section of fence over the road now boasted a shiny new gate.

Lightly colored, freshly disturbed gravel contrasted the entire length of the path to the front end of a black van. The rear of the van disappeared into the building at the bottom of a ramp leading to some kind of garage door into the basement.

Concrete walls lined the ramp and protruded a few feet above the ground's surface. On the left waist-high wall leaned a dark figure with a combat submachine gun slung over his shoulder so that the weapon hung on his stomach. A glint of red flared from his lips, followed by a plume of smoke that rose quickly in the chilly weather.

Oz noted the man's choice of unfiltered cigarettes and then put the observation out of his head as he heard Lyon's voice in the earpiece the size of a hearing aid.

"Paloon, status?"

"Net's up," the Grey Wolf hunter replied from his command post in the van two blocks down the street. *"All freqs have been passive for twenty-eight minutes. Registering twenty-nine beings; five are piolant."* Paloon sent mental commands for sensory data. *"All piolants appear armored and armed or very close to a weapon. Of the natives, eleven are carrying or near weapons,"* Paloon switched systems to connect to the camera in Lyon's cannon, *"including the one you're looking at."*

"Hitook, Larin, are you in position?" Lyon requested.

"Roger."

"Affirmative."

"Ky, are you with me?"

"Check."

"Paloon, what are the level readings?"

Two ticks later, the answer came. *"There are three on the surface, including the one outside. The rest, including all piolants, are in the basement, concentrated toward Larin's position."*

"Larin, what do you see?"

"Nothing. The windows are boarded or pitch black."

"Give me a schematic."

Paloon obliged and sent his signal to the knight.

A green-outlined form of the building appeared in the left side of Lyon's glasses. It rotated from three dimensions to a flat blueprint of the first floor. A few seconds later, it shifted back to three dimensions as it lowered to the basement before going flat again.

Lyon scanned the entire floor, taking note of stairwells, doors, windows and the life signals. *"Okay,"* he commanded as the image disappeared.

"On my mark, Larin and Hitook, enter and take Paloon's directions to neutralize the two targets on the first floor. Ky, get ready to catch my target."

Without hesitation, Lyon squeezed the trigger. A silent snap of the head and the guard began to collapse, the cigarette tumbling from his mouth.

"Go."

Before Oz could hear Lyon's command, a thin, all-black figure appeared in less than a blink to catch the falling guard with a knee and arm. The free hand plucked the cigarette from the air and fluidly crushed it in her palm. Ky gracefully lowered the corpse to the ground as Lyon signaled for Oz to follow him.

The two rose to a crouch and scampered across the supply yard to the new fence. Lyon slid a pen-sized device from his black vest. Oz noticed an infrared beam ran from the tip to the fence. In an arc, the beam sliced an opening as the now loose fence collapsed to the ground in a rain of partial links.

With another silent motion to Oz, Lyon led him through the opening, along the shadow of the small hill and to a position next to Ky.

Some well-placed cuts by his particle cannon allowed Larin to slip into the rear corner entrance of a stairwell. The rolbrid paused as his eyes adjusted to the shift in light. He glanced down the stairwell, but nobody waited at the bottom. The basement would have to wait until they had cleared this floor.

Across from the stairs, walls covered in rusted, grey lockers snaked to the left. Larin slowly proceeded and halted as he turned the corner. Large hallways opened to his left and straight in front of him. At a little more than half the length of the building down the hall, light danced. Hues of red, blue and purple swirled about the hall from a room lined with windows that opened into the building.

Larin glanced to his left. As expected, Hitook entered the building through a side entrance near the front. The rolbrid raised a hand to signal to Hitook to freeze. With a few more silent hand signals, Larin explained that there was something ahead and for the liqua to circle around.

In agreement, the two moved out, gradually moving closer, watching for any changes in the shadows and listening for the slightest noise.

Light, gradual steps led Larin down the hall of severely scuffed, speckled brown flooring. Walls not covered in dilapidated lockers gave way to windows and doors that offered peeks into the abyss-like pitch of the vacant rooms.

The hall gave way to a large intersection on the left that sported a staircase to the second floor. Larin carefully peeked around the corner before proceeding to the rear of the stairs and closer to the light source.

Above music that could be faintly heard, Larin picked up on whispers of phrases and what sounded like giggles. The rolbrid looked around the far corner of the staircase and was surprised to see Hitook had moved so close without the slightest noise. In a reflexive motion, Larin's arm jerked forward to signal for the liqua to halt.

Larin set himself on the floor and scooted across the hall to the wall that supported the windows that glowed. With a silent flick, he detached a particle cannon from its holster. Once its computer came online with his internal mechanisms, he disengaged the rotating arm support to give him more flexibility as he slowly raised the barrel over his head and just above the ledge to peek into the room.

The weapon's inter-barrel camera gave Larin a greyish, daylight view of the room. Obviously an office of some kind once, the otherwise barren room seemed to object to the squatters now occupying the floor. Sitting cross-legged on a pile of disheveled blankets, a man and woman took turns leaning over a small, mirror-topped table as lines of white power disappeared through a straw they shared. Against one wall, a globe of ever-changing light sent long shadows across the room and randomly lit a midget boom box radio.

The rolbrid dropped the weapon then signaled for Hitook to hold his position. Larin inched farther down the length of the wall to line the shot. Once in position, he popped the weapon up again, aimed for the man's head and waited for the female's head to rise from the table.

With a dull "thoom" a bolt vaporized a hole in the glass window along with two skulls, the owners of which collapsed with muffled thuds.

"Scratch two," Larin remarked as he quickly double-checked his weapon's reloading meter and holstered it.

Lyon responded. *"Paloon, can you confirm?"*

"Stand by." The atlantian worked his sensor systems. *"Confirmed. The first floor is clear."*

"Check." Lyon adjusted himself. *"Proceed to your entry points, and wait for my go."*

Ky quietly leaped to the top of the stairs to a single door next to the garage entrance. She then slipped in almost as if the door didn't exist.

Lyon began approaching the far side of the van sitting in the wide door at the bottom of the ramp until he noticed Oz. The terran held his arms locked in a V in front of him, hands almost in a death grip on a type of pistol he'd never seen before.

"First thing, relax," Lyon corrected as he grabbed the top of the pistol and pushed toward Oz until he loosened his elbows. "You'll be lucky if you shoot anything if you're that tense." A flick of his thumb activated a blue targeting dot that didn't seem to emanate from anywhere on the pistol. "That will help; just don't shoot me in the back."

"I don't plan on it," Oz replied.

"Neither do I. Deal?"

Before Oz could answer, a succession of messages from the others came into his earpiece that they were ready.

Jerking his head for Oz to follow, Lyon glided down the ramp along the side of the van and into the darkness below. Once there, the room didn't seem so dark to Oz. What he took to be the antiquated boiler system stretched away from them along the wall as they rounded the rear of the van.

Light glowed from the windows that formed the top half of the walls around a worker's office, which appeared more like a break room. A football game flickered from a small TV sitting on top of a refrigerator in the corner, but the sound came from a radio, possibly on the floor. Of the two round, mismatched tables, one was home to a card game that obviously required a degree of trash talking.

"Ky, I have two targets. Can you neutralize?"

"Let's see," was all she said.

She leaned over the rail at the top of the stairs to see the light coming from the opposite side of the janitor's office. Ky took a few steps down then kicked her legs over the banister in sequence. With her feet firmly between the rods of twisted wrought iron, she fell forward to end upside down and the top of the banister hooked into the bend of her knees. Slowly she lowered until her eyes made it past the bottom of the stairs so she could see into the office.

Ky scanned the situation before giving an analysis. *"Give me a minute."*

To what, brush her hair? Oz thought. Lyon didn't seem bothered, but that just encouraged Oz to give him a what-in-the-hell look. Slightly shaking his head, Lyon pointed a finger at his eyes then at the two terrans playing cards.

Almost like a chastised dog, Oz cringed a bit and looked on, expecting to see something but seeing nothing. At what felt like a minute later, still nothing.

With a slight twitch, the two terrans collapsed right before the light went out.

"Neutralized," Ky commented as Lyon approached the offices. Oz scrambled a bit to catch up, still unsure of what, if anything, he just saw.

"Twelve armed targets remain, no sporadic movement," Paloon reported to explain that their presence hadn't been detected.

Oz's vision adjusted as he followed Lyon through the old janitor's break room. Slumped over the blood-splattered cards strewn about the table, each corpse sported two quiver-like bolts: one in the throat and one in the forehead. He had no way to tell whether the hits occurred simultaneously.

Exiting the other door, Oz noticed Ky crouched under the stairs. She tapped a finger first at her throat then at her head as if to answer Oz's thoughts. He then wondered if she had even moved from the shadows. Reason won. Oz deemed that Ky had to have moved; otherwise, who had turned out the light?

Lyon approached and stood next to Ky but moved as if he did not notice her. The knight looked down the hall to see Larin against the wall at the far end of the building.

"Paloon, target locations."

"From your position," the hunter replied to Lyon, *"ahead turn right, and the next two doors on your right open into a room with one piolant, who has been dormant. The next two will open into a room with two armed natives. Then at the far end is a room with two dormant piolants.*

"Between Larin and Hitook is the hive. There are three piolants, one dormant; three armed natives and all the unarmed natives."

Lost in thought, Lyon began to slightly rock his head then stopped. *"Wait, you said there were twelve armed targets. Where's the other terran?"*

"Oh, shoot, sorry. He's in a room off the hallway that runs a bit off center between the two main focuses. You'll see it after turning right, just past the center stairwell, the hallway will stretch to the far room that's housing most of them."

Lyon went back to thought. Only Oz seemed to fidget while wondering what the alien wacko had so demanding on his mind.

"Ky," the knight began with his orders, *"take the piolant in the room to the right. Hopefully, he'll be sleeping and it will be quick. Oz and I will take the two terrans in the room next to it. We'll meet up and charge the room at the far end, but expect them to be awake by then."*

Lyon's voice shifted. *"Larin, Hitook, enter opposite ends of that room. Hit them hard and fast, surprise will be your key, which is why we will have to be quick. Our window of surprise won't last for long. Any questions?"*

"What of the one in hallway?" Ky didn't feel good about the lone gun.

"Take him out if we have time, or we can do so on our way to help Larin and Hitook if need be. He'll be no match for us. The piolants should be our main focus."

"Any restrictions?" came Larin's voice.

"Short of blowing holes in the exterior walls or crashing the building down on us, everything goes."

"That's a little restrictive."

"You'll live." Lyon adjusted the grip on his particle cannon and double-checked its status. *"If that's it...go!"*

Chapter 18

Ky slipped through the door and into the dark room where Paloon had identified the life signs of a piolant. Lyon and Oz watched the door quietly close before proceeding to the next door.

Lyon turned the knob but kept the door closed until he could feel the bolt slip past its housing in the jamb. He threw it open and charged into the room, Oz right behind. Lyon leveled his particle cannon at the one terran who heard the intruders.

In a black sweater jacket left unzipped to reveal a red shirt with a large, two-digit number, the man leapt from his chair, where he had previously been staring at a laptop. It took a second for the situation to soak in before the terran lunged for his small, submachine gun on the table. Before the terran's hand could breach the plane of the table, a searing bolt bored an inch-wide hole through his head.

As the body flew head first into the far wall, Lyon turned to see Oz holding his pistol at an angle to the floor and just watching the other terran. Bathed in light and clothed in a tasteful plaid shirt, the terran bobbed his head to the loud music seeping from beneath the tiny ear-buds connected to a radio on the desk. Next to the radio, various stacks of paper currency formed a wall stretching to another laptop computer.

Finishing his count with mouthed numbers, the terran began placing the next stack when he froze, gazing at the two men standing before him. Oz instinctively raised the pistol but did nothing.

"Look, Oz," Lyon's mental voice came through Oz's earpiece, *"the rules are simple: Kill him, or he kills you. Hesitate and die."*

Still nothing.

"Let's try it this way: Kill him, or you're a liability, and I'll kill you."

Oz wanted to turn and confirm the truth he knew must have been in Lyon's eyes, but before he could, the terran immediately stood. Another instinct fired the pistol.

No louder than a puff of air and with a recoil barely strong enough to harm a fly, Oz wondered if the weapon had fired at all. As he began to gaze at the weapon in his hands, the results suddenly seized his attention.

The man before him gaped like a zombie, stumbling a bit before blood came bursting from the massive hole torn through his chest. The body hit the floor with a wet thud.

"In the heart." Lyon cringed. *"That's nasty."*

Heavy weapons fire sounded from outside. Lyon grabbed Oz's arm and jerked him toward the far door to the next target.

"We don't have much time." Lyon let go and gripped the particle cannon with both hands, charged the door and kicked it open.

On the command, Larin crept forward, peeked around the corner to his left and took in the full scene in a fraction of a second. As he had suspected from the light on the floor and noise from a radio, the door stood open.

A local, in a long white coat and with his back to the door, walked away toward a bank of refrigerators. The outline of another large being made for a menacing backdrop. By the nasty looks of the weapon cradled in thick arms, the big one must have been a piolant with a face of a local.

To the right towered thick, brown cabinets that came two feet shy of touching a high roof. On the other side, long tables striped the floor. Various beakers, tubes and mechanical contraptions sprouted from tables, each working as feverishly as the locals slumped over them. Every worker breathed through a white mask that matched the long coats and skull caps.

Larin had seen it before: a slave line. He couldn't tell what they were being forced to make, but he doubted it was anything good.

At the far end of the room, three locals appeared to be in a conversation with two piolants, who attempted to pass themselves off as locals from this planet. One piolant stepped away from the group toward the far door as if finished with all he had to say.

Larin flew back around the corner, absorbed the scene and plotted his move. The exiting piolant was about to walk into Hitook, meaning the rolbrid probably wouldn't be able to expect assistance any time soon. So his plan had to be massive and quick.

With another darting peek around the corner, Larin saw a local bending down into an open refrigerator. The piolant jerked as if noticing Larin but remained unsure of exactly what he had seen, if anything. No time left.

Larin grabbed the doorpost with his left hand and whipped the particle cannon around with the other, aiming for the piolant. Instead, the bolt caught an unaware local in the left shoulder. Stepping away from the refrigerator and standing up, the local unknowingly put himself in the line of fire. The tray he had retrieved flew upwards, sending tiny glass vials and blue power into the air.

Expecting return fire soon from the target he should have neutralized, Larin pulled back, strengthened his grip on the doorpost, engaged the geomagnetic unit in his combat pack and half leapt into the air to plant his feet on the wall. In short, quick movements, he scuttled up the door frame like a nimble monkey. It was none too soon.

The piolant began punching six-inch holes in the wall with his cannon. Each shot made an awful-sounding whump as three snakes of blue-white light writhed in a tight screw then soared through the wall with no more difficulty than a clipper cutting waves.

All the way at the top of the doorframe now, Larin noticed the multiplying holes tearing away at the wall to the point that it appeared incapable of supporting weight. With all his experience he had no idea what kind of weapon this was, which didn't sit well with him.

With plans A and B out the window, it was now on to plan C. Larin just wished he had made a plan C.

Paloon didn't notice the movement in time to warn Hitook.

The piolant pulled the door open and strode forward, down the hall in front of him, with such focus he remained unaware of Hitook withdrawing into the shadows. Just as tall and wide as the furry liqua, the being had a terran face but reeked of piolant scent. An odd weapon rested along the creature's back.

Hitook hedged his bets and began a light-footed quickstep to get close enough to snap the neck without being detected. When he neared within inches, a piercing-wet crackle of energy from behind Hitook sent reverberating sounds throughout the basement floor.

The being turned and moved fast to take advantage of the small window of Hitook's distraction. With two hands and a foot suddenly pounding into his chest, Hitook flew backwards, feet skipping off the floor, until he crashed into the wall with enough force to dent it a bit.

Light flashed from down the hall to Hitook's right. Obviously the weapons fire kept Larin busy, but the nearby door opened again, and a small team of armed terrans moved as if to exit the room. Hitook's right hand grabbed the barrel of the pointing weapon, and without turning his body, he pounded a heavy foot into the assault team. The terrans tumbled into one another.

With a flick, Hitook slammed the door shut, just in time to look back at the charging piolant. The electronic terran mask now gone, either due to distraction or futility, large red and green eyes burned with anger as the beast braced for ramming.

Hitook swung the rifle with the speed, power and grace of a professional golfer. When the butt of the weapon connected to the piolant's chin, the gun cracked in two but not before stopping the charge and knocking the attacker back a few steps.

But this piolant was no stranger to close-quarters combat. If the strike to his chin hurt or distracted him, it wasn't for long, and he hid it well.

Hitook didn't hesitate either. With a flick of his wrist, he sent the remaining half of a weapon spinning upward. As it spun, he snatched the magazine of rounds from inside of the rifle and shoved it forward. As he did, mental focus compressed the energy around him into a thin, yet strong, invisible wall between his right palm and the weapon. Other energies gathered in his left fist, and as soon as the magazine and wall were in alignment, Hitook threw the energy in his left hand forward.

Each round in the large magazine exploded simultaneously, turning the remains of the weapon into a large fragmentation grenade. The shield protected Hitook but sent chunks of metal into the piolant before throwing him to the floor.

Hitook had hoped the explosion would have knocked the piolant out, but just as he leapt forward to check, one of the piolant's massive legs snapped up to wrap around Hitook's throat. As if a spinning axle, the piolant twisted his body with enough force to bring his other leg over Hitook's head and into his gut.

Hitook crashed into the wall of metal lockers as the piolant finished the move by planting his feet and propelling his body vertical. An arm shot from Hitook in retaliation, but the piolant just grabbed it and launched a roundhouse with his other arm into Hitook's neck, sending the liqua head-first and deep into the wall of lockers.

The piolant clamped onto the lockers. Bolts screamed and popped as the tower of metal came down, driving Hitook to the floor.

Victor of the battle, the piolant stomped on Hitook's arm, exposed from below the lockers. In piolant, he declared, "Nice trick, cop. But your furry hide is going to have to do better."

Hitook had it together enough to wonder how this piolant knew he was from the Corps, but he knew it wouldn't take much to put the pieces together. The thoughts disappeared when the piolant jumped and landed on top of the lockers with deadly pressure.

Lyon stuck his head out the door and instantly heard sounds of a very loud scuffle coming from the room Ky had entered. The door exploded in wooden splinters as the blur that was Ky's body shot down the hall like a cannonball.

A massive being with a terran face plowed through the fragments of the door. When sounds came from Lyon's right, the face shifted to that of a piolant, one that noticed Lyon. But Lyon couldn't help from turning to see what the noise was.

A door had opened to reveal two more piolants. Instinctively, Lyon stuck his weapon out and at the more menacing target. As he released bolts at a now closing door, he mentally commanded, *"Oz, shoot at the far corner by the door!"*

Both cells spent, Lyon pulled in to let them recharge and impaled Oz with his eyes. "Now!"

The urgency in Lyon's voice alone seemed to pull the trigger as Oz began to fire away, putting large holes in the wall and causing a large cloud of drywall power to fill the area.

As distractions go, it wasn't much, but it worked well enough.

Ky grunted as she pushed herself through the hole in the drywall. Her face mask and hood looked as if rescued from a rabid badger. Several loose flaps partially covered her view, so she yanked if off her head, letting her hair flow loose as she charged back down the hall.

Along the way, a door to her left began to open. *The lone terran,* she thought while seeing a weapon slowly extend from the door as if its owner was afraid he might find something. Ky wondered for a moment if the weapon might be pointing at the piolant, who was getting pummeled with bits of the exploding wall. That gave her an idea.

Ky lunged forward, grabbed the weapon with her right hand and the terran's exposed wrist with her left. With a solid foot against the door so as not to let it open too much, she yanked hard, pulling the terran forward. A heavy, wet thud sounded before the body crumpled to the floor.

She cradled the rifle, and just as her tail pushed the door closed behind her, Ky pulled the trigger. A burst of lead soared into the piolant, although she knew it would take more than that to put down such a massive, plate-covered being. But she kept firing bursts as she walked closer.

Larin regretted his choice of shooting so blindly, but he didn't have the time to identify the finer points of the mistake. The remaining time to act grew increasingly small. Still crouched on the wall, he shuffled over to the farthest side of the door frame, away from the wall that was being quickly vaporized.

He sneaked the barrel of the particle cannon around the edge of the frame, aimed and fired.

Green, glowing flat shards of allaric crystal spewed from the under-barrel mount like it was a super-fast mechanized playing card dispenser. The difference was these cards flew at high velocity and shattered into mini grenades upon impact.

The piolant's body armor appeared to hold as each crystal bounced off of the chest plates and exploded, destroying everything except the intended target. A few of the fragments even tore through the thick cabinets and began nicking the locals cowering under their tables.

Larin let off long enough to readjust his aim to the wall just behind the piolant's head. Another pull of the trigger emptied the magazine. This time the allaric slats exploded at the right angles and sent hundreds of razor-sharp blades of crystal into the back of the piolant's head.

The display of flying green disks sent the other would-be attackers on the far end of the room diving for cover, but they hesitated just long enough for Larin to finish the attack. As he shuffled back to the top of the wall above the door, the other piolant opened fire, taking chucks out of the wall where Larin had been. Over the thumps of the piolant's weapon, Larin could hear weapons fire from what must have been the locals.

Soon both walls would be nonexistent. This left his options limited.

Larin kept one hand gripping the frame's molding as he holstered the cannon, then rotated it sideways in its holster. He yanked out the allaric magazine and slammed it into the bottom of his combat pack for reloading, then grabbed another from the same location.

His weapon re-armed, Larin unhitched a palm-sized square from the bandoleer across his chest. He stuck the cube in his mouth as he grabbed another.

Fingers already in place, he triggered the buttons and chucked the first one into the room. He grabbed the other from his mouth and did the same.

In a split second, the first one triggered with a bright strobe of light; the other followed to catch anyone who blinked. Then dense, black smoke billowed everywhere to give Larin the blind he would need.

Larin bounced off the wall like a basketball coming off a backboard, hitting the floor in a crouch. His right hand grabbed his primary cannon, then his other hand unholstered the additional cannon strapped to his left leg. In a snap they came online, and he activated the arm rests that rotated around the bottom of the pistol grip from their standard forward positions.

Two short pipes extended from the top of the combat pack to peek, one each, over his shoulders. The cloud of black disappeared into a silvery vision in Larin's eyes as the ultrasonic sensors came online. When they did, he charged forward.

Through the dense smoke, two-round bursts of green crystal sheets spewed from both weapons targeting the areas around anything that moved. Keeping the angles correct, Larin ensured the crystal explosions aimed the resulting shards away from him as he kept moving forward.

Screams on top of screams intertwined with the shattering of glass, fracturing of concrete, splintering of wood and cracking of tile. Soon, slivers of crystal permeated almost everything in the room.

As the last rounds flew, Larin noticed the crippled piolant stumbling over the mushy remains of the locals he attempted to hide behind. The rolbrid brought both cannons to bear, targeting crosshairs lining within his eyes. Smooth pulls of the triggers unloaded all four cells of the two particle cannons into a barrage of shots, decapitating the piolant from the chest up.

Hitook fought to brace himself against the constant pounding. Even pacing his breathing between bashes didn't seem to help him mentally focus.

Then the piolant stopped slamming himself down of top of the lockers piled on Hitook and walked away. With the weight gone, Hitook gathered the strength to lift himself enough to see from under the fallen lockers what must have distracted the piolant: particle cannon bolts farther down the hall. Soon white light returned fire.

The piolant walking away, unhitched the weapon from across his back and took aim. Hitook knew, body and soul, that he had to act fast.

Focusing, centering, the liqua worked quickly to forget everything, shedding the world around him like oversized clothes. Behind closed eyes he became one with the All and the Void, unity, balance, connection.

Rebar snapped with deep thuds as concrete screamed. At the speed of a locomotive, an entire wall of previously untouched lockers, to include the wall itself, blasted from one side of the hall, plowing into the unsuspecting piolant and flattening him against the far wall as if he were no more than a leaf under a boulder.

Lockers flew off Hitook as he scrambled from underneath and charged toward the piolant, whose hand and wrist poked from between the wreckage on the wall.

Hitook grabbed the hand and yanked the piolant free, only to greet him with a heavy fist to the face. Still shocked from the sudden attack and force of the wall, the piolant weakly attempted to defend himself.

Hitook's right hand shot forward and wrapped around the piolant's head to jerk him over a rising knee. The knee didn't target the gut but lower and popped the piolant at the correct angle to release his feet from the ground, flipping the piolant in the air. When he came down, so did Hitook's foot, into the piolant's neck.

Cracks exploded as the piolant's neck plates and vertebrae shattered under the force of a dozen jackhammers.

Wired on adrenaline, Hitook didn't hesitate to move on. *"Paloon, target?"*

Automatic fire came to a ringing silence as the bolt slammed and locked to the rear as the final brass case whizzed from the ejection port. Faint smoke trailed from both. The target, an armored beast of a being, took all thirty rounds, not counting any rounds from Oz, and stammered from the jolt. The shock wouldn't last for long; Ky knew it. Piolants had a nasty habit of not going down easy.

Ky dropped the rifle, which clattered to the ground as she blasted into a charge.

"Oz, cease fire!"

On his second magazine, Oz still couldn't tell what he was supposed to be shooting at through the wall or why. Considering the current situation, he figured it had something to do with staying alive long enough to realize he really had to use the restroom. Ky's order blared from his earpiece loud enough to make him pull his weapon from the target just out of shock.

At least it worked because Ky neared to within inches of an arm's length not even a second later. Her eyes locked onto the staggering piolant's neck. With one solid swipe, she'd claw the piolant's neck to shreds. So close to her target, so close to finishing this, Ky didn't noticed the brief realization in the piolant's eyes.

Unsuspecting reaction matched unnatural speed as the piolant's arms flew out, and massive paws clamped on to Ky's neck. Still shaking off the effects of the earlier assault, the piolant picked Ky off the ground and out of her range.

Instinctively, Ky grabbed for the thick arms in a feeble attempt to keep the piolant's hands from crushing the breath out of her. She flailed a bit like a wild animal before planting her feet in the piolant's chest and attempting to push away, but the piolant's grip held firm and grew tighter.

As if an epiphany reached her from the heavens themselves, Ky realized she might not be within arm's reach, but she was within leg's reach. After all, she had her feet on the piolant's chest. In rapid succession, Ky began kicking the piolant's face from side to side like a vicious game of close-quarters table tennis. The effort stressed to Ky the need to breathe again; she would have to change tactics to get the results she needed in time.

Ky planted both heels in the creature's jaw line as she sent her tail on a back-up mission, in case this failed. Before she could push in an attempt to break the neck, his muscles locked as a four-lipped smile cracked across the piolant's face like an ugly flower. Luckily, her tail had found was she believed she had previously seen on the wall.

With a deep, hollow thud, a red, metal canister pounded into the piolant's head. Stunned, the beast relaxed his grip enough for Ky to pry loose. Her tail dropped the fire extinguisher as she pulled her legs into a fetal position. Using the piolant's arms for a springboard, she bounded up into a cannonball over the piolant's head.

On the far side, Ky exploded, plowing her legs into the piolant's shoulders and sending him to the floor, face first. Without hesitation, Ky dove for the plates on the back of the piolant's neck. Her hands locked on a plate, then she planted a foot into the piolant's back and tore the plate free.

Once the plate came free, Ky flipped it in her hands in a fluid, textbook motion and shoved it sideways into the opening, sliding it past the muscle bands protecting the vertebrae to sever the main nerve cord. Instant death.

⋞♦♦♦♦♦♦♦♦⌖♦♦♦♦♦♦♦♦⋟

Lyon sat on the floor with his back against the door as he leaned out for a look. The fight to his left drew his attention, and he saw Ky locked in a choking grip. He prepared to aim his cannon at the piolant's exposed side when the two piolants on the other side of the building starting sending rather unwelcome reminders that they were still alive.

In two shots, the kinetic energy pulverized the wall and barreled into the door with enough force to snap the top of the door off and into Lyon's head before tumbling across the room. Lyon hit the floor, partially because of being hit with the debris, then looked to Oz. *"Hey, Oz, how's it going over there?"*

Still at the far corner of the room, Oz appeared to be outside of the firing pattern as bright beams of light shot over Lyon's head. Given Lyon's sudden desire to chat, Oz wondered if the door had hit Lyon a bit too hard in the head.

Oz attempted to say something, but the endless thumps from the piolants' weapons fire muffled his voice. If the weapons had to recharge, neither noticed.

Lyon tapped a finger to the back of his ear and yelled, "What!?"

"Fine...considering!"

Lyon nodded appreciatively. "You have any gum!?"

That did it. Oz knew Lyon had lost it, and it showed on his face. "No!" After purposefully staring at the bolts soaring over Lyon's head, Oz asked, "You going to do something about this!?"

Lyon simply shook his hand toward Oz as if to indicate he'd get to it when he had a moment to spare. Meanwhile, he attempted to analyze what he was up against. But like Larin, Lyon had never seen or heard of weapons that created a twisting triple-beam of light. Years of half-forgotten classes could only conclude one remote possibility that super-heated, liquid plasma might have the properties to allow a similar continuous distortion. The odds of Lyon being correct wouldn't tempt even a risk-taking gambler; however, betting would soon be irrelevant if the knight didn't do something about the risk.

During short pauses between rounds, Lyon flipped like a fish onto his belly. Granted the last time Lyon saw Ky, she didn't seem to be doing so well, but he trusted that she was a big enough girl to take care of things. He had more pressing problems.

Along the floor, Lyon slid his particle cannon out the door. Purposefully aiming high, he fired a few glowing green slats of crystal into the room, just enough to startle the attackers. Lyon abruptly pulled the weapon to his chest and rolled. As the piolants recovered and began opening fire, dismantling the corner of the room, Lyon popped up on one knee at the far side to fire a particle bolt into one of the piolant's legs, followed by a few more allaric rounds.

Slamming to the floor and rolling, Lyon ended with a repeat of the measure catching the other piolant in the shoulder. During Lyon's third attempt, Paloon barked, *"Lyon, cease fire!"*

He paused with his face to the ground only to notice a deep, nasty black mar in the flooring. *"Why should I? I'm just getting warmed up."*

"You're about to find out," Paloon replied bluntly.

An explosion roared from the room and shook the building. Lumps of concrete, twisted bits of metal, splinters of wood and streams of piolant blood shot out the doorway, closely followed by projectile smoke that traveled several feet before billowing to the ceiling. Oz swore someone had decided to dynamite a new mine shaft from the abandoned school's basement. Yet he still wondered if that was the case.

Lyon hopped up on his knees and gazed through the holes in the wall like an alert prairie dog. He didn't know what to make of it.

"Those were the last two," Paloon reported. *"All's clear."*

Lyon stood and stepped out the door to notice Ky uncurling from the defensive ball she went into at the sound of the explosion. A mist of fine white particles still filled the air making it difficult to see anything near the source of the explosion.

Approaching still somewhat cautiously, Lyon came upon another scene to his left where it appeared something ripped the wall out and pushed it across the hall. His thoughts began to toy with ideas on how that happened, but the answer came when he made it to the next doorway.

Another wall had found itself on the opposite side of the room than it should have been. Between it and its companion wall, which showed sign of giving a bit under the pressure, were hundreds of items: mangled metal bed frames, crumpled bedding, something resembling a squished locker and two dead, and rather flat, piolants. In the hole, where the wall should have been, stood a heavily panting Hitook.

Tense muscles wrinkled his forehead as if undergoing severe migraines. Droplets of saliva blasted from the sides of Hitook's mouth with each heavy breath. Eyes closed, the liqua struggled with calming down.

Lyon watched Hitook for a moment then soaked in the scene before holstering his cannon. "I guess this proves finesse is overrated."

Chapter 19

Acidic dust burned in Lyon's nose and left a bitter taste in his mouth. Mechanisms torn open by the firefight left strips of metal strewn amidst bits of glass from the hundreds of shattered vials and tubes. Coating it all was a blue dust that glinted in the light.

In the wreckage, one container seemed intact. Lyon pinched the long-necked vial and lifted it to look at the blue dust in its bulbous bottom. As he slowly stirred the vial in tiny circles, the dust flowed about as if liquid.

Lyon stopped long enough to turn to Paloon. "What is it?"

A rectangular device about twice the size of Paloon's hand flashed through several screens, and the hunter watched attentively for a few more moments before acknowledging the question. "In short, I don't know. Apparently there's nothing like this on file."

"Are you sure it's not just some kind of designer drug?" Oz questioned while shaking a bottle of blue capsules that rattled.

Paloon glanced about again at what remained of the little makeshift factory. "It's possible, but it could also be a biological weapon."

Uneasiness settled on Oz's face as he slowly put the bottle back on one of the tables.

"Oh, don't worry," Paloon reassured Oz with a nonchalant flick of his hand. "If it is a bio weapon, it's probably only the dormant part of one; otherwise, we'd be dead by now." He paused to think about it a bit more. "Or it's just really poorly made and will end up killing us slowly over the next several years."

Oz gulped hard as Lyon glanced from under an arched brow at Paloon. "Aren't you just a joy to have around?"

"I try."

"Is the net down?"

Paloon nodded. "Yes." He had taken the drones out of action after confirmation of the last neutralization.

"Mac," Lyon began, *"can you patch into this spectroscope and send the data to the Corps for matching?"*

"Yes, and no."

"Mac, stop playing around."

"I'm not, honest," the computer defended itself. *"Could I? Yes. But the last I heard was W'Lowe telling us to ix-nay on the ommunications-kay until they contact us."*

Accurate as the computer may be, Lyon contemplated countering that order. Maybe his shortsighted desires blinded him, but he found himself disagreeable yet strangely compliant.

Suddenly a loud thud pounded as one of the piolant's weapons compressed the air in the room and flashed in bright light. All three, to include Oz, drew weapons and aimed across the room in the direction of the source.

"Figured it out," Larin declared from the floor.

As the others put away their weapons, Lyon nodded to Paloon. "Do what you can."

Oz followed Lyon who navigated around the tables and bodies. At the far end, a piolant corpse lay on its back with various probes in its body, its hand loosely gripping one of those weapons across its belly. Larin yanked the probes out of the body, snatched the weapon and stood.

"Obviously it's still functioning, right?" Larin pointed at the weapon before aiming it down the hall and pulling the trigger. Nothing. "But it doesn't want to play." He loosened his hold on the weapon to point to a connection plate in the grip. "So it must need a bio signature from its owner." Larin knelt, placed the weapon in the dead piolant's hand and pushed the piolant's finger on the trigger. Nothing.

He dropped the weapon before reinserting the probes. "It must need something more." The first two needle-like devices slid into the being's right chest. "So if we make the heart pump to create at least a mild pulse," Larin explained as he inserted another into the neck, "and run a mild current through the nervous system, we can simulate life signs."

Larin remounted the weapon in the piolant's hand and fired another shot out the door and into the far wall.

A short, guttural yelp sounded from that direction as Hitook poked his head around the corner. He had almost stumbled into the line of fire but now just gave everyone a quizzical look. No one paid attention.

Larin dropped the weapon and the piolant's hand. "Only when fired by its 'live' owner will it work."

"That's a little odd." Lyon screwed his right cheek. "Can you guess why?"

"Well," Larin said as he stood and mindlessly tapped the corpse with his toe, "the turenese did something like this once, in this detail that is. The goal, simply, was to ensure any enemy could not use their weapons against them. They did it to everything: pistols, rifles, vehicles, mechanized armor. Everything.

"After the Belanegniz Conflict erupted, the turenese quickly discovered one major problem," Larin continued. "Sure it worked as they had hoped, but it worked both ways. There's no efficient way to reprogram these weapons on the battlefield, so once the owner was dead, the enemy couldn't use it, but neither could anyone in the Turen Army. Soon they were left with just useless hunks of metal, often just abandoned on the battlefield because they couldn't haul it all back for reprogramming."

Though appreciative of the informative history, Lyon just wanted the facts surrounding the current situation. "So is this a turenese weapon?"

"No, frap no." Larin shook his head. "I've never seen anything like it, but it's definitely not turenese."

"Then is there a point to your story?"

"Sure," Larin sounded as if it should be obvious, "whoever wired these weapons either never heard of the situation with the turenese or they have and just don't care. In either case, evidence of one thing is present: paranoia. Of what or why exactly, take a guess."

What did that mean? Lyon knew his mind would spend days speculating. Nothing could stop his subconscious at times. He let his mind follow that path wherever it may lead, but he didn't stop exploring more trails. "What did you find out, Hitook?" he asked without taking his eyes off the dead piolant at his feet.

"Living quarters, temporary at best." Hitook came around the corner and entered the room. "The piolants stayed here for maybe a week at a time. There might have been some rolbrids here. The quarters for the terrans are on the other side of the building. By the looks of it, they may have lived here in longer stretches but with fewer amenities."

"Slaves?" Oz couldn't believe it.

"Possibly." Hitook's face showed no emotion. "Indentured servitude, maybe. Could even be choice due to ignorance."

Oz, mouth slightly agape, turned to look at the piles of dead terrans, then back to Lyon. The knight threw up a finger. "Don't even go there." He adjusted to briefly match the glare. "Either way, they were part of this operation. Their condition does not excuse their acts. No remorse, so don't ask."

Lyon shifted to Hitook. "How did you pick up on rolbrids being here?"

Hitook's head barely jerked toward the door. "There's a box of chur roots under the rumble."

"Frapping-A!" Larin jumped from the floor and bolted to the door. "It's just what I need."

"After you get your fix," Lyon yelled after the rolbrid, "see if you can get these weapons useable."

"Yeah, sure, all over it," came the fading response.

Lyon gave a light sigh, then pointed to Oz and Hitook. "You two, search these bodies for any kind of identification, terran or otherwise." He slipped past Hitook and out the door. "Report what you find to Mac and have him run whatever searches he can."

Confidence. Authority. Something in Lyon's voice pulled at an unseen, yet amenable, cord deep in Oz. Maybe memories of the smart sting from his mother's switch of dogwood teaching him to respect his elders caused it. Alternatively, years of military influence may have bred such non-questioning reactions. He responded agreeably with a start but caught himself in the reaction and stopped to question it.

Had all the recent events happened too quickly to allow him to think clearly? Why should he be doing this at all? He still wondered whether he should trust any of them. Nothing could keep him from feeling like he was in a prison without chains, kept at bay by a threat of the unknown. After all, they had just slaughtered an entire building of people. About that, something was askew. In all that had occurred, not once did he sense anger from his captors. Nor was it a cold, detached, methodic killing. The closest description came to him in a vision of a farmer stepping on ants while crossing a field, a kind of detached, unknowing disregard. No acknowledgment of the lives lost, yet no hatred or gratification. This left him with bewildering thoughts of what it all might mean.

Hitook approached him from his left. The beast of a creature smiled mildly with a slight nod. "Undesirable as they may be, some actions must be taken to ensure the safety of everyone on this planet."

Had Hitook just read his mind? Oz wondered as the question appeared on his face despite an attempt to hide it. "But...?" His question trailed off, not knowing what to say.

"Some enemies are unforgiving," Hitook continued. "Therefore, extreme actions may be required to ensure the sanctity of the whole. It is as the forester who carefully burns away underbrush so it does not later provide the tinder of an uncontrollable fire."

Hitook continued, before Oz could speak, once again as if to respond directly to the terran's thoughts. "True, beings, regardless of planet, are not to be treated with the disregard of twigs beneath our feet, yet they have become involved. 'How' doesn't change the situation. Whether they know little or much, what they know must be contained to ensure the safety of this planet. It is the best we can do for now."

Oz blinked but never stopped looking Hitook in the eyes. Black orbs returned the gaze with the calm alertness of a grazing animal. A feeling of knowing the truth in the liqua's words rapped against Oz's psyche, demanding to be respected and accepted.

Soft strands of fur fluffed along the liqua's face as Hitook jerked his muzzle to point softly into the room. "Now we have to do what we must. Their identities may provide understanding of how deep this infestation runs."

That same thought blared in Lyon's head as he pulled open a door to see a terran invisibly pinned against the wall and gasping in wheezes for air. Unlucky enough to be the only one left alive after Ky took his weapon and knocked him out, his neck gleamed with a hundred bloody scratches. The blood had begun to congeal but not before seeping enough to mix with sweet and soaking a plaid shirt down to the third button. The resulting stench forced Lyon's nose to twitch.

Across, but facing the terran, Ky sat erect with the insides of her feet splayed flat on the floor with her legs together and hands on her bent knees.

"Did you do this to him?"

"If you're talking about the blood," Ky responded without opening her eyes, "no. He did that, fighting to remove a nonexistent physical restraint."

The terrified terran's eyes shakily rotated in their bulging sockets to see the new arrival, obviously not a rescuer.

"What have you got?"

Ky sniffled a bit before answering. "Much of what we already had. Recruited about a year ago, he works for a yakuza, most likely the same one. He thinks these piolants are actually yakuza 'royal guards,' whatever that means." Ky rubbed the back of her neck. "That substance they're manufacturing, it's being directed by the yakuza leadership but under the piolant's supervision. This one," she didn't stop her rubbing as she jerked her head toward the struggling terran, "thinks it's a kind of drug, but he doesn't know. The stuff gets shipped away with piolants who return with the payment, in local currency."

"What is he doing here then if the piolants are running the show?"

"Glorified babysitter, apparently. He and his companions are responsible for handling the slave workers and transporting them when needed."

"That's it?"

"He's rather low in the structure and too dumb to even be curious."

"Does he know—"

"Lyon," Paloon shouted through the team's internal communications system, *"we've got inbound."*

"Locals?"

"No, it looks like a slow-moving yofeeti signal packing a multi-dimension carrier wave, and it's headed to this building."

Lyon knew a yofeeti signal most likely meant a matter transmission. If aimed here, somewhere in the building was the receiver. *"Find the target receiver. Everyone else, follow Paloon."*

Lyon bolted for the door. Ky stood but didn't let her prey go. "What of this one?"

"Don't need him."

As the two joined the quickly moving pack down the hall, the terran gasped his last breath, eyes rolled back in flickering motions before only a mortal shell crumpled to the floor.

Paloon used his internal communications feed with the van outside to patch into Mac, who had much more access to triangulate the trajectory of the incoming signal. Tracking it with a map of the building that filled his vision, Paloon busted into the room before realizing it was the same location in which Ky had got into a tussle before getting thrown through a door.

The group clustered just inside the door. Pulling up the rear, Oz felt for and found a light switch. Dangling from cords, naked, clear white bulbs blared to reveal a sunken floor, square-shaped with large, flat steps leading to the center. Golden plates covered the center floor as tubes of the same metallic substance created mini towers at the four corners. This was the receiver; Paloon just knew it.

Each tube crackled to life. This brought everyone a bit farther into the room, but they stayed back with the mild attention of a crowd waiting for the ringmaster to step into the light and begin the show.

Multi-colored fireflies of light appeared from nothing and began to accumulate in the center of the room, only a few at first, then hundreds and even more. Within the confines of the four tubes, space itself began to warp inward as if to create a perfect globe, leaving the surrounding area unaffected.

Oz's brain struggled with what he was seeing. He couldn't help but blink quickly, then hard. Pain ached in his head. It looked as if two realities coexisted. The effect had no basis for understanding in Oz's certainty of what was real. Struggling to make sense of it all pushed his brain into a migraine.

Points of light increasingly connected with each other. The resulting cloud began to take shape. A lack of light framed an uncertain form of the object. Lyon gazed upon the show the way a rubbernecking driver might squirm while studying a bloody vehicle accident. All other options eliminated, the truth about what the inbound object must be came to him much like an ugly kick to the groin.

Lyon's particle cannon flew from its holster. His team followed immediately and silently, each taking positions in a semicircle around the transporter. A bit slow, Oz joined in with the pistol Lyon had handed him earlier.

As the final molecules came together, disbelief reeked from the room like it was highly acidic feline urine. For there, being transported, intact, in front of their eyes, was a piolant. Alive!

The final atom in place, the globe of warped space wobbled back into place with an appearance of gelatin. Instantly the piolant knew he had picked a bad time to return to work and went for his weapon with a start.

"Don't!" barked Lyon.

Few theorists thought it possible, but every test to teleport a live creature failed. Yet before their eyes, a matter reconstructor had pieced a living being back together without killing it. Of all, Paloon had the most interest in the possibility. "How is—"

"That's not important now," Lyon cut him off. The knight slowly moved, never dropping his aim, to get the piolant's attention. He had it.

"There's no out," Lyon began. "This can be easy, and you can live. Or we can get ugly, so don't be stupid."

The piolant's stern face didn't change, except for a flicking flinch of his lower right lip, which resembled a leaf briefly catching a small breeze. His burnt-orange eyes glided over the other occupants in the room with methodic attentiveness.

"I'm Knight Kendrick with the Dragon Corps." Lyon seized the piolant's attention again. With so many dead piolants, the rolbrids found in the other building and what the dragoon said, this mission really began to reek of a renegade Korac faction. "We want Horwhannor, so where is he?"

Expecting to see at least the slightest widening of the eyes, Lyon watched but spotted nothing. The piolant might as well have been an iron statue. Yet the piolant broke the mold and allowed one dual-pupilled orb to slowly swivel independently back to scrutinize the largest object in the room: Hitook.

Both of the piolant's eyes gleamed healthily like sheets of glass at dusk. Cold stillness radiated from the glare and helplessly infected the room. Even the air grew stale.

There! If he had blinked, Lyon would have missed the faintest of glints, the kind that came from deep understanding, a touch of the ethereal knowing of what was and what must be. As fast as it showed itself, it retreated into the depths for camouflaged protection.

Quietly wishing it not true, Lyon had to acknowledge what he knew it meant regardless of how futile. "This isn't your fight."

Deaf now to all but the voice in his head, the piolant smoothly and quickly reached for his weapons. Multiple beams of light exploded into his chest, hammering muscle and bone into a cavity of mush. Several seconds strolled by until the soulless vessel thumped with a slight flop to the floor.

"Frapping devoted idiot," Larin half-mumbled as he mildly kicked the dead piolant's leg.

Lyon lowered his weapon and stepped forward, inspecting the confrontation's result. He knew the time came for the decisive action that all true leaders face.

"Check the vehicles," Lyon directed to all whom could hear, "and get all the weapons and equipment you can carry."

Chapter 20

"This is suicide," Ky stated for the third time.

Lyon couldn't avoid it any more. "Staying on this rock and waiting for the Corps to get off its ass to do something is suicide. I, for one, am going to the source of this, so I can get out of here and live to see next year."

"They'll be waiting for us."

"Doubtful." Lyon adjusted the straps on his legs, firmly securing some newly acquire gear. "This guy," he jerked his head toward the dead piolant in the corner, "didn't expect us. We go now, or they *will* expect us next time."

"But teleporting live beings is impossible; it'll kill us."

Lyon drifted to a halt and stood. "Ky, I understand your worry, but I also know what I saw, what we all saw. How they do it, I don't know; I'm not going to pretend to know. But it must be how they are moving around this planet, and our job is to stop them. Luckily enough, we have a great team with the skills to pull this off. But to make that happen we need you focused."

Bashful anxiety uncharacteristically softened the edges of an otherwise cheery face. Even the tips of her ears seemed lower somehow as her tail rested still on the floor.

Hitook and Oz entered the room, each holding one end of a long, preformed crate of sorts. Inside, stacked like plates in a dishwasher, were enough combat packs, the type Larin favored, for everyone else in the room. When they placed the crate on the floor, Lyon gave the next set of instructions.

"Larin, give Oz a full cannon, suit him with a pack and give him at least enough training to protect himself."

The rolbrid sat against the wall with one of his cannon's guts open. He looked up and shot in two bursts, "What? You're joking!"

"Every manned gun we have going in better be worth at least one more dead renegade. As much as I would love to have two of you, we don't. So could you at least do what you can with him?"

It wasn't just the logic that intrigued Larin but the challenge. He sprung from the floor with ease as he slammed his weapon shut and holstered it. "I'm not promising anything."

"I'm not asking you to," Lyon replied and shifted his attention elsewhere, leaving Larin to approach Oz.

Squinting one eye, the rolbrid scanned the local from toe to head, much like a boxer sizing up the competition. "Other than today, what weapons experience do you have?" Larin asked before rummaging through a crate.

"Um," Oz sputtered a start, "I hunted with my father when I was a kid, and I've fired standard issue rifles in the military."

"Marksman?" Larin asked while continuing to rummage.

"No."

"Ever see combat?"

"Not really."

"That's not an answer; either you have or haven't."

"No."

Larin turned as he pulled a particle cannon from a formfitting case and cradled the weapon in his arms without acknowledging it. "Ever kill anything?"

Oz slipped into thought, trying to remember something and feeling half ashamed.

Larin sensed it. "Not even when hunting?"

Oz shook his head. "Today was the first time."

This left Larin wondering how to proceed, then he reminded himself that his rolbrid hide could be on the line. "Well, you're in luck." His voice even genuinely sounded cheery. Hitook suspiciously watched from the sidelines.

Larin proffered the cannon with one hand and slapped it with another. "This will practically kill everything for you."

Oz lifted the weapon from Larin's hand and attempted to get comfortable with it as the rolbrid ran down the basics.

"This is the Dragon Corps' standard weapon, technically called a particle torque laser; it's simply a compact particle cannon with a torque barrel." Larin pointed out the parts. "This thin collection grid wrapping around the back end is where it feeds. In dense atmospheres, its fire is near continuous; on this rock it takes about twenty seconds to fully charge one of its two cells." With a tap on the top rear of the weapon, he continued. "The micro-fiber battery is so dense that it'll keep the molecule accelerator running at top speed for an entire day in continuous operation."

Larin grabbed the top of the weapon and twisted it a bit in Oz's hands to better show the rest. "This contraption along the bottom is an adjustable arm rest, but don't worry about it; you won't need it. The rest of this under the torque barrel is an allaric launcher."

He pulled the magazine free from it perch just in front of the trigger guard and turned it toward Oz. The terran only saw a hollow squarish container.

"It's empty," Oz remarked.

"No, it's full." Larin thumped a finger on the top layer of translucent crystal. "You'll only have standard clips, thirty rounds apiece. The allaric slats act like mini-grenades, to use something you might be familiar with, so be careful. Now, you won't have a direct interface with the weapon, so slide this button forward to fire the allaric, and...here," Larin took the weapon, wrapped his hand around the grip, reprogrammed the weapon and handed it back, "now you're set to fire half cells with the cannon and single shots with the allaric. If you need it adjusted later, one of us will need to do it.

"Half-cell shots mean if we confront armored targets, aim for the head, neck, joints, any spot with no or weakened armor; otherwise,"

Larin's voice dropped sarcastically low, "you soon won't have anything to worry about."

Larin returned the allaric clip and slammed it home. The weapon emitted an electronic buzz as it prepared the rounds for firing. One-handed, the rolbrid reached back into the crate and retrieved a device about as wide and long as Oz's thigh. "This is a stock for the Zeus."

"Zeus?"

"We informally call this weapon 'Zeus.' It's a nickname of sorts, but," Larin tapped the device he now had, "this is a five hundred series combat stock. It's not the top of the line but an efficient modifier."

Oz noticed two more clips like the one used for the allaric launcher protruding from the bottom of the stock. Larin pointed them out. "These are your immediate replacement magazines for the launcher. That'll give you ninety on the weapon, and the combat pack carries enough to refill all the clips once, giving you one hundred and eighty allaric rounds in all." Larin took a moment to shoot Oz an emphasizing, and somewhat knowing, look. "If you use a hundred and seventy-nine rounds, don't forget to save the last one for yourself."

Creepy vibes squiggled up Oz's spine in response to the way Larin shared that last bit of information. Oz couldn't tell if the rolbrid was sarcastically joking or giving genuine advice that he'd give anybody else.

Without asking, Larin took the weapon from Oz's grip, coupled the stock behind the particle cannon and jammed them together with a solid snap. In motions as smooth as mercury, Larin jabbed a finger into the groove along the top spine of the stock and yanked back as he pointed the weapon forward with the other hand. Small paddles ratcheted back, opening ports to tubes that ran lengthwise along the front half of the stock. Oz had no doubt his teacher had performed the move a thousand times.

Next, Larin slid a black stick from one of the three pouches of flexible fabric on each side of the stock. About an inch square and a foot long, the object sparkled as if made from highly compact coffee—solid, black coffee. "These are Brock sticks." He fitted the stick into one of the open ports and butted it against the associated paddle that he had previously pulled to the rear. Then he retrieved another stick and duplicated the procedure on the opposite side. "They're a specialized mixture of condensed matter, which comes in extremely handy in light atmospheres or in intense combat situations."

A light pounding on the top rear of the stock sent the paddles shooting forward and slamming the Brock sticks in place so hard that it would constitute rape on most planets. "By lining both sides, the weapon's buzzard field can instantaneously feed from the sticks to fill sixteen cells. With half-cell shots, that'll give you thirty-two rounds per set of two sticks. You'll have three sets on the weapon, and the pack has another twelve sticks. So that's a hundred and forty-four cells or two hundred and eighty-eight half-cell shots.

"If you can't reload or you go through all the sticks, the open slits on the sides of the stock will allow the field to pull from the atmosphere. The recharge speed will degrade quickly as it depends on the density of the air wherever you are, but it will still work." Larin spun the weapon around in another highly proficient move and handed it, butt first, back to Oz. "Try it out."

Instantly Oz remarked at the lack of weight. "Whoa!" As if gyros or another mechanism were at work, the weight seemed precisely balanced and manipulated as to feel not as heavy as it should.

Larin nodded. "Yeah, I know. Just don't point it at anyone here. Speaking of which," Larin slapped the raised platform on the front top of the stock, "this is your sight. It connects through the stock to the main targeting system here. It's what we call an inter-core targeting system, in other words, you're looking right down the barrel. It's one of the more accurate systems. The laser-screen monitor will provide you a three-dimensional image so you'll know when the barrel's straight. Now before we fit you with a pack, let's get you a sidearm."

The rolbrid turned to find Lyon across the room. The atlantian had one hand on each of Ky's shoulders in a reassuring gesture and appeared to be in the middle of a pep talk to the sullen dextian. Larin didn't care if he interrupted, so he did. "Do you want him to have a Katarei or let him keep that lame Tempest?"

Many words have been used for the Tempest—conventional, traditional, low-tech—but this marked the first time Lyon had heard someone call the Silver Knight's royal sidearm "lame." Being interrupted further intensified his scowl. "He can keep my sidearm for now; he's familiar with it already."

Larin shrugged and commented to Oz, "Your loss. Now, let's get to the pack." Hitook had already hoisted one from the crate.

With a reassuring pat on Ky's shoulder, Lyon stepped away to let her collect herself. "Paloon, what's the status?"

The hunter sat cross-legged with cables running from his arms and the back of his neck to the golden-metallic tube that marked the southwest corner of the reconstructor pad. Distracted with his invisible work, he attempted to answer. "I'm still not sure. I think I have identified the coordinate pairs and folded them, yet the strange structure of the subcarrier signal is keeping me from verifying the signal's integrity."

Maybe Lyon understood, but he wouldn't bet on it. "But do you think it will work?"

Paloon visibly stopped and snapped his focus to the physical plane. "It shouldn't work, period. Call it spirit, soul, karma, chi, Gaia, life force, whatever, no reconstruction technology has been able to move a living creature and keep intact whatever it is that keeps them alive. It's practically an unbreakable law."

Lyon tossed a thumb at the piolant carcass in the corner. "Then how do you explain this unfortunate bastard's appearance out of thin air? We didn't experience a miraculous birth of life. If we did, I think it'd feel different. He came from somewhere, and I'd bet he came from one of those vessels."

"How could a bunch of renegades, regardless of who's leading them, develop the technology to pull off what even the most advanced races have failed to accomplish?" Paloon shook his head at the ground. "Ironic nonsense."

"For the sake of argument," Lyon offered, "let's say teleportation of living matter is a scientific possibility and this device can do it. Can you reverse the signal?"

Paloon looked up, folded his arms and calmly, quietly replied, "I think I have."

"That's all we can ask of you." Lyon turned. "Let's hurry up with the gear; I want an insertion in five minutes."

Rushing to strap on the last bits of gear naturally opened the internal valves, allowing adrenaline-like substances to take over their systems. Concern about the unknown lost to heightened concentration and a focused survival instinct that would let them be prepared for anything. They scrambled about the slippery selvage of a waterfall emptying into an unexplored abyss. Averting their eyes, even for the next five minutes, from the discouraging void offered relief more vital than they had time to realize.

Systemically securing the final pieces of weapons and gear, each one gravitated to the center platform like mindless gnats indirectly making their way to a bug-zapper. In Harquebus fashion, or maybe it was just Larin's personal style, the rolbrid sported weapons of all shapes and sizes from about every exposed section of his uniform. Strangely enough, Ky ran a close second in that endeavor, and the rolbrid noticed.

Larin eyed Ky oddly as he watched her holster two large pistols into a V-formation down the small of her back, touching just below her tail and the tips of two swords, the hilts of which protruded over her shoulders. Just as Ky noticed the peculiar admirer, Larin calmly, yet slyly asked, "You wouldn't happen to have a holdout pistol hidden in some unmentionable region, would you?"

"Shut up, you puny pervert!" the dextian snarled.

Larin laughed in a way not too different from a hundred shattering windshields. He took small pleasure in goading Ky. Something about her personality just begged for it, or he secretly found her attractive. If the latter was true, he wouldn't admit it—to anyone, including himself.

A click sounded the release of a black cable from one of the golden pillars in the corner. Paloon coiled the wire in his hands as he unplugged the other end from a jack in his arm.

"Ready?" Lyon asked.

"Thirty seconds, and it fires."

Nervous tension rippled through the room, forcing the sweat out of everyone's hands, or paws, as the case may be. Yet Larin didn't flinch. He shifted around loading his dual particle cannons with Brock sticks. Nearby, Oz twitched and wondered why he couldn't remember what had led him to this point. Larin noticed and couldn't pass up the chance.

"Don't you people have this phrase, 'Reality is stranger than fiction'?" the rolbrid asked with a nudge to Oz's hip in a way that didn't stop Larin from readying his weapons.

"U-um, yeah," Oz stammered as his thoughts briefly let go of his fear. "It's, ah, actually it's 'Truth is stranger than fiction.' So what?"

"Well," Larin spoke around a chur root that flicked about in his mouth, "either way, if this works, your reality is about to get really frapping weird."

Intense worry strangled Oz's face as the terran fought to keep his stomach calm.

"Five seconds," Paloon commented.

Larin whipped both cannons forward and stepped in front as the others also tensed their grips on weapons. Then silence.

Time sidestepped, allowing space to waltz with gravity in an electrically fabricated, eleventh-dimensional, quantum ballroom. Everything inanimate and alive simply disappeared.

Chapter 21

Matter displacement is not too different from the universe's scariest roller coaster. But much like falling from a great height, it's not the trip but the sudden stop at the end that's a bitch.

Screaming at millions of miles a second, the quantum cart zipped forward on electric wheels, riding rails of gravity, only to smack abruptly and violently into a particular intersection of space-time.

The jolt jerked Lyon, Paloon and Oz forward as they buckled before emptying the contents of their stomachs onto the floor. Larin winced as he fought the pain but couldn't help falling forward on one knee, barely keeping one eye open to provide a strategic view of the room he couldn't get from his weapons' cameras.

Ky stumbled but caught herself and looked about quickly, just in time to notice Hitook's eyes roll back as the massive beast began to collapse. She let her crossbow fall to her side as she grabbed Hitook's collar and yanked him forward so he'd fall on his chest. Luckily, that patch of floor was free of bile. She fished about Hitook's leg pouches until she found the finger-sized tube she sought. Once placed against the liqua's rear thigh, the device hissed. Ky returned the empty canister as mumbled noises announced Hitook's slow return to consciousness.

Wiping acid from his lips, Lyon spit as he asked, *"Status?"*

"Clear." Even mentally, Larin grunted as if unable to breathe. *"I think."*

"Yeah, it's clear," Ky confirmed as if unfazed from the recent dance with dimensions not yet explored by most beings in the universe. She crossed the room to the closed double doors and placed a hand against the metal surface. Eyes closed, she commented, *"The area outside is clear for now. I'd advise that everyone gather themselves before an unsuspecting technician strolls in here."*

It took considerably less time to say than actually accomplish. Ky continued to monitor the hall outside, sounding warnings as people approached and passed by the room, which was good since the initial slow response from the team would get a good, collective belly laugh from even the most poorly trained military unit.

Hitook continued to press a paw against his left eye, then rubbed his temples as he watched Paloon approach the large screen on the other side of the room. The hunter ran his fingers along the left edge of the massive monitor as if sensing through the wall. Paloon's fingers stopped as he pulled a tool from a pocket, pausing to shudder as a silent bubble of internal gas crept up his throat to burn his nasal cavities.

Attempting to forget the nauseating moment, Paloon proceeded to pry a panel from the wall. Wires coiled through the wall's innards only slightly masking the rapid flickering of electrons soaring through crystalline circuit boards. Paloon began making his own connections with wires that ran from the sleeves of his coat.

"You have the equipment to remote in?" Lyon asked.

"Yeah, but I wouldn't—"

"I need you mobile." Lyon knew Paloon would have concerns about becoming a liability if on the move while attempting to remotely get access to the vessel. *"We'll have to ghost in as far as possible to reduce the time any prime targets have to egress the ship and increase the time we have to find an exit. I can't risk leaving a security detail to protect you and can't guarantee your safety. So,"* Lyon concluded matter-of-factly, *"you're coming with us."*

Paloon lightly tongued an eyetooth as he contemplated the situation, then nodded and removed the needed equipment from his coat.

"Larin," Lyon mentally spoke as he turned, *"you're on point. Hitook, you're advance, and you'll double as Paloon's guard, when needed. I'll back up Larin as lead, followed by Paloon running recon. Ky, that puts you on rear."*

"What about the local?" Larin asked as he thumbed toward Oz and continued to munch on a root.

The thought stalled Lyon. Sure, he had insisted on bringing Oz along and swore he would control him. Now he had no option but to admit that he hadn't planned on what to do with him in such a situation. Granted, the current predicament could easily be viewed as unpredictable, so adapting to the situation was what leaders had to do. But the others were Corps-trained; he knew what they could do, and he could trust them to do it. The terran posed an unknown.

Throughout the evening, Oz had become somewhat accustomed to listening to the others through his earpiece, even when their mouths didn't move. But now he grew more uncomfortable the longer the silence continued and finally felt compelled to say something. He didn't yet know what.

Lyon noticed the growing uneasiness on Oz's face and cut in, *"First, don't speak unless an absolute must."* The knight noticed Larin's habit and stepped forward while continuing to speak to Oz. *"Since you don't have the same internal microphone as the rest of us, we don't need the excess noise giving away our position."*

On the last word, Lyon reached over and pushed the crackling chur root farther into Larin's mouth. *"Swallow if you must, but get your fix quietly."*

Larin grimaced but did as directed, turning to aim his disdain at the floor. He didn't doubt the request was reasonable but couldn't decide if he was mad more at Lyon or at himself.

Lyon followed his instincts and pointed at Oz, *"You're on rear with Ky."*

The dextian finally lost concentration from the hallway outside. *"I swear,"* she retorted with thick tones of anger, *"if he stumbles or glitches, I'll execute him."*

Oz released a worried, "Wha—"

A raised hand from Lyon silenced him. *"Fair enough."*

Oz attempted to protest again, when Lyon follow with a warning. *"Just don't fuck up."*

"Paloon?" Lyon queried to change the subject.

"Almost," came the reply.

Meanwhile, Ky glowered to emphasize her warning to Oz before returning to her previous task. Bewildered, Oz couldn't read this elfish cat creature. Her demeanor and grace at times were reminiscent of fabled royalty, yet at other times, she snapped with the subtlety of a foul-mouthed pirate who'd rather disembowel an ally than share his ill-gotten loot. Not for the first time in the evening, Oz wanted to go home, but now he didn't really know where he was. He had a guess but felt it best not to ask.

"I'm in," commented Paloon, who didn't speak again until he had replaced the panel and turned to the group. On the wall-sized screen, controls for the transporter disappeared to reveal schematics of a large vessel. *"We're on the Rodayne. It's an Ujik class, combat destroyer belonging to—or at least once belonging to—the Korac Council. The full crew complement, including ground and air support forces, is one thousand six hundred and eighty-seven, or two thousand six hundred and ninety-six with war crewing."*

"What are we facing?" Lyon asked.

"Unknown. I haven't found that information yet, but using the ship's internal sensors, a quick guess is it's packing about two-thirds of a standard crew."

"Is Horwhannor here?"

Using the ship's computers to comb through data files faster than he could think, Paloon never missed a beat. *"No signs of him. But there are reports that indicate he favors the Trioki."*

That changed everything, again. They most likely spent their last ounces of luck on making it through the transporter alive, and asking to have the prime target handed to them would be a bit much. However, it didn't stop Lyon from feeling like Fate had ruled against him again. Locating and subduing Horwhannor could have provided a bargaining chip. Now, the options were limited.

True. They could attempt to take command of the vessel, turn it against the rest of the fleet and maybe, just maybe, hold the Trioki at gunpoint to negotiate surrender. While the odds appealed to Lyon's desire for a challenge, common sense forced him to consider the reality that such a futile attempt was tantamount to suicide.

Suddenly aware of the weight of the eyes upon him, Lyon wondered how long he had been in thought and felt compelled to make an instinctive reaction. *"We blow it."*

No one responded, each lost in contemplation. Lyon added for clarity, *"Find a weak point and get us there. We'll rig a bomb. Then get us to the flight deck and out of this coffin. If we can't get Horwhannor, we're going to hamper his operation."*

Slow acceptance lit Paloon's eyes as he came to agreement. He then looked about as if expecting an answer before asking. *"Outside of the native, has anyone been on an Ujik class destroyer?"* No response.

"I could have used the help, but in this case, here are my guesses." He pointed to them as dots appeared on the schematics, which moved about. *"But this is most likely it. It's a regional maintenance compartment that just happens to be located above a secondary injection conduit for the tertiary drive system."*

"What's the system?" Larin asked, knowing that such a job of rigging a bomb rested with his expertise.

"Vectored thrust using an edchinal mixture of seven to one. Can you do it?"

"Yeah," Larin replied with a confident lack of concern. *"A sneeze could set that off; just get me there."*

"Sure, it's two decks down and about eight hundred meters toward the left bow." Paloon pointed behind the group toward the transporter they came from. *"That's if we go direct."*

"Can you lock it down?" Lyon asked hopefully.

Paloon shook his head negatively. *"They've got security protocols running. If I go after it, I'll have to go deep and someone will need to drag me. I might be able to do two or three nearby doors at a time though."*

"What about our exit?" came Ky's voice off the metal wall she faced. She knew she should handle the confrontation more boldly, because unless she was in the right mental state, she could become a hindrance to the team. *"I don't want to leave our only possible means of a return trip unless we've got our escape planned."* At least, that's what she wanted to believe.

Paloon nodded. *"From this location,"* the schematics on the wall began to move again, *"one deck up and four hundred meters out is a flight deck with shuttles big enough for all of us. All we'll have to do is take the flight deck by storm. We'll be out of here before they know what happened."*

"Works for me." Lyon knew the risks, but he continued to chide himself. He pushed it aside and decided to deal with his choice. *"Okay, we'll do this segments at a time. Paloon, point us in the right direction; do what you can."* Lyon raised his cannon and jerked his head toward the door. *"Let's go."*

"Not yet," Ky replied faster than Paloon. *"Approaching, two from the left, one from the right. Casual."*

Impatient and eager to get the job started, Lyon gave the order. *"After they pass, Ky, neutralize them; Larin, secure the corridor; Hitook, get those bodies in here. What direction?"*

"Right," replied Paloon.

In Ky's mind, visions of beings glided along the hall. She sensed presence, mood and surface thoughts. A lone rolbrid and two doludgians approached each other with only casual acknowledgment. The doludgians' chatting reinforced their own opinions on how much they disliked a particular co-worker. The two groups crossed slightly off center of the door. Ky waited for the rolbrid to get just one step past the maximum opening point.

Without warning her teammates, she tapped the door release. It slid open, and she popped out with her crossbow. In a blur, Ky shot the rolbrid first, then the two doludgians, her auto reloading and cocking weapon keeping up and making sounds no louder than whispers. Ky was back inside before the bodies could crumple almost simultaneously to the floor but not before Larin was at the door with a particle cannon pointing in each direction.

"We're clear," Paloon commented, but it didn't keep Larin from taking his time.

The rolbrid crossed the hall, his face pointed to the far wall but eyes focused down both halls by watching through the weapons' internal cameras. Halfway across, his arms went from their wide V formation to snap in opposite directions, his left arm across the front and right arm around his back. Then Larin spun clockwise to put his back against the wall while never losing his fields of fire down both halls.

Hitook had the first body in the room before Lyon decided to stow his weapon along the side of his combat pack and help move the other bodies. With the hall clear, Ky grabbed Oz by the shoulder and yanked him along into the hall to guard the left as Larin turned and started advancing down the right corridor.

Leaving the only immediate means of escape behind, the team had no choice but to advance.

Just short of a miracle was how Oz viewed it. They had made it to the maintenance room undetected. Hitook did have to sneak up on two creatures and snap their necks and impale a third upon the team's descent into the room from a duct-like system between the floors. From the internal communications and the pounding on doors, Oz deducted that Paloon had used his connection into the vessel's computer system to keep locking doors long enough for the team to move into the next hall, room or hatch without being stumbled upon by unsuspecting residents.

Along the short trip, Oz also finally admitted to himself that the people, beings, creatures or whatever his traveling companions were honestly believed themselves to be on a vessel full of hostile enemy. Oz had previously been half distracted, swinging in and out of realization and recognition of the truth before him. Going through the motions in an extended state of delirium only took one so far. Clarity came to him like slowly heated water. Now it raged in a roaring boil threatening to deafen him with the noise.

"You all right?"

Oz looked up to Hitook. "Yeah," he lied.

Just moments ago, Oz watched this massive, hairy beast thrust a two-bladed sword down another creature's spinal column. Then Hitook nonchalantly wiped the blades clean with his fingers, flicking the blue, gelatin-like substance to the floor. He now spoke with the gentleness of a lamb.

Oz wanted to be sick. His mind raced at nervous speeds trying to sort through the meaning of his recent epiphany. Stuck on an enemy ship in orbit around his planet, a situation that should scare him. It did. He paused to notice that he could feel the adrenaline rushing through his blood, but his stomach wasn't twisted, his palms were dry and his ears didn't feel warm. The thought distracted him. He was scared but without all the regular side effects.

"How thick?" Larin asked as he rapped the floor with his foot.

"About two meters," Paloon responded from his sitting position against a rack of large metal plates. *"Olum-sil alloy."*

Larin searched about until his eyes stopped on a tall, thin door-like panel. He opened it. Hanging garments filled the inside. The rolbrid sounded acceptance as he leaned his particle cannons against the wall and withdrew the GK from his combat pack

"Larin," Lyon intoned with tension. Here was not the place to be lobbing CNG grenades.

"Relax." The rolbrid detached the magazine, knelt and thumbed out five rounds, which clattered on the floor. *"You wanted a bomb, so I just need some explosives."*

Larin slammed the magazine home and twirled the rifle over his left shoulder and back into its place against the side of his combat pack. Still kneeling, he began arranging the canisters, standing them on their ends in a wide circle on the bottom of the locker. *"Ky, you still have that Quietus?"* He had seen her strap it to her leg before they jumped, but he still asked.

"Yes." She stopped monitoring the activity outside one of the room's doors long enough to poke her head around a rack.

Lyon noticed and quietly motioned for Hitook to take the other door.

"I need it."

"Why?" She argued but still proceeded to unholster the pistol from her right calf.

"I just need a couple of rounds; I'll give it back." He waited until he heard the weapon sliding along the floor then caught it with his foot before continuing. *"I don't know why you brought the thing."*

"If I run into a piolant again, the fucker's getting a couple of shots of that in his face." Bitter rage growled, even in Ky's mental voice.

Originally the acid pellets were created to be a solution against beasts with thick hides or plates, but in warfare the use became impractical. Larin couldn't deny, however, that planting a few rounds in a piolant's face would allow you enough time to get to a weak spot. He unclipped a flash grenade from his chest bandoleer. From the grenade's back, he slid off a thumb-sized wafer of plastic. Then he set the square grenade in the center of the CNG rounds. *"No wonder you're armed to the teeth, you got whooped, and now you're out to make a point."*

"And the reason you're toting that massive CNG launcher is to compensate for your own inadequacies."

Lyon coughed a chuckle and turned away in an attempt to hide it.

For once, Larin responded, *"Don't encourage her."* He shook his head, amazed at his loss for a retort, as he detached the wide magazine from under the Quietus's barrel and peeled off two glass rounds. As green liquid bubbled inside, Larin rested the rounds on top of the flash grenade and stood as he returned the magazine to the pistol and gently closed the locker door.

"It's set."

"What did you do?" Lyon asked, unsure of what had just happened as he watched Larin walk over and hand Ky her pistol.

The rolbrid turned back and held out the wafer of plastic he pulled off the grenade. *"I flick this remote switch, the grenade goes, enough to shatter the housing around the ammoi zeririol. Now that acid is flammable, and when it burns, it burns hot, hot enough, that it will melt through the floor, dropping the CNG rounds into the conduit. Meanwhile, the heat will set off the nitro in the rounds, which in turn will cause a CNG detonation, which will travel through the conduit into the edchinal tank. Then everyone in this death trap is just not going to feel so well."*

Troubled, Lyon wondered if all rolbrids felt the desire to create witty comments. *"What if it doesn't burn all the way through?"*

"Oh, it will. Even if the floor's solid alloy, this stuff will burn right through, no doubts."

"So you've done this before?"

"Um, no."

"How do you know it will work?" Impatience filled Lyon's mental voice. He didn't want them to be wasting their time; he wanted this ship destroyed.

"Look, it's not like people are constantly inviting me to ship destruction parties. 'Here, see if you can blow up my ship with just the weapons on your back.' But theoretically, it will work."

Lyon stopped himself from replying to the sarcasm. Instead, he chose the path of least frustration and decided to trust that the lieutenant knew what he was talking about. *"Fair enough."* The knight turned and approached Paloon to nudge the apparently sleeping body. *"Paloon. Paloon!"*

"Hey, not so loud," Larin retorted as he shook his head. *"We hear that too."*

Lyon rolled his eyes before noticing Paloon spring to life.

"I was out doing recon in the flight deck systems." He stood and blinked hard. *"I also went a little deeper into the security net, and everything is still calm."*

"Good." Lyon adjusted his grip on his cannon again. *"Gather yourselves. It's time to leave."*

Chapter 22

Mild blue walls snaked about mostly at right angles. Through the gloss coat shimmered a touch of gunmetal grey. The only mar on otherwise seamless walls came as a wide black streak that ran parallel to and about three feet above the floor. Every so often the dark line would break into vertical rows of marks resembling something between kanji and hieroglyphics.

Paloon reported that the other side of the door was clear, and the team proceeded again, turning right, then left.

"How far is this maintenance hatch?" Lyon asked.

"Not too far," Paloon paused to check the systems again. *"It's just up ahe—wait!"*

The team froze. Larin stopped at the bend as the hall took another turn to the left. He peeked down the passage to see nothing as Lyon inquired, *"What is it?"*

"Something's not right." The hunter's voice trailed for a moment. *"I think I'm being shadowed."* At the end of that thought, Paloon cursed as his body shook. It took all of his will to force his back to the wall so he could slide down somewhat safely.

Tensions heightened but not soon enough. With an electrical crack, a bolt of energy ripped down the hall and tore off a small chunk of Larin's left bicep. His weapon immediately fell from his weakened grip, but the rolbrid reacted as if nothing happened. He spun with the momentum of the shot, quickly bringing the particle cannon in his right hand around, aiming down the hall and blasting four bolts. Still wishing to hit anything, he knew the volley had missed the assailant as he kept spinning another half turn out of the line of fire.

"It's on!" Larin barked as he crouched to retrieve his other weapon.

Oz followed Ky's lead the best he could as they positioned themselves to shoot anything that might come out of the door they just left. Hitook leapt over to help Paloon to the floor as Lyon slid next to Larin and gave the rolbrid a small nod.

Larin knew what it meant and hoped he could keep the grip on his weapons as his arm started to throb. But the circumstances called for action or death. Pain didn't have a voice in the matter. Both of Larin's cannons came high around the corner and began an alternating barrage of fire down the passage and into the far corner of the cross intersection about thirty paces away.

Under the cover, Lyon's legs split as he threw his right foot toward the base of the far wall. As he landed, he crouched low and aimed for the opposite corner of the intersection. Seeing someone's shoulder, he released a solid bolt, tearing flesh and throwing blood against the wall. Lyon powerfully extended his now bent right leg and, almost like a frog, jumped out of the hall.

Larin, too, sought cover for what little he had exposed as return shots cracked down the hall and pounded dents in the bulkhead. After several waves, the volleys ended long enough for Larin to return covering fire and Lyon leapt into the hall again.

This time, as he expected, no target remained within his line of sight. A mental switch activated the under-barrel mount, and two bursts of green crystal sailed down the passage, aiming to crash into the far wall and fill the perpendicular hall with shrapnel to remove any remaining threats in that direction. With the shots fired, Lyon jumped back before he could see what Larin witnessed.

The allaric crystals smashed into an invisible wall, sending the shards back in the direction they came from. Larin's cannons received nicks as he barely made it out of the hall in time. Razor-sharp crystal slivers whistled by his face as they raced to pepper the already dented bulkhead in a cacophony of screeching thuds. The result resembled a bed of nails standing on end, but with much deadlier nails.

Lyon first thought that their attackers also fired, but Larin knew what had happened. *"We have a teek!"*

Only a teek, or a telekinetic, could have produced enough force to shatter the crystals early and send the resulting shards in the wrong direction. Whether a random patrol or not, the lethality of the assailants ratcheted up several hundred notches on Lyon's personal scale.

The knight dove toward Ky, tagging her on the shoulder. *"Take care of it."*

Ky peeled away, joining Hitook in moving to the front. Oz watched the exchange as Lyon took Ky's place at the rear. Lyon kept his weapon's stock to his shoulder and didn't look or acknowledge Oz, but he did point two fingers to his eyes then back at the door Oz was supposed to be helping Lyon watch.

"Incoming!" Larin warned, but Hitook had already sensed the movement and mentally caught the grenade as it sailed around the corner. Hitook pushed it as hard as he could against the opposing wall of force as another grenade then another flew around the corner. Barely noticing them in time, Hitook couldn't push them back but did stop them half way down the hall.

Wedged between mental walls of force, the grenades thunderously exploded in rapid secession. A wall of fire pushed outward until it forced the mental fields to bulge under the pressure. Strain drove sweat from every pore on Hitook's nose as the liqua began to growl, but he held it until he knew he could safely drop the invisible wall and rest for a moment. Any teek maintaining the wall on the other side would also be too mentally fatigued to attempt anything soon.

As Hitook knelt on one knee, Ky brought her focus to a close. She had been standing, fingers intertwined into an oddly shaped tent before her, and her a gaze focused on the opposite side of the bulkhead. Probing through the walls of metal, her mind used the flowing of energy to seek out the enemy teek. Steady. Focus. The explosion weakened the teek's mental defenses, and Ky uttered a grunt as her arms shot forward. A spike of mental energy soared like a drilling arrow through the piolant's brain.

"Go!" Ky commanded.

Larin snapped around the corner, holding his cannons in at wide angles. Bursts of allaric soared down the passageway, past where the invisible wall had been and into the far bulkheads of both intersecting halls. The rolbrid twisted out of the way while green light flashed in strobes as each round shattered, filling the hall with more razor-sharp shards.

"Forward!" Larin barked.

Hitook was already on the move. Too fatigued to attempt any mental combat, he knew he'd have to rely on physical training. Racing down the hall, he tried to relax his body. As he appeared in the intersection, on his right, a piolant with his plates littered with shards had already begun to stand with weapon in hand.

Tough, Hitook silently complimented as he beat the piolant at speed. He gripped the piolant's wrist, pulling the weapon off target and the arm up, revealing probably the only area not covered in shards. In a flurry, Hitook repeatedly pounded his foot into the piolant's side as he pulled on the arm. As he heard plates begin to crack, Hitook also heard a grunt behind him. He turned to see a doludgian somehow summon enough energy to begin picking herself off the floor.

With his free hand, Hitook snatched the weapon out of the helpless piolant's hand and threw it with grace and power. The misshapen missile buried itself in the doludgian's skull. A stunned pause later, the being collapsed to the floor again, this time for good.

Turning his attention back to the piolant he held captive, Hitook noticed a dazed vemulli gradually pushing its fur-covered body up the wall. Hitook wanted to wonder how they had survived the barrage of allaric rounds, but he didn't have time.

He kicked for the piolant's legs, sweeping the creature off its feet and forcing it to the floor face first. He brought his foot around and aimed for the best shard-free location, which just happened to be the piolant's neck. The boot came down solid and heavy as Hitook twisted and pulled on the arm to stabilize himself. Cracks and snaps fired from the neck and shoulder with Hitook's full weight shifting to allow his other foot to arc around and into the vemulli's jaw, careful to dodge the maw of sharp teeth.

The kick was weak, but it connected. He brought his left foot down as he spun backwards. Hitook's right foot came off the now dead piolant and whipped around with much more force square into the side of the vemulli's head. The neck shattered as the head twisted and bounced off the wall, orange goo splattering from the corpse's mouth.

Larin arrived, his head jerking about as he surveyed the damage Hitook had done. *"Frapping-A!"*

"What is it now?" Lyon asked.

"Oh, nothing," Larin replied as he gazed at Hitook's calm eyes and reeled a bit. *"We're clear; we're very clear."*

"Good. Hitook, get back here. We'll need to carry Paloon."

Lyon and Ky had already swapped places again. Lyon knelt next to Paloon's twitching body. He knew the hunter must be locked in an electronic fight for his life. Most likely, they zeroed on Paloon's connection to the ship's system in hopes of holding it open long enough to force a deadly shot of feedback into Paloon's brain. There were risks, but Lyon needed help.

Hoping to get a signal through all the static in Paloon's head, Lyon unleashed a forceful backhanded slap across Paloon's face. "Paloon!" Another hit, and Lyon repeated, "Paloon! We need to know where the nearest flight deck is!"

Hitook arrived and immediately scooped Paloon off the floor. In the motions, Paloon's face seemed to shine more whitely than possible.

Lyon needed to get through to Paloon. "Pa—"

"Straight...a...head." The words came as struggles. "Ele...vator...up...one...stay...left." Paloon collapsed again, hanging off Hitook's arms like wet pasta.

Time didn't haggle, so Lyon reacted with what little information Paloon was able to get through. He slapped Hitook on the biceps and barreled around the corner toward Larin. *"We're moving, now!"* Straight through the intersection, past Larin and to the far door, Lyon punched the release.

Another short hall extended in front of him before opening into a circular room. The walled, round core must contain the elevator. But luck was running true to form and the doors weren't facing their direction. As Lyon approached where the hall emptied into the round room, he noticed the edges of two more hallways on the far edges on both sides of the center structure.

The combat tactician in him didn't like the position this put his team. Obviously, ship security knew they were here; security might have been watching them for a while. The thought should have been unsettling, but Lyon's frustration and desire tipped the scales. He halted at the edge to provide as much cover as possible. *"Get in and seal that door."*

Ky pushed Oz back with one hand as she also backed in through the door. Then she slammed her hand on the release. As the door slid down, Larin raised one cannon. Tiny vents on the sides of the allaric magazine spouted green fire as Larin discharged a few of the rounds of uncharged, clear, solid slats of allaric. Three rounds into both sides of the door embedded themselves half in the door and half into the bulkhead.

Larin hadn't completed the task before shots fired from Lyon's cannon.

"Incoming, flanking positions, armored."

Lyon's status report sent the team in motion. Ky spun, her tail bringing the crossbow around, and she began firing to the left. Hitook laid Paloon against the wall and tried to ready his barely refreshed mind for another possible teek attack. Lyon crouched and fired alternating shots of bolts and crystal, but the allaric would have less of an effect as he could easily see that these responding forces came suited in armor. It could explain the slower response time, but that didn't matter at the moment.

Larin finished and joined in with both particle cannons blazing, half trying to eliminate targets and half just trying to keep the attackers from getting any good shots.

"Out of bolts," Ky notified. *"I've got the left."*

Oz who still hid in the far corner, his mind racing on what to do, watched Ky reach over her shoulders and unsheathe twin short swords from around her back. Light gleamed on the shiny, vaguely blue blades as Ky leapt for the far wall. In short runs along the curved bulkheads, she bounced between them as she barreled down on the doomed guards turning the corner.

An arc of energy fizzled in front of Larin's face. The rolbrid correctly assumed that Hitook had starting running defense from the incoming fire. After the energy dissipated, Larin noticed the responding forces weren't advancing. Instead, they pulled back, sticking close to their cover and only taking the most defensive of shots.

Lyon had also noticed. *"This isn't good."*

"Yeah, I know." Larin quickly looked about remembering the few words Paloon had been able to get through earlier. *"We need to go up one floor, right?"*

"Yeah," Lyon snapped as he sent another series of shots before pulling back against the wall to replace his cannon's Brock sticks.

"Fine." Larin stepped around a cross-legged Hitook, snarled at Oz and pointed at the weapon he held. *"Are you going to use that?"* Larin didn't wait; he grabbed him by the shoulder and pulled him up front. *"Cover me."*

"But—"

"I don't give a frap if you hit anything, just fire."

Sparks exploded in Oz's face, startling him into a yelp and tossing him painfully on his butt.

"Hitook is protecting you, but you had better get firing to keep their heads down. I'm going to be busy."

Larin turned his back to the firefight and spun his dual particle cannons until they pointed down and the stocks were cradled under his arms. He slammed them home at odd angles into his hip holsters. They clicked securely. With that, Larin reached down for the barrels and pulled them up as he fell back. The butts of both stocks fell solid on the floor, finishing the whole contraption that held Larin in place.

In smooth but quick movements, Larin slid the Warmonger weapon from the top of his combat pack. Snapping the plank-shaped weapon down then up, he extended the components, grabbed the barrel, yanked to lock it in and didn't wait for the matter field to ready. Metallic light exploded in booming waves that immediately became deafening reverberations for a couple of seconds until the beam stabilized into twisting arcs of electricity that ate away at the ceiling.

Two soldiers recovered from the previous assault of crossbow bolts only to turn the corner and be amazed at the fast dextian bouncing between the walls. They attempted to target Ky, but before they could fully raise their weapons, she was above them. She tightly somersaulted off the wall, slicing one blade through the weapon and hands of the soldier on the right and ending her twirl by firmly pounding her feet into the head of the one on the left. Clattering armor couldn't cover the screams as the two crumpled to the ground, and Ky used the resulting momentum to spring to the far wall.

One guard decided to break from the group farther down the circular hall that had been attacking the rest of Ky's team. The guard, for whatever reason, thought it wise to leave his squad to help the others. But Ky noticed and had a strategy. Metal screeched as she thrust one sword into the wall and curled herself in as if working parallel bars one-handed. She planned to swing down and torpedo herself into the approaching guard. A flash of light from her left changed those plans.

She dropped, releasing her sword seconds before it began melting into the wall, the result of being struck by a bright, white beam fired by the new forces coming down the hall that shot off the circular room to the left. Ky rolled toward the new target and sprang up, cutting the weapon in half with the sword in her left hand and driving her left foot in a high kick to the attacker's chin. She hadn't forgotten her initial target, and now with her right hand free, snatched one of the machine pistols from the small of her back and fired a short burst of rounds.

A hair's width behind each other, the three explosive bullets seemingly detonated simultaneously. Bits of armor twinkled in the comet trail of blood and tissue as the guard lifted from the floor and arched backward to bounce limply to a halt.

Ky ducked to dodge another shot, re-holstered the pistol, rolled to miss another round, then, with sword now gripped with both hands, gutted one guard like a small, defenseless woodland creature as she sprang up. With methodical precision, the skilled assassin proceeded to blaze a swath of death through the newly arrived platoon. The blitzkrieg came to a stunned halt when the door at the far end opened.

Eternity droned in the few seconds it took Larin to slice three sides of a rectangle out of the ceiling. Larin wished it hadn't taken so long as he was just as eager as everyone else to exit. With a powerful, yet quick, set of flicks, the molecular destabilizing weapon collapsed back into its plank shape about a third of its extended length. Larin slid it back into the top of his combat pack as he mentally engaged the pack's magnetic displacement unit.

The rolbrid flew to the ceiling and clamped onto it through the new opening. Throwing the pack in reverse, Larin came down in screams. The pulling on his left arm murderously agitated the wound he received in the initial stages of the earlier firefight. He unconsciously released his grip but had pulled the ceiling down enough to soar back up and come down on the thick tongue of metal with both feet.

Metal crashed as the tab of ceiling hit the floor. *"Express stairway out of here,"* Larin grunted and jerked his nose at the newly formed ramp to the floor above.

Lyon took a peek over his shoulder and nodded approvingly. *"Ky, get back here, we're moving."*

"Good." A slight tremble in her tone flagged of a potential problem. *"Because we have mechs."*

"Ah, hell no!" Larin belted.

Ky bolted in an expeditious retreat as two globule distortions blew past her back and loudly crashed into the bulkhead.

Larin unholstered both particle cannons and went to twirl them over his shoulders to attach them to his combat pack, but the clear blood draining from his sleeve and now covering his left hand sent one cannon flying forward. He attempted to fling blood off his left hand as he peeled the square-shaped grenades off his bandoleer with his right hand. Clicks sounded as he threw them like misshapen disks down both halls.

"Fire in the hole!"

Ky spun to help Hitook maintain a wall of protection as the concussive force compounded within the enclosed space of the halls.

Lyon reached down for Larin's previously lost cannon, and now aimed one cannon down each hall. *"Get Paloon, and get up that ramp!"* Once the smoke no longer seemed pressed against an invisible wall, Lyon released tight, alternating volleys of bolts and crystals down the halls for covering fire.

About half way up the ramp, Larin added to the barrage of covering fire the best he could as Ky ran past. Hitook, cradling Paloon, came next, closely followed by Oz, but Larin pushed the local up the ramp. *"We're moving,"* Larin yelled at Lyon who began backing up.

By the time Lyon made it to the top of the ramp, Larin had the Warmonger out again and promptly cut into the floor to finish the rectangle he had started. Shrieks pierced the air as the last bit of metal tore loose under the weight, and the metal slab thudded to the floor below. Amidst everything, wisps of smoke whispered a warning.

"Incoming!" Larin barked.

Ky's inertia delayed her turn back but didn't keep her from catching the grenades just as they popped through the hole in the floor. Any remaining fragments of physical hearing seemed to take a vacation upon yet another thunderous explosion, which left the team a bit stunned.

As they gathered themselves, Lyon pointed down the hall. *"Ky, take point; keep to the left; look for what may be a hangar; get moving."*

Twanging whistles ended with tinny clanks. Lyon and Larin careened their necks to see multiple cables shooting through the hole in the floor, as magnetic clamps on each one secured the cables to the ceiling. Such a large hole would keep ground troops from coming down the hall even if they did use the elevator, but the pilots of those compact combat mechs seemed determined to pull their death machines onto the upper floor and continue pursuit.

"Move!" Lyon reiterated with determination.

A glass factory exploded in Larin's throat, as the rolbrid vocalized a growl of frustrated anger. He gripped the Warmonger tighter as needles of light shot from the sides of the tip and a ball of light crackled into existence. Cutting the cables wouldn't do, so Larin charged boldly to the selvage. "Not on my watch!"

Atoms exploded as light raced from the weapon and stuck the first mech below. Larin pulled wide, dragging the destructive beam across the two combat droids that had gathered. Under the blossoming fountain of errant electrons, both pilots screamed in terror as the beam moved so quickly as to decompose only parts of their bodies. One pilot, however, still held on to enough sanity to ensure his death would not be without repercussions.

Hissing air sent a wide, thin block of glowing red rods soaring up from the rear of the last mech.

"Get down!" Larin belted as he halted his attack and threw himself to the floor.

Damaged, the core detonated prematurely, violently shaking the entire area of the ship and bathing the hole in the floor with a liquid florescence. Heavy heat peeled Oz's eyelids back so he could see from his supine position the light giving way to thick blankets of cobalt fire rolling in torrents along the ceiling. Lime curls whipped about as if tasting the heated air.

Even counting the accident that claimed his friend's life and almost killed him, Oz had never been in such fear for his life. Muscles ached as he slammed his eyes closed and clenched tightly. He didn't want to open them again but did so without thinking when someone tapped his boot.

Oz shifted to see Ky beginning to stand and motioning for him to move. His eyes darted to the ceiling, but the massive fire had receded. Either it was short lived or Oz had blacked out from fear.

Recovering like a band of rapidly sobering drunks, the team rose from the floor to stumble into a weak run. Keeping left at the Y-shaped intersection, they continued on and repeated the direction choice at the next interchange, which opened into a long hall.

Ky, a sword still in her hand, pointed at the wall and read the sign. *"There are escape pods ahead."*

Lyon unevenly wobbled his head. *"We're going to need something faster. Keep looking for a hangar entrance."*

Several feet ahead of the others, Ky scanned farther down the hall and aimed her blade at two wide doors on the left. *"Is that it?"*

"Yeah," came the muffled response followed by a string of mumblings.

Everyone turned to see a squirming Paloon weakly attempting to wrestle free from Hitook's thick arms.

"Let me go." Paloon's shaky voice contradicted the hunter's attempt to be strong.

Hitook obliged and lowered Paloon to the floor as delicately as one would handle a newborn. Moans accompanied the rubbing of fingers in the spikes of his grey hair.

"Welcome back, dirty dog," Larin snipped sarcastically. *"You've conveniently dodged all the fun."*

"Not now!" Lyon annoyingly scowled at Larin.

Paloon didn't have the energy to care what Larin thought. But Lyon knew, or at least had a good idea, what Paloon must have gone through in the electronic realm. Such battles, if they didn't kill you, could leave you wishing it had.

"We don't have much time." Paloon moaned as he stumbled against a wall, swatting away Hitook's offered hand for support. He began shuffling across the hall toward the door. *"I have us a ship that's prepping itself now, but we're stranded if someone figures out what I've done."*

"Can you get us in?" Lyon questioned, feeling helpless as he watched Paloon struggle to move on his own.

"I embedded an access code before they sent another wave of attacks; they're probably too busy trying to find me to look for buried code."

Static raised the fine fur on Ky's back. A look of recognition passed Hitook's face, and she knew he felt it too. Neither had to communicate. Ky lunged across the hall and pushed Oz to the floor.

Getting Oz out of the way didn't leave her with enough time. *"Inbound."*

Hitook had it. Wrists together, the liqua caught the stream of white energy as an array of long, wildly whipping sparks streamed from between his fingers. The same rounds that had melted metal and punched holes in walls now stopped dead in Hitook's grip and were forced to dissipate into the surrounding air.

Until Paloon could open the door, the team had very few options. The shooter saw the lack of effect, and Ky saw the shooter before he ducked back around the corner down the hall to the left.

"He's mine."

Ky slid her sword toward Oz and withdrew her pistols as she darted down the hall. Quickly reaching speed, she ran onto the wall and to the opening. Timed wonderfully, her toes griped the edge, helping to throw her across the opening. Dual pistols came down, immediately barking three-round bursts through every target that moved: a running guard, a crouched guard, a slightly unaware guard—a mech?

Surprise flushed Ky's face as the first slug of transparent kinetic force smashed into her left leg. Still in air, Ky could feel her body began to spin like a weathervane, but the sensation was short lived as a second shot plowed into her right shoulder. Together the rounds halted Ky's flight and drove her forcefully across the hall and into the bulkhead.

Shrieking whines from the mech's cannons drew the team's attention to the intersection and into a surreal warp as they watched Ky's body bounce off the wall. Before her body rebounded two inches from the wall, a second, tightly packed volley of distorted space pummeled Ky's chest. Streams of blue blood shot from Ky's mouth as the air escaped her lungs. In the short eternity her body seemed held against the wall, moisture began to coat the cloth around her chest before her body flopped to the floor.

Hitook roared and bolted forward as Larin and Lyon raised their weapons, but they lacked a target. A shrieking whine echoed again. Lyon knew what that meant.

"Get that door open!"

"I'm trying," Paloon muttered as he fumbled with the keypad to enter the bypass code he had implanted.

Larin and Lyon dove for the small bit of cover the inset door offered as the mech turned the corner, cannons charged and ready to fire again. Reality broke in on Hitook's emotions. Too much distance, he'd never make it to the mech in time. He scrambled a retreat and noticed Oz had just begun to pick himself from the floor, putting himself in the line of fire.

The massive liqua collided with Oz and held him tight as Hitook felt the pilot pull the trigger. Two rounds hammered into Hitook's back. A deep, resonant growl accompanied jets of saliva from clenched teeth.

Simultaneously, Lyon and Larin popped around the small indentation in the wall and launched shots first at the war machine then at the troops attempting to breach the corner. Amid the salvo, Lyon quickly scanned Ky's unmoving body and the growing pool of blue blood. The sight steeled his rage that might have exploded had not the sound of the opening hangar door forced him to react.

Oz belted startled objections as Lyon yanked him by the arm away from Hitook and through the now open door.

"Hitook, get Paloon and get to that ship!"

Bestial rage glowed in his eyes as Hitook's head snapped toward Lyon.

"She's dead." Lyon forced the words past the tightest in his throat.

"And you will be too if you don't move your furry hide," Larin added, knowing the risks and not caring as he continued shooting.

In the past few moments, Lyon witnessed some interesting events. He couldn't explain them all yet and didn't have the time to think about them. But he doubted Hitook would go down easily if he decided to give his life trying to pull Ky's body out. Either the realization that the action would be suicidal or the shrieking whine of the mech's kinetic blasters recharging sent Hitook forward, snatching the weak Paloon off his feet and into the now closing door. Lyon grabbed Larin's shoulder and pulled him in.

Save for a long window along the right wall, dark grey metal formed the rectangular hangar. Evenly spaced beams pushed against the ceiling. From the large doors that flanked the opposite wall, metal grates snaked about the floor and around long indentations.

Around one of the dips in the floor, two beings stopped looking into the pit and stood perplexed at the new arrivals.

Being the first to arrive, Oz felt abandoned and offered an uncomfortable smile. Wrapping fingers around the weapon he still carried, he became aware of the possible situation and tried to smooth things with a, "Hi."

The rest of the team bolted through the door as it slammed shut.

"Second one on the left," Paloon pointed from his cradled position in Hitook's arms.

As the two headed for the ship, massive bolts of kinetic energy pounded into the door, bulging the metal. Woefully unprepared for the event transpiring before them, the maintenance technicians dashed for the opposite door, only to reel when it opened too soon and a mech charged through.

"Shit!" Oz yelled and dove for the nearest pit. Air left his lungs and pain filled his body as he landed on unforgiving metal.

Lyon dove in after him but landed in a prepared crouch. Larin planted himself behind a nearby pillar and watched two globules of distorted space sail over Hitook's head as the liqua and Paloon leapt into another pit.

Peeking above the floor to take pot shots would be suicide, yet Lyon needed to get himself and Oz to the next ship over. *"I need covering fire!"*

"So do I," Larin blasted back. The warrior heard the kinetic cannons charging as the rattle of boots signaled that the hangar was filling with guards. He didn't have to see to know it.

"I need my other cannon!"

Lyon took a second to think about which of the two cannons he had was the one he picked up then tossed it out of the hole toward Larin. White beams raced in their direction as Larin snatched the weapon from the air and pitched his other cannon in return.

Mumbling prayers rattled in Larin's throat as he swapped out the allaric magazine and used his sub-dermal connection to the pistol grip and activated this weapon's modification. One deep breath through the nose, Larin calmed and whispered, "I hope you're right."

The rolbrid snapped around the corner, sweeping the weapon and holding the trigger back. Neon green slats spewed forth in a glowing arc. At half the distance, the slivers of crystal prematurely exploded, sending a hailstorm of deadly sharp daggers.

"Go!" Larin yelled as he emptied the magazine, then followed with red bolts from the particle cannon.

Lyon leapt from the pit, half dragging Oz along. Scampering to the next pit, Oz saw the light from an open hatch at the base of this hole and found himself being pushed into it by Lyon.

Larin yanked back against the pillar. The magazine fell from the weapon and clattered to the floor. Retrieving another magazine from the bottom of his combat pack, Larin's reload came shaky as two hammers of force buckled the beam he hid behind. The mech pilot's message came clear: He still remained a very viable threat.

Even with the mech still operating, most of the responding guard force took serious causalities. Larin had gotten Nux's idea to work. Using the cannon's range finder to calculate the distance and patch it into the allaric charger, the weapon could precisely overcharge each round to explode early. The result created an indiscriminating multitude of shards without the need to strike a surface first.

Two more rounds pounded the pillar. Larin felt the metal buckle into his back. The next pair would blast the beam from its moorings.

Rushing for the ship, Larin sprayed the already peppered hangar with crystal and landed two bolts into the mech to keep the pilot busy. He ended with a roll down the hole and into the hatch. The floor slammed shut, banging the hatch closed.

Hitook finished securing Paloon to the pilot seat then pushed against the ceiling to hold himself in place as the ship rocketed from the docking clamps. The others lost balance and tumbled about.

"Buckle in," Paloon warned.

"A bit late, space jockey," Larin grunted.

"Just get us out of here," Lyon commented as calmly as possible while pulling himself into one of the swiveling chairs and hooking his arms through the seat's harness. Turning to Oz crumpled in the back, Lyon nodded to an empty seat. "*Better get off your butt and strap in.*"

Metal peeled away from the outside of the glass cockpit to reveal a dark chamber highlighted by streaks of red light glowing from the room's waistline. Lifeless ships of various designs clung to the ceiling where there had previously been pits in the floor. This new floor instead had a ribbed trench that came closer before disappearing under the ship Paloon piloted.

He banked to face a tight hole in the wall. From the mouth stretched a tube lined with similar rib-like structures, but these ribs pulsed with blue light in a sequence so rapid that Oz found it blindingly captivating.

Hitook straddled the copilot's chair then slid into it as the ship eased forward at a gradually increasing rate.

Nearing the port's event horizon, Paloon let out a deep breath. *"Cross your fingers."*

"What do—"

Larin's comment fizzled as the electromagnetic rings snatched the ship and flung it forward at a frantic pace into the pitch, which disappeared in a flash of fire. Explosions jarred the tiny vessel and the tube assembly, but the rail launcher indiscriminately chucked the ship through the blaze into the openness of space.

Paloon punched the thrusters, lurching the ship forward.

"What in the hell was that?" Lyon half yelped.

"That, as I had hoped, was the emergency system blowing the hatch." Paloon seemed calm and preoccupied.

"So you couldn't open the hatch?" Trembling slipped into Lyon's voice. "You could have killed us."

"Sure, it was a gamble, but blowing your own hatch versus having it ripped off is cheaper and quicker to fix; I had hoped they would have taken that into account during the ship's design."

Larin was about to join the chastising, when Paloon cut back in, *"Now, this ship's scanners suck; I need your eyes. Tell me what you see."*

Each passenger found their own trails along the glass roof, but all eyes locked on to the sight behind them. Hundreds of vessels glittered like black gold sprinkled with tiny lights. Even in the shadow of the moon, they couldn't miss the massive outline of the Trioki flanked by slightly smaller vessels but each as menacing as the darkest of demons.

The words came slowly from Oz. "Holy shit."

"Yeah," Larin huffed, "tell me about—ah, frap!"

Pinpoints of light blinked, a few at first, from the destroyer they had just left then hundreds blazed from all the massive vessels. They were fighters, lots of fighters.

"Please tell me we've got weapons," Lyon begged.

"You wanted seating room and speed," Paloon snapped as the tiny ship jumped forward, its thrusters giving all they had. *"You either get that or a fighter, and for now this—"*

The first rounds of bolts seared past the glass cockpit. Paloon sent the ship into random movements hoping to stay out of the fighters' target scopes.

"Blow it," Oz belted then scowled when no one seemed to pay him any attention. Louder, he yelled, "Blow the damn bomb!"

Realization smacked shock on Larin as the rolbrid reached for the switch in his vest. Flipping his thumb, the switch clicked in an odd moment of silence, soon followed by incoming fire.

"They're getting closer." Hitook calmly observed as Paloon jerked the ship about like a hummingbird on amphetamines.

Oz now wished he hadn't opened his mouth because his stomach wanted to puke but couldn't tell through which end to empty its contents as the ship corkscrewed, arced and flipped simultaneously.

In the small pauses between the jerking motions, Lyon's words came in puffed grunts. "Your bomb will work, right?"

"It'll work," Larin reassured himself more than answering the question. Yet Paloon's brutal control of the ship seemingly dragged on. "Maybe."

Overwhelmingly bright white light scorched the darkness of space as the Rodayne ballooned into a luminescent orb larger than its original form. The fusion sun expanded to consume fighters that had previously attempted to join the pursuit.

Paloon's passengers had to keep their eyes shut for what felt like minutes until the brightness lowered to a tolerable level and then winked from existence.

The fighters still rapidly approached, but Paloon kept a straight path as the pursuers floated by, lifeless. Drones. Without the Rodayne to give commands, the once deadly fighters became lumps of space debris.

Paloon hooked the ship around the moon, out of sight from the shaken armada, and pushed on to the planet below. No one spoke for the rest of the trip.

Chapter 23

Two hundred and forty thousand miles of silence; they were the quietest two hours of Oz's waking life.

Landing in a remote field, they found the van waiting nearby. Oz couldn't tell if Paloon had quietly called for it or if Mac had driven it there. Everyone just piled in with no complaining about the insufficient seating.

As the van pulled away, the craft they arrived in began a Paloon-programmed set of instructions, launching and darting toward a nearby lake to bury itself. It would have been another six hours of quiet if not for the occasional request to find a public bathroom.

Slightly damp air hung still in the dark basement. A tinge of electricity tainted the air's odor with a mild tang, as if it too sensed the future.

A loud bang echoed as Larin dropped a small chest on the floor and, with a heavy boot, kicked it across the room to ricochet off the base of the stairs and spin into the lockers with a clattering racket. The rolbrid sulkily stomped to the workbench against the wall, withdrew one of his weapons and began mindlessly tinkering with it.

The others gradually filed into the room with a pace of emotionally drained mourners leaving a fresh gravesite.

Lyon slumped into his chair, his face almost striking the tabletop. "Something alcoholic, just make it strong."

Light bounced until it formed a tall, narrow glass of liquid onyx: koj, or pasteurized and fermented brains from a squirrel-like creature found on Pio. Dreary eyes fell onto the concoction and vaguely winced. Koj was best served ice cold—it helped kill the taste—but Lyon didn't care. He soon snatched the tall shot, threw it down his gullet then slammed the glass down for a refill. Mac obliged, and Lyon downed it too. When the glass hit the table again, the light filled it with koj, but Lyon slumped back in his chair to let his body adjust to the first two.

Paloon limped into the room next. Either he hadn't quite recovered from the mental attack while plugged into the Rodayne's system or the injury was physical, a result of Hitook handling him a bit too rough. Paloon wouldn't say, but Hitook followed nearby, ready to help in case the hunter faltered on his way to a chair.

He almost sat next to Lyon when Paloon noticed the signature glass of koj resting in front of Lyon. Paloon sidestepped to the next chair to put at least some distance between him and the rancid odor that will, with time, start slowly creeping about like a patient predator.

Hitook continued to the other side of the table but stopped short of sitting. Instead, he rested his hands on the back of the chair and let his head gradually drop his dreary gaze to the table.

Noticeably bringing in the rear, Oz tensely stepped into the room, afraid to make too much noise. Leaning against the back wall, he privately hoped to disappear. Deep in his mind he felt, even sensed, as if he was being executed without a trial. Granted, everyone occasionally had strange thoughts, maybe even like this, but Oz couldn't shake it. In waves it came at him as if it were a thing he knew; it just lacked a why. His mind translated it into visions of watching a jury nod their collective heads in agreement as a prosecuting lawyer gave an obviously emotional closing statement. But Oz was unable to hear a word of it. Deaf as to why he faced a death penalty, Oz twisted his face in concentration to think of something, anything, else.

Motion in the room gave Oz a brief respite. Hitook started for a return path through the tunnel.

"Where are you going?" Lyon gruff voice startled everyone. So throaty the question, everyone mistook it as anger.

"To meditate," Hitook calmly replied with closed eyes. He silently waited and prepared to offer further thoughts before Lyon roughly huffed and jerked his head lazily as if to excuse Hitook from the room. The liqua slowly resumed his path.

Before the blanket of mournful reverence could smother the room again, Larin's building abhorrence exploded into a suspiciously audible grumble. "That'll help."

"Ignore him," Paloon slipped toward a departing Hitook.

Larin paused his clanking fidgeting. "Frapping bite me, space boy!"

"We could do without your general distaste of everything for just a few moments," Paloon returned with increasing agitation.

With his back to Paloon, Larin's head jerked rapidly as if mocking Paloon.

Frustration peaked within Paloon, who didn't care that he let his next thoughts be heard. "Childish prick."

"Frap off!" Larin belted as a particle cannon whipped around, pointing its suddenly larger-than-life bore at Paloon's face.

Oz and Paloon jerked in shock, but Lyon seemed unfazed, mostly due to the koj that was already starting to "faze" him rather well. Had he been a shade more exhausted, Paloon figured he might have wet himself. Larin always seemed an unstable trigger nut. His records already showed he disliked anyone of higher rank. Just maybe, this assignment finally snapped this psycho.

Such contemplations fizzled as Paloon noticed the battery compartment at the top rear of the weapon was empty. Crazy? Yes, Larin was crazy, but Paloon didn't doubt that Larin was also a pro. He wouldn't have drawn a weapon without a battery and expected to use it. Paloon slid his eyes from the weapon to Larin's eyes. What unstable emotions wrestled in that rolbrid mind?

Larin knew the battery lay on the table behind him. But emotions called, and he answered. With weapon pointed, he wallowed in the dream of it being ready, of him pulling the trigger and of feeling the rush of satisfaction of distantly dispensing pain. Or was that dissipating pain? His psyche marveled at the thought, which dissolved behind the torrent of thoughts racing through Larin's mind. One made it to the surface, and Larin kicked the weapon up then dragged it back around to the table. Clattering of tools and metal continued, as did the mumbling.

Paloon shook his head in infuriating puzzlement. "We *all* could really do without you being a jerk to everyone, for at least a day."

"Bam!"

In a millisecond, Oz now found himself staring down the moon-sized barrel of Larin's cannon. His body slammed itself flat against the back wall as his mind raced for ideas but kept crashing into the fact that regardless of what Oz decided to do, Larin could pull the trigger faster.

The noise came from the chair Larin had kicked from under himself and into the lockers. Larin landed firm and with a steady aim.

Paloon flew from his seat so fast to send torrents of pain through both legs. "Put that away, damn it! You're crazy." Then Paloon heard it. A faint whine rang from the cannon in Larin's hands. It peaked then faded from existence before starting again. Somehow, in the blur of motion, Larin demonstrated how much of a pro he was and reloaded the battery while bringing the weapon to aim. Paloon suddenly regretted the "you're crazy" comment.

"Calmly think about this." Paloon took his time with the words as if to force the tension in the room to bend to his will. "He's not worth it. He hasn't done any—"

"He's a liability," Larin snapped as anger even further contributed to the stress visible in his face. "I have all rights to terminate this...pet before he fails to perform again and gets another one of us geeked. Liabilities are highly expendable."

It wasn't being called a "liability" or "expendable" but the rolbrid's tone with the branding of "pet" that reeked of derogatory defamation. So strong came the title that it lunged and clamped a death grip on Oz's gut. Immediately, Oz took it personally, very personally, as if someone just showed everyone in the city a photo of Oz having sex with his own mother. He was pissed.

"One damn minute, you short shit!" Oz blasted back without a second's thought.

"Shut the frap up!" Larin's shout assaulted Oz with so much force and determination that it shattered what little protection Oz had recently built to shield himself from the immense fear of dying in the next few seconds. "You disgusting local. You shouldn't even be here. I shouldn't even be wasting my time with this backward frapping rock. You're not even in an alliance. Let the p'tahians wipe you and your kind from the emptiness of space. No loss. It's the least that should happen."

"Larin," Paloon started again at a pace to counter the rolbrid's fast rant, "what do you think he has done? I don't recall him ever do—"

"That's because you were out of it, but I saw the whole thing." Larin audibly breathed for a moment. "More of a liability than helping, this spineless local hindered the entire operation. He failed to pay attention to what he should have been watching, so she—"

A gurgle rang from Larin's throat as his face grimaced. Paloon almost didn't believe it: Larin choked a bit. This hard-lined warrior actually had taken Ky's death rather hard, more than anyone would have guessed. This changed the matter considerably.

Larin steeled himself then yelled, "Ky died trying to save your frapping skin!"

"Put the weapon away." Each word came as a composed stillness. Lyon hadn't moved his slouched head when he spoke them. He braced himself on the table, caressing the shot of koj.

Larin peered over his extended arm at their dormant leader.

"You can't stop me this time, knight. You know I'm justified."

A realization hit Paloon, and the hunter suddenly doubted Larin's confidence. If Larin had felt himself so justified, Oz wouldn't still be alive.

"I said," Lyon stated, "put the weapon away. If you kill him, I will impale you with the barrel before your finger can release the trigger."

Interwoven in those words ran strings of unwavering verity, not a cold, detached proclamation that people spout to psych themselves or scare threats bigger than themselves. Paloon could tell. He had heard the latter too many times. The words that Lyon spoke stepped into being, stood tall and emanated a nonchalant truth, as if to say in passing, "Water is wet." It needed no explanation; it just was, and everyone knew it.

Lyon did not want to intimidate Larin; he simple stated an undeniable truth.

Larin squinted. He'd had it with their leader's antics. Dragging a local around with him wasn't advisable, and Lyon's continued defense only reinforced Larin's belief that their leader didn't want to admit his failure.

Mild movement from Lyon startled Larin, but the rolbrid quickly recovered and snapped his weapon arm even tighter. Oz swore he also saw Larin's finger squeeze the trigger a tad tighter. Lyon slowly stood with Larin's eyes intensely watching every action.

Lyon stumbled a bit as he got to his feet. Paloon wondered for a moment if Lyon could have performed his previously announced action with this amount of koj in his system. Inebriation aside, Lyon gradually made his way to Larin's side then leaned to speak into the rolbrid's ear.

Together, they stood motionless. Neither Paloon nor Oz could hear what was said, if anything. Lyon's mouth barely moved, but a good minute passed before Lyon slowly reached for the weapon and removed it without a struggle from Larin's loosening grip.

Larin dropped his arm and walked away. Lyon rose from his stooped position and watched Larin gather the chair he had previously knocked over and sat back at the workbench, face in hands.

Paloon and Oz locked eyes, sharing a look of bewilderment. Paloon figured Lyon must have just further threatened Larin with death.

Oz guessed, with much dismay, that Lyon agreed with Larin but reserved the right to kill Oz himself. Both were far from the truth.

"I too want revenge," Lyon said to anyone who wanted to hear his slightly slurred words. "But Ky's killers are dead. They died when Larin blew up their ship. But that doesn't keep me from wanting revenge. It's more than our mission; I want Horwhannor dead."

Control wrestled with hatred in Lyon's tone.

"Paloon," Lyon shifted his focus, "how do we get back up there?"

The hunter reeled at the thought. He didn't want to think about it. Suicide did not rank high on his list of things to plan. But Lyon's eyes beckoned for an answer.

Paloon threw an arm in the air as if to motion, "What the hell?"

"We could retrieve the ship we stole, go back up there and try to sneak aboard, but they'll see us coming as soon as we leave the planet." Paloon let air hiss from a snarl as he scanned a few more thoughts. "If the transporter is still intact at the school, I might be able to probe for more signals. But even with the right frequency, we'll need the launch codes, and there's no guarantee I could hack it."

As if waiting for Paloon to finish, the next words came in a lifeless monotone drone, "Not feasible."

The voice's lack of direction meant it must have been Mac, but it didn't sound like him. For a second, Paloon wondered if Mac, too, was mourning.

"Why?" Lyon asked.

"Local police have responded."

Lyon smirked. "Figures."

"What about the restaurant?" Oz's voice cracked a bit as he pushed himself from the wall.

Contempt briefly tightened Lyon's face, but he never turned to allow Oz to see the reaction. "What restaurant?"

Oz heard something unidentifiable in Lyon's tone and instinctively swallowed. "Back when you guys had those yaks screaming at the tops of their lungs keeping me awake, I vaguely remember them screaming about a restaurant." Doubt slipped in. "Didn't they?"

Lyon and Paloon briefly made eye contact, a moment of realization.

"Yes," Paloon admitted. "But it's a restaurant, a place they own and operate like a safe house, nothing more."

"But it's something." Oz stepped forward. "Look, I'm sorry about what happened, but we shouldn't be calling this quits. If you are cops as you claim to be, then here's a lead. Shouldn't we follow it?"

Annoyance closed Lyon's eyes and dragged his head down. He didn't need to be lectured, and he retorted out of spite, "It's just a restaurant."

Paloon, however, changed his tone. "He's got a point."

Disdain blazed from Lyon's eyes, but Paloon continued. "Somehow Horwhannor and this yakuza organization are linked. We can either charge into Horwhannor's front door or shake this yakuza tree and see what falls."

"Honestly," Larin finally spoke but didn't move, "I'm for charging down that piolant's throat."

"But that's sure suicide." Paloon began gesturing as he spoke. "We had one shot, and we took out a destroyer. We had enough surprise on our side to take out an *entire* destroyer. That's damn good. But we'll need a whole lot more than karma to pull that off again. Not only do they know we're here but they also know that we know they're here."

Oz rolled his eyes as his mind twisted that phrase around and then he nodded approvingly, but no one had asked him.

"What about the Vendetta?"

Paloon knew what Lyon must have been contemplating. "Yes, we could get the Vendetta and possibly sneak off the planet without being detected, but I won't be able to get it aboard one of those ships without attempting to use an access code, and that will announce our presence. And it's not a breach ship. If we make it up there, we'll be able to look around and pick our noses. We don't have that kind of time."

As if grudgingly accepting fate, Lyon steadily nodded. "Fair enough." Lyon faced Paloon. "Nine hours. We move in nine hours." He started toward the stairs. "Mac, we need recon completed in eight." Then he added in a mild whisper. "Revenge is not over."

A few steps up, Lyon paused as if he had almost forgotten something. "Paloon, lock Oz in his room. He stays here."

"Bu—" Oz impulsively rebuffed. "Why?"

Lyon shifted completely around, which startled Oz enough that he tensed. During the motion, Lyon's sight landed on the remaining shot of koj. He descended the stairs, snatched the shot and pounded it down. The stinging burn racked his face in pain.

"You're still responsible for NeNa's death," Lyon coughed as he spun unsteadily and trudged up the stairs, the door closing behind him.

Larin rotated in his chair to face the room. "Who in the frap in NeNa?"

Paloon shrugged.

Chapter 24

Faint mist persistently fell but remained mostly invisible. Only in the pale glow of the street and traffic lights did the moisture sparkle as it glided down. The lack of traffic fueled the dark streets with an even more stark aura. Initially, he thought that seeing so few vehicles in the last hour seemed odd, but Lyon shrugged it away, chalking it up to the hour. However, that didn't explain the restaurant.

Down one block and across the street, the restaurant had a nice corner lot. The long front of the establishment faced a small side road. A gold-trimmed emerald awning covered the sidewalk in front of the ornately carved, dark-red wooden doors. Five gold kanji characters arched the front of the green fabric; below, the words "Kyoto Steak & Sushi" were written in the same color. Lyon assumed the kanji meant the same but couldn't tell since he never had the time to learn the difficult language well enough to read it.

Across the street from the overhang, a three-story parking garage faintly glowed from the distantly spaced dingy yellow freckles that passed for pseudo illumination. Paloon positioned the surveillance van on the open top deck. For about two hours, he reported that not much changed around the restaurant.

Hitook reported the same. The liqua waited on the roof of a defunct electrical appliance store. On the verge of being destroyed, the structure sat across and on the far end of a tiny alley running behind the restaurant. A garbage disposal truck would barely be able to navigate to the few dumpsters, but the gap gave Hitook a view of the restaurant's rear entrance, valuable even with Paloon's drones spying on all corners of their target.

It was this utter void of activity that troubled Lyon. Light traffic at this time of night, Lyon could buy, but absolutely no one went in or left the restaurant. Unless the restaurant normally closed before the sun set—and it didn't, Mac checked—this didn't feel right.

"They just closed shop," Larin declared from the station wagon's driver seat. *"They started getting too much heat from recent events and figured it would be best to reduce their presence a bit. There's nothing here."*

Lyon brought his attention back to the display screens in front of him in the passenger seat. He had Larin drive so he could comb through all the data Mac could gather on the place. With an unenthusiastic finger, Lyon rubbed his chin. *"Paloon, anything yet?"*

Tapping holographic buttons, Paloon flicked through the images from the drones. *"All the ravens are still blind."* Something was keeping the drones from penetrating the structure. Whatever it was, it was definitely alien to this world and most likely resided in the restaurant. *"Sure, Horwhannor might have provided a jammer just as he did the weapons, but that doesn't mean they don't leave it running all the time. Larin could still be right."*

Lyon had been hoping for more. He needed more. He needed another chance to find Horwhannor, at least cripple his operation. An empty restaurant just brought them back to square one.

"Thinking about it isn't going to change the situation any," Paloon said.

Lyon lost track of how long he had been silent, but it must have reached irritating levels among his team. After all, they had been waiting already for more than two hours.

"Look," Paloon resumed his scolding, *"there might not be anything here, but are we at least going to do something? The only thing worth finding might be a bowl of rice, but there's at least some illegal jamming gear in there that we can seize for now. Either way, let's go in or go home."*

Serendipitously Paloon unknowingly got into Lyon's mind like a second subconscious. Lyon wanted to curse it, mostly because he couldn't deny the logic.

"You're right." After a deep breath, Lyon smacked palms onto his legs. *"Let's do this. Hitook, get into the alley and to the rear door. Larin and I will take the front. Wait for breach on my word."*

Shortly before Lyon started, Larin had already opened the door to exit the car. He had jogged across the street before Lyon finished. Lyon shook his head in minor disbelief before stepping out of the vehicle, adjusting his long, brown duster and circling around to the front of the station wagon.

A taxi in an apparent rush sped by, splashing water on Lyon before he could make it completely into the street. It left him standing, staring as his legs, at the taxi turning a corner, then back at his legs. The few inches of his pant legs not covered by the duster were now soaking wet, thanks to the one vehicle in the past twenty minutes that just had to be here when he finally decided to cross the street. The irony almost made Lyon scream. To himself, Lyon swore if he ever physically met Fate, he'd be sure to give it a good, swift kick in the nuts.

With a slow shake of his head, Lyon tried to shrug it off before sprinting across the street to catch up with Larin. But the rolbrid had already made it against the wall to the right side of the green awning. Without his seemingly ever-present combat pack, Larin unzipped his black jacket to expose a solid grey shirt. He then detached his particle cannon from its leg holster and waited for Lyon.

Steps from the door, Lyon reached into the folds of his duster and withdrew his cannon before positioning himself on the opposite side of the doors.

"Hitook, ready?"

"Affirmative."

Lyon nodded to Larin, who responded by positioning himself in front of the doors, cannon held down.

"Paloon?"

"Nothing's changed."

"Go."

Larin raised a heavy boot and kicked the solid wooden door. It gracefully flew inward, crashed into a glass picture frame as it thudded into the wall, then flew back to crack Larin in the knee.

Stifling curses, Larin bounced about on his left foot while kicking his right, as if that would help the pain.

It didn't, but it helped Paloon. Seeing the whole scene from one of his drones, Paloon's laughter blurted uncontrollably. Even through the echoing noise in the vehicle, Paloon heard gravel shift near the front of the van.

Lyon's hand extended to catch the door on its second return then slowly pushed it in, scanning the area with his cannon before taking his first steps in.

Two rice paper walls that extended a short distance into the room flanked the entry. On the left, remains from a framed drawing of a mountain hung precariously by its corner. A lectern sprouted between the two walls. Lining the far wall, glass and chrome formed an internally lit sushi bar.

Farther in, Lyon peered to his left. Chairs encircled two marble-lined grills, the far one on a slightly raised platform. Along the wall, burnt orange lanterns flickered as if containing open flames but without the smell.

Larin finally dared to walk on his injured leg. As he limped inside, Lyon motioned for him to search the left side. The rolbrid hobbled away as Lyon took the right.

To the other side of the sushi bar, another stone-rimmed grill sported a very aristocratic air with its mini pagoda roof over the grill and seating area. It pointed out for Lyon just how high the ceiling was to allow the two-tiered red tiles even a few feet of clearance after they peaked.

The restaurant circled around to the left, as low tables encircled with pillows spotted the tiny bay windows along the outer wall. Lyon noticed some strange lighting arrangements in the next room as he approached the pagoda, then he felt it and smelled it.

He tightened the grip on his weapon. "Identify yourself before I kill you."

Hitook approached the rear door, waved a hand over the primitive lock with just a short pause. After a click, he pushed the door in.

A tinge of refrigerant pierced his nose as he entered the darkness. Hitook's thoughts returned to just unlocking the door; his mind drifted further to remember Ky's look of distaste when he demonstrated that ability before.

After crossing the room on auto-pilot, Hitook froze when he opened the door. He felt it but couldn't stop himself from opening the door. He knew now it wouldn't have helped.

"I'm your friend." The tone in the obviously terran voice carried an unspoken "for now," which didn't go unnoticed by Lyon. "I do not wish violence, only to talk."

The calmness of the voice matched the open door and otherwise stagnant restaurant, Lyon knew that whoever they were, they had been waiting. It made him question who had been watching whom. But if they had wanted him dead, they would have already attempted something. Lyon took the risk and stepped forward.

Low tables continued to line the outer wall to Lyon's right. Mahogany formed a bar that ran the length of the left wall then doglegged to the right. Racks of international spirits covered the walls. In the corner, behind the bar, light bounced off mirrors to silhouette a full suit of samurai armor and crossed katana, which radiated a menacing omen.

Spotting the center of the room, a round table glowed from a single source of light from the ceiling. Of the two chairs, the far one held a calm man dressed impeccably in a suit that just screamed wealth. Massive guards flanked him, with a third farther back in the room. A fourth rose from behind the bar, blocking a bit more of the light from the armor display.

Their faces looked terran, but judging by their sizes, Lyon guessed them as piolants, except for the scrawny one behind the bar; he was terran. Each steadied heavy kinetic throwers—pointed at him. Sure those weapons could be considered non-lethal by piolant standards, but they would pound Lyon to mush in seconds.

Contemplating his options, Lyon knew he could take two, maybe three, but the others would roast him before he hit the floor. Besides, he couldn't tell what weaponry the immaculate gentlemen at the table might have near him.

"Hitook?"

The liqua visually counted three armed beings in front of him. Behind him, in the darkness, he could sense three more. He hoped for a possible crossfire situation if he made the right move, but that vanished as he ran the trajectories in his head. Each stood at precise angles to allow for the widest berth to prevent fratricide. At the same time, it allowed each person to be covered by at least two other gunners. If he made a move toward anyone or in any direction, he'd never see the morning. For now, they seemed comfortable by just waiting.

"I'm pinned. I'm not shot, but I will be if I move."

"Paloon?"

Slowly taking the passenger seat, the atlantian glanced back at the cannon toting piolant out the driver's side window then back to an identical threat in front of the van. He silently wished he hadn't investigated the noise.

"I currently have two rather irritated piolants visiting me." Paloon smiled but stopped when the terran-masked piolant in front of him readjusted his aim.

That only left Lyon with Larin, but he knew the warrior had already been making his move. As if to read Lyon's thoughts, the terran at the table spoke.

"Your friends will be unharmed as long as you remain peaceful."

Lyon let his frustration flare in a snarl.

The man continued. "Please have your other shorter friend step around peacefully. He'll find all the remaining doors locked."

Lyon wanted to kick himself for walking into this trap. All that reassured him was the possibility of walking away alive. *"Larin, you heard him. Don't try anything. Just holster you weapon and slowly walk in here. Stand behind me to my left."* He just knew Larin would hesitate following the order, so he added a bit of reassurance of a plan. *"You cover the piolants on the left and in the rear and the terran behind the bar. I've got the one on the right and the terran at the table; I want him alive."*

That wasn't a plan; that was suicide, and Lyon knew it. However, it worked. Larin gradually emerged from the other room, weapon holstered but his hand remained on the hilt.

As if to return the gesture of good faith, the finely-dressed gentleman briefly raised his left hand. The terran behind the bar strolled to the door at the end of the bar. He opened it while lying flat against the wall. Lyon leaned a bit to his right to see what he guessed was there.

Stooped to fit in the door, Hitook remained motionless, eyes darting back and forth from his potential attackers.

"As I said," the gentlemen resumed, "your friends will remain unharmed—"

"You never answered my question," Lyon half-growled. Obviously their *hosts* wanted something. Lyon also wanted something: information.

"Please forgive my rudeness. I am Yabuki Yumiro." Yabuki motioned to the empty chair. "Please take a seat."

As Lyon holstered his weapon, easing the nervous tension of the piolants, and took the seat, Yabuki continued.

"My men will not harm you as long as you do not openly threaten us. You have my word on that." Yabuki paused as if waiting for a reply. Lyon didn't oblige. Yabuki just nodded. "May I have the honor of your name?"

Interesting. For as much as Lyon initially thought they knew, they, too, remained in the dark on many things.

"You may call me Lyon."

"Fair enough. You may call me Yabuki." Yabuki relaxed a bit, as if on purpose. "You have a very interesting name. Slow, methodical yet powerful."

Lyon twitched his nose at the attempted compliment. He couldn't help but to turn the tables. "And your given name is rather unusual. Are you good with a bow?"

"So you understand my language. Impressive. Very impressive."

With the repeated word, Lyon highly doubted it. He sensed that he had further surprised his guest—every chance to keep the scales shaking, the better.

"Who names a child as such?"

"I do." Yabuki calmly replied as if discussing it was the purpose of the meeting. "Being an orphan gives one a degree of flexibility. You learn to be independent, to take care of yourself. But to do that, one must shed those skins given by other people, such as names."

Lyon scanned Yabuki's finely tailored suit. "You seem to be doing well for an orphan."

"That I am." Yabuki smiled at the boost to his ego. "Hard work and perseverance pays off for anyone with desire. Even an orphan can gain the influence required to lead powerful organizations."

This terran, flanked by aliens, couldn't know who held the cards here. Yabuki lived in an illusion. Lyon's distaste for this terran grew with each word. "Somehow I doubt that."

Yabuki sensed the disgust. "Please do not misunderstand me. I'm here to help because only my organization can."

"It's not your organization." Lyon glared. "Regardless of your calm demeanor, you view me as a threat; otherwise, you wouldn't require such firepower. Yet you didn't know who I was until you asked for my name. You still don't really know. If you really are the local yakuza boss, you're taking an awfully big chance for our first meeting."

Yabuki's eyes widened for a moment at the mention of "yakuza." It was the reaction Lyon wanted. Now was the time to go for the gut.

"My guess, you're a third tier peon."

Bulls eye. Irritation flared in Yabuki's eyes as his face tensed. The terran fought to bring his anger under control, but frustration remained in his voice.

"Very perceptive, Lyon-san." Seriousness steeled his eyes. "I may not lead them, but do not doubt my influence; it could be your downfall."

Lyon smirked at the weak attempt to turn the tables.

"And I recommend that you don't assume to know me." Lyon glanced at the piolants in the room. "How are Takahiro and Takehiko doing? They still enjoying prison? Please let them know that I enjoyed our little talk."

This time Yabuki's surprise didn't show.

"I wish I could. Tomo had an unfortunate accident with an industrial strength dryer, and Taka bumped into several sharp objects during a food fight." Yabuki forced a shrug as if he didn't care. "Seems that their license-plate-making days are over."

Lyon huffed from his nose. "That's too bad; I kind of liked them."

"I doubt that," Yabuki replied calmly.

"You still don't know me." Lyon raised his head a bit more. "Regardless of what your *handlers* may have told you, I seriously doubt that you really understand who we are." Lyon raised a brow. "You'd be surprised."

"I doubt that, too," Yabuki quipped, but an uneasiness flashed in his eyes before they returned to cold orbs. "But we can discuss that when you have a gun pointed at my head."

Lyon tensed. He wanted to fly from his chair and indulge the weasel but kept his emotions in control. He barked, "What do you want?"

Yabuki clasped his hands and tapped his index fingers against the bottom of his lower lip. "You have something we want."

It sounded like some rehearsed line that had run through Yabuki's head for the past week, and he instinctively used it in a pathetically predictable instance.

"No shit," Lyon snarled. "That's why I asked."

"It would be to your best interest, Lyon-san, to watch your tone with me."

What a weak-willed worm, Lyon thought. All's better if he could keep Yabuki irritated, so Lyon had no plans to stop.

"Can we please get to the point? I have a roast in the oven."

Yabuki's eyes narrowed. He wanted to give the signal for those royal guards to waste this scum. But he had his orders.

"You're in the possession of a human." Yabuki waited to recognize the surprise in Lyon's eyes. "We want him...alive."

Maybe this weasel did know more than he let on. How did they know he stole Oz from a hospital? Why would the yakuza care? Then he looked to the piolant to Yabuki's right. Horwhannor. It had to be. But why would that renegade pirate care about a terran? What was it about Oz that made him so darn valuable to someone? Obviously he now needed many more pieces to complete the puzzle.

"Who?"

"Do not fain ignorance," Yabuki smiled greasily like a used-car salesman, "it's doesn't suit you."

Fuck you, Lyon thought. He again contemplated killing Yabuki but stopped when the realization that two if not three members of his team would be dead before the first piolant hit the ground. This scum wasn't worth it.

"Why do you want him?"

"There is no need for you to worry about such matters. We simply require him intact."

"Why should I?"

The piolant to Yabuki's right stepped forward. Larin must have tensed because the other piolants reacted. Lyon peered to the left and held up a hand, requesting Larin to remain calm. The approaching piolant kept his eyes on Larin as he set an object on the table. Silver and shaped like a neutered teardrop, the object had no markings, but the piolant touched something before returning to his post.

Lasers shot up in a repeating twirling pattern, increasing in intensity until they formed an image. A being was pinned to a wall with clamps holding each limb out to their extremes. Torn, blood-soaked clothes hung loosely from the thin frame. Lying weakly on the chest as if broken, a head rested at an obscuring angle. As if on cue, a massive hand reached to grab a tuft of long, blood-matted hair and lifted the head.

Recognition flashed on Lyon's face, and Yabuki responded.

"She's still alive."

Lyon couldn't disguise his frustration as he glowered at Yabuki then returned his attention to the video.

Suddenly, he noticed the tail, which was so dark, possibly from blood, that he had thought it a seam in the wall. Then Ky's eyes opened and rolled about a bit as she moaned. Her face looked as if it had met the business end of an avalanche. The fist let go, Ky's head dropped, and the video vanished.

Lyon fought back the mounting urge to rip out this dick's throat. Sensibility barely won the battle. If he wanted Ky back, he'd have to play their game—for now.

Gloating in the situation, Yabuki grinned. "All we ask for is a simple swap: him for her."

Chapter 25

Blurred memories became fuzzier with each bout of pain that crashed in her head. At least the pain let her know she was alive, but with such unrelenting torment, she would gladly have taken death.

Jumbled bits of recent events flashed in her mind as if someone with a nervous twitch kept flicking a channel changer. Amidst the confusion of events, she had waited for the advancing security forces to leave her for dead. With their attention elsewhere, she summoned all her remaining strength to scuttle down the hall and flop herself into an escape pod. Thumbing the hatch closed, she finally heard someone exclaim that her body went missing.

Ky almost didn't have enough energy left to pull the activation handle. When it did go, she collapsed completely, rolling like a rag doll as the tiny capsule blasted from the side of the destroyer. Life pods didn't offer speed or stealth, but life-preservation instincts could only operate on what options remained.

Several hundred meters from the vessels, the pod began leveling for prolonged flight. The sensation relaxed Ky, but she choked it down as she struggled to remain conscious. She had to at least guide the ship to the planet and cross her fingers. Then concussion waves buffeted the pod, slamming Ky around until darkness dragged her under.

The stench of crusted blood and moldy fur assaulted her nose. Familiarity allowed her to recognize the odor as her own. Not a pleasing thought, but it failed to compare to her increasing realization that she was strapped to a wall. Attempting to test those bonds, she tensed muscles, triggering an agonizing burning in her chest. For now, Ky held little hope that her body could come to her aid if needed.

Grey light seeped into her eyes as Ky struggled to force them open and raise her head. Blurred outlines hinted that the tiny room was empty except for a small table, behind which sat a yellow-skinned doludgian with a stubby beak and bald neck. Light glowed from a screen on the desk.

Ky thought her movements went unnoticed until the doludgian folded the screen into the table and stood. He just stared with unblinking green orbs that resembled large, marbled peas. The lack of further movement snagged Ky's interests. Spells of pain forced her eyes to temporarily close in convulsive twitches, but it failed to keep her from monitoring the doludgian, who acted more like an obedient robot waiting for its next order.

The answer came when the door across the room from Ky swooshed open. In stepped a massive frame backlit from the hall. Klaxons roared in Ky's head. A few more steps into the room's light allowed reality to confirm the conclusion of her psyche.

Bronze skin glinted with a fine sheen of moisture. Hard plates ironically gleamed a soft green around the head. Detached coldness eked from the twin, black pupils almost collectively large enough to hide the eyes' jade color. Overwhelming all she could barely see, death preceded him like a fog rolling off a rotting swamp. She couldn't smell it, not physically, but the ethereal realm now reeked of decay.

She didn't need to see the singed scar under his right eye to know him to be Horwhannor or that she wanted nothing to do with his ilk.

"How happy I was," the piolant began in thick sarcasm, "to hear that Her Highness had awoken."

Horwhannor approached close enough for Ky to smell his not-so-clean breath. His jaw tensed as his four lips rippled in and out of a purse, similar to the effect of a rain drop striking violently into a pool of still water.

"That's right, Muilo," apparently talking to the doludgian in the room but keeping his piercing eyes drilling into Ky's, "we're in the presence of royalty."

Rocking his head back, Horwhannor retreated a few steps as if to assess the entire scene of Ky pinned on the wall. "A forty-second Adian, correct?" He continued without waiting for an answer, not that the thought even crossed Ky's mind. "Do forgive me for not bowing, as I fear the kind gesture would not be returned." Horwhannor glanced at Ky's shackled wrists. Ky just stared through the tops of her eyelashes. "How's your mother? Well, I hope."

She doubted it. Only a small-minded person would start such a conversation just to boost his own ego. So he had access to information on her and her family, big deal. She refused to acknowledge him, a larger annoyance than she realized. Horwhannor kept his temper under control, for now.

Shifting his eyes from the floor to Ky and back, he began a slow pace of the small room. "Yes, I know much about you." Ky wondered if Horwhannor could literally read her thoughts or if she was that transparent. "I am quite intrigued as to why a dextian royal would join the Dragon Corps, but you dextians were never much of a match in true combat, so I guess it's not much of a worry."

This jerk had the audacity to bring up his "victories." The Nuvulm Incursion wasn't a battle or a campaign; it was a bloody slaughter, the worst loss the dextians faced in the War. Calling that event a fair fight would be the gravest injustice possible to the millions who died that day. How could someone sleep with that holocaust on their soul? Ky's mind would have found more peace if she had shot an innocent, unaware paralyzed blind man in the back with a bazooka.

Yet, here, in front of her, Horwhannor gloated about it. This wasn't the quiet *war hero* she'd heard so much about. He was nothing more than a self-righteous blow hard who required combat and death to fuel his need to feel useful. Pathetic.

"I am, however, quite interested in why the Dragon Corps is here." Horwhannor halted and narrowed his eyes at Ky. "Did you come all this way just for me? Or is there something else going on?"

Minutes slipped by, Ky believed, with Horwhannor not moving an iota.

"Still not talking?"

Ky read into the tone that Horwhannor had tried to interrogate her before. She began questioning how much time had passed and wondered what she may have already said. It could just be a childish ploy to fool her senses, so she refortified her emotions.

"Tisk, tisk, my princess." Horwhannor waved a finger before her face. "Don't get tight-lipped; that's rude." Gracefully, his thick digit stilled then gravitated toward the blood-soaked rip under Ky's left breast. He smirked as his finger plowed into the wound.

Ky screamed uncontrollably as her body attempted futilely to withdraw from the source of the pain. The squirming increased as Horwhannor hooked his finger and twisted it slowly as if attempting to engage a stiff lock. He withdrew, but Ky continued to scream for moments afterward, then slumped forward, exhausted.

"So what's it going to be? Are you going to make me believe that the Drags actually followed me all the way here?" Horwhannor snarled with a huff. "I doubt it; no one on that side of the universe could." His eyes narrowed. "So why are you here?"

"To collect your pathetic carcass!" Ky emphasized her unhappiness with a shotgun of spit.

With a wince one moment and anger the next, Horwhannor clamped a hand on Ky's shoulder and dug his finger in with enough pressure to almost break the skin.

Shrieks echoed in the room until reaching deafening levels, forcing Horwhannor to yell. "Lies! If the Drags wanted me dead, I'd be destroying armadas right now and not dealing with the pathetic likes of you!"

He released, but the howls undulated into background noise.

"This is my planet, my system, and your kind are not welcome," Horwhannor placed a thick, sharp fingernail against her left biceps. "So tell me, what are the Drags interested in here, or I'm going to kill you."

Ky's thin brows crashed together, spit flew from her snarled fangs and her eyes snapped into a feral stare. "Fuck you!"

Blood exploded from Ky's arm as Horwhannor drilled his finger straight through to the wall. Ky cried for death as her captor clamped onto her arm and squeezed to intensify the pain.

The quick withdrawal sent more waves of pain, keeping Ky oblivious to Horwhannor wiping his blood-coated finger on the tatters of her remaining clothing.

Leaving his prisoner to scream, Horwhannor turned to the doludgian. "Prep her for surgery. I need her ready by—"

Air cracked at the speed of Horwhannor's hand as it flashed to seize an invisible rod of energy that now existed where his head had been a millisecond ago. From its new, askew position to dodge the attack, the piolant's head slowly rotated, as snarls steadily increased in ugliness to match the level of dread in the room. As Horwhannor's body finally spun, he swapped hands, never losing grip of the mental spike that floated in the air.

Bulging eyes glowed from Ky's face. A mixture of pain and shock held her in suspense. How did he sense the attack in time to dodge it? No reports indicated that Horwhannor was mentally astute. She had put all her last energy into this attack. How could he actually grab a force spike and in such a way that she couldn't pull it back? How powerful was he? Was it because she was just too weak?

Horwhannor cared little about Ky's self debate, and now his voice stank of hate. "Do you really think you're the first assassin to try that?" Horwhannor used the force spike's mental connection to Ky and began stabbing it back into her brain, slamming her head into the wall. With each thud, more blood splattered and Horwhannor belted "I've killed better" in pauses timed to the pounding.

Holding the spike in his right hand, Horwhannor ratcheted back his left hand before plowing it into the spike. A massive bone-chilling scream exploded from Ky's throat as the invisible energy shattered into fragments that tore chunks from her life force.

Anger continued to boil in Horwhannor as his prisoner went limp in the wall shackles. He spun and drove a fist into the wall before charging out the door while ordering, "Fix her."

Prismatic flecks glinted as they swirled about the deep blue. Another jolt sent the twinkling bits streaking about in orderly ribbons of fury before each dot winked from existence.

Through the dark liquid, an eye blinked.

"What does that mean?"

The plain-clothed scientist lowered the test tube and slid it into place among the rack of matching vials on the table. With a quizzical hum, the scientist contemplated for a moment before answering the eye's owner.

"I don't know."

"Well, do you have a guess as to what it is?" Agent Kim held out for some hope as he dragged a gloved finger across the tabletop. Blue power glittered on his black leather.

"It's just going to take time and more tests."

Kim didn't buy the forced confidence in Mike's tone.

"Don't give me that. You've had half an hour; you should have at least narrowed it down by now." Kim held out his power-coated finger. "It's not a natural substance is it?"

Challenges riled Mike like nothing else. The solution existed. He just needed the right test. And condescending words fueled his frustration. "You want a guess? Maybe it's some kind of experimental narcotic. Why don't you lick up a few doses, and if you live, I'll tell you what it did."

Kim frowned as he flicked the dust from his finger. "Touchy."

The agent stepped over a body while quietly excusing himself from Mike's presence. Hanging around would only irritate the situation. Let the man work.

On the way out of the room, Kim blankly watched more technicians examine the smooth grooves cut in the wall. Streaks of polished gypsum shined from the sheared edges of the drywall.

Dismay shook Kim's head. As he made his way across the basement of the once abandoned school, wonder filled his thoughts. This job only got harder with time. Soon it would take more work than was possible. He just didn't want it to be on his shift. He didn't want to be the failure.

"You okay?"

Burn's voice snapped Kim back to reality. He had made it completely into the far room on cruise. Kim raised his eyes to see Burn sitting on a tiny, folding chair behind one of the golden canisters that guarded the floor's metal mat.

"Hello?"

"Uh, yeah." Kim blinked hard and momentarily gazed at the floor. "Lost in thought."

"Not much luck then," Burn guessed before returning her attention to her own problem.

No one noticed Kim shake his head or barely hear him say, "No."

Burn's attention immediately snapped back to the screen on her laptop. Sitting cross-legged on the floor next to her, another female agent clacked away one-handed on another laptop; her other hand nudged the joysticks of what appeared as the remote to a toy car.

Kim thought about just waiting patiently and politely but correctly surmised that if he did Burn would not say another word for some time.

"How about you?"

A moment more went by before Burn lifted her gaze from the screen. Then her shoulders sank in defeat as she exhaled. She lowered the screen as her lips twisted. "Not much."

She slipped the computer from her lap and set it on the floor before standing. Then she crossed the room in part so she didn't feel like she would have to yell at her partner and, in part, to just step away from her frustration for a moment. "We might have finally located its power circuitry, but just as with the others, it's still erratically different from any other piece we've found."

Discomforting worry increased as Kim revisited his previous thoughts. "Do you feel that?"

"What's that?"

"Losing control." Kim's face remained still. "The frequency is increasing and the complexity has just become more confusing lately. I mean, what do we have here?" Kim mindlessly waved an indiscriminate arm at the carnage strewn about the school's basement. "Is it some kind of gang war or highly armed vigilantes?"

Burn wanted a cigarette. "I try not to think about it and just focus on one task at a time." Concern raised her brow. "I'd recommend that you do the—"

"Excuse me."

Burn leaned to the side as Kim twisted, both now looking at Detective Logan Morgan standing in what remained of the doorway. An unkempt mop of dirty brown hair capped a long face and slender features. He'd been on loan from the local police department and at the scene for at least the last twenty-four hours and looked it.

Tired eyes lazily gazed at the two agents as he offered a cell phone. "Someone wants to talk to the person in charge." With the words, odor of burnt tobacco filled the room.

Burn retrieved the phone and half whispered, "Who is it?"

Logan shrugged. "Don't know, don't care."

Burn squeezed past Logan as she placed the phone to her ear.

The detective adjusted himself under his heavy black coat. "Got something for you though."

"Yeah," Kim slipped as he gradually returned from his thoughts, "what's that?"

Logan spun and jerked a finger for the agent to follow. As they made it down the hall, a pair of agents hauled some equipment around the corner. Logan watched for a moment before leaning against the wall, withdrawing a cigarette and lighting it. In a low voice, as if to keep a secret, he spoke unsettlingly. "Remember the mush face we found in here." He jerked his head toward the door to his right then glared at Agent Kim. "You asked about possible yak connections. We didn't find any, at first. He's got a list of minors, nothing organized. It took shaking some squealers to hear that he was interested in joining the yaks, but that stopped. Now rumor puts him as some kind of yak gofer."

Kim expected that and found some form of relief that at least something linked the events.

"So what is this, some kind of yak war?"

Protocol kept Kim's mouth shut. Though his eyes might have communicated something different, Kim wished it was that simple.

"You're not going to believe this," came Burn's voice as she rounded the corner and tossed the phone to Logan. She nodded a knowingly look to Kim. "Guess who that was."

Chapter 26

Ridges of clouds covered the sky, looking like inverted puffy mountains with dark tips and white valleys. The air stank of ozone from the recent rain that now covered the concrete.

Lyon stepped from the driver's seat of the station wagon. His eyes followed the wet stone across a barren landscape to a row of dilapidated hangars. The closest appeared to be in the best condition. He doubted that many locals knew such a secluded place existed so close to the city. Though the rarely used runway now felt stark, Lyon could tell by the patched tarmac and visible hangar repair that it hadn't achieved abandoned status...yet.

Oz and Larin began exiting the vehicle. In short order, the rolbrid had an opinion.

"I don't like this."

Lyon agreed; dread hung in the air like the smell of rancid beef in a hot meat locker. But he remained silent as he closed the door.

The van came to a halt behind them. As Hitook lowered himself from the passenger seat, his nose sniffed loudly then again to confirm what he sensed. Paloon heard it even over the sound of his closing door.

"What is it?"

"Confidence and fear," Hitook answered, "and it's not us."

"At least they're scared." Larin attempted to emphasize his statement with a nod, but Hitook ruined it.

"There's considerably more confidence than fear." Hitook looked at the surroundings for a moment but failed to find what he expected. "It's a dangerous mixture."

"So are we," Lyon added to keep the courage of his team high. "Let's just get this over with."

The knight stepped off toward the hangar. The others followed. Oz received rude assistance from Larin, who spun around to the terran's rear and jabbed him in the back with the barrel of a particle cannon.

"Hey," Oz yelped from his new bruise, "you don't have to be so rough."

"You're the prisoner, remember?" No love lived in Larin's gruff voice. "Now move." The rolbrid underscored the command with another jab.

"Ow, damn it!" Oz jerked forward. "You don't have any friends, do you?"

"Not needed."

"Figures."

Contrasting with the massive metal doors of the hangar, a tiny wooded one sported spots of baby blue under chipped and marred red paint. Tarnished brass formed a knob that reflected Lyon's tense face. He stared as if half expecting the door to open on its own.

He peered at the guys behind him before returning to the door. It reeked of a cliché-riddled movie script. Because it might say something about their host, Lyon doubtfully searched for more pieces to the puzzle.

"Paloon, what do you have?"

Immediately upon Lyon's request, the other atlantian switched between the feeds from his pre-positioned drones. A small screen in his left eye flicked with video images from multiple angles. The process was slower than it would be if he could be patched directly into the van's computer, but he didn't have that option this time. The deal was that everyone had to be at the meet.

"Still nothing." Suspicion seeped into Paloon's mental voice. More likely than not, Horwhannor was more than prepared for any of Paloon's tricks.

Lyon breathed in, straightened his back and opened the door.

The smells of motor oil, diesel and solvents assaulted his nose as he stepped over the high entry. Light dropped from the high windows to barely illuminate the center of the barren, stained concrete. Metal grates formed a maintenance catwalk that circled the interior just below the massive windows, which were formed from collections of small squares.

Larin push Oz into Lyon to move the knight farther into the room to allow everyone else to enter. Paloon had the caboose, and though he didn't plan on closing the door, its unevenness allowed gravity to handle the task.

Darkness shrouded the far end of the hangar due to the angle of sunlight. Lyon squinted as his eyes studied the faintest of outlines for any clue. *"Paloon, what now?"*

Lyon's head remained silent for too long. *"Hitook, can you see anything at the far end?"*

Again, no response. He turned to see puzzlement on his team's faces, especially Paloon, who fought to break the jamming signal that kept him from receiving anything from the drones. Defeat drooped his shoulders as Paloon dropped his arms.

"We're being jammed." Paloon's voice echoed in the hollow building. "We've lost internal communications and the link to the drones. I can't even get Mac."

"Well then, voice it is." Lyon scanned the surroundings again as he proceeded across the expanse of smooth rock. "Stay blue and report anything."

All five sets of eyes roamed the floor, walls and ceiling, but each one failed to notice the faint glimmer until it was too late. Cloaking shrouds slipped from thirty armed beings who popped into existence along the entire catwalk. Lyon's team members each reached for their weapons but held short, except for the weaponless Oz, who just held up his hands and exclaimed, "Shit!"

"Don't draw your weapons if you wish to live."

The voice spoke in an intergalactic standard language, and though Lyon couldn't tell which one spoke it, he knew the statement to be true. If Horwhannor wanted them dead, he would have kept his gunners cloaked and just turned the hangar into a kill box. Why hadn't he? Lyon glanced at Oz. Was this terran so important that protecting his safety was a priority for Horwhannor? If that was the case, his team's safety would immediately be put into question once Oz left their custody.

"That includes the stump," a different voice came from the shadows on the far end of the hangar floor. "Holster that weapon, traitor."

Now, Lyon knew who owned that voice. "Larin, put it away."

The rolbrid huffed but complied.

"Good, obedient pet."

Slipping from the darkness, an eight-foot high piolant approached with an aura of twisted charisma that could only belong to someone as warped as Horwhannor. From neck to foot, a think, black duster covered his bulk, and Lyon could only guess at the number of armored layers concealed within.

"Such a disgrace to see someone from a Council clan now a Kingdom puppet."

"Shut the frap up," belted Larin as he whipped around Oz and tensed the grip on his holstered cannon. He didn't need Hitook to plant a massive paw in his chest to hold him back, but it helped. "You're the traitor, asshole."

"Larin, please," Lyon requested as calmly as he could.

"Yes," Horwhannor added with a threatening step forward, "please."

"We are not here to address your peeves, Horwhannor." Lyon knew he had to keep tension in his voice to stand up to a warrior like Horwhannor. "So let's get to the point."

The piolant tilted his head toward Lyon and scoured the atlantian with his eyes. "So you're the Corps' head bitch? Didn't you get the order not to come armed?"

Lyon's eyes flashed glances at the armed warriors on both sides. "Obviously you didn't think we would be that stupid."

"I guess not." Horwhannor had given them some credit but not the respect due a fellow warrior. "Why don't you just leave this planet?"

"Can't do that."

"Why not?"

"I can't leave without you."

Horwhannor's head plates scraped against each other as he raised a brow. "Is that so? That little slut of yours told me about as much, but she wouldn't tell me why."

"Do I really need to spell it out for you? Your precious Council wants your ugly head on a platinum platter."

"*I'm* the true Korac Council, now," Horwhannor half yelled as he jabbed a thumb in his chest. "Those weaklings no longer have the strength to restore the glory to the Council like I do."

"Then why are you here?"

"I should be asking you that, shouldn't I?"

Lyon just stared, silently trying to guess what was going on in this demented piolant's brain case.

"I know you didn't follow me here." Confidence gave Horwhannor's voice life. "Not even the Corps could have made the advances I have. I've learned a lot and would love for you to call in your Corps buddies so I can show you pukes all that I've gained. Soon, even the Kingdom will fall."

Fragments of pieces. Lyon needed more but couldn't tell how far he could press before this delusional nut cracked. He needn't have worried, because Horwhannor didn't give him the chance.

"But first, I need something you have, and I have something of yours." The piolant's eyes briefly widened. "Let's trade."

"You first."

"You are stupid. As long I have the high ground, you're going to play by my rules. Now give me this dirt-borne aborigine, before I kill you all."

Something sparked in Lyon's head, something about how Horwhannor referred to Oz. It was how he didn't specifically refer to Oz. Lyon had assumed Horwhannor knew who Oz was, but obviously he didn't. Although Lyon had only his assumption, he went with it as he fought to control the sweat in his palms.

"I wouldn't trust you to take a leak and not piss on yourself."

Lyon's teammates began to wonder if their leader had just lost it. None of them desired to die today and didn't appreciate having someone play with their lives by threatening a known killer.

The knight locked his eyes with Horwhannor. "Sure, we may not get out of here, but you might not either. You're facing four battle-trained marksmen." Minor exaggeration, yes, but Lyon needed the deception. "Odds are one of us will get you before going down. Want to test your luck?"

Anger pulled Horwhannor's lips into a snarl, creating an even uglier appearance than Lyon thought possible. But the knight kept his composure, and since he still stood, Lyon ratcheted the tension a level.

"Your move, fuck face."

Paloon wanted to leap the six feet to Lyon and box him in the mouth. That thought kept him distracted so much so that the tension caused him to jump when Horwhannor belted out laughter. The four lips flapped about as if the piolant's mouth had exploded. Lyon wondered if he sensed admiration in that laugh, but that thought came to a halt when amazement took over.

Horwhannor crammed the side of his left hand into his mouth and clamped down until something cracked. Bluish goo coated the piolant's ugly grin as he spit a glob of it on the ground and pounded it with his boot.

"I swear on my blood that if you give me the aborigine that I'll give you the princess."

A blood oath. Lyon had heard about them, and Larin had only seen two others in his life. Piolant warriors were a twisted lot, but such an act made the oath law. Lyon shrugged then motioned for Oz to go. Larin jabbed his fist in the terran's back.

"Sorry, but this is goodbye."

"Asshole," Oz snapped as he fought to keep his balance. From one captor to the next. This was bullshit. He turned to Lyon. "Thanks a whole fucking lot for nothing."

Lyon refused to acknowledge the terran's existence.

Horwhannor jerked his head, then another, shorter piolant came forward pushing Ky into the light.

Cleaned of blood and now in new clothes, Ky only looked at the ground. Anticipation trickled through Lyon. He had expected her to be on a gurney or, worse, dead. It took mental strength to keep him from yelling to her.

Worry crossed Oz's face as he studied Ky, then Horwhannor. He gulped and forced his feet to move and his mind not to think about where he was going.

As if in tune, Ky began stepping forward. Matching footfalls slowly and rhythmically echoed in unison to Oz's heartbeat. He could feel his heart in his head as he watched a grin grow on Horwhannor's face. Oz broke the gaze to look at Ky who neared being level with him in the exchange.

She finally lifted her eyes to meet Oz's. Pain, sorrow and fear clashed to form water in Ky's eyes as tension squeezed her face until it began shaking. A spark of horror jumped the gap and shot down Oz's spine, forcing sweat to explode from every pore. Something was terribly wrong.

The terror also struck Hitook like a mana wall. Instinctively he mentally reached for Ky. *"What's wrong, Ky?"*

She tried to keep from doing it, but the dextian faced Hitook. Ky could no longer contain the flood as tears streaked down her face, and Hitook could sense her thoughts. *"Goodbye...friend."*

Terror shook Hitook into action. He leapt forward toward Ky and screamed, "Something's wrong!"

Thunder clapped, and the back of Ky's head exploded, propelling her body forward into Hitook's fast approaching arms.

"Noooo!" was all anyone in the hangar could hear as the liqua screamed.

Horwhannor snapped an arm out to grab Oz and tossed him like a rag doll to the hangar's rear. The guards on the catwalk readjusted their weapons that resonated in a multitude of clicks, whistles and hisses. All the weapons were malfunctioning.

Shock startled Lyon, Paloon and Larin, and they had barely enough time to find cover and draw weapons as some guards withdrew sidearms and opened fire.

The firefight failed to disturb Hitook as he held Ky's head in the crook of his left arm and stroked her hair with his right paw. Weapon fire ricocheted off an invisible bubble around Hitook as he closed his eyes and lowered his friend's body to the ground. Anger gripped Hitook's jaw until the emotion morphed into a desire for revenge.

His eye's popped open, not to the black orbs that had been there moments ago, but to glowing, refracting crystalline sheets that locked on to the sight of Horwhannor retreat. Hitook's mouth snapped open in a scream as energy shot from his body in the form of visible, prismatic pins that soared toward Horwhannor like a tidal wave of hate.

The mixture of the energy amassed during the attack and Hitook's scream forced everyone in the building to buckle as if taking on ten times their weight while daggers penetrated their skulls.

Sensing his impending doom, Horwhannor spun to face his death. The cloud of pins slammed into the piolant, then through him. Chunks of plates, skin, meat, tissue and bone flew away in a shower of blue blood.

Pounding his fists into the floor, Hitook leapt into the air. He withdrew his twin hand-blades from his back as he soared even faster to slam down onto Horwhannor's corpse. Hitook stood with Horwhannor's head impaled on one hand blade, the other whistling through the air to slice the remains of the piolant's body in half.

The psychic assault threw Lyon off balance during his slow race to the left wall. Now, he crashed into it but held his balance. Retrieving a sidearm from the small of his back, Lyon began running down the length of the wall as he blasted away with it and the particle cannon while dodging rounds that bored holes in the wall behind him. Oz's body lay somewhere ahead, but the vision of Hitook elevating his trophy kill disturbed Lyon and distracted him from finding Oz.

Paloon, being out of his element, threw as many rounds into the fight as he could force out of his cannon as he struggled to keep behind a moving Larin, even though the rolbrid didn't offer much cover. Paloon wasn't a coward; he just figured it better to be behind Larin than in front. He was right.

Larin snatched his other particle cannon from its holster and commenced launching streams of glowing allaric crystal. In mid flight, each rectangular slat of crystal fractured, sending thousands of razor-sharp daggers along the length of the far catwalk.

As the first couple of attackers thrashed about under the onslaught, the others abandoned their mission in order to get out of the way. But they failed. Each collapsed like limp dominos.

"Frapping-A!" Larin jeered from clenched teeth then released his grip on the triggers as Hitook joined the fray.

The massive beast spiked Horwhannor's corpse like a game-winning football before cannon-balling his way straight up through the bottom of the far catwalk. Immediately upon breaching the opening he created, Hitook extended his legs and planted his feet with enough force to threaten taking down the entire structure. Using the shock to his advantage, Hitook planted twin blades into a rolbrid's face and caved in the chest of a doludgian with his rear foot. He then brought that foot around to kick the headless rolbrid into a missile toward a piolant.

Recovering faster than Hitook had hoped, the piolant knocked the body aside and countered Hitook's lunging attack with a punch to the liqua's spine. Unfazed, Hitook wormed his elbow around the piolant's rear then whacked his left palm into the attacker's back. At first, the seven-foot creature just froze as if paralyzed, then he dropped to his knees, and blue goo exploded from his mouth.

Hitook ignored the retching stench and charged toward the last attacker standing, a piolant wounded by Larin's previous attack.

Lyon couldn't see Oz's body anywhere in the main hangar, so he darted for a half-open door against the far wall. In mid-trip, Lyon leapt to the side as Hitook soared down with a piolant's body under his feet like a skateboard. Upon impact, Hitook's massive feet flattened the piolant's chest sending an explosion of innards in all directions.

The knight felt too rushed to notice the crystallized rage still within the liqua's eyes, so Lyon compensated and kicked the door open, throwing out both arms with a weapon pointing down each end of a dark hallway. Light snuck past Lyon to highlight the crumpled body of Oz, who clenched his stomach with each shallow cough.

Lyon relaxed his arms, stepped forward and knelt. "Are you all right?"

"Fuck no," Oz spat between coughs. "What happened to protecting me?"

"Sorry," Lyon unemotionally responded. "Shit happens." The knight glanced around in the darkness, listening for the slightest of noises. "See anything?"

Saying another word would just mean more pain, so Oz jerked his head toward a faint crack of light at the end of the hall.

Lyon blasted toward what soon faintly appeared as another door. Hollow metal rattled in response to Lyon's kick as he waited a moment for his eyes to adjust to the light outside. He charged outside to find himself facing the two tree-trunk-sized barrels of a pulverizer cannon.

"Damn, Mac, back off!"

The remote computer guided the levitating station-wagon tank back a few feet and lowered it a bit. *"Sorry about that."*

Though glad that their internal communications systems were back, Lyon had more important problems to focus on. *"See anything?"*

"Behind you."

Bone slivers, tissue clumps, plate chucks and an entire piolant's worth of blood coated the gravel and outside wall of the hangar. At least the piolant most likely didn't have enough time to even feel pain.

"A tad overkill, don't you think?"

"What would you have preferred I do, flash my brights?"

Lyon ignored the computer's mockery. *"Have you seen anything else?"*

"Nothing. It's dead out here."

"Well, he had to be running to something. Search every bit of this ground at least five hundred feet out. There's got to be a ship around here somewhere."

The tank leaned to one side and peeled away.

"Paloon, get those drones in the air; we need to find their ship."

No response. Apparently Horwhannor had somehow focused the jamming to everything inside the building. Lyon only had enough time to give it a moment's thought before re-entering the building.

Oz had braced himself against the wall in a crippled stance. He leered at the knight as Lyon aimed his face toward the door to the main hangar.

"Larin, status!"

"Clear!"

Lyon holstered one weapon and opened the door before holstering the other. Corpses littered the floor and catwalk, all seemingly joining a mesmerized Larin and Paloon in watching Hitook cradle Ky's body in the lap of his folded legs on the floor.

Globs of tissues slid down syrupy strands of blood dangling from Ky's head. The concoction poured onto Hitook's arm, which cradled her neck. With the other hand, he mindlessly petted the length of her body. Tears welled within Hitook's normal black orbs.

Paloon noticed the glance from Lyon and responded by shaking his head. No amount of even the most advanced surgery could save someone from a cranial bomb. Horwhannor obviously never intended to allow Ky to live.

Lyon approached but at a distance so as not to disturb Hitook's mourning any more than needed. "Paloon," he started in a half whisper, "I need you outside, away from whatever is jamming this building. Get the drones searching for a ship in waiting. Mac is already looking. There has to be something out there, and it can't be far."

Paloon nodded, stepped back then moved away toward the door.

Lyon moved farther into a corner and motioned for Larin. When the rolbrid approached close enough, Lyon began quietly. "What's next? There's now an armada of Korac Council pirates in orbit without a leader."

Larin exhaled deeply through his nose. "Hope there's a well-established chain of command. That'll keep them from doing anything too spontaneous. But if there isn't," Larin peered through his brow at Lyon, "and I'll bet there isn't—once they find out that Horwhannor is dead, there will be a fight for power, and whoever wins will exert his strength in a show of power with the first thought that enters his mind."

"Unpredictable." Lyon's comment almost sounded like a question.

"More like volatile." Larin corrected. "We might have just pulled the pin from a grenade." The rolbrid looked back at Hitook still caressing Ky's lifeless shell. "I say we find their ship, fly up there, pretend to be them, take over a warp-capable ship, get somewhere safe and call for an evac."

Anyone could have guessed that would be Larin's plan, so Lyon let the rolbrid talk. But seeing Hitook hold Ky's body forced the knight to wonder if the importance of this mission could possibility outweigh a further lose of life. Gradually, Lyon's thoughts began to accept the legitimacy of Larin's statement.

Those views disappeared when Hitook snapped his head as Oz finally entered the room. At first Lyon wondered if Hitook blamed Oz and would kill again, but then Lyon felt it too. The atmospheric pressure in the building was changing, quickly. Then something unexpectedly crashed through the ceiling.

Chapter 27

The force of the impact knocked everyone to their knees as heated wind whipped around as if frustrated in seeking the quickest way out of the building.

Grey smoke pouring into the hangar from a point high above an opening in its ceiling formed a thick column. Undulating curls coated its surface in ceaseless ripples that rushed to the floor. The cloudy column roared with such speed that the entire building should have been filled with blinding smoke in seconds, yet the tempest maintained at rolling billows at the base of the smoky pillar. Not even the faintest wisps of dust escaped the crisply defined borders that outlined the rolls of vapor.

"Are you guys all right?" screamed Paloon's excited mental voice, which continued without waiting for an answer. *"What's going on in there?"*

"We're fine," Lyon replied, but he wasn't absolutely sure as he got back to his feet and looked around for the others. *"I think."*

"What's going on in there?" Disturbed excitement dominated the tone of Paloon's repeated question, and he seemed not to acknowledge Lyon's reply.

"Stop frapping yelling," Larin fired back as he stood. The rolbrid glanced at Lyon and joined him, staring in wonder at the moving, yet stationary, column of smoke.

Peripherally, Lyon noticed Hitook and Oz also rising from the blanket of dark clouds on the floor. The realization that the impact must have knocked out whatever had jammed their internal communications slipped into Lyon's mind only momentarily; there was too much in there for it to stay long.

Lyon coughed as if sublimely affected by the sight of the smoke. *"What do you see out there?"*

"What I see," Mac interrupted impudently, *"is a sky full of some really pissed off clouds that just stomped a foot in your ass."*

"And the weather is becoming increasingly unstable," Paloon added. *"It's like nothing I've seen before."*

"Well," Larin chuckled, *"other than a cloud's foot, the weather's rather lovely in here. Want to join us?"* Silence answered. *"Didn't think so."*

"What in the hell is going on?" Oz yelled from the other side of the column.

As if to answer, an oval of light glowed from inside the smoky column as a deep voice boomed into the room.

"Behold, for I will bring evil upon you."

An aura gleamed around the outside of the cloudy pillar but appeared to be extending from the glowing light in the center. Together, they pulsated in beat to the voice.

"You bring with you the inequities of your father's father's father and your blood's lineage within my midst." The voice forced the walls to rumble as it continued to speak indirectly. "Unclean is your presence. It is naught but shame and defilement. Prostrate yourself for thy sins."

"What is that?" Paloon yelled again. *"I can hear that all the way out here."*

"Shut up," responded a rather agitated Lyon. *"If you want to find out, then you're more than welcome to join us; otherwise, please be quiet; that goes for you too, Mac."*

The computer thought about it, then decided it would be best to remain silent.

Lyon walked sideways, staring at the illuminated pillar of smoke as Hitook backed away from it. Maybe it was sentient. It wouldn't be the oddest creature Lyon had ever met. Maybe something lived within it.

"Who...what are you?"

Wind pounded about the large room as the voice rumbled with anger. "I am Yahweh, Hashem, Jehovah, Adonai, Elohim, Master of Legions."

Larin squinted with one eye and glowered with the other. "Who?"

"Um," Lyon fumbled at first not believing he was about to say this, "it *claims* to be *the* God."

"Blasphemy!" The word roared as the aura collapsed into the light then exploded with enough force to knock everyone off their collective feet and blow all the grey smoke back through the hole in the roof.

Warm light continued to float in its oval shape, then rise near the destroyed ceiling. The light intensity changed rapidly. As it dimmed, it birthed a silhouette. Details formed as the light blinked from existence.

Irregular black spots freckled a cocoon of grey feathers. Ripples tossed away a few fluffs of baby feathers as whatever lived inside moved about. With a whoosh, the feathers tore open into two massive wings, uncovering a humanoid figure clad in silver medieval chest armor and a white tunic rimmed with gold pomegranates and bells.

A smaller set of grey wings uncoiled from around the creature's bare legs. Yet another tiny set of wings retreated from around the face. Longer than shoulder-length brown hair flowed freely from what was an ordinary terran face, if not for the anger that glowed red from within the eyes. Its mouth opened to reveal normal teeth that morphed into fangs then back again as if both sets coexisted in the same place.

Without any further movement from the mouth, the voice cracked like thunder. "Behold the wrath of the Lord thy God."

From over its shoulders, the seraph unsheathed two swords. Each hilt brandished perpendicular blades ridged with curling hooks of red-hot steel as if fire itself licked from the edges.

With a flick of the wrists, the angel spun the swords around then plowed them like meteors toward the ground. Both weapons pierced the earth, which shrieked in pain. All remaining fragments of glass in the building shattered into dust, and the concrete ground exploded. The earth shook as its maw opened in a jagged line that ripped the hangar building in half as the ground pulled apart.

Resurgent tremors rippled through everything as the team members attempted yet again to get on their feet.

"Holy cow," Mac belted into everyone's head, *"that was a seven point two."*

"Mac," Lyon yelled back, *"we don't need a report, just find this being's damn ship."*

His voice trailed as he watched the creature, without an apparent use of its wings, soar over the gorge and land near Ky's body.

Bewilderment twisted in its eyes. The seraph raised its head and stared down at Lyon, Larin and Hitook in a line. "Give ear, where wanders the stray?"

Hitook stepped forward, making the angel's size exceedingly apparent. At what must have been a height of at least thirteen feet, the beast watched Hitook's approach as if a minor amusement.

"You are not son of man."

Hitook kept his head level. "Who are you, and what do you want?"

"We let the truth be known, yet the flock forwent the seal to the covenant. Bring forth that which has lost favor, an offering to the mother, and purge yourselves from my chosen."

Forgetting he still wielded his hand-blades, Hitook shook their points like accusing fingers at the seraph's gut. "You're fooling no one, so I'm not going anywhere until you answer my questions."

Larin joined Lyon in gulping. Neither thought Hitook's sudden boldness would help the situation any.

Anger inflamed the angel's eyes as smoke began to trail from the edges of its enlarging mouth. The walls shook to the beat of the panting seraph, knocking bits of loose metal from the structure. Then its voice pounded, "Get six steps hence for I am God!"

On the deep emphasis of the last word, Hitook's body launched like a bullet into the back of the hangar.

"Ah, frap no," Larin barked and drew both particle cannons.

Paloon must have entered at that moment as Lyon could hear him shout "What the...?" as Lyon joined Larin in drawing weapons.

The knight felt he had to do something. Glancing at a traumatized Oz collapsed against the far wall, Lyon returned to the immensely formidable adversary. It showed no effort in tossing an eight foot liqua around like a leaf in a typhoon. Somehow, Lyon felt responsible.

"We came for the renegade Horwhannor, whose corpse lies amid this rubble." Lyon readjusted his aim at the angel who never flinched even the slightest. "If you are with him, then we have no choice. But if not, then explain yourself."

The seraph lowered his head toward Lyon. "As you have forgotten, you have fallen. Gird yourself for retribution is nigh."

Two bolts blasted from the cannons of an annoyed Larin, but the cylinders of light held short as the seraph raised a hand. With that motion, all remained still. Time halted. No one could move. Lyon couldn't even force his lungs to breathe, yet he continued to think and feel. The sensation started giving Lyon a true notion of fear.

"What in the hell did you do, Larin. I can't move." Fear in Paloon's voice meant most likely they had all been trapped in...something.

"I didn't do a frapping thing!" Larin exaggerated his anger to compensate for the terror he too felt. *"I wasn't going to let this overgrown bird just start tossing us around."*

"Quiet, both of you." Lyon wondered how they could still communicate, but other more immediate factors demanded attention. *"Unless you have something constructive to add, silence."*

Across the frozen landscape beyond his outstretched arms, Lyon noticed all the still particles in the air between him and the hole in the far wall. *"Hitook? Hitook, are you alive?"* Silence prompted Lyon to mentally curse across the team's communications channel. *"Oz—"* Lyon stopped when he realized the terran couldn't transmit mentally.

All was forgotten when the seraph finally moved, unhindered in the frozen time. The eight wings folded around once again until completely encasing the angel, then they exploded in a cloud of deep grey feathers. At the epicenter stood an immaculate, normal-sized terran.

Amid a clear complexion with just the right tint of sun, a large, genuine smile flashed, temporarily distracting from the big hair. Dark blond locks curled around while interweaving with bushy sideburns to seemingly create a natural pouf top and airy bangs. Something about the style hinted that it would take hours and a case of hairspray to perfect the look.

A white silk shirt shined brighter than seemed normal against the black suit with purple pinstripes that matched perfectly at every seam. Tiny sequences subtly caught the light from their strategically placed pattern along the white lines of a purple silk tie. Even the perfectly folded peaks of the silk handkerchief shimmered from the top of the breast pocket.

Capping the look, a thick, diamond-crusted gold ring gleamed from his right hand.

Without losing the cheerleader smile, the man gasped. "Bringing myself to your level is so irritating, like trying to breathe under water." One at a time, he reached up each sleeve to tug on the gold and diamond clasped cuffs. "At least this way, I experience less stress." He navigated around the rubble as if afraid he'd scuff his shiny loafers at any moment. "I hope this form is more amiable." Though the creature's lips now moved when he spoke, the perfect set of pearly whites never stopped smiling.

He pranced about a chunk of concrete to arc around Lyon's cannon-wielding arm. With a cock of his head, he peered at Lyon with a child-like gaze. "Why have you returned?"

"What is he talking about?" Paloon fired.

"I don't know."

"Just get him to frapping restore time," Larin injected, *"and I'll personally stomp his ass."*

"Fools." The comment went generically as he carefully stepped back. "I do not require a link into this communication system of yours to know your thoughts."

The well-groomed man retrieved a golden coin from his pants pocket and daintily held it in front of him. He then let it go. It simply remained still within the air.

"This thing you perceive...this time." He held out his palm under the coin as if serving it to anyone who could see. "Maybe for you it seems to have stopped, but this *time* has...taken a walk. It's actually rather irritating." He lowered his hand only to wave it about the room. "To you, existence has stopped, yet I move and you continue to think and perceive. None of this is needed."

"Just answer our questions," Lyon demanded mentally since, unlike his pompous captor, he couldn't move his jaw. *"Who are you, and what do you want?"*

"You still don't get it." He continued to smile in such a perpetually exaggerated way that it grated on Lyon's nerves.

The well-dressed man held up a finger. "I am here." He pointed over his shoulder to a clone in the far corner. "I am there." The hangar floor filled with his copies and claimed in unison, "I am everywhere." They all disappeared. "And nowhere."

His voice kept going, "I am all and none. I am what was, what will be," a ghostly visage of him shimmered before Lyon then snapped into corporeal being, "and what is. Simply, I am."

Lyon so wanted to punch this arrogant bastard in the face.

"Tisk, tisk." The man waved a finger like a mocking metronome. "You have no right to be angry. It is I who should be angry." However, the smile never changed. "Your ancestors betrayed us, yet they sent you back to steal what they discarded. Thou shall not steal, Lyon Vulgrin Wolfen son of Kendrick. Now where is that which you stole?"

For some unexplainable reason, Oz's name popped into Lyon's mind. As if responding, the overly happy man turned to see Oz's frozen body. In less than a thought, he stood by the terran. Like a rag doll on puppet strings, Oz's body jerked off the floor then froze, as the one person who could move encircled Oz while looking him over as if peering through his brain.

Oz's mind filled with about every curse he could contrive, even a few he never used before.

"So that is why we could not find you." He turned briefly toward Lyon. "Trying to outdo the master? Bravo." Resuming his scan of Oz, the man whispered enough for Oz to hear, and for once, malice crossed the immaculate face. "Oh, how I would love to slice open your soul and taste its ether."

Never before had Oz so much wanted to piss himself, but the lack of time wouldn't allow it.

"What do—" Lyon mentally yelled.

"What is it, worm!" The man flashed from across the room and back into Lyon's face like a military drill sergeant, the happy smile a distant past. "You are nothing but a mere worm, a worm in my fruit, distracting from the sweetness that is life, so out with it worm!"

Lyon steeled himself and took a guess. *"Are you the one who sent Horwhannor to retrieve him? Why? Why is this terran so important to you?"*

"Oh," mockery filling the man's voice, "'No one can do the job better than I,' is that what you want to hear? You have done nothing less than defile the art. You want the seat back that bad? Not even if you begged for it. He can't even return to the flock after what you've done. Steal the lamb, pay the penitence.

"Is this what you desire?" he continued with arms raised. "Have you returned only to interfere and receive a wrath due you so many years ago? So be it. I am a vengeful god."

"What are you talking about?" Lyon challenged. *"You're not making any sense."*

The man calmed, lowered his arms and squinted at Lyon. "It that true? Is it that you are but an ignorant gnat pissing away its meaningless existence by blindly falling prey to a bug zapper? Could you possibly not know—"

The words sputtered into coughs and gurgles as the man lifted from the floor. In flickering bits, Hitook took form behind the god-being who now had the liqua's massive paw buried in his back.

"I'm not part of your well-oiled machine," Hitook grunted as the sound of a wet crush crackled from the god-being's stomach, and two particle cannon bolts sizzled into the ceiling as the golden coin fell to clink on the ground.

The visage of an immaculate terran slipped away into ether, revealing a wiry thin humanoid body covered in blue-grey skin. Long fingers dangled from short legs and long arms. What had been a cranium now resembled white mush in Hitook's paw. With a weak thud, the corpse hit the ground followed by splats of white chucks flung from Hitook's shaking paw.

"Don't tell me that was a p'tahian." Paloon said while running across the floor to get a better look, hoping fervently this was not the case.

"Appears so." Lyon knelt to poke the body with the barrel of his cannon.

"Frapping hell," added Larin. "So much for not getting noticed."

"Couldn't you guys tell?" Calmness returned to Hitook's voice. "It's been a telepathic mind trick ever since he arrived."

"Well, that's just nice and fancy for you." Larin holstered his cannons. "I guess that's why we keep you around, so what took you so long?"

"Look," Lyon waved around the cannon in his hand, "that's not important. If the p'tahians are already here, then why are we still breathing?"

"Um, guys," came an uncertainly excited Mac, *"this might be your answer."*

Cracking thumps from the tank's pulverizers dully made their way into the hangar's interior. The team reached for weapons as Paloon cursed himself for failing again. A blink and the screens were in his vision.

He yelled, "Incoming!"

"No, shit!" Mac snapped. *"Now get out of the building."*

Hitook, Larin and Paloon headed for the front door as Lyon jumped across the tiny cannon and raced to grab a urine-scented Oz. Then whistles cracked as hunks of metal flew off the building to the rhythm of the exploding earth.

Chapter 28

Chaos dulled the senses and filled the air itself with dull shock waves strong enough to level buildings. Ringing replaced hearing, and lungs gasped for breath in the fluctuating atmospheric pressure. Physical laws took a holiday as flashes of light sent the surroundings into color negative ribbons of themselves with each disorienting green blast.

Bass tones thumped in Paloon's skull as consciousness took its time returning. Faint screeching got lost in the pain racking his body. Then the bass returned, snapping Paloon to consciousness. *"Mac,"* he groaned while picking himself off the ground and ignoring the fire in his knees, *"pick up on my position."*

"I can," Mac grunted as two more thuds sent cylinders of white light into the air, *"handle it."*

"Get your ass over here!"

Time left no room for arguments, and Paloon shifted his attention to his drones as he waited for Mac to comply. However, each feed returned nothing but a black screen within his vision.

"I've lost them," he shouted to all.

"What's there to lose?" Larin rolled on to his back and pointed to the sky. *"It's right there."* Then the rolbrid's extended arm jerked about trying to keep up with a point of light in the sky.

Blue filled the recently created hole in the clouds, and from it twinkled a white fleck that darted about like an attention-deficit firefly with a twitch. It zipped about in straight lines only to suddenly stop just long enough to blast to a different direction. The flashes of perpetual movement set Paloon's eyes to aching as he doubted the ability for any being to withstand such dramatic shifts at those speeds. Thinking stopped, and instinct took over as two glints of green light left the white speck.

Larin cursed and scrambled to his feet only to be lifted by his collar by a running Hitook while Paloon bolted in his own direction. The ground behind them roared and spat dirt and pebbles at the retreating prey.

Skidding to a halt on his back, Paloon wondered why he failed to notice the orange fire engulfing what remained of the hangar.

"Lyon!" Paloon's hand slipped around his bloody knee as he picked himself up. *"Lyon!"*

"I need guns," fired Larin as he scrambled off his feet toward the van.

"Lyon!" Urgency electrifying Paloon's call.

"Breathing," the knight responded as he wheezed. *"Oz is out cold."*

"Where are you?"

"Under some rubble but not bad. Should be able to get out. Situation?"

"One ship that—"

The white speck blinked a set of green eyes.

"Get out of the building!"

Paloon slammed himself into a ball, but his guess was wrong. The penetrating green blast bypassed the rumble of the hangar and plowed into the side of the van.

Violent forces tore through the vehicle like a rampaging freight train. Ribbons of deteriorating metal sent whistling spears in all directions, as if a porcupine had exploded leaving a ten-foot crater.

Smoke and orange fire washed over a transparent globe surrounding a traumatized rolbrid with yellow eyes the size of lemons. In one hand, Larin held a combat pack. From the other fell the less than half a pack that had made it into the barrier before the explosion.

The only possible explanation gradually dragged Larin's eyes across the crater's edge to blink at an exhausted Hitook. As the liqua fell to one knee, the barrier popped and sent a screaming Larin falling into the crater.

Paloon almost ran for the crater when two pounding thuds rumbled in his left ear.

"It won't sit still," Mac rationalized his poor aim as he pulled along side Paloon.

The hunter threw himself into the tank and immediately started slamming connections onto his skin and kicking Mac out of the system. *"I'm going after it."*

Lyon couldn't rebut before the tank shot into the air. *"That's suicide."*

"So is trying to fight them from the ground," barked Paloon.

"Larin, cover fire," Lyon ordered as he cleared the building and aimlessly started sending rounds from his particle cannon into the air.

"Give me a moment." Larin grunted, even mentally, as he scampered up the crater's wall, resting a moment to catch his breath with his arms holding him on the selvage. He wanted to laugh at the sight of particle cannon shots flying into the air. *"You're just drawing attention."*

"I know that," Lyon belted, grabbed Oz's leg and sprinted across the taxiway dragging the terran's body. *"Got a better idea?"*

Larin glanced up to see Paloon flip the tank in a sideways corkscrew to dodge two more rounds. One slammed into the position Lyon had been firing from; the other soared off into the distance woodlands to give a squirrel family a really bad day.

"Actually, I do." Larin activated the geomagnetic units of his combat pack and flew from the crater. He withdrew the Warmonger from the top of the pack and had it fully extended and ready by the time he made it above Lyon. *"Catch."*

Lyon rolled on to his back to see it in time to catch the falling weapon.

"Short bursts, then run, repeat," Larin ordered.

"Keep them busy and guessing, I get it." Lyon sounded patronized.

"And," Larin emphasized as he soared off, *"if you hold down the*

trigger, it will pound you into mush."

The dogfight remained rather one-sided. Regardless of how close Paloon got, the enemy ship never stayed still long enough to allow Paloon to get a shot or to allow anyone else to look at it long enough to describe it as anything other than a point of white light. Wherever Paloon fired, the light always blinked out of the way a millisecond after he had pulled the trigger. Though the light's weapons were powerful, they apparently took time to charge and had no internal guidance, which always gave Paloon time to dodge.

Short streaks of multi-colored light entered the fray, one buzzing by Paloon's window as he attempted an inverted dogleg sweep under the light.

"Who else is firing at me?" In a second, Paloon had an idea. *"Larin, is that you?"*

"It's me," Lyon responded. *"Sorry about that. Just trying to—shit!"*

The p'tahian ship fired one missing round at Paloon and another screamed toward the ground.

"I have you," came Hitook's voice as debris ricocheted off the force barrier around Lyon.

"Thank you."

"Just keep moving," Hitook politely advised. *"I'm not sure I can protect you from a direct round."*

"And aim away from me next time," Paloon injected. That reminded him of something. *"Where is Larin anyway?"*

"Just got into position."

"Where's that?" Worry crept into Paloon's voice.

"Don't worry about it. Just keep that frapping thing busy and over the hangar."

Flying just above the cloud line, the rolbrid reached back and spun the GK off the side of the combat pack. Connected to the weapon's computer, Larin aimed the scope at the cloud opening over the hangar and selected the dispersion program he wanted, which appeared as a series of target arcs in his vision. With each pull of the trigger a click and a whirl chucked a carnagearenos grenade into the air.

Klaxons sounded in Paloon's brain, distracting him so much that he almost ate an incoming green bolt of light. Still unable to breathe from the near hit, Paloon gasped again as his scopes lit up with ten inbound warheads.

"What are you doing?" The tension peaked in Paloon's voice.

"I said, don't worry about it." A mental command ejected the magazine, which fell into the clouds, as Larin yanked open the rear door of the stock, slid out another magazine and slammed it into the weapons. *"Keep it there, but be ready to run when I say so."*

Soon, nine more rounds started arcing their way toward the lights of the dogfight. Then Larin leveled the weapon, armed the next round and yelled, *"Run!"*

Paloon kicked the tank's rear in a reverse pitch and punched the throttle as the last round rocketed at full velocity directly toward the falling warheads. Once at the center, the final round detonated into a rapidly expanding ball of fire radiating blast waves that triggered the nineteen other rounds now scattered about the sky. A cacophony of relentless explosions rolled until catching the very edges of the clouds on fire in the voracious chain reaction feeding off whatever molecules it could consume.

Boom after thunderous boom pounded the air and the ground in such rapid succession that it quickly became impossible to tell actual detonations from the rebounding echoes. A mini eternity passed before anyone could register that the detonations had stopped, leaving only shadowy dins of their former selves in everyone's ears.

As their senses returned, everyone gazed upon the fading veil of fire. Underneath, the previously attacking point of light blinked, twitched, then blinked. Otherwise, it remained motionless for once.

Finally, it jerked forward again, causing everyone to curse. However, this time it only went half its previous sprint lengths before falling in a streak of sparks that, in a twinkle, became a huge orange fireball, which didn't last long before exploding in twirls of green smoke with tongues of orange fire.

"Now, that wasn't so frapping difficult," Larin boasted, leaving Lyon wondering if the rolbrid did it to just ease the tension everyone else felt.

Lyon's muscles trembled as he stood again allowing the massive weapon to fall to his side. With a deep breath, he closed his eyes. *"Mac, get a—"*

"Already on it," the computer replied. *"The Corps is apprised of the situation."*

"Any chance of retrieval?" Larin asked.

"The issue didn't come up."

"Paloon," Lyon blasted before Larin started griping to everyone, *"get down here, we need to get out of here fast."* Lyon glanced across the parking apron toward Oz's body, which just began to twitch with signs of life. Then the entire series of events flashed through his head. *"I have a funny feeling about this...a dreadful funny."*

About two miles away from the ending battle, glints of light sparkled on a hillside. The binoculars lowered to reveal calm, brown eyes deep in thought.

Agent Kim dropped his arm to allow the binoculars to fall to his side. He really wished he knew what conversations had occurred in that hangar. The agent turned to face his partner and the informant. "Who are they?"

Yabuki puffed from his cigarette. "That? I wish I knew."

The trio stared holes in each other trying to read thoughts. Fruitless, true, but Kim at least attempted before going the obvious path.

"You say they're responsible for the destruction of your dock warehouse and possibly your factory, so why lead them here, only to let them destroy a private airport?"

Yabuki removed the cigarette from his lips and dropped his head to peer over the top of his sunglasses. "Don't shit me. You saw the same thing I did. That was a firefight, not some random act of violence."

"Against whom?" Agent Crisostomo prodded.

"A mutual enemy." Yabuki calmly returned the cigarette to his lips. "Someone brought disgrace upon my family. We merely made arrangements to level the playing field so they could repay their debt by helping us repay for past sins."

"It seems like they're the threat." Kim glowered at Yabuki, calmly irritated at the yakuza lieutenant's confidence. "So you know these people?"

"Only that their leader calls himself 'Lyon.'"

"If that's all you know, then why should we help you?"

"Do we still have a deal?"

"Yes," Burn replied, "the deal still stands. However," she accentuated the words with a slender finger, "we want all the weapons you have."

"Can't do that. You should know that. We will continue to protect our own."

Kim shrugged his shoulders. "Then the deal's off, and you'll see a cell for killing Francisco Imondi."

"Regardless of what you may think about the yakuza, *agent*, we still hold true to our honor. Against my judgment I brought you here because I sense honor in you. And whatever is happening is bigger than both of us. Call whomever you must, but don't feel that there's a threat here."

"Looks like they took care of that."

Yabuki snickered. "It's not over, and I'm going to bet you already know that."

Burn sneered. "If you think we're part of some government conspiracy to keep this under wraps then why risk telling us what you know."

"Miss," Yabuki stomped on the butt he flicked to the ground, "if you believe the world of intelligence is solely the realm of government agencies, you are terribly misinformed."

Yabuki spun and headed for his car.

"Yabuki," shouted Kim, "I can't let you leave."

A red spot flashed on to Yabuki's back, but he never needed to turn to know it was there.

"And yet, you will, Agent Kim."

Similar red dots blinked into existence on the two agents' chests.

Kim spied the dot on his chest, huffed and slowly glared at Yabuki. "I expected nothing less."

"Then we have a deal. You know where to reach me."

Kim watched Yabuki drive away before the laser lights from hidden snipers disappeared. For a moment, Kim and Burn exchanged glances. Then as Kim adjusted his sports coat, Burn unfolded a cell phone and made a call.

"Scramble a full containment team on my location," she calmly ordered. "We have a level two breach."

PART FOUR

DIPLOMATIC DESTRUCTION

Chapter 1

She fought to keep from succumbing to thoughts of despair, but her greying dark brown ponytail swayed as she shook her head vigorously. “This is crazy.”

Lyta wanted to say much worse. She had an entire crew, the largest she had ever commanded, to think about. Fear on her part could cause her to make a mistake, risking those souls. If it weren’t for that, she would have said much, much worse.

Captured in her brown eyes, space ship schematics floated above her desk. Each highly classified image spouted every fragment of data the Dragon Corps could gather on the currently displayed p’tahian ship.

She flipped to the next image but wasn’t surprised by the stats. No race had been able to detect the vessel outside of using the old-fashioned eyeball. This, Lyta knew from many years of experience, meant her chances could range from holding her own in combat to getting thoroughly trounced in the blink of an eye. Modern space combat relied on multiple computerized sensors to track all the data. Even when consolidated, automatically prioritized and graphically represented, it still took five full-time watchers to effectively monitor every possible threat. Maintaining complete visual surveillance would not only be impractical but impossible.

This little crippling factor might have been why the Federal Kingdom kept the Bafomet in secret. After the Purusha’s destruction during the Twin Quasar War, everyone thought they had seen the last of the Horizon class starship that was so powerful it could be stopped only by a black hole. What no one considered was that every ship had an experimental model. Now, not only did Lyta sit within a cabin on that ship, she commanded it.

Two days ago, she didn’t even know the Bafomet existed, and now she had at her disposal the most powerful space ship known to anyone under the Dragon Corps’ jurisdiction. But when Lyta looked back at the holograms of p’tahian ships, she began to doubt that claim. If the Bafomet couldn’t electronically find the p’tahian ships, the multitude of cannons would be firing practically blind. Even with a captured white dwarf powering the massive ship, the shields could only hold for so long under a constant barrage of fire from vessels it couldn’t target.

However, Count Jeffs Dorin continuously touted his support of this mission. The orange trillig had a cabin just down the hall from Lyta. Something about him made Lyta uneasy. He held himself with an air of confidence that reeked of smugness. He was a manipulative snot, Lyta could just tell. Being manipulative was probably what allowed him to weasel in as the Corps representative on her ship.

Sure, Dorin's record contained nothing but academic praises: triple doctorates in psychology, law and atlantian history. Every time Lyta thought of that last one, her mind strayed in bewilderment as to why a trillig would be so fascinated with another race's past. Leader Kawka said Count Dorin was some kind of eminent expert on the mission. But it didn't matter; that little fur ball was gunning for a promotion to duke, and she could smell it.

Allowing herself to get infuriated, she firmly punched two fingers at the hologram to flip to the next section. The information it presented failed to improve her mood.

Following the data on p'tahian ships, a classified report explained all known contacts with the p'tahians, from the ber to the First Cloister's recent plea.

The ber were the first known race to cross into p'tahian "territory." They did so unknowingly, but there were no signs of civilization or claims to ownership in the systems they found. After a few millennia and several thousand ber outposts, the p'tahians found them.

The few surviving reports remain riddled with contradictory information. At first the p'tahians were friendly and mildly timid. The ber gladly shared information about themselves and all the other races they had befriended. Soon, however, the p'tahian-ber relationship soured. Moving from shyness to hate, the p'tahians demanded that the ber abandon all their outposts and leave the galaxy.

This drastic shift sent the ber reeling. Never before had something such as this occurred in their encounters. The ber offered resource sharing agreements, but the p'tahians would have nothing to do with them. Their demand stood.

As if an undeclared deadline had passed, the p'tahians began attacking the ber outposts. Simultaneously, each station came under overwhelming firepower that simply burned the ber's existence off each planet. The ber sent forces to defend the remaining stations. They achieved a few successes, but those wins just further irritated the p'tahians, who responded with even more powerful ships.

These newer vessels packed so much firepower that one reportedly crushed an entire ber fighter wing without taking a scratch. The ber felt they had to evacuate all outposts to save as many lives as possible, but they found themselves in a fighting retreat. P'tahian ships blasted away at everything, even humanitarian shuttles. It became a mad dash to leave the galaxy for the safety of the ber's home. That notion proved to be naïve.

At this point, the p'tahians wanted more than to just get rid of a few trespassers. They wanted death. So the p'tahians stealthily followed the retreating ships for years until the ber reached their home galaxy. Then the p'tahians resumed the genocide. During the next decade, the p'tahians conducted a methodical, surgical eradication of the ber.

From planet to planet, the p'tahians killed every form of life they found in the ber's galaxy, with complete disregard that the galaxy was home to more than just the ber. Many life forms quickly became extinct. Even the intelligent races, most still experiencing the budding advancement of civilization, became the unfortunate victims of an unmitigated holocaust. The ber had secretly sheltered these other races for centuries, but now they couldn't even protect themselves.

Other races attempted to come to the ber's aid but had their space armadas obliterated on the outskirts of the galaxy. Every time the p'tahians destroyed a fleet, a verbal warning would go to the owning government: "Our conflict with the ber does not concern you. Stay away or face our wrath."

Allies and enemies alike helplessly listened to distress signal after distress signal. In mass desperation, the ber pleaded for the p'tahians to stop the slaughter. The years of pleas finally fell silent.

Another year led to the p'tahians broadcasting a self-declared manifesto that sounded more like an ultimatum. The statement established borders and a simple diplomatic policy: Any race that crossed the border would meet the ber's fate.

Lyta yelped, startled from her trance. She jerked so hard that her reading glasses jumped from her nose to land with a hollow thud on the head of the creature now in her lap. From under a mop of cotton-like dreadlocks, two eyes of coal gleamed questioningly at being conked. After a few pets, the event was forgotten.

"Kunta, you scared the lights out of me."

The tailless creature mewed and started rubbing against Lyta's stomach.

"You are incorrigible."

Kunta ignored the comment, lost in the ecstasy of being petted.

Lyta smiled as she retrieved the glasses that had bounced onto her lap, folded them and placed them on the desk. As she did, Kunta sat back on her rear and began purring hard enough for Lyta to feel it in her legs. Eyes closed and the tip of her baby blue tongue visible, Kunta basked in just being next to Lyta. The scene had a strange calming effect and loosened Lyta's tense shoulders.

"So what should I do?" Lyta's voice opened Kunta's eyes for only an extended instant. "I have a ship of over four thousand souls hoping I know what I'm doing; well, I have no idea what I'm doing."

She sighed. Lyta knew her orders, so she knew what she had to do, but she felt helpless. It was hard to do otherwise. Optimism told her not to worry. She'd meet with her subordinate elders on the ship later; together, they would devise a plan on how to best confront the p'tahians and then they would brief the entire crew on it.

She just hoped that this Sangraal was the universe's largest cannon because they'd need all the firepower they could get.

As if reading her thoughts, a faint bong sounded.

"Yes," Lyta answered.

A flash bloomed, startling Kunta, who leapt from Lyta's lap in a fury and darted for the nearest hidey-hole or extra-dimensional portal, which was where Lyta swore the creature disappeared to at times. Regardless of how many times it happened, Kunta didn't like spontaneous holograms.

Meanwhile, the light solidified into a full-size hologram of Lyta's lead operations officer, Hunter Ulf.

With a slightly deep voice for a trilom, Ulf reported. "We have arrived." As he spoke, Ulf's tiny beak-like head wobbled as if balanced precariously on the top of his giraffe-styled neck. Grey tentacles twitched in their states of being, folded in front of a short torso propped on stubby legs.

"Anything on the scopes?"

"Negative," Ulf replied. "Shall I begin the protocol?"

"Yes," Lyta agreed as she stood. "Might as well. I'm on my way."

"Affirmative." Ulf nodded before the hologram flattened itself into the ceiling.

Lyta tapped her desk, sending the floating image of the data into oblivion. She turned and walked through the wall, which melted away to grant her access. Once she completely entered the hall, the wall reconstituted itself.

Peering down the corridor, Lyta mindlessly watched a few people traverse the path, each nodding as they passed. Dread and hope formed an odd mixture of pessimism and optimism in her gut. She started down the hall anyway.

The trip to the bridge wasn't long, but lately it had become increasingly painful. For once she wanted to make it somewhere without—

"Good day, Elder Vinci."

Lyta halted, closed her eyes and breathed deeply. She knew the owner of the voice, and it was the person she had wished to avoid. But as if on cue, there he was. *What? Is he watching me through the walls?* Putting the thought away, she turned.

"Good day, Count Dorin," she responded as if the count's presence didn't irritate her.

Resting on top of an orange and white beard sat a perpetual smile. Lyta wanted to reach out and smack the lips right off that smile, but she stifled the emotion, spun on her heels and resumed her previous route to the bridge. She knew Dorin followed. He had been on her heels like a lost puppy from day one of this mission. Being in her room offered the only bit of sanctuary in which the count wasn't somewhere nearby. She mentally wrestled with how to tell him to piss off, but irritating the only Corps representative onboard would only make this mission harder and life miserable.

"Isn't this exciting?"

Lyta's brow furrowed a bit before forced tact took control. "What's that?"

"We've made it."

"You seem to be well informed. I just found out myself."

"Yes, well, I do work hard on keeping informed, so I've been monitoring our progress quite closely."

Too closely, if you ask me, Lyta thought but said nothing.

"After all, if the protocol works, we will actually see the Sangraal. Do you know few have even seen it and even fewer know what it is? This is an exciting time, is it not?"

Lyta knew Dorin only wanted confirmation, but she couldn't help but wonder what form of manipulation slumbered in that query. So she neutralized her response. "For a historical scholar, such as yourself, maybe, but as you know, I'm more concerned with the safety of my crew. I'd feel better if this thing we've come to retrieve was five armadas of combat vessels rather than a mythical relic, especially if we are to have a chance against the p'tahians."

"But if the myth is true—"

"Myths aren't true; that is why they are called myths."

"It appears the Myth of Terra is true. That is why we are here after all."

Lyta didn't get time to respond. A few yards from the bridge, Lyta saw her executive officer burst from the door.

"Something is docking into the hangar," the rolbrid half shouted as he grabbed Lyta's arm and nearly pulled her off her feet as he rushed back toward the entry to the bridge.

Always easily excitable, Hunter Illion Gavtin often reacted from gut instinct instead of contemplated thoughts, due in part to his seemingly endless energy. Ceaselessly fidgeting with something, Illion came off as a perpetually coiled spring that sprung at everything only to quickly coil and spring again. This made many wonder if encasing him in an immobilizing cocoon of steel would result in an explosion triggered from all the twitching.

Lyta had seen past the jittering to reflect that funneling all that energy through proper mentorship and into helping Illion learn all he could would make him an indispensable administrative assistant. She was right. Now when Illion reacted in a blink, it came from well-informed instinct and almost always proved to be appropriate, though often a bit overly energetic.

"Is it a vessel?" Lyta grunted loud enough that Illion let go.

"Unknown. Scanners are getting nothing. Ulf is working on getting visuals." Illion stepped through the door and skittered forward as if he were a child encouraging his parents to hurry and enter a toy store. "Almost immediately after sending the messages per the protocol, we received a response of simply, 'Prepare to be boarded.' Then something started boarding on its own."

Lyta entered her bridge without fanfare and scanned the arc of holograms that presented a condensed view of the space outside the vessel. Behind the transparent images, the blast shields were up since the protocol dictated every portal on the ship had to be covered.

"What do we have?" Lyta asked, heading for her command chair.

Illion began, "There are—"

"We have," Ulf interrupted, "distant visuals, no details, and we are running diagnostics to troubleshoot the sensors. Whatever it is, it effortlessly took control of the docking computer, and it has begun the landing sequence in the aft hangar." The operations officer did not care for anyone outside of his direct staff briefing Elder Vinci on operations; that was especially the case with Illion, who, Ulf felt, never knew when to keep quiet.

"Let's see it," Lyta ordered as she seated herself in a massive chair that almost dwarfed her. It began gliding about on gyroscopic-controlled bearings as it precisely adjusted to her weight.

Ulf, who stood on the bridge's lower level between Lyta and the massive holographic display, took his seat at his command deck, which formed the center peak for five other command consoles lined in an arc in front of the holograms. As Ulf worked on patching in the display, Dorin took his seat to the right, behind Lyta, as Illion quietly moved behind the command chair to take his small station resting about half a level down to Lyta's left.

The apex of the arced hologram melted into a much flatter image of the star-speckled edge of the Ir Ha'Emet Nebula. As rendezvous points go, this wasn't the safest; one freak burst of ultraviolet radiation or massive ion discharge could temporarily cripple a vessel for weeks, if not months. Bright green capped the jagged edge of a mountain range formed by a haphazard web of red lighting bolts.

Amidst the still beauty, a light speck flickered and shifted a bit to the left. Just as Lyta noticed the movement, the hologram encased the point with a blue circle topped with an inverted red triangle.

"Is this the closest we've got?" Lyta asked.

"Affirmative," Ulf replied. "This view is off the number five cannon in the below starboard aft battery. Its movement over the past couple of minutes indicates a small object or craft."

"Count, is this it?" Lyta half hummed in contemplation.

"It is possible."

Dorin's unwavering tone didn't fool Lyta; the count likely knew less than she did.

"I want a security detail waiting outside the hangar."

"Already done," responded a red huyin in a Harquebus uniform who was hunched over a console so steeply that it appeared as if his granite-like slab of a body would snap at any moment.

"Thanks, captain. Start clearing the block."

"Aye," Captain Wrentin responded.

During the next couple of silent minutes, the object changed colors several times—blue, orange, white, red, green—reflecting the light from the nebula's ionized gasses. During the light show, the object grew until the faint edges formed a vessel. Soon it became apparent that calling it a vessel was an extreme exaggeration. The squat craft was nothing more than a tiny planet skipper barely large enough to hold ten people. Such shuttles couldn't support long duration trips, and they were far from any colonized planet.

This did not go unnoticed by Lyta, who started scanning everything visible in the image. Somewhere out there hid another larger vessel.

"Anything on the scanners yet?"

"Nothing," Ulf response almost discouragingly, "and all diagnostics keep checking clean."

Lyta tapped her fingers on the arm rest as her lips twitched a bit. "Get the meet and greet team to the hangar."

"On it," Gavtin responded excitedly as he activated his internal communications unit and relayed the order. Then he paused, "Are you joining them?"

From the corner of her eye, she glared at her executive officer for a moment. "No thanks, I don't feel suicidal today."

The sarcasm was wasted as Gavtin resumed his task with a formal reply. "Got it."

Silence fell upon the bridge once more. Those not busy working at their consoles watched the center screen. Over the course of about six minutes, the view switched to a camera inside the hangar as the white shuttle with mirrored cockpit windows entered, rotated to face the door it just came through then softly lowered itself to the deck.

"It," Ulf stumbled while still analyzing the data coming in, "appears to be atlantian in design, but there are no visible markings."

Lyta silently wished she had more information. Just as she started to get lost in contemplation, her executive officer interrupted.

"Lone Verseum requests permission to enter the hangar."

Lyta exhaled a shallow breath. She liked Lone Ning Verseum and hoped she wasn't about to send him to his death. They had no idea who or what was onboard that shuttle or if this entire mission was a trap. A realization struck her that if this shuttle had the ability to hack the Bafomet's computers in order to land itself then there was little she could do to protect this ship and her people. Strangely, this gave her comfort.

"Granted," she said while studying the stationary image of the shuttle in the hangar. It still refused to offer any clues as to its origin or purpose. "Security, have the detail enter but stand back, holster weapons and only draw them when a direct threat presents itself."

"Aye," Wrentin replied.

From the lower left of the screen, Verseum crept into view. His face remained hidden at this angle, but the rest of his body language broadcast nervousness. Wearing the Force Grey Wolf formal solid grey uniform with the three, silver V-shaped chevron on the sleeves, he looked like a tower of dust undulating in the nonexistent wind. That tower almost exploded when the side door on the shuttle popped open then slowly folded down to form steps into a darkened interior.

Demonstrating some master voice control by keeping his edginess from being audible, he began the formal greeting. "On behalf of this ship's commander, Elder Lyta Siobhan daughter of Vinci, I welcome you to the Bafomet. I am Lone Ning son of Verseum. Do you require any assistance in disembarking?"

Silence. Both in the hangar and on the bridge.

Then Verseum cocked his head as if listening to something, but the bridge crew heard nothing over the audio channel. He suddenly strolled forward and entered the shuttle.

"What is he doing?" Lyta barked.

"Permission to ingress, extract," Wrentin requested.

"Hold fast." Lyta shifted to her exec, "What is—"

Illion raised a hand and gazed into the floor. "He...he is okay," he began with his concentration split between his boss and the internal communications he had with Verseum. "He re-...responded to a...request from...an ambassador, he thinks."

"Is he out of his mind?"

Illion relayed the query then fumbled with summarizing Verseum's response. "He is...aware of the risk, but—" Disbelief and confusion contorted Illion's face as he leaned back and turned to Lyta. "Something *made* him feel calm and unthreatened."

Lyta screamed, "What the hell?" Movement on the screen distracted her from yelling more.

Verseum exited the shuttle, immediately noticed the tension in the security team and motioned for them to relax. As he stepped onto the hangar's deck, the shuttle's three occupants began following in a line that led out of the hangar. The screen continually shifted to new cameras to keep the arrivals in view.

"Have the security detail follow at a safe distance, and I want bridge security before they get here." Lyta ignored the confirmation as she studied the trio that followed Verseum.

All wore hooded cloaks that kept their faces from view of every camera. About a foot taller than the other two, the first's black cloak was loosely tied with triple strands of gold rope knotted on the left with tassels hanging low. Green light flashed from under the bottom of the cloak.

Similarly dressed in black cloaks and silver rope without the flashes of green light, the other two carried items. One carried a dark brown, almost black, chest with both hands holding the bottom. Lashed in rusting strips of iron, the chest appeared rather heavy, but the carrier's arms never adjusted or quivered under the weight. The final cloaked figure walked with a tall oak staff topped with a mesmerizing headpiece. Fine cords of a milky yellow metal knotted themselves in endless loops to take the three-dimensional form of an apple. Though an almost white yellow, the metal gleamed a bright reddish gold.

This trick of physics entranced Lyta so much that she did not notice the arrival of the bridge's security team or that the group had neared within seconds from the threshold.

"Elder Vinci," Verseum began as he entered, "I am pleased to introduce Samurai Sophia True daughter of Tenjin." Verseum continued with the formal introductions, but Lyta tuned out.

Samurai Tenjin stepped forward. Jade flashes again flickered from the bell of the cloak. Through an opening in the cloak, Lyta noticed a large emerald slab hanging from a chain of gold loops around the samurai's waist. Lyta thought she noticed some form of inscriptions in the tablet, but before she could take a second look, she was distracted by the samurai's delicate fingers gracefully removing her hood. *Young. So young,* Lyta thought.

Shoulder cropped hair glistened with an inky sheen as large ebony dots glowed warmly from ivory eyes. Pinkish skin barely wrinkled as pale red lips smiled with the comfort of a thick quilt on a chilly day.

"You may call me Sophia if you wish." Her serene voice intoned with a pious benevolence.

Lyta felt compelled to stand. As she did, she glanced at Sophia's companions who now flanked her. Shock struck Lyta for the second time in almost as many seconds. *They're just kids.*

"You may call them Yeshua," as she nodded to the boy at her left holding the staff, "and Miriam." Returning from nodding at the girl holding the chest at her right, Sophia continued. "They are my keepers, and when they speak you may trust it as my word."

"Thank you," Lyta found herself saying.

"I trust you have orders to our final destination."

"We do." Lyta paused and half stopped her head from cocking to one side. "Pardon, but we have little information short of the protocols we used to contact you. Will you be joining us on this mission?"

"Yes." Sophia spoke without tone. "We require little and will not be a burden."

"I understand; however," Lyta nodded to Verseum standing behind the group, "we will have quarters ready for you shortly."

As Verseum made silent calls, Sophia nodded with her eyes closed. "Thank you." Then with an unwavering tranquility, Sophia requested, "We should depart soon as time may be our greatest obstacle."

Lyta nodded in acceptance then halted. "We are prepared to depart as soon as the Sangraal is aboard. How may we help?"

"That won't be needed." Sophia smiled. "We may depart."

If it wasn't for Sophia's unflustered tone, Lyta would feel challenged. Instead she once again scanned the objects the trio carried. Concerned doubt crept in Lyta's voice. "Then the Sangraal is in your possession."

"It may not be possessed," Sophia replied calmly. "And these objects are only tools."

Vague conundrums had a way of irritating Lyta like nothing else, and more times than once had she wished Dorin would pick up on that peeve. Lyta fought to paralyze her face from wrenching in tension as she took a deep breath. "I do not wish to sound rude, but I have my orders. We must have the Sangraal before we can depart."

"Then depart." Sophia's voice increased in volume and suddenly carried a pitch of exalted authority. "I am the seventh daughter of the seventh daughter. I am that which you seek. I am the Sangraal."

Chapter 2

Neon blue characters streamed by in a circle within the dome-shaped room. Short of the bright letters, the place was pitch and featureless, but it *felt* like a dome. Next to him stood someone else watching the flying words. This companion seemed familiar, but he didn't have time to discern who it was, the mesmerizing streak of letters kept seizing his attention.

As if in some torturous loop, the characters clumped together to create what he guessed to be words in a language not only foreign but like nothing he had ever seen. Then the translation would zip by before the characters would return as the strange hieroglyphic letters. It left him struggling to make sense of it all and straining to find meaning to this obviously important message.

Then the room shook violently with three distinct booms that temporarily sent the neon characters vibrating into multiple images of themselves. Startled, he searched the empty room briefly before his eyes snapped back to the scrolling marquee floating above his head. The three booms returned, and this time, the entire scene popped out of existence.

Wearily, Lyon fumbled out of bed and barely kept himself from collapsing into an incoherent, crumpled hump on the floor. Machine gunning blinks gradually refocused his eyes as three muffled knocks echoed from somewhere downstairs. His eyes darted about behind squinted lids as his mind raced to guess from where the noise came.

Lyon hopped up to stand on his bed and peer through the high window above the headboard. Below, the door to the rear parking lot stood wide open to allow access for the refrigerator truck backed up the to building.

What? Lyon thought as his mind still struggled to piece reality together. Then it hit him so hard his eyes popped open, and he pushed the window out a bit too forcefully and yelled, "Hey, Derrick, I'll be down in a minute!"

As Lyon fell from the window, he heard mumblings from outside and wondered if, for the first time, he had upset Derrick.

This began to worry Lyon. Never had he ever seen Derrick in an even mildly grumpy mood, and Derrick never spoke a cross word about anyone or anything. Lyon had always quietly admired that quality.

During that thought, the scene he had just noticed out his window finally registered. It wasn't early morning; the sun was already many degree off the horizon. The thought that Derrick could be several hours late never had a chance of entering Lyon's mind, which could only mean one thing: Derrick, unable to wake him earlier, went ahead and finished the rest of his rounds and came back. This was based on the unlikely possibility that Derrick had been knocking on the door for the past three hours. But then again, Lyon had no idea how long Derrick had been knocking.

Derrick always had shown a type of persistent determination, almost to a fault, when it came to work. Lyon experienced it a few times and compared it to a cheetah with the throat of a gazelle firmly in its jaws. Short of the threat of immediate death, Derrick would not waiver from completing a job he started, and the only result could be the gazelle coming down, breathless. Lyon found himself admiring that once, until he thought about a few situations in his job where that kind of ethic could needlessly get people killed.

But for Derrick it worked, and it never seemed to bring him unhappiness, until now. However, it didn't keep him from smiling when Lyon opened the back door.

"Good day," Derrick began with a tip of his hat and not the slightest tone of discomfort. Maybe Lyon had imagined the muffled grumbling.

"I'm sorry, Derrick," Lyon blurted, almost stumbling on his words. "I hope you weren't out here—"

Derrick silenced Lyon with a raised hand. "I'll hear nothing of it. It's part of the job, so let's get to it."

Without a word, the duo swapped out all the dairy products since even the freshest one had expired yesterday. As Derrick drove away, Lyon waved before closing the gate and stepping back into the rear of the building. He stood in the dimly lit storage room for a while, wondering why he should even bother with the store. He and his team should be fighting to get off this rock while there was still time. Then he strolled forward, lost in thought, and uncontrollably peered into the freezer again.

Grey meat glared back at him.

Lyon's shoulders fell loose as a sigh wheezed through his nose as if the universe's most despicable failure had resulted from his ineptitude. An unaimed hand reached around the corner behind him and began slapping the wall until it struck the phone, almost knocking it completely off the rocker onto the floor. A flurry of finger fumbling jostled the phone in an air ballet of graceful chaos that somehow landed the handset square in his palm, due largely to a freakish bit of mindless luck.

From memory, his thumb dialed the slaughterhouse. Lyon didn't care about the extra fees for same-day delivery. "Just send me my full order," he stated.

As the phone clanked back on the receiver, his mind wandered even further into desperation. He sighed again as he closed the heavy freezer door, half wanting to bash his head into it. Strolling into the next room, Lyon kept his eyes down as his mind remained wrapped around rhetorically asking where his life had gone wrong. Then Fate found a new way to increase his burden.

"Why me?" he exhaled in a barely audible tone. Then he yelled, "Why fucking me!?"

The brief release of stress offered Lyon enough control to wrestle his mind back into a phantasmal padded cell as he gazed before him. The entire produce section looked more like a long forgotten penicillin experiment than a salad bar. He even doubted the usefulness of adding the fruit carcasses into a mulch pile. The possibility of the mounds of fuzzy, blue-grey mold feasting on dead vegetation to survive long enough to achieve intelligence was too great a risk, regardless of how remote.

His shoulders drooped further as he dragged himself into to the storage room for some gloves and a bucket. Back at the produce counter, Lyon started removing the rotten plants by the handfuls. Such rough handling irritated the mold, which retaliated with some of the foulest smelling microscopic spore clouds known to man. Lyon didn't notice; he had already drowned the stench with thoughts.

Twice, his actions had gotten someone killed. Why else would he have volunteered for such a remote assignment? Wasn't he just running from the burdens that came with making decisions? Or did his bosses covertly steer him to this assignment once they recognized his blunderings, thinking it best to bury him in a remote location for a while? Lyon hoped it was the first but started doubting it.

Was it the same clumsy leadership that led to NeNa and Ky's deaths that made his current troops react more like members of an immature high school class than a cohesive team? And was that a bad thing? He couldn't decide. Though something intangibly tried to make him think so, he refused to believe it entirely. This sent him into another spiral of doubt. If he truly suffered from maladroit leadership skills, then how would he know?

How irritating, he thought.

From the depths of this self-feeding pity tornado, a disturbing thought rose eerily like the demented shadow of a demon struggling to free itself from a supernatural plane of perpetual pain: Had he already been flagged in the Dragon Corps personnel system as a washed-up has-been? Was that why his commanders ignored his reports? Was that why the dragoon so quickly turned down his request for an infiltration team?

It made an ugly bit of sense that came stocked full of uncomfortable, eye-opening realism, as if he had just sent to his superiors an irretrievable and self-incriminating message that would eventually lead to his gangland-style assassination.

Lyon's gut took a holiday.

The resulting void had no bottom and no edge, just pitch. Had his entire career, all he had ever known, finally come to an end? Or did his life in the Corps end long ago, and his supervisors were just waiting for him to see the reality?

Gradually, Lyon acknowledged the world around him, but the first thing he focused on was the last bit of rotten vegetables clenched by his gloved hand.

Have I really come to this? he mentally asked. *Is this all I'm good for?*

With an exasperated sigh, he chucked the mess in the bucket and sulked out the back door, where he silently cursed the stench from the dumpster as he emptied the pail. A forest of mop and broom handles clattered to the ground when he flung the bucket toward the corner of the storage room before half stomping off toward the front of the store.

At the far end of the second aisle, he found the only line of room deodorizers he had and yanked a box away with each hand. As he turned to head back, Lyon was faced with a shadow in the front window. He squinted until the figure finally registered in his disheveled mind as a person with cupped hands around his head peering into the window.

"Is somebody in there?" came a slightly muffled male voice. "Hey, are you open, man?"

Lyon huffed, this time in anger, as he marched up to the check-out counter and slammed the air fresheners down. Fury sounded with every flick of the locks on the entrance, and Lyon flung the door with no less fervor.

With a glance at the stacks of pilfered newspapers, Lyon kicked at them and barked, "What!?" His tone shocked him into inhaling deeply and trying to relax his face.

Whether the gentleman had noticed or sympathized remained unknown. "Yeah, are you back open? I just wanted to know before I walk all the way down to the Super Mart again."

Another deep breath breezed through Lyon's nose as he clenched his eyes. "Yeah, sure." Lyon half heartedly held the door open as he stepped back into the store, and it wasn't long before he let go.

The reluctant customer found himself scrambling to the door and stopping it only inches from completely closing. Squeezing through as if not allowed to the open the door any more than necessary, he entered, pushed his shades onto his bald head and whiffed the aroma of decay. "Something stinks, man."

Lyon froze, an empty air freshener box in one hand and its contents in the form of a plastic tower in the other. If the knight's stare could ever be verbalized, the words alone would have a high probability of mortally wounding, if not permanently debilitating, the recipient of the communication.

Startled from being an unwilling participant in the volley of anger, the bald man jerked back a step.

Lyon flicked the empty box at the floor behind the counter and slammed down the air freshener. "Aren't you a smart one?" He opened the second deodorizer. With both in hand, Lyon faced his victim. "Let me guess, you've got a Ph.D. in observation." Lyon stepped around him and headed to the back. Even though his voice became more muffled, he didn't stop. "Thanks. If it wasn't for you, I wouldn't have come to that conclusion."

The gentleman, who epitomized the definition of tolerance, leaned a bit while scanning the butcher counter freezer. "Do you have any rib-eyes?"

"Hmm," Lyon vocalized loudly, the volume increasing as he began his return trip to the front of the store. "I don't know. Let me check." As he stepped in the main room, he joined in leaning and gaping at the empty freezer. Then he shook his head purposefully. "Nope. Guess not." He headed for the stool behind the cash register. "Must have all went bad. Won't have any until later today. There's always frozen meals in the other room; they should still be good."

With a shrug, the customer left for the other room and returned with a couple of frozen pizzas and a box of sodas. After paying for his items, the gentleman hefted his food then paused with genuine concern on his face. "I hope your day gets better, man, because you're not a very nice person at the moment."

He tapped his shades, which slid off his head onto his nose, and quietly left, oblivious to the death stare Lyon bore into his back. Before the door closed, Lyon started mumbling incoherently like a deep-throated kettle letting off steam.

Sitting on the stool, frowning, Lyon sulked in a pit of volcanic hate. In just a span of several minutes, he had gone from bewildered and mildly frustrated to full-blown anger at life. He disliked himself for his failures, both in and out of his control, and was royally miffed that Mac hadn't wakened him.

His head jerked back as the thought struck him. For the first time in a long time, Mac wasn't pestering him.

"Mac!?" Lyon let a few moments of silence go by before a smidgen of worry tweaked the fringes of his voice. "Mac!?"

"Um, yeah." The words oozed from the speaker below the counter in a drawl that just sounded pitiful. Lyon even envisioned Mac's three-dimensional visage downstairs, sitting on a holographic metal-framed chair upholstered in tattered and stained floral-print vinyl, with an almost empty half-gallon rum bottle in one hand and a shotgun in the other, just moments away from a self-ventilated brain case.

This startled Lyon into forgetting his fabricated misery. "What's up, man? You don't sound so well."

The computer snorted. "Ain't that something? Have you even listened to yourself? You aren't sounding so peachy yourself, bud."

"No," Lyon trailed off in thought for a second, "I guess not." He was eager to change the subject. "What have you been up to? I kind of missed you this morning."

After a bit of humming, Mac answered, "Thinking. I've been thinking." A bit more thought enlightened the computer and enhanced its current demeanor. "Hey, what do you mean 'missed' me? It took you nearly an hour to even notice. That kind of shatters your attempted condolence, doesn't it?"

Mac seemed a bit bitter, but Lyon couldn't blame him. He just shrugged. "Guess I was lost in thought." Lyon rubbed his forehead and stared into the distance at nothing for a moment. "So what have you been thinking about?"

"What do you think!?" the computer yelled. "Losing her once was bad enough. What!? Do you think the second time made it any better?" Tense silence stretched for a good minute, but when Mac returned he had calmed considerably. "I don't like these emotions. Why can't you take them away?"

Lyon hadn't thought about how quickly his computer companion could get attached to someone else. For the first time, Mac was experiencing the loss of a friend. "I wish I could, buddy, but to get one, you get them all, even the bad ones."

"But...?" Mac wandered off into more thought. "What do I do?"

Lyon guessed at what the computer meant, but he didn't have to try too hard because he was sharing the same thought. "Nothing." Lyon dropped his head. "There's nothing anyone can do. Pain like this doesn't go away; it doesn't change. The only thing that can change is your perception of that pain, and that takes time, sometimes years."

"I don't think a decade will change this feeling."

"It seems like it never will change, at first. You'll just have to trust me."

Mac released a displeased huff.

He couldn't force the computer to understand, and he knew it. But Ky's death was the last thing Lyon wanted on his mind, and it would take work to achieve that goal. Glancing about, Lyon noticed the newspaper racks, which reminded him of the stacks of papers he had kicked outside the door. This sent him straight to work, doing anything to keep his mind occupied.

Lyon couldn't tell how many people had helped themselves to the papers, but by the multiple popped bindings and wads of advertising inserts between the papers and the wall, passersby had done so for days. He doubted they were criminals; petty thieves tend to not read newspaper. More likely than not, people had left money, but even in this neighborhood, a stack of nickels wouldn't last more than half an hour out in the open.

The chore filled less than ten minutes of Lyon's day. Returning from throwing away the old papers, he swiped a can of soda from the freezer and opened it as he approached the front of the store and called out to Mac. "Where are the others?"

"What do I care?"

The caustic tone froze Lyon in mid-gulp for a moment. Before he could clear his throat to question his computer's motives for the statement, Mac continued.

"No, really. Why should I care? There is no reason, so I don't. You want to know where they are? Then go find them yourself."

Mouth open, seconds from responding, Lyon stopped himself and shut his mouth. It would do no good and would most likely just fuel the situation. The computer needed its time to discover its own way to deal with these new emotions.

Back behind the counter, Lyon just perched himself on the stool and stared out the window. Being left to his thoughts appeared to be his destiny today. He considered napping the day away, but the resulting dreams offered potentially worse torment. Now, lost in the textured grey of the building down the street, Lyon fought to keep from thinking about Ky's death and what it meant. But the more he fought, the more he thought about it. Soon he drowned in depressed contemplation.

Not once but twice Fate had presented him with a chance to correct the error that led to NeNa's death. Three mistakes, two deaths and a lifetime of distress. Again and again, his mind played out every detail, everything he had missed, every opportunity that he had passed over, every scenario that should have been and would have led to Ky still being alive, as if to repay for NeNa's death. Nothing would, but he liked to think that something could. That was his curse.

With that realization, Lyon shook himself from the trance. Glancing behind him, his eyes locked on an oddity. Sitting on the counter rested two dollars and thirty-five cents. It wasn't there a moment ago, but then again, what was a moment? How long had he been lost in thought? And how deep? Had he been out of it so much that someone had entered the store and bought something with him not so much as noticing the slightest of noises?

Lifting the money from the counter, Lyon just paused with it clutched in his left hand as he slipped into another trance. This time the bell above the door snapped him out of it, stuttering at first but soon punching the cash register door open and putting the money away.

As he did, he noticed his next customer. "Good morning, grandma."

The elderly lady rose from unfolding her cart to grip the side of her glasses with two fingers and a thumb. Readjusting the lens to ensure she saw clearly, Mrs. Franklin gazed at the clock on the wall. It was well past three in the afternoon, but she politely said nothing about the error. "Hello."

"I'm sorry," Lyon began, "but all the meat went bad, I won't have any until maybe later tonight or in the morning."

"That's quite all right," she comforted without a worry in the world as she started up and down the aisles. "You've been closed for some time." Lyon tried but couldn't tell if she was upset. "Not knowing when you might open again, I took the bus to that fancy, new market where Gerald's hardware store used to be. I still have me enough meats to last for a few more days."

Guilt twisted Lyon's gut. He knew how much she hated taking the bus, especially to shop. She must have stocked up a bit so she wouldn't have the take the trip too often, but hauling all that food on the bus must have been trying. Fewer people seemed to help nowadays.

"I'm sorry I've been closed. The ride wasn't too bad, I hope."

"The ride was fine," she said while scanning the side of a rice box. "This nice young lady named Jill helped me on and off the bus. Such nice people," she muttered while moving to next aisle. "It was the store that was nerve racking. So many people and blasting all kinds of noise over the speakers; there was so much racket I couldn't hear myself think."

She paused long enough to pick a bottle of dish soap and place it in her cart. "I like that you have only one kind of dish soap, just like Al did. Have you been in that store up there? There are enough brands of dish soap to fill this room. I remember ever since I was knee-high to my mother, bless her soul, all we would need was dish soap. When she first saw all these brands, she looked at me and said, 'Alessa, it's all just soap.' That's still true today. It's all just soap. It doesn't matter if it's made with herbs or fruits or foams; it's all soap. I just need it to clean my dishes, not smell nice or look a particular way. It's all just soap."

She finally ended her rant and continued her shopping as if the previous frustration never existed.

As in all the times before, grandma's words left Lyon wondering. Was she somehow manipulating him to compare all the worries in the world with all the brands of soap in the world? It doesn't matter the kind or flavor of worry, it's all just worry. One simple thing that's easier to deal with than the hundreds of thousands of types. Or was he seriously over thinking this? Maybe grandma was just talking about soap.

She approached the counter, unloading the items as Lyon added them. Paid for and bagged, the groceries went from Lyon to grandma to the cart. During the process Lyon tried to apologize again.

"I am sorry about being closed. I guess I've just been too busy to pay attention. I should have had the store open for you."

"Oh." Grandma stretched out the word as she gently pumped an open palm as if to say, "Shush, I'll hear nothing of it."

"Don't worry your pretty little head about it," she said softly. "After all, I'm not long for this world."

The comment sent Lyon's head reeling. Such talk did not set well with him, regardless of how distant a future it might reference.

It was her next set of words that turned Lyon's world upside down. "Not many around you are."

Dread imploded into his mind, and darkness shrouded his vision. Her raw psychic abilities, regardless of how bewildering they could be, always made Lyon wonder how much she could see. He wondered if she could see his real identity, and if she could, would she say anything?

However, this talk of death, so bluntly, heightened Lyon's senses and put him on the defensive. How much did she know? What did she know about the future, especially this planet's future, that she wasn't telling? At least she wasn't telling directly. She kept leaving vague bits of clues.

Then it hit him: Maybe this was just another chance to correct his wrongs. Rules and regulations be damned, he had to know in order to save lives. "How will—"

Grandma immediately shook her head.

Lyon stopped, wondered and tried again. "But who—"

Grandma shook her head again. "It is not how, or who, but why."

She quietly left the store, leaving Lyon wallowing in a murk of mystique.

Chapter 3

Beyond the edge of shattered and upheaved concrete, only a bottomless black void existed. Along the way down the crevasse, jagged bits of stone protruded from the walls in disorganized clumps. The light glimmering from their glossy surfaces contrasted with the pitch below that seemingly stretched to eternity.

The deep darkness came to him laced with dread. He couldn't stop from wondering if the endless pit resting just past the selvage at his feet represented, in some sickly twisted way, his inevitable future.

Recent events had created the second major shift in his perceptions of reality during his life. The first came with accepting his current job. The initial shock dulled over the years, but this second climax came with more of a persistently nagging, almost mocking, foreboding.

Agent Kim rolled a toothpick around his mouth as he took a deep breath and then instantly coughed out the toothpick. Sulfur saturated the air with its unmistakable taste that nearly brought him to regurgitation.

Subconsciously registering the toothpick falling into the cavern, Kim snapped his head. "Hey!"

Near the outlying skeletal remains of the burned out hangar, a full-body black biological suit switched off a humongous torch contraption held around its hips and turned to reveal a yellow-bordered faceplate sporting a large, cylindrical filter attachment.

"You think you could tone it down a bit for a while?" Kim yelled to ensure his message got through the suit.

The guy behind the mask responded with a curt, unintelligible phrase muffled by the suit.

Kim wondered momentarily if he was being cussed at but ignored the incident when the guy moved away to scorch burnt alien body parts off of what remained of the building.

His attention back at the gorge, he rose from his crouched position. Another breath disappointed. It would take time for the sulfur stench to dissipate to tolerable levels. Then his lost toothpick came to mind.

For some reason his mind played back, in slow motion, a vision of the toothpick tumbling away. Then the sliver of wood morphed into a likeness of Agent Kim and kept tumbling, end over end, down into the ravine until it was swallowed by the darkness.

With a huffed smirk, he had to admit the hallucination reflected exactly how he felt: He was trapped in an unavoidable spiral toward a dark, dark future. He didn't know how dark, but the signs all around him failed to offer much hope for a positive outcome. Regardless of how drastic, there was no turning back now; he couldn't. That was the one thing in his life that was an undeniable certainty.

"Hey, Kim!"

He looked over his shoulder at his approaching partner who was cradling in her arms a weapon almost as long as she was tall.

"Anything interesting?" Agent Crisostomo asked with a jerk of her chin toward Kim's way.

Kim returned to the crack in the ground and grimaced briefly. "Interesting? Yes."

"Any idea what caused it?"

His face tensed again as he replied, with an extra layer of disappointment, "No." He paused. "The edges are vitrified, as if from a plasma cannon, but the cavern walls are uneven, not cut smooth as weaponized plasma would do. Instead, it's as if something forced the ground to split on its own just before the plasma jumped in and melted it." Momentarily Kim's eyes wandered to stare at nothing in particular before gradually making it back. "I have no idea what could have done it."

"Well," Burn offered with a tinge of cheer, "I think I found Yabuki's reference to leveling the playing field."

That had Kim's attention. "Really?"

He spun as Burn whipped around with well-practiced grace the weapon she had been carrying. A flick spun a connection ring until it unlocked the butt of the weapon. Weighted by a box-shaped magazine in the rear, the bottom half of the stock dropped, sliding on internal rails as it did. She snapped the rifle parallel with the ground sending the weighted half of the stock over to land on top of the weapon. Holding that part in place with one hand, she spun the rifle upside down with her other.

With both hands occupied, she just held the weapon on display as Kim squinted at it. He had no idea what to look for and knew Burn wouldn't hint; she was a bit peculiar that way. So he was left with just scanning the exposed, narrow circuit board and wiring. Then his eyes stopped, and Burn noticed it.

"See it?"

"I...think."

One link in the circuit board had a mild mar running a bit deep. If it wasn't for the type of weapon, it would seem to be nothing. But in a rail rifle such as this one, the only moving part was the mouse-sized slug of metal being propelled from the rear magazine through a series of electromagnetic tracks. But the slugs were too blunt to cause such a surgical slicing, even by accident.

"What caused this cut?" Kim asked as he reached to feel it with a finger tip.

"That's the question of the day," Burn remarked. "That cut doesn't sever the connection, so a diagnostics check runs clean. However, it is deep enough to keep a full charge from ever passing through the circuit, which would trip in the regulator and keep it from firing. Whoever did this knew *exactly* what they were doing."

Kim crossed his arms, closed his right eye and hummed inquisitively. "How would the yaks know how to do this?"

"I'd like to know that too," she stated while closing the weapon with similar deft movements as the ones she used to open it. "One better, I'd like to know if they had help and, if so, from whom?"

"I'm not sure I'd want to know that answer."

"Me either, but how else did they disable, by my estimates, some twenty weapons of various types with the same skill?" She slammed the butt of the weapon on the floor and let the question go unanswered.

"I can confirm one thing we saw," Kim offered.

"What's that?" Burn asked, willing to temporarily forget her previous frustration.

Kim held out a palm toward the ground at an angle and began walking in shaky staggers as if being led by a divining rod. With the spot found again, he stopped and pointed at the ground. "A presence touched down here."

Burn knew Kim saw the same thing she did. What else would descend from the sky and enter a building as a cloudy column? Of course it was a presence. The true question had yet received an answer. "What would bring it down here?"

"Exactly," Kim remarked. "Why? What could be so important for it to risk becoming so vulnerable?"

"Wait a minute." Burn's eyes darted around then she spun and roughly pointed the barrel of the rifle toward were she felt the catwalk must have been. "So these guys weren't setting up an ambush; they were running protection."

Kim blanked for a moment before nodding in agreement. "They might have been bodyguards." He thought about it for a moment and huffed, "So much for that. At least it wasn't us."

Burn snapped her head over her shoulder. "We weren't here, as far as I'm concerned." She turned back and scanned the scene of biological suits scorching everything in sight before adding in a trailing voice, "They don't need to know."

Undoubtedly, Kim agreed. He had no desire to file it with his report. There were too many unanswered questions to be offering unrequested answers that would only place their collective butts in a sling. They already faced one ass chewing.

"How are we going to explain this Lyon guy that...?" Kim found himself stumped on how to vocalize his thoughts.

"There's nothing to explain," Burn stated. "We tell the chief what we know, and the rest will come with time."

"That's not quite what I mean."

"So you mean—"

"I mean, how did they get here? We're supposed to catch such traffic, but they got right by us. If *they* did it, how many more have?"

"What? Do you think we're perfect?" Burn understood Kim's thoughts, every agent wrestled with them at sometime, at least the agents who cared. "We're good. We're damn good, but we're not perfect. However, there can't be too many more of them, or we would've noticed."

"Are you sure?" Kim questioned. "If you didn't notice, they

weren't returning fire with standard-issue firearms. And at least one wasn't from the neighborhood. And what of that one who flew on his own and that craft they had?"

"What about it?" Burn restrained annoyance from entering her voice.

"Maybe we should recommend scrambling the Nubius to run cover and respond to any unusual activity in hopes to catch them."

"Kim," Burn twisted her head forcing her neck to pop, "this is as nice as I can tell you, but you need to get your head back in the game."

Kim was taken aback a bit, but he knew she wouldn't say that if she didn't mean it.

"I'm not ready to admit failure, and the Corona projects are the fail-safe. Showing our hand too soon will get it cut off, then we'll have nothing. But for now, we have the high ground; I want to keep it."

Kim squinted at his partner. "What high ground?"

Burn let her lips release a smirk. "We know about them, but they don't know about us. And while the trail is still fresh, let's find them before they get seven billion people killed."

Chapter 4

Wrinkles marred the bridge of Kurosawa Tetsuya's nose. In his brown eyes, disappointed frustration fueled a fire that flickered with reflected images from the massive screen protruding from the floor in front of his desk.

Invisible lines distinctly segmented the display into several images. The left two-thirds of the screen formed two rows of three pictures each. Each window housed a different face. Two were actively yelling, apparently at each other. One aggressively responded in waves while one seemed to calmly hold a private conversation with no one. Of the remaining two, one tried to politely interject only to be orally stepped on, and the other remained still, only blinking occasionally behind round glasses.

This is madness, Kurosawa thought.

Takeuchi Katahi and Uesugi Masaru had been at each other's throats for the good part of ten minutes. Adachi Ryuunoskue vehemently disagreed with both. Sumeragi Nori refused to cut his response short due to the childish antics of others and continued to speak until he was finished. Murakami Yuuma felt some points on all sides were quite valid, but no one gave him a moment to finish a sentence. The calm eye of the storm, Saionji Noboru, patiently waited with an uncanny ability to tune out the cacophony of idiocy for the moment, assured sanity would return to the debate.

"We have no other choice," blurted Takeuchi. "We need a new oyabun."

"I'm tired of repeating myself," Uesugi yelled. "Our rules are clear: We must first know the whereabouts of our oyabun."

"We don't even know where to look."

"That doesn't change our laws."

"...from established procedures to proceed...," Sumeragi continued with his voice now audible between short pauses.

Murakami began to open his mouth, but Adachi beat him to the point. "Takeuchi, you are crazy to suggest rewriting the laws over this."

"Hai," Uesugi chimed in agreement.

"Both of you are crazy," Takeuchi blasted. "This is not a normal situation. We must choose now before it is too late."

"Too late for what?" Uesugi sneered. "Are you going somewhere?"

Unintelligible yelling resumed, and Kurosawa subtly shook his head, briefly looking at the normally placid image of Saionji, who pushed the center of his glasses with two fingers. Attempts to maintain self-restraint continued to fail. Kurosawa could feel his control slipping.

The family should not be like this. It had not been this divided for many years.

"Gentlemen," Kurosawa pleaded, but he only grabbed some of the attention. Takeuchi and Uesugi kept at it. "Gentlemen! Please!"

Kurosawa swore he felt blood in his throat from yelling so loudly. The outburst halted Uesugi, but Takeuchi only gradually lowered his voice before deciding to end with one final curt phrase, "We must vote."

Refusing to acknowledge the remark, Kurosawa began calmly. "I did not wish to bring chaos into the family with this meeting. It is only that I have concerns that have recently surfaced. My earlier question was merely based on those concerns."

Saionji finally spoke. "As true as that may be, your concerns about the oyabun's whereabouts must have some justification to bring them before us so boldly."

The mild chastisement in that statement did not go unnoticed. Kurosawa admitted he deserved it. "I called upon you six because I consider you more than brothers in the family; all of you are dear friends, friends whom I know personally. I cannot say the same for the oyabun."

"Careful," Sumeragi warned, "you tread a dangerous path."

"Yes, I do." Kurosawa knew exactly what he was getting into. At least he hoped he did. "I can conclude from everyone's statements that none of you have recently received contact or been able to contact the oyabun."

Kurosawa paused for rebuttals, but everyone remained silent. "Has anyone personally met the oyabun?"

Another round of silence answered the question.

"Not one of us, for the past eight years, has seen the oyabun in person." At first, Kurosawa's voice carried mild notes of doubt, but it soon steeled. "However, each of you met Ishiguro-sama." Kurosawa knew personally that each of them had drunk sake with the previous oyabun, Ishiguro Shinji, shortly after he assumed the title. "We have not disrespected the family, yet 'royal guards' are sent to watch over us. This does not sit well with me."

Takeuchi jerked as if about to blurt his opinion, but he held short and slumped into a similar pose of contemplation assumed by the others. Clearly, Kurosawa's friends had thoughts much like his own. The thickest loyalty did not keep them from noticing the obvious: Something had run afoul in the family.

"I trust each of you with my life. I would not have asked you here otherwise. Your oath to the family is without question. This is why I must now test that loyalty." Kurosawa tapped a few keys until a video window appeared in the blank space to the right of everyone's screens. "Prepare yourself."

Kurosawa's warning was an understatement. Little could have prepared them for the video as it began to play. Yet just as Yabuki had captured it, the scenes gave all a peek behind the mask of a royal guard. Awe, confusion, bewilderment, shock—all of it struck the watching faces, even after the video stopped. A few key taps rewound the images to stop on the alien face.

Kurosawa let it sink in a bit before cutting the uneasy silence. "Something has veiled the truth from us. Perhaps that veil has now silenced its owner."

"As amazing..." Uesugi stumbled, "as amazing as this is, this is not proof that the oyabun is aware."

Takeuchi agreed. "What if the oyabun also uncovered this...this truth," he didn't want to say it, "and it has now led to his death?"

"Or worse," Sumeragi added, "what if the oyabun is nothing more than a puppet?"

"That would mean," Murakami's thoughts disturbed him to the point of tripping over his words, "we're nothing more than puppets of a puppet."

"Hell if I'll be somebody's puppet," Takeuchi blasted.

"Too late." Uesugi did not intend for that to come off as a challenge, but Takeuchi took it as such, thanks in part to Adachi's loud laughter.

"Speak for yourself, Masaru-chan."

Before another round of yelling between the two could resume, Saionji shared his insight. "What if the oyabun is not and has not been that which he has pretended to be?"

This scenario hit everyone like a brick wall in the chest, even halting all breath, except for Kurosawa, who already had the time to give plenty of thought to the video's possible implications. "I came to the same uncomfortable probability."

"But that would mean...." Murakami trailed off as he lost the words to say what he felt.

Takeuchi gave up waiting for Murakami to finish. "What the hell is this anyway?" he asked while thrusting a finger at the image of the unmasked royal guard.

"We don't know," Kurosawa responded. "But after a few hours, all your memories of the interactions you've had with them and with the oyabun himself will become suspect. For example, three of our facilities that had special protection from the oyabun's royal guard have recently been attacked; one of them has vanished, literally.

"We believe these attacks are linked to and, possibly caused by, a group, which includes other strange creatures, that appears to be attracted to these activities."

"What are you talking about, Kurosawa?" Adachi barked. "Do you really expect us to believe that the oyabun is an alien and is under attack by other aliens? That would put us in the middle."

Kurosawa motioned for Yabuki to step out from behind the screen, where the yakuza solider had been waiting patiently. "I want you to meet Yabuki Yumiro." Kurosawa relinquished his seat to Yabuki, who reluctantly sat down. "Tell them."

During the next half hour, Yabuki detailed all the events from the spy at the warehouse to the firefight at the airport hangar. As the story progressed, the gentlemen on the screen became more uncomfortably agitated. There was no time for questions as their minds attempted to process the extraordinary events being described. Once finished, Yabuki relinquished the seat to Kurosawa.

"For redemption, we require uncommon alliances and even more uncommon actions." Kurosawa knew he didn't have the authority of the oyabun, and only that authority would move the family to mass action. However, he had to try. "It may be best that you do what we have done. Bring the family in tight. Protect yourselves. And kill any royal guards."

A few subtly nodded, but Adachi failed to accept the last statement. "Only the oyabun can order that. Even if they are puppets, these royal guards are...." Logic finally reached Adachi, stopping him short.

"They are not yakuza," Kurosawa stated. "They're not even human. We have lost many kobun attempting to take down the few remaining royal guards, even with the newly acquired weapons."

Sumeragi added, "We have an obligation from the machi-yokko to protect the weak. We should turn to that duty, and we best not falter."

"But what of an oyabun?" Murakami asked. "We need a leader, a trusted leader, to orchestrate our actions."

"How about Kurosawa?" Adachi offered.

Now it was Takeuchi who laughed, but Uesugi nodded in agreement with Adachi's recommendation. But Kurosawa wanted nothing of it. "Now is not the time for such things. We each need to take individual actions to secure our assets and restore the family."

"True. It is the only way," Saionji agreed. "Working independently will allow us flexibility and agility during what will likely be a rapidly changing situation. We know what we must do. For now, that is sufficient."

The wisdom soaked in. They all concurred. Then in silence, they disconnected from the teleconference.

The screen slipped into the floor as quiet descended into the room. Kurosawa gazed out the window for a minute before standing and heading for the door. "Follow."

Yabuki obeyed and trailed behind as Kurosawa made his way to the roof.

Covering almost the entire span of the large roof, multiple types of traditional gardens blended into a flow of tranquility. A hanging garden, tea garden, sand and stone garden, strolling stream garden—a balance of Zen and conflict.

Yabuki followed Kurosawa in removing his shoes and placing his feet in one of the provided sets of wooden sandals. Along the winding stone path, Kurosawa tried to see all the ferns, trees and flower species, but the rare plant life was not Kurosawa's goal today.

He strolled to the dark maple bridge, braced on its four corners by stone lanterns lit with a strong fire. At the bridge's apex, he gazed down at the flowing water, made possible by a pump and filter system. In the current, large white Koi fish with black flanks swam only strong enough to stay fixed in their positions.

Strange how Kurosawa could relate. But he continued across the bridge to the rock garden island and the wooden bench on which he sat, Yabuki standing quietly to the side.

Frozen in the sand, the waves of a calm sea yielded to the ripples radiating from a stationary stone no larger than Kurosawa's fist. Once again, he related. Regardless of the consistent ebbs of one life, there would always be unavoidable disturbances. However, it was the stray contemplations that came with such thoughts that disturbed him. Other people may have avoided them with distractions, but Kurosawa welcomed them. He wanted to be disturbed by the consequences of his actions, past and future. It was how he grounded himself in reality through mental penitence.

Yabuki wondered why Kurosawa had come here to say nothing. There was a purpose to the visit, maybe even to show Yabuki something. But he felt the lesson would be unspoken, only taught through self-realization. Kurosawa would lead Yabuki here, but only Yabuki could learn the lesson on his own, in his own way, in a way that had meaning to him and him alone. Even that notion failed to help Yabuki. Continued analysis only impeded his mind from releasing its bonds and accepting the moral infused in nature.

In a clatter over the bridge, Naoko rushed, obviously not caring for the noise from her unskilled motions in wooden shoes. The secretary halted and bowed deeply.

"Kurosawa-san, greatest apologizes, but Kido-san wishes to see you. He says it is of the greatest importance."

Kurosawa watched as Naoko never raised her eyes to meet his, then turned his focus to the sand once more, allowing a minute to slip by. "Very well. Send him."

She bowed even deeper before clattering over the bridge again.

Calm moments of thought slipped by until Kurosawa turned to notice Kido waiting quietly. Kurosawa had no idea how long Kido must have stood there, but such skills were a prerequisite for the job.

Standing at five-ten, Kido Osamu's wide shoulders filled his tailored suit. His tan face remained still during his bow; however, his shoulder-length black hair swayed with the motion. During the movement, the ridge along the top right of his scalp became more apparent. Initially, most wrote it off as a part in Kido's hair, but closer examination would reveal the scarring from hastily applied stitches.

At first, Kido allowed society's values of appearance to affect his attitude toward himself. Years of self-loathing brought him to a brink at which an epiphany saved him from suicide: He was lucky to be alive, lucky that the bullet didn't slice his skull wide open instead of only deeply grazing it. Or was it skill rather than luck that saved him? At least his opponent at the time wasn't so lucky.

"Be quick."

"Hai, Kurosawa-san," Kido began immediately. "As expected, the agents called in additional forces; however, their actions appeared to be focused on destroying the scene, mostly by fire, such as burning the carcasses."

Kurosawa twisted his head briefly, bemusement sweeping over his face, but looked past Kido before returning his gaze to the sand garden. "Is that all?"

"Several people in the agents' cleanup crew appeared to be abnormally comfortable in handling the special weapons found." Kido breathed as he contemplated his assumption one more time. "They had handled such weapons more than once before."

Kurosawa trusted Kido's opinion. Otherwise, he wouldn't have directed Kido to stay behind at the hangar for as long as it took to monitor the results. As always, his reports and answers were direct and without all the frivolous details that the insecure spout in repetition, serving only to insult a listener's intelligence.

"Very well," Kurosawa commended. "See Ayumu. There's another situation that needs your attention."

"Hai." Kido bowed and departed.

Tranquility returned to the garden. Kurosawa's mind, however, was far from undisturbed. He wondered if he had misjudged these agents. Had he shown too much of his hand, too soon, to the wrong person? That thought didn't sit well.

Whose side were these agents on? The agents' seemingly persistent interest in his organization had Kurosawa drawing conclusions that the agents were hunting down these creatures posing as terrans. But now, the agents might be trying to hide the existence of these creatures.

"Twice now, I have been deceived," Kurosawa calmly stated. "My actions have done nothing more than to bring further dishonor."

"Your intentions are of the most honorable," Yabuki attempted to console.

"Don't patronize me, Yumiro-chan," Kurosawa barked. "You're better than that. My intentions fall considerably short of balancing the results of my actions. I must be wiser in my choices to restore honor."

Yabuki waited to ensure Kurosawa had finished. "My apologies, Kurosawa-sama. I meant to say that your intentions are correct; however, we have failed to provide you with sufficient information to choose the proper path to honor."

Kurosawa felt another chastisement surfacing until he realized the tone in Yabuki's voice. "What are you thinking?"

"If the agents are not exactly what we had hoped, there's always one more player."

Kurosawa forced himself to not immediately reject the idea. After a few moments of thought, he asked, "Do you trust him?"

The question froze Yabuki in a quick bout of second-guessing. He had only met him once, and that was a brief encounter. But he didn't want to leave his boss waiting for an answer. "I would have to say, yes. His words had truth." Another thought distracted Yabuki. "I believe he even tried to warn me about the royal guards."

Kurosawa's eyes remained locked on the sandy ripples. Even without the trust, the one thing certain was that they now had a mutual enemy.

"Find him."

Chapter 5

A few hundred thousand miles above the planet, a hexagonal crystal blinked into existence. Only slightly larger than two feet long, it floated motionless until finally realizing it had arrived.

Its gunmetal sheen began glinting with star light as it gradually started a slow and steady spin. During the motion, one of its pointed tips gravitated toward the planet below until locking into place, as perpendicular as an elongated item could be to a curved surface.

Something wasn't right. It didn't like where it was. A sensor failed to meet the requested parameter. To fix the issue, the crystalline object blasted away at miraculous speed from the plant. Even with no visible form of propulsion, the tiny drone could easily give the fastest space fighter a good chase. Instead, it only headed in a straight line at nothing.

Then it stopped.

Hours slipped by.

It only floated, slowly rotating.

Blinding light exploded under the crystal and flashed away just as quickly. Where the light once was, a large cube levitated calmly for a few seconds before an internal mechanism began unfolding the metallic box until it formed a very long plank. Another pause accentuated the phases of transition as it began to unfold again. This time, slivers, only minute fractions of the main plank's size, unfolded from the bottom to form an octagonal tube.

After another break, the wafer thin planks detached and seemingly drifted away without losing the octagonal shape. When they reached a diameter of several hundred feet, they halted. The transformation had taken place ahead of schedule, so there was nothing to do but wait.

Then an orange ring of light shot down the tube until it spat out a silver orb. Once again, under no visible propulsion, the orb veered away just as another orange ring produced a twin to the first orb that took a separate path.

About a mile away from the original formation of objects, the globes came to a standstill, then began transforming. Liquid movements turned the spheres into inverted bowl-shaped webs of metal crowned with a ball one-fourth its original size.

This time there were no pauses between steps. The equipment had finally aligned with the precision timing of arrivals.

Balls of light formed under the nets in preparation to safely catch the inbound spikes. As the light intensified, the jump tube went into a seizure of orange rings, ejecting drone fighters in nonstop rapid succession, with hundreds inbound.

As they arrived, the fighters equally split to defend their assigned catcher stations. Just as the number of drones reached a tad more than a hundred, the blinding light under the stations winked away to unveil a Grey Wolf battle cruiser under one, and a battle destroyer under the other.

At the helm of the cylindrical-like battle destroyer Chaos, Elder Åentøn Żev screwed the brow above his reptilian beak. The huge terese being then squinted his large eyes and fired orders.

"Weapons?"

"Forward battery ready. Others coming online. Net up in less than two."

"Screen?"

"Clear."

"Nearest hostile target?"

"About two point seven light-seconds direct, approaching at about point six miles a second on a current trajectory distance of eight light-seconds."

Almost perfect, and it should be safe enough. At least Åentøn hoped so. "Launch the Cappadocia."

From the lower forward launch tube shot a tiny grey Kanytelleis class scout that sprouted wings a blink before rocketing toward the planet below.

"The Cappadocia reports all systems blue and full control."

"Good," Åentøn breathed, a bit relieved. "Engage auxiliaries and patrol to the eighth sector and anchor. Launch Second Squadron, First on standby and Third on alert."

As a score of fighters shot from the Chaos' bays, the small spaceship gracefully pulled away from under the catcher station. As it did, another ball of light formed to receive the next inbound war ship.

A few miles away, the long, thin battle cruiser Sheshach prepared for combat. The entire battery of blaster turrets along the top of the cruiser unfolded their barrels, which then screwed into place. When completed individually, the turrets began sweeping around as the gunners function-checked the systems.

Under the Sheshach, the cruiser's two massive rail cannons, which stretched one from the stern and one from the bow to overlap in the center, steadily rotated from their stored positions to point toward their respective sides of the craft. During the trip, both of the double barrels extended to full length as blue light flickered from the barrels while the magnetic system came to life.

Sitting in the heart of the beast, Elder Nathaniel Deven son of Picaron monitored the progress on the large screens around the bridge. From what could be gleaned from the displays, it appeared they had arrived as predicated.

"Come about to twelfth sector at cruising speed."

The vertical plank of a craft began listing to the right as the bow lifted just before the auxiliary engines pushed it forward.

"Launch Siska Wing. I want defensive formations."

Nearly a hundred fighters began pouring from the cruiser to create packs of three that dotted an invisible oblong sphere about a mile away from the Sheshach's surface. A few lone fighters zipped about to check on the status of everyone's positioning.

"Has the Shingi arrived?"

"Aye, sir. They report some stress fractures in the crow aft, but otherwise, they are intact with no injuries."

Nathaniel had feared worse, so tension released from his shoulders. Spiking a dreadnought into the middle of a solar system, though within operating limits, always came with difficulties and risks, to include complete destruction of the massive craft.

No catcher station could handle an inbound dreadnought. The only option was to spike the craft several million miles off the system's orbital plane. But being so close to the star had made Nathaniel nervous. If the gravitational forces tore the Shingi apart, he would be in charge, and he knew they had no chance without at least a dreadnought on their side. Even then, victory would still probably be a matter of luck.

"What's their arrival?"

"About twenty-seven hours."

"Fair enough," Nathaniel mused. "Notify Chaos that we have Den Control until the Shingi arrives."

"Done, sir. Also, the Chaos reports the successful debarkation of the Cappadocia."

Nathaniel was about to acknowledge the statement when another crew member spoke.

"Sir, Hell's Comet has arrived at Catcher Station Bravo and is requesting orders."

"Good." Nathaniel scanned the schematics of craft locations for the ideal location for the combat frigate. "Have them anchor and start construction in sector ten, and tell them we need that jump point operational in twenty hours."

"Aye."

The Grey Wolf elder forced himself to sit back in his seat. Rest, even of the slightest variety, would be a rare commodity in the coming days. He should seize it when he could. Just as that thought surfaced, it left.

A large holographic screen with an image of the first catcher station flashed. He didn't need the crew member on the operations floor to tell him that the combat destroyer Trafalgar had arrived. Nathaniel had a battlefield to prepare.

Chapter 6

He felt as if he were on trial. In some sense, he was, but Lord Jordan son of Haddox found it irritatingly ironic. Normally, as the senior judicial magistrate of the Dragon Corps, *he* oversaw trials. At least his were organized and planned, unlike this spontaneous lynching, which spawned from an innocent-enough meeting with racial delegates.

Such drastic shifts, however, happened far too often in the political worlds that so irritated Haddox. So long ago, he had decided to become a lawyer to fight political corruption with the black and white word of the law. It didn't take long before the letter of the law became a blurred mix of grey. The more he studied, the more grey it became. Finally the black and white at the extreme ends of good and evil disappeared, succumbing to nothing more than a darker or brighter shade of grey. Regardless of how good something appeared on the surface, the law always allowed for it to be viewed as evil, and vise versa.

Even joining the Dragon Corps failed to ease Haddox's torment. Operating under stricter laws had not saved even the Dragon Corps from opinionated interpretation of the rules. Though all the governments had agreed on the Corps' charter, here they were now, bickering about it and questioning Haddox's decisions on using the Corps authority.

"What gives you the right to weaken the enforcement in our Quabent Parsec?" demanded Efton Wu Nolpic, the chancellor of the marselian race, as all four of his blue fists flew about wildly in frustration. "The smugglers and raiders are barely being held in check as it is. They'll abuse the lack of immediate Corps presence." He sighed then huffed, "This is just unacceptable."

Haddox adjusted his stance a bit but tried not to appear to shift his weight as he stood. In front of him, dignitaries from almost every walk of life crowded into the room and waited for a response. His reply hadn't changed much regardless of how each politician attempted to ask the question in a new way. The game frustrated him, but Haddox internally fought to keep his emotions out of it.

"I apologize if I sound repetitious." The Dragon Corps lord attempted a slight smile without appearing to be condescending. "But our charter, as agreed to by all races we protect, gives us the authority to readjust our assets to best meet needs—"

"Yes, yes, yes," injected Chief President Burtune Kerald from the trilligs, "you said that numerous times, but what could possibly be more important? What exaggerated misunderstanding could possibility be so poorly interpreted to falsely justify ignoring so many criminal-infested districts?"

Haddox, while momentarily wondering if the calico fur ball had just blurted a subtle triple negative, responded calmly. “I’m afraid I cannot share that information.”

“Exactly why is that?” belted Kaiser Telyen Hamshirton.

Haddox uncontrollably squinted briefly at the rolbrid leader. At first, Haddox thought the kaiser only injected to throw anyone off the trail, but Hamshirton had fired the charge with such force that Haddox began to wonder if the kaiser truly didn’t know.

Haddox gathered his composure in a breath. “A governmental body has requested our assistance and asked for complete secrecy. We are going to honor that; it’s the same right that we would give to any one of you.”

“But does it truly deserve such force as to undermine the security of so many parsecs elsewhere?” challenged Prime Minister Si’Con-Bernardic of the su-vol.

“We have evaluated the request in great detail and believe that such a realignment of forces is needed, at least for now,” Haddox answered.

“ We only have your word on that, Lord Haddox,” Prime Minister Bernardic spat back, his hood of blue feathers glimmering in waves as tension shot down his neck. “The agreement is for the Dragon Corps to equally serve all, not bend to one government’s whim just because they have sold you on a good story. You’re allowed to work outside of our government’s control so such things don’t happen, but they have. And this is deplorable.”

Murmurs launched several simmering discussions. The subjects might have all been directed at Haddox, but it was the tone that threatened him the most. To justify his position, he may have to add more fuel to their distrust.

“We need the extra forces,” Haddox began forcibly to gather the leaders’ attentions, “because this critical mission has forced us to contact the p’tahians.”

An uproar of furious exclamations exploded into a cacophony that could almost be felt, much like a bass beat rumbling from a speaker. After the wave hit, some still attempted to yell over each other while some bickered in agreement and only a few remained calm. Haddox couldn’t make sense out of any of it. Only a few words made it through the din of yelling, and those words had no love for the Corps at the moment.

When the yellers collectively paused for a breath, the terese leader, Supreme Goddess Łønnæ Ꞙrệdrïcķ, thumped the flat end of her blocky, green fist on the table and calmly inserted, “You have doomed us all.”

Varying degrees of agreements erupted, but Chief Czar Warnon, from the piolants, made it through the noise as the loudest. “What gives you the right to take such drastic measures?”

Haddox wondered if the tone he detected in the piolant leader’s voice was guilt or a note of bitter responsibility. The lord tried to respond, but the chief czar hadn’t finished.

“Nothing can justify taking such actions that risk us all,” Warnon rattled, his dual-pupilled, lime-green eyes full of worry on how to damn such actions without pointing the finger at himself. "This is unwarranted, uncalled for and intolerable."

Prime King Grégoire Dakota son of Gavin briefly stood, scepter in hand pointing at Warnon then to Haddox. "I have to agree with the czar: Under what authority do you think you have to threaten us all with such a brash action?"

"The BU-nerry Protocol," Haddox stated.

"The what?" exclaimed High Commissioner Kornee san-Citor of the doludgians.

"Yes, commissioner, the protocol is named after the expedition your people led to try to save the ber from p'tahian extinction." Haddox tried to keep his voice respectful for all those who died in that effort. "The BU-nerry Protocol dictates when and how the Dragon Corps may make contact with the p'tahians if ever warranted as critical in accomplishing our mission. It has been part of the Corps charter since its creation."

"Yes, but how could hun—" Chief Czar Warnon froze after almost giving away too many of his secrets. He then scrambled to recover. "How could any task asked of you require such an action?"

"You will have to trust us." Haddox's answer ignited another commotion, and he realized he needed to calm the mob and put the czar at ease. "However, the government requesting our assistance, which required the current realignment of forces, did not know and did not request us to activate the BU-nerry Protocol. Other factors are at play."

"Tell us all for sake of our very existence," clacked the jexan dictator Premier Emperor Ge Nvum as his antennae flicked about in agitation. "Speak to justify."

Haddox wanted to kick himself for allowing this to get as far as it had. Now he was forced to dance around topic after topic. "Ladies and gentlemen, please understand I am bound by my duty, and I cannot share that information."

Rebellious grunts of disdain rumbled around the room. Haddox felt a coup brewing and mentally struggled with ethics to decide how much to say. Then relief came.

Dextian Queen Kyria Adian rose, gradually quieting the room, and she waited for the silence. "Do these secrets involve my daughter's death?"

Haddox sighed as he closed his eyes. He was afraid that the reason Queen Adian came to this meeting instead of the royal queen herself was to challenge him with such a statement. He lifted his head to look at her mournful, green eyes. "Yes."

"Then," Queen Adian firmly stated, "for my daughter's sake and for our family, why?"

Pain for the queen's loss hit Haddox harder than he had expected, weakening the last remnants of will. "We have been secretly watching an entire race living within p'tahian territory for some time. They are mildly civilized but woefully underdeveloped. We have a classified charter that charges the Dragon Corps to protect these people. Since they are in p'tahian territory, it has been an extremely delicate matter. When this other government had asked us to hunt down...," he searched for the words safe enough to use, "a dangerous fugitive, that search crossed paths with protecting these people, and now, it appears to have drawn the attention of the p'tahians."

"Once again," Prime King Gavin shouted, "these people cannot be so important as to risk us all."

Haddox started to get infuriated. Sure, the atlantian king had no idea that this revolved around the Myth of Terra, but that didn't excuse his short-sighted rudeness.

"Your highness," Haddox blurted with enough force to be curt, "we cannot turn our backs on these people. Have we not learned anything from history? We turned our backs on the ber. Sure, we tried, but when it got hard, we ran. Whether right or wrong is moot. But undeniably, the ber are worse for it. They have been wiped from the universe."

Haddox had everyone's attention quietly wrapped in regretful pity. "You created the Dragon Corps to defend what is right, regardless of territory or government and to protect those who cannot protect themselves. Every member in the Corps takes that charge seriously, and we're not going to back down."

Stillness swallowed the room for the first time since the start of this meeting. Haddox wished he hadn't been so assertive and wondered what the leaders might be contemplating. Maybe they would call for his resignation or just arrange a political coup to reorganize leadership and control of the Corps. The only thing that brought Haddox peace was that he spoke his mind.

The vemulli's Exalted Sovereign Hec Yun iDur slipped into the silence with calm wisdom. "We should prepare ourselves."

In a wave, the other leaders began nodding.

"Correct me if I'm mistaken," Queen Adian spoke up from her now seated position, "but the Corps is in need of as many forces as possible?"

Haddox nodded before answering, "Yes. But we are doing our best to leave enough forces behind to meet our other obligations."

As the queen shook her head, the tips of her ears poked through the short white hair that caressed her head like two cupped hands. "That's not quite what I meant, but I understand your concern. The Dragon Corps has always helped the Dext Royal Family in times of need. Maybe it is that unwavering dedication that drew the attention of my daughters. Regardless of my decision, Ky followed her heart. To honor that, I relinquish the Dragon Corps fleet in our Beiyon Parsec from its obligations and duties to the Dext Royal Family. May they aid you in the absence of my daughter."

"Your highness," Haddox half gasped, "I appreciated the gesture, but such a move is too risky. The pirates in that sector are among the most violent. It—"

"I insist." The queen's face froze; she would hear nothing of it.

"We will take care of our own the best we can. My daughter trusted in the Corps, and so shall we. We will sacrifice our request for forces in hopes that you may put them to better use. And for the sake of us all, I wish you luck."

Nearly an hour later, the meeting concluded with rounds of formal farewells before each leader blinked away into a pile of quickly dissolving pixels. As relieved as one in Haddox's shoes could be, the meeting had at least ended with a mutual understanding between all parties. Now, he had his own part to fulfill.

"Jerry." Haddox had no need to lift his face toward the raised cab in the Cube.

"Yes, my lord," Earl Harrington's voice returned.

"Put the entire Corps on full alert, Batcon One. Call the others and tell them I want the Cube manned for full operations to monitor Terra Four activities, and they had better be here in fifteen minutes. And on the way, tell Dars to order the Nebuchadrezzar's battle fleet to pull out of Beiyon and expedite directly to Terra Four. They may resupply if they can, but it had better not slow them down."

The command and control director went straight to work without reply. The desks and chairs lowered into floor and rose in a different formation, as the screens came to life and a hologram of Terra Four engulfed Haddox were he stood.

"And get me a stiff drink," Haddox demanded. "Real this time, I don't want any of that synthetic shit."

"Yes, my lord."

Chapter 7

Three mounds of black cloaks marked the points of a triangle on the floor of the suite's common room. Marking the center of the invisible image was a leather chest stripped in rusted iron bands. Chants in a near-dead language came from the larger mountain of ebony fabric and harmonized with the air, which willingly hummed in response.

Hours of meditation neared a culmination, as it had for thousands of years. No one knew exactly who had discovered the traditions or why she had the need to seek them. She may have stumbled upon them. Perhaps she was simply born with a sight like no other and used that ability to teach others. Yet while the custom remained true, few were trusted with the rituals.

The chant ended with a soft fading tone as the largest figure lifted her hooded head and extended her arms to place one hand on each side of the hide and metal chest. Still speaking the archaic language, Sophia Tenjin spoke calmly toward the object. After her final word, the chest's square latch clicked. Sophia opened the lid to reveal an internal coating of plush, purple velvet caressing a small pyramid made from tiny silver bricks.

She scooped the object in both hands as if holding the most delicate egg and rose effortlessly. After a few steps back, she faced the opposite direction from the chest on the floor and walked forward, around a wrought-iron lectern and toward a shoulder high, cylindrical pillar of bronze. Grooved flutes ran its entire length, up to the scroll-shaped capital. A sheet of plush black cloth crowned the top, and it was upon this that Sophia gently set the silver pyramid.

She offered a few more words of gratitude in the old language before stepping back again and turning to face the lectern. From a ring at the crest of the lectern's slanted top to a groove at the three-footed base stood the oaken staff topped with a reddish gold apple made of knotted strands of lemon yellow metal. It glowed happily as Sophia quietly acknowledged it with a nod.

She reached into her cloak to detach a short chain of golden loops and pulled it from under the layers of cloth. At the other end of the chain dangled an emerald slab. Sophia placed the tablet on the lectern and ran her left hand down its face, her fingers fondling the etched letters, before placing both hands on the object.

Chants resumed. The spoken words sang with a melody that resonated with the essence of life throughout the universe. The green crystal slab initiated a vibrating reply that buzzed under Sophia's fingertips. The slab's pulsation peaked at barely being audible when the object's inscription flashed with a golden light, and the room filled with the sound of a click, much like the sound of a glass rod being snapped in half. The chanting stopped.

Sophia fingered the left edge of the tablet and lifted the top layer to open the slab like a book. She continued, one page at a time, gently separating them and delicately placing them on the right side. About a quarter through the emerald book, Sophia stopped to place her two fingers in the upper right corner of the right page. As her fingers glided right to left, the invisible letters shimmered a white gold, fading as Sophia spoke the words.

Across the room, Sophia's keepers remained still, hunched in their unnatural appearances. They listened intently as each word spoke to them differently. Each term had a hundred possible interpretations, each expression a thousand, and each phrase a million. Regardless of how many times spoken, every sentence was heard anew, unveiling another of life's secrets.

Sophia stopped and lifted her eyes to the far wall. Her sight trailed down the wall toward the room's main door and stopped for a moment. She stood back from being bent over the reading as she scooped up the right side, closed the book and centered it on the lectern.

At her glance, the keepers leaned forward to close the lid on the chest, lifted the object and carried it out of the room in tandem with one another.

When they departed, Sophia stared at the door a bit longer before mentally signaling for the door to open, catching a shocked but smiling Count Jeffs Dorin a bit off guard, just moments away from finally pushing the door's call button.

"Oh, hello, Samurai Tenjin," spoke the white bearded orange trillig. "I hope I'm not interrupting anything."

He was, but the count's statement did not require a reply. So Sophia just stood and watched Dorin until he grew mildly uncomfortable, but he hid it well.

"Do you mind if I come in?"

"No." Sophia's reply held neither tension nor comfort.

Dorin dipped unnecessarily as he entered, taking his time glancing about the room, attempting to stealthily take note of all he could see. However, Sophia did not need to be astute to spot Dorin's covert inspection; she had detected his intentions while he walked down the hall outside the room.

"I hope all the accommodations are to your liking."

"They are more than I need." Sophia doubted the count's concern and disliked his misplaced credit, as if he would dirty his hands with such degrading chores.

"Is there anything we can do for you?"

Sophia lifted the hood off her head with two hands. Her black hair glistened to a grey-white in places. "The living air is all I need."

During her answer, Sophia noticed Dorin's grey blue eyes scanning her cloak, neck and everything in the room, including the artifacts. Though it took only a few seconds, when he returned to face Sophia he realized how noticeable his actions might have been.

"I couldn't help but notice that you do not carry with you the traditional dress or markings of a samurai in House Bravo."

"My rank is a title only." Sophia's pale lips parted only enough to speak the words. "It allows me to further my studies."

"Well, even as a member of House Bravo, you might be interested in knowing the initial fleet has arrived and House Bravo has sent its messenger."

"I am aware of the House's actions."

Dorin's smile relaxed slightly as he probed Sophia's ink-black eyes; he could not find even a fragment of emotion. He refused to allow this to disturb him as he resumed a full smile.

"What studies concern you, if I may ask?"

Sophia watched Dorin move across the room, perhaps to get a better look at the objects on the lectern and column. "I seek truth."

"Truth in what?"

"I seek all truths."

"Yes, but is there a specific subject?"

"All subjects." Sophia accepted the questioning, and Dorin continued to smile. "I seek truth in all forms of life."

"As in the meaning of life?"

"That is a broad category, but yes, among other things."

Dorin clasped his hands behind his back. "Some may say there is no understanding to the meaning of life, at least not without faith."

"Truth never requires faith or belief." Sophia's head turned away briefly as her eyes blinked slowly, then she resumed speaking as if nothing had happened. "All truth is tangible, nothing more than a lost animal. Just because it cannot or chooses not to find you does not mean it is not there. It is the path that is obscure."

"Then why hasn't someone by now found this path and shared it with others?" Something in how Dorin enunciated the words lifted Sophia's left brow.

"Many have, but the path to each truth is different for each person. The paths I find will only lead someone else to falsehood."

Even with the perpetual smile, Dorin's eyes gave away that Sophia's words disappointed him. "Then how do you know you've found truth and not a falsehood?"

"The truth speaks to you like nothing else. Once you've experienced it, the call is unmistakable."

"You are on a path now and bringing people with you?"

"My current journey does not involve seeking truth."

"So why agree to the Dragon Corps' call?"

Sophia narrowed her eyes momentarily. "I am not without a sense of duty."

Dorin cocked his head sideways in thought then straightened. "It is just that many agencies and governments have requested the presence of the Sangraal numerous times, often to honor the Sangraal, but only rarely has the Sangraal ever appeared. It is almost as if the Sangraal wishes to be a fabled legend. So why choose now?"

"The time has arrived." Sophia's tone held no bitterness to Dorin's increasingly condescending tone.

"Which time has arrived, if I may ask?"

"There was a point in history that will come to pass." Sophia blinked slowly. "I wish to be there. At times the end of one thing is just as important as the birth of everything."

"Is it destruction you seek then, not truth?"

"I seek neither."

"Is that why you speak of future history and an end? Do you already know the future?"

"The future may not be known, only understood."

"You claim then to predict the future?"

"No. The future may not be predicted, only understood."

"Yes," Dorin dipped his head for a second, "you've said that. Maybe I'm not comprehending your meaning of understanding the future."

"With each choice, Fate dictates the consequences, each leading to its respective set of choices. Such is the cycle of Fate. These choices and consequences are written into future's infinite boundaries. One may understand the future, but at any moment the present choice may recast the future."

Dorin's hand moved to his face and stroked his orange-striped beard in one methodical movement. "What is it that you understand about the future that brings you here?"

"That is not for you to know."

Dorin peered at Sophia's inanimate face. "It would be beneficial to everyone involved to know if there is something they should avoid or a weaknesses that could lead to death."

"Pray to Avalon that it does not come to be."

"Excuse me?"

Sophia calmly repeated herself.

"So the revered Sangraal would keep secrets that could save lives? That doesn't sound very noble."

"Such information only hinders. It would not help."

Sophia's placid emotions to even his underlying accusations irked Dorin more than he liked, but the average person would not detect it, hidden behind his smile.

"Pardon my forthrightness," Sophia requested, "but what is it that you want?"

If Dorin's smile could get wider, it did. "That's quite all right. Maybe I should be as direct. I'm an aficionado of atlantian history and culture; therefore, all aspects of atlantian history pique my interests. But there is nothing more intriguing than the elusive Sangraal.

"It is not often that someone of my learning has the opportunity to meet the almost mythic Sangraal. Some tales refer to you as the fount of knowledge, unmatched by any other sage, but this is hard to confirm as you seem rather taciturn with the knowledge. Maybe evasive is a better word.

"Even these items from atlantian antiquity," Dorin said as he pointed a paw at the lectern and column, "I can only guess, but I believe I remember references to these. Still, those histories are elusive, and even when found, they are vague.

"I guess what I'm trying to say is that it can be difficult for one of my race to truly understand atlantian history, especially culture, because of natural apprehension. However, it is undeniably my passion. Ergo, I seek knowledge."

Sophia lightly shook her head negatively. This left Dorin flabbergasted.

"I know you more than you know yourself."

Dorin screwed his furry face. "How so?"

"Your desire is not knowledge but manipulation and control. You egotistically quest for advantage, inconsiderate to those even closest to you."

Dorin dropped the smile. Frustration flared in his eyes. "Miss Tenjin, such statements are unwarranted, deceitful and border on treasonous."

Concern, of any variety, failed to shade Sophia's face, but pity glinted in her ebony eyes. "Does your soul truly torment you so?"

"Do you only wish to infuriate me?" Dorin bellowed. "Is the almighty Sangraal nothing more than a manipulative spoiled brat who treacherously enjoys angering those she declares are beneath her?"

"Anger does not destroy. Ignorance does."

Tension gripped Dorin's face into a hard frown. She had just called him an idiot; he was sure of it. He had come here in hopes of sharing knowledge and learning from the legendary Sangraal, only to be dejected with abject humiliation.

"Ridicule is an inferior replacement for dialogue." Dorin spun on his heels and marched out the automatically opening door.

Sophia watched the count depart. When the door closed, her eyes followed across the wall until reaching the corner. Emotionless, she slipped the hood back over her head.

Chapter 8

In the hush that followed the opening and closing of the large metal door, Lyon lumbered down the stairs, each footfall thumping hard on the wooden steps. He felt drained. The day hadn't offered any challenges or a strenuous workload, yet it served as a vampiric poison to his energy and mood.

As he pounded his way down, Lyon noticed Larin slumped over the left side of the workbench on the left wall. The rolbrid's odd angle made Lyon wonder if Larin had fallen asleep at work, but that thought disappeared when the short man twitched.

On the lighted table to the right, a rebellious, snot-nosed teenager clad in leather and chrome, sporting chin, lip, nose and eyebrow piercings and topped with a short, neon-green mohawk sat studiously in a tiny one-piece chair and desk. A few feet away, a holographic wall held a miniature black chalkboard, which unnaturally displayed video images from an unknown source. Lyon noted captions writing themselves in chalk below the picture, erasing and starting again.

The thought that his computer companion had willingly decided to watch television without the sound seemed strange, even for Mac. Larin must have yelled at Mac. It fit with Lyon's thoughts, which meant Mac might be in one of his strange moods. Lyon didn't wish to deal with it, so when he reached the basement floor, he grabbed a chair, spun it around and faced Larin instead.

"Hey, Larin, what are you up to?" Lyon jerked at hearing the unintentional indifference in his voice but lacked the energy to correct it.

Silent minutes slipped by, but Lyon didn't mind. At least Mac hadn't acknowledged him either, so it gave him moments to rest his mind, which failed to relax. Instead it tormented him with the same thoughts it had worked over for the past couple of days.

"Working," Larin finally responded, giving Lyon relief from his thoughts.

"Working on what?"

"A pistol."

Lyon pushed himself out of the chair toward Larin. "What are you doing to my pistol?"

"Trying to improve it."

Lyon made it to Larin's side and finally noticed the cable running from the back of the rolbrid's neck. The other end of the cord was stitched into a makeshift circuit board that sprouted another line that wired itself into a tiny, open panel on the side of the sidearm. "That pistol's fine as is."

"Sure, but I'm trying to make it better." Larin's voice halted for a moment to let him focus on another delicate part of the task. "Remember that modification I made to my particle cannon, the one that allowed me to detonate the allaric slats early? Well, I'm trying to do the same to this pistol, but it's proving more difficult. I'll most likely have to create an external range finder, but the internal coding is extremely complex. These weapons are very set in their charging routines. The subroutine is not the issue, it's creating and incorporating the right set of variables to pass to and from the subroutine without causing the rest of the program to crash."

"You had better not ruin my weapon," Lyon stated forcefully without yelling.

"Relax." Larin never moved from his position; his zoned face never showed expression. "As I said, it's a subroutine. You'll be able to turn it off or on as you see fit. I've finished all the other particle cannons; they're working fine. So I thought I would try this pistol."

Lyon twisted his face. "What do you mean you finished all the other particle cannons?"

"I modified the allaric launchers to do the same as mine."

"I didn't say you could do that."

"You didn't have to. I'm the Harquebus here, so the weapons are my concern. If you've got a problem with that, fire me. I'd love to get kicked off this frapping rock."

Larin's comment sent Lyon back to his previously undesired line of thought. So he ignored the rolbrid's defiance and strolled over to slouch in his chair.

"Besides, what do you expect me to do?" Frustration dully infested the rolbrid's vibrating voice. "I'm bored."

Lyon mistook the tone for apathy. He expected nothing less.

"This whole hullabaloo should be over." Larin's agitation grew stronger in a bid to be recognized properly. "That traitorous bastard is dead. Mission accomplished. So why aren't we on a shuttle home?"

"What of the terrans?"

"What about them?"

"There should be some sense of duty to protect them after what we did." Lyon kept his eyes closed as he slouched. "If that truly was a p'tahian ship we destroyed, then we've got their attention. We've doomed these people."

"Why should I care? The Corps doesn't care. Of all the blessed crap, they don't even care about us. It's been days since we reported Horwhannor's death, but what do they say?"

Lyon knew. It privately disturbed him. He didn't need Larin to rub it in.

"Good job." Sarcasm and cynicism twisted Larin's words. "Report received. From this point forward, stay off all channels until you receive your next set of orders."

Larin rolled his chair around to slump over the other side of the table. "What does that mean to you?"

Lyon didn't want to discuss his interpretation. He felt it best to keep his mouth shut at the moment or risk sounding like a traitor himself.

"I'll tell you what it means: a frapping write off. That's right. We're expendable."

"Knock it off!" Lyon barked. "I'm sick of hearing about your conspiracy theories. From now on, keep them to yourself."

Lyon slowly closed his eyes again as he ignored Larin's bickering mumbles.

Larin had a way about him that irritated Lyon so quickly, as if the rolbrid knew exactly what buttons to push. If it wasn't for the rolbrid quickly proving himself invaluable in a firefight, Lyon might have executed him by now. Strange how he had grown fond of the bitter little man.

The situation could be better, sure, but Lyon sat, helpless to do anything about it. His thoughts trailed toward Ky's death, and he spent the next several minutes wrestling with them. He refused to be dragged into another pit of despair without a fight. The effort floundered every time he glanced at the door to the right, behind which rested Ky's body in a cryogenic coffin.

In the end, Lyon won, but in doing so, he made a sacrifice. The only thought more overwhelming was a Larin-like level of pessimism at the team's current prospects. Moments stretched on as Lyon wallowed in the dark thoughts of how this might be his last day. It took depression to a new level for Lyon. That feat tripped a mental circuit breaker so that his next thought—*This is a load of shit*—sent his mind off in an extreme, unnatural tangent.

His mind happily tossed the idea around and played with it. The contemplation so occupied Lyon's mind that he ignored the mild grunts coming from somewhere behind him. Instead, he marveled at why this thought never came to him before.

Absent-mindedly, Lyon slipped, "Ever think about the first things you touch after wiping your butt?"

Larin faintly shook his head but harshly dismissed him with a forceful downward wave of his left arm. Not only did the question sound stupid, he still harbored bitterness from the previous chastisement.

"I'm serious." Lyon pushed himself up from his slouched position. "One of them is the soap or the soap dispenser. The cleanest thing, or what you would think to be the cleanest object, is actually the dirtiest. Think about it. The only time someone touches the soap is when their hands are dirty. Soap is some foul stuff."

Larin powerfully snatched a handful of wires and yanked them from both the weapon and the back of his neck then began sounding off as he spun in his chair. "Look, I don't have to frapping listen—"

The rolbrid's brow tensely dropped low as anger blazed in his eyes. "If I could choke you, I would!"

Lyon reeled. "Me?"

Larin flashed a confounded look at Lyon. "No." Then he jabbed a stubby digit at the hologram table. "Him."

Lyon leaned to peer around the back of his chair to finally notice the spectacle Mac was making of himself. Wedged in and weighted down by the scholastic desk and chair combo, Mac's punk persona futility attempted to leap from his seat while frantically waving his right arm around, propped by the left hand. The antics came delivered complete with accompanying "Oooh! Oooh!" surges mixed with various unintelligible grunts.

"For the love of reason," Lyon pleaded, "what is your problem?"

"You've so gotta check this out, dude." Mac whipped a leather-and-stud wrapped hand around to point at the video screen in the chalkboard.

Lyon turned his seat around as he squinted at the tiny picture. Instead of even bothering to strain his sight to read the captions, he ordered, "Audio."

"...from about thirty miles from there, when he caught this amazing footage."

The image disappeared before Lyon could make sense of it. In its place appeared a slightly elderly gentlemen with dyed hair and a grey suit with just enough pin stripes to make the stuffy uniform appear somewhat casual. "That's why we turn now to our senior space analyst, Doctor Heinrich Freeman. Doctor, these images have captured the world's attention. What are we seeing here?"

The picture switched to an image of an even more elderly gentleman with a full head of white hair and round glasses. His name appeared momentarily for those who had forgotten it already.

"I have just recently talked to my colleagues in the government's space administration, and they confirm my initial theories that these flashes of light, amazing as they may appear, are nothing more than the light of a pulsar finally reaching our planet."

For what was likely the hundredth time, the video played. In a cloudless night sky, a flash, brighter than any of the stars, appeared. Another appeared after a few seconds.

Lyon flew from his chair and grabbed the holographic screen, pulling it closer and stretching it larger. The degree of energy drew Larin to hop off his stool to get a better look.

"Some of our viewers are writing in, asking if these are pulsars, then why didn't anyone detect and report the light of a super nova? And some are claiming these lights are extraterrestrial in origin."

The older gentlemen snickered at the anchor's comments.

"Doctor, could you explain to the other viewers what a super nova is and how it might be connected to a pulsar?"

"Sure." He stifled his laughter as the camera zoomed in. "Pulsars have been mistaken to have intelligent origins since they were first discovered. They begin as stars that collapse in an explosion called a super nova. This creates—"

"Kill the audio," Lyon directed.

Larin beat him to the punch. "Those are spike and jump flashes."

"Damn right they are." Lyon poked his head around the enlarged screen. "Mac, scan all the other stations. Give me anything you can find."

Soon, the entire hologram became spotted with eight feeds from news stations. Mac added a new one about every ten seconds and then unnecessarily remarked, "This is starting to break around the world."

Lyon ignored the computer and fingered the images, enlarging those with the most interesting images.

"Look at that," Larin exclaimed, indicating a moving point of light. "That thing's huge. Is that a dreadnought?"

"Maybe. I just hope it's ours." Lyon switched to a new image as Mac added it to the mix. "Mac, can you get us some direct images?"

"I'm trying, but traffic on all the satellites is nearing maximum capability. It's tough fighting through it, and with so much activity, there's little chance of going undetected even if I do make it through."

"It's a bit frapping late to worry about being covert," Larin accurately summed the situation.

"Very," the words came slowly as Lyon thought, "very good point." Lyon stepped back to take another assessment. "Mac, put out a low-powered, audio wide-broadcast on Corps channels for a 'Terra Den Control' and see what happens."

"On it."

Another image slipped onto the now crowded screen. A different feed started showing images of riots.

Lyon pointed at it. "This isn't good."

"Figures," was all Larin muttered.

"This is Den Control," blasted into the room as Mac struggled with turning the sound down. "Who is this?"

Pleased shock jerked Lyon's head back. "This is Knight Lyon Vulgrin Wolfen son of Kendrick on assignment on Terra Four. Are you our evac? It seems a bit excessive."

"Stand by."

Lyon and Larin shared bewildered glances, losing a bit of their focus on the multitude of images in front of them.

"Knight Kendrick?" asked a new voice.

"Yes."

"This is Duke Mular Chichiq onboard the dreadnought Shingi, I have jurisdiction."

Lyon noted the distinctly huyin accent that colored the unusually well spoken voice. The concern on his face came from the fact that a Corps dreadnought was actually in orbit. "Pardon my words, but isn't this a bit overkill for an extraction? It's seriously upsetting the balance down here."

"I have no such orders, and societal woes concern me not."

Lyon caught the faint whistles of Larin's aggravation reaching its boiling point, so he silenced the rolbrid with an extended hand.

"Then may I ask, why are you here?"

"It cannot be discussed on this channel. Stay off all channels until your emissary arrives."

"Once again, excuse me, Duke Chichiq, but—"

"The channel's dead," Mac interjected.

"What the frapping hell does he mean he doesn't have orders to evacuate us?" Larin stomped around in a tiny circle to help release his frustration. "I'm not some frapping local to be discarded on some back-ass rock. What did they come here for, war?"

Lyon knew Larin meant the question sarcastically, but the knight had already considered it. "Maybe that's exactly what they've come here for."

Larin froze and stared at a stolid Lyon.

"Holy shit, guys," bellowed a running Oz, who blasted into the room from the under-street tunnel. When he stopped, he grabbed his waist, bent over and tried to point upwards with the other hand, gasping. "Have you seen outside?"

"Yeah." Lyon jerked a hand at the displays. "Just finished talking with a Duke Chichiq. Apparently the Corps has vessels in orbit, and it's making the news, even causing riots."

"No," Oz huffed, "I mean, right outside. Something's landing."

A bemused expression streaked across Lyon's face. "Mac, give me the outside cameras."

The news broadcasts disappeared in a flash, replaced by the street outside disturbed only by a tiny, black scout vessel finishing its landing sequence.

Lyon bolted up the stairs with Larin close behind. Oz lazily rocked his head about, wishing he was in better shape, before trotting after the duo.

The front door almost came off its hinges as Lyon rushed into the street. Larin, weapon unholstered, stood back, taking note that Paloon had already positioned himself on the other side of the street, also armed.

With a pop, the vessel's dark canopy opened and hissed as it retracted. Everyone watched intently. When the canopy cleared, staring back at everyone was Ky's face.

"Mind if I borrow your garage," she smirked. "This thing's a bit conspicuous sitting in the middle of the street, don't you think?"

Chapter 9

A single, low wattage light embedded in the wall dimly lit the tiny bunk room aboard the combat cruiser Chimera. With her feet propped on a footlocker, a dark-skinned atlantian sat in a flimsy chair and hunched over her knees. Light purple dreadlocks covered her face as she fidgeted with her toes.

Baggy grey sweats hung around her legs, and a tight white shirt with sleeves so small as to be nearly nonexistent dipped low enough in the back to reveal an upright pentagram at the base of her neck. Additional tattoos marked both arms: a winged goddess on one and a snarling wolf's head on the other.

The military style quarters remained strangely quiet for the activity under way in the vessel. She could faintly hear the humming of electricity and bubbling of some unknown liquid in the bulkheads. But Lone Wakanda Kamaria daughter of Kameko liked it that way. Without at least a mild constant noise, she'd never be able to wind down after a long, strenuous shift.

The tiny metal door flew open in a clatter.

"Hey, Wakanda!"

"Damn, man," she exclaimed, dropping her dagger.

A muffled "huh" seeped from the pile of blankets on the top bunk.

"Go back to sleep," Wakanda tried to comfort, "it's just Lyloda being his same old rude self."

The pile of blankets complied as Wakanda lifted the dagger off the floor and pointed it at the over seven-foot tall marselian dipping deeply and turning sideways to fit through the door. His sleeveless, black and red vest laid bare four muscled, blue arms, one marked in black with the same, though larger, snarling wolf's head as the one on Wakanda's arm.

Waiting for her mech partner to fully enter the room would not be her style. "Hey, while you're here, check this out." She stretched her right foot forward. Etched into the purple-coated nails of her first three toes were replica images of the dagger she had used to carve them.

"Sweet, huh?"

"Cool," Lyloda replied.

The response lacked the emotion she wanted. "Why do I even bother with you?"

"Because you like me."

"Doubt it." She dropped her feet as her small, brown eyes looked up.

The bunk room already felt small. Every time Lyloda Minsa, of the lycan rank, visited, his immense size reduced the room's mildly uncomfortable confines to near stifling levels.

"Is that why you're here?" She pointed the blade at the scroll of papers Lyloda had been mindlessly thumbing in his bottom set of hands.

"Yes." Delight drew Lyloda's smile wide as his eyes squinted into vertical lines of deep black. "Take a wild guess what the stratosphere for the planet below us if full of."

She shrugged her shoulders annoyingly. "I don't know, poison?"

"Close. Ozone."

"Big deal."

"No, not that synthetic crap. This is true, naturally occurring ozone, completely pure."

She half turned her head and glared at Lyloda. "The nine hells you say."

"I'm not kidding." The massive beast knelt down and began unrolling the papers along the top of the footlocker. "These are some of the biometric readings."

"How in the hells did you get these?"

"Tala."

"Tala? Tala just gave these to you?"

"She knew I'd be interested."

"But she just *gave* these to you?" Wakanda leered at her partner. "What did you have to do?"

Lyloda dipped his head a bit. "I agreed to five...*dates*."

"Dates!?" Wakanda laughed. "You little whore. Whatever." She dismissed the slander with a wave. "As long as you can live with yourself."

"Hrm." Lyloda curled his lip. "At least this might actually be worth it this time. Look at these levels." He tapped a thick blue digit at some numbers on the papers. "And check out the compositions and quantities. There's enough here to keep every marselian in the universe high for the next ten generations."

"So what's your point?"

"This," he wagged a finger at her, "we rig the Wrath with tanks and collection vents. If we get fired down there, we pop the vents just as we enter the stratosphere and take our fill of pure-grade ozone. There's room in that mech to store more than enough ozone for both of us to retire."

Wakanda chuckled. "Yeah, and where are we going to get a dealer?"

"Taken care of." The coldness in Lyloda's black orbs made Wakanda wonder what nefarious deeds lurked in her partner's past. One thing for sure, Lyloda was dead serious.

She gave it a bit more thought then started nodding her head. This was doable. She stood and held out her hand. "I'm in."

Lyloda smiled wide and smothered her hand in his. "Outstanding."

"The fates be damned!" she exclaimed.

Another "huh" filtered through the blankets on the top bunk.

The team replied in unison, "Go to sleep."

Far above the planet's surface, the jump station commenced another spasm of lights as all three tubes disgorged a continuous stream of fighters until nearly four score clouded the area. Each slightly long and flat craft sprouted from the rear an arc of metal, almost as long as the fuselage, that curved down. Twin, thick tubes capped the end. On top, near the nose, sat an oblong canopy of faceted, smoked glass.

In the formation's lead, a worn grey fighter with haphazard arrangements of black blemishes sported an otherwise immaculate paint job. A small, white bird graced both sides of the fighter's nose, but these birds had fire in their eyes and lightening bolts in their clutches. Splashed above them in thick, red letters, the galactic-standard words read "Demonic Dove."

A matching stark-white face peered from behind the now transparent canopy. Instead of red, these eyes gleamed a cobalt blue, same as the tiny plates that symmetrically spotted the snowy face in such a pattern that any su-vol would think him handsome. His cape of metallic green feathers glinted in the starlight as Hunter K'lib G-Vin leaned forward to check his readings from the rest of his fighters.

"Den Control this is Theta Wing; we're in the box and glowing blue," K'lib mentally informed.

"That's a roger, Theta," returned a disembodied voice. *"We've got you with a clean jump. Welcome to the war."*

The controller paused to double check the formation plans. *"From the system plane, patrol to sector five eight. Report to the Trafalgar. Warm 'em up and keep 'em hot."*

"You heard it," K'lib turned his communications to his wing mates. *"Engage primary and secondaries and put auxiliaries on the go. Flash and ready by the numbers in three...two...one...flash."*

In a systematic wave, the main thrusters on the butt end of each of the fighters' main fuselages blasted yellow lights and specks of particles that glinted in the darkness. G-Vin waited for the final fighter to cleanse its injection system, after which he initiated the next wave of changes.

Part of the fuselage and the arc of metal under the craft split in half and spread to create an inverted V shape, stopping when the angle reached ninety degrees. This time, G-Vin didn't wait. Doors under the new wings slid open, allowing weapon pods to drop and lock in place.

When the final craft reported all systems online, G-Vin shot forward and veered toward their target trajectory. His fellow Grey Wolf fighters formed defensive positions that placed some pointing in abnormal directions while still keeping the same flight path as their leader.

Various ships zipped by, darting from any of the multitude of cruisers, destroyers and frigates that now started filling the space above the planet. In the distance, G-Vin's target lingered. The destroyer only had a few fighters of its own flying nearby for protection.

G-Vin scanned the hull and immediately identified the Trafalgar as a combat destroyer. Such models incorporated any mix of mechs, drop ships, bombers and fighters, but normally, they only had a squadron worth of fighters, two at the absolute max. G-Vin commanded three in his unit. Rotational schedules offered the only solution, but with only one squadron docked at a time, this was going to be rough duty.

The su-vol began relaying as much to his squadron commanders when a glint on his displays caused him to flick his controls and, in a snap, invert his fighter. Looking down through the top of his canopy, he watched the nearing approach of the dreadnought Nebuchadrezzar.

Its tremendous size made G-Vin's wing of fighters appear like gnats next to a small car. With the Shingi just point two light seconds away, the neighborhood suddenly felt decidedly cramped.

"The Cappadocia reports a safe landing and location of the target without incident," announced a controller on the operations floor of Shingi's bridge.

In the command chair, Elder Rior Kyston turned to her left to glance at Duke Chichiq to ensure he heard. The granite-colored duke turned from tapping away at his screens and bent the top half of his flat body to answer the dextian's silent question.

Then the lanky being stood and approached Kyston's side. "In that case, let's not dawdle," his tiny mouth moving rapidly as he spoke.

The pale dextian relinquished her chair to the duke and strolled over to position herself against a railing to watch the coming events.

"Open all known Korac channels and prepare for broadcast," the duke ordered the controllers below as holograms on the two-story domed screen displayed numerous assorted collages of data and images of the Corps vessels in the area. "Begin."

Waiting for a faint, short whistle, he started. "This is Duke Mular Chichiq, duly designated jurisdictional representative of the Dragon Corps. This is to the rogues who are currently in illegal possession of the Korac Council's Ranklin station and Eighth Space Force." He didn't anticipate a reply, especially not so soon, which was why he didn't wait for a hailing acknowledgment before making the announcement. However, he took a moment for the likely disorganized command structure aboard the Ranklin to rouse itself enough to listen intently.

"By the authority of the Dragon Corps, I hereby order for your unconditional surrender. Close all weapon ports and allow for the peaceful boarding by our forces, which will escort you from this restricted galaxy to face your fair, yet swift, trial. There are no negotiations in this matter. The only satisfactory agreement is for your complete capitulation; otherwise, we will use extreme force to achieve these results—even if it means your absolute annihilation."

The last of the ultimatum echoed in the bridge. Not even a breath left Chichiq as he remained completely still and minutes went by. He expected nothing less. Any remaining rogue leaders were likely bickering among each other while racing to display power against the least dedicated members of their crews in hopes of preventing a mutiny. While a delicate balance, the latter bit would accelerate the process, hopefully enough to cause them to make mistakes.

"Trying to take us would seal your doom." The declaration sounded freakishly calm, not what the duke expected at all.

"With whom I'm I speaking?" Chichiq inquired.

"I am Gor'vium."

"May I assume you represent the entire rogue force in orbit of the planet known by us as Terra Four?"

"Since I am the senior commander of the true Korac Council, you may."

The name and accent pointed vigorously at the owner being a piolant. Yet this piolant's tone held a strangely tempered purpose. The duke put this to the test.

"In that case, you must have successfully succeeded Horwhannor following his recent execution?"

Gor'vium didn't give in to the attempt to fluster him with the Dragon Corps' awareness of his previous leader's death.

"Also, you must be aware of our presence and that the Corps has an entire armada here to discharge intergalactic law by force if necessary."

"You are going to need more than an armada to take us."

Chichiq bottled the confusion fueled by the unperturbed piolant.

"You are currently in restricted space," Chichiq stated, "in p'tahian territory. It would be to your best interest to surrender now and—"

"What?" Gor'vium fired. "Do you think we would be afraid to attract the attention of the nearest p'tahian fleet? To the contrary, we're counting on it."

This declaration accelerated Chichiq's thought process like nothing he had ever experienced. Just when he prepared to give Gor'vium credit as a sane negotiator, he turned out to be suicidal. Maybe Gor'vium saw no escape and hoped to achieve victory, even if it meant sacrificing his fleet to obliterate his enemies.

"Did I baffle you?" Gor'vium injected after moments of silence. "See, the p'tahians are businessmen. For a minor trade of information and manual labor, they allow us to stay here. They have also given us a few new trinkets. We will be more than happy to entertain you with these toys if you so much as even flinch in our direction.

"Now," Gor'vium continued, "it may be in *your* best interest to leave."

"Can't do that," Chichiq replied, as irritated as a poker player who just bet it all and had someone call his bluff.

"No one lives forever," Gor'vium taunted. "I guess we get to stare at one another until my friends arrive."

Chapter 10

Chains rattled as Paloon closed the garage door. The space shuttle barely fit into the slot, but its size kept it from fitting down the elevator, so here it would have to stay.

As Paloon worked on finding a way to climb over the vessel, the others headed downstairs.

"So you're Ky's twin?" Oz directed at the team's new visitor.

"Not exactly," she replied, "at least not how you likely mean it."

Julie reached the basement floor and turned to flash her ebony eyes at Oz. Her shoulder length black hair swayed as if a solid silky sheet.

"We are birth mates; we were born at the same time. There are five of us. Only two were female. Needless to say, that bothered mother." Julie went back to following Lyon as he navigated through the tunnel to other side. "I guess there's only me now, and I'm not all that keen on being queen. Mother might actually try to give birth again."

"So you're born in litters, kind of like dogs." Oz hadn't felt uncomfortable about the thought until he spoke it.

Julie halted and spun in a tight circle to take a stern stance. "What did you call me?"

Oz scrambled. "I'm sorry; I didn't mean it like it sounded. Really, I'm sorry."

"You had better be," she frowned at him. "Where are you from anyway? You kind of look atlantian, but you're not."

"Here. I mean, I'm human; I'm from this planet."

Julie didn't believe her pointed ears and squinted one eye before she spoke. "What?"

"I'm—"

Lyon rushed back to interrupt and get Julie's attention by lightly grabbing her arm, but she shot him a harsh look of disapproval, and he released her.

But he continued with his verbal interruption. "It's a long story. We saved him from a severe radiological burn and a possible cranial bomb."

For a bit longer, Julie watched Oz, who nodded and added, "I guess they did at that."

"So much for saving my sister from a cranial bomb."

Shame, irritation and offense simultaneously crashed into Lyon. "Hey, we couldn't get to her in time." The events leading to Ky's death uncomfortably rushed through his head. "And we didn't even know Horwhannor had wired her with a brain bomb."

"Relax, man," Julie chuckled while giving Lyon's shoulder a quick punch, which hurt. "I'm just having a little fun. I don't mind having this local around as long as you're fine with it, but," she paused while dragging her head around toward Oz, "why are you hanging around? Don't you have somewhere else to be?"

The questions stumped Oz, and confusion blanked his face. He had no idea how to answer her or, for that matter, himself. Why did he stay? He thought that maybe it was due to Lyon's threat, but he no longer felt threatened. Maybe he could willingly leave now, but he wanted to stay.

"Hello?" Julie called as she rapped a fist on Oz's head. "You still here?"

Oz jerked away as if snapping awake. "I-I don't know. I guess I don't have anywhere else to go. I've always been kind of a loner. Besides, if I leave now, the military would eventually find me, and I doubt the explanation of my absence would keep me from getting thrown in prison. Plus, things are rather interesting around here."

"Well," Julie squinted, "if you start acting squirrelly, I'll kill you. Speaking of which," Julie turned to Lyon, "where's her body? Mother didn't send me here for a vacation."

Lyon's eyes darted about a bit as his mind raced, trying not to think about how much his shoulder now hurt. He blinked it away and resumed escorting Julie into the main room.

Larin, who became distant the moment Julie introduced herself, had long since returned to the workbench, putting all his focus into the pistol. As for Mac, he now stood on his chair to look over the chalkboard-clad wall and watch Julie with the look of intense befuddlement that was only possible from a teenager trying desperately to feign disinterest.

Julie noticed the tiny boy standing in his chair. She briefly watched from the corner of her eyes, confusion twisting her brow, until Lyon spoke up and pointed at one of the rooms to the right. She acknowledged with a nod. "Give me a moment," she stated before slipping into the room.

Minutes later, a one-sided, muffled conversation began seeping from the room. A seated Lyon glanced between Oz and Paloon, who had since returned and taken a seat. None of them knew what to do, so they just shrugged at one another.

"Yes, mother," blurted into the room as the door opened. Stepping through, Julie held a tiny screen in her palm. "Continue with the proceedings. I'll—" Julie abruptly ended the thought as she closed the door. "No, I don't, but that will be my first priority. Until then, proceed without me." Julie watched the tiny screen. "Yes, mother. Bye-bye."

Julie exhaled deeply as she put the palm screen away and half mumbled to herself, "Ky was always her favorite."

She straightened and froze when her eyes saw the new image on the table. Lyon turned to see what had caught Julie's attention then snapped his head away, half ducking it in shame.

At the far end of the table, Mac, in a persona twice as tall as the last, leaned against a graffiti splattered dark-red brick wall. He wore pointed eel skin boots, a leopard-print long coat, a white silk shirt ringed with three gold chains, and a red fedora.

Mac scanned Julie from top to bottom as he sucked air through his teeth. "Dang, girl, you sure are packing a fine trunk of junk in that badunk-a-dunk."

"What did you just say?" Julie asked.

"Uh," Larin injected without moving his head from his work, "I think he said you have a fat ass."

"What!?"

"Whoa, he—" Lyon threw his hands forward and shook them as if to wave off Julie's hostility. "He meant it in a good way." Lyon shifted to point a palm at Mac then faced Julie. "He picks up all these terran phrases and doesn't know when to turn them off. In this case, it's just some kind of obscure introduction or greeting."

"Excuse me?" Julie didn't need Larin's quiet chortle to sense the truth. She pointed a finger a Lyon. "I'm going to beat you. What kind of greeting is that, and how do you tell someone they've got a fat ass in a good way?"

Lyon quickly lost a sense of control over the situation and wondered if the dextian was serious about this threat.

Then Julie leered at Mac's holographic image. "Wait, he's got emo chips. Why did you go and build a computer with emo chips? Are you out of your mind?"

Lyon felt an urge to stand but kept his seat. He fumbled in responding, not that Julie was waiting.

"I hate emotional computers." She glared at Mac. "They're dangerous. Heck, I'll bet you had something to do with my sister's death. Did you?"

When Julie jerked forward with the last question, Mac threw up his ring laden hands. "Yo, you best step off out of my biz, bitch."

"Mac!?" Lyon screamed just as Julie lunged forward.

Paloon barely intervened in time, using all of his strength to hold Julie back. She went into a tirade of verbal attacks while Larin had a good laugh, listening to all the turmoil.

"Mac," Lyon shouted, "apologize, right now!"

"Geez, if that woman can't take a compliment, I don't have to—"

"Drop it," Lyon yelled then pointed. "This is Ky's sister, and you will respect her! Now, apologize!"

Reluctance curled Mac's lips as he tried to stare down Lyon but lost. "Julie," all tone dropping from Mac's voice as he removed his large hat, "I'm sorry."

"Now, go away," Lyon ordered.

The image disappeared, Mac's pouting face the last thing visible before dropping through the table's surface.

"C'mon, he's gone." Paloon tried to sound calm but couldn't hide the tension. "He's just a childish computer; it's not worth it."

"I know that," Julie barked as she pushed away from Paloon. "Don't you think I know that? I just didn't expect to be welcomed so rudely."

Lyon attempted to apologize for his computer, but Julie showed no sign of acknowledging the regret. Instead, she began pacing, breathing heavily through a fanged snarl. She closed her eyes, placed her hands on her hips and inhaled deeply a few times, ignoring Larin's supportive comment on the need for the computer's demise and Lyon's resulting chastisement.

"Is this the entire team?" Julie asked calmly, eyes still closed.

"No. Hitook is not here," Lyon replied then looked about inquisitively. "By the way, where is he?"

"He's still meditating," Paloon informed.

"What?" Lyon's disbelief sounded like displeasure. "It's been, what, two days now?"

Paloon exaggerated a shrug. "What do you want me to do about it? If he wants to sit still for two days, that's his problem."

"Either way, I would like for him to be here now."

Distaste swirled in Paloon's eyes as he stared at Lyon. Though reluctant, Paloon finally gave in and departed to go disturb Hitook.

Julie remained motionless, and such a lack of outward action ratcheted up Lyon's concern. To break the tension, he started talking about the one thing he observed since Julie's arrival.

"I notice you mention your mother a whole lot more than Ky ever did."

Julie huffed a light chuckle. "Yeah, we can be like that sometimes; we got it from mother. Work for work time and family for family time, and never shall they meet. Or so mother keeps proclaiming."

"So your mother is the reason why you're here, I mean, for your sister?"

Julie huffed another laugh, a bit harder this time. "Mother?" She finally opened her eyes. "Well, yes and no."

She walked toward the far end of the table to sit at the very top of the chair back, feet firmly planted onto the front of the chair back and her black tail hanging free. " Mother can be quite influential in the royal queen's dealings, but even being second in line for the throne does not give her complete authority. Therefore, I'm fulfilling another role on behalf of the Corps so as not to solely be an escort for my sister's body."

"Then you're the emissary Duke Chichiq told us to expect?"

"Yes," a shade of seriousness colored Julie's tone, "but I'll discuss that when your last team member arrives."

Silence returned to the room, making Oz rather uncomfortable. Larin didn't care, leaving Lyon and Julie lost in separate paths of thought. Time strolled by until Paloon returned to the room and took his seat without fanfare.

Lyon froze and stared questioningly at Paloon with brief glances toward the room's entrance. The grey-haired hunter refused to acknowledge the non-verbals; he wasn't Hitook's babysitter. Lyon began to open his mouth but halted as Hitook piously entered.

The massive beast hung his head low with his hands clasped in front and lumbered with the speed and enthusiasm of a zombie. Gradually nearing the table, Hitook peered forward without lifting his head. The sight of Julie gave the liqua pangs that forced the light in his black eyes to shimmer as they twitched with spasms.

"I am sorry for failing to protect your sister."

Julie nearly blared, "Who the hell are you?" But Hitook's words came so timidly, she stopped with her mouth agape.

The wimpish tone boiled Larin's irritation into a gurgling grumble. Folding his arms and looking away, Paloon silently agreed: Ky's death was no one's fault; Hitook should stop being so self-loathing. Oz, however, pitied Hitook for the torment he suffered. Lyon leaned toward Oz's line of thought but forced himself to not show it.

Realization struck Julie, who finally closed her mouth but raised a finger and immediately began talking again. "You're the one Master Incana mentioned, the one who met Ky before she left for this mission?"

Hitook barely nodded affirmatively.

Julie leapt from the chair top, darted toward Hitook and with little resistance yanked one of his paws free to shake it. "It's a pleasure to meet you." She slugged him in the arm with the side of her fist. "What are you sorry for?"

"I killed your sister by failing to protect her."

She dropped the paw and took a step back while glaring at Hitook. Julie half turned toward Lyon with her head making the rest of the turn a moment before returning her eyes on the eight-foot-high mound of fur. "What's he talking about?"

"Just what he said," Lyon replied. "He blames himself for Ky's death more than anyone else here." Lyon shrugged. "I guess they were close."

Larin grumbled again as Julie reared her head back. After another suspicious scan, Julie began chuckling. "You? And Ky? I doubt it. She's just not the freaky type." She laughed lightly while noticing Hitook maintaining his solemn expression, refusing to even flinch. Everyone here was taking her sister's death far too serious for Julie's taste.

An impression overcame Julie, forcing her to stifle her humor. Another critical examination of Hitook's stance confirmed Julie's sensation. This beast waited for chastisement or some kind of corporal punishment for this self-fabricated failure.

She aimed to place a hand on Hitook's shoulder but it fell short and landed on his chest. She sighed for a moment. "Look, I don't need to know the circumstances of my sister's death to know she wouldn't blame you. Ky just wouldn't do that." Hitook still refused to show any signs of acknowledgment, so Julie expounded, "On behalf of Ky and our crest, I relieve you of all responsibility in relation to her death."

Julie held her hand on Hitook for a while longer, hoping for a reaction. Nothing came, so Julie grew tired of this line of thought, left Hitook to wallow and resumed her perch on the chair at the opposite end of the table. Before finishing the task, she began, "Now that you're all here, let's get to business."

"Listen up," Lyon shot toward the workbench, compelling Larin to stop his tinkering to turn and face the table.

"As we speak, Corps forces are undertaking a large movement to this planet in order to escort the remaining rogues out of this galaxy as quickly as possible."

"We kind of guessed that from the news reports," Lyon commented.

Interest perked Paloon's brow. "What news reports?"

"Just some terran television news reports of lights in the sky," Lyon remarked with a wave as if the details weren't important. "But how many vessels are we talking about?"

"The last count I heard was twenty-one."

"Look," Paloon changed thoughts and orally attacked Julie, "that's only a fleet. Horwhannor's pals have more than an armada's worth of combat vessels; bringing anything less is suicidal."

The misdirected challenge bounced off Julie, leaving her unfazed in both stance and tone. "I don't make those decisions. I'm sure they're doing the best they can."

"Can't be all that great," Lyon added. "The arrival is already all over the news. Don't tell me that our mission is to try to keep this quiet? That's impossible at this point."

"No," Julie shook her head, "they don't expect us to keep it quiet. It is actually to the contrary: They expect it to get worse. As you already know, these guys are not going to leave peacefully, and the resulting battle is going to be far short of invisible. That's where this one tiny problem comes into play, and we are tasked with fixing it."

Julie let the tension hang, which left four people who just wanted the answer and one who, reluctantly, already knew it.

"The Corps doesn't have jurisdiction," said Lyon, resignedly.

Julie pointed at Lyon. "Exactly. And that is what we have to fix."

"Wait one minute," Paloon exclaimed while almost leaping from his chair, "what do you mean the Corps needs jurisdiction? They sent us here. Jurisdiction didn't bother them then."

"Don't be naïve." Julie curled her lips and glanced pitifully at Paloon. "You were expendable."

"I knew it!" Larin flew off his raised chair, thudded to the ground and charged the table, thrusting a stubby brown finger at Paloon. "I frapping knew it! I tried to tell you, but you didn't want to hear—"

A crash sounded from Larin's throat, thanks to a speedy thump from Julie's tail. The surprise action sent the rolbrid off balance as Julie pushed Larin back with her tail.

"Back off and shut up," Julie ordered. "Nothing is going to change it. Matter of fact, we are still expendable. We are not getting off this planet until we get that jurisdictional approval."

"You said, 'we,'" Lyon commented.

"That's right. I'm not allowed to risk a departure flight, so I'm part of your team until we either die or get that jurisdiction."

"How are we supposed to do that?"

"You tell me," Julie replied to Lyon. "You're the expert on this planet. All I know is that we need to have the senior representative of this planet's government agree to protection from the Dragon Corps."

Paloon huffed. “That hasn’t stopped them yet. Why do they need it so bad now instead of getting us off this rock?”

“For the same reasons you already mentioned,” Julie answered. “They’ve only been able to sacrifice half an armada to do this. However, if this planet agrees to Corps jurisdiction, then the lord can activate article two hundred and thirteen of the charter and pull every vessel, even without government approval, to help remove the renegades as quickly as possible.”

“Why not try to get the jurisdiction first?” Lyon inquired.

“The situation has already become too unstable with Horwhannor’s death. The Corps decided to move immediately and hope we can get the jurisdiction in time.”

Oz broke his silence. “But from who?”

“Excuse me?”

“Who are you going to get this approval from? You said it had to come from some kind of representative from this planet’s government. There are hundreds of governments in the world.”

Astounded, Julie had to challenge. “You’re going to tell me that you don’t have a single planetary government?”

“No, we don’t.”

Julie shook her head and blinked hard. “I’m surprised you haven’t killed yourselves.”

Lyon jerked his chin toward Oz. “What about that organization that all countries are a member of?”

“What the United Nations?”

“That’s it. What if we go to them?”

“And what?” Oz threw up his hands. “Even if we could stroll right in, what do you expect me to say? ‘Good day, secretary general. These aliens kidnapped me and threatened to kill me, but they turned out to be okay people who really want to protect us, and they would like your approval to help protect Earth from an extremely powerful alien race that wants us dead.’?”

“That’s a nice start,” Julie commented.

Oz was irritated by the lack of appreciation for his sarcasm. “Look, not every country is a member, and even those that are members, they don’t trust one another. It’s far from a planet-wide government. It’s more like a bureaucratic bickering machine.”

“Well,” Lyon injected in a way to show that he agreed with Oz’s assessment, “it’s all we have.”

“Then how do you expect us to get their attention: shoot your way to the assembly floor?” Oz looked away and failed to stifle the next mumble. “That seems to be all you do.”

Lyon scowled as Oz got a contradicting double shot from Paloon—“That was uncalled for.”—and Larin—“Frapping right; let’s blast our way in.”

“We’re not blasting our way in,” Lyon fired seconds before worry strangled his thoughts. “However, we will need some kind of compelling reason to get in.”

The room’s occupants tried to think about this, but every idea required days of explanations. No one knew if they had that much time and wished for better answers. Those solutions never came as the attempts were disrupted.

"Lyon," Mac's disembodied voice called bashfully.

"What?" belted Lyon, still irritated by his computer's previous rudeness.

"We have a visitor."

"A visitor? Where?"

"Out front."

"Let me see."

A holographic monitor popped into existence in front of Lyon, and it displayed a waiting trio calmly facing the store's entrance. At the lead stood Yabuki Yumiro.

Chapter 11

In the center of Delphi, copper seamlessly formed four walls, a ceiling and a floor to create a rather plain room. A brass triangular table rested a tad off center. Brass slabs at least a foot thick rose from the floor, each just a few feet away from the center of each of the table's three sides. They stood at a slight, yet noticeable slant. Two similar objects unceremoniously leaned against the far wall.

At the pointed head of the pyramid-shaped table rose a rectangular golden platform. Standing on the platform, a similar slanted slab of gold sprouted flat, plain wings half as thick as the slab.

Facing the triangular table and leaning against the raised slab of gold, Quirinus gazed at nothing in particular, his large, black eyes only occasionally blinking with transparent eyelids. The large blue-grey face barely held in the massive, almond-shaped eyes, leaving just enough room for a small mouth. Thin arms and legs ended with four spindly digits each. A white toga wrapped his frail-looking body, the loose cloth clasped on his right shoulder under a gold and red disk marked with a p'tahian symbol for authority.

A corner of the room unfolded to create a temporary doorway through which four p'tahians quietly stepped into the room. All wore similar clothing to the first occupant, yet with different symbols on their right shoulders. The first two took their places at the table, leaning against the slabs there. The last two p'tahians rested against the slabs on the wall as the door refolded to restore a seamless corner.

"Dire words have reached us," Rhaderon began from his position at the table. His greenish brown skin showed no wrinkles, and the tiny mouth only barely moved. "Pyridamanthys has fallen."

"Hark," Quirinus exclaimed as he lowered his head, "this marks a sad day indeed. Our thoughts shall be heavy with lamentations." The leader raised his eyes as their gaze locked with the elderly p'tahian against the wall, his grey skin a shade darker than his greying eyes. "Achodel, through time you have always proved wise in counsel and true in deeds. Will you honor me by filling Pyridamanthys' position as a trusted flamen?"

"My days may be short, but as you request, it shall be my deference." Achodel stepped forward to lean at the once empty position at the table. "My heart for you."

"It pleases me so," Quirinus replied. "Spite the jubilation from sorrow, give ear, for much remains to be discussed. Infer the shepherd slain for Pyridamanthys to undertake such great risks only to perish. This stray proceeds to leave our grasp empty."

"We may seek, but not find. That time is bygone," petitioned the blue-green Asphlegethon, the third priest at the table. "We let the truth be known. Natheless, as it happened on the sixth, they heeded not.

They have turned a rebellious shoulder. In as much, we must feel forced to turn an exquisite land to devastation."

Rhaderon agreed by nodding faintly and slowly. "In the recent they summoned and spoke to me saying—"

"Do not name the keepers," injected Asphlegethon.

"Trust that the keepers have despoiled us and fouled my words so much as their name shall not be spoken," Rhaderon assured his companion before resuming. "The words of the remnants came to me saying they plead for concord as if in hopes for alms. Confronted with their ears that are hard of hearing, they answered and said unto me that they do not favor the clash of swords. They have two faces with two mouths. For behold, the signs betoken their failure to uphold the bond of our scripture. Where it was said to them to shun from such proximity or assay our wrath once more, alas as we speak, they befoul what is ours."

"We must exclaim to throw open our nation's doors of battle," Asphlegethon pleaded in support of Rhaderon's comments.

Quirinus slightly raised a long hand, an act asking for a moment of silence. Then he spoke. "Achodel, what say you of these words?"

"As said before, the failure rests at our feet; the blood mars our hands. For our nation, we must take for ourselves the honor in their eyes and seal the covenant."

"And what of the flock?" Quirinus questioned.

"Save them through the hands of their sanguinary arbiter," Achodel stated without hesitation.

Quirinus let silence take the room as he contemplated the situation. The army would not be ready, but few alternatives remain now.

"This anger fills me with a great rage. My thoughts are storm-tossed." Quirinus's voice did not change in flux or volume. "As I called and they did not listen so shall they call and I not listen. Hitherto, I move my hand against them. It will happen that in this place it shall be their end days. Then they will know truth, a righteous and mighty truth."

The other occupants in the room simultaneously folded their long fingers and placed them on their seals that marked their right shoulders.

"Plead to Asgard," ordered Quirinus. "We have demand for its strength."

Chapter 12

"Two dogs, loaded, and a large beer," Gabe requested, his voice slightly louder than normal in hopes that his order would make it through the cacophony of the crowd and the bustling mayhem behind the counter.

The redhead in a uniform red-and-white-striped polo shirt and whatever jeans she had put on this morning nodded while tapping at a register before slipping into the chaotic foot traffic around the food and drink dispensers to retrieve the order.

"Dude," Dalton groaned, "why do you do it?"

"What?"

"Two?" Dalton threw his open hands forward and opened his mouth as if to further question his friend's choice, then gave up. "Whatever, man. If you get sick again, you're dragging your own ass to the stool this time."

Dalton, deep down, knew he would still help his friend, but he wanted to appear stronger than he really was.

"I can't help it." Gabe smiled slyly. "I like how they taste. It's not my fault if my stomach doesn't agree with me. Besides, the beer will help me to not remember."

Dalton shook his head, bewildered by his friend's strange logic and stranger digestive chemistry. Onions always triggered in Gabriel the most amazing gastric grenade with a three-hour fuse, which emptied everything in his stomach. By that point, it would mostly be bile until the dry heaves kicked in. But his body had an even harder time with alcohol in any form. Fermented anything always sent his mind into the blissful world of blackouts.

Some might consider such repercussions as curses, but not Gabe. To him, they were circumstances that could be twisted to his benefit. After all, the result always made others envious.

Gabe dropped the smile and jerked his head toward a dark-skinned man navigating the stream of people pouring into the stadium. Dalton turned to notice his approaching co-worker holding a humongous pretzel and sucking on a straw stuck into a clear plastic tumbler containing a thick orange liquid.

"A pretzel and orange juice?" Gabe asked with disbelief in his voice. "Do you realize how gay that looks? Please tell me it's at least spiked."

Kazi shook his head negatively without moving his lips off the straw until he needed them to speak. "Actually, it is an orange and banana smoothie." The thick accent placed his boyhood home somewhere not on the current continent.

Gabe prepared to respond but was cut off by the concession stand attendant. "Your order, mister." He spun to pay the lady.

"Ignore him," Dalton requested of Kazi. "He's nothing more than a redneck wannabe stuck in the big city."

"Hey," Gabe returned with two overflowing hot dogs precariously balanced in one hand and a half-gallon of beer in the other, "I resemble that remark."

After a round of automatic mild chuckles, Dalton lowered his large soda to lift the tickets from his shirt pocket. "If everyone's ready, we're in section double D, row forty-six."

They entered the coliseum and toward their row. While side-stepping to their seats, they caught the eyes of three attractive women dressed in the same team's paraphernalia. The two trios exchanged a few glances before one of the ladies spoke up.

"Kazi? Kazi Franklin?"

"That's me," Kazi responded with the same phrase he always used when someone spotted him in public.

The three ladies, who appeared to be at least ten years too old to squeal, squealed. Then the same lady asked, "Will the weather be in the Jackal's favor today?"

"It'll be a beautiful day," he responded generically and smiled as he sat while the girls smiled back and giggled.

Gabe leaned forward and gazed pleadingly at Kazi until he could handle it no more. "What the heck, dude?" Gabe half whispered.

Kazi just shrugged and sipped his smoothie.

"Don't be modest," Dalton injected, then he turned to Gabe. "Even being a fourth chair TV meteorologist has its perks. This guy's a mini celebrity, which makes him great to take to bars."

"You make it sound like I'm a chick magnet." Kazi tried to sound humble, but his smirk gave him away.

Dalton shook his head. "This guy darn well knows what his local fame can bring him."

Kazi shrugged as Gabe looked back at the women again and cussed.

"What?" Dalton asked.

"They're married."

"You sure?"

"Yeah." Gabe took a swig of beer. "The rocks on their hands would cost me two *years* salary."

Just as the announcer began introducing himself and advertising the game's sponsors, a mobile food vendor strolled closer to the three, barking his wares. Gabe turned slowly toward Dalton and smiled the most mischievous smile possible.

"Come on, man, don't," Dalton pleaded.

"I'm going to," Gabe prodded.

Dalton only huffed as he closed his eyes.

Gabe threw up a finger. "One bag of roasted nuts."

After paying the man and taking the bag of peanuts, Gabe took the bag and nearly pushed it into Dalton's face. "How would you like some roasted nuts?"

Gabe's smile seemed as loving as a baseball bat to the face. He chuckled as he retrieved the bag and began eating the peanuts by the handful.

Kazi glanced between the two, knowing he had missed something. "What was that about?"

Gabe froze in mid chew and asked through a full mouth, "You didn't tell him?"

Dalton only screwed his face as his eyes cringed as deep into their sockets as possible.

Gabe laughed so hard a few bits of peanuts shot out before he could cover his mouth. Wrestling with laughter and chewing proved nearly impossible without several swings of beer. He finally got things under control enough to explain to Kazi. "See, Dalton here doesn't like to hear 'roasted nuts' because of a really nasty incident with a propane barbecue grill." Gabe raised his brow high as he shot Kazi a "you get me" look.

"Gabe," Dalton belted, "you're an ass!"

Gabe kept the look as Kazi's mind raced to connect the innuendoes. Then it hit him as a painful look raced across his face. "No!" Kazi didn't want to believe it.

"That right." Gabe sat back, popping a few more peanuts in his mouth. "Burned those bad boys so bad, they don't work no more."

"You're a real ass," Dalton muttered.

The murmur of the gathered audience had been gradually getting louder. When the noise started to include screams, it grabbed the attention of the three guys who started looking around. A few people began pointing to the sky.

Only a speck moments ago, the white dot grew rapidly in size and in seconds became a big as a bus and was getting bigger. Whatever it was, it was landing right on the stadium. Everyone instinctively threw up their hands and screamed.

That's when Gabe, Dalton and Kazi failed miserably at holding up a hundred tons of interstellar steel.

"Commander, the last mechanized unit reports a successful and uneventful touchdown."

Gor'vium sat erect in the command chair aboard the space station Ranklin. Not even a flinch from him acknowledged the deck hand's statement. The closest he came to recognizing the report was his next order. "Has the Corps responded?"

Another deck hand from across the command floor answered. "That's a negative. The Corps has made no aggressive movements and appears to remain in defensive formations. Even communications remained calm...considering."

"It appears," came the voice of the piolant deck officer standing behind and to the left of Gor'vium, "that the p'tahian technology is working as promised. We have reached the surface undetected; stealth will secure us surprise."

“Do not celebrate quite yet,” ordered Gor’vium. “We need more than surprise to survive. Whether detected or not, we have made the first move. Though I do not trust the Dragon Corps, neither do I trust the p’tahians. While I am not one to surrender, this move many only serve a p’tahian objective. Of all things in this universe, it is only that thought which scares me.”

Chapter 13

From the shadows, Lyon watched intently while mentally drawing the scene. Across the street, Paloon and Larin would be in their firing positions with Hitook on the roof. Julie half dragged Oz with her to the roof of the store but not before he caught a tossed particle cannon. As for Julie, at one moment she had nothing; the next, she wielded a battle sword as long as she was tall. Lyon couldn't deduce where the blade had come from and mentally noted to ask her later.

The knock came again for the third time since Lyon made it to the back of the store. As before, Yabuki just calmly reached a fist forward to rap on the door. Neither Yabuki nor the two who flanked his rear spoke a word. Except for the knocking, the trio remained as still as the large, black car parked against the curb behind them.

Lyon wondered how this yakuza punk found him and why he dared show his face here. Lyon contemplated killing Yabuki for whatever part he might have played in Ky's death. The intrigue, however, kept Lyon at bay. This wasn't a chance encounter. Yabuki's confident stance and persistence spoke loudly. The yakuza lieutenant knew where he was, which, though disturbing, meant Yabuki was more than aware of how vulnerable he was at this moment.

Such boldness in the face of the enemy changed Lyon's initial view on the situation. At first it appeared to be a showdown, now it felt like an arranged meeting someone had failed to tell him about. Instead of drawing his weapons and barking orders from well-protected seclusion, Lyon changed his mind and decided to confront his enemy face-to-face.

The inside door opened to reveal Lyon's face through a screen.

"Well, well, well, if it isn't the man whose father really must have wanted a girl." Lyon paused to see if poking fun at Yabuki Yumiro's name would spark a reaction. It didn't. "While I appreciate your patronage, the store's closed."

"I didn't come here to shop."

"Is that so? In that case, give me one reason why my friends behind you shouldn't bore a hole in your head."

The yakuza agents failed to flinch even the slightest. Lyon expected them to and half wanted to see the reaction, but there was nothing. Instead Lyon saw the cold emotion of a true killer.

"It appears, Lyon-san, we find ourselves with a common enemy."

"Ha," Lyon ejected. "Did you come just to amuse me? Please. Save your breath. That arrangement of yours was a hell of a setup, and it led to my friend's death. Therefore, you see, my remaining companions, who barely made it out alive, don't care for you much. And they very much would like a bit of revenge."

Not even a bead of sweat marred Yabuki's stone-like face.

Lyon continued, with a nod toward the two standing behind Yabuki, "I see you found some replacements for Taka and Tomo. Do they know how coldly their boss talks about his previous companions' *accidents* in prison?"

"Rin and Taichi are aware of Taka and Tomo's failures, but that's not important now."

At the mention of the names, Lyon scanned to two body guards. The slender female with a tight pony tail and a granite expression must be Rin. In contrast, Taichi had a confident yet simple-minded smirk, as if he was clueless and knew it. Outside of the idiot expression, Taichi's build was more fit for a sumo ring. However, Lyon didn't doubt the large man's speed.

Shifting back to Yabuki, Lyon questioned, "Then why are you knocking on my door at one in the morning?"

"Did you not say that I didn't know you? Neither did we know our 'handlers,' as you put it." Yabuki let the statement sink in. "I had offered to discuss it when you had a gun pointed at my head, so let's discuss it."

"Nice speech. However, I may not show you the same compassion I did earlier unless you start giving me a reason and quick."

"Our royal guards, and likely the impostor oyabun, were not human, and I'm going to guess that you are not either, Lyon-san."

"Yet you somehow managed to track me down, and now, here you are. It's not the smartest move you ever made."

"We realized our error too late, Lyon-san, but not too late to aid the enemy of our new enemy."

Lyon glared at Yabuki. "What are you getting at?"

"You didn't notice?"

"What?"

"In that hangar, you faced a firing squad armed with malfunctioning weapons. We couldn't stop the meet without showing our hand, but we sabotaged those weapons in hopes that it would give you enough time to destroy our new enemy."

Lyon's right brow peaked. "Aren't you full of surprises?" Lyon breathed loudly. "This doesn't make us friends."

"Maybe not, Lyon-san, but I did come to offer a truce."

"A truce?" Lyon fired. "You're kidding, right? I have no reason to make peace with an ignorant foot soldier who sends me to an ambush, then claims to have saved me from it."

"Think of us what you like, but we take our honor seriously and plan to restore it with or without you."

Lyon huffed a laugh. "How do you plan to do that?"

"We have gathered the yakuza bosses and informed them of how we have been fooled. Together, we are conducting a systematic eradication of these...things."

"Piolants."

"Excuse me?"

"Piolants," Lyon repeated. "those guards of yours are members of a race called piolant."

"Well, these...piolants infiltrated our organization, and now they are dead."

"Piolants are generally pretty tough, battle-hardened warriors. And you just calmly killed them, did you?"

"True, it wasn't easy. We lost quite a few doing so, but at least we had the weapons we needed."

"Ah, yes. I've been meaning to ask you guys about that, but you see, every time I get shot at or blown up it slips my mind. Now that we have time, how about you tell me your part in this whole weapons smuggling business."

"Distribution," Yabuki stated as an all-inclusive answer.

"Distribution? That's it?"

"Basically." Yabuki smiled briefly. "Our black-market network has delivered shipments to nearly every point on the globe."

"Who are they going to?"

"From what we can tell, there is no person on the other end. Each shipment went to stockpile locations, as if creating armories around the world."

"I doubt it is that simple."

"As do we."

Lyon folded his arms and leaned against the doorjamb. While he contemplated options, from killing Yabuki to closing the door and pretending the meeting never took place, Lyon kept returning to the one that he knew he'd have to choose. He fought the implication that it was that simple. Yet he toyed with the idea again.

Outside of what hand-to-hand skills they might know, the trio before him had no weapons; Mac's earlier scan confirmed it. Even the driver, who still remained seated behind the smoked glass of the windshield, possessed nothing with which to protect himself or his employer. Such accepted vulnerability struck a cord of admiration with Lyon. With his eyes now closed, Lyon hoped he wouldn't regret this.

Lyon pushed the screen door open. "Fine, you're in."

When Yabuki caught the door, Lyon sprung from the wall. "However, if you walk through this door, you play by my rules." Lyon spun and headed to the back of the store.

Yabuki watched Lyon slip into the shadows and pause for an answer. Turning around now might be his death warrant, but so could walking through the open door before him. But Yabuki had given his word, so the choice wasn't his. With a deep breath he entered the door. "I'd rather not do this, Lyon-san, but my new oyabun wishes for me to do whatever it takes to protect this city."

"There's more than just this city at stake," Lyon replied as he walked away to lead the trio of yakuza soldiers to the basement.

As they entered, a tiny version of Yabuki clad in black from head to toe and wrapped in a black, leather duster greeted them. Mac pushed his sunglasses up his nose with two fingers.

Lyon motioned a hand toward the vacant chairs. "Have a seat." As they complied, Lyon shifted his attention to the computer. "Mac, go away, call the others in and bring up the scans of the pirate armada."

The image flickered to life as Lyon pointed at it. "I'll try to make this quick."

Plastic slapped as Yabuki closed his phone.

"Done."

"You're kidding!" Lyon's doubt overshadowed his confidence.

"In eight hours," Yabuki explained, "our contact will be waiting in a parking garage ten blocks from the United Nations. He'll be prepared to make badges for everyone here, then he'll lead us in as a maintenance team. He assures me he has access to maintenance doors that bypass the security screens."

Lyon stood, silent in disbelief. He struggled to accept the luck, but it came too easily to be trusted. He looked to Julie for a reaction. She shrugged as if to say, "It's better than nothing." Then she went back to keeping watch on their new guests, who were still quite calm despite sitting in a room full of extraterrestrials and being told their world might get destroyed in an epic war.

Oz leaned back in his chair and yawned while trying to force a sentence, reverting to just repeating himself. "Then what, hold every delegate at gun point?"

The mention of weapons sent Lyon's gaze toward Larin, who, out of utter frustration at their guests, immediately immersed himself in tweaking the pistol on the workbench. Larin refused to talk to anyone, even when asked a direct question. On the whole, this was a good thing, but Lyon feared the rolbrid would, at any moment, spin around and ventilate Yabuki's skull. Yet Larin remained still, so Lyon answered Oz, "That's just impractical."

Another thought finished in Lyon's head. "Mac, what's the agenda look like?"

Mac responded without holographic fanfare. "The general assembly doesn't meet again for another week; however, the security council is meeting later this morning to discuss peace and security in the Upper Guinea."

"We don't have a week," Lyon half mumbled to himself as he started pacing. "The security council will have to do."

"Wait one darn minute," blurted Paloon, who obviously was still irritated at Yabuki's presence, and he, once again, directed his frustration at the yakuza solider. "The six of us are just going to stroll in as maintenance workers? Am I the only one who thinks that such a gaggle would be a bit suspicious?"

"Actually," Yabuki calmly corrected, "it will be nine, twelve if you count our contact and his assistants."

"Who said you're going with us?" Paloon barked.

Evenly, Yabuki stated, "This is not open for debate."

Paloon jabbed a finger at Yabuki but looked to Lyon, who hadn't really paid much attention. "They're not going!"

"We are willing to help in order to restore our honor, but this help comes on our terms." Yabuki tilted his head at Paloon as if chastising a child. Then he straightened. "We have spent many years cultivating and training this contact, and this risks crippling our ability to use this asset again."

"Hello?" Julie interrupted melodiously with just a shade of sarcasm, "in case you missed that bit in the briefing just now, the future risk to your assets would seem to be of little concern when your planet is about to be destroyed."

"Quite true," Yabuki bowed his head toward the pointy eared creature perched on a chair across the table. "However, the conditions of our offer stand firm."

Another rebuttal surfaced in Paloon, but Lyon capped it. "Skip it, man." Lyon turned his attention back to the group. "They're in."

Amid Paloon's more vocal grumbles, Julie remained composed and asked, "Are you sure?"

With tiny nods of his head, he breathily replied, "Yeah." Now sold on the decision, he justified it. "We need as many guns as possible on this one. So what's your plan?"

"We have three teams," Yabuki began, "each representing different maintenance companies, which arrive at staggered times. Once all are in, we meet and make our way to the assembly floor. That is if you can get us there in eight hours as you promised."

"That's not a problem." Lyon wagged a finger then tapped his chin. "Mac, see if you can get some schematics of that complex."

"On it."

"Paloon," Lyon spoke loudly to shatter his fellow atlantian's frustration and get his attention, "I need you and Larin to start loading whatever gear you can in the tank. Pull out the weapons control station and put in another chair."

Paloon stared at Lyon for several moments until he released his held breath. "Fine, fine. It's your call." He navigated around Lyon to go shake Larin out of his reclusive hobby.

"With that," Lyon turned to Julie, "I need you and Hitook to rest the best you can and prepare—"

"Lyon!"

Everyone jumped at Mac's booming alarm. Lyon prepared to chastise harshly but froze as the hologram table created a large screen with an image that made his blood run cold.

"I-I'm sorry," Mac stuttered an apology. "I wasn't paying attention and just stumbled on to it."

"Just give me audio."

"...refusing to talk to us, but from what we can see, it appears all their efforts against the metal beast seem futile."

Towering two hundred feet into the night sky, an alien mechanized artillery platform stood on humanoid shaped legs in the rubble of a sports stadium. Fire raged among the stadium's remains and everything nearby. Destroyed vehicles, including responding police cars, fire trucks and ambulances littered the scorched ground.

A missile roared into the scene and bloomed into a fiery explosion with a distinct concave shape about a hundred feet from the mech. As the camera man fumbled to shift the view to what was attacking the invader, the stubby barrel on top of the robot's horizontal torso rotated in its turret toward the aggressor. The cameraman barely got the fighter jet in view before it erupted into a green fireball.

"I don't know what to say," the reporter stammered. "Once again, the military's attempts seem futile. This seems to be the same situation throughout the country since these robots have landed in every—"

"Mac, get the duke on the line," Lyon ordered. "As soon as you have a connection start piping in the feed and get as many news feeds on this as you can."

"I-is—" Oz hesitated, searching for what he wanted to say. "Is this the p'tahians?"

"No," Lyon corrected, shaking a finger at the screen. "This is a Korac mech."

"A D-M-F model," Paloon injected, "a fourteen twelve, to be exact. A tad old, but these locals don't have a chance."

"Knight Kendrick, you have jurisdictional approval?" came Duke Chichiq's voice as his granite face sparked to life on a smaller screen floating above the larger one, which now included multiple news broadcasts of similar scenes in cities worldwide.

"No, my duke, but I need for you to watch the feed we're sending. It appears Horwhannor's bunch has landed."

The duke tapped the feed, and in seconds, anger appeared on the huyin's face as his three purple eyes created an inverted arch. "How did they arrive on the surface without us detecting them?"

"I don't know, but they're here." Lyon glanced at the larger screen containing ever-changing images from around the world. "And they're here in mass. Jurisdiction be damned; they're digging in. If we don't do something quick, soon they'll—"

"Get that approval!" Chichiq roared, as much as his shrill voice would allow. "We will address this. We are operating in a legal grey area until we have jurisdiction, so do not call again unless you have it."

The image disconnected and vanished.

"Tell your contact," Lyon forced while pointing a finger at Yabuki, "to speed up that time table. We roll in less than fifteen."

Chapter 14

Klaxons blared at near annoying levels as strings of green light flashed in rapid sequence down the crowded hall. Wakanda squeezed through the gauntlet of beings yanking gear out of their lockers and putting on their combat suits.

She thought less about her own tardiness as she noticed from a distance that Lyloda's locker remained closed. Now in a small clearing and at arm's length from her own locker, she started to verbalize her dismay that her partner was late, but a shouted warning distracted her.

"Look out below!"

Wakanda jumped away just in time for Lyloda to slide down the ladder against the wall. He landed with a thud. A grey bodysuit covered him from neck to toe. On the left side of the collar glowed two v-shaped silver chevrons. Before she could ask how he got suited up so fast when the others were just finishing, he slapped a black and grey tube in her hand.

"What's this?"

"Our maps," Lyloda answered with a smile. "I figured you'd forget yours again, so I rushed to get a copy."

Wakanda scowled and tossed the tube back. She *had* forgotten, again, but she didn't like being told she was predictable, especially in a bad way. A punch to the locker popped it open, and she began slipping her suit on over her clothes because there was no time to change. Similar to Lyloda's uniform, her rank of three chevrons marked her collar.

Slapping the last clasp into place, she yanked out her helmet, slammed the locker shut, snatched the map tube from Lyloda's hand and started running down the hall with her partner in tow. A couple of zigs down the hall led to a door about to close before she pushed it open again.

In front of her, the large launch bay stretched. Flashing green lights created strange shadows within the standard illumination around the line of command housings protruding through the floor. On each, the back hatch stood open as maintenance crews scrambled around conducting the final launch checks. Several yards in front of each open hatch stood the crew pairs, except for number nine, toward which Wakanda and Lyloda rushed.

A door embedded in the metal wall to Wakanda's left opened seconds before she could get into her position and stuff the map tube in her chest pocket. From the opening floated Hunter Hikkola. A black uniform coated his tiny limino body and four arms. The three chevrons capped with the profile of a small wolf's head rested on his left chest and reflected in his four black eyes. With his entrance, the sirens in the bay halted and the lights went to a solid green.

"Listen up, you dogs!" barked Hikkola as he started floating down the line of mech crews. "Those chicken-shit pirates have somehow landed on the surface without getting detected by our flyboys. It's our job to fix it. These scum have had several hours to position and dig in, so expect resistance.

"Our mission," Hikkola spun and retraced his levitation, "is to protect this planet by any means possible. These bastards are our sole target; there will be no firing on the indigenous population or wanton destruction. Put your arm down, Wakanda," he commanded without looking toward her as she complied. "I'm not an idiot. They will not like you. You will be just more invaders, and they will likely wish you dead and may do anything to bring about that end. But I repeat, no firing on the indigenous population. Protect yourselves the best you can, but you best do it with the minimum amount of force necessary or your ass will answer to me."

Hikkola stopped and faced the line of officers. "Now," he rotated his long head as he scanned up and down the line, "these bastards want a war; we're going to give them one. So begins," he inhaled deeply and roared, "the hour of the wolf!"

Everyone in the bay roared in reply as the crews donned helmets and charged into their respective command stations as the maintenance technicians closed and sealed the doors.

Wakanda yanked the map tube from her pocket and slammed it into the waiting port next to her chair as she sat. Flicking the port cover closed, she began securing the six-point harness around her body. To her right, Lyloda already had his hologram system up. She hurried and slammed her head a bit hard into the back of her chair, pulling on the cables that ran from the chair to her neck.

Holographic displays popped into existence around Wakanda's position. She mentally initiated a self diagnosis program and started sifting through manual systems checks.

"How's our ammo?"

"Full," Lyloda replied.

"Matter generators?"

"Operational."

A screen blinked in front of Wakanda. The diagnosis returned with positive responses from all systems.

"Engaging primary reactor in three...two...one...engage."

A flicker in the systems coincided with a faint hum that increased in pitch until it created a familiar and comforting background noise.

"Chimera Control, Wrath."

"Go ahead, Wrath."

"We're blue and ready for launch."

"Stand by."

The next few moments stretched to eternity as Wakanda vocally chastised her fellow pilots who couldn't hear her colored encouragement.

"Stand by," returned the voice from combat cruiser Chimera's control room.

Wakanda and Lyloda leaned back into their seats.

"In five."

The crew felt the vibrations as the chute doors opened below them.

"Three...two...one...purge."

A muffled clank released the mech to float freely but only briefly before the dock's thrust cannons fired, blasting the armored giant from the side of the cruiser. Clear of the bay, Wakanda mentally ordered the blast windows to lower. They revealed a black sky speckled with hundreds of mechs launching from the Dragon Corps vessels in orbit. Each glittered in unprotected sunlight.

There were various types, but the closest were just like Wakanda's craft: humanoid with very robotic accents and a neckless head that sat off center to its left shoulder. But Wakanda's craft proudly displayed its uniqueness in the form of intergalactic letters scrawled at an angle across its chest below its head, and they read "Tranquility's Wrath."

Wakanda lifted from the seat as much as she could to peer through the windows and look at the dark orb below. She relaxed back into the seat and brought into view her entry path. With her confirmation, Wakanda and Lyloda's chairs rotated so they faced the deck below them. As the seats locked in place, the holographic screens, which now floated below Wakanda, began counting down. Upturned rockets attached to mech's locked arms fired, rapidly plowing the mechanical beast into the planet's atmosphere.

The screens morphed into a three-dimensional representation of all the mechs as they, too, began speeding toward the planet below.

"Fire the plasma shell," Wakanda ordered.

After a few taps, Lyloda replied, *"In place."*

Moments later, a bowl of red flames bloomed into existence and gradually increased in intensity until nearly a clear blue.

"Two minutes," came Lyloda's voice into the pilot's head.

"Until landing?" Wakanda doubted it; it seemed way too fast.

"Until the stratosphere."

"Oh," breathed Wakanda, then shock hit her. *"You finished the retrofit?"*

"Barely. But I had to lose the ammo mags in the legs."

"What did you do that for?"

"I cut the tanks wrong."

"Well, I hope we won't need them."

"As do—"

The mech shook as the now spent rockets peeled off to drift away from the protection of the plasma shield and burst into fire. With precise grace, their chairs rotated back to their original positions.

"Shit," Lyloda blurted from his startled state. *"That gets me every time."*

"Don't be a pansy; give me the status."

"We're in standard range in thirty seconds."

"Targets?"

"Nothing," Lyloda replied. *"It's clear."*

"Express, Wrath," Wakanda radioed as she leaned at an angle to

see her partner mech, Hades Express, about two miles off her left side. *"We're clear on targets. Confirm."*

"Confirmed," replied a rough rolbrid voice.

The flame shrouds cupping both craft dulled to a bright red then faded from existence. Wakanda leaned forward again to see what she could make out of the world below when the craft shook as its descent slowed drastically.

"What was that?"

"I programmed the intake valves to open as soon as we hit the stratosphere," Lyloda answered, then excitement entered his voice. *"We're already at forty percent, wait eighty ... damn that was fast! We're full."*

Wakanda also doubted the speed and, for the sake of all it promised, hoped the tanks weren't just full of standard air. *"Is it pure?"*

"Wrath," called the pilot from the Hades Express, *"are you all right? You're slowing down up there."*

"We're fine," Wakanda shot back, possibly a bit too curtly, then she shifted her attention back to Lyloda. *"Well?"*

The marselian shook his blue head in disbelief. *"The filters worked. The sensors are reporting one hundred percent pure ozone. I can't believe this."*

Lyloda rested back in his chair struggling with the reality that he was now in possession of enough pure-grade natural ozone to be set for life. But that would have to wait. Energy shot through him as he lunged forward and began rerouting the oxygen systems.

Wakanda noticed with a suspicious eye. *"What are you doing?"*

"I've got to try it."

"What!?"

"Just a little hit." Lyloda almost sounded as if pleading for acceptance, but he didn't stop making adjustments. As soon as the systems were rerouted, Lyloda pressed the overflow button on his mask, squealed in ecstasy and collapsed.

"Well, ain't that just fucking grand," Wakanda belted. She was in the middle of an insertion and her gunner just got high and crashed.

She pulled her mask down to confirm the air in the cabin was breathable before leaning over and yanking the mask off Lyloda before he overdosed. With Lyloda's mask in her hand, she stared at it for a second. Then curiosity got the better of her. Before she had thought it through, Wakanda put the mask to her face and inhaled deeply.

Spastic coughs contorted her body as she chucked the mask. The coughs morphed into spitting as she also found herself breathing forcefully out her nose in weak attempts to purge her body of the foul gas.

Her brain kept spinning as she finished her spitting and leaned back. Wakanda silently cursed herself while blinking hard and rolling her head around. What's a drug for one race was poison to another, and she knew that, but she sure felt high. Tingling sensations coursed over the surface of her brain as if it were being teased by feathers, and the light entering the cockpit played with all spectrums as it danced.

The radiant masquerade drew Wakanda to the window.

Just off the horizon, the planet's sun sent ripples of orange light that reflected differently on the layers of quilted clouds. Each sprouted billowing mounds of blue-white cotton that peaked with golden-pink tips. On one particularly tall stack of clouds, a thin, steady rainbow encircled the rippling shadow of her mech.

She smiled at the sight then looked up to notice a ribbon of pink streaking the blue-grey transition from sky to space. Below, veins of concrete and arteries of water striped the green landscape, freckled with white and grey buildings.

Wakanda couldn't help but view the city, which was still so far below, as a considerably easy target. Instead of destroying, she had to protect it, whether the citizens there wanted it or not. But with such a large place, her job just got more difficult.

Lost in the view below, Wakanda almost didn't notice the smoke trail coiling up toward her mech until it had been joined by several others.

"Incoming," barked the pilot of the Express. *"Multiple missiles, no lock on their mother."*

Adrenaline kicked Wakanda into overdrive. She snapped her head to notice Lyloda still collapsed in his seat. Mentally she engaged his seat injectors as she tried to find the origin of the missiles.

A tiny needle pricked Lyloda's skin, and within half a second, he lunged forward, puking his guts out. Projectile vomit shot straight through his holograms onto the bulkhead and part of the window.

"We've been acquired," the Express reported. *"Thirty seconds until contact."*

"Don't do anything foolish," Wakanda pleaded. Any mech pilot knew trying to engage in combat during descent was suicide. The best way was always to just hope you make it to the ground.

"We're already dead."

"We can call in support!" Wakanda realized how weak that logic sounded.

"There's not enough time."

Wakanda could see the Hades Express below her. Its right hand gradually moved to withdraw its mini cannon as bright blue light bloomed under its feet, and the thrusters attempted to compensate for the shift in weight.

"Get a fucking lock!" Wakanda screamed at Lyloda, who had already came around enough and was in the middle of calling the strike.

"...off my coordinates. Give me a laser," Lyloda demanded.

The Hades Express' mini cannon roared to life peppering the ground at the base of the smoke trails with hundreds of explosive shells. In the midst of the chaos, a blue beam shot from space.

"Left three, up one," Lyloda ordered.

As the beam moved, Wakanda noticed another shift in the Hades Express, which now raised its left hand.

"He's going to fire the xenon," Wakanda shouted.

"Can't he wait?" Lyloda bellowed, mostly upset that his work would mean nothing in just a matter of seconds.

At the tip of the mech's left arm, three prongs protruded in an inverted pyramid shape. In their center, a purple fire flared until it encased all three prongs.

"He's not waiting," Wakanda reported. *"He's going to kill himself."*

"Halt," Lyloda ordered the space-based crew. *"Lock and fire with two."*

As Lyloda finished, a purple beam shot from the Hades Express into the barrage of shells, but the mech's thrusters couldn't compensate for the kick that sent the metal beast into a head-over-heels spin. Before it could make one rotation, a missile slammed into it, exploding into a green sun. The other missiles whistled past with one catching the explosion and igniting into another fireball.

The blast waves pushed the Wrath around as a few other missiles tore past it in a series of rectal clenching near misses. During the onslaught, two shells from the space-based rail cannons screamed past. The first crashed into the planet, throwing up a mushroom cloud of debris and blowing a hole in the ground. The second round only added to the pandemonium.

"Shit!" Wakanda exclaimed, not at the resulting devastation but at being distracted and not noticing how close they were to the ground. She engaged the landing sequence, which launched a metal plate off the back of her mech's legs. The plate zoomed to the ground and planted itself.

"This is going to be rough," she warned.

Though the landing plate had enough electromagnetic juice to soften the mech's landing, she had fired too late, so it wouldn't have all the time needed to achieve the best result. She ignited the jump thrusters and kept her mental trigger finger on the button to unlock the mech's joints.

For the last several miles, the Wrath plummeted with a tense crew shaking about as the thrusters fought to perform in a way they weren't designed. The effects of the electromagnetic pad finally became noticeable.

"Three," Wakanda began the countdown, *"two...one."*

She released the lock as the mech pounded the landing pad into the dirt while buckling at the knees and hips. Soon the mech's fists also hit the dirt, forcing the elbows backward.

As soon as she could gain control, Wakanda threw the reactor into overdrive and fought to stand. The mech resisted at first but soon gave in. On their feet, Lyloda immediately engaged all weapons systems as Wakanda launched the drone.

On the right side of the mech's back and resting at an angle, form-fitting panels popped open to release a tiny jet with diamond-shaped wings. It blasted without hesitation out of its holster and into the sky.

"BARD away," Wakanda reported as she ordered the battle assistance reconnaissance drone to search for the source of the missiles that took down her battery mate.

"All weapons online," Lyloda announced.

While the drone was launching, the Wrath's right hand disconnected the thirty millimeter mini-cannon from its hip. Over the left shoulder, near the head, a rack of four medium-range missiles rose slightly from its vertical position against the mech's back but stopped short of rotating to a more horizontal position for launching. Two chrome barrels extended above the right shoulder, which was much wider due to the offset position of the head. With the barrels fully extended, the entire cannon structure rotated like a conch shell over the shoulder to point forward.

These weapons combined with a full-sized external particle laser on the outside right arm, a left arm that was nothing more than a xenon laser, anti-personnel grenade launchers in the legs and a chest full of three types of missiles and a close-range anti-mech cannon to make the Citadel mech the best armed defensive mech in the Dragon Corps arsenal. Wakanda eagerly wanted to put it to the test against whatever shot down the Hades Express.

In seconds, which felt like minutes, the scene of the rail cannon strikes came into view on her holographic screens. The deep cone-shaped craters each turned half a city block into little more than ash and dust. Though nothing was on fire, several fire trucks were on the scene; their placement, however, made Wakanda wonder how long they had been there.

A sequence of colors flashed from the monitor as she flipped through the filters. The multi-colored strobe stopped as a once unnoticeable chunk of black glowed yellow. Wakanda zoomed in and studied it for a moment. Panning the view around, she failed to find any matching pieces, which could only mean that Lyloda had called in a darn-near exact hit.

"You got it."

"Yeah, I know," Lyloda responded calmly.

Wakanda knew how good Lyloda was; she wouldn't have picked him as her gunner if he wasn't that good. But she just couldn't let him get away with such a cocksure statement without at least a little ribbing. Opening her mouth in preparation to have some light-hearted fun with the marselian's emotions, she stumbled into Lyloda's interruption.

"I'll bet they're not here to thank me for what I did."

Wakanda glanced to her right to notice her partner pointing out the window. She turned her eyes forward, looked beyond the holographic screens and noticed a few tiny vehicles racing down a road toward her. They compounded all the wailing noise they made with flashing lights that bounced off the nearby buildings. Stopping several hundred yards short, the vehicles whipped sideways as the occupants bailed to take cover.

Immediately, the mech's systems identified the responding police officers as a minor threat, outlined them in yellow and engaged the anti-personnel grenade system.

"Turn that damn thing off," Wakanda ordered.

Lyloda did so just seconds before the mech's automatic defense systems would have made quick work of the small force. *"It's off,"* he reported, *"but now what? They don't look particularly happy."*

"Now," Wakanda said, *"we talk."*

She engaged the loud speaker and closed her eyes while focusing on the training she received in native languages. First contact was always delicate; she had to get this right the first time. The phrases circled in her head, and she mentally read them again and again, hoping she'd get the pronunciation correct.

Opening her eyes, she took a deep breath.

The drone's screen flashed green. It found a second target: a completely intact model fourteen-twelve DMF. And it was headed her way.

From outside the Tranquility's Wrath, the nervous police officers jumped when they heard an unmistakable female yell come from the towering metal beast.

"Shit!"

The creature then stepped out of the hole it had made upon landing, turned and started walking in the direction of the destroyed stadium while ignoring the salvo of small arms fire from the cops, who didn't know what else to do.

Chapter 15

Deep under the desert floor, a once polite conversation had just became uncomfortable. A dark wooden desk stood before a seated man dressed in an olive-green bag of a uniform with two blue stars on each shoulder. He held a phone to his ear and grimaced.

Shifting in his seat, he glanced at the newly arrived papers on his desk then up at the pilot waiting patiently for his orders. The young, healthy man was covered in black from head to toe and held a black helmet under his left arm. A hose ran from the helmet to a box on his chest. Though the outfit had no marks of standard military insignia, the tight cut of light brown hair gave the pilot away.

"All I'm saying," the general spoke into the phone, "is that this exposes a highly classified project, and doing so has some serious consequences."

"Rat's ass, general!" The voice over the phone blared unusually loudly for such a strongly scrambled signal. The general pulled the phone away, and though the pilot heard it, he didn't flinch. "I don't care if this exposes you as a transvestite prostitute! You have your orders!"

The slamming of the phone nearly forced the general's end to vibrate. With a deep breath, the general sifted through some choice words but chose to keep his composure in his present company and lightly returned the handset to the receiver.

With another grimace and a snort, the general lifted the stack of papers off his desk and removed the orange bordered cover sheet. All capital letters formed a nearly consistent chain of acronyms for several pages. Following the military message traffic, a few photos captured high-angle images of a few of these invading machines.

The general's thoughts were mixed. He wondered where they came from and what their intentions were, but he also wondered about why, if these things were all over the place, only a few were to be targeted instead of all of them.

He huffed and tongued his bottom teeth. Then he stood, closed the stack of papers and handed them back to the pilot.

"Son, I'd wish this on no one." His earnest voice trailed with a bit of country twang. "But if there's anyone who could do it, you can. So give 'em hell."

Boots smacked together as the pilot snapped to attention and saluted. As soon as the general returned the gesture, the pilot spun and charged out the door and down the hall toward the octagon-shaped aircraft bay.

Yellow light roamed the glass walls as a horn blared an annoying set of two tones. Crews scrambled to get equipment carts off the bay floor while a few disconnected cables from the bottom of the triangular silver craft. From the low-profile cockpit canopy, a long pole descended to the floor, sprouting pegs every several feet.

It was to this ladder that the pilot dashed, then he stopped to fold and stuff the papers he held into a chest pocket and don his helmet. He climbed into the seat, and as the canopy slid over his head, the ladder folded itself into a self-closing compartment in the side of the fuselage.

The few remaining people on the bay floor dragged the last of the cables away from the craft. As soon as everything was clear, the floor jerked and then began its smooth ascent.

On the surface, the doors of a large hangar opened. From the maw blasted the silver craft, which needed no runway to take flight, and it climbed into the sky.

Larin yanked open another locker and started pulling weapons and placing them in Oz's waiting arms.

"You guys are not going to believe this," Mac spoke to everyone, even those not in the room, "but new mechs have landed, and they appear to be Corps mechs."

"About frapping time," Larin belted audibly as well as through the team's communications link. "Little late to the party."

"Well, if they're here already," Oz asked, "then what does it matter if we get this approval they want so bad?"

"They're likely here just as a defense measure and to help level the field a bit," Paloon injected mentally from across the underground compound.

"Won't that make our task a bit harder?" Oz's point made Larin snort as if to say such situations were common.

"It just means we need to hurry even more," Lyon commented from somewhere on the surface. *"It doesn't change the fact that we need jurisdictional approval, even if it's after the fact."*

With that, Oz turned with his arms full of weapons and headed for the tunnel. As he approached, a strange sense of dread snuck from the recesses of his mind and flared, sending a shiver down his spine and forcing his face and hands into a cold sweat. It was just fear of the unknown getting the better of him; at least, that was what Oz tried to tell himself to get control of it, but before he could, he screamed and crumpled to the floor, sending the weapons clattered in every direction.

"What was that?" Lyon yelled back.

Paloon and Julie also heard it and ran into the tunnel from the other end.

"Oz has collapsed," Paloon reported.

"Why?"

Julie scanned the area to try to find an answer for Lyon. "I don't know. I'm not picking up anything." Then she looked down at Oz. "Whoa! He's hot—I mean as in active. His brain is in overdrive."

"I knew it," Larin commented with the same sincerity he showed by refusing to respond to Oz's screams. *"We should have killed him."*

"Knock it off, Larin," Lyon ordered. *"Julie, can you help?"*

"I don't know." She faintly shook her head while studiously peering into Oz's brain. "It's a jumbled mess in there right now."

Faint images flashed through Oz so fast as to blur into mutated impressions that could not be rooted in reality. The overall theme seemed centered on his work on that classified aircraft. However, it all came too fast to make sense.

Gradually, Oz regained control and tried to stand.

"Are you all right, man?" Paloon offered a hand.

Oz stammered, "I don't know."

"What are you seeing?" Julie inquired softly.

Oz shook his head. "I don't know. It doesn't make sense. It's just this extremely strong feeling that something very terrible just happened."

"Welcome to the frapping war, kid. Terrible things happen."

"Larin," belted Lyon, *"this is your last warning: Shut up!"* He calmed his voice before addressing the others. *"Can you help him into the tank?"*

"Yeah," responded Paloon, who already had Oz on his feet.

"That means, Larin," Lyon returned, *"that you're taking his seat with the yaks, and if you complain, I'll have you follow them on foot."*

⋖♦♦♦♦♦♦♦♦♦⌖♦♦♦♦♦♦♦♦♦⋗

Agent Kim closed his cell phone and stuffed it, with his fist, in his overcoat pocket.

"The Nubius should be on the way," he reported.

Across the roof, Burn never lowered the binoculars she gazed through.

"It had better be," she stated. "That general is one step away from being fired, and I'd happily do it personally." Her voice trailed as she resumed concentrating on the skies.

Kim turned to look in the same direction as his supervisor. He didn't need the magnification to see the huge mechanical beast appearing between the gaps of the skyscrapers and strolling through the streets as if it owned the town. This second wave was unexpected. Kim stopped himself. Maybe it wasn't a second wave; maybe they had nothing to do with each other.

"Who are they?" he asked.

"If I knew that, I wouldn't be so irritated." Burn thought about that statement. "I take that back; I just might be. But one thing's for certain, they are peeing in my pool, so they've got to go."

For a moment, Kim watched Burn, who continued to gaze through the binoculars at the Dragon Corps mech marching about so confidently.

"We've done all we can for now," Kim stated and stared toward the distant mech. "There are other issues at hand."

Burn lowered the binoculars. Her partner spoke the truth, so she had to stifle her frustration for now.

"Your informant had better be telling the truth," she stated.

Kim nodded. "He's legit." He stuffed his other fist in his coat pocket and raised his right brow at Burn. "Now we have the chance to succeed where the others failed."

"In that case," Burn commented while heading for the rooftop door, "let's go say hello."

Kim quietly followed.

On the outskirts of the city, traffic on a highway bypass screamed to a standstill. At the head of the traffic jam were multi-car accidents caused by rubbernecking drivers who couldn't pull their eyes off the two, large, weapon-toting robots taking a stroll down the median of the eight-lane highway.

The one in front moved cautiously, with its hand-cannon at the ready. The other walked backwards to watch the rear. Both were bluish silver and sported Grey Wolf logos painted on their upper left arms.

This particular battery of light Dragon Corps mechs had made it to the surface intact. But on the way down, they had seen movement.

"Where is it?" called the pilot of the rear mech. *"My scopes are blank."*

"I don't care what our scopes say," the battery commander in the lead replied, *"I know what I saw."*

To the left of their position, across four lanes of stalled traffic, a tall wall of fabricated rock plateaued into a series of large buildings flanked by a small park. From behind the front building of red brick, a metallic brown mech stepped around and launched a volley of missiles but not before the battery commander noticed the movement. He dropped his lead mech to its knees, and an electronic shield flared from its left arm.

As the missiles erupted into a torrent of fire and concussion waves that pushed around the halted vehicles on the road, the commander whipped his hand-cannon around and let several score of rounds rip into the general direction of the attacker, who ducked back behind the building.

"Coward," the commander cussed as he stood and leaped over the traffic, his partner immediately following.

When they reached the wall, fire gushed from their feet, sending them up to the higher level.

"I've still got nothing on the scopes."

"Forget about the scopes," the commander ordered. *"They're obviously blocking them."* He eased his way toward the corner of the building where the attacker had appeared. *"Looks like we're going to have to do this the old fashioned way, so keep your eyes up and open."*

The side of the building exploded into a chunky rain of brick, glass and steel followed by hundreds of high-velocity rounds that pounded into the chest of the second Dragon Corps mech. The attack sent it flying off the plateau and toward the lower mass of vehicles and people, who wisely decided to stop gawking and run.

The commander moved to take advantage of the situation, and he jumped around the building and released his entire chest-load of missiles. The pirate mech shot straight into the sky, and the missiles zoomed on by as if nothing had ever been there. The missiles continued for a couple of blocks before they obliterated an office building that none of its employees liked working in anyway.

Before the commander could wonder why the missiles didn't lock, he found himself vulnerable. He dropped to one knee and threw up his electronic shield in time to stop most of the rounds from the enemy mech that now floated to the ground. He rolled out of the line of fire, sprang to his feet and leapt to the top of a building. As he charged down the length of the roof, he fired blindly into the alley with his cannon. He reached the far end and looked about for his target.

A bolt of blue tore from the sky and crashed into the commander's back. The force sent the mech over the buildings and toward the highway below. The commander's partner rolled out of the way just in time for the mech to plow, head-first, into the dirt of the median.

As the two toppled mechs fought to regain their feet, a silver triangle zoomed overhead.

"What's that?"

"A nasty pest," the commander replied as he struggled to get out of the crater, his mech visibly shaking. *"That shot darn near fried all my circuits."* When he looked up to see the ship in the sky, he turned to his partner who was now sitting on his butt, leaning against the wall. *"Well, don't just sit there! Shoot the damn thing!"*

He let two rockets fly, but they soared past their target when the silver triangle made an unnaturally sharp turn and returned, belching another blue lighting bolt. The second mech got its shield up in time, but the attack seemed nonstop.

"Mayday, mayday," the commander called on all Dragon Corps frequencies, *"this is Vagrant Battery Charlie Niner, we are in a world of shit."*

"Charlie Niner," came the reply, *"this is Citadel Battery Tango Four, could you be more specific? What does the shit look like, and where is it?"*

"Within two hundred meters of my position, we have one ground mech and one aircraft. We are unable to lock on either. We have one mech crippled; ammo is running low."

"Stand by, Charlie Niner. Help is inbound."

On the command deck of the Tranquility's Wrath, Wakanda turned to her partner. "What in the hells are you doing?"

"You heard them," Lyloda replied, "they need help."

She glared forcefully at him then pointed out the window. A couple thousand feet down the road, the mech that had flattened the stadium was now recklessly charging toward them.

"We just found him." Urgency filled her voice. "*I* need your help."

"So do they." Lyloda glanced at the charging enemy. "Keep him busy for a moment."

"What?" she spat then yelped as the attacker sent two highly explosive greeting cards flying her way. Wakanda turned the Wrath backward to present a flat profile and then backpedaled into a cross street, taking out several cars, a vacant newspaper stand and one screaming idiot who was too busy filming the scene with his cell phone to get out of the way.

The missiles rocketed past and tore out the side of a glass skyscraper. As they did, two of the six doors marking the center of the Wrath's lower chest popped open and burped forth a pair of bobsled-shaped missiles. Both dropped a few feet before sprouting wings and roaring to life. They rose high and arced to the right on their piloted path to the edge of the city.

At the missiles' destination, the commander of the Vagrant battery had a difficult decision. His partner was under a ceaseless onslaught from the flying triangle and getting pushed into the ground.

"I'm about to red line."

"Hang in there," the commander encouraged. With resolution he lifted his hand-cannon toward the craft and fired several bursts in its direction.

As he expected, the aircraft deftly dodged the rounds with several sharp jerks, but it also stopped firing. It shot farther away, dropped low and zoomed up the highway toward the crippled commander. His mech didn't have enough energy to get out of the hole fast enough, so he held his ground and activated his shield. The sheet of electrons only came to life in splotchy patterns that exploded when the bolt of lightening struck.

From the Wrath, Lyloda piloted his missiles using the holographic screens in front of him. If the target couldn't be detected by scans, then he'd have to rely on the missiles' onboard cameras. Besides, with quantum antimatter missiles the key wasn't precision but vicinity.

Lyloda's screens shook as he rocked around in his chair. "Hey, you think you can keep it a bit stable? I'm flying here."

Wakanda scowled. "Bite me, blue boy."

She slid the Wrath to a stop from its jog down the street. A few blocks down the road, the enemy mech glided into place without missing a beat and launched a few missiles. She ducked the Wrath behind a building, which took the brunt of the attack but not before having a really bad day.

"You know, you could help."

Lyloda glanced beyond his monitors then back. "You're doing fine. Give me a moment."

About to cuss at Lyloda, Wakanda switched and cursed her attacker who appeared in front of her again.

From his screen, Lyloda could see the distressed mechs in the distance as one detonated into a shower of metal and fire. The attacking aircraft dragged the lightening bolt across the ground and traffic toward the other mech that had just weakly gotten to its feet before getting bashed into a concrete wall from the bolt's force.

Lyloda engaged one missile's afterburners sending it shrieking toward the silver triangle, which halted its attack and darted away, but not it time. Lyloda detonated the missile, which was replaced by a globe of multi-colored sparks that consumed everything within a thousand feet, to include the highly advanced terran aircraft.

"Splash one," Lyloda reported.

After that, the ground mech wasn't hard to miss. It had been standing in the tiny park watching the battle below in amusement, but with the ship destroyed, it ducked behind some buildings.

Lyloda tapered his remaining missile's yield down to several hundred feet and sent it rocketing over the highway then whipping around the building's corner and right up the retreating mech's ass.

"Splash two."

The resulting explosion sliced divots into the nearby buildings and the street, but that was a small price to pay, considering.

"Thanks," came the remaining Dragon Corps mech.

"Not a problem," Lyloda replied. *"Sorry I couldn't make it sooner."*

"Look," Wakanda barked as she fired a volley of heavy bullets toward the corner of a building, behind which the enemy mech dodged, "if you're done playing, I could use your help over here."

Chapter 16

High above the planet, the travel-weary crew of the dreadnought Nebuchadrezzar patiently watched the scanners and listened for any additional direction from the Shingi. Since the Nebuchadrezzar had trekked from dextian space with its entire battle fleet, the Shingi felt it best to pass recommendations rather than orders to the ship's skipper.

"The Shingi requests that we to assume formation Comet Five to fill the top of their Nebula Three," reported an officer from the operations floor.

"Make it so," the skipper ordered.

The officer relayed the command to the Nebuchadrezzar's fleet as others continued with announcements.

"Sir, reports are coming in that almost all ground forces have made violent contact."

He knew the pirates must also be aware of that situation, which meant they would be positioning themselves and watching the Dragon Corps fleet. If they did, they would see the fleet breaking its previous fixed orbit and moving closer toward the moon.

"What is the status of the rogues?"

"No change," reported an officer. "They remain in formation behind the moon."

This didn't make sense. They were either blind or up to something. Were they planning to use the moon as a shield? If they did, they would be as good as trapped. There had to be something else, but what?

"Are you sure?"

"I've tripled checked the systems, and nothing has moved in the past three hours."

"How soon until we clear the apogee?"

"Five minutes. Shall I raise shields?"

"Not yet. Raise them in four. Let's save as much energy as possible while we can."

"Sir! I have an energy peak directly in front of us."

"How far out?"

"Undetermined."

The crew had run out of time to react. At the very edge of the blue-and-white marble below, the planet's atmosphere split open and spewed forth a large, blue beam of fire that raced straight for the massive warship, splitting the Nebuchadrezzar cleanly in half.

Amidst the quickly dispersing fire blooms and glittering bits of wreckage, a few life pods started launching from the severed halves of the hull. However, not many fighters cleared the chutes without crashing.

"Bloody hell," exclaimed Elder Kyston from her command chair aboard the Shingi. "They shot straight through the atmosphere."

Her shock had brought her to the edge of her seat. She had never seen anything like it. Heck, she didn't even think it was possible. But there, in one shot, she had just lost nearly a quarter of her firepower.

"I'm rightly pissed off!" She stood and started barking orders. "Did they move?"

"Negative, ma'am. Scans show the entire enemy fleet directly behind the moon."

"Right good those scans do us. Guess we'll do this the old fashioned way." Her eyes momentarily tensed in concentration. "Flank and raise the cruisers. Have them fire as soon as they see the glint of metal. Send the destroyers in low and fast. Have them hold short for the cruisers' fire."

"Aye, aye!"

Aboard the Trafalgar, Theta Wing commander, Hunter G-Vin, stared out a portal window in irritated horror at the destruction of the Nebuchadrezzar. Flashing green lights and klaxons blended with the chaos behind him, but G-Vin didn't care. He wanted revenge.

"Trafalgar control, this is Theta Wing command," the su-vol called through his internal radio, *"request to launch and act freely."*

"Request denied, Theta Wing," replied an indifferent voice. *"Hold fire, repeat, hold fire, wait for command and fighter instructions."*

"Fuck command," G-Vin shot back, but no one replied.

Gunner crews watched intently at the very edge of the white-lined blue planet below, and it came. A shimmer. The entire pirate fleet was far from where it should have been, behind the moon. In fact, the fleet was much closer and ready for war.

Every rail cannon on the six Dragon Corps cruisers blasted in rapid fire, each hurling large metal pellets to hammer to death anything in their paths.

G-Vin could sense the vibrations through the hull of the Trafalgar at it sailed under the shelling cruisers. He immediately opened another communications link.

"Trafalgar control, this is Theta Wing command."

"Go, Theta Wing command."

"Request permission to launch and act freely."

"Denied, Theta Wing. Other fighters are defending the Trafalgar. We do not need Theta Wing at the moment, rest and wait for orders."

G-Vin stormed down the corridor. He had never taken well to "no" as an answer to any request in his life.

"Trafalgar control, this is Theta Wing command, reconsider my request for launch."

"Standby, Theta Wing."

The now mildly irritated voice of the controller cut off for several minutes. Another speaker returned.

"Theta Wing command, this is Trafalgar command, please remain on standby at your post. We do not—"

A door to the bridge flew open, and through it stormed the short, green-feathered G-Vin.

"Don't shit on me, Dave!"

Elder Dave Killian rose just in time to stare down at G-Vin, who stopped just inches from his chest. G-Vin's smaller height didn't make him appear any less menacing.

"Look, K'lib," Killian began, "I can't let you go. I don't have the order, and I want to keep you here until needed."

"In case you didn't get the invitation, there's a war out there," G-Vin half yelled. "I don't give a damn about waiting for orders; they need as much firepower out there as possible. Now, I'm taking my wing, and we're heading out there. Either open those launch doors or I'll blast them open."

G-Vin headed back for the door but halted and faced Killian again. "You best launch everything you've got and start joining the fight before you get your crew killed." With that, he spun and bolted for the door and sent the order, *"Theta Wing, prepare for launch."*

Back in the Trafalgar fighter bay, crews scrambled at such a frenzied pace that a few even resorted to leaping over crouched workers in order to take more direct routes to their next locations. Some fighters were already piloted, prepped and raised to the flight deck; others were not far behind.

G-Vin jogged to his fighter, the Demonic Dove; snatched his waiting helmet from the hands of his crew chief and leapt into the cockpit almost without the need of the ladder. He immediately went through his own series of systems checks, disregarding any advice from his crew chief. G-Vin felt he knew his craft better than anyone and could perform the procedures in less than half the time.

Without warning, he engaged the platform and raised himself to join his waiting wingmen on the flight deck. None of them would even consider disrespecting their commander by not offering him the first launch and lead in the formation.

G-Vin lifted his fighter from the deck and pivoted toward the launch tube. *"This is how it's going to go down,"* he radioed to his entire wing. *"Fire at will. If you need to break off to help someone else, so be it; however, do your best to stay with me. Keep your eyes up and off your screens, don't second guess your natural reaction and you'll make it back. Now let's show these punks how our pack does business."*

Multiple howls roared into the team's communications channel as G-Vin's Demonic Dove blasted toward and through the launch tube.

The darkness of the tube gave way to the brightness of the battle. Hundreds of beams, lasers and missiles painted deadly webs around which the multitude of fighters had to navigate as they shot at one another. Explosions from confirmed kills added to the visual mayhem, along with the multi-colored flashes from the larger vessels' shields as they absorbed hits or prematurely detonated missiles. But not all shields succeeded.

The constant pounding from the rail cannons finally made it through the Ranklin's shield and hammered the hull. The result sent the pirate station tilting just as it was finally charged and ready for its second shot. The blue bolt veered from its intended target and started cutting an angled swath through space, wiping out fighters from both sides and inadvertently cutting a different Dragon Corps cruiser in half.

G-Vin scanned the scene as quickly as possible. It appeared that the Dragon Corps cruisers were almost completely focused on firing at the space station, but it was the massively lurking Trioki that gave G-Vin a chill that shot down his feathered spine. The Envoy class battleship was even larger than a Dragon Corps dreadnought. The Trioki currently had a Corps cruiser and two destroyers locked in combat while taking out any fighter that came within a hundred miles.

By the look of it, the cruiser and destroyers wouldn't last too much longer, after which the Trioki would continue until it could get a clean shot at the Shingi. If that happened, the battle would be minutes away from lost.

The situation was not new to the pilots of Theta Wing. As an independently operating fighter unit, they were continually in and out of conflicts, not too different from hired mercenaries. When they weren't fighting, they were training on how to fight. While they had never faced an Envoy before, their leader had a plan.

When the last fighter reported a successful launch, G-Vin relayed his thoughts. *"Engage all systems. Go in fast then drop low on my lead. Give me a flat indigo formation. On my mark, hold fire and break for the flanks. Pop for a transom approach. That big guy's ours."*

A round of various confirmations was muffled by the hundreds of thrusters roaring to full power in seconds. In a few seconds more, Theta Wing was dodging fire. Over the years, G-Vin had learned not to rely on his screens. Now, by just the tones in his head, he could instinctively tell what kind of incoming fire his fighter had detected and from what direction. While it could be deafening for the uninitiated, fighter pilots either learned to live with it or die.

With one hand on each of the horizontal control sticks that protruded from the walls of his cockpit, G-Vin fought to keep forward momentum as he ducked and dodged fire from both enemy and friendly forces. Though it sent him and the Demonic Dove in nearly every direction in all positions, evading long-distance weapons fire was the easy part. His eyes soon locked on to something far more dangerous, and he barely had time to shout, *"Incoming,"* before the enemy fighters began firing.

Theta Wing immediately returned fire and began chasing the enemy fighters, which resembled flattened tin cans. It quickly became apparent that Theta Wing's fighters had superior maneuverability as they picked off the approaching force while only taking one loss in second squad and one in the third.

G-Vin heard those squadron commanders call out for search and rescue forces as he noticed the enemy leader kicking in the hyperthrusters and diving to try to avoid Theta Wing. He opened the top-rear thruster and the two lower-forward thruster to pitch his ship to track his firing.

"Make a hole," he ordered as the enemy broke the lower plane of Theta Wing's formation.

His fellow fighters split as G-Vin dragged his laser fire up to meet the fleeing craft, which bloomed in a quickly dispersing orange fireball.

G-Vin half yawned as he spun his fighter around in time to notice the last of the enemy fighters succumbing to his wing's firepower. It had been easier than he expected. He wondered that if during his time in the Dragon Corps the Council had put too much emphasis on combat vessels and had ignored fighter development, but those thoughts disappeared as another off-aim blue bolt from the Ranklin shot overhead and passed to take a chunk out of the top of the Trafalgar, sending the crippled craft in a deadly spiral toward the planet.

Suddenly higher than he wanted to be, G-Vin banked low and steep while continually dodging the latticework of fire. What he saw through the mesh was a pleasant surprise. Nearly two wings of heavy pirate fighters that resembled cross-shaped rods were hugging the planet. Someone had beaten G-Vin to the idea.

They must be heading for the Shingi, he thought. *Too bad for them.*

"Sierra Six," he ordered, as his fighters quickly complied.

Two squadrons formed a cross as the other two formed an X. As one leg of the cross slid snugly in an open gap of the X, G-Vin took his position on the opposite side of the X.

The enemy fighters still hadn't noticed them, so G-Vin couldn't help but release a mildly maniacal laugh as he gave the command to fire by discharging his own weapons. Soon the entire wing rained laser fire. If it wasn't for trying to keep formation while still dodging fire between the larger vessels, it would have been too easy.

A few were able to respond in time to get off a couple of lucky shots, but the last enemy fighter took a shot through the canopy as Theta Wing broke through the ceiling of heavy weapons fire to replace the enemy formation that had been there just moments ago.

As he hit the upper atmosphere, G-Vin ordered, *"Break."* He pulled his fighter up and level as the wing broke in two. Each part clustered in diamonds of three ships each and began their paths around the crown of the planet.

The canopy of combat continued to flicker above as one Corps cruiser finally shot off one of the firing prongs of the crippled Ranklin, but they were still taking damaging fire from the station's other weapon systems. Some Corps destroyers attempted to move in for the kill, but they were soon confronted by a few enemy destroyers that had been hiding behind the station, apparently for this very purpose.

A flash of white drew G-Vin's attention to his left. He could barely make out the sides of the Trioki as he circled around underneath it. The dissipating beam of light came from the front of the Trioki.

Amid the cacophony of radio chatter, G-Vin heard, *"The Shingi has been hit; it's not responding."*

Those words finally sent G-Vin's adrenaline pumping as he

slammed the throttle open to send the Demonic Dove skipping over the surface of the atmosphere in flashes of fire. He risked damaging his lower thrusters but didn't care.

G-Vin fought with the shaking craft until he could no longer see the side of the Trioki, then he shot straight up from the planet. With that momentum keeping him going, he spun his fighter around to face the rear of the Trioki.

Its massive thrusters were still ignited in their struggle to move the enormous ship, and that was just what G-Vin had hoped for. As he came to stop directly behind the Trioki, he looked to the left to watch two of his squadrons lift up and level with his craft. With a look to the right, he saw his other two squadrons doing the same.

A devious smile crept across his stark white face as he looked forward again, then he released a battle yell as he charged forward, leading his entire wing directly into the blaze of the Trioki's thrusters. Just as the heat started to make the Demonic Dove's metal skin glow, the entire wing blasted away to force the emergency valves on the thrusters to close. But by this time, they had snuck past the shields and fanned out.

"First and third, cover fire. Second and fourth, mine it," G-Vin directed as he popped over the rear edge of the Trioki then dropped to closely follow the hull but not before the ship's anti-aircraft batteries had turned around and opened fire on this wing. A few fighters lost it early, but the rest quickly adapted, swishing back and forth as they returned fire.

Soon the cannon blisters that protruded from the hull started erupting in fire at a more rapid rate than the wing's fighters as G-Vin led the formation in a corkscrew pattern around the mammoth ship. The fighters in the rear squadrons dropped large canisters from their bellies in a chaotically methodical pattern that followed the twisting flight path. Instantly, the bombs magnetically clung to the hull.

"Mines away," reported the second squadron commander.

"Second and forth, take lead. First and third, finish."

The rear formations bounded over and took some losses as they adjusted to returning fire.

Approaching the lower bow of the Trioki, G-Vin noticed a larger-than-normal blister of metal that wasn't spewing blaster fire. It had to be the command center.

He let the rest of his wing continue with the mine laying as he jerked on the controls and yanked the Demonic Dove into a hard circular bank to the left. G-Vin pulled it in tighter and tighter until he planted a ring of mines around it.

As the second report of *"Mines away"* rang in his head, G-Vin leveled and snapped straight up to face the planet below.

"Pull out," he ordered and shot forward into the atmosphere.

G-Vin spun around to make sure the remainder of the wing was out of range as he sent the detonation signal. Slowly at first, then in rapid succession, the mines exploded in a fiery ring that nearly dissected the immense vessel. Immediately, hundreds of panels shot in all directions then the compounded effects of the mines cut off entire chunks that began helplessly floating away. As a finale, G-Vin's tightly packed mines flared into a column of fire that almost burned through to the opposite end of the hull.

He had lost nearly half of his wing, but seeing the lights and blasters of the crippled Trioki fade from existence made it worth it.

Chapter 17

Hitook and Larin sat across from Yabuki and Rin in the back of the large car, the driver and Taichi sitting in the front. Regardless of Larin's questions, Rin never reacted except to quickly look at Hitook every time the large beast shifted. Even though the car's backseat was designed for six people, Hitook's presence made it mildly cramped.

The car came to a stop as Yabuki finished talking on his cell phone. Since the entire conversation had been in Japanese, Larin could only understand a few words.

"So was that your boss?" Larin asked.

Though an innocent question, Yabuki felt irritated. "Yes."

Yabuki's curtness was lost on the rolbrid. Larin was about to ask another question when the front passenger door opened.

"What is it?" Yabuki called to the driver.

"There is a traffic jam, Yabuki-san," answered the driver. "There are also some fires ahead; Taichi-san is taking a look."

"Yabuki-san," Taichi cried out, then stuck his head back into the car, "we might have a problem. Traffic has stalled in all lanes, and there appears to be some kind of rioting up ahead. Cars are overturned and set on fire, and it's blocking all traffic."

"What's the deal?" Lyon asked wirelessly.

"Apparently a riot," Larin replied.

"Mac, do you have anything?"

The computer responded to Lyon. *"The police frequencies are full of reports of violent riots, looting and general mayhem throughout the city; this appears to be the case around the world as well. There's an overall 'end-of-the-world' fear that's growing with every flash in the sky and every report of fighting between large robots."*

"Is there any way around?" Yabuki asked, oblivious to the mental conversation.

"There doesn't appear to be," Taichi replied before retreating to the outside once again. "No. Cars are turned in every direction trying to get out, and no one's moving."

"Larin," Lyon called, *"how far away are we?"*

Larin translated the request to Yabuki. "How far until we reach your contact?"

"About eight blocks," Yabuki answered. "Why?"

Larin ignored him. *"Eight blocks."*

"Is his contact still there?"

"Can you confirm that your contact is still waiting?"

Yabuki leered for a moment then started dialing. The conversation turned to Japanese and soon seemed heated, but Larin couldn't tell if it truly was an argument or just the emphasis on how the words were pronounced.

"He is still waiting for us," Yabuki replied as he slid the phone into an inside pocket of his suit coat. "There is some rioting nearby, but he reports that the parking garage is still safe."

As Yabuki spoke, Larin thought the words so he could relay them back to Lyon in as near to real time as possible.

"I need directions."

Larin verbalized Lyon's need. "How do we get there from here?"

"West two blocks, south two blocks then west again for four blocks."

"Got that," Lyon stated. *"Now I need a name."*

"What's the contact's name?"

"Igarashi Shiro."

With that information, Lyon began giving orders that Larin spoke for his current company's benefit.

"Lyon says that they are going to go on ahead, and that we are to dismount and proceed through the traffic on foot."

Before Larin finished, Hitook already had the door open and exited the cramped space to stretch.

"I'm not being left behind," Yabuki stated. "If they're getting around this traffic, so are we."

Larin pointed to the sunroof. "Unless your car can do that, we're going on foot."

As Yabuki glanced up to see Paloon fly the station wagon tank overhead, Larin followed Hitook out of the car and toward the truck to retrieve their gear.

Normally the crowd would have taken notice of Hitook's abnormal size, but this time, the attention of amazed eyes and agape mouths was directed instead to the flying station wagon.

As Paloon piloted them overhead, Oz leaned as close to the window as possible to gaze down at the mayhem. Some stalled drivers and passengers watched in wonder, others ran for it, and a few mindlessly joined in the sprints, only to fail miserably in their attempts to hurdle the nearby cars. While some just seemingly ran amok with no direction, setting fire to anything they could like free-range pyromaniacs, others systematically worked together to break into stores and haul away as much as they could carry.

"This is insane," Oz commented, just as someone leveled a shotgun at an unsuspecting looter carrying a stack of boxed laptop computers. "Oh shit! He just shot him in the back; they're going nuts down there."

"That's expected," Paloon calmly stated with a tone that assured anyone listening that he had seen such things many times before. "It's only going to get worse until we can—Hey!"

Sparks sprang from the vehicle's front right fender.

"Are they shooting at me?"

Lyon took a nonchalant glance out his window to see someone on the street with a rifle pointed in their direction. "Looks like it."

"Idiots," Paloon muttered as he pulled the tank up and banked to the left to fly over the buildings.

As they rose above the roofs, Julie was the first to notice the horizon filling with smoke from a few large fires scattered about the city. "Working to get jurisdictional approval seems a moot point. This place is already a war zone, jurisdiction or not."

With that, Oz leaned to his left to see what he could out Julie's window. Lyon also casually glanced to his left, but he had already started to respond. "We still have our orders, and we'll carry them out." His voice trailed slightly as he took in the meaning of the devastation around the city. "I just hope this contact is still there and can get us into that building."

"Heck," Julie snidely replied, "let's hope this building is still intact and these leaders haven't buried themselves in some secret hideout."

The vehicle dipped as Paloon announced, "We're here." Then they hit the top deck of the parking garage a little hard, but the shocks took the brunt of the landing as the tires released short squeals.

"Well," Paloon commented to no one, "I've had better landings."

As he hooked the vehicle around and headed down the exit ramp, Paloon slowed so everyone could follow their instinctive reactions and inspect every inch of the structure for anything suspicious. Even at slow speeds, the tires squawked as Paloon turned down the next ramp. The noise echoed around the empty concrete structure.

"This may just be me," Oz began, "but does anyone else feel like this place is unusually barren?"

"What do you mean?" Lyon genuinely asked.

"Well, for a parking garage in the middle of the city, there's not one single car."

Julie injected, "Don't forget there's a war going on, half the city is on fire and the population likely thinks it's the end of the world."

"What's that mean?" Oz didn't see the point.

Paloon answered. "It's a common reaction. It doesn't matter the race or planet, most beings will run for the hills, I believe you call it, when they think they are being invaded by some unknown alien force."

"The first thing they did was jump in their vehicles and ran toward anywhere but here," Julie clarified.

"Hold up," Paloon called as he turned the next corner and pointed toward a shadowed figure leaning against the back of a dark van. Behind it, a grey van sat, and several parking spots closer to the team, a white van rested. "Is this it?"

"It's the third deck." Lyon observed the white number in a green square next to a red stairwell door. "It must be."

Paloon slowed to a stop. As Lyon stepped out, the figure leaning on the van sprung vertical to face his guests.

Lyon spoke. "Are you Igarashi Shiro?"

"Everyone out of the vehicle," was the only response.

"We're friends of Yabuki Yumiro."

The stranger repeated his demand.

Lyon paused to evaluate the situation and determined the request as reasonable. "All right guys, come out and join me."

The rest of the team exited the vehicle; as they did, the stranger made another demand.

"Now take five steps forward from the front of your car."

Lyon delayed as he gave it a bit more thought, but he eventually complied.

When all four were finally in a line, another request came.

"Now, slowly unholster your weapons and place them on the ground with the barrels facing away from me."

"What's the point of this?" Lyon had serious reluctance toward surrendering his weapon. "We're friends of Yabuki Yumiro, who sent us here to see Igarashi Shiro. Yabuki is caught in traffic and will be here soon."

"I'm only looking out for my safety," the man said. "Now, please place your weapons on the ground with the barrels pointing away from me and take five steps back."

Lyon glared as he released a silent huff before unwillingly drawing his particle cannon from its thigh holster and placing it on the ground in the prescribed manner then stepping back. The others slowly followed.

"Now," Lyon began gruffly, "may we speak to Igarashi Shiro?"

The doors on all three vans exploded to disgorge a slue of hired guns. In seconds they had the team surrounded and didn't waiver. keeping their weapons trained on the group.

Lyon tensed his brow. "This best be a joke."

"It's no joke," the man assured. "I'm Igarashi, but—"

"But he doesn't work for Yabuki," came another voice from a man who stepped from behind a concrete pillar. Dark shades covered his eyes, his hands were hidden in the pockets of a black trench coat and his loafers echoed as he stepped. "Igarashi actually works for me. It's through loyal people such as Igarashi that we can keep tabs on certain activities."

"Who the hell are you?" Lyon challenged.

"Agent Kim, but you may call me Kim."

"Well, Kim, if your beef is with the yaks, you've just screwed yourself. We're not yaks, just acquaintances. So why don't you go take your investigation elsewhere."

"My interests in the yakuza are only to monitor the activities of much more interesting groups, such as your own." Agent Kim stepped closer to get a better look at Lyon's team. He stopped to look down at the row of particle cannons. With his right shoe, he indifferently pushed one behind him.

"What do you think you know about us?" Lyon demanded.

"Little, actually. You weren't my primary assignment, but it appears that your little band here made short work of their leader. Which is impressive, to say the least," Kim chuckled mildly.

Lyon failed to see the humor. The words had a deep meaning. Whoever this person was, he was too confident in knowing about his team and about Horwhannor's group. "Whom do you work for?"

"That's not important. Besides, you should know this already. If you don't, then that's just another reason why I'm in this position and not you."

"I hate this vague shit, so just tell me what you want so I can get to the post office before it closes."

"You're bold; I'll give you that." Kim took another step toward Oz. "I believe it is you I'm after, Manuel Ozuna."

Oz reeled, but it was Lyon who objected. "Wait one fucking minute; why in the hell is everyone after this terran?"

Agent Kim removed his glasses and gradually turned his head to lock gazes with Lyon. The entire team immediately noticed it, but it was Oz who spoke first.

"You're not human."

Kim turned back to Oz. "Neither are you, technically. But it doesn't matter what they've done to you; now is the time to return you to the flock."

As Kim began to reach for Oz, Julie jerked and lurched forward, only to find the barrel of a very large-muzzled weapon suddenly in her face. At the far end of the barrel, Agent Crisostomo's smiling face beamed back.

Kim disengaged his attempt to seize Oz. "Everyone, meet my partner. We just call her, Burn. She's quite quick when she wants to be, and she's a bit trigger happy."

It was obvious that Burn wasn't terran either. Julie growled at her, but Burn just smiled back with the calm pleasantness of a serial killer. "Don't push your luck." Burn pounded the point of the weapon into Julie's chest. "Get your fuzzy butt back."

The dextian gradually complied but didn't drop the fanged snarl.

Overall the situation appeared more grim every second. Lyon raced for ideas and went with his gut. *"Mac, patch in a line to the Shingi. Meanwhile, set up while I keep this jerk talking."*

"You're not taking him anywhere," Lyon nearly yelled, "until you tell me why everyone is after this guy."

Kim clenched his lips and breathed through his nose. "I wish it hadn't been like this, but you can only blame yourselves. If your kind," Kim shifted his gaze to Paloon then back to Lyon, "hadn't turned tail and betrayed your creator then there would be no need for me."

"What do you mean?"

"Oh my." Kim leaned back on his heels. "Don't tell me you didn't know we were working for the same team all this time. I guess they do like keeping their soldiers in the dark."

Lyon didn't believe it, but he asked anyway. "You're atlantian?"

Kim couldn't help but laugh. "Yes but no, not like you mean it."

"What's that supposed to mean?"

Stress began to line Kim's face. The subject had a special place in Kim's heart, and the emotion showed. "We're your replacements. We're the new breed—improved over your inferior kind, which turned down the job and ran to the stars like the cowards that you are."

None of this was making any sense to Lyon. "What in the hell are you talking about?"

"Look," Kim charged Lyon and approached a little too close, "let me educate your ignorant self. Take a wild guess what 'atlantian' means in the native language."

"I don't know what you're talking about, and would you please back off?"

"It means 'slave master.' That's right, you cowards are running around the universe calling yourself slave masters, and you don't even know it." Kim finally took a couple of steps back and forced himself to calm. "However, we're the only true atlantians any more."

Confusion made Lyon glance around for a solid thought to grasp. As he did, a voice blasted into his head.

"Shingi Control here."

Lyon visibly snapped as he recalled why he had called the ship.

"This is Knight Kendrick, I need to speak with Duke Chichiq."

"Stand by."

"What?" Kim inquired upon seeing Lyon jerk. "Is it coming back to you, or are you just shocked that you were replaced?"

"Neither," Lyon fumbled in his voice and thought. "You've still lost me on this whole 'slave master' bullshit; we don't make slaves of anyone."

"Not any more; your ancestors turned down the job. Weren't you listening?" Emotion, again, infused Kim's words. "But we're better than you. We love the power granted to us by our creators, and we do our job now by integrating with the slaves. We don't hide away like your kind did. We're in the thick of it.

"Granted," Kim continued. "I'll give your ancestors credit for the commandments and prophecies. They were strong and worked on this planet for several thousand years; they even still work somewhat to this very day, but they didn't completely hold. So we had to extend our reach beyond the church. With time, we infiltrated the educational systems to control what they learned and didn't learn. We gave them what they felt they wanted and used it against them. We pushed them to develop television then learned to influence them through that medium, and we're getting darn good at it. Now, we didn't abandon all that you did. We did learn from you and put someone with temporal lobe damage into a position of power from time to time, just for kicks, so we could sit back and watch the resulting war. Besides, it helps boost their technology toward being more capable."

Kim smirked as he reminisced. "It wasn't easy. We may have deviated a bit from complete blind obedience in wait for the city's return, but we did what we had to do. They ran amok after your cowardly departure, but we've returned control and kept the flock in check. In those whose logic overrode the programming, we nurtured complacency so that they don't even care about what's going on around them and feel that they can't change it. It's cleverly beautiful, really. Until you arrived, they were well on their way to fulfilling their destiny."

"Oh, is that so?" Lyon's sarcasm was wasted. "And what destiny is that?"

"To serve as the Army of the Gods," Kim stated matter-of-factly. "And they're so close to being ready; however, they are to be approached on our terms, not yours. They must serve their true creators as they were designed."

"Army of the Gods!?" Lyon refused to believe what his mind was concluding. "Gods!? What gods?" Lyon paused, leered and lowered his voice. "The p'tahians?"

Kim growled, "You're not worthy of even uttering that name."

Lyon's eyes widened. "You're crazy, legitimately certifiable."

The implications made the rest of Lyon's team visibly uneasy, and the conversation had infuriated Kim so much that he missed the sign, but Burn pointed it out.

"Check out the human," she directed with a jerk of her chin.

Kim looked, but it took a moment before he recognized the significance of Oz just standing there with only a shade of confused fear in his eyes.

The agent tongued his teeth as he snickered. "Aren't you a precious one? I can see now why they want you back."

Curiosity overpowered fear and twisted Oz's face. "What?"

Kim faintly huffed a laugh. "At the mention of that word you should be dead, at the very least in an irreversible coma, but there you are, very much alive."

"Why wouldn't I be?"

"It's part of what makes you not quite human and the next evolution in creating the obedient soldier, but you've resisted the programming somehow. We need to know why and correct that."

"I'm not your soldier, and I'm not going to be."

"We'll see about that, but either way, we've got the upper hand. Soon, the Gods will return, they'll finally get their revenge on the betrayers, and you'll either reintegrate into the army or die. The choice is yours."

"Duke Chichiq here," blasted the voice into Lyon's head, *"you had better have that jurisdiction."*

"We've run into a snag, and I need clarification."

"What possible clarification would you need?"

"The source of this jurisdictional approval, will the most informed agent of a government do?"

"Maybe, as a minimum, I don't see why not."

"Well, it's going to have to do."

Lyon spoke up, "Manual Quiet Storm Ozuna, as the duly designated agent from one of the leading governments on Terra Four, do you hereby authorize the transfer of jurisdiction of this planet and system to the Dragon Corps for protection and security?"

"Hey," Kim reached out and grabbed Oz, "you can't ask him."

"Why not?" Lyon challenged. "He's the only completely informed and untainted representative of this planet. Well, Oz, what's your answer?"

"Absolutely," Oz replied.

Lyon smirked. "Looks like you've just been usurped. Take him."

Kim's head bloomed into a mushroom of blood, bone and grey matter. Simultaneously, Taichi and Rin jumped into the scene to efficiently and effectively disarm each mercenary as they worked their way through the group. From behind, Hitook blasted from the stairwell with his twin blades in each hand and roaring at the top of his lungs; the shock allowed him time to close the distance and slice through the would-be attackers. The confusion gave Lyon, Paloon and Oz the opportunity to jump for their weapons while Julie sidestepped, grabbed Burn's weapon and rammed the butt into Burn's neck. As the agent stumbled back, her head also exploded.

In a few seconds the team had annihilated the threat.

Across the street, on the roof of a bank, Larin and Yabuki stood from their prone positions.

"You're not a bad shot," Larin complimented as he cleared and stored his weapon.

"Thank you," Yabuki replied as he also cleared his weapon. "And thank you for letting me have the first shot."

"Not a problem. You made it sound like a personal issue."

"It has been personal for some time now; he just proved to be more of a jerk than I had thought," Yabuki stated before leading Larin down the fire escape and across the street to the parking garage.

In the structure, Lyon re-holstered his weapon. *"So duke, there's your jurisdictional authority. Now get us off this rock."*

"Understood, you deserve it," Duke Chichiq replied. *"We'll dispatch a retrieval team to your location."*

"Hey," Mac injected, *"what about me? You just going to use me, abuse me and leave me?"*

Lyon sighed and thought. *"Duke, have the team meet us at my base."*

"As you wish, just get that government agent back here alive."

Chapter 18

The Shingi's bridge staff scrambled about in a ballet of controlled chaos. The shot from the Trioki had fried circuits and drained the ship's power supply in seconds, and its lifeless hull hid a frantic crew fighting to get systems back online.

Elder Rior Kyston's patience grew thin, but it was all she had. She leaned in her chair, her right cheek propped on a fist and her tail thumping against the left armrest of her command chair. Lost in apathetic irritation, she reacted slowly when the emergency lights flickered on.

"Ma'am, we finally have seventy percent auxiliary power," came the voice of one deck officer.

"Then get the displays up, and give me a status on the main systems," Kyston ordered.

As the hologram projectors fought to come to life, another officer offered, "We've found another blown conduit node. We've already depleted the supply; it's going to take a while to build a new one."

"Ma'am," came another voice, "we have a priority call for Duke Chichiq."

"It'll have to wait," she replied as she gradually leaned forward in her seat and attempted to make sense of the pixilated images on the hologram screens. "Get a line out. I want a status."

"Already on it, ma'am, and here it is."

"Elder Kyston?" a voice boomed with crackling audio. "Is your crew safe?"

"Yes, we're here and alive. Who's this, and what's your status?"

"We're so glad you're all right. This is Elder Picaron from the Sheshach. Right now, the Ranklin has been disabled and boarded. The Trioki has been fatally crippled and is in an uncorrectable descent. We've taken severe losses, however. In addition to the Nebuchadrezzar, we've lost the Aethiopia, Callicles and Trafalgar. However, we've crippled most of all the remaining major enemy vessels. The exception is a cruiser and two destroyers, but the North Star, Chimera and Chaos have them locked in a non-kinetic stalemate. We expect to have them boarded soon."

"Then," Kyston inquired as she grimaced at her screens, "why can't I see anything?"

"Oh," Picaron replied, "the Tikvah has been broadside at your bow to shield you since you went dead."

Kyston stood and evaluated the situation. With the battle nearly over, she allowed her thoughts to unfocus and her attention to drift slightly—until Duke Chichiq inched into view on her left. She shifted her dissociated gaze to Chichiq's general vicinity.

"May I take that call?" he asked.

A slight nod conveyed her consent as she casually scanned the bridge and holographic displays. The wrath of battle left deep, unavoidable wounds. Now, she had to face Fate.

"Move the Tikvah, so I can see."

The officers on the bridge quietly complied by transmitting the order. After a few moments, the long cruiser complied by firing its bow-side thrusters, swinging the vessel away like a door.

Where there was once a latticework of laser fire now was a sea of glittering debris. Dead fighters tumbled aimlessly, occasionally colliding with the remaining chunks of the metallic carcasses that had been larger combat vessels. The once mighty Trioki pitched forward in its uncontrolled descent as internal fires flickered through the few remaining port windows.

In the distance, she could discern the shapes of a handful of vessels, which must have been the remaining forces locked in a standoff. Even farther out, a few groups of Dragon Corps fighters continued to pick off the last of the pirate fighters as soon as they violated a request to cease fire and surrender.

A flash drew Kyston's attention to the planet below. The Trafalgar began to burn in the upper atmosphere as a few of the last life pods fired from the hull. She knew some would stay and fight to save the vessel, and they would surely die. All she could do was hope that all of this death had been worth it.

"Sheshach," she called, "what's the status on the surface?"

"We've suffered forty percent losses and estimate about five cities remain in pirate control. We're in the process of regrouping and moving a phalanx into each city. Estimated repossession is within twelve hours."

To the lower left, a couple of frigates moved into view to recover the life pods from the Trafalgar. As she watched, Kyston lost track of time. She snapped from her trance when the Shingi's main lights and systems kicked in.

"Ma'am," a deck officer needlessly reported, "the reroute worked. Power is restored to about eighty percent. All main systems are powered."

"Good. Launch everything to get out there and help," she ordered.

"Will do," returned multiple voices, as the bustle resumed.

"Elder Kyston."

The dextian turned to face the duke in response to his hail.

"We have jurisdiction," the flat faced huyin stated. "I need a retrieval team to secure the delegate."

A lot of good jurisdiction does now, she thought, but she conceded. "So be it. Launch the Beowulf and find some escorts from the stranded fighters. Priority two."

It only took seconds for the crew to the respond.

"Beowulf underway."

"Theta Wing has volunteered for escort."

"So be it," she half muttered, then cleared her voice. "This jurisdiction," she announced toward the duke, "is it worth all this?"

The question went unanswered, and she expected as much as she retuned to her chair. Before she could sit down, collective yells and calls jerked her attention to the screens.

From apparently nowhere, a gargantuan object appeared in orbit over the planet. The object was the size of—and looked a little like—two mountains, one inverted and connected at the base to the other.

On the bottom half, metallic blue crystalline pillars formed a tightly packed upended pyramid of haphazard design. Glittering streaks zipped about as if just under the surface of the crystal, yet every so often, they would leap from one semi-transparent, faceted pillar to another.

In juxtaposition to the apparent technology, the top half was a stone city with a smooth texture as if carved directly from a solid marble mountain. Fluted and twisted columns, supporting capitals engraved with vines and leaves, surrounded the complex structure that exponentially grew in height toward the center. The towers, spires and stacks of buildings all had an intricate network of external stairs and alleys that connected to the main system of roads that encircled the heart of the medieval metropolis.

The entire object glowed with a faint golden sheen. As it floated, a doppelgänger image of the object peeled from the original form, then rapidly flew away at great speed until no longer visible.

From the object came a resonance that penetrated every corner of all the ships in orbit down to the deepest cavern of the planet with a crisp, heavy voice.

"From the halls of Delphi to the streets of Asgard, your Gods have returned."

In a hundred different languages from millions of beings, the voice received a collective "What the fuck?" Though aware of the replies, the owner of the deep voice did not stop its pronouncement.

"You, who are so bold as to ignore and return, your actions hath arose us from our holy abode. In virtue of your sins, you have lost favor; therefore, return not, for you have touched evil, only to touch others.

"As you have forgotten us, we have forgotten. We, the true Gods, whom you have spurned for these millennia, shall now eat from the table of vengeance but not be sated. In this oath, you shall be cast into Tartarus."

The words of the ultimatum still slowly seeped in as everyone fought for meaning. Some did so through prayer, others with logic, and others allowed shame or fear to consume them so rapidly that all they could do was cry.

For Lyon's team, which had collectively scrambled to the top of the concrete parking garage to stare at the sky, the voice held a special foreboding. They shared glances among themselves and toward the object, which was even visible in the daytime sky.

The voice returned. "Behold, the plague of Erebus."

A shower of lights sprang up from the bottom half of the object and arced down toward the planet. Reflexive jerks fired a few Dragon

Corps cannons, which prompted every manned gun to join in. Though only a shade of its former brilliance, the barrage lit the darkness on its way toward the object, but not a single shot made it. Laser rounds, missiles and even approaching fighters, each, at varying distances from the object, just slipped into nothing, allowing the silvery rain to continue unhindered on its path to the planet below.

For the team on the surface, the white showers quickly became demonic as each drop burst into a fireball. The fiery rain only increased in speed as the drops screamed toward the ground turning the once blue sky to an eerie green peppered in streaks of red.

"What is going on?" Lyon slowly asked.

The collective silence broke with a keen observation from Hitook. "Those are vehicles."

"What?" Lyon couldn't believe it. "What kind of vehicles?"

Hitook kept his gaze skyward and just shook his head. "I don't know."

"Please tell me these are your boys," Oz pleaded.

"Sorry," Paloon replied, "we've got nothing like this."

"They're frapping insects."

Everyone shifted to see Larin with his long rifle raised and peering through the scope.

"They're shaped like insects," he described. "And they're metal."

"Mac," Lyon called, *"what have you got?"*

"Armageddon, man! It's freaking the end of the freaking world, man!" the computer screamed with the energy of one who was scampering around aimlessly.

"Mac," Lyon began to chastise, *"now is not—"*

Images appeared in the minds of most of the team.

"Just look at the freaking pictures, man," injected Mac. *"This is it, man. We're all going to die, man."* The computer trailed off in mumblings about how he couldn't believe it, that he was too young and something about never smoking enough pot.

Lyon lifted his sleeve to watch the screen on his arm computer. As he did, Oz approached, soon followed by Yabuki, to see what had everyone else standing stunned. They soon matched the expression.

The large object in orbit had finally ended its attack, and still not a single round fired at it landed, though the last vessels of the Dragon Corps armada continued to try.

"Frapping hell, this ain't good," Larin commented.

"Thank you, Doctor Obvious," Julie quipped. "But what are we going to do about it?"

"Whatever we do," Yabuki stated, "it had better be quick."

The others looked up to notice the fireballs just seconds from impact.

"Take cover!" Lyon yelled.

The top of the parking garage offered little in the way of protection, so a few immediately went prone, and those who didn't found themselves slammed to the ground when one of the fireballs crashed into the street nearby. As soon as they could pick themselves up, everyone bolted to the edge of the building where Hitook already waited, watching the crater below.

Fire and smoke dissipated to reveal a slim, sled-like craft resembling a flat, legless grasshopper that floated several feet above the bottom of the crater. It began gliding from the crater. As it did, shifting dust and a glimmer of light hinted that a transparent orb surrounded the craft. The way it moved out of the crater confirmed it. Though free to move independently inside, it rolled onto the street's surface as if trapped in a marble.

"I know what to frapping do," belted Larin as he flung his sniper rifle onto his backpack and withdrew the carnagearenos grenade launcher. Before the rolbrid could level the weapon, the craft shot forward at breakneck speed. "Where in the frap is it going?"

"Look," Paloon exclaimed as he pointed.

In the distance, a Dragon Corps Citadel was running toward the scene. Though seriously undersized compared to the towering mech, the craft bolted straight for it by banking to the left but doing so by first arching up the side of a skyscraper on its right. At the apex, it paused as streaks of light shot from the craft and blasted away the corner of a building across the street. Then it rolled down to the pavement, darted for the building it shot and used the collapsed roof as a ramp. Airborne, it unloaded a barrage of laser fire into the approaching mech.

The Citadel stumbled back under the unexpected salvo as its pilots fought to get a target lock, which continuously failed. Blind fire became the only option.

With the familiar sound of a deep hissing whistle followed by a vacuum of silence ringing in their ears, Lyon's team ducked behind the concrete railing seconds before a condensed beam of purple fire blasted from the Citadel's three-pronged left fist. The pilots dragged the xeonic laser through the air in hopes of hitting the assailing craft, but the metallic grasshopper hit the ground, ceased fire and sprinted around the street too fast to track manually.

When it had a moment, the enemy craft halted for a second, fired one beam at the left arm's joint then returned to zigzagging down the street, impetuously flatting everything and everyone in its way.

Fire spewed from the Citadel's left arm joint as a crack reverberated from snapping hydraulic rods. Though still connected, the arm went wild, and the pilots couldn't turn off the laser. Just as they prepared to fire the arm's emergency disconnect charges, the attacking craft fired on the Citadel's knee joints, compounding the difficultly of remaining balanced.

A few gawkers misjudged the towering beast's height and halfheartedly retreated, only to die in a bloody mess as it fell back on them. The fall flung the xeonic laser up, sending the beam down the street and diagonally across the skyscraper next to the parking garage.

Windows exploded as concrete blocks became dust that immediately burst into flames, adding to the heat from the purple laser as it cut clean through the building and its support beams. Eerie creaks overpowered the sound of the explosions and drew the attention of Lyon's team on top of the parking garage, allowing them to helplessly watch the top of the skyscraper fatally slide down the new cut and crush them.

Not even the Citadel could have saved them from the concrete coffin. After the mech crashed to the street, the approaching craft accelerated and rolled over the Citadel, flattening it from groin to head. In the process, the mech's fusion collider went critical and bloomed into a blue and white dome that razed every nearby building, while the silver grasshopper just rode the blast wave into the air. When it hit the ground, it darted off for its next target, killing everything in its path.

Meanwhile, events in orbit failed to offer much hope. Though the Dragon Corps vessels continued a ceaseless bombardment, the object just calmly floated as if to yawn as each round fired at it slipped into a personal void.

"Witness," boomed the voice, "before all, the wrath of your own doing."

Flakes of matter seemingly appeared from nowhere in front of the object and increased in number until they coalesced into a thick cloud. In less than a blink, the entire cloud funneled into a star-bright shaft that shot straight past the Tikvah and unceremoniously slipped into the hull of the Shingi. Previously flooded with light from the beam, the blackness of space returned as if nothing had happened. Seconds ticked by as spectators watched, dumbfounded. Then one panel at the very tip of the Tikvah rocketed away from the hull.

That micro explosion triggered a wave of rapidly propagating blasts that ripped down the side of the Tikvah. At increasing speed, the rampaging explosion ate away half of the vessel until the rear thrusters blasted into bits just a second before the Shingi exploded, destroying what little was left of the Tikvah and obliterating many of the tiny ships nearby.

Waves from the brilliant cataclysm banged the other vessels around. Elder Picaron aboard the Sheshach barely held himself in his command chair as he fought to keep his thoughts from wallowing in despair. With the destruction of the Shingi and Tikvah, he had command, but command of what?

Down to less than a quarter of their original strength and facing what he could only guess was a p'tahian battleship, how could he possibly win? He pushed the pessimism aside to die with dignity.

Since the blast had shocked the gunners to silence, he ordered, "Keep firing. Bring the Chaos about to sector five. Pull the fighters back to commandeer the pirate vessels. Have the—"

Another incandescent streak of light split the heavens.

Chapter 19

With no apparent origin or destination, the light beam attracted bubbling waves of distortion that rippled toward it from all directions. Dimensions split at the lip of the glowing streak and detached a molecule-thin sheet of space-time.

From the abyss of the undetectable opening emerged the tip of a cross-shaped hull that grew rapidly in size and, in seconds, dwarfed everything in orbit. The Bafomet competed with the nearby moon in size, but the moon had nowhere near the gravity-inducing density. On the planet below, clouds shifted as tides uncontrollably reversed.

The crew had no chance to react. Deep inside the Bafomet, something had already gone to work long before the ship even began to leave the dimensional slip. On its plush, black pillow, the udjat had sensed that it was home and began calling. The tiny bricks of the small, silver pyramid flashed in a coded sequence, paused, repeated and kept repeating it.

Through the hull, across space and down to the deepest crevasses of the planet, invisible waves called for a response. In time, it came. Old systems set to passive modes thousands of years ago finally registered the signal. In the pitch black, a matching miniature pyramid began glowing in time and sequence to the code.

The return signal pushed its way up, getting stronger until it reached the udjat, at which point the frequencies resonated to audible tones that sounded in time to the glowing sequence and penetrated the ears of every creature in the solar system.

From her meditation, Sophia's eyes snapped open as the udjat, glowing and beating out its song, began floating from its pedestal behind her. Destiny had finally arrived.

Time folded. And it folded again until it nearly unraveled the universe. Frozen in place, the crew of the Bafomet could do nothing but feel the pounding wave pass through them on its way to the planet below.

Through the clouds and across the ocean, the tones soared, seeking their home, crying out for a reply. Deep in the darkness, another ancient mechanism answered.

A stone pillar pulled down then laid flat before pushing itself into another pillar to complete the connection. From a nearby cannon, an iridescent, faceted orb blasted through the water's murky depths, broke the surface and headed for space, all the while flashing and beeping to the tones emanating from the Bafomet. The orb eked past the outer atmosphere, slowed to a halt and basked in the sun's radiation.

With a thunderous crack, a shaft of light exploded from the multicolored sphere and headed toward the sea below. The clouds parted, and the light slipped into the water. From that intersection point, a large, circular wave sped away abnormally fast while carrying with it twin, expanding rings of golden light, one inside the other, which floated just below the surface. At about five hundred kilometers from the center, the wave stopped, leaving the golden rings in place. Golden pictographs individually flashed into existence between the two rings and filled the circumference, forming a near solid disk.

A second wave shot from the center carrying a matching set of golden rings, stopping, this time, at about three hundred kilometers. It, too, soon filled with a unique set of pictographs of light that, like the rings, floated just under the surface of the water.

Visible concussion waves rippled from the orb as a surge rocketed down the shaft of energy, pounding out a round wall of water that rampaged with tsunami strength in all directions. But the golden rings and glyphs never wavered.

Then a third double ring left the center and stopped about a hundred kilometers out, only to fill with ancient symbols.

When the last hieroglyph blinked into existence, the orb sent through the shaft of energy another surge that slipped into the waters below. Deep rumbles vibrated throughout the planet as the outer golden disk shifted counterclockwise. As it rotated, the symbols it contained began flashing in sequence. Soon the second ring began spinning in the opposite direction followed by the innermost circle matching the rotation of the outer circle. With the final disk in motion, the tremors throughout the planet increased in strength.

As the spinning rings reached speed, a barely visible energy wave bolted from the center, triggering a massive round wave behind it. Though seemingly not possible at first, the disks spun even faster. The hieroglyphs in the rings finally blurred into a faint sheet of gold that continued to gain velocity.

The fuzzy images began to clump into splotches that slowed until giving the illusion of gradually rotating backward as another wave of energy blasted from the center. Additional acceleration reversed the illusion, pushing the hazy golden patches forward again until distinct images began to form. Where once there were pictograms, the rapidly spinning disk now contained unfocused characters of a different language. The letters became more distinct as the rings spun faster.

Another wave rocketed from the center, then another, and another, until they came too fast to count. With the last shock wave, a large dome of ivory broke the water's surface and gleamed in the light from the orb high above.

It rose to reveal a trim of silver that stretched into a greater roof and flared into high arching buttresses. As the silver arches came down, they gave way to columns of milky yellow metal that curiously gleamed a crimson gold. The same metallic substance coated the structure's walls that gave way at the corners to small alcoves housing golden statues.

Continuing to rise, the stadium-sized building soon found itself entrapped in a golden fence that encircled far more than the building.

When the ground finally rose above the surface of the water, it was covered in a fine mossy green turf lined with walkways made of the same metal that formed the building's walls.

The walkways encircled the expansive grounds that continued to ascend and swell to form the top of a massive hill that threatened to become a mountain. From the sidewalks, steps of golden silver poured down the hill in multiple directions, stopping in regular intervals to ring the hill, which began revealing small buildings, benches, lookouts and outdoor stadiums as it climbed out of the water.

This continued in tiers as the gigantic mound rose higher and higher into the sky. Just before the base of the hill escaped its watery tomb, a massive city exploded from the water. Temples, outdoor gymnasiums, meeting halls, bath houses, fountains, schools, courtyards and libraries all sat at the foot of the hill. Though made mostly of native stone, all the public buildings displayed trimmings of gold, silver and the mysterious metal that gleamed with a different aura than its true color.

The ground expanded farther at it rose then dropped sharply into the sea just as the sea unveiled two massive outer rings of land, the first smaller than the second but identical in appearance. Small houses of plain adobe speckled what was obviously age-old farm land in well-manicured sections. Brick bridges trimmed in gold and silver linked the rings to each other and the inner island.

One segment of the inner island formed a port that sat at the head of a system of canals through the rings to the outer sea. Platinum gates capped each of the canal's ends, flanked by bricked walls of ebony topped with a layer of scarlet stones. The arrangement continued to the sea and equally blended into the enormous wall that surrounded the outer ring and thereby encased the entire acropolis. Above the black bricks, the ground-level ring of red gave way to twenty feet of thick cinders of ivory crowned with a silver gable. Huge doors of carved platinum under an arch of silver and gold at the mouth of the port was the only entry into the wall, which was ribbed at equal distances with towers that rose slightly higher than itself.

Aftershocks finally began to wane across the planet. Most terrans could only wonder what had happened, but a few along some of the world's coasts could barely see the colossal structure but then only barely. If it wasn't for the beam of light pointing it out, they, too, would have never noticed it. However, from space, no one could miss it. Where there was once just water now floated a glowing city the size of a small continent.

Time continued to feel murky as Elder Vinci pushed herself from the chair.

"Target that orb," Lyta began her orders that sounded as if she spoke through water as time had only begun to unfold and release its hold. "Launch all squadrons and phalanxes, and find out where that noise is coming from."

The reverberating tones hadn't stopped repeating their sequence since the Bafomet's arrival.

Just as one of the bridge officers responded, "It's coming from us," the tones stopped and time unfolded with a snap.

"What was that?" she demanded.

Just then, the shaft of light under the orb blinked out. As if someone had yanked away its supporting column, the faceted sphere fell to the planet below in a perfect descent toward its launch tube. As it slipped in, mystical green energy blasted through copper veins that wove throughout the city, setting fire to flameless torches, lamps and sconces. Through pipes over the bridges, the green energy reached the outer wall and rippled through veins to each of the towers, which responded with their silver roofs shooting up and pulling into existence a very top column of glass.

"Ma'am," a bridge officer aboard the Bafomet exclaimed, "we have unregistered departures."

"What?" Lyta barked. "How's that possible? Who's missing?"

"It's Samurai Tenjin and her delegation."

"Check the shuttles, and send security to her room."

"Ma'am, all shuttles are accounted for; they just disappeared."

Miles below, deep in the newly exposed city, a shallow rectangular pool greeted its recent arrivals.

Leaning over, Sophia held in both hands the udjat. As her keepers lifted their hands from the top of the tiny pyramid, Sophia rose to scan the city ending with a gaze at the gilded building on top of the hill.

"In the fullness of time, we have returned home, to Avalon." Sophia glanced down at the two children. "The prophecy calls."

With that, she placed the udjat in the waiting hands of the one called Yeshua and took the large staff offered by the one called Miriam. The Sangraal clasped the staff in both hands in front of her, bowed her head and began quietly chanting. The two keepers turned and headed down the length of the reflecting pool toward the huge mound in the center of the city and the large stone doors that faced them. As they stepped from the water, each flanked to take a corner and turned to face the Sangraal as she lifted her head and lightly tapped the staff on the ground three times.

Tremors shook the area as the ground rose below Sophia's feet and lifted her into the air until she stood on top of a towering monolith of black stone. Similar monoliths scattered about the inner island also rose from pools, sending one final shake through the island as they locked into place.

Sophia lowered the apple-shaped headpiece of knotted metal to a mere hair's width from the top of the monolith and started tracing a clockwise circle. As she did, the green energy that flowed through the city entered the monoliths, filling three-dimensional cores visible from their exteriors. When she completed the circle, full-sized ankhs glowed brightly from deep within the black monoliths and sent colorless waves of energy radiating throughout the island.

Moss-covered patches became plush lawns of grass. Manicured plats of dirt bloomed into furtive farms. And the barren parts of the island transformed into thick forests from which the sound of animals soon began to emanate. Bountiful life thrived again, as it had so many thousands of years ago.

The invisible energy waves flapped her cloak about as Sophia's ink-black hair danced in the air. With one hand, she unclasped the emerald slab from its golden chain around her waist. She flung the slab into the air and let it go to. The slab simply floated, riding the waves of energy. With a wave of her hand, the slab split open and clanged as the pages flapped rapidly. A flick of her finger stopped the book as energy flowed into the pages setting all the letters glowing at once.

Just as the p'tahians' ultimatum had, Sophia's voice now boomed throughout the solar system.

"Behold, the Age of Aquarius is nigh. As my ancestors had fought you before, now is retribution."

Sophia began reciting the ancient chant from the emerald book as the alien object in orbit spewed another shower of sparks twice as thick as its last. She sensed the impending attack but didn't falter in her incantation. With her last words, she spun, planted the staff on the top of the monolith and pointed the headpiece toward the large stone doors in the mound. Blue energy jumped from the headpiece and bolted for the doors, pushing them open.

Waiting at the foot of the new entrance, Sophia's keepers appeared like ants in comparison to the colossal doors, but as soon as the portal had opened enough, they entered. Light filled the stone corridor not from the blue bolt of energy but from the far end, deep in the ground, where a dark red wall glowed like flowing lava.

Stone stairs on the left led the duo high up to a platform that protruded toward the center of the lava wall.

As Yeshua held the udjat, Miriam stepped forward.

"Fenrisulfr."

Blasting through the sheet of lava and stopping within inches of Miriam's face charged the enormous head of a wolf whose eyes glowed with a fiery gold and whose agape maw of fangs snarled with a salivating growl. Without hesitation, the tiny girl reached past the fangs and snatched the black stick that had propped the wolf's jaw open. The fangs snapped like a steel trap.

Unharmed, Miriam held the smooth, slightly curved stick and gazed pitifully upon the beast. Gradually the growling subsided to snarling as the demonic monster peered into the eyes of the child before him. There, in those eyes, was an unmistakable sign.

"Why have you come?"

"It has been a long time," Miriam responded. "As promised, we have returned."

"But why?" snarled the giant wolf. "You have left me here to rot for an eternity. You feared me so then; why face me now?"

"It was never fear." Miriam glanced at the stick as she rolled it in her palms. "It was pity. Your rage, unchecked, would have been your downfall. We had to find a way to bind you before you destroyed yourself too soon."

"You think I had rage before, just let me go so I can swallow you whole."

"You won't harm us," spoke Yeshua.

"Would you bet your life on that?"

"I know you better than you do." Yeshua stepped forward. "You won't harm us."

The monstrous wolf glared at Miriam's companion and saw the truth. "Damn you."

"Now, Fenrisulfr," Miriam chided, "that's no way to be. Hold out your right paw."

Through the sheet of black and red lava, the creature dragged his massive arm forward revealing the silky green ribbon that kept him bound. With a flick of her thumb, Miriam split the stick and unsheathed the sword inside. Performing the slightest movement, Miriam severed the bonds as if they had been made of nothing more than a whisper.

As Fenrisulfr glanced down at his free paw, Miriam commented, "It must hurt to know your key to freedom was with you this whole time."

Growling sounded from the deepest part of his throat as the wolf leered at the tiny torturer.

Miriam only pointed the blade in the general vicinity of his other paw. "Come, Fenrisulfr. Fate waits for no one."

Outside, Sophia stood on top of the towering ankh watching the second wave of fiery rain make it through the atmosphere and begin its attack upon the citadel. From the glass tops of the outlying towers, green beams shot into the sky blasting away at the invading vessels. The defenses would hold for now, but she knew time grew short.

As she watched, a gust of moist air pushed into her. She smirked and turned to be face to face with the beast her keepers released.

"You," he growled. "I should have smelled your blood from my prison."

"Fenrir, my child, it is your own tainted blood that shrouds your sense of me." Sophia smiled and approached the edge, closer to the beast to place a tiny hand on his gigantic muzzle. "It has been too long."

"Then why come for me now?"

Sophia smiled wider and gazed into the creature's eyes. "Ragnarök has arrived, dear Fenrir." She placed her hand under the beast's jaw and lifted his head toward the heavens.

High in the sky, the alien object continued to release its shower of attack craft. Recognition burned bright and set Fenrir's golden eyes on fire. "Asgard!" he growled.

Sophia leaned forward and half whispered, "The gods and giants fight once more. Vengeance awaits."

Chapter 20

Elder Vinci, temporarily mesmerized by the cloud of enemy craft headed for the planet, further found herself boggled by the response of green beams from the new island. Lyta changed her initial thought of the isle being an additional threat.

"Whatever, that is," she stated, "it's obviously got the p'tahian's attention, so let's open her up." Lyta shifted her attention to the floating object and its continuing ability to absorb incoming fire. She engaged her command voice. "Charge the main cannon, target that city, ship, whatever the hell that thing is, and fire at will. Let's see what this thing can really handle."

"Will do," answered the Bafomet's command crew in unison.

The vessel's cross-shaped hull retracted in the center to reveal three massive magnetic rings rotating around a bright blue speck of light that powered the massive ship. The crew released the brakes, sending the rings flying faster in orbit around the star and collecting near maximum power. That energy began rippling as it raced down the Bafomet's hull toward the bow, where it crashed into a colossal stream snapping like a whip toward the p'tahian ship.

As the beam neared the stone city, closer than any previous fire had, anticipation brought the Bafomet's bridge crew to their feet, but like everything else before it, the blast finally slipped into nothing. As the energy poured into a bottomless void and darkness returned, collective sighs filled the bridge.

"Wait," Lyta yelled to silence her crew, "it moved." She was sure of what she saw. "That shot pushed it. That means it's not invincible. Charge and fire again."

"Will do!" The crew took their seats but one remained standing. "Ma'am, what's that?"

From the planet below, a silver streak, larger and brighter than the previous ones, shot toward the object instead of from it.

"Zoom in," she ordered.

As the holograms raced to enlarge the picture, Lyta couldn't believe her eyes, and her bewilderment formed three distinct words. "What the hell?"

Surrounded in a prismatic aura, a giant bipedal wolf shot straight through Asgard's defenses and hooked over the rim to land at the base of a circular outdoor amphitheater. Upon touching down, he rose to his full height and could almost see over the top seats as he looked around. Columns capped with a ring of marble encircled the amphitheater, but little else was in view.

Fenrisulfr strode up the bench seats carved into the stone and entered the medieval city by squeezing between two columns and ducking under the ring of marble.

Before him, cobbled stone entrapped a rectangular courtyard of plush grass and several large trees. Benches rimmed the immaculate garden at enough distance to signify that no one should walk on the lawn. Elsewhere, well chiseled boulders expertly placed in interlocking positions formed the store fronts, homes and meeting halls of a very viable but barren city.

"Yahweh!" Fenrisulfr yelled. "Show yourself! Want to play a nice, violent game of tag? I'll even be it!"

Silence.

"Oh, I'm sorry."

He wasn't.

"I forgot."

He hadn't.

"You don't like people to use that name, do you?" the wolf taunted. "What's your ego going by these days? Ra? Allah? Odin?"

"He is no longer with us," came a voice from nowhere and everywhere at once. "It's Quirinus now."

Fenrisulfr looked around for any sign of life. Nothing. "It's not going to matter." Stepping off to walk around the courtyard of trees, he continued to goad his prey with every heavy footfall. "Do you fear me? He did. You should. I'm the bastard seed created by your kind breaking the very rules you set. Now your fate comes calling."

Nearing the far end of the rectangle-shaped yard, Fenrisulfr increased the intensity of his voice. "When I find you, and I will, I'm going to kill you and your entire Empyrean. Every last one of you self-righteous pricks."

That threat sparked something; Fenrisulfr could sense it. He stopped and scanned the barren plaza. At the T-junction ahead, three alcoves marred the high wall. In the center rested a large stone statue of a bare-chested man sitting, his legs crossed and his arms resting on his knees. In the flanking recesses stood tall, armored warriors clad in tunic-covered chain mail and wielding upright swords on the outside and, on the inside, holding body-length shields, each engraved with a Maltese cross.

Fenrisulfr leered at the scene. Then he sensed it again and glided his line of sight to his right.

There, in a wide niche in the wall, stood the statue of a woman with four arms. If it wasn't for the long garland of skulls around her neck, she would have been completely naked. In her raised upper arms she held a sword in the left hand and a trident in the right. The other two hands were in front of her. The left gripped the hair of a severed head while the other held below the head a chalice fashioned from a skull.

The wolf furrowed his brow and slowly peered to his left.

As he expected, another cavity in the wall housed a sculpture, this one of an elderly but fit man wrapped in a toga that barely covered his chest. His hair and beard flowed long with curls as he clasped a spear, held diagonally across his chest.

Fenrisulfr's muscles rippled as he tensed. "Is this the best you can do?"

The statues exploded with flying flakes of rock and light, leaving live versions of themselves that began to advance on Fenrisulfr.

The wolf snarled as he clenched his fists. "Bring it."

Sheathed in fire, the evil rain evaporated the clouds and cooled to unveil points of light that zipped about in straight lines but at sharp angles. Soon the sky was full of them as they darted like supersonic fireflies toward the risen acropolis.

With the increase in the number of attack ships, each tower around the city began firing multiple green beams. Avalon's defense systems were reaching their capacity, and some of the p'tahian ships were starting to adapt and dodge the grid of anti-aircraft fire.

The image was reflected in Sophia's ebony eyes. She, as the Sangraal, had to do something soon and could only trust that her training had prepared her.

"Seek refuge," she commanded.

Miriam resisted. "This is our fight."

"But it is my fate," Sophia stated as she turned to face her two keepers waiting on the ground. Then the Sangraal softly jerked her head toward the building on the mound. "Go. Protect the hearth."

Sophia watched Yeshua and Miriam jog toward the nearest set of stairs winding up the hill before turning to notice some of the fighters finally breaking through. Their bolts of blue laser fire exploded as they struck the ground around her. A few rounds even soared straight for Sophia's head, but she stared them down as they fizzled against a shield surrounding her.

"Taste the wrath of my blood."

In a counter-clockwise spin, with the staff almost touching the top of the monolith, more energy flowed from the black stone. At the end of the circle, she spun the staff in her right hand before landing its base square on the monolith. Three bolts of energy jumped from the generator to the knotted strands of metal on top of the staff, which stored the power like an unlimited capacitor. With it charged, she tipped the staff down to her left then swung it to the right while arcing to the rear then snapping the headpiece toward the sky.

A flare of energy blasted from the headpiece and crashed into one of the ships, shattering it into pieces. With the ship's destruction, the excess energy chained in multiple directions seeking and finding nearby fighters, sending them careening off course to explode.

Sophia released a devilish grin. "So sweet."

As she repeated the ritual, people took notice from several thousand miles up.

"There it is again," Lyta commented on the flash of light that had distracted her from the actions aboard the p'tahian vessel. "Zoom in on that point."

The image rapidly enlarged at a speed that would make the uninitiated woozy, then stopped with a top down look of Samurai Tenjin firing away bolt after bolt of energy and stacking quite a count of downed p'tahian fighters.

"How in the hells did she get down there?" exclaimed an astute bridge officer.

A silent Lyta wondered the same, but she soon became more interested in how the samurai summoned her attacks with such lethality.

Lyta motioned with a "well then" nod and shrug. "It doesn't matter; she seems to be doing fine by herself."

On another screen, a brown plume mushroomed from the stone city that topped the p'tahian object.

"Did we hit it?" Lyta asked with a tone of stifled hope.

"I don't think so," replied a busy deck officer struggling to split his attention between his commander and finding the cause of the explosion.

The scene snapped to a close picture of a rubble pile that had been an adobe building moments before. While the dust was still thick in the air, Fenrisulfr dug his way out of the debris.

"You puny piss ants are starting to tick me off," Fenrisulfr declared with obvious annoyance. Finally free from the wreckage of the ruins, he pushed down the remains of a wall fragment to step into the street. "I was too naïve before to have truly thought I could kill any of you, but I'm starting to warm up to the idea."

Down the street, the two armored crusaders stood shoulder to shoulder, nearly covering the entire width of the path with their immense size. In trained unison, they locked shields, threaded their swords through the dips along the top and charged.

Fenrisulfr scowled and braced for impact, only to spring up at the last moment and soar above the blades while reaching down to plant a cupped paw on top of each of the guards' heads. With a firm push, he sent them stumbling forward to the ground while propelling himself to the next target.

Landing on one knee, Fenrisulfr shifted to the left to grab the hand holding the trident that barreled for his head. As he succeeded, he shifted again to repeat the move, catching the sword arcing down for his shoulder. With both wrists firmly in his grip, Fenrisulfr rose to confront the placid face of the four-armed goddess.

"Ha," Fenrisulfr exclaimed, "I've got you."

Dangling from one of Kali's other hands, the severed head spoke. "Who's got whom?"

Tossing the head to the side, she downed the bloody contents of the bone chalice in one gulp. She let the empty goblet fall to the ground as fire set her eyes ablaze and a freshly formed smug grin revealed a fiendish set of fangs.

With her now-free hands, Kali pounded for Fenrisulfr's belly, gripping the wolf's flanks and burrowing her thumbs into his gut, breaking skin and tearing muscle.

Fenrisulfr howled in pain and nearly lost his grip on her other arms. It was just enough for her. With a firm grip on her victim, she fell back in a controlled roll, pulled her feet in, then pushed out, sending Fenrisulfr flying in a wild arc.

In a crumpled heap, the wolf smashed into the pavement and started skidding to a stop, which came early at the heel of Buddha's foot.

Wordlessly, the huge man bent down and grabbed Fenrisulfr by the legs. With a snap, he flung Fenrisulfr up and down repeatedly as if beating the dust from an old rug. The ground sufficiently cratered, he flicked the wolf into the wall on the right then threw him across the plaza.

Trees splintered in countless pieces as Fenrisulfr helplessly plowed through the courtyard on his way toward granite columns that, in turn, reluctantly shattered under the wolf's momentum. The far end of the indented amphitheater finally succeed in halting the furry cannonball.

Fenrisulfr quietly wished there had been more trees. At least they were softer.

Looking much like an elderly man with arthritis, Fenrisulfr struggled to peel himself off the sharp-angled rock seats of the amphitheater and get on his feet. He reached to massage his back, but a burst of pain from his torn abs stopped his paws short as he gripped his blood-soaked gut and howled.

Over the raised horizon of the amphitheater, the toga-covered elder used his spear as a walking stick as he strolled into view. With crystal blue eyes full of wisdom, he peered down at the wounded wolf.

"Nothing smart to say this time, you malformed abortion?"

Fenrisulfr just glared at his age-old enemy.

Zeus gazed at Fenrisulfr and calmly stated, "You were our worst mistake. We should have never allowed your birth, and our fear should not have kept us from correcting that mistake."

Zeus lifted his spear in the air as it flashed into a lightening bolt. "Looks like we had nothing to fear after all."

He hurled the bolt at his injured prey, but Fenrisulfr released the grip on his stomach in time to catch the entire flare in his paw.

Fenrisulfr smirked at the reeling Zeus.

"I might be ostracized, but you can't deny that the blood of your kind also courses through my veins." Fenrisulfr lowered his paw, with the lighting still crackling at all angles in his tight grip. "You have much to fear."

Squeezing tighter, Fenrisulfr bent the energy to his will until multiple bolts jutted from between his fingers. A snap of his wrist sent the salvo of bolts flying into an unprepared Zeus, lifting him into the air and throwing him across several buildings to finally crash and create his own private plum of dust.

Full of renewed vigor, Fenrisulfr rushed up the far end of the amphitheater to see the charging crusaders flanking him from both sides of the garden in the courtyard. When they scampered to a stop, moments ticked by as they watched each other, attentive to the slightest flinch.

From the right, a crusader lunged. Fenrisulfr stepped to the side and took hold of the warrior's shield from both sides. Using the attacking momentum, Fenrisulfr sent the crusader in an ungrounded spin for several rotations before halting hard, dislodging the knight from the shield and sending him flying into Buddha. As both crashed into a wall, Fenrisulfr shifted to the other crusader that he knew had already started to stampede toward him.

Fenrisulfr flicked the shield in his hands toward the crusader's feet. Dexterity failed as the warrior tried to jump over the flying shield and accidentally landed on it. Balance lost, he fell toward at a waiting Fenrisulfr.

Seizing the sword hand and knocking the shield out of the way, the huge wolf lunged and sank his fangs into the soldier's neck.

The creature, once made of flesh, instantly reverted to its previous stone incarnation and exploded into a million pebbles, leaving a tiny blue-grey p'tahian, nearly cut in half by the force of the bite dangling from Fenrisulfr's jaws.

High-pitched squeals forced Fenrisulfr to tense his jaw and silence the annoyance. Half of the lifeless p'tahian fell with a wet flop followed by Fenrisulfr spitting out the rest of the putrid creature.

In the distance, Kali crouched in a stance similar to a spider primed to attack, then lolled her tongue in a hiss.

Fenrisulfr sneered at the counterfeit deity and pointed a finger.

"You're next."

Chapter 21

In the pitch black, the stench of smoke assaulted his nose as dust coated the inside of his mouth. Each attempt to breathe just sucked in more of it. The air he couldn't see was obviously full of a foul-tasting fine power. He coughed to try to clear his lungs, but every cough led him to inhale, filling them with more smoke and dust.

The darkness reluctantly retreated under a bright point of light that turned the inky air into a muddy brown.

"Are you okay?"

"My lungs are on fire," Oz coughed.

"Good," Paloon commented. "That means you're alive."

"You're welcome," came Julie's straining voice from the shadows.

Paloon shifted the glow from his flashlight around until he found Julie braced as if holding up the newly arrived roof by sheer strength alone.

"Don't just sit there gawking," Julie quipped. She grimaced as dust rained from the cracked roof and muted creaks blended into rumbles as weight shifted in the building that had fallen on them. "It's taking all my psychic energy to keep this building from crushing us; I can't hold it forever, so you had better start finding a way out of here and quick."

Paloon began crawling around as he called out to the rest of the gang. Oz forcefully restrained his hacking as he joined in the search. Fumbling in the dark, Oz finally found someone's leg, but when he shook it to wake them up, the leg came loose. With a scream, Oz fell back and instinctively tossed the leg, which hit Paloon.

"What the—" The hunter halted his chastisement of Oz to inspect the unwelcome gift. "Looks like one of Yabuki's friends didn't make it. Now, quit playing with the dead and find the others."

Trying to help, Julie visually explored her area and discovered an unconscious Larin lying behind her. With a sharp whip, she thumped the rolbrid in the head with her black tail. Only grumbles responded, so she slapped him again.

"Wake up!"

Enraged from being so rudely awakened, Larin growled, "Do that again, and I'll rip it off!"

"Touch my tail, and I'll kick you in the groin so hard you'll be spitting piss for a year. Now get your lazy ass up and make a hole so we can get out of this coffin."

Anger held Larin's face tense as he muttered a protest, but he reluctantly complied. He rarely passed a chance to make something explode.

As the others gathered away from Larin's preparations, Hitook struggled in the tight confines to slide closer to Julie.

"Let me take it," he pleaded with a tinge of contriteness. "I can handle it. You should get out first."

Julie snarled. "Shut your feed hole. When that rolbrid finishes, you'd best—"

"Fire in the hole!" Larin yelled.

Everyone barely had time to cringe before the shaped charge blasted a hole in the wall, allowing the outside light to flood the dust-filled cave. Lyon shuffled to the entrance and gazed down. It was about ten feet down before a pile of debris haphazardly tapered at uneven intervals into the street.

"Let's go," Lyon said as he motioned with one hand and helped Yabuki out of the opening with the other. Paloon followed.

Lyon looked back at the stalled liqua. "That means you too, Hitook. Move it." With a jerk of his chin toward Julie, Lyon added, "Are you going to be okay?"

Julie twisted her face briefly and grunted. "Just get out before I change my mind."

Barely covered in tattered clothing, Rin finished her search and pulled up to the exit. Lyon scanned her quickly to make sure the patch of blood on the side of her head was only minor. "Anyone left?"

"No. Taichi didn't make it," Rin calmly replied and began climbing down.

Mildly surprised at her icy emotions, Lyon shifted his attention back to Hitook, who had barely moved. "Hitook!"

He ignored Lyon's call and directed his concern to Julie. "I'm not going to leave you."

"That does it!" she barked. "What's your deal? You're creeping me out. Now, get out that hole before I drop this roof just for a chance to kick your furry ass. Now move!"

Stunned like a scolded puppy, Hitook gravitated to the opening and rolled out. Lyon followed but not before motioning to Julie with a nod that silently wished her luck.

Outside, Lyon noticed that the streets were strangely barren except for multiple pools of blood and the mixed rubble that had fallen next to the collapsed parking garage. At the base of the debris heap, the others gathered and sporadically coughed while looking about, mildly confused about how they had survived. Lyon followed their gazes to the collapsed remains of the skyscraper that had crushed the parking garage as if it was nothing more than a cardboard box.

An explosion rocked the building as it further imploded. A billow of dust and rocks blasted from the makeshift exit moments before a pointy eared bullet with a tail shot from the hole, heading for the tall office building across the street.

Clinging to the brick façade, Julie shouted, "Whoo, that was close." Peering down, she began descending. "And it was actually kind of fun."

"In that case," Larin piped up, "how about we shove your scrawny butt back in there and you can have another frapping go at it, this time blindfolded?"

"How about I phone your mother," began Julie as she leapt down, "and inform her that she unknowingly gave birth to a soon-to-be eunuch?"

Larin, at a loss for a quick comeback, just leered.

Lyon hopped down from a large chunk of concrete and patted Oz on the back, who was bent over coughing. "Well, we only lost one—sorry about that Yabuki—but it's pretty good, considering." With a thumb over the shoulder, he pointed at the wreckage of two buildings that had an unexpected and sudden collision. "The unfortunate bit is that our transportation is in that mess somewhere, so we get to hike it back on foot."

Others grumbled. Yabuki retrieved his cell phone, opened it then cussed. "No signal."

"Look, people," Lyon said as he walked past everyone and headed up the street, "we're not making any headway just standing around. Let's get out of here before this world goes any more to hell."

Struggling slightly, the group followed unhurriedly, trading glances at one another with thoughts full of questions but nothing to say. In the distance, gunfire sounded, not pot shots but fully automatic weapons. It was followed by the clamor of multiple rocket launches, and then by thunderous explosions. Yells and screams blended in rhythm to the pandemonium.

They turned a corner, and a woman carrying a child clutched close to her shoulder ran past with no care that a few dust-covered alien creatures were strolling down the street. Lyon noted the lack of reaction with mild interest, then noticed the crater.

Starting less than half a block away, a deep void created a clean basin that stretched about two blocks in diameter.

"What in the hell happened?" Yabuki stood baffled.

"The Citadel," Paloon commented, "it must have gone critical. Good thing it wasn't any closer."

The distant noise of weapons fire had also gotten noticeably louder but still stayed at an unobservable distance, buried in the city somewhere beyond the crater.

Oz jerked his head in a general direction of the noise. "I wonder what's going on."

"Welcome." Larin snapped sarcastically. "We're at war; where have you been? Glad you could join us."

"Whatever it is," Lyon answered, ignoring the rolbrid's chiding, "we're not equipped to handle it. But if we're careful enough, we'll get out of here without contact, which is the current priority." Lyon's voice tapered as he glanced around then darted for an alley across the street. The others followed.

They moved through alleys for a few blocks, navigating around the crater. Along the way, they noticed that each street was spotted with pools of bloody mush but otherwise remained barren.

Finally, on a street that offered an intact path past the crater, Lyon led the others down the road. As they moved, he kept scanning the vicinity. Across the street to the left, muted red bricks speckled with errant black and grey ones reached high and even covered its previous windows. Several stories up, multiple layers of white letters had faded into incomplete words from a long-gone business.

To his right, brown bricks with a head-high ridge of jutting grey cinders encased a black metal garage door that displayed a faint yellow warning, "No Parking." Waist-high, yellow-striped black posts flanked the door.

After the second post, an alley broke to the right. Lyon began to pass it as he glanced down the alley. Lyon froze and jerked backed against the metal door, making more noise than he cared.

"What is it?" Paloon asked.

"We've got company." Lyon jerked his head toward the alley. "One of those insect things is sitting at the far end, in the other street."

"Did it see you?"

Lyon inched closer to the edge, being careful not to expose himself too much. "I don't think so, but I think we should—" Lyon turned to talk to the team and then noticed Julie wielding a massive battle sword as tall and wide as she was and likely heavier.

"Where'd that come from?"

"What? This little thing?" Julie held out the mighty blade and glanced between it and Lyon. "I just keep it around in case of emergency."

"But where did it come from? Where have you been hiding it?"

"Can't a girl have her secrets?"

While bemused expressions came from the rest of the group, Larin just scanned the dextian from top to bottom and back, rolling his tongue around his teeth and wishing he had been paying more attention to that little trick.

Lyon crept to the edge to see if the craft had moved, while Julie glared at Larin, who failed to stop gaping at her as if she was a porn star.

"Pervert." She followed it by smacking Larin's face with her tail.

"I told you not to do that again; I'm—"

"Shit," Lyon shouted as he retreated from the opening. "It's moving up the alley. Spread out and—"

Confirming the presence of its prey, the craft blasted from the alley and shot across the street to stop on a car it had just flattened.

The few who could draw their weapons in time got in a couple of ineffective shots before finding themselves running and diving out of the way as it chased them down. The weapons fire just bounced off its invisible globe of a shield, but those who could do so kept firing.

The vessel turned on Yabuki, and Rin darted to push her boss out of the way, only to splatter her blood in all directions as the craft sped over her. Hitook vocalized his anguish at the sight, unintentionally attracting the ship's attention. It banked hard and charged the liqua, who only had time to throw up a quick personal psychic shield.

When the two connected, the impact punted Hitook into the air and implanted the furry beast into an apartment building.

"Hey, fuck face!"

The ship halted and spun around to face Julie, who strode up the street while dragging behind her the gargantuan sword that threw sparks as it cut into the asphalt. She came to a standstill. "Care to try me?"

Without hesitation, the ship broke at full speed toward the dextian. She swung the sword around and hefted the blade level with the charging craft. Sound barriers nearly broke when the vessel connected and came to a standstill at the sword's point. Julie tensed and grunted as she forced her energy deep into the earth, but the craft proceeded to gradually gain ground, pushing Julie back. Nuggets of road showered from her feet as they cut groves in the pavement at an increasing rate.

Julie screamed as her energy flowed into the visible spectrum. The result sent a spray of sparks much like iron against a grinder as the shield kept spinning to push Julie back.

A wild crack echoed off the buildings as the battle sword finally pierced the shield, which completely evaporated as Julie plowed the point into the head of the silver craft and pushed it to the ground. With the momentum of her previous tension, she rushed forward, dragging the blade down the length of the vessel to cut it in half.

At the far end, Julie fell to her knees, panting and covered in sweat. "I hope I don't have to do that again."

Larin approached, squatted next to the craft's remains and poked at it with his particle cannon. "Look at this frapping crap." He poked some more. "It's biological."

The others gathered. Though the thing had a distinctive metal shell, the innards were a twisted mess of wet guts that seeped out into a sloppy mess.

"I'll be damned," Lyon mumbled as he kicked the thing's metallic exoskeleton. "I've never heard of such a thing. Is it an animal or a machine?"

"Incoming!" warned Paloon as he grabbed Yabuki by the collar and half jerked him toward the alley before letting go.

Soon, no one needed encouragement. The ground starting exploding as laser bolts rained from the sky.

"Frapping hell," exclaimed Larin as he dropped to one knee and returned fire. "This ain't looking good."

Lyon could deduce that piece of wisdom on his own from the number of p'tahian aircraft that had apparently been attracted directly to his team. "Get into the alley." He ran over to Julie to pull her to her feet. "Paloon, scout ahead and find us a subway or something better for cover. Oz take—shit!"

One of the fighters dropped low on a strafing run down the street. As it did, it zoomed past Hitook, who climbed out of his hole in the apartment building just in time to see the ship open fire. Julie summoned the last bit of her strength to block the shots with her battle sword. By the time the fighter pulled up, it had knocked Julie down and unconscious.

Infuriated, Hitook jumped the seven stories to the street. Transparent waves of energy flared from his aura as if it was on fire. With his forearms clasped, one on top of the other, Hitook rose as he gradually dragged his arms apart, and sparks began jumping between them. When his palms met, the sparks flared into a thick bolt that flowed back and forth.

Hitook extended his hands wide, stretching the bolt as if pulling taffy. Then with a roar, he poured more energy into the bolt until it neared uncontrollable levels. Finally he slammed his paws together, crushing the lightening into a ball that shot from his paws into the sky. It sought out the ship that had fired on Julie as it banked to the right to circle around for another bombardment.

On his feet long enough to see his attack home in and blast the fighter to bits, Hitook collapsed.

Previously trying to pull Julie to safety, Lyon handed her off to Larin. "Get her into the alley." He raced to his other fallen comrade. "Hitook!" Though initially calling to ensure his teammate was alive, a new sense of urgency entered his voice when he saw another fighter streaking to their position. "Hitook! We've got to go, and now!"

Lyon lunged for Hitook and attempted to yank him to his feet. It was like trying to pull an ancient tree out of the ground, but Lyon fought more desperately as the fighter lined up for the shot then exploded. Through the flames flew another fighter, a Dragon Corps fighter, Kanytelleis class, Lyon was positive.

"Are you Knight Kendrick?" The question came on the team's internal communications channel.

"Who's this?"

"That depends. Are you Knight Kendrick?"

"Yes. Now who are you?"

"Glad we found you. I'm Hunter G-Vin, commander of Theta Wing; we're your retrieval party. You weren't at the pick up point, so we came looking."

"Well, we ran into a bit of interference."

"Figured as much. Stand by as we secure the zone."

The rest of Theta Wing had already started the dogfight before G-Vin had made the comment.

"Paloon," Lyon called, "get back here and help me get this brute on his feet."

Larin gave a similar order to Oz after just getting Julie awake then noticed Yabuki squinting down the road. "What is it?"

"I'm not sure." Yabuki hesitated. "But it looks like more of those metal insects."

"Another frapping one," Larin cussed as everyone looked down the road to confirm what Yabuki said next.

"Not one, a whole damn army."

"Um, hey, Theta, that rescue had better come soon," Lyon transmitted. *"We've got multiple ground targets, and they're moving fast."*

"We're kind of busy at the moment," G-Vin quipped. *"Can't you hold them off for a minute or ten?"*

"I'm sorry to disturb you, but no. We won't be alive long enough for the extraction if you don't help us now."

"Got'cha covered," came another voice, a female voice.

"Who's this?"

Far down the street, as the rolling vessels crossed an intersection flanked by skyscrapers, a large metal foot flew into view and kicked the lead ship, planting it deep into a building.

"Goal," the Citadel screamed excitedly as it swung around the corner and its massive hand cannon roared to life. The thirty millimeter rain kept the attackers at bay as the Citadel backed up to create some distance. *"The name's Wakanda, this here's Tranquility's Wrath, and you're welcome. Now get moving. We'll take care of this."*

"I'm not so sure about this," Lyloda called to his companion as his marselian eyes watched the wave of craft zip about, including up the sides of buildings, to dodge the fire.

"All hells! They want to be difficult." Wakanda's purple dreadlocks flung about as she snapped her head around to gauge the situation then, mentally unlocked the safeties. "Unload the chest."

Lyloda didn't argue, and Wakanda fought to keep standing as the Citadel stumbled when thirty-nine missiles of three types launched simultaneously from its chest. Each sought targets in its own way. Many hit their targets, but most just further destroyed the city in a most spectacular display of mixed explosions.

"Oh, you little pests," Lyloda belted as he checked the matter generator gauges and didn't like it. They didn't have five minutes to wait for the first reload.

"Try this." Wakanda brought the xeonic laser up and fired short bursts in random patterns, then the hand cannon spun empty. "Fuck!"

"On it," replied Lyloda as he ejected the next tubular magazine from the right leg.

Wakanda moved the Citadel's arm to allow the hand-cannon's empty magazine to fall to the ground and reloaded from the new one, then resumed fire. But the unyielding ground attackers forced Wakanda to back up even farther. "Fire the neutralizers," she ordered to Lyloda before pleading to G-Vin's crew. *"Theta, you best get that retrieval under way. I'm not going to be able to hold these fuckers off for much longer."*

If G-Vin did respond, it was drowned by Wakanda's cheering as she flattened one craft with the xeonic laser, followed by the dull thumps of the twin barrels over the Citadel's left shoulder. Whistling as they soared, fat capsules sparked to life before clanking to the ground. Some of the attacking craft moved a little too close and found themselves uncontrollably sucked into the neutralizer pellets' magnetic pull. But the others adapted quickly and started navigating around them.

A block behind Tranquility's Wrath, the Beowulf finally landed. Lyon's team members gratefully dragged themselves the best they could toward the box-like craft with high wings and a rear hatch that lowered as the ship landed.

"Shit, I'm spent," cried Wakanda as she emptied the magazine from the hand cannon.

Preoccupied with trying to improve the firing pattern of the neutralizer cannons, Lyloda announced, “That was our last mag.”

“Well, fuck,” Wakanda blurted and flung the useless weapon, which sailed until it flattened a small corner diner.

Wakanda then started firing the massive particle cannon strapped to the outside of the mech’s right arm, but she knew she couldn’t beat the wave of craft back with just that and the xeonic laser. Even though she still got in a lucky shot from time to time, she’d be overrun in seconds.

“I’m serious; get out of here now,” Wakanda bellowed as she retreated even farther, within feet of the Beowulf.

One insect craft shot up the side of a building and tried to bolt around the Citadel, but Wakanda batted it off the wall with the mech’s right hand. The drastic shift in weight forced Wakanda to stumble back.

As the Beowulf began taking off, Oz saw the movement through the still-open hatch and screamed, “Holy shit!” just before Tranquility’s Wrath smashed into the Beowulf. The Beowulf banked sharply as the pilot fought for control, but Oz had already gone into a free fall toward the exit before crashing onto the cargo floor and sliding out the hatch, getting an undesired full view of the ugly scene below.

“I kind of wish we had another magazine,” Lyloda sighed.

“I wish we had those grenade shells,” Wakanda snipped. “Shit!”

A couple of the attacking craft sprung to pound into the Citadel’s chest. Wakanda engaged the close-range eighty millimeter, multi-barreled chest cannon, but the kick just helped the attackers tip the war machine back.

Finally realizing that he was actually pulling away from the scene and not approaching it, Oz looked up to see Yabuki pulling him back into the Beowulf’s loading bay.

“We humans need to stick together, right?” Yabuki offered a slight smirk before turning his head. “We’re clear; close it.”

As the door lifted, the team collectively sighed in relief.

“That was a frapping close one.” Larin sounded mighty proud of himself.

“But,” Oz turned back as if to look at the Citadel through the closing hatch, “what about—”

“Hold on!” the pilot shouted before pulling the plane hard to the left.

Outside of the cockpit, a colossal fireball, with a strange streak of silver, raged from space on a path directly for the city’s coastline.

On their back, the crew of the Tranquility’s Wrath fought to get the machine to stand but knew death neared.

“It was nice knowing you, Wakanda.”

“I wouldn’t have it any other way, brother.”

Bright white light filled the sky, followed by waves of yellow and red, and a thunderous crash cued a blast wave that flipped the Citadel and propelled it into a violent tumble through quickly obliterated buildings, freeway intersections and a park before it landed in a large pond.

With distinct words, a seriously disoriented Wakanda summed the feelings for both of them. "What in the blessed hells was that?"

Lyloda just shook his now throbbing head and rubbed it, but then froze. Wakanda saw it too.

Gliding into the view from their cockpit, a large fur-covered paw offered to help the Citadel to its feet. The face of the paw's owner also came into view.

"Need a little help?"

Stunned, Wakanda mindlessly accepted the help from the towering wolf and took its paw.

As they got the Citadel on its feet, the crew saw a massive fire raging where the Asgard had crashed into the planet. Standing next to them, Fenrisulfr peered over his shoulder at the Tranquility's Wrath, smirked then jerked his muzzle toward the conflagration.

"So much for the coming of the second city."

Epilogue

Along the apex of a rich, blue sky, a faint, semi-transparent line streaked from horizon to horizon. His eyes barely detected it or the pentagon shape at its summit.

Though it had only been there for a little over a year, he couldn't remember seeing the sky without the planetary defense system in place. How it came to be named "Alessa" he'd never know, but he had been told it was a fitting memorial for another guardian angel. It was a curious but reassuring feeling as he stood on his balcony.

"Ambassador Ozuna," a feminine voice called from inside his office.

Without turning, he could see in his mind's eye his assistant in a sharp black and white dress skirt, and shoulder-length, curly brunette hair enter the room behind him.

"You have a call from the Dragon Corps' regional command."

He glanced at his gilded watch. "Thanks, Emma. I've got some time; patch it to my desk."

After another glance into the sky, he straightened his finely pinstriped business suit and stepped inside. As he sat at his large oak desk, a red light blinked on his phone.

"Answer."

Pixels jumped from his desk until they formed a full-screen image of a face he had almost forgotten.

"Oz, man, how's it going?"

"Lyon?"

"One and only." Lyon smiled. "How long has it been? Two years."

"Something like that," Oz commented as he noticed a change in Lyon's uniform. "Looks like congratulations are in order."

"What? This?" Lyon asked as he pinched his high collar emblazoned with a circular figure of a winged dragon. "Guess it's proof that they'll promote anyone in this outfit."

"Well, Wyvernnaire Kendrick, heard from the rest of the team?"

"Not lately." Lyon shook his head. "Paloon is still teaching, I think, but Larin did get that chief engineer position in weapons development, despite his captain's reluctance."

"I bet he's enjoying it though."

"He is." Lyon faintly nodded his head for a moment. "And, as you can guess, Hitook graduated to ninja, but he's refusing to go anywhere and is staying on with the school's staff. I haven't heard anything from Julie since she retired."

"Retired?"

"Yep. She'll make a fine queen one day."

"I feel sorry for her court."

Sharing a short laugh, Lyon tapered into a lower voice.

"Hey, how...how's he doing?"

Briefly perplexed, Oz lightened with understanding. "Oh, he's doing all right. He seems to enjoy his new life."

"I'm glad he's doing well." Lyon trailed in thought and went silent.

"Hey," Oz pulled Lyon out of his funk, "I'm sure you didn't call just to reminisce, what's up?"

"Well, with this new rank, I'm now in charge of a task force that's being formed to take a closer look at the p'tahians."

"What for? They haven't bothered us since the battle. Why open the wound?"

"Basically," Lyon raised his brow, "you aren't the only Terra in the neighborhood, and it looks like the Corps wants to take a closer look at those operations to see what the p'tahians are really up to."

"That's like poking a sleeping dragon."

"True, but dragons, sleeping or otherwise, are still dangerous. Hopefully, we can learn enough now to counter whatever the p'tahians might try next. Many of us have just been waiting in nervous anticipation."

Oz couldn't discount the concern. "What's the plan?"

"Use your Terra as a springboard to the other Terras."

"What?" Oz was visibly upset. "How am I supposed to sell that? I'm having a hard enough time with the recruiting efforts, not to mention the religious extremists; those crazies will kill anyone, including themselves, just to have a shot at proving a point."

"Just sic Fenrisulfr after them."

"I wish I could, but he won't leave Avalon." Oz leaned back, his tension bleeding off. "Not like I can blame him after what they tried to do to him. I just wish *I* could retreat to a nice sanctuary, too"

"Oh, you'll come up with something to make everyone understand how important this is for everyone's safety, not just for your planet. You're good at it." Lyon pointed an open palm at Oz. "After all, you're the ambassador to the Dragon Corps."

"I'm only here because of you."

"It wasn't all me. Besides, I'm sending you a team to meet you and discuss the details. They'll help."

"Like hell," Oz huffed. "The last time you brought a team to my planet, you darn near destroyed it."

Lyon chuckled. "Guess the Sangraal will just have to save my ass again."

Oz shook his head in disbelief, but it reminded him, and he glanced at his watch.

"Oh, damn."

"What?"

"Speaking of Sophia, I'm supposed to meet her at the General Assembly; we're scheduled to discuss the process of finally bringing this planet's laws in compliance with interstellar law. It'll be another fight."

"Good luck with that."

"Yeah, we'll need it."

"Take care, man."

"See you around."

The screen exploded into pixels as Oz hit the disconnect button, stood and headed out.

Emma met him at the door, began walking with him into the hall and handed him a briefcase. "Here are the copies of the presentation and abstracts of the required changes in order of importance. Also, your security detail is waiting and—"

"Tell Yabuki that he worries too much and to stop sending me with an army everywhere I go."

Emma gracefully bowed as Oz stepped outside into a cordon of sharply dressed men with suits tailored to hide automatic weapons.

"You're relieved, men. Go home."

They glanced at Emma. With her nod, they bowed and departed down the steps that led to the roadside and a white car. Leaning against the hood, a medium built man with a smoky-grey golf cap and a five o'clock shadow from two days ago chewed on half of an unlit cigar. Dressed in a worn brown leather jacket, buttoned-up denim shirt, white undershirt, faded blue jeans and scuffed work boots, he glanced up from a hand-held TV before putting it in his coat pocket and opening the car door as Oz approached.

With a tip of his hat, the incongruous chauffeur, in a gruff accent, greeted his employer. "How's it going, Mr. O?"

"Pretty good," Oz replied as he entered the car. "Yourself?"

"Absolutely fantastic."

"Why's that?"

"It's Wednesday." With that revelation, the chauffeur closed the door and entered the driver's seat.

Intrigued, Oz asked, "What's special about today? Is it your birthday?"

"Nope, Mr. O." As the car started and began moving forward, the driver glanced in the rearview mirror at Oz. "Wednesday is the only day that begins with W, so what's not to be happy about?"

Oz just smirked and chuckled. "That's a very good point. I guess it is a very good day."

"Exactly." The driver chewed his cigar for a big more. "Hey, Mr. O, I've been doing some thinking."

"About what?"

"About everything that has happened since that battle with those p'tahian things and what the existence of Avalon and Fenrisulfr and the Sangraal and all that mumbo jumbo actually means."

Oz remained silent for a while, but his driver failed to elaborate. "Did you come to any conclusions?"

"Yeah, I did."

Silence returned, making Oz smile as he glanced out the window for a moment then back to the mirror. "And what's your conclusion?"

"That someday, I'm going to start my own religion so that when I die, I'll have my own mythology: the mythology of me."

Oz couldn't restrain the laugh.

"You can't die, Mac. You're the best built android I know."

"Well, a computer can dream, can't he? Even a computer can dream."

About The Author

Dale Yates has a mild fascination in seeking the meaning of life through the study of everything from theology, mythology and folklore to astrophysics, quantum mechanics and eleven-dimensional string theory. He spent seventeen years, in his spare time, slowly piecing together this, his first book. During the hobby, he never truly knew how or if the book would end, but luckily, it did.

He lives with his wife, daughter and brother-in-law.

Made in the USA